BOW STREET SOCIETY:
The Case of The Fatal Flaw
By
T.G. Campbell

All characters in this novel are fictional. Any resemblance to persons living or dead is purely coincidental.

Cover illustration by Peter Spells
Bow Street Society Logo by Heather Curtis

Text & artwork copyright © -
2025 Tahnee Anne Georgina Campbell

Edited by Susan Soares
All Rights Reserved

Printed by KDP

ALSO BY THE AUTHOR

The Case of The Curious Client
The Case of The Lonesome Lushington
The Case of The Spectral Shot
The Case of The Toxic Tonic
The Case of The Maxwell Murder
The Case of The Pugilist's Ploy

The Case of The Shrinking Shopkeeper & Other Stories
The Case of The Peculiar Portrait & Other Stories
The Case of The Russian Rose & Other Stories
The Case of The Gentleman's Gambit & Other Stories
The Case of The Fearful Father & Other Stories
The Case of The Scream in the Smog & Other Stories

The Case of The Devil's Dare
in
Criminal Shorts
a
UK Crime Book Club anthology sold for the benefit of
The Red Kite Academy in Corby, Northamptonshire, UK.

The Case of The Contradictory Corpse
in
The Brumology: The Author City Birmingham Anthology

Dedicated to my beta reader Kim J. Cowie and my Nana Eileen

ACKNOWLEDGEMENTS

Thank you to all my readers, including my beta team, for your unerring enthusiasm and support. It keeps me going in moments of self-doubt and pushes me to be the best writer I can be. Also, thank you to my sister for her faith in me and unconditional support, my editor, Susan Soares, for her professionalism and keen eye for detail, my illustrator, Peter Spells, for his wonderful artwork which graces all Bow Street Society book covers, and my friends and family who listen to my writerly ramblings with grace and patience. I greatly appreciate all you've done, and continue to do, for me.

I'd also like to thank David Luck, archivist at Bethlem: Museum of the Mind. The research sources, information, and advice he gave me about Bethlem Hospital in the late nineteenth century were invaluable. They helped me to create a realistic and believable depiction of this famous institution in *The Case of The Fatal Flaw*. A depiction I hope will dispel the cliches and challenge my readers' preconceptions about the treatment of illnesses of the mind in the Victorian era.

I'd also like to thank the West Midlands Police Museum. The information they gave me about Birmingham City Police in the 1890s was also invaluable. It helped me pinpoint the headquarters of the Birmingham City Police to a real location, thereby allowing me to create a vivid sense of time and place for my reader.

Finally, I'd like to thank my friend Matt for allowing me to loosely base the character of Detective Inspector Matthew Rupert Peter Donahue on him in the short story *The Case of the Contradictory Corpse* and now *The Case of The Fatal Flaw*.

TABLE OF CONTENTS

Acknowledgements	6
Prologue	9
One	16
Two	28
Three	35
Four	42
Five	50
Six	58
Seven	66
Eight	78
Nine	86
Ten	98
Eleven	109
Twelve	117
Thirteen	124
Fourteen	132
Fifteen	140
Sixteen	146
Seventeen	151
Eighteen	159
Nineteen	170
Twenty	182
Twenty-One	192
Twenty-Two	201
Twenty-Three	213
Twenty-Four	222
Twenty-Five	232
Twenty-Six	242
Twenty-Seven	254
Twenty-Eight	263
Twenty-Nine	273
Thirty	280
Thirty-One	293
Thirty-Two	305
Thirty-Three	314

Thirty-Four	323
Thirty-Five	335
Thirty-Six	344
Thirty-Seven	351
Thirty-Eight	360
Thirty-Nine	367
Forty	377
Forty-One	386
Forty-Two	395
Forty-Three	403
Forty-Four	415
Forty-Five	424
Forty-Six	432
Forty-Seven	440
Forty-Eight	453
Forty-Nine	463
Fifty	473
Fifty-One	482
Fifty-Two	493
Fifty-Three	506
Fifty-Four	515
Fifty-Five	527
Fifty-Six	535
Fifty-Seven	541
Fifty-Eight	554
Epilogue	562
Glossary of Terms	575
Notes from the author	578
Gaslight Gazette	591
Sources of Reference	592

PROLOGUE

5th January 1897

It was early morning and Detective Inspector Caleb Woolfe had been sitting in his office overlooking Bow Street for over an hour. The bridge of his nose ached, and the corners of his eyes were heavily bruised, obliging him to self-medicate with whisky. If a constable had had his nose broken by a single punch, his fellow officers would've derided him for weeks, if not months, afterward. Yet, Inspector Woolfe's status and reputation was such, no one dared to remark upon his injury.

Hearing approaching footsteps in the corridor, Inspector Woolfe returned the bottle of whisky to his desk and stood. He greeted his visitor with a sombre expression and outstretched hand. "Good morning, sir."

"Good morning, Caleb." Detective Chief Inspector Jones removed his bowler hat with one hand whilst his other gave Inspector Woolfe's a firm squeeze. His brown hair and moustache were neatly trimmed and combed, whilst his midnight-blue double-breasted suit with matching waistcoat and tie fitted his slender form like a glove. An open knee-length, black overcoat and burgundy scarf kept it largely hidden from view, however. His hazel-brown eyes cast an appraising glance over Woolfe's dishevelled brown suit, unkempt black hair, and bloodshot eyes. Frowning, his gaze lingered on Inspector Woolfe's broken nose and bruised face. "That looks nasty."

"It's better than it was." Inspector Woolfe indicated the vacant chair opposite. "May I take your coat, sir?"

"No, I shan't be staying." Chief Inspector Jones put his hat on the desk and sat.

Inspector Woolfe returned to his own seat. Despite being anxious to learn the reason for his senior officer's visit, he knew it would be rude to not make polite conversation first. "Was your Christmas a merry one, sir?"

"Yes, thank you. I gather yours wasn't, though."

Inspector Woolfe gave a small grunt. "Our cells were full by midnight."

Chief Inspector Jones recalled the pleasant day he'd spent with his wife Clara and their son Michael, who was home from boarding school. He knew Inspector Woolfe was unmarried and, as far as he was aware, childless. Nevertheless, he'd hoped the man had some relative to spend the day with. "Forgive me for prying, Caleb, but don't you have family in London?"

Inspector Woolfe thought of his younger sister who was a maid in a big house down Sussex way. She always spent Christmas Day with the other domestics, and he'd not spoken to her in years, besides. "No."

"I wish I'd known. You could've spent Christmas Day with us," Chief Inspector Jones said with genuine regret.

Inspector Woolfe couldn't envision himself in the finery of Chief Inspector Jones' Mayfair home. A vague memory of Inspector Lee accusing him of 'soiling' his carriage simply by sitting in it flitted through his mind. "Thank you, sir, but I don't mind keeping an eye on things here."

"Very admirable of you."

Inspector Woolfe gave a dismissive grunt. "I'm only doing my duty, sir."

Reminded of why he was there, Chief Inspector Jones' expression turned grave. "I'm glad to hear you say so, Caleb, because it is your sense of duty I'm here to call upon."

"You have it, sir."

"Good. For I have news of great import that warranted more than the impersonal communication of a letter."

Inspector Woolfe leant forward, his folded arms upon his desk, as a feeling of dread descended upon him. Was he about to be dismissed, without notice, pay, or pension? In his mind, he replayed the incident between him, Mr Farley, and Mr Skinner. He couldn't think of anything he'd done to break the police code or law. Recalling his last meeting with Chief Inspector Jones about his discovery in Inspector Conway's house, he felt his dread intensify. Had it been proven Conway was corrupt after all? Feeling his mouth turn dry, Inspector Woolfe swallowed and wet his lips.

"Detective Inspector Conway is being reassigned to E Division upon his return to active duty," Chief Inspector Jones stated. "Detective Inspector Lee will be taking his place as head of the Mob Squad at A Division."

Inspector Woolfe stilled, and his limbs froze. Staring at Chief Inspector Jones for several moments as his mind produced only blank thoughts, Inspector Woolfe's body then went into overdrive. A tight knot formed in his stomach, and he suddenly felt light-headed, both of which caused him to feel nauseous. His thoughts also swirled too quickly for him to follow, making him feel dizzy as well. "Wh-what did you just say?"

"Detective Inspector Conway is being reassigned to E Division and Detective Inspector Lee is taking his place as head of the Mob Squad at A Division."

Inspector Woolfe sat back in his chair, struggling to focus. "What?" The memory of discovering the envelope in Inspector Conway's house leapt into his mind, confusing him further. "You think John's guilty?"

"Certainly not," Chief Inspector Jones rebuked. Of all the people he'd told, he'd expected Inspector Woolfe to be the one to question it—aside from Inspector Conway, of course.

"And Lee, the new head of the Mob Squad? Are you mad?" Inspector Woolfe challenged. Remembering who he was addressing, he hastily added, "No offence meant, sir."

Chief Inspector Jones' features tightened. "I know this must have come as a shock to you, Caleb, but I expect you to abide by my wishes and trust my judgement."

"I do, and I will, but Lee was the one who put the money in Conway's house, sir."

"We have no proof of that."

"No, but I'll swear it was him until my dying day," Inspector Woolfe insisted. "Putting him in charge of the Mob Squad will let him think he's won." He looked away and mumbled under his breath, "making him even more of an arrogant bastard."

"Inspector Lee is none of your concern," Chief Inspector Jones stated in a firm tone. "Your duty is to Inspector Conway. I want daily reports from you about how he is spending his time here. If you have any concerns about his behaviour, or others', I want to be notified immediately, do I make myself clear?"

Inspector Woolfe felt the tight knot reform in his stomach. With a heaviness to his voice and expression, he replied, "Yes, sir."

* * *

6th January 1897

Chief Inspector Jones took a puff from his pipe and, exhaling the smoke, watched the cloud dissipate. The din of muffled footfall and garbled conversations coming from Scotland Yard's corridors provided a constant accompaniment to his thoughts. Sitting in a comfortable armchair by the fire in his office, he recalled the conversations he'd had with John and Caleb. Things had gone relatively smoothly so far, and there was just one more thing to do. Yet, the entire plan relied upon getting this last step right.

Hearing a knock upon the door, he moved to sit behind his desk. "Come in!"

When Detective Inspector Gideon Lee walked in, he had his hat in one hand and his walking cane in the other. In his fifty-eighth year, he was twenty-five years Jones' senior. Aside from some crow's feet in the corners of his striking dark-blue eyes, his clean-shaven face bore no signs of his advanced years. His manicured nails and tailored fit of his open, ankle-length black fur coat, and dark-brown suit and waistcoat were in-keeping with his self-proclaimed status as a gentleman. His face, shoulders, and salt-and-pepper hair were damp from the rain he'd been obliged to walk through between his carriage and the Yard.

"Good morning, sir," Inspector Lee greeted. "You wished to see me."

"Yes. Please, make yourself comfortable."

Inspector Lee recalled he'd been denied such an invitation the last time Chief Inspector Jones had given him a dressing down. The summons to Scotland Yard so soon after Christmas had taken him unawares, however. Therefore, he remained braced for a scolding as he put his hat, coat, and cane on the hat stand and sat in the chair before Chief Inspector Jones' desk.

"How was your Christmas?" Chief Inspector Jones enquired.

"Pleasant. Thank you," Inspector Lee replied with caution.

"You seem on edge," Chief Inspector Jones observed, taking a puff from his pipe.

"I'm keen to hear the reason for your summons, sir."

"Quite." Chief Inspector Jones emptied his pipe and returned it to its box. "I've completed my investigation into the allegation of corruption you made against Inspector Conway and found it to be utterly baseless."

Caleb mustn't have gone to Jones about his discovery after all, Inspector Lee inwardly mused. It both angered and disappointed him, but his expression remained grave as he said, "Sergeant Gutman swore he witnessed Miss Trent and Inspector Conway exchanging envelopes, sir. I stand by his testimony."

"I gave you my assessment of his testimony at the time, Gideon. I shan't repeat myself," Chief Inspector Jones dismissed.

"Yes. Sir."

"Also, my conclusions about your behaviour still stand."

Inspector Lee bowed his head to hide his displeasure as he shifted his weight within his chair.

"Yours hasn't been the only hostility toward Inspector Conway within the service, however," Chief Inspector Jones continued in a regretful tone. "The scrutiny given to his conduct by the board has led to a weakening of trust between him and his fellow officers. Many are questioning his loyalty."

Inspector Lee lifted his chin. "Including me, sir."

Chief Inspector Jones' eyes narrowed. "Yes. I'm aware of your thoughts on the matter." He averted his gaze to a document on his desk. "To alleviate tensions and monitor Inspector Conway's behaviour, I've removed him as head of the Mob Squad and reassigned him to E Division at Bow Street." He met Inspector Lee's gaze. "Furthermore, I've ordered Inspector Woolfe to provide me with daily briefings about Inspector Conway's activities, and to notify me immediately if his behaviour, or others', cause him any concern."

Inspector Lee felt his heart leap in his chest at the news. If he had been alone, he would've cheered. As it was, he fought to suppress his delight. "I see."

"Naturally, someone must take his place as head of the Mob Squad to continue our surveillance of the Bow Street Society. I've decided it is to be you, Gideon."

Inspector Lee's features lifted with a broad smile.

Chief Inspector Jones' jaw tightened at the sight. He had suspected securing the position of head of the Mob Squad away from Inspector Conway had been Inspector Lee's aim all along. Yet, to have his suspicions confirmed by this blatant show of delight was almost too much to stomach. Unwilling to jeopardise his plan by openly scolding Inspector Lee, he opted for stating facts, instead. "I haven't made this decision lightly. John is a very old friend of mine."

Inspector Lee's smile faded. He was unaware of the connection but, upon reflection, thought it went some way to explain Chief Inspector Jones' previous reluctance to act against Inspector Conway. He assumed a serious expression out of respect. "I understand, sir."

Chief Inspector Jones found he believed him. "I'm glad you do." He picked up the document and gave it to Inspector Lee. "The list of undercover detective officers assigned to the Mob Squad. You will start immediately."

Inspector Lee studied the list. "Yes, sir."

"I've already arranged for your affects to be brought from Chiswick to the Yard. You'll be in Inspector Conway's former office on the first floor. Sergeant Gutman will be your direct subordinate." Chief Inspector Jones knew the sergeant's loyalty to Inspector Lee was as strong as his to Inspector Conway. Yet, if he was going to succeed in giving Inspector Lee enough rope to hang himself with, he needed him to feel secure in his position. Giving him Sergeant Gutman would go some way in achieving that. Chief Inspector Jones picked up his pen and pulled over a blank piece of paper. "You may tend to your new duties."

Inspector Lee stood and held out his hand. "Thank you, sir."

Chief Inspector Jones looked from Inspector Lee's hand to his face and back again. Although it turned his stomach to do so, he gave it a firm shake. Determined and hopeful for his plan to be successful, he warned, "Don't disappoint me, Gideon."

ONE

The cold morning air prickled Miss Trent's face as she crossed the porch. Although the grandfather clock had chimed six-thirty when she'd passed, it was dark when her dark-brown eyes glanced up and down Bow Street. In mid-January, the sun wouldn't rise for another hour or so, which was why she'd chosen to venture out at this time. Her plans had the potential for both humility and humiliation; emotions she tried to avoid. Therefore, if she had them thrust upon her this morning, she could rely upon the darkness to hide her embarrassment.

Lifting her dark-brown, A-line skirts as she descended the steps, she felt the benefit of her brown tweed jacket upon stepping into the open street. The thick leather of her heeled boots protected her feet, whilst her woollen stockings kept her legs warm. Tossing her plaited, chestnut-brown hair over her shoulder, she felt her nose and cheeks turn numb.

The sudden thud of a door pulled her attention to the police station. Catching sight of two figures, she saw the faces of Inspectors Caleb Woolfe and John Conway pass by the white lamps. Despite the slight bruising around the former's eyes, she could tell his gaze was straight ahead. As if sensing Miss Trent's eyes upon him, the latter looked at her and gave a subtle nod before following his friend into the back of a waiting horse-drawn van.

The sound of its door slamming reverberated around the street. Although its driver was plain clothed, Miss Trent suspected he was an undercover policeman. Thus, it was likely the trio were embarking upon a covert operation—something Inspector Conway had had ample experience of during his time as head of the Mob Squad.

She still couldn't believe what had happened. *"Jones' just lookin' out for me,"* he'd told her by way of explanation. She hadn't known Chief Inspector Jones for as long as Inspector Conway, but she was certain she'd formed a fairly accurate picture of his character. She found it inconceivable he would intentionally slur Inspector Conway's name at Scotland Yard without a *very* good reason. Yet, he appeared to have done precisely that by reassigning him to Bow Street. She knew Inspector Conway wouldn't have blindly agreed to it, so she was convinced he was hiding the truth from her. *But not for long*, she thought.

The sound of cartwheels on cobblestones pulled her from her thoughts. Looking to the source, she did a double take upon seeing Mr Snyder sitting atop a vehicle that wasn't the Society's cab. In fact, it was more akin to the traders' wagons she'd seen in Tonbridge. It had four large wheels, a cast-iron frame & axles, and two benches, one in front of the other. Although padded, they were the only "luxury" on a vehicle without doors, walls, or roof. There wasn't much of a floor either. A single layer of wood separated the riders from the road. Finally, a slanted panel of wood, topped by a vertical one, shielded the driver's and front passenger's lower limbs.

Recognising the horse as Red-Shirt at least, she had a burning question waiting to be asked when Mr Snyder had brought the vehicle to a stop. "Where is the cab?"

"The livery," Mr Snyder replied in his East London-accented voice.

Miss Trent cast a second appraising glance over the vehicle. "I thought you were teaching me to drive this morning?"

"Yeah, and this here's the best thing to learn in." Mr Snyder patted the top of the panel in front of him. Aside from his head and hands, his entire body was covered by his heavy, black cabman's cloak. The large brim of his hat was pushed upward, thereby allowing the weak gaslight of the nearby streetlamp to illuminate his brown eyes, black whiskers, and weathered features. Although almost a month had passed since the boxing match against Inspector Conway, Mr Snyder's face was bruised, still. "A dog cart."

Miss Trent refrained from stating the obvious. "Did you learn to drive in one?"

"I did." Mr Snyder leant across and held out his hand.

His answer, and the immeasurable trust she already had in him, was enough to convince her. Putting her right foot on a metal step protruding from the cart's side, she took his hand and allowed him to pull her up with a wince as she lifted her left foot into the vehicle.

"How are you feeling?" Miss Trent enquired once she was settled beside him.

Mr Snyder patted his side. "Gettin' better every day." He glanced at the porch. "No Toby this mornin'?"

"I decided to let him sleep."

The sixteen-year-old pot boy had been brought to the Bow Street Society's house following the inevitable closure of his former workplace and home. The arrangement had been temporary at first, but he'd gotten along with her and the Society's members so well, she'd decided to make it permanent. His help cleaning the Society's house, and the wage he brought in from his work at the underground railway bar, were also appreciated.

"How's his readin' with Miss Hicks goin'?"

Miss Trent repressed the urge to roll her eyes at the mention of her former lover. "Well."

Mr Snyder smiled. "We'll get him to Oxford yet."

"Getting him reading and writing is more important, Sam," Miss Trent said. "It will give him a better chance at a well-paid trade to keep him out of the workhouse." She knew there were plenty of honest tradesmen in the workhouse, but it didn't mean they shouldn't gift Toby with a good education.

Mr Snyder offered her the reins.

Miss Trent looked between them and his face. "*Here?*"

"No reason not to."

"Except my nerves," Miss Trent mumbled but nonetheless took the reins.

Mr Snyder chuckled. "Don't be daft, lass." He looked to her hands. "Hold 'em in your left hand."

Miss Trent transferred the reins.

Mr Snyder arranged the near rein over her forefinger and the other under her middle finger, thereby putting two fingers between both. He gently lifted the former rein. "This 'ere's your near rein." He gently lifted the latter rein. "And this 'ere's your off rein, or what you'd call the right rein." He straightened her forefinger and moved her thumb closer to the near rein. "Keep 'em like that." He tapped her forefinger's knuckle. "And the near rein close to this. You'll be able to move Red-Shirt left or right better."

"How?"

"Turn the back of your hand up for left and down for right." Mr Snyder withdrew his hands. "Keep the reins loose and your elbows in."

Miss Trent nodded. "And how do I get Red-Shirt to stop?"

"Pull the reins to you, but gently, or he'll rear."

"Right," Miss Trent said with a hint of trepidation.

"Ready?" Mr Snyder enquired.

Miss Trent quietly breathed in and out as her heartrate quickened. "Yes."

Mr Snyder looked to the horse. "Walk on, lad."

Red-Shirt bobbed his head as if in agreement and moved forward. Miss Trent instinctively tightened her grip on the reins.

"Easy, now." Mr Snyder gently opened her thumb and forefinger whilst keeping his gaze upon Red-Shirt. "Like that."

Although they were travelling at a snail's pace, Miss Trent felt exhilarated at being in control of a horse and cart. Her mind was filled with ideas for journeys she wouldn't have to rely on others to make. Additionally, she could step-in for Sam if he became indisposed. With all these thoughts and feelings swirling inside her, she forgot about her fear and looked forward to her newfound freedom.

* * *

The van rocked from side to side as it drove over the uneven cobblestones at considerable speed. Aside from the candlelight coming from a pair of Davey lamps hung on either side of the doorway, the van's interior was in darkness. Although it had solid walls and door, the cold had still penetrated the space, causing Inspector Conway's chest to ache. It was over a month since his ribs were fractured, which should've meant they were almost healed. Yet, as with other breakages he'd sustained both in and outside the ring, the pain had lingered in the form of an ache exasperated by changes in temperature. The fact Inspector Conway was obliged to sit on the floor and grip a shelf above him whenever the van turned a corner didn't help, either.

Inspector Woolfe wasn't faring any better. His six-foot-four-inch, broad-shouldered frame was squeezed into the narrow space, causing his bent legs to cramp and his back to hurt. The twin of Inspector Conway's shelf above him meant he also had to perpetually lean forward with his wrists resting upon his bent knees. Barely distinguishable in the dim lamplight, his mouth formed a hard line, whilst his black, bushy eyebrows were pushed together. He hadn't uttered a word since they'd left the police station.

Inspector Conway shifted his weight as he felt pain in his lower back. At the same time, he reached into his overcoat and took out a box of matches and a couple of cigarettes. He gave one to Inspector Woolfe and put the other between his lips. Lighting each with a match, he took a pull from his for as long as his ribs would allow. Exhaling the smoke, he turned his dark-blue eyes to Inspector Woolfe who took a much longer pull.

A violent coughing fit ensued, its ferocity causing his upper body to turn rigid and his free hand to clench into a tight fist. Suddenly hyper-aware of his friend's distress, Inspector Conway forgot about their task as deep concern and a desire to help overtook him. The only thing keeping him silent was the knowledge Inspector Woolfe loathed being fussed over. When the coughing fit eased, Inspector Conway felt only marginally relieved; it had been one of many he'd witnessed since being reassigned shortly after the new year.

"Bloody cough," Inspector Woolfe muttered under his breath.

Inspector Conway took another pull from his cigarette and, tilting his head upward, exhaled the smoke whilst keeping his gaze upon Inspector Woolfe.

"Winter always does my chest in," Inspector Woolfe added, taking a much shorter pull from his own cigarette, and exhaling the smoke with a few, much weaker, coughs.

Inspector Conway bent his leg and rested the heel of his cigarette-holding hand upon his knee as he turned his head away from his friend.

"Stop it," Inspector Woolfe growled.

Inspector Conway bowed his head and put his cigarette to his lips. "I've not said anythin'." He exhaled the smoke.

"But you're thinking it," Inspector Woolfe retorted. "Loud enough to hear."

Inspector Conway met his gaze. "Can't a bloke be worried about his mate?"

"*No*," Inspector Woolfe growled. "Not this one."

"You're not right, Caleb."

"It'll pass," Inspector Woolfe dismissed, finishing his cigarette with a final pull, followed by a few more coughs. "Just as soon as the weather warms."

Inspector Conway parted his lips but closed them, again, when he felt the van slow. He pinched the end of his cigarette to extinguish it and, holding the butt in his closed hand, got to his feet. Although he gripped the shelves on either side, his body continued to gently rock until the van came to a complete halt. At which point, he unlatched and pushed open its rear door and climbed out. The butt was also discarded into a nearby drain.

"Leg's gone to sleep," Inspector Woolfe growled as he clambered to his feet. Obliged to remain bent over, he shuffled his way to the door and caused the van to lower onto its rear axle as he climbed down. "We're getting a cab back," he announced, slamming the door.

"We'll have our bloke by then, so we'll have to," Inspector Conway pointed out.

The van had brought them to the entrance of a short, dead-end street in Whitechapel. It was deserted at this hour, the workers having left already, and the dossers being asleep, still. Having previously given their instructions to the plain-clothed constable to wait with the van, Inspectors Woolfe and Conway strode down the street to the third building on the right.

A former lodging house, it had two storeys above the ground floor, each with a pair of sash windows. The ground floor had four: two either side of the front door. All had their curtains closed. The façade of the narrow building was stained with a mixture of damp, soot, and grime. The couple of steps leading to its front door were warped and had an unconscious, drunken vagrant sprawled across them.

Inspectors Woolfe and Conway stood at their foot as the former reached over and struck the door with his fist several times. Waiting only a few moments before repeating the action, he stepped back and glanced at the ground floor windows.

"Wait…" Inspector Conway gripped Inspector Woolfe's arm as he went to strike the door for a third time. "Someone's comin'."

They heard the sliding of a bolt and the turning of a key before seeing the door open a few inches. A woman in her mid-forties with black hair, large, hazel eyes, and a fair complexion peered out. "We're closed."

Inspector Woolfe pushed the door as he put his foot on the top step, obliging the woman to move out of the way. Entering, Inspector Woolfe strode into the hallway and turned back to her, whilst Inspector Conway followed and closed the door. Able to see her fully now, they saw she wore green slippers with a matching velvet dressing gown and a white nightdress.

An open archway on the hallway's right led into a large room. It was filled with plush dark-red sofas and loveseats, and purple chairs. Round tables littered around the room had bowls of grapes, walnuts, and other delectable foods arranged upon them. A closed door on the hallway's left was marked *Private*, and another to the left of the stairs presumably led to the kitchen and backyard. The walls were decorated with a lilac and plum damask floral paper, and the floors were covered by a dark-red carpet throughout. Pictures depicting the nude female form in a variety of poses, some of which Inspector Conway didn't think possible, hung on the walls. The remaining furniture consisted of plain side tables, potted plants, and a couple of bookcases.

Inspector Woolfe began, "We're—"

"The girls are asleep." The woman folded her arms.

"We're not here to put coin down, Mimi," Inspector Woolfe growled.

Inspector Conway had recognised Madam Mimi's name during Inspector Woolfe's earlier briefing. He'd never met her, but Mr Elliott of the Bow Street Society had during the Maxwell case. It had amused Inspector Conway to think of the uptight lawyer in a cat house.

Madam Mimi ran an admiring gaze over Inspector Conway. "Are you a copper like this one?" She gave a sideways nod to Inspector Woolfe.

"Yeah," Inspector Conway replied.

"*Two* of you. My, we *are* honoured," Madam Mimi said with blatant sarcasm. "Is this a raid, Caleb?"

"We're not here to hurt you," Inspector Conway reassured. "We just wanna get our bloke and go."

Madam Mimi turned expectant eyes to Inspector Woolfe.

"That's it," Inspector Woolfe confirmed.

"What's he done?" Madam Mimi enquired.

"Nothing you need to know about," Inspector Woolfe warned.

Madam Mimi's features tightened. "I've got a right to know if my girls are in danger."

Inspector Woolfe narrowed his eyes. "They were in danger the moment they got in with you, Mimi. How many girls is it now you've beaten black and blue?"

"Only the insolent ones," Madam Mimi replied in a matter-of-fact tone. "But they'll all be awake, soon, and if you're going to drag a customer from their bed, I'd rather you did it when no one could see." She looked to Inspector Conway. "What does he look like?"

Inspector Conway showed her a black and white mugshot of a man with short, curly hair and large nose. He was wearing a dark-coloured bowler hat, waistcoat and tie, and light-coloured shirt. There was a large grin on his face as if being photographed by the police amused him. "Jack Jerome, thirty years old, from Birmingham."

Madam Mimi glanced at the photograph. "He's with Colette." She turned amused eyes to Inspector Woolfe. "You remember which room is hers, don't you, Caleb?"

"Remind me," Inspector Woolfe growled.

"Room nine," Madam Mimi said with a smirk. "Second floor. Third door on the right."

"Thanks." Inspector Conway put the photograph away.

"Stay here and be quiet," Inspector Woolfe warned Madam Mimi as he and Inspector Conway crossed the room. Ascending the stairs at a brisk pace to begin with, Inspector Woolfe soon slowed as he became out of breath. Maintaining his forward momentum, though, he reached the summit first and continued down the narrow corridor ahead of them. Locating room nine with ease, he tried to turn its knob but found it was locked.

When he moved back in preparation of ramming it, Inspector Conway put his arm across his chest. "I'll do it."

"Suit yourself," Inspector Woolfe muttered, switching places with him.

Inspector Conway turned his shoulder toward the door and launched at it, a sharp pain searing through his chest as he did so. The door shook in its frame but remained in place. Moving back as far as the corridor would allow, he threw himself against the door a second time. Again, a flare of pain exploded in his chest. The door burst open, though, obliging him to grip the frame as he stumbled inside. Upon righting himself, he saw Jack Jerome clambering out the window.

"Oi!" Inspector Conway yelled. He ran across the room and, reaching through the window, grunted as Mr Jerome kicked his hand whilst clinging to the drainpipe. Shaking the pain from his fingers, Inspector Conway looked down and saw their prey was a third of the way down the drainpipe already.

Inspector Woolfe also stuck his head out. "That's never going to hold your weight."

"'Ere, what's goin' on, Caleb?" a woman's voice enquired from behind them.

"Get back in bed, Colette," Inspector Woolfe replied as he and Inspector Conway returned inside.

Colette was in her early twenties with waist-length, chocolate-brown hair, brown eyes, and rose-pink lips. She was also naked.

"Miss," Inspector Conway greeted, his head down, as he ran from the room.

"I said 'get back in bed,'" Inspector Woolfe warned, both looking and pointing at her as he followed Inspector Conway from the room. It wasn't the first time he'd seen her naked, and hopefully, it wouldn't be the last.

"You go out the front, I'll go out the back!" Inspector Woolfe shouted after Inspector Conway as they ran down the corridor, toward the stairs.

"Right!" Inspector Conway descended the stairs as quickly as he could.

Inspector Woolfe, with his long stride, overtook him in seconds, and they parted at the bottom.

Whilst Inspector Conway left via the front door, Inspector Woolfe ran to the rear. His face was as red as a beetroot, with sweat covering his forehead and cheeks, when he emerged into the cold air. Panting hard from the run, he was immediately gripped by a violent coughing fit from the sudden change in temperature. Nevertheless, he entered the yard proper and, turning around upon the spot, scoured the area for any sign of their prey. When he saw none, he moved sideways and leant his shoulder against the damp wall. His chest felt like it was on fire as he fought to bring his coughing and breathing under control.

The gate on the other side of the yard opened, and a red-faced Inspector Conway entered. Audibly out of breath, he announced, "The bugger's scarpered."

Inspector Woolfe pushed away from the wall as his coughing finally eased.

Inspector Conway watched his friend approach with deeply concerned eyes. "Caleb—"

Inspector Woolfe shoved him aside and growled, "Get off my back, John."

Inspector Conway glared after him as he left the yard but knew it was futile pursuing the conversation any further. Releasing a soft sigh, he wiped his forehead with his sleeve, glanced up at the house, and followed his friend with a closing of the gate.

* * *

Miss Trent slowly brought the dog cart to a halt outside the Society's house. When her lesson had begun, she was convinced she'd be moved to tears with relief by now. In reality, she'd found she wanted to continue.

"You're a natural, lass." Mr Snyder's smile filled his face.

"I have the best teacher." She returned the reins to him. "Thank you, Sam."

"We're not done yet. You've gotta get more hours in."

"And we will." Miss Trent climbed down from the dog cart and onto the pavement. "But I must prepare breakfast before Toby resorts to chewing the wallpaper."

Mr Snyder chuckled, glancing at the rising sun. "Lad's probably still asleep."

"Probably."

Mr Snyder touched the brim of his hat. "I'll come by later."

Miss Trent stepped back and waved him off as he drove away. Turning toward the house, she caught movement out of the corner of her eye. Upon looking down the street, she saw the silhouette of a man briskly walking away in the opposite direction. Although it could be coincidental, this was the third time she'd seen a man loitering around Bow Street with no apparent business to tend to. They'd all chosen spots near to the Society's house as well. Naturally, she had her suspicions about what—or more precisely, who—was possibly behind these incidents but had no evidence to substantiate them. "For now," she muttered, watching the man until he was out of sight.

TWO

Mother falling. Father's face. Mother falling. Father's face.

Mr Percy Locke pressed his thin palms against his green eyes, trying to dispel the horrific visions.

Mother falling. Father's face. Mother falling. Father's face.

"Percy." Dr Lynette Locke's gentle voice slipped into his ears like an angel bringing salvation. At the same time, her tender touch eased his hands from his face, and he saw her dark-blue green eyes fix him with an unwavering gaze. Her dark-blond eyebrows were also drawn together. "Everything is fine. You're safe."

Mr Locke lay back, but the tightness in his shoulders prevented him from resting flush against the tin bath's side. His hand also instinctively gripped its edge, causing his knuckles to turn pale, whilst his breathing came in short, sharp breaths. The water's heat had already increased his blood pressure enough for him to feel his heart thumping in his ears. With the added fear brought on by the visions, he felt certain his heart would burst forth from his chest. "I do not feel… safe," he panted, sweeping a shaky hand across his forehead to wipe away the sweat. More plagued his pink face and chest.

Dr Locke moved her stool to sit behind her husband. "You need to relax," she said in a gentle voice as she massaged his shoulders. "Close your eyes."

Mr Locke looked up at his wife. Dark circles and a grey tinge marred her eyes and complexion respectively. Yet, the remainder of her appearance was well-maintained and impeccable. Namely, the mass of dark-blond curls upon her crown and her tailor-made attire of dark-blue skirts and a pale-blue blouse with small, dark blue flowers. With a halo of gaslight behind her, she looked every inch the angel she was. "I do not want to. Every time I do, I see Mother falling."

Dr Locke carefully prised his fingers free from the side of the bath and, taking his other hand, laid them atop one another on his chest. "I know." She returned to massaging his shoulders. "But try to relax anyway. Let the bath do its work."

Mr Locke gave a curt nod and, putting his hands under the water, closed his eyes. In his late twenties, his once-healthy, slender form had become painfully thin. Although a strict regime of force feeding rich foods to him had allowed Dr Locke to restore some weight, there was still a long way to go before he was back to his former self. He still had his short, blond, curly hair, at least, which Dr Locke adored.

Running her fingers through it as she stroked his head, she couldn't help but reflect on their ordeal. From their ongoing war against his heroin addiction, to the relentless assault from his inner demons. He'd deceived her and, at times, she'd felt like she was torturing him with some of the treatment methods she'd implemented. She'd lost count of the times he'd hurt her emotionally. Yet, the time he'd struck her remained the hardest to swallow, and the most impossible to forget. He'd been in a fevered frenzy at the time and thus, was oblivious to his actions, but neither of them could excuse the act to this day.

With the recollection still too painful to dwell upon, she turned her thoughts to their previous attempts to wean him off the drug. She wanted to hope this time would be different but dared not to. He had disappointed her far too often before. She felt her heart harden at the reminder, but it melted, again, with a simple glance at him. Despite all rational thought, her love for him conquered her anger, grief, and fear. She longed for the Percy Locke she'd married like the desert longed for rain. She could never abandon him, nor contemplate such. Quite simply, he was her world. Unfortunately, that world could be as hellish as it was heavenly.

Feeling as though she were at risk of her emotions getting the better of her, Dr Locke went to work laying her husband's clothes out upon the bed. These comprised of a black waistcoat with a vertical dark-green pinstripe, white shirt, dark-green frock coat, and black trousers. To them, she added a dark-green cravat, and gold pocket watch with matching cufflinks. Feeling her self-control restored by the task's end, she adopted a formal tone as she announced, "It's time to get dressed."

Mr Locke looked over at her. "May I have a few minutes more?"

"No." Dr Locke retrieved a towel from the washstand. "You know the schedule."

"But—"

"Must I fetch Claude?" Dr Locke warned.

Mr Locke shrank back in the bath. He loathed and feared the attendant in equal measure. Thankfully, he was now only called upon when Mr Locke was—in his wife's words— 'being difficult.' "No," Mr Locke quietly replied. "I will get out of the bath."

Dr Locke hated resorting to threats, but at times like these, they were the only things which worked. She put the towel with her husband's clothes and offered him the use of her arm. "Come on, then."

Mr Locke frowned, but there was gratitude in his eyes as he took a firm grip of her arm and the side of the bath and leant his weight upon both as he stood. Transferring his grip to her shoulders whilst stepping out of the bath, he looped one arm around hers and allowed her to help him to the bed.

* * *

"I've decided to take the opportunity of today's visit to discuss your proposal," Miss Trent said, alluding to Inspector Lee's daily visits. She sat at the head of the table in the Bow Street Society's meeting room, whilst Inspector Lee sat on its left side, facing the door. Glancing at Mr Gregory Elliott, who sat directly opposite the policeman, she added, "With this in mind, I invited Mr Elliott here as the Society's legal representative."

Although identical in age to Miss Trent at twenty-eight, Mr Elliott dressed like someone much older. His choice of a black frockcoat over dark-blue waistcoat and black trousers was conservative attire usually reserved for elderly businessmen. His shirt was a crisp white, though, and complemented his flawless, fair complexion.

Arriving after the solicitor, Inspector Lee had chosen this spot to allow him to admire Mr Elliott's luxurious, dark-brown, wavy hair, green-brown eyes, and plump, red lips. Inspector Lee's gaze lingered upon those lips as Mr Elliott said in his usual monotone, "I've read the proposal and concluded there are neither legal nor practical grounds to justify putting a plain-clothed detective officer in this house."

Inspector Lee's gaze shifted to Mr Elliott's. "Please, elaborate."

"E Division's police station on Bow Street adequately serves the Society," Mr Elliott said.

"Because Inspector Conway has been reassigned there?" Inspector Lee probed.

Miss Trent's features tightened. "Inspector Conway no longer has any contact with the Society."

"Fortunately," Mr Elliott interjected.

Miss Trent cast him a black look. "He isn't the *only* policeman at Bow Street, either." She looked to Inspector Lee. "The police station is filled with able-bodied officers whom we may call upon for assistance or protection. Having yet another working from this house would serve no purpose other than to keep the Society and its members under constant surveillance."

"The Bow Street Society's activities oblige the Metropolitan Police to spend a great deal of manpower and resource on protecting its members from themselves," Inspector Lee said. "Case in point: Inspector Woolfe sustaining a broken nose whilst protecting Mr Callahan Skinner."

"He chose to intervene," Miss Trent pointed out. "Mr Skinner can protect himself."

Inspector Lee cast a hard glance at her but addressed Mr Elliott as he went on, "Placing a plain-clothed detective officer in this house will enable us to maintain our protection of the Society's members whilst reducing the cost to the service as a whole."

"The rules of the Bow Street Society clearly state *no* policeman, on active duty or otherwise, may become a member," Miss Trent said, firmly.

"I'm fully aware of the Society's 'rules,'" Inspector Lee said, drily. "And I'm not proposing he become a member but an in-house protector."

Miss Trent pursed her lips and exhaled deeply through her nose to calm her anger. "Whatever you call him, he's still a policeman, and he simply *being* here would be enough to deter anyone who's lost faith in the police from seeking the Society's help."

"Unless that is your intention?" Mr Elliott challenged. "To bring about the forced closure of the Bow Street Society."

The corner of Inspector Lee's mouth twitched. "Not at all."

"You speak of 'cost to the police,' when it isn't *us* who are arranging surveillance of me and this house," Miss Trent pointed out. "I saw *another* of your men loitering around the street this morning. If you want to reduce the amount of manpower and resource spent upon us, I suggest you start by reassessing your own practices."

"I don't have to," Inspector Lee said. "My senior officer is responsible for such things, and he has found my 'practices,' as you so quaintly put them, more than satisfactory." He took his time in having another sip of tea to irk Miss Trent further. As he carefully replaced the cup upon its saucer, he nonchalantly enquired, "By the way, how was your driving lesson with Mr Snyder?"

Miss Trent knew he was trying to provoke her, but she refused to rise to the bait. "Very well, thank you. I'm having another tomorrow morning."

"What you're doing amounts to police harassment," Mr Elliott stated.

"Observation," Inspector Lee corrected.

"Are you 'observing' the members, too?" Mr Elliott enquired.

A twinkle entered Inspector Lee's eyes. "I'm not at liberty to say."

"Which means you are," Miss Trent interjected, annoyed.

"On what grounds?" Mr Elliott demanded. "Do you suspect the Society of criminality?"

Inspector Lee smirked. "Our investigations are ongoing."

"We *demand* you cease *at once*," Mr Elliott insisted, his voice uncharacteristically impassioned.

Inspector Lee leant forward, thereby closing the distance between himself and the solicitor. Catching the scent of lavender carbolic soap coming from Mr Elliott, Inspector Lee felt even more attracted to him. Cleanliness was next to Godliness, after all. In a gentle tone, he said, "If you have nothing to hide, you have nothing to fear." He ran his gaze up and down Mr Elliott. "Do you have something to hide, Gregory?"

"No," Mr Elliott replied, his hard gaze fixed upon Inspector Lee's face. Noticing how he looked him over, he was reminded of the time Inspector Lee couldn't keep his hands to himself. "Do you?"

"We all have our secrets," Inspector Lee replied, brushing his foot against Mr Elliott's calf.

Mr Elliott moved his leg away with a jolt, stunned by the uninvited contact.

Unaware of what had occurred beneath the table, Miss Trent could nonetheless see the way Inspector Lee looked at Mr Elliott. It was like watching a hungry cat who'd cornered a mouse. "If you don't stop your harassment of me and the Society's members, I'll have no choice but to complain to Commissioner Bradford and, if necessary, the Home Secretary," Miss Trent warned. "You've heard our answer to your proposal and our reasons behind it." She stood. "Now, I'm asking you to leave, Inspector."

"Even Miss Trent has her secrets," Inspector Lee said with a smirk as he rose to his feet. Collecting his hat, gloves, and walking cane from the chair beside him, he headed for the door. "I suggest you ask her about them sometime." He retrieved his coat from the hat stand in the hallway and put it on as he returned to the meeting room's doorway. "As for making a complaint: it would only make us scrutinise you and the Society further, Miss Trent." He put on his hat. "I'll see you tomorrow. Good day."

THREE

Miss Trent returned her notebook and pencil to their drawer in her desk. The click of the lock when she turned the key provoked the memory of Inspector Lee's ominous statement, however: *Even Miss Trent has her secrets.* Becoming still as her focus turned inward, onto visions of Chief Inspector Jones, she didn't notice Mr Elliott enter the room.

"Is something amiss?" he enquired in his usual monotone.

Miss Trent's focus snapped back to her surroundings with an instant lifting of her head. The moment she saw Mr Elliott standing in the doorway, her mind registered his question. With a wry tone, she replied, "Only Inspector Lee's visits." She slipped the key into a pocket concealed within her skirts. "I think we were successful in quelling his ridiculous proposal," she gave him a knowing look, "despite his efforts to the contrary."

Recalling Inspector Lee's uninvited contact beneath the table, Mr Elliott averted his gaze whilst crossing the room to the fireplace. "His arrogance knows no bounds." He turned to face her with a rigid posture despite a conscious attempt to force himself to relax. "The revelation of his surveillance of the Society's members was particularly disturbing."

"But not entirely unexpected," Miss Trent muttered as she tidied her desk.

Mr Elliott recalled Inspector Lee's statement regarding the clerk. "What did he mean by even you have secrets?"

Miss Trent kept her gaze upon her task. "I haven't the faintest idea." She stole a glance at him as she sat behind her typewriter. "He was just trying to sow the seeds of mistrust." She loaded a sheet of paper into the machine to appear nonchalant. "When I said I'd lodge a formal complaint about his conduct with Commissioner Bradford and the Home Secretary, I wasn't making an idle threat. I shan't allow him to bully me." She recalled the predatory way Inspector Lee had looked upon Mr Elliott. "Or anyone else."

"Nor I," Mr Elliott stated in a firm tone.

Mr Elliott was the most unforgiving of the Bow Street Society's members. She knew he'd be swift to terminate his membership and their friendship if he ever discovered Chief Inspector Jones' connection to it.

"I'm sure Inspector Lee has plenty of secrets of his own," she said as she typed. "We know very little about his life beyond his work, after all."

Mr Elliott considered his own knowledge of the man and realised it was limited despite his past encounters with him. "I think it's time we remedied that."

Miss Trent halted in her typing to fix him with a firm gaze. "We mustn't do anything to provoke him unnecessarily. We don't know what information *he's* gathered about *us*." She knew he would understand what she was alluding to.

"My enquiries will be discreet."

Miss Trent considered the risks but concluded Inspector Lee's arrogance would likely make him blind to the possibility of the Society investigating him, albeit on an unofficial basis. "Very well." She struck a key to start a new line. "Let's play the game his way."

* * *

"Is it true?" Dr Percy Weeks enquired, his voice quieter than usual. His Canadian accent was also more pronounced.

Standing in the doorway of Inspector Woolfe's office, his attire of a knee-length brown overcoat, off-white shirt, and brown trousers were rumpled and unwashed. Black circles around his eyes gave him a gaunt appearance, whilst his lank, jet-black hair clung to his clammy forehead. The strong stench of bodily odour mixed with stale alcohol also came off him in waves as he visibly sweated. It was certainly the worst state the policeman had ever seen him in.

Putting his pen down, Inspector Woolfe rested his arms upon his chair's and sat back. With their last meeting fresh in his mind, he had a good idea what Dr Weeks was referring to. Glancing at Inspector Conway's unoccupied desk on the opposite side of the room, he knew their mutual friend would return at any moment. Therefore, their time was short if they wanted to avoid explaining the situation to the ignorant man at its centre. He knew he did, and he was quite sure Dr Weeks felt the same. "Yeah, since Christmas."

Dr Weeks' face turned ashen. "And Lee's...?"

"The new head of the Mob Squad."

Dr Weeks turned his back upon Inspector Woolfe and slowly ran his hands through his hair before gripping it tightly at the back of his head. He muttered, *"Jesus Christ."*

"Sit down."

Dr Weeks threw down his hands and glared at him over his shoulder. "I don't wanna sit down!" He paced as he shook his head and muttered about Inspector Lee under his breath.

Suddenly, the door opened and, as Inspector Woolfe had anticipated, Inspector Conway walked in. Dr Weeks abruptly halted at the sound and stared at his friend. Yet almost immediately, he downcast his eyes and hurried past Inspector Conway to exit the room.

Watching his swift departure with parted lips and a dumbfounded expression, Inspector Conway turned to Inspector Woolfe. "What's the matter with 'im?"

Inspector Woolfe averted his gaze to his report as he picked it up. "Forgot to get his old lady a Christmas present." Inspector Woolfe knew it wasn't the most convincing lie, but it was the first thing to come into his head. Besides, it was plausible where Dr Weeks was concerned.

"That don't surprise me."

"Me neither." Inspector Woolfe was relieved his friend had accepted the lie.

"I'm gonna get a cuppa. Do you want one?"

Inspector Woolfe glanced at him. "No. Thanks." He cleared his throat and, listening to Inspector Conway's departing footfall, worried about the state Dr Weeks would be in by the time they met again. *If only the bugger had stayed long enough for me to explain*, he thought. As things were, he didn't know when he'd be able to pay the surgeon a visit without Inspector Conway. After all, Inspector Conway's welfare was Inspector Woolfe's top priority, at least for the foreseeable future. Dr Weeks would just have to fend for himself.

* * *

Mr Locke chewed the piece of bacon whilst staring at the mound of food remaining on his plate: sausages, eggs, kidneys, and kippers. Several pieces of buttered toast with marmalade had also been piled upon a small side plate. He'd already eaten three strands of bacon, two sausages, two boiled eggs, a kipper, and half a kidney, all washed down with two cups of sweet tea. As a result, his stomach felt angry and strained. Yet, he continued his slow consumption, frequently glancing at Claude in the process.

The attendant stood just a few feet away, his muscular arms folded across his white shirt, black waistcoat, and tie. In his mid-twenties, he was six foot seven inches tall with a bulbous nose, chestnut-brown hair, and a lean yet muscular build. His deep-set hazel eyes followed Mr Locke's fork as it moved from the plate to his mouth.

"After breakfast, we will take our stroll around the garden," Dr Locke announced from the table's opposite end. Having eaten only two boiled eggs and a piece of toast, she was now reading the letters which had arrived in the morning post: hers and her husband's. She came to the end of the current correspondence and, putting it face down upon the table, moved onto the next. "Then, you will spend a few hours reading in the lounge before joining me for a light luncheon." She put the letter face down and moved onto the next. "Some new models of locks have also been delivered. You'll enjoy fathoming their flaws."

"From Mr Holland?" Mr Locke enquired, alluding to his locksmith friend who had a stall on the Whitechapel Road.

"No." She set aside the bill she'd read, mindful to keep it separate from everything else. At the bottom of the pile was the new edition of *The Era* newspaper. Colloquially known as the Actor's Bible amongst those in the theatrical profession, it contained a wide variety of segments. Including advertisements from actors and actresses seeking work, reviews of new productions, and articles about the latest scandals and divorce court proceedings.

Like his peers, Mr Locke was an avid reader of the publication and relied upon it to keep abreast of trends and developments within the industry. Since his relapse, though, Dr Locke had vetted each edition before passing it to her husband. She feared an article speculating about his absence, and the connected fortunes of the *Paddington Palladium*, could send him back to the opium den. Thus far, there had been no such article.

Yet, as she flicked through the pages this morning, a headline caught her eye. It read: *THE GREAT LOCKE'S DISAPPEARANCE: PADDINGTON PALLADIUM'S POPULARITY PLUMMETS.* Feeling a heaviness form in her breast as she read it, she felt it intensify as she swiftly read the ensuing article. In brief, it speculated on the circumstances surrounding her husband's sudden and prolonged absence from the theatre that had been his life. One theory was he had succumbed to illness. Another was he had gone bankrupt but had somehow managed to keep the case out of the law courts. The article's writer was conclusive in their scathing review of, what they termed, *mediocre performances from forgettable singers and clumsy routines from heavy-footed dancers*, though.

Dr Locke closed the newspaper, her mind racing with questions of how Mr Locke's business manager could allow such an article to be written, let alone published. She felt sick but mostly enraged. The *Palladium* meant the world to her husband, and the promise of performing there, again was one of the few things which kept him focused on his recovery. Tucking the newspaper under the pile of letters so he wouldn't see it, she resolved to call upon the business manager later that day.

Trying to keep the news from her husband but nonetheless hearing the irritation in the tone of her voice, she continued to outline his schedule. "We'll have a light dinner at the usual time, followed by our walk. Finally, a warm bath and glass of hot milk should help you drift off to sleep." She gathered up the pile as she stood and tucked it under her arm. Picking up the bill with her other hand, she looked at her husband's plate and frowned. "You've hardly touched your breakfast."

Mr Locke's grip tightened upon his knife and folk as he bent forward, hoping to hide the offending mound of food. "I cannot eat any more, Lynette."

Dr Locke and Claude exchanged glances.

"We've discussed this, Percy," Dr Locke said. "You can't regain your strength if you don't regain some weight, and you can't regain your weight if you don't eat."

"I *have* eaten," Mr Locke nudged his food around the plate with his knife and fork. "See?"

Dr Locke strode over and compared what was left to what she'd put on his plate. He'd clearly made a valiant effort, but she needed him to eat more, still. The article in *The Era* had only highlighted further the urgency of him returning to full health. Taking his fork from him, she stabbed a piece of kidney with it and held it to his lips. "A few more bites."

Mr Locke's lips curled in disgust as he looked at the morsel. "I cannot, Lynette. Please. I shall vomit if I do."

Claude's arms suddenly slid under Mr Locke's and pulled them back, causing him to drop his knife. Mr Locke immediately shot his wife a wide-eyed, pleading look whilst trying to wriggle free. "I *cannot*, Lynette!"

A pained expression passed over Dr Locke's face as she gripped and lifted her husband's nose, forcing him to lean his head back. When he clamped his mouth shut, she tightly pinched his nasal passages and waited. Within moments, his oxygen-starved body compelled him to take a large gulp of air. At which point, Dr Locke shoved in the piece of kidney before clamping his chin with her hand to prevent him from spitting it out.

"Swallow," she ordered.

Mr Locke panted hard through his nose but complied, nonetheless.

Dr Locke stabbed another piece of kidney with the fork and held it to her husband's lips. "Again."

This time, Mr Locke accepted the morsel without coercion, albeit with a small gag.

Dr Locke presented a third piece of kidney to his lips. "Again."

Mr Locke took the morsel and, fighting against his gag reflex, swallowed it whole.

Dr Locke tossed the fork onto the plate with a clatter. In a voice strained by emotion, she said, "I *despise* doing this, Percy, but you give me no choice." She gave a curt nod to Claude, who immediately released her husband. To the latter, she said, "I expect you to do better at luncheon."

"I will, I promise," Mr Locke said feebly, unable to meet her gaze.

FOUR

Mr Morris Thurston pushed his brass-rimmed spectacles up his nose whilst keeping his gaze fixed upon Miss Mina Ilbert. Sat before her desk, he reclined against the low backrest of his chair but immediately sat forward. With his elbows upon his knees, he clasped his hands before his face as he darted his hazel eyes between the script on the desk and Miss Ilbert's expression.

In his mid-thirties, Mr Thurston was approximately five feet five inches tall with a slim build. His triangular-shaped nose dominated his oval-shaped face, whilst his naturally narrow eyebrows were barely visible behind his spectacles. Gifted with a high forehead, the line of his chocolate-brown hair was uninterrupted against his skin. A cream tie with a dark-gold floral print hung loosely around the stiffly starched Eaton collar of his white shirt. His mud-coloured jacket was faded at the edges and largely hid his dark-brown cotton waistcoat from view.

He gestured erratically at the script when he saw the blue pencil in her hand. "It *is* finished." When she proceeded to cross out some dialogue, he added, "*My* draft of it." He shuffled forward in his chair and, lowering his head, kept his gaze upon her as he held up his open palms. "Now, the story of the Red Barn Murder is well known, I grant you. But I *promise* you, Mr Van Cartier's 'interpretation' at the Cabbage cannot show itself to *mine*. Why, his Captain Macfluffer was *beyond* belief and—"

"I shall form my own opinion, thank you."

Mr Thurston repeatedly nodded as he clasped and unclasped his hands before his face. "Y-Yes. I know." He clasped his hands tightly and leant forward with a contrived smile. "I *bow* to your theatrical prowess, Miss Ilbert."

"I am not a blowsa-bella, Mr Thurston. Nor was I born with a sneer. I simply know what I like and, by joyful happenstance, what *I* like is also liked by our darling patrons."

In her early forties, Miss Ilbert had flowing, shoulder-length, golden-blond hair loosely pinned back from her face. Her striking blue eyes could pierce a man's heart with a single look and condemn a fool by the same measure. Her red-velvet bustle dress followed the contours of her corseted torso perfectly as her golden jewellery glinted in the gaslight. Superficial characteristics aside, she was also a formidable businesswoman. Within a year of becoming its lead actress and manageress, she'd turned around the fortunes of the *Crescent Theatre*, Strand, London—much to her critics' disappointment. To Mr Thurston's mind, it was little wonder the theatre had become a success under her leadership. As the theatre's prompter and super master, he'd seen firsthand how the 'Lily of the Lyceum' had tamed the actors' unpredictable, artistic temperaments. She had also ensured others who worked in the microcosm society of the theatre knew their worth. Furthermore, their worth was not only understood but appreciated by the management.

Holding his tongue to allow her to read in silence, Mr Thurston ran his gaze over his surroundings. Miss Ilbert's office was on the theatre's ground floor and was linked to both the foyer and backstage areas by a corridor. When standing at the door to the office, Miss Ilbert's desk was directly opposite, facing inward, with a window behind. It was littered with piles of documents, including play manuscripts, account ledgers, and promotional postcards of Miss Ilbert in her pantomime fairy queen costume. A small wooden clock sat on the desk's edge, facing Miss Ilbert. On either side of the clock was an ornate brass inkstand and pen and a small vase containing flowers purchased at the Covent Garden market.

A bookcase filled with play manuscripts, play bills, musical scores, costume designs, past copies of *The Era* newspaper, and numerous literary works was within reach of Miss Ilbert's desk on the left side of the room. As Mr

Thurston shifted his gaze from its shelves to the wall behind, he was surprised to see mauve-coloured wallpaper with an intricately painted white floral design. Despite his many visits to this office, he'd never noticed it, but was pleased he had now, for it was very handsome.

Pushing his spectacles back up his nose, he turned his head to regard the rest of the room. In the corner directly to the right of the door was a smaller desk belonging to the theatre's business manager, Miss Emmaline Kimberly. Sitting upon it was a Salter 5 typewriter, inkwell, and pen, and an unused pile of paper. A hat stand containing both ladies' coats, hats, and umbrellas was directly to the right of the door. All the furniture was made from dark wood to match the varnished floorboards.

Mr Thurston checked the time on his pocket watch and considered leaving Miss Ilbert to her reading. He dismissed the idea as soon as it had appeared, though. If it was this agonising to wait for her to finish reading his play when he could see her, the agony would be tenfold if he couldn't. Shifting within his chair to get comfortable, he resigned himself to passing the time any way he could, including counting the flowers on the wallpaper.

Thirty long minutes came and went.

Finally, Miss Ilbert closed and put down his manuscript.

Mr Thurston held his breath. Two years' work rested on this moment.

All at once, Miss Ilbert's mouth turned upward in a closed-lipped smile, her features lifted, and she released a brief yet gentle hum as she ran her hands and gaze over the manuscript's cover.

"It is wonderful, Mr Thurston." Her smile grew with the parting of her lips. "The tragedy of the tale leaps from the page and into my breast. The humanity betwixt the words and characters leads me by the hand down the story's twisting road."

Mr Thurston stared at her, stunned, as his wildest hope came hurtling into reality. Naturally, he'd imagined this conversation numerous times, but which writer does not pray for their work to be praised by those they admire most? Unable to fully comprehend the situation, he spoke before considering his words: "The story is in the barn."

Miss Ilbert put her hand upon his clasped ones and gently teased, "You look like I have insulted your mother."

Mr Thurston sat bolt upright with wide eyes. "Oh no. No. Not at all, Miss Ilbert." He gave a feeble smile. "It is simply... always I had *hoped* but never did I *believe* you would give my work such high praise."

"It merited it." Miss Ilbert looked down at the manuscript, again, as her gaze turned inward to a rapidly forming vision of it on stage. "This will be our little theatre's next production."

"After the pantomime's run, you mean?"

Miss Ilbert stood, prompting Mr Thurston to do the same. "Yes. Provided the play is permitted by the Lord Chamberlain, of course." She returned the script to him. "I've made a few necessary alterations and annotations. Please implement them and ensure the leading part is given more dialogue. I want to read the revised draft in the morning before rehearsals so it may be submitted to the Lord Chamberlain as soon as possible."

"Certainly."

Miss Ilbert glanced at the clock as she plucked a well-thumbed script from the pile. "We shall discuss the details of reparation another time." She strode around the desk and allowed Mr Thurston to open the door for her as she enquired after the extra cast members, "Have the supers arrived?"

"They are in the auditorium."

"Good."

As they entered the corridor, Miss Kimberly stepped forward to greet them with some letters in her hand. In her damaged, husky voice, she said, "This morning's post, Mina."

Approximately five feet eight inches tall, Miss Kimberly had curly, brownish-red hair pinned atop her head in a tight bun. At forty-one, she was Miss Ilbert's junior by two years. Her attire of a fitted, dark-green cotton jacket with matching bustle skirts over a black, high-necked blouse complemented the forest green of her eyes.

"Thank you, Emma." Taking the first of the letters, Miss Ilbert tore open its envelope and read its contents. Dictating a brief response to Miss Kimberly, who swiftly transcribed it in shorthand, Miss Ilbert returned the letter to her and repeated the process with each of the remaining correspondence.

Whilst the two conducted their business, Mr Thurston couldn't help but revel in the memory of Miss Ilbert's praise. The arrival of Miss Kimberly had also caused his heart to swell further. To him, her beauty was unsurpassed, even by Miss Ilbert.

"Good morning, Miss Kimberly," he warmly greeted.

"Mr Thurston." Miss Kimberly replied in a formal tone. "A telegram for you, Mina."

Miss Ilbert accepted the telegram, read it, and slipped it into the script.

Miss Kimberly referred to her notebook. "The wardrobe mistress would like to speak to you about the supers' fairy costumes, and Mr Akers has written to confirm he and his assistant will be here this evening as you proposed."

"Please tell Mrs Hightower we shall have our discussion after the super rehearsal," Miss Ilbert said.

Miss Kimberly noted the instruction. "Luncheon at two?"

"*Please*." Miss Ilbert had been working since dawn, but there was still a considerable amount to do. Sustenance was a necessity, but its arrangement was a luxury she could ill-afford. "Could you—?"

"Our usual table by the window?" Miss Kimberly interrupted in a knowing tone.

"If possible," Miss Ilbert replied.

"I placed the reservation this morning," Miss Kimberly said.

Miss Ilbert's features lifted. "*Wonderful*!"

The ladies embraced.

Keeping her hands upon Miss Kimberly's upper arms as she looked lovingly into her eyes, Miss Ilbert enquired, "*Where* would I be without you, Emma?"

"In the super rehearsal," Miss Kimberly reminded her.

Miss Ilbert released her. "Indeed!" She strode down the corridor. "Mr Thurston!"

The moment she was out of sight, the rigidity left Miss Kimberly's face, and she gazed upon Mr Thurston with great fondness. "Are we dining tonight, still?"

"Nothing would give me greater pleasure." Mr Thurston kissed her knuckle.

"Nor I." Miss Kimberly agreed, her eyes shining with delight. "I look forward to hearing all about your meeting with Mina."

"Mr Thurston!" Miss Ilbert called in the distance.

"Yes, Miss Ilbert!" Mr Thurston kissed Miss Kimberly upon the cheek and hurried after their employer.

* * *

Mr Locke's feet scraped the ground as he ambled along the dirt path that ran the length of the narrow garden at the rear of his house. The heat escaped his sweltering core in the form of a bright-red complexion sheened with sweat, whilst his breathing came in short, sharp puffs. Putting almost all his weight upon his wife's arm, he used the ebony walking cane in his other hand to maintain his balance. Feeling his lower legs growing heavier with each step, he fixed his gaze upon the bench at the end of the path and resolved to reach it.

"Once more around the garden," Dr Locke instructed.

"*No*," Mr Locke insisted with a gasp, shaking his head. "Sit. I must… sit."

Dr Locke noticed he'd begun to drag his feet and so guided him to the bench. "Can you manage?"

"I believe so." Mr Locke shuffled around until he felt the cold wood at the back of his knees. Gripping his wife's arm and his cane to maintain his balance, he dropped onto the bench with a loud grunt and immediately reclined against its backrest. He closed his eyes and took a few moments to allow his breathing to slow and the fire in his lungs to weaken. Pulling his handkerchief from his pocket, he mopped his brow and pressed it against each cheek in turn.

Dr Locke sat beside him and reached over to loosen his cravat. He pushed her hand aside, however, and snapped, "Leave me be for *one* moment, Lynette."

Dr Locke withdrew her hands as her face adopted a pinched expression. "Very well." She moved away from him to sit rigidly upon the corner of the bench, facing the garden.

Closing his eyes, Mr Locke took a deep, pained breath whilst pinching the bridge of his nose. "Darling, *please*." He dropped his hand to his lap and stared at the back of her head, waiting for any hint of a response. When none came, he lowered his gaze to his hands and absently rubbed his wrist as he said in a quiet voice, "I apologise. I know you were only trying to help. It is simply, at times, I feel as though you are only my doctor and," his voice cracked with emotion as he finished, "my wife no longer."

Dr Locke's shoulders stiffened. In a calm, yet adamant tone, she stated, "When you cease being only my patient, I will cease being only your doctor." She stood and offered him her arm. "It's time to go inside."

Mr Locke gripped his cane between his knees and, slumping forward, rested his full weight upon it. Not daring to look at her for fear his tears would fall, he watched a rat scurrying across a flower bed opposite instead.

A pained expression passed over Dr Locke's face as she swallowed her hurt and anger at his perceived ungratefulness. "Stay out here, then. *Freeze* to death to spite me."

"You know I did not mean–" Mr Locke began, his voice breaking with emotion.

"You haven't meant many things, Percy. Yet we are still picking up the pieces." She turned her back to hide her trembling lips. "I've an appointment this morning." *To save your theatre,* she thought. "I'll be home by luncheon." She hurried away. "Claude will keep you company."

Mr Locke's vision blurred with tears the moment he heard the back door slam.

FIVE

"I shall *not* be *silenced*!"

Hearing the yell as he neared the corridor's end, Mr Thurston recognised the male voice at once. His suspicions were confirmed when, upon entering the foyer, he saw the Reverend Ananias Mullins. The Church of England clergyman was in his early sixties with bushy whiskers and receding yet wavy hair, both of which were salt and pepper in colour. The top edges of his black cassock and white collar were the only parts of his attire visible beneath his ankle-length black coat. He stood with his legs planted wide, one behind the other, as he thrust out his chest and clutched a sheet of paper before Miss Ilbert's face. There was a tightness in the corners of his hard eyes as, with a reddened face and high chin, he stepped into Miss Ilbert's personal space and declared, "Woe to those who scheme iniquity, who work out evil on their beds!"

Miss Ilbert jerked her head back at the sudden intrusion but immediately resumed her stiff stance. Narrowing her eyes, she projected her voice as she commanded, "That is *quite* enough, Reverend. I shall not be intimidated or insulted in my own theatre." She looked past Reverend Ananias at the young male ticket office clerk. "Nor shall I permit you to intimidate my employees." Her gaze hardened as it returned to Reverend Ananias. "This is the third time this week we've had the *displeasure* of your company, and it will be the last. Even saints were human once, and I, like they, have reached the limit of my patience." Miss Ilbert stepped forward, obliging Reverend Ananias to retract his front leg and place it beside the other. "You, sir, are an intolerant zealot who has no right to call himself a man of God."

Reverend Ananias' face flushed a darker shade of red. "And *you*, Miss, are a vile *harlot*!" Returning swiftly to her personal space, he brandished the sheet of paper in her face so ferociously, it struck her several times. "*You have corrupted every young man at Hampstead School!*"

Miss Ilbert lifted an arm to defend herself whilst turning away abruptly. Striding from the foyer and into the auditorium in the vain hope Reverend Ananias may leave, she sighed upon hearing him rush after her. Spinning around to face him, thereby halting him in his tracks, she thrust her arm past his shoulder and pointed at the doors they'd passed through. "*Leave* now, or I shall have you removed!"

"You may toss me asunder, but God shall not be so easily defeated!" Reverend Ananias warned. "He will strike down the wicked, and *you* are the *wickedest* creature I have ever known! Your seduction of these boys, through your *evil* spectacle of *iniquity* thinly disguised as 'art' shan't go unpunished! For the lips of a harlot are like a honeycomb dropping, and her throat is smoother than oil. But her end is bitter as wormwood, and sharp as a two-edged sword. Her feet go down into death, and her steps go in as far as hell."

"Is there a problem, Mina?" a male voice casually enquired behind Miss Ilbert.

"No," Miss Ilbert curtly replied. "Please, return to your duties, Mr Stone."

Mr Ronald Stone looked to Mr Thurston who indicated Reverend Ananias with his eyes. The super master and prompter stood behind the clergyman and was therefore out of his eyeline.

"At *once*, Mr Stone," Miss Ilbert demanded, casting a glare at him over her shoulder.

Mr Stone was in his late forties with deep set, dark-blue eyes, and thick, black hair. Approximately five feet eight inches tall, his attire consisted of a dark-grey double-breasted suit with a matching waistcoat, white shirt, and dark-red bowtie. A smile danced across his lips as he stood beside Miss Ilbert. "I think my duty lies with you." He turned his head to address Reverend Ananias directly, "I'm

Mr Ronnie Stone, the stage manager here at the *Crescent Theatre*. What seems to be the problem, Reverend?"

Reverend Ananias strode forward and gave him the sheet of paper. "I discovered Master Granville Norton, a scholar at Hampstead School where I preach, writing this filth in the library when he ought to have been at prayers."

Mr Stone began to read the letter but Miss Ilbert abruptly cut him short, snatching it from him. Smirking as he allowed his arms to fall naturally to his sides, he relished the look of utter irritation in Miss Ilbert's eyes as she turned away and read the letter.

"This is a harmless expression of his admiration for my acting ability, Reverend," Miss Ilbert dismissed once she'd finished. Tossing the letter at him, she added, "I get many more like it every week. Whilst I do not solicit such attention—"

Mr Stone gave a soft "humph."

Miss Ilbert shot him a fierce look. "I appreciate the recognition of my talent and hard work."

"There is a simple solution to all this." Mr Stone picked up the letter and handed it to Reverend Ananias. "I'll have all young men removed from the stage door." There was a hint of sarcasm in his voice as he enquired, "You don't object, do you, Mina?"

"Not at all, Ronald," Miss Ilbert replied in a derisive tone, knowing he disliked his first name being uttered in full.

Mr Stone's features tightened as spots of colour entered his cheeks. Turning his back upon her, he enquired, "Are you satisfied now, Reverend?"

"No," Reverend Ananias replied, firmly.

Miss Ilbert momentarily bowed her head as she supressed her amusement.

"They are prohibited from entering this theatre by the headmaster of Hampstead School, and he expects his orders to be obeyed," Reverend Ananias stated. "As do I."

Mr Stone gave a weak laugh. "We couldn't possibly deny entry to every young man who comes to our doors, Reverend. We'd be bankrupt within the month."

"And the world would be rid of another den of iniquity," Reverend Ananias said.

"But—" Mr Stone began.

"Would you not prefer the boys to be safely inside the theatre where there is a police constable?" Miss Ilbert enquired from Reverend Ananias. "All manner of things could befall them on the streets."

Mr Stone gave Miss Ilbert a sideways scowl. "Such as meeting a prostitute."

Reverend Ananias drew his head back quickly as his eyebrows rose and his eyes widened. "These are mere *boys* of *sixteen*, Mr Stone!"

Mr Stone gave a one-sided shoulder shrug. "I was fourteen when I found the pleasures of the flesh—"

"For the one who sows to his own flesh will from the flesh reap corruption! *You* are as *corrupt* as *she*!" Reverend Ananias pointed at Miss Ilbert. "And I have had all I can stomach of this wicked, *vile* place!" He strode from the theatre, slamming the auditorium door against the wall as he did so.

Miss Ilbert turned fierce eyes upon Mr Stone. "To my office! *At once*!"

* * *

Inspector Lee held the cup close to his lips to take intermittent sips of tea whilst studying a mass of documents. Affixed to the wall of his office at Scotland Yard, they included reports, statements, photographs, and newspaper articles. The contents of each related to the Bow Street Society in some way. On a separate wall were the typed biographies of the known Bow Street Society members based upon what he, Inspector Woolfe, and Sergeant Gutman had discovered thus far.

His gaze shifted to Dr Weeks' biography. He'd

intentionally hidden the truth about the Canadian's parentage from his colleagues to maintain his hold over the surgeon. Yet, the state he'd seen him in earlier gave him cause for concern. Inspector Lee had been entering his private carriage outside the Society's house when he'd caught sight of Dr Weeks leaving the police station. Dr Weeks' dishevelled clothes and troubled demeanour hinted at an internal conflict potentially connected to Inspector Lee's blackmail. The only other possibility was Dr Weeks was concerned for Inspector Conway following his reassignment. Either way, Inspector Lee thought Dr Weeks looked close to breaking point. If the worst were to happen, Inspector Lee needed to be in a position to extinguish the flames of turmoil before they could spread.

Inspector Lee set down his cup and turned to Detective Sergeant Ethan Gutman. His subordinate occupied a smaller desk in the darkest corner of the office. "I want you to keep Dr Weeks under surveillance. His membership of the Bow Street Society and close friendship with Inspector Conway makes him a risk to our security and reputation."

"Yes, sir." Sergeant Gutman glanced at the clock on the wall. "Now, sir?"

In his late twenties, Sergeant Gutman was clean-shaven with neat, dark-brown hair and brown, almost tan, coloured eyes. His attire consisted of a shop-bought dark-green suit with matching tie and white shirt. It was a million miles away from his undercover garb and even his sergeant's uniform.

"When we're finished here." Inspector Lee picked up his teacup and resumed his study of the information on the wall. "Has your search of the police records yielded any new results?"

"Not yet, sir, but Mr Hargreaves keeps on at it."

It was a tremendous task—searching the Metropolitan Police Force's entire archive for the smallest mention of the Bow Street Society and its members—so Inspector Lee wasn't surprised that progress was slow. He hoped the list of known members they'd sent to the divisional stations across London (apart from Bow Street) would yield better results.

His gaze drifted to Dr Colbert's biography. He'd had no contact with the mole in weeks, partially due to making himself intentionally unavailable, and partially due—he suspected—to Inspector Woolfe's influence. He had recruited Dr Colbert, after all. The fact remained Inspector Lee needed the details of the Bow Street Society's bank account, however, and only Dr Colbert could get them. From the list of depositors, Inspector Lee could identify the likeliest suspects for Miss Trent's mysterious employer. Anything Dr Colbert may see or hear during his visits to the Bow Street Society may further add to the picture, too. Thus, whether Inspector Woolfe approved of it or not, Inspector Lee intended to rebuild his bridges with Dr Colbert.

Drinking the remainder of his tea, he set the cup aside and turned his thoughts to the morning's meeting with Miss Trent and Mr Elliott. She had been as formidable as ever, and he as attractive. Despite his best efforts, Inspector Lee often found himself thinking of the man. A passing thought here, a recalled memory there. They never lasted long, but their frequency had increased since he'd put Mr Elliott under surveillance by a Mob Squad detective. He'd put many of the other Society members under surveillance, too, but none had fascinated him as much as Mr Elliott. Picking up the detective's report into Mr Elliott's background, he read it with interest.

The detective could find no trace of any relatives, leading him to suspect Mr Elliott was either an orphan or had become estranged from his parents and any siblings some time ago. Mr Elliott's legal practise appeared to consume his every waking hour. Furthermore, he appeared to have no friends beyond his fellow Bow Street Society members, and the detective had found nothing to suggest he was romantically connected to anyone. In short, Mr Elliott's existence appeared to be a rather dull one.

Until Inspector Lee neared the end of the report. In its last few lines was the revelation the detective had discovered whilst making discreet enquiries with Mr Elliott's small army of legal clerks. One of them, a Mr Warner, had given the name of a clerk who'd left Mr Elliott's employment under murky circumstances. Mr Warner was unable to provide further details, except it had occurred at most two years ago. Mr Elliott also forbade any of them who'd known the clerk to utter his name in his presence.

"Fetch Caulfield," Inspector Lee instructed.

"Yes, sir."

Sergeant Gutman left the room, returning with their colleague a short while later.

In his early twenties, Sergeant Aiden Caulfield had short, dark-brown hair and wide, round, brown eyes. His attire consisted of a cheaply made, yet impeccably kept, dark-grey cotton suit and tie and cream shirt. Having requested reassignment to the Mob Squad at A Division following his promotion from constable, he'd been delighted to work for Inspector Conway. When Inspector Conway was reassigned himself, though, Sergeant Caulfield's request to be reassigned with him had been refused. It had left a bitter taste in his mouth, evident in his pinched expression as he stood before Inspector Lee. Unlike his previous senior officer, he had little to no respect for the new head of the Mob Squad.

"You are to learn the whereabouts of a Mr Homer Fairbairn," Inspector Lee began. "He's aged approximately twenty-five. His last known employment was as a legal clerk at Mr Gregory Elliott's law firm." Inspector Lee wrote down these and the remaining details about Mr Fairbairn from the detective's report before offering the sheet of paper to Sergeant Caulfield. "Inform me as soon as you have them."

Sergeant Caulfield's jaw visibly clenched at the order. Aware he could be charged with insubordination if he refused, though, he took the piece of paper and slipped it into his notebook. "Yes. Sir."

"You may go," Inspector Lee dismissed him with a wave of his hand.

Sergeant Gutman smirked as he watched Sergeant Caulfield leave the room. *Serves him right for supporting a traitor,* he thought.

Inspector Lee's thoughts had already moved on, however. "The Bow Street Society refused our proposal, as we knew they would." He referred to his list of plain-clothed Mob Squad detectives. "Who is between assignments at present?"

Sergeant Gutman peered over Inspector Lee's shoulder at the names. "Sergeant Jude Perry, sir."

"Introduce him to the owner of the shop opposite the Bow Street Society's house and station him in the front bedroom as agreed."

Sergeant Gutman collected his things from the hat stand.

"Then commence your surveillance of Dr Weeks."

"Yes, sir—oh, who would you like to check in with Sergeant Perry?"

"I'll make the necessary arrangements, just get him in there as soon as possible."

Sergeant Gutman grinned. "Yes, *sir*!"

SIX

Miss Ilbert strode into her office and turned abruptly, thereby obliging Mr Stone to take a sudden step back. She pointed at him, her fingertip close to his nose. "You were *deliberately* trying to provoke him." She lowered her hand but continued to glare at him.

Mr Stone's mouth twisted into an ugly sneer. "Reverend Ananias is an old fool."

"That 'old fool' could pour his lies into the ear of a journalist on Fleet Street, and my theatre would be in the newspapers for all the *wrong* reasons."

"And the people who condemn us over their toast and marmalade would be the same people queuing up for our next performance." Mr Stone pulled back the chair before her desk and sat. "People love a scandal." He lounged upon the chair and lit a cigarette. "My theatre thrived on the tripe written about it."

"Not in the end, it didn't," Miss Ilbert muttered under her breath as she went behind her desk and sat.

"What did you say?" Mr Stone had heard it clearly enough but wanted to see if she had the gall to repeat it.

"I said 'not in the end, it didn't.' But there wasn't much of a theatre left, was there?"

Mr Stone took a pull from his cigarette but kept it close to his lips as he exhaled the smoke. "I lost everything in the fire."

Miss Ilbert averted her gaze. "I know."

"And I'm 'grateful' for what you did for me, Mina," he said with a sardonic edge to his tone. Taking another pull from his cigarette, he slowly exhaled the smoke. "Out of the 'kindness' of your heart."

"My kindness has limits," Miss Ilbert warned. Hearing a knock on the door, she called, "Yes, what is it?"

The door opened, and an eighteen-year-old woman poked her head into the room. She was approximately five feet six inches tall with shoulder-length mousy-brown hair parted in the centre. Her attire consisted of a midnight-blue V-necked jacket with black A-line skirts. Beneath the jacket was a plain, midnight-blue blouse. She darted her light-brown eyes from Miss Ilbert to Mr Stone and back again. "Forgive me, Miss Ilbert, I didn't know you were with Mr Stone."

"We've finished our discussion," Miss Ilbert stated. "What is it, Joanna?"

Mr Stone stubbed out his cigarette against its case and slipped both into his pockets as he stood. "*Quite* finished." He approached the door and waited for Miss Joanna Hightower to hurry inside before leaving.

"Mother has sent me to fetch you," Miss Hightower replied once they were alone.

"The super rehearsal is first." Miss Ilbert joined her by the door. "I'll be along to speak to your mother about wardrobe afterward."

"Yes, she knows, Miss Ilbert, but she said it mustn't wait because she cannot continue with her work until she has an answer from you."

Miss Ilbert pursed her lips and released a deep breath through her nose. "Very well. Come along."

* * *

"I'm afraid there isn't anything to tell, Inspector," Dr Neal Colbert admitted.

"No new cases?" Inspector Woolfe enquired.

They stood amongst a cluster of dense bushes at the rear of Bethlehem Hospital. The wet and cold conditions meant the patients were restricted to the indoor areas. Consequently, Dr Colbert and Inspector Woolfe were alone in the grounds.

"Not since the Grosse case." Dr Colbert studied the bruises in the middle of Inspector Woolfe's face. "Speaking of which, how is your nose?"

"Sore."

They continued their walk along the grounds' periphery.

"But healing without complication, I hope?" At only five feet seven inches tall, Dr Colbert was obliged to tilt his head to look Inspector Woolfe in the eye. His dark-blond eyebrows were also drawn together, whilst his chocolate-brown eyes mirrored the concern in his voice.

"Don't fuss over me, doctor," Inspector Woolfe warned, punctuated with a cough.

"Forgive me. It's a professional habit of mine."

In his early thirties, Dr Colbert's appearance bore the signs of his overnight shift at the asylum. He'd roughly combed his dark-blond hair with his fingers and smoothed down his split dark-blond moustache with a thumb immediately prior to greeting Inspector Woolfe at the entrance. His off-white shirt, black waistcoat and tie, and frockcoat were also dishevelled, whilst dark bags marred his eyes.

"Have you got the name and address of the bank where the Society's account is?" Inspector Woolfe enquired, recalling the conversation he'd had with Dr Colbert and Inspector Lee back in December.

Dr Colbert tilted his head down and frowned. "No. The opportunity hasn't presented itself without searching Miss Trent's office."

Inspector Woolfe recalled Dr Colbert's account of finding Dr Weeks in the same room. He'd used the words 'trying to open the desk,' meaning it was likely she kept the desk locked. Therefore, a casual search was not only dangerous but liable to fail. "Too risky. Tell her you want to make a donation to the Society and need the name and address of its bank to make the deposit. You've earned her trust with your work on the Grosse case, so she'll give them to you."

"I'll try it." Dr Colbert slowed as they came to the front of the hospital. "To whom should I give the information? You or Inspector Lee?"

"Me." Inspector Woolfe lowered his voice. "Don't tell Inspector Lee anything."

Dr Colbert halted mid-stride. "Why not?"

Inspector Woolfe faced him as he also halted. "We're not working together anymore."

"Yes, I presumed as much, but why?"

"It doesn't matter," Inspector Woolfe growled.

"I've risked my life and my reputation becoming a member of the Bow Street Society," Dr Colbert firmly reminded him. "I have a right to know if the men I am working for are in conflict."

"Just do what I've asked, doctor," Inspector Woolfe snapped, the force of emotion in his voice bringing on a coughing fit immediately after. Turning away as his face went red from the strain, he released a growl as soon as he caught his breath.

Dr Colbert watched the spectacle with pursed lips and a knitted brow.

"*I'm* the one you come to with any new information," Inspector Woolfe stated in a gruff voice. "That's all you need to know."

"So be it." Dr Colbert indicated Inspector Woolfe's chest. "How long have you had the cough for?"

Inspector Woolfe sniffed hard, cleared his throat, and sniffed again. "A few weeks."

"Come inside." Dr Colbert turned toward the building.

Inspector Woolfe narrowed his eyes. "What for?"

Dr Colbert looked over his shoulder. "I want to examine you."

"I told you not to fuss over me," Inspector Woolfe growled.

"And I told you I want to examine you," Dr Colbert said, firmly. "Inside, please."

Inspector Woolfe glared at him but, when Dr Colbert didn't so much as blink under his gaze, he muttered a curse and entered the asylum ahead of him.

* * *

"I don't want to be told problems, Mr Cokes, but solutions," Dr Locke said as she paced the floor of his office, changing directions multiple times. With one arm holding her stomach, she kept her head turned away whilst her fingertips rubbed her forehead.

Mr Natan Cokes was in his early fifties with thick dark-grey hair, narrow whiskers, and alert light-blue eyes. Attired in a burgundy frockcoat over a white shirt, burgundy tie, and burgundy waistcoat with gold embroidered roses, he looked every inch the showman he was. For the past three months, he had been the business manager at the *Paddington Palladium*, however. It was a personal favour to the Lockes, with whom he had been friends for many years. His gaze followed Dr Locke from behind his desk. "Percy at the top of the bill *is* the solution, Lynette."

Dr Locke gave a curt shake of her head. "Quite out of the question."

Mr Cokes indicated *The Era* newspaper she'd thrown onto his desk upon her arrival. "As unpalatable as this is, it's the truth. People come to the *Paddington Palladium* to witness astonishing magical feats by the Great Locke. Without him, it's just another mediocre theatre."

"We pay you to ensure it isn't." Dr Locke glared at him but continued to pace.

"Yes, but, unlike Percy, *I'm* not a magician."

"You aren't amusing."

"And I'm not trying to be." Mr Cokes stood and moved around the desk to intercept her as she passed. "If this theatre is to survive, it *needs* the Great Locke."

Dr Locke pressed her fingertips against her forehead as she bowed her head. "No."

"He could announce the acts, introduce and end each show—"

Dr Locke's head shot up. "I said *no*." Her hard, unblinking eyes bore into him. "Percy is *not* to set *foot* upon this stage until *I* allow it. Do you understand?"

"Yes, but—"

"Then it's settled." Dr Locke tossed *The Era* newspaper into the fire. "I expect to see a swift increase in takings, Mr Cokes." She met his concerned gaze with a stern one. "Or it will be *you* seeking employment in that rag's classified pages."

Mr Cokes returned to his seat with a deep sigh. "I'll do my best, Lynette."

Perceiving the sincerity in his voice, Dr Locke immediately felt ashamed of her behaviour. This was swiftly followed by a sense of despair as she realised how far the situation with Percy had driven her away from her former self.

"Thank you," she said, softly.

Mr Cokes lifted sympathetic eyes to her. "And be sure to tell Percy the same."

Dr Locke gave a sad smile. "I will."

* * *

Standing in the wings, Mr Thurston polished his spectacles with his handkerchief. Meanwhile, the supers—the additional actors who provide texture and numbers to a production—were conversing in groups upon the stage. Neither they nor Mr Thurston dared to proceed with the rehearsal without Miss Ilbert's presence. Spotting Mr Stone entering the auditorium, Mr Thurston put on his spectacles and hurried down the steps at the side of the stage to intersect him. "Where is Mina?"

"With Mrs Hightower." Mr Stone walked past him.

Mr Thurston side-stepped to block his path. Lowering his voice, he demanded, "What was that about earlier?"

"Just Reverend Ananias' usual ranting."

"No, I meant—"

"I *know* what you meant, Morris."

Mr Thurston lowered his voice further. "You shouldn't be so unfeeling toward Mina."

"Whyever not?" Mr Stone enquired in mock confusion.

"W-Well, she's kind, intelligent, has a marvellous business mind—"

"Vindictive. Beef-headed. Lucky," Mr Stone corrected. At the shaking of Mr Thurston's head, he challenged, "You're only defending her for the sake of your play."

"That isn't *true*."

"Yes, it is." Mr Stone smirked. "You're so readable, it's a wonder you're not a librarian."

"You're wrong." Mr Thurston lifted his chin. "She's already agreed to have it as the next production."

Mr Stone's smirk vanished.

"So, you see, my defence of her is sincere," Mr Thurston continued. "As is my recommendation you end your scheme with Mr Jerome."

Mr Stone's features tightened. "I hope you're not threatening me, Morris."

Mr Thurston stilled. "No." He gave a brittle laugh. "I wouldn't ever—"

Mr Stone moved in close, cutting him off. "If we're discovered, I'll make certain the only play *you'll* be writing is the nativity in Newgate."

Mr Thurston gave a feeble smile. "Honest, Ronnie, I didn't mean anything by it."

"I hope not." Mr Stone tightened Mr Thurston's bowtie. "For your sake."

"Mr Stone!" a woman's voice called.

When Mr Stone and Mr Thurston turned toward its general direction, they saw its owner at the doors leading into the foyer. Approximately five feet seven inches tall, she had brownish-red hair pinned tightly against her head beneath a broad-brimmed maroon hat adorned with a flourish of features, red berries, and dark-green foliage. The slenderness of her hourglass figure was accentuated by her tight corset. Her attire consisted of a high-waisted, maroon-coloured jacket with matching A-line skirts and a frilled white blouse. A dark-brown fur stole wrap was draped over her elbows and around her waist. Her ebony upturned semi-circular eyes were the most striking feature of her dainty face. With perfect diction, she enquired, "Where may I find mother?"

"In the wardrobe department, Miss Lily," Mr Stone replied, flashing her a smile.

"Thank you." Miss Lily Ilbert shifted her gaze to the other man. "Mr Thurston."

"Miss Lily," Mr Thurston greeted politely.

Once she'd returned to the foyer to take the corridor backstage, Mr Stone muttered in a lustful voice, "What I wouldn't give to have her beneath me."

Mr Thurston's jaw dropped, and he stared at Mr Stone, stunned.

"Don't forget what I said, Morris." Mr Stone smiled upon seeing his expression. He tapped his cheek. "Close your mouth, or you'll catch flies."

Mr Thurston clamped his mouth shut. After a moment to gather himself, he mumbled, "I shan't forget, Ronnie."

"Good boy."

SEVEN

Dr Weeks drank the remaining beer from his glass and set it down on the bar before Miss Polly Hicks. With his crossed ankles resting against the bar's base, his hips resting against its side, and his bent arm resting upon its top, he leant forward and lifted bloodshot eyes to meet his lover's disapproving gaze. "Get me another, darlin'."

In her late-twenties, Miss Hicks had her loosely curled, blond hair tied back from her face with a dark-brown ribbon. A mixture of soot, grime, and sweat spotted her delicate cheeks and nose, as well as her well-worn dark-brown dress. Her corset increased the curve of her waist and simultaneously compacted and lifted her breasts. Although she stood on the raised floor behind the bar, her heeled boots increased her height further. Consequently, she not only towered over Dr Weeks, but she could see the entire underground railway bar at any given point. In an East-London accent, she cooly stated, "You've already had six, and it ain't even lunchtime."

Dr Weeks nudged the glass closer. "I *said*: get me another, darlin'."

Folding her arms and audibly inhaling a long breath through her nose, she lightly poked the inside of her cheek with her tongue as she considered whether to serve him.

"Please."

Miss Hicks audibly exhaled the breath and picked up the glass. "I ain't carrying your sorry arse." Walking down the length of the bar, she met Toby by the beer barrels.

Barely five feet tall, the sixteen-year-old Pot Boy had lank, mousy-brown hair, and a disproportionate build. His comfortable lifestyle, courtesy of Miss Trent and the Bow Street Society, showed in his considerable weight gain and the healthy pink hue in his fair complexion. The group's financial generosity toward the boy was also plain to see in his new white shirt, dark-brown trousers, and sturdy boots. Using his arm to hold some empty glasses against his stomach whilst putting more on the counter beside the barrels, he glanced past Miss Hicks at Dr Weeks. "Your mate's coppin' the brewery, ain't 'e?"

"It's the only thing *he'll* be coppin' tonight," Miss Hicks said.

Toby put down the other glasses and, reaching over to the bar, picked up another. Noticing the movement out the corner of his eye, Sergeant Gutman looked up from his *Gaslight Gazette* to watch Miss Hicks and Toby whilst listening to their conversation. He'd chosen this spot to avoid making eye contact with Dr Weeks. Thus far, his judgement had proven sound, and neither Miss Hicks nor Toby had recognised him besides. Concerned the pair might sense him watching them, though, he returned his gaze to his newspaper whilst sipping his beer and keeping an ear on their conversation.

"Want me to toss 'im out?" Toby enquired.

Miss Hicks laid a gentle hand upon his cheek. "No, love."

Whilst waiting for his drink, Dr Weeks replayed Inspector Woolfe's words in his mind. This was immediately followed by a vision of Inspector Woolfe revealing the truth to Inspector Conway, and the latter's reaction. Dr Weeks had been friends with Inspector Conway for years, but he knew the sanctity of friendship wouldn't be enough to dull Inspector Conway's hurt-filled rage at the betrayal.

Pulling his shoulders in and holding his elbows tight against his chest, Dr Weeks put his head in his hands and dug his fingernails into his forehead. The visions persisted despite the pain, though. Some depicted Inspector Conway walking away from him in disappointment, whilst others depicted Inspector Conway beating him black and blue. There were even some fleeting ones wherein Dr Weeks demanded that Inspector Lee reveal himself as the true mastermind behind the diabolical plot to sully Inspector Conway's reputation. Yet, as much as Dr Weeks feared Inspector Conway's reaction, he couldn't muster the courage to risk his other shame being exposed to the world.

"This is the *last* one, love," Miss Hicks warned as she served his refreshed pint.

"Whatever ya say, darlin'," Dr Weeks mumbled, taking a large mouthful.

Miss Hicks held out her hand, prompting Dr Weeks to search his pockets.

Another feminine hand suddenly dropped the correct amount into Miss Hicks' hand, however. In a broad Canadian accent, its owner said, "Here ya are, child."

Dr Weeks stared at the middle-aged woman beside him. Taking in her dark golden-brown hair, hazel eyes, strong chin, and prominent nose, he ran his gaze over the rest of her form. Her forest-green bustle dress was largely hidden by a fitted brown cotton coat trimmed with real black bear fur, and a brown felt hat with an overabundance of berries and foliage sitting forward on her head. Her voice, face, clothes, and perfume were so familiar to him, he'd recognised them in an instant. Yet, despite this, his mind couldn't process the reality of her being before him. All he could muster was a quietly uttered, "Jesus Christ…"

Miss Hicks looked from her lover to the woman and back again. It was plain to see he knew her, but she was a stranger to Miss Hicks. A pang of jealousy erupted in her breast as she thought this woman might be one of Dr Weeks' former lovers. A glance over the woman told her she was too old, though, even for someone as well-sexed as him. Remaining intrigued and unnerved by the woman's identity, she demanded, "Ain't you going to introduce us, Perce?"

"'E's jus' a little shocked to see me, child," the woman explained with a smile. "Evangelina Breckenridge."

Miss Hicks cast a questioning look at Dr Weeks.

Miss Breckenridge followed her gaze. "Percival's mother."

* * *

"Whilst I agree the additional leaves make the skirt voluminous, their positioning shall encumber the legs when she is pirouetting," Miss Ilbert stated as she attempted to free the layers of dark-green teardrop-shaped fabric. They were caught between the knees of Miss Abigail, a super, who was modelling Mrs Hightower's latest fairy costume design. Standing on an overturned soap box within the small, square storage room that doubled as the wardrobe department, she'd held the same position for almost an hour. Feeling her feet ache, she shifted her weight from one foot to the other.

"Stop moving, or I'll prick you," Mrs Naomi Hightower warned as she folded the first layer close to its seam and pinned it. Taking a pin from the cushion strapped to the back of her hand, she repeated the process with the next layer.

The chief wardrobe mistress, to give Mrs Hightower her official title, was in her early forties with a slender build, mousey-brown hair pinned into a bun atop her crown, and dark-brown eyes. Her attire was understated considering her profession: an unembellished chocolate-brown dress with long sleeves and high, rounded collar. As she moved around the soap box, the hem of her A-line skirts brushed against the floor, gathering dust.

Whilst her mother and Miss Ilbert had their discussion, Miss Joanna Hightower tidied the fabric table. Hearing the gentle creak of the door nearby, she did a double take upon seeing Jack Jerome's hazel eyes peering through the gap. They had a mischievous twinkle in them, whilst his large, close-lipped smile caused their corners to wrinkle. Glancing at her mother to find her deep in conversation with Miss Ilbert, still, Miss Hightower slipped from the room and closed the door.

"*Jack!*" she cried in a whisper, "You're not allowed back here."

Mr Jerome's smile grew as he rested his large hands upon her waist. His abundant, dark-brown, curly hair, with sun-bleached blond highlights, prevented his brown bowler hat from sitting flush against his skull. In a broad, Birmingham accent, he explained, "Oy missed yow, didn't oy? Give us a kiss."

Miss Hightower giggled as he kissed her neck. "Stop it."

Mr Jerome kissed the opposite side of her neck. "But yow like eet so."

"Mother is in there." She pinched his bowler hat and put it on. "What do you think?"

Mr Jerome chuckled. "Eet's too big for yow." He took it back and put it on. "When can oy see yow, eef not now?"

"Tonight, after the show."

The initiation of a song from Miss Lily drew their attention to the stage. Although she was hidden from view by the scenery, the rapt gazes of the supers they could see alluded to her position. Mr Jerome and Miss Hightower listened for a few moments before the former briefly touched the latter's cheek to get her attention. When he had it, he softly enquired, "Ees old man Benton 'ere this after?"

Miss Hightower averted her gaze. "I don't know."

"Yow sure?"

Miss Hightower gave him a feeble smile. "Why wouldn't I be?"

"Joanna!" Mr Stone called from a short distance away.

Miss Hightower's heart leapt into her throat at the sight of him. "Yes, Mr Stone?"

Mr Stone strode over. "Who is this?" He glared at Mr Jerome. "Who are you?"

"A friend, sir," Miss Hightower replied. "Who's leaving. Aren't you, Jack?"

Mr Jerome grinned. "Yeah."

"Get back to work," Mr Stone ordered, prompting Miss Hightower to immediately return to the wardrobe department. Once alone with Mr Jerome, he moved to stand before him and lowered his voice. "You're *early*. Mr Benton isn't due to arrive until five."

Mr Jerome continued to grin. "Don't worry, Ronnie. oy know my business." He tipped his hat. "Tarar-a-bit."

Mr Stone's glare bore into Mr Jerome's back as he walked away toward the stage door. Yet, Mr Jerome didn't increase his pace beyond a leisurely stroll. Paranoid the arrogant lad might put on a show of leaving so he could slip back to Miss Hightower, Mr Stone followed him. After watching him leave via the stage door as promised, he double bolted it and returned to the backstage area.

"Sing the one about the girl with the golden hair," Mr Stone heard a super call out just as he was passing the rear of the scenery.

"Yes!" a second super cried. "*Please*, Miss Lily!"

Mr Stone emerged from the wings to see Miss Lily standing before the small audience of supers kneeling upon the stage. Mr Thurston, beyond them, sat up upon seeing Mr Stone. Mr Thurston watched Mr Stone closely as he retrieved a stool from the wings and sat within a few feet of the group. Recalling Mr Stone's earlier remark about Miss Lily, Mr Thurston felt anxious on her behalf, but his sense of self-preservation overrode any desire to protect her. Instead wishing to avoid Mr Stone, he made himself appear smaller by leaning forward, pressing his elbows against his sides, and turning his shoulders inward.

Moving her arms as if she were a swan spreading its wings, Miss Lily leant to the right and sang in a mezzo-soprano operatic style. "There was once a country maiden came to London for a trip, and her golden hair was hanging down her back." She leant to the left and put the knuckles of her right hand against her forehead. "She was weary of the country, so she gave her folks the slip," she switched sides and hands, "and her golden hair was hanging down her back."

Mr Stone opened his legs slightly, his gaze trailing over her feminine form, as she centred herself and swept her hand across her brownish-red hair. She sang, "It was once a vivid auburn, but her rivals called it red, so she thought she could be happier with another shade instead." She exaggerated her movements as she tiptoed across the stage. "And she stole the washing soda," she stopped and made a rubbing motion with her hands close to, but not against, her hair, "and applied it to her head." She turned her back to the group and, pulling an ornate comb from her hair, allowed it to topple loose. "And her golden hair came streaming down her back!"

The supers laughed and applauded. Yet, their gaiety was abruptly cut short by Miss Kimberly demanding in a deepened tone, "*What* is going on here?"

All eyes, including Miss Lily's, turned to the business manager standing in the stalls' right aisle. With an obvious tightness to her expression, she fixed Miss Lily with a stern gaze whilst advancing toward the stage. "*This* is a theatre, *not* a music hall. Mr Thurston, why has the super rehearsal not begun?"

Mr Thurston quickly got to his feet. "We're waiting for Miss Ilbert." He glanced toward the backstage area. "She's with Mrs Hightower."

Miss Kimberly climbed the stairs and walked onto the stage. "I'm certain she'll be here soon. Have the supers take their positions."

"Yes, Miss," Mr Thurston said and clapped at the group. "On your feet."

The supers did as commanded, exchanging nervous glances as they did.

"Tired, Mr Stone?" Miss Kimberly enquired in an ironic tone upon seeing him sitting on the stool.

"Only of people who spoil joviality," Mr Stone replied as he departed into the wings.

"What an *impossible* human being," Miss Kimberly stated quietly. To Miss Lily, she said, "You are an actress, not an athletic droll."

"Yes, Aunt Emma," Miss Lily said, dropping her gaze and tidying her hair.

"Are the supers ready, Mr Thurston?" Miss Kimberly called over.

"They are," Mr Thurston replied.

"Good, I'll fetch Mina—" Miss Kimberly had been walking toward the rear of the stage when Miss Ilbert emerged from behind the scenery, causing her to halt. "I was just coming to fetch you; the supers are ready for their rehearsal."

Miss Ilbert walked with her business manager to the group but changed course when she caught sight of Miss Lily's unhappy expression. "What is the matter, child?"

"Nothing, Mother. I was just singing the golden hair song to the supers."

Miss Ilbert lifted her chin and, casting a knowing glance at Miss Kimberly, said, "Ah." She lowered her voice. "You know how much Emma disapproves of it," she smiled, "despite your rendition being *rather* amusing." In her natural volume, she continued, "Such vulgarity has no place in my theatre." She slipped her arm around Miss Lily's and escorted her back to the supers. "And does not befit an actress of your beauty and talent. Emma…" She waited for her to join her before leaving the stage via the steps and sitting in the front row of the stalls. "We are already behind schedule, so I want us to work especially hard at perfecting the dance from the second act," Miss Ilbert instructed the supers. Her gaze shifted to Miss Lily. "Make your mother proud, child." She darted her gaze to Miss Kimberly, who handed her the pantomime script.

* * *

Miss Hicks jerked her head back, stunned. "His mum?"

"Yes," Miss Breckenridge replied.

Sergeant Gutman closed his newspaper and sipped his beer as he listened intently to the conversation unfolding between Miss Hicks and Miss Breckenridge. Stealing a glance at the latter, he thought she was both similar and dissimilar to how he would've imagined Dr Weeks' mother to be. Similar because she seemed to share a tactlessness with the surgeon, and dissimilar because she seemed to be the more dominant of the two. Yet, regardless of his own thoughts, he knew Inspector Lee would be very interested to learn of this latest development.

"Yer supposed to be in Toronto," Dr Weeks said, addressing his mother. "Why ain't ya in Toronto?"

"Because I can't be in two places at once," Miss Breckenridge replied.

Dr Weeks' gaze hardened. "Ya ain't sent a *damn* word about this."

"She's your mum," Miss Hicks reminded him. "She don't have to tell you anythin'."

Miss Breckenridge smiled. "Thank ya, child."

Dr Weeks picked up his pint and, cursing, took a large mouthful.

Miss Hicks put her hand on her hip. "Ain't you going to introduce me?"

Dr Weeks gestured to Miss Hicks and, in between swallows of beer, said, "Mum, this 'ere's Polly Hicks, my lady."

Miss Hicks beamed. She loved it when he called her that.

Miss Breckenridge's face lit up. "So, yer the one who's been tryin' to make an honest man outta my Percival. 'E mentions ya a great deal in his letters. It's a pleasure to finally meet ya."

"The same to you," Miss Hicks said. Glancing at Dr Weeks, she teased, "Percival?"

Miss Breckenridge placed a gentle hand upon her son's arm. "I know he don't like me callin' him that, but that's what I named him, so that's what he'll be when I'm around."

Dr Weeks pulled away from her and, taking another large mouthful of beer, glared at the bottles on the shelf opposite.

"Can I get you sumin' Mrs Breckenridge?" Miss Hicks enquired.

Dr Weeks bowed his head to hide the shame in his eyes.

Miss Breckenridge's smile faltered. "Yes," she regained her composure, "thank ya. A sherry, if ya please."

Miss Hicks glanced at Dr Weeks and went to pour his mother's drink.

Miss Breckenridge moved closer to her son as she ran an appraising glance over him. The stench of beer coming from him was overpowering. Yet, she put her lips close to his ear and rested a gentle hand upon his. In a low, tender voice, she said, "Yer right: I should've told ya I were comin'." She reached to straighten the knot of his tie, but he pushed her hand away. She tilted her head to look him square in the eye. "Ya smell like a bum-boozer," she observed in a sombre tone. "Is yer Polly takin' good care of ya?"

Dr Weeks kept his steely gaze firmly on the bottles opposite.

Miss Breckenridge drew her eyebrows together, concerned. "When were the last time ya had somethin' to eat?"

"I ain't hungry," Dr Weeks mumbled, taking another mouthful of beer.

Miss Breckenridge pointed at the glass. "How many of them have ya made disappear?"

"Not enough," Dr Weeks mumbled.

Miss Breckenridge frowned. "Ain't ya supposed to be at work?"

"Ain't ya supposed to be in Toronto?" Dr Weeks flung back. He lifted the glass to his lips, "and not buggin' me."

Miss Hicks served Miss Breckenridge her sherry. "The *Coach & Horses* pub is Perce's local. They make a lovely ale and kidney pie. We could get some tonight, if you'd like, Mrs Breckenridge?"

"I'd love to, child, but Percival and I have an appointment." Miss Breckenridge briefly touched her son's arm.

Miss Hicks turned accusing eyes to Dr Weeks. "First I've heard about it."

"Ya and me both," Dr Weeks said.

"Don't be silly, Percival," Miss Breckenridge said. "Yer've been enough times."

"When?" Dr Weeks challenged.

"Last year," Miss Breckenridge replied. "And the year before that and the year before that." She took a sip of sherry. "The date should be etched in yer mind."

The meaning of her words struck Dr Weeks like a lightning bolt, causing him to freeze and his stomach to somersault. His initial instinct was to assume his mother was mistaken. Yet, a swift check of the date in his mind confirmed she was correct: today *was* the day he dreaded. Feeling his already debilitating sense of self-loathing intensify, he frantically wracked his brains for a way out of the appointment. In his desperation for a solution, though, he'd completely forgotten about his lover's presence.

"What's special about today?" Miss Hicks enquired, looking between them.

Dr Weeks' head shot up like a startled rabbit.

"It's—" Miss Breckenridge began.

"*Nothin'*." Dr Weeks interrupted.

Miss Breckenridge parted her lips but was prevented from speaking by her son suddenly taking a firm grip of her arm and pulling her away from the bar.

"I'll see ya later, darlin'," Dr Weeks called to Miss Hicks.

Noticing he'd abandoned the last few swallows of his pint, Miss Hicks realised he was more desperate to leave than she'd thought. Keen to discover why, she hurried after them but lost them soon after in the burgeoning crowd of the busy platform. Thus, she was left wondering what the devil was going on as she returned to the bar.

Having watched the entire scene unfold, Sergeant Gutman had also followed Dr Weeks and his mother into the crowd. Unlike Miss Hicks, he was far more experienced in these matters, and so managed to keep them in sight until they'd boarded a hansom cab in the queue outside the station. Boarding the cab immediately behind, Sergeant Gutman instructed its driver to follow its counterpart.

EIGHT

A heavy mustiness hung within the small archive room at the *Gaslight Gazette* offices. The smell, combined with the lack of fresh air, irritated the back of Inspector Woolfe's throat, compelling him to clear it between coughs. A small, dark-brown glass bottle was on the corner of the desk at which he sat. Containing the medicine gifted him by Dr Colbert, it was already a third empty. Feeling the familiar tightness in his chest heralding another coughing fit, he uncorked the bottle and took a sip of the foul-tasting mixture. It invariably caused him to gag, but it was a small price to pay for the relief it provided. Feeling the tightness subside, he replaced the cork and set the bottle aside.

Since beginning his investigation into the Bow Street Society, he'd been told on a few occasions that Miss Trent had applied for the position of its clerk by answering an advertisement in the publication. Miss Amoretto, an actress at the *Paddington Palladium's* lodgings, and Mrs Louise Snyder, the wife of Mr Sam Snyder, had been the sources.

The latter had revealed Miss Trent had returned to live with the Snyders after she'd secured the clerk position. He was confident this had occurred in November 1895 as it was the month Miss Trent had leased the office above *Derby's Stationers*, Endell Street, with the assistance of her solicitor, Mr Calvin. Mrs Snyder had also revealed Miss Trent had brought the advertisement to the Snyders for their opinion prior to her returning to live with them. On this basis, he planned to search every morning and evening edition from 1st October until 30th November, 1895. The edition currently open before him was from the morning of 12th October and formed part of a large, leather-bound volume.

Turning to the classified section, he scanned its columns for references to the Bow Street Society. He was also looking for advertisements seeking clerks where the company name was omitted. Thus far, he'd found only two examples of such advertisements. He would get the names of the people who'd placed these, and any others he may find, once he'd completed his search.

He checked the time on his pocket watch and found he was nearing the last of the thirty minutes he'd allocated for today. His obligation to Chief Inspector Jones meant he couldn't be away from Inspector Conway for long. Whilst Inspector Woolfe trusted Sergeant Bird to give detailed reports of Inspector Conway's comings and goings during his absences, he also knew Sergeant Bird shared other officers' mistrust of their colleague. It concerned Inspector Woolfe that Sergeant Bird's prejudice could cause him to misconstrue Inspector Conway's activities as suspicious when they weren't. In short, Inspector Woolfe knew he could only rely on the facts he witnessed firsthand.

He recorded the page and number of the edition he'd searched in his notebook and returned the volume to its proper place on the shelf. Pulling on his fur coat, he dropped the medicine bottle into one pocket whilst taking some coins from the other. These were discreetly put into the hand of the *Gaslight Gazette's* archive clerk as he left to guarantee the man's silence about his visit.

* * *

"I gave instructions not to be disturbed." Dr Colbert stood behind his desk.

"By anyone or only me?" Inspector Lee enquired in a sardonic tone.

"I'm sorry, doctor," the head attendant said as he entered behind the policeman.

"By anyone," Dr Colbert lied. "Not to worry, Mr Corwin. You may book an appointment for the inspector to see me tomorrow morning at ten."

"Yes, doctor." Mr Corwin went to leave the office but halted upon seeing Inspector Lee remove his hat and gloves. "Sir?"

"The matter cannot wait," Inspector Lee warned Dr Colbert as he put his gloves into his hat and set it down upon the desk. Taking his walking cane from where he'd tucked it under his arm, he fixed Dr Colbert with a sombre gaze.

Mr Corwin also looked to him for further instruction.

"Return to your duties," Dr Colbert said. "And close the door, please." Sitting whilst the head attendant obeyed his request, he invited Inspector Lee to make himself comfortable.

"I'd like to begin by apologising for my prolonged absence." Inspector Lee leant his walking cane against the desk as he sat in the vacant chair before it. "There were matters which demanded my undivided attention. Since we last spoke, I've been reassigned to A Division at New Scotland Yard."

"You're no longer at Chiswick High Road?"

"Correct."

Picking up a pencil, Dr Colbert sat back. Holding its ends whilst resting his elbows upon the broad arms of his leather chair, he considered the merits of asking his next question. Concluding he wouldn't have peace of mind without the answer, he enquired in a cautious tone, "May I ask whether your reassignment was connected to your conflict with Inspector Woolfe?"

"There's no conflict between us."

Dr Colbert sat forward. "There isn't?"

"Conflict is defined as a prolonged struggle between opposing sides. Inspector Woolfe has made it clear he doesn't want my help in bringing about the Bow Street Society's end. In line with this decision, he has also ceased all communication with me. Hence, there's no conflict between us, but rather an absence of cooperation."

"I see." Dr Colbert continued to hold the pencil whilst resting the heels of his hands upon the desk. "May I ask why?"

"We disagree on the character of Inspector John Conway."

"The man who fought Mr Snyder?"

"Yes. I believe he is corrupt and in league with the Bow Street Society. I detest him for these reasons. Inspector Woolfe, on the other hand, believes he is honest and has been wrongly accused. He is also close friends with him. You can now understand why a reconciliation between us hasn't been made."

"Indeed, I can." Dr Colbert frowned. "From what I've heard said about him, Inspector Conway is a controversial figure amongst the Society's members. An alliance between them and him would be tense but not enough to place it beyond the realm of possibility." His frown deepened as another possibility occurred to him. "Do you suspect Inspector Woolfe of colluding with Inspector Conway and the Bow Street Society?"

"I believe it's a strong possibility, yes. Especially as Inspector Conway is now assigned to Inspector Woolfe's police station at Bow Street."

Dr Colbert dropped the pencil. "He is? But what if Inspector Woolfe tells him about me? About what I'm doing at the Bow Street Society?"

"Inspector Conway would undoubtedly inform Miss Trent who would undoubtedly terminate your membership."

Dr Colbert stood and momentarily turned toward the window. "Do you think he would? Inspector Woolfe."

Inspector Lee joined Dr Colbert. "Inspector Woolfe is fully aware of Inspector Conway's suspected loyalty to the Bow Street Society. He appeared to have retained his determination to continue his investigation into their affairs when I last spoke to him." He gave a reassuring smile. "No, I don't think he would. At least, not for the time being. If he is obliged to choose between his loyalty to the law and his loyalty to Inspector Conway, though, I fear he will choose the latter."

Dr Colbert furrowed his brow. "What can be done?"

"Precautionary measures." Inspector Lee gathered up his things. "We—that is, you and I—shall continue our investigation into the Bow Street Society. You will also keep me informed of all new information and developments. If the worst should come to pass, and Inspector Woolfe betrays you, you will have an ally in me, still. Naturally, this plan will only be effective if we don't disclose our ongoing cooperation to Inspector Woolfe."

"I agree," Dr Colbert walked to the door. "The more workings of the Bow Street Society I see, the more I'm convinced it is a poor excuse for wilful vigilantism." He offered his hand. "You may rely upon my assistance and discretion."

Inspector Lee firmly shook Dr Colbert's hand. "Excellent."

* * *

Mr Jerome took a few puffs from a cigar as he rested against a cold, brick wall opposite the *Crescent Theatre's* stage door. His head was down with his bowler hat pulled forward, thereby keeping his face in shadow. On either side of him, also leaning against the wall, were two men of similar age. The first had his head bowed and the collar of his old coat pulled up to hide his face. The second wore a flat cap with its peak pulled down over his forehead and a dirty neckerchief over the lower half of his face.

It was almost five o'clock, and the noise from the Strand traffic filled the air. The passageway in which the trio were ran perpendicular to the theatre from the Strand at the front to the service alleyway at the rear. Although open, its four-foot width meant the tall buildings on either side kept it in perpetual gloom. The added complication of nighttime had also descended in the past hour, thereby plunging the passageway into near pitch-blackness. The only meagre light came from a candle-lit lantern suspended above the stage door.

Deeper in the passageway, concealed by the darkness, was a sixteen-year-old boy with short, dark-brown hair parted at the side and hazel eyes. Wrapped in a knee-length black coat, he had a dark-blue scarf covering his neck and chin, black trousers, and old, worn boots. His cheeks and nose were red from the cold.

Having arrived some time ago, before the three men in fact, he was conscious his continued presence depended on his ability to be quiet. With this in mind, he'd kept his movements to a minimum and his breathing shallow. The last thing he wanted was for the men to either rob him or, worse, expel him into the street.

Hearing a cab come to a stop on the street, the boy stepped out of his hiding place to peer down the passageway. Mr Jerome and his associates did the same, and they all saw a figure emerge from the vehicle and pay the driver. When the figure turned into the light and revealed themselves to be a man, though, the boy slipped back into the darkness. In stark contrast, Mr Jerome led his associates up the passageway to intercept the newcomer as he entered.

"Good evenin', Mr Benton," Mr Jerome greeted with a grin.

In his mid-forties, Mr Luthor Ellis Benton was approximately five foot eleven inches tall with severely receding oak-brown, wavy hair, and an impressive, bushy moustache. His angular brow and narrow, yet thick, eyebrows gave him a serious-looking natural countenance. This increased tenfold when his brows came together, and his brown eyes narrowed upon seeing Mr Jerome and his associates. Striding down the passageway, he turned sideways and went past them, heading for the stage door. As he did, he boomed, "*Not* tonight. *Thank* you!"

"But yow've not given us what we want," Mr Jerome said, swiftly putting himself between Mr Benton and the stage door.

"And you're not going to get it," Mr Benton said, glancing at the two men as they came up beside and behind him. "I've had enough of these demands. Do you hear me? *Enough.* You shan't get another penny from me."

Mr Jerome's smile faded. Taking the cigar from the corner of his mouth, he blew its smoke into Mr Benton's face. Watching him cough and waft it away, he warned, "Eef yow don't pay, we'll give yow the bird."

"Then give it," Mr Benton retorted. "I'm an actor—an *artiste*. I shall rise above your yells and give the greatest performance of my life regardless. Now," he lifted his chin and looked down his nose at Mr Jerome, "move aside."

Mr Jerome grinned, taking a few more puffs of his cigar.

Mr Benton's gaze hardened.

Mr Jerome blew the smoke into his face, again.

Feeling his anger explode at this rudeness, Mr Benton attempted to grip Mr Jerome's shoulder and shove him aside. Yet, the younger man was quick to swat his hand away and swing at his jaw. Blindsided by the sudden impact, Mr Benton stumbled sideways with Mr Jerome moving swiftly after him, his cigar still in the corner of his mouth. Neither they nor the other two men saw the boy emerge from the shadows, dart past them, and run down the passageway.

"I'll have you arrested for assault!" Mr Benton bellowed as Mr Jerome grabbed him by his coat's lapels and shoved him back against the wall to hold him there.

"Yow saw him hit me first, didn't yow?" Mr Jerome enquired from his associates.

"Yeah," one replied.

"They'll never believe you," Mr Benton warned.

"Three against one," Mr Jerome pointed out. "But eef yow give us our money, we'll say nowt about eet and let yow be an artist tonight."

"And again, tomorrow night, and the night after that, and the night after that," Mr Benton countered. "*No* more, I *say*!" He pushed against Mr Jerome with all his might, thereby forcing him to stumble backward.

"Yow!" Mr Jerome yelled, raising his fist to strike Mr Benton again, only to be interrupted by the sound of the stage door opening. Looking sharply across to it, his fist held in midair, he dropped it upon seeing Mr Thurston emerge.

"What is going on here?" Mr Thurston demanded without conviction.

Mr Jerome stepped back from Mr Benton and, taking the cigar from his mouth, blew the smoke in Mr Thurston's direction. "Nowt." He grinned. Walking backward down the passageway with his associates behind him, he gestured to Mr Benton. "Oy wanted his autograph."

Mr Thurston turned concerned eyes to the actor who pushed past him into the theatre. When he looked back to the passageway, though, Mr Jerome and his associates were gone. Pursing his lips as he contemplated what could've happened if he'd not intervened, Mr Thurston was relieved he had—despite the consequences. Glancing up and down the passageway, he returned inside and closed and locked the door.

NINE

Standing hunched over in the hansom cab whilst gripping its side, Dr Weeks looked along the street in both directions. Seeing neither man nor beast, he stepped out onto the pavement and instructed the driver to wait for them.

"Help yer mother, son," Miss Breckenridge said with a few pants after scooting along the bench. Holding out her arm, she waited for Dr Weeks to take her hand before attempting to pull herself to her feet. Immediately dropping back onto the bench, she held out her other hand for him to take. Only when he leant back and pulled her toward him did she finally manage to get to her feet. Breathless, she released one of his hands. "Yer shoulder."

Dr Weeks turned sideways and allowed her to put her full weight on his shoulder as she stepped down from the cab. Pressing his lips together, he felt a tightness forming in his jaw and facial muscles as he watched the debacle. He curtly enquired, "Are ya out?"

"No, I'm still inside," Miss Breckenridge retorted in a sardonic tone.

"Ya don't gotta be sarcastic."

"And ya don't have to be rude." Miss Breckenridge gave him a warning look.

"I wouldn't be if ya hadn't made me come 'ere." Dr Weeks crossed the pavement and climbed some steps.

"It's *once a year*, Percival." Miss Breckenridge stood behind him on the steps.

Dr Weeks released a loud sigh and, knocking on the door, muttered half-seriously under his breath, "Call me Percival again and ya'll be walkin' home."

The door opened directly to reveal a gentleman in his late forties with dark, chestnut-brown hair, bulbous nose, and green eyes crowned by caterpillar-like brows. His attire consisted of a black frockcoat over a plain, navy-blue waistcoat with matching tie, white shirt, and black trousers. A silver watchchain hung across his rotund middle. He moved back and stepped aside upon seeing Dr Weeks and Miss Breckenridge.

The narrow hallway beyond was dimly lit by a kerosene lamp placed by the semi-circular window above the door. All doors leading off the hallway were shut except one, and it was to this the gentleman indicated once his visitors were inside. As he closed the front door and secured the latch, a second hansom cab turned into the street and slowed to a stop several metres ahead of the first but on the opposite side. Inside, Sergeant Gutman looked up and through the narrow opening in the roof to meet the driver's gaze. "Wait here."

"I'll stand on me 'ead if the money's righ'," the driver said in a gruff voice.

"Waitin' is enough for now." Sergeant Gutman climbed out, crossed the street, and walked along the pavement.

After leaving the underground railway bar earlier, he'd followed Dr Weeks and his mother to the surgeon's home. They'd stayed there awhile, thereby compelling Sergeant Gutman to loiter in the bitter cold, before emerging to walk to the nearest cab rank. He'd followed and crept up to their cab just as they were giving the street name to their driver. Deciding on this basis to give them a small head start, he'd instructed the driver of his cab to wait before setting off.

Now, as he strolled past the other cab, he recognised its driver as the one Dr Weeks and his mother had hired. Stopping under the pretence of lighting a cigarette, he blew out the match and turned to stroll back the way he'd come. With his hands in his trouser pockets, he moved his head as if he were simply taking in the scenery.

He soon caught the glint of a brass plaque in the streetlamp's gaslight. Stopping for a second time, he noted the building was opposite Dr Weeks' cab. Plucking the cigarette from his mouth and exhaling the smoke, he read the words engraved upon the plaque: *T.I. Fry, Esq.*

Solicitor. Committing this to memory, he took a few more pulls from his cigarette as he strolled back across the street. Tossing the cigarette into a puddle in the gutter, he climbed into his cab and instructed his driver, "We'll wait 'ere for a bit."

Inside, Mr Tristan Ingram Fry stood by his desk with Dr Weeks, whilst Miss Breckenridge sat on a chair by the fire, the room's only source of light. The curtains were also drawn, and the clock on the mantelpiece neared seven o'clock. The after-hours appointment was intentional. It meant Mr Fry could maintain strict confidentiality on behalf of his client without cultivating suspicion and intrigue amongst his employees.

"The terms and conditions are quite clear, Dr Weeks. Neither you nor your mother are permitted to communicate with Lord Weeks under any circumstances, or by any means," Mr Fry said, firmly. "Including through his legal representative."

"He'll want to hear what I've got to say," Dr Weeks insisted.

"Which is?" Mr Fry enquired in a condescending tone.

Dr Weeks raised his voice. "His damn name printed in every rag in Fleet Street."

"Are those your intentions?" Mr Fry enquired, maintaining his tone.

"The *hell* they are!" Dr Weeks shouted, throwing up his arms as he turned to pace the room. "I'm tryin' to stop it!"

"Then who?" Mr Fry enquired.

Dr Weeks stopped pacing, his back to Mr Fry. "I can't tell ya."

"Why not?" Mr Fry enquired.

Dr Weeks spun around. "'Cause the sonofabitch will get it printed as soon as ya leave his office!"

Mr Fry glanced at Miss Breckenridge who was either not paying attention or had chosen to have temporary deafness, as she warmed her hands as casually as if she were at home. He returned his attention to Dr Weeks and pointed out, "Then a visit from Lord Weeks would have the same effect."

"Yeah—" Dr Weeks began.

"Therefore, a meeting between him and you would not only be in breach of the terms and conditions set down and agreed upon for many years, but would be utterly pointless," Mr Fry interrupted.

Dr Weeks' features tightened as he felt his anger rise at the solicitor's pompous arrogance. "I ain't wantin' him to talk to the sonofabitch. I want him to talk to the fellas who employ him, so they'll search his place and get the documents back."

Mr Fry's chin lifted a fraction, as did his tone. "What documents?"

Dr Weeks smirked at the small triumph. "A record of my birth and a statement from the midwife."

"Have you seen them?" Mr Fry enquired, his expression and tone turning grave.

"For a couple of minutes," Dr Weeks replied.

"So, there's a chance they could be forged?" Mr Fry enquired.

"Yeah, but he ain't the kind to—" Dr Weeks began.

"Blackmailers are a great many things," Mr Fry interrupted with a raising of his voice. "Being honest is not one of them." He went behind his desk and unlocked a drawer. "If you only saw the documents for a couple of minutes, it is highly likely they were forged. Yet, even if they weren't, I would advise Lord Weeks to insist they were if the unthinkable were to happen and the British press learnt of their existence. It would make for an uncomfortable few days, but he would weather the storm, and the press would soon lose interest."

Dr Weeks advanced upon him. "Am I s'pposed to 'weather the storm,' too?"

"Yes," Mr Fry replied firmly. "That is *precisely* what you should do." He tossed two red velvet money pouches onto the desk and laid out identical copies of a typed agreement. "In addition to denying Lord Weeks is your father, of course."

"The hospital's board ain't stupid. They don't like scandals, either. They'll see the documents are genuine and toss me out on my ass," Dr Weeks said.

"That isn't Lord Weeks' concern," Mr Fry dismissed.

"I'm his *son*," Dr Weeks growled.

"*Bastard* son," Mr Fry corrected. "Who should be grateful for what he receives." He adopted a hard tone. "Now you are of age, Lord Weeks isn't legally obliged to continue your allowance. He chooses to do so because he is a generous and honourable man."

"I don't want his damn money!" Dr Weeks picked up a pouch and tossed it across the desk. "I want his support!"

"The money *is* his support," Mr Fry said. "Or as much of it as you are going to receive from him."

Dr Weeks turned sharply away and put his hands on his head. "I don't believe this."

"Miss Breckenridge, please talk some sense into your son?" Mr Fry requested.

"I weren't able to when 'e were in the womb. What makes ya think I'm able to now?" Miss Breckenridge replied in a wry tone.

"Very well. You both leave me with no choice." Mr Fry put the money pouches into the drawer. "If you refuse to accept the terms and conditions of Lord Weeks' generosity, neither of you shall receive your allowance."

"Ya can't do that!" Miss Breckenridge cried.

"I can, and I shall," Mr Fry replied.

"Percival! Speak to the man!" Miss Breckenridge pleaded.

"You shan't convince me otherwise, Dr Weeks," Mr Fry warned. "Either you accept the terms and conditions and sign the agreement, thereby securing this year's allowance for you and your mother, or refuse and leave here without a penny and, quite possibly, destitute."

"Percival?" Miss Breckenridge enquired, her eyes wide with panic.

Dr Weeks fixed Mr Fry with a fierce glare. "Yer a cold-hearted bastard."

Miss Breckenridge stood and gripped her son's sleeve. "Percy, *please*."

Dr Weeks looked at his mother and, seeing the desperation in her eyes, exhaled heavily through his nose. If she were to become destitute because of his stubbornness, he knew he'd never be able to forgive himself. Despite the fact she insisted on calling him Percival. Putting his arm around her shoulders, he pulled her in for a gentle sideways hug. "Don't worry, Mum. I'll take care of ya." He released her as he approached the desk. Taking the pen from Mr Fry's inkstand, he tried to ignore the nausea building in his stomach as he signed his copy of the agreement.

Mr Fry smiled. "You've made the right decision."

* * *

A solo flute filled the air with a gentle melody as Miss Ilbert glided across the stage with a line of young ladies following. Miss Ilbert's green and gold costume of a fairy queen, and those of the ladies playing her fairy subjects, sparkled in the stage footlights. With their arms spread so their fingertips were almost touching, Miss Ilbert and her dancers curved their line toward the scenery before curving it again to glide back across the stage.

Constructed in the shape of a horseshoe for better acoustics, the auditorium had a lower floor of stalls and pit that extended under the dress circle to the back and side walls. The balconies of both the dress circle and circle wrapped around and above the lower floor. Three private boxes, stacked one atop the other, were located at the ends of these curves, adjacent to the stage.

Every seat was filled, with the richer patrons occupying the boxes. The auditorium's newly installed electrical lights were also fully lit. As a result, the faces and expressions of everyone in the audience were clearly visible to the performers. Everyone's gaze was fixed upon Miss Ilbert, following her around the stage. Compliments and favourable remarks, uttered loudly over the flute, came from various points in the audience.

Miss Ilbert's delight grew with each she heard, however. As the violins joined the flute, thereby increasing the depth and drama of the musical accompaniment, she and the other dancers increased their speed. The circle which their line formed also tightened until, at the music's crescendo, Miss Ilbert leapt onto a metal plate in the centre of the stage and threw up her arms. The moment she did, the tiny lights which dotted her crown and costume illuminated a bright white. A gasp of awe erupted from the ladies in the boxes at the sight. A round of applause immediately followed, spurring Miss Ilbert and her dancers to gracefully leave via stage right.

As the applause died away, Mr Luthor Ellis Benton strode onto the stage from stage left. His costume of pale-blue silk britches, white tights, pale-blue silk frockcoat, and white lace cravat was reminiscent of an eighteenth-century aristocrat. Upon his head was a powdered wig, complete with pale-blue ribbon. The developing bruise on his jaw, courtesy of Mr Jerome, was hidden by the white powder covering his face. His cheeks were also rouged, and his lips painted red.

With his chest puffed out and his head held high, he walked to the centre of the stage whilst projecting his booming voice into the audience. "Such a glorious morning as this must not be witnessed by mere mortals, for Heaven's beauty abounds in its blue skies and the richness of innocence abounds in its golden sunlight. All the while, the scent of feminine grace abounds in the flowers' scent. What a glorious morning to be alive! I—"

Unabated hissing tore through his words. Turning sharply to gaze into the stalls, Mr Benton saw Mr Jerome and his two associates standing two rows in. They had their hands cupped around their mouths and were only stopping their hissing long enough to take a breath. The audience members in the immediate vicinity looked between them and Mr Benton with a mixture of surprise and amusement.

Mr Benton's anger was ignited by the disruption, but he kept it contained to a brief chewing of his tongue. Turning his back upon the group, he walked across the stage and attempted to continue his monologue. "What a *glorious* morning to be alive! I—!"

"Get off the stage!" Mr Jerome shouted, continuing his hissing immediately after.

"A quackin' duck could do better than this old cove!" Mr Jerome's associate shouted.

"*I dare not blink, for fear the dream in which I walk may end*!" Mr Benton bellowed, his words accompanied by the constant hissing of Mr Jerome and his associates.

"Get off the stage!" Mr Jerome demanded, again.

An audience member in front of Mr Jerome turned and enquired, "Can you not leave the poor man alone? He is trying his best."

Mr Benton's neck bent forward before stiffening again as he demanded, "Are you being *serious*?!" He jerked his head back and lowered it, again. "My *best*?!" He lifted his chin and glared down his nose at the audience member. "*I* am an actor of the *highest* calibre!"

"Could of fooled us!" Mr Jerome shouted.

"And *you* are nought but a hissing snake, sir!" Mr Benton shouted back, drawing a ripple of laughter from the audience.

"Better to be a snake than an ass!" Mr Jerome retorted, drawing a second ripple of laughter from the audience.

Mr Benton darted his gaze around the auditorium at the sound.

"Get. Off. Get. Off. Get. Off." Mr Jerome shouted. His associates also resumed their hissing.

"Get off the stage!" cried the audience member who'd tried to defend him earlier.

"Yes, we want to see *talented* actors! Not buffoons!" another audience member shouted from the back row of the stalls.

"Get. Off. Get. Off. Get. Off." Mr Jerome shouted with, to Mr Benton's horror, the rest of the audience joining in.

Feeling his heart pounding, his leg muscles quivering, and a heat flushing through him all at once, Mr Benton clenched his teeth and hands until his body became so tense, he thought it might snap in two. The chant, shouted by over a hundred voices in unison, engulfed him as completely as if he'd fallen into the ocean. Darting his gaze from the stalls to the dress circle to the circle and back to the stalls, he turned sharply to look at the boxes on the left and right. Every face was angry and, in the cases of some of the men, fists were being thrown down in time with the chant's beat. Mr Benton took one step back, then another, and another. Finally, he turned and ran off the stage, causing the audience to instantly erupt into rapturous applause.

* * *

"Ya could write to him," Dr Weeks mused aloud.

"Pardon?" Miss Breckenridge enquired, his sudden words taking her by surprise. They'd travelled in silence since leaving Mr Fry's office.

As the gentle motion of the cab rocked him, Dr Weeks turned his head to meet her gaze. "Yer've got yer money now. Ya could write to my father and ask him to see me."

Miss Breckenridge put her hand on his as regret entered her voice. "I'd love to, but—"

"But ya ain't goin' to." Dr Weeks pulled his hand away and glared into the road ahead.

Miss Breckenridge tutted. "Ya *know* I can't, Percival! Yes, I have the money, but 'e could jus' as easily take it back." She adopted a sympathetic tone. "Maybe all this will blow over, if ya jus' give it time?"

"It ain't goin' to blow over, Mum." Dr Weeks leant forward and, resting his elbows upon the tops of the doors, held his head in his hands.

Miss Breckenridge put a gentle hand upon his back. "Look, son. Even if the worst *does* happen, ya'll always have a home with me." She leant in close. "Ya could come tourin' with me, like the old days."

He ignored her as imaginings of his acquaintances' disgust upon learning the truth of his parentage bombarded his mind. These were swiftly followed by imaginings of Inspector Conway and Miss Trent's reactions to this fact, alongside everything else. Dr Weeks' stomach lurched. The possibility of losing his few close friends sickened him more than losing his reputation and position.

Lifting his head, Dr Weeks put his hands together as if he were praying and rested his nose in the gap between them.

He needed a drink.

* * *

"*Never…* in *all* my years have I—" Mr Benton's voice, already heavy with emotion, broke. Sat on a chair backstage, holding a glass of brandy, he put his fingers against his temple as he tilted his head sideways. His eyes stared at the floor, but his gaze was turned inward, focusing on the memory of the audience chanting for him to leave the stage. A sensation of heat rose from his core as he fought to fend off the tears which threatened to fall. 'Humiliated' couldn't begin to describe his feelings. Speaking so quietly it was almost a whisper, he said, "I shan't step foot on stage again."

"*Yes*, you *shall*, Luthor," Miss Ilbert said, firmly. She sat on another chair beside his. "It was those *pests* who turned the audience into a mob, not you."

Mr Benton lifted sad eyes to Miss Ilbert and Miss Kimberly standing behind her.

The music accompaniment of the next scene reached them from the stage. Miss Ilbert had decided for Mr Benton's understudy to perform the remainder of tonight's pantomime, as much as it had pained her to do so.

"They have been causing trouble for Mr Benton at the stage door for almost a week now," Miss Kimberly said, an edge of irritation to her voice. "We have attempted to dissuade them by altering Mr Benton's arrival time each day. Yet, they somehow know it anyway."

Miss Ilbert pivoted in her chair to look up at her business manager and friend. "You suspect someone within the company is warning them?"

"I'm merely saying it's a possibility," Miss Kimberly replied.

"A very *good* one, I'd say," Mr Benton interjected.

"Mr Stone," Miss Ilbert called as the stage manager walked past. "Have you seen those pests with anyone from the company?"

Mr Stone smiled. "I have, as it happens."

"Who?" Miss Ilbert enquired.

Mr Stone replied with mock reluctance, "I don't want to get anyone in trouble—"

"*Who* was it?" Miss Ilbert demanded.

"Miss Joanna," Mr Stone replied, suppressing his delight.

Miss Ilbert stood and, with Miss Kimberly and Mr Stone following, went straight to the wardrobe department. Miss Joanna and her mother were surprised to see their manager, business manager, and stage manager enter without knocking. They were visibly alarmed by the hard gaze Miss Ilbert fixed Miss Joanna with.

"Have you been telling others when Mr Benton will arrive at the theatre?" Miss Ilbert demanded from Miss Joanna.

"No," Miss Joanna replied. "I-I do not know when Mr Benton—"

"I saw you with one of the men who drove Mr Benton off stage," Mr Stone interrupted.

Miss Joanna stared at him, stunned. "Jack… drove Mr Benton…?"

"Have you been seeing that no-good Jack Jerome again?" Mrs Hightower demanded. "Your father isn't going to be happy, my girl."

"I am *far* from happy, too," Miss Ilbert stated in a hard tone.

"Miss Ilbert, I swear on my life, I never told Jack anything," Miss Joanna insisted.

"I shall leave the disciplining of the girl in your husband's hands, Mrs Hightower," Miss Ilbert said, addressing the wardrobe mistress. "If I discover she has lied to me, though, you will both be dismissed." She left the wardrobe department, followed by the others.

Upon returning to the backstage area after parting company with her and Miss Kimberly, though, Mr Thurston intercepted Mr Stone. In a low voice, the prompter warned, "You shouldn't have done that to Miss Joanna, Ronnie."

"I wouldn't have had to if you'd left things alone, Morris," Mr Stone said.

"They were going to hurt him," Mr Thurston squeaked.

"To persuade him to pay, but *you* ruined everything."

"It's not fair. None of it."

"Life isn't fair."

"I don't want the lives of innocent people ruined," Mr Thurston insisted.

Mr Stone's brow flattened and, in a cold voice made even more menacing by its softness, said, "I hope you're not threatening me, again."

"N-No, never, Ronnie."

"I didn't think you'd be stupid enough to try." Mr Stone moved into Mr Thurston's personal space, his hard eyes boring into his. "But people can surprise you."

Mr Thurston swallowed hard and quietly replied, "Yes, Ronnie."

TEN

Running perpendicular to Bishop's Road in the northwest and Westbourne Crescent in the southeast, Westbourne Terrace was also a short walk from the Lockes' home on Cleveland Terrace. This proximity made it the ideal place for Dr Locke to take Mr Locke for his nightly fatiguing walk. Residences of Westbourne Terrace were also of the same social class, thereby allowing the Lockes to be inconspicuous and undisturbed for the duration of their visits.

With pink cheeks and a sheen of sweat covering his forehead, Mr Locke halted to catch his breath. Their nightly aim was for him to walk a full loop of the Terrace's avenue of trees without stopping. Although he had yet to achieve this, he was walking a little further every night. Tonight, he had walked nearly the avenue's length before needing to rest. Tucking his walking cane under his arm, he mopped his brow with his handkerchief and scanned the immediate area for somewhere to sit. Alas, there was nowhere.

Dr Locke looked behind them to gauge the distance they'd walked. It had taken Mr Locke over a week to get this far. The thought of spending another eight nights trying to get him to also walk the length of the avenue's opposite side filled her with frustration and sadness. If he'd only push through the fatigue, he'd regain his stamina and strength much sooner. She turned cold eyes to him. "You must keep going."

Mr Locke lowered his walking cane and leant upon it. "After a time, my body becomes a lead weight, and every step feels like I am walking through mud. The time grows longer each night as I feel myself growing stronger. I walk until my legs tremble, and I am on the brink of collapse." His voice hardened. "In short, Lynette, I am doing my best."

"As am I. Do you think I enjoy seeing you so weakened?"

"No."

"Then do not speak to me as if I were your enemy, Percy." Dr Locke's gaze softened as a tinge of sadness entered her voice. "I'm painfully aware of how brutal the treatments have been, but your recovery isn't possible without them."

"Lynette." Mr Locke took her hand in his. "*I* am wholly aware of what *you* are going through at my hand." He furrowed his brow and lowered his head as a pained expression gripped his features, and regret laced his voice. "Words do not suffice to express my burden of guilt and shame." He lifted his head, and there was hope in his eyes. "But my actions may express my undying gratitude for all you have done and continue to do for me. My progress is slow, but I give you my word. I shall recover and become the man you married."

Dr Locke felt her heart ache at his earnest determination, for she'd heard it all before. "I truly hope so, darling."

Mr Locke understood and accepted her hesitation. His relentless desire for the drug had compelled him into employing deceitful and manipulative methods to procure it. Consequently, he'd repeatedly broken his promises to her and her heart. Yet, he'd resolved this time would be different and, thus far, it was. Giving her hand a gentle pat, he offered his arm. "Shall we?"

Dr Locke afforded herself a small smile as she slipped her arm around his, and they continued their walk.

"A lock had me thoroughly perplexed this afternoon." Mr Locke had a twinkle in his eye as he added, "When I had fathomed its rather basic flaw, I was quite embarrassed at my own stupidity."

Dr Locke chuckled. "You are losing your touch, darling."

Mr Locke smiled at her with affection in his eyes. "I do not think so."

Dr Locke returned his smile and held him closer as they walked.

* * *

Sitting in the middle of a sofa with her spine flush against its back and her arms folded, Miss Lily tightly clutched her jacket draped over the latter. Poking a finger down the side of her corset as she fidgeted in her seat, she glanced at the clock on Miss Ilbert's dressing table. "When may I go home?"

"Soon," Miss Ilbert replied, putting on some rose-scented perfume. Sitting before her dressing table's mirror, she had changed back into her red-velvet bustle dress. Her stockinged ankles were crossed beneath her stool as she leant forward to inspect her complexion. "The longer you wear the corset, the quicker your body will adapt to it."

"Yes, Mother." Miss Lily laid her jacket across her knees and, bowing her head, held her hands in her lap whilst toying with a doll-shaped charm on her bracelet. "Mother?"

"Yes, dear?"

"Why were those men so beastly to Mr Benton?"

"It can happen on occasion."

"But why? I thought Mr Benton's performance was wonderful."

Miss Ilbert turned upon her stool to face Miss Lily. "Sometimes ignorant people do beastly things. One is more exposed to it in the theatre, but one shouldn't allow it to stop one from pursuing one's art."

Miss Lily clasped her hands in her lap and met Miss Ilbert's gaze. "What should I do if they are beastly to *me* on my debut?"

Miss Ilbert put a gentle hand upon Miss Lily's cheek. "They shan't be."

"But if they are?"

Miss Ilbert withdrew her hand. "You conduct yourself with dignity and grace." She released a soft sigh. "As justified as Luthor was in his reaction to those men, his rudeness lost him the good will of the audience."

A knock on the door caused them to look up.

"Come in," Miss Ilbert called.

The door opened, and Miss Kimberly entered. "The company is gathered on the stage as per your instructions, Mina."

"Thank you, Emma. We'll be along in a moment," Miss Ilbert said.

Miss Kimberly glanced between Miss Ilbert and Miss Lily. Catching their sombre expressions, she enquired, concerned, "Has something happened?"

"We'll be along in a moment. Thank you, Emma," Miss Ilbert said, firmly.

"But I may be able to help," Miss Kimberly said.

"It's a private matter between me and my daughter," Miss Ilbert said.

Miss Kimberly's posture visibly stiffened as her mouth flattened.

"We'll be along in a moment," Miss Ilbert repeated.

Miss Kimberly was rigid as she turned and slammed the door upon leaving the room.

* * *

"I thought I'd find you 'ere," Miss Hicks said, sitting beside Dr Weeks on the bench.

The surgeon had put himself in an alcove by a latticed window of the *Coach & Horses* pub. Located on St John Street, it was a stone's throw from his rooms above *R.G. Dunn Pawnbrokers*. Given the hour, its bar room was filled with most patrons obliged to stand. Dr Weeks had only managed to secure a table because he was a well-paying regular and friend of the landlord. Three empty pint glasses littered the table, whilst the fourth he was drinking from was already half-finished.

"I was worried." Miss Hicks looked between him and the glass as he took a large mouthful. "Don't you think you've had enough today?"

"Nah." Dr Weeks lifted the glass to his lips and, leaning his head back, drank the remaining ale. Adding the empty glass to the others with a thud, he pulled the money pouch from his pocket and took out a few coins. "Get me another, darlin'."

"When you've told me what's goin' on," Miss Hicks said, firmly.

"Nothin's goin' on." Dr Weeks shoved the coins into her hand. "Get me another drink. A pint. Ale."

"I ain't stupid, Perce." Miss Hicks put the coins down in front of him. "You was drinkin' like a beer-eater before, and 'ere I find you doin' it, again. It ain't like you. So sumin's the matter, and I wanna know what it is."

Dr Weeks rested his elbows upon the table and bowed his head low. In a rough voice, he said, "I told ya: nothin's wrong."

"If that's the truth, I'm a nun," Miss Hicks countered, sardonically. "What 'bout the appointment with your mum?" She lifted the money pouch an inch off the table and dropped it. "And where's this come from? You rob someone?"

Dr Weeks snatched the money pouch off the table and stuffed it into his pocket. "If yer not goin' to get me a drink, leave me in peace."

Miss Hicks pursed her lips and exhaled loudly through her nose. Despite her irritation at his lack of cooperation, she was worried about his deteriorating state. He'd been a heavy drinker since she'd met him, but this was different. He was usually a happy drunk. This was drunkenness born from despair. Taking a gentle hold of his arm with both hands, she tried to coax him to his feet whilst saying in a soothing voice, "Come 'ome, Perce."

Dr Weeks pulled his arm free. "I ain't goin' anywhere 'til I get another drink."

Miss Hicks glared at him. "Ge' it yourself." Getting up from the bench, she muttered, "Ungrateful bastard."

Dr Weeks flinched at her unfortunate choice of words. Mr Fry's voice also crept into his mind: *Bastard son. Who should be grateful for what he receives.* Followed swiftly by Inspector Lee's: *Your parentage certainly explains much of your behaviour. The drunkenness. The rudeness. How does it feel, carrying the burden of your mother's shame? Knowing your father never wanted you?*

A strangled sob escaped Dr Weeks' lips. Wiping his face with his hand as he gave a loud sniff, he glanced around but saw Miss Hicks was gone. Snapping his fingers at the landlord, he lifted his empty glass to indicate his order. At the landlord's nod of acknowledgement, he put the glass down and lit a cigarette with trembling hands. The subsequent smoke he inhaled took the edge off the weight in his chest, but only the drink could sponge it out completely, albeit temporarily.

Sitting a couple of tables across from him, Sergeant Gutman finished his ale and kidney pie and wiped his mouth with the back of his hand. Putting some coins down by way of payment, he stood and left the pub in time to see Miss Hicks loitering by the door to the rooms she shared with Dr Weeks. The way she looked into the shadows hinted at a conversation with another.

Intrigued, Sergeant Gutman crossed the street and walked along the pavement past *R.G. Dunn Pawnbrokers*. As he did, he saw a man in his mid-thirties with unkempt chocolate-brown hair and a bushy moustache standing in the doorway of the stairwell to Dr Weeks' rooms. His deformed ears and nose hinted at a profession in the boxing ring. A suspicion supported by his thick neck and broad chest. He was attired in a knee-length, blue coat and trousers and thick, light-grey woollen jumper. When he spoke, it was with a broad Belfast accent. "If 'e wants to soak 'eself, let 'im be."

Miss Hicks held herself. "I've not seen 'im like this before, Noah."

Sergeant Gutman stopped to light a cigarette and eavesdrop.

The man cupped Miss Hicks' face in his hands. "'E don't deserve you." He slid his hands to her waist. "And if e's not comin' home…" He leant down to kiss her.

Miss Hicks turned her head away. "I can't."

The man gently lifted her chin between his thumb and forefinger. "You can."

He kissed her, lightly at first, before slipping his tongue between her lips and wrapping his large arms around her. When the kiss eventually broke, he held her tightly against him, and she was breathless whilst gazing up into his eyes. Her face had also flushed a bright pink. "If 'e comes 'ome, you've gotta go."

"Like a thief in the night," the man said, smiling broadly.

Miss Hicks put her arm around his waist as he released her to put his arm around her shoulders. Sergeant Gutman watched them until they'd entered the stairwell to Dr Weeks' rooms. When the door closed behind them, Sergeant Gutman glanced back at the *Coach & Horses* pub.

He debated whether he ought to fetch Dr Weeks so the surgeon could see what his good woman got up to whilst he was losing himself in the bottle. Realising it would give him and his surveillance activities away if he did, though, he decided to report the development to Inspector Lee instead. Continuing on his way to the nearest cab rank, he calculated how much expense money the Yard owed him whilst finishing his cigarette.

* * *

Every part of the stage was occupied. The small army of workmen, including carpenters and pulley operators, stood in rows at the back. In front of them were the ticket office employees and the conductor and musicians from the orchestra. The supers were gathered in a group on stage left with Mr Thurston. The members of the pantomime's main cast were gathered on stage right with Mr Benton. Mr Stone and Miss Kimberly stood front and centre of the crowd, with Mrs and Miss Hightower behind.

When the auditorium doors opened, and Miss Ilbert entered with Miss Lily, all conversations died away. The crowd's attention became fixed upon the theatre manager as she walked down the aisle and onto the stage. Sensing the tension in the air by the hush alone, Mr Stone fought the impulse to roll his eyes. The atmosphere was blatantly what Miss Ilbert had had in mind when she'd issued the cryptic summons via Miss Kimberly. It was as manipulative as one could get, and it both amused and irritated him that everyone had fallen prey to it.

"Good evening, everyone," Miss Ilbert began once she and Miss Lily were stood before the crowd. "You are no doubt wondering why I have brought us all together tonight."

Mr Stone snorted.

"Do you have something to say, Ronald?" Miss Ilbert enquired.

Mr Stone turned aside and dismissed the question with a wave of his hand.

"Good." Miss Ilbert returned her attention to the others. "You're all aware of the incident during this evening's performance." Several people nodded and muttered their assent. "In addition to his unacceptable behaviour earlier, the leader of the group, a man named Jack, has been blackmailing Mr Benton into paying him to avoid such incidents."

Several jaws dropped amid many gasps. This was immediately followed by people turning to their neighbours and expressing their disbelief and shock. These exclamations soon evolved into full conversations which grew in volume and intensity as everyone tried to process the news.

"*Silence!*" Miss Ilbert cried, projecting her voice across the stage.

Again, the conversations died away as all eyes turned to her.

"As shocking as this revelation is to most of us here, it shan't come as a surprise to some," Miss Ilbert continued, her gaze drifting to Miss Joanna. "For they are Jack's co-conspirators in the blackmailing of Mr Benton."

Miss Joanna's face crumpled, and she ran into the wings, her hand clamped over her mouth as tears fell down her cheeks. Those surrounding her stepped aside and watched her flee with a mixture of shock and confusion. One enquired from their neighbour, "Is Joanna involved?"

"It is unknown who is involved at present," Miss Ilbert said over the subsequent murmuring. Once the group's attention had shifted back to her, she added, "But I shall find out soon enough." She stepped back and addressed the company as a whole, "There is a wolf amongst us who threatens to ruin not only our pantomime but the very reputation of our beloved theatre." Her gaze drifted to Mr Stone. "I cannot allow that to happen."

She paused to take a deep breath and brace herself for the reaction she suspected would come once she'd finished her next speech. "Jack's co-conspirator, or conspirators, have until this time tomorrow night to come forward and admit their guilt. The deadline also applies to anyone with information that could lead to the identification of those responsible. If no one volunteers themselves or their knowledge, I shall have no choice but to dismiss everyone in the company."

Several people swivelled their heads slowly as they glanced between Miss Ilbert and their neighbours. Others stared at her with dull eyes. Everyone remained silent, however. Yet, as the minds of the company members registered the ultimatum and conjured visions of what it could mean, they moved and expressed their alarm, shock, and confusion to their neighbours.

Miss Kimberly, who'd been as ignorant of the ultimatum as the others, came forward with a pallid complexion and wide eyes. In a voice strained by emotion, she enquired, "Does this also apply to me, Mina?"

A pained look entered Miss Ilbert's eyes. "It applies to everyone, Emma."

"And Lily?" Miss Kimberly enquired, her eyes becoming damp.

"And *I*?" Mr Benton demanded, stepping forward.

"To *everyone*," Miss Ilbert replied to them both, her voice filled with regret.

Mr Thurston went over to Mr Stone and hissed into his ear, "Say something, Ronnie!"

"I'm not admitting anything to that witch," Mr Stone hissed in return.

"*But it will leave everyone destitute*!" Mr Thurston hissed in desperation. "*Including you*!"

Mr Stone glared at him. "I'll get another theatre soon enough." He shifted his glare to Miss Ilbert. "We'll see how far she gets with no company, and no one willing to work for her once word gets around." He walked off into the wings.

"Please stay here for the technical rehearsal if you are required. The rest of you may go home," Miss Ilbert ordered over the din. "I ask *all* of you to give serious consideration to my words and the future welfare of your fellow employees." The conversations died away, again, as angry and fearful eyes turned toward her. With deep concern in her voice and expression, she went on, "I hope whoever is responsible is decent enough to protect the company and the lives within it. For disbanding it and sending you all into destitution is what I have always striven to avoid. Yet, those responsible have given me no choice." Her breath hitched in her throat. "I am truly sorry and pray to God I am not forced into taking this horrific action. Thank you."

With an exchange of worried, angry, and sad glances, the company gradually dispersed across the stage, either to wait for the technical rehearsal or to depart for home. Unable to look them in the eyes as they passed, Miss Ilbert instead allowed Miss Lily to take her to her office for some brandy.

ELEVEN

Miss Trent checked the time on her pocket watch as she crossed the landing. Finding it was almost ten thirty, she eased open the door to Toby's bedroom and peered inside. His sleeping face was illuminated by the glow of the kerosene lamp on his bedside table. Lying upon his side, he had his cheek resting upon his hands and the blankets wrapped tightly around his body. The sound of loud, steady breathing told her he was in a deep sleep. Careful to avoid the loose floorboards, she crept inside, extinguished the lamp, and crept out again.

Going downstairs at an easy, unhurried pace, she tilted her head side to side and gripped the back of her neck as she went into the kitchen. Her features softened when she saw Inspector Conway pouring some hot water into the teapot. He stopped what he was doing upon seeing her. "It was whistlin'."

She took the cast-iron kettle from him. "Sit down. I'll finish this."

Inspector Conway pulled out a chair from under the table and sat. "Was 'e asleep?"

"Sound." Miss Trent added tea leaves to the pot and stirred them.

"Have you thought about what I said?"

Miss Trent put the lid on the teapot and laid out the cream, sugar, and cups upon the table. "Yes, and I've decided to let Toby live here." She gave him a warning look as he parted his lips to argue. "The workhouse would be the worst place for him, and you know it."

"A bit of 'ardship never done me any 'arm."

"You told me you were on the wrong side of the law when you were a boy." She smirked, a twinkle of mischief in her eyes.

Inspector Conway cleared his throat as the back of his neck warmed. "Yeah… but that was different." He nodded toward the pot. "Is it brewed yet?"

Miss Trent's smirk grew into a wide grin at his discomfort. It was a reaction she'd rarely seen in him, which made it even more amusing. She stirred the leaves, again. "Almost." She sat beside him as her expression became serious. "Anyway, Toby has had his fair share of hardship already. If the Bow Street Society can provide him with a safe and loving home, I see no reason why it shouldn't."

"What does Richard think about it?"

"He agrees with me." Miss Trent checked the strength of the tea, stirred it one last time, and poured it into their cups. "Speaking of Richard," she looked at him sideways, "what are you two up to, John?"

Inspector Conway averted his gaze to his tea as he added cream and sugar. "Nothin'."

Miss Trent watched him with expectant eyes.

Inspector Conway picked up his cup and met her gaze. "Don't give me that look."

"Richard wouldn't have reassigned you to Bow Street without good reason."

Inspector Conway put the cup to his lips. "I told you what 'e said." He took a mouthful of tea.

"I know there's more to it, John."

Inspector Conway put his cup down. "Like what?"

"You tell me."

"There's nothin' more to tell, Rebecca."

"I'll ask all night if I have to."

Inspector Conway knew she would, too. Drinking the rest of his tea, he set his empty cup down beside the teapot whilst considering the best way to approach the matter. Casting his memory back to when Chief Inspector Jones told him about his reassignment to Bow Street, he remembered his words about Miss Trent: *"Inspector Lee is less likely to suspect a conspiracy if her reaction to his new assignment is genuine."* Miss Trent knew of Inspector Lee's new assignment, now, though. *Richard's got what he wanted*, Inspector Conway thought. He maintained strong eye contact with her as, in a steady, low-pitched voice, he admitted, "You're right: me and Richard are up to sumin'."

A visible tension gripped Miss Trent's neck, shoulders, and arms. She fixed him with an intense, cold stare as her emotions fluctuated between disbelief, hurt, and anger. The memories of her meetings with Inspector Conway and Chief Inspector Jones, together and separately, also swept through her mind in a blur. In a hard tone, she enquired, "What?"

"Richard made Lee head of the Mob Squad to let 'im get closer to the Society, and 'e put me at Bow Street to keep an eye on 'im."

Miss Trent's expression tightened, and she turned her head away. "And I thought I could trust you."

Inspector Conway stared at her in disbelief. "You can."

"So, why wasn't I told?" Miss Trent demanded, turning hard eyes upon him.

Inspector Conway parted his lips with a sigh, went to speak, but thought better of it upon reconsidering his words. Closing his lips with a frown, he knew no explanation he could give would ease her justifiable hurt and anger. Nevertheless, she had a right to one. In a steady voice, he said, "Richard said Lee would get suspicious about bein' made head of the Mob Squad if your reaction to it wasn't genuine."

Miss Trent's brow lifted. "And neither of you remembered I was an actress?"

"I—" Inspector Conway cut himself short as he realised it hadn't occurred to them. Feeling a warmth sweep up from the back of his neck, over his ears, and across his cheeks as his complexion flushed pink, he cleared his throat and looked down, unable to meet her gaze. In a subdued voice, he admitted, "No… we, erm… we forgot about it."

Miss Trent stared at him, stunned. Rather than feeling angry, though, as she'd expected, her next emotion was amusement as she envisioned the pair of them whispering and worrying about keeping their plan a secret from her. A smile crept over her lips, and she burst out laughing. Resting an arm across her stomach and an elbow upon her arm, she pressed her fingertips to her mouth but continued to chortle.

Inspector Conway looked at her, confused. "What's so funny?"

"You," Miss Trent chuckled, "and Richard." Her eyes sparkled. "*Some* detectives you both turned out to be." She allowed her laughter to flow freely, much to Inspector Conway's surprise, and put a hand on his arm as she tried to calm herself. "Oh, John." She grinned. "What am I going to do with you?"

Feeling relieved and reassured by her laughter, Inspector Conway was more than happy to be the butt of the joke if it meant salvaging his friendship with the clerk. He could also see the funny side. He smirked. "Go to the theatre?"

Miss Trent leant her head back and laughed.

* * *

"It is an *outrage*, Mina. An *outrage*!" Mr Benton bellowed. Standing before her desk whilst she sat behind, he threw his hand up in a sweeping motion whilst turning upon his heel as he continued, "*I* am the *abused* party!" He walked away a few paces before turning upon his heel, again, to face her. "Does my support, my *affection*, mean nought to you?"

Miss Ilbert stood. "It means a great deal, Luthor." She walked around the desk and closed the distance between them. "But someone is trying to ruin this theatre, to ruin me, and I cannot allow it."

Mr Benton withdrew his hand and held it aloft as she reached for it. He lifted his chin and peered down his nose at her. "*I* should be *above* suspicion."

Miss Ilbert's features tightened. "No, you shouldn't." She rested clasped hands against her skirts. "I cannot be seen to be taking sides in this matter. Either we all suffer or none of us do."

"The scoundrel shan't come forward, you know."

Miss Ilbert gave him a questioning look. "And why not?"

"If he cared for this theatre, he would not be attempting to ruin it." A small tremor entered Mr Benton's voice. "I care for this theatre, Mina, and I care for you. A great deal. Do not abandon either of us for the sake of your pride."

"Regardless of what happens here, my feelings for you have not changed, Luthor."

Mr Benton's eyebrows gathered in as he studied her face. "Nor has your mind."

Miss Ilbert's hands fell to her sides. Stepping back from him, she maintained strong eye contact whilst holding her chin high, exposing her neck. "No."

Mr Benton's expression slackened, and he gave a small nod. In a low yet steady voice, he warned, "On your head be it, then."

Miss Ilbert's own expression slackened as she stared at him in stunned disbelief. Swivelling her head to allow her gaze to follow him as he left, she parted her lips to call him back, but he was already gone. A wave of nausea swept over her as she replayed his words. It wasn't what he'd said, but rather how he'd said it. *On your head be it, then*. She realised he hadn't been speaking of the danger to the theatre, but of the danger to her. For the first time in many years, she felt frightened.

* * *

Dr Weeks finished his last pint and added the glass to the others littered across the table. With laboured movement, he slid across the bench and swung his legs out with the intention of standing. Feeling his head swim at the sudden motion, though, he sat a moment and waited for it to settle

113

before leaning on the table and unsteadily getting to his feet.

Two men in their early twenties sat at the next table. The taller of the two had unkempt dark-brown hair and beard, a crooked nose, and brown eyes. His attire consisted of an old brown cotton jacket, faded black trousers with thinning knees, off-white shirt, and brown neckerchief. The shorter of the two men had grimy light-blond hair, a pointed nose, and pale-blue eyes. His attire consisted of a dark-blue coat torn on the left elbow, light-brown trousers, dark-brown high-necked shirt, and dark-brown flat cap.

Shortly after taking his seat an hour prior, the tall man had seen Dr Weeks taking coins from the money pouch. He'd nudged his short friend who'd turned and also seen the pouch. They'd since kept a close eye on the surgeon and his pouch to determine how much money he had. An eventual glimpse of bank notes had had the men wetting their lips and formulating a plan to get their hands on them.

Now, as Dr Weeks swayed on his feet, the tall man tapped the short man's arm and nodded toward their quarry. The short man turned to look, again, and watched Dr Weeks half-stagger, half-shuffle to the door. With a glance at the tall man, the short man stood and left the pub behind the Canadian. A heartbeat later, the tall man also stood and followed his friend.

Once outside, Dr Weeks' eyes had struggled to focus due to a combination of the cold night air making them water and his severely inebriated state. As a result, the once-familiar surroundings of St. John Street had become a mass of blurred colours and shapes. He couldn't even be certain which direction was home. Leaning against the pub's external wall with one hand, he squinted into the darkness, confused. Yet, almost immediately, he decided to go right, with no greater basis for his decision than it seemed to be a good idea at the time.

Having crossed the road upon leaving the pub, the short man had waited for the tall man who'd joined him just as Dr Weeks had started to shuffle along the pavement opposite. The men exchanged glances and, whilst the tall man walked up their side of the street to cross the road ahead of Dr Weeks, the short man crossed where they were to follow the surgeon. Within moments, they were in their desired positions with Dr Weeks in between.

The short man reached into his coat and gripped the club concealed there.

At the same time, the tall man took a cigarette from his trouser pocket and openly held it where Dr Weeks could see it as he blocked the surgeon's path. With a flash of a smile, he enquired in a broad East End of London accent, "You ain't got a match, have you, mate?"

Dr Weeks stopped abruptly, the act causing him to sway. Seeing only a blurred, dark silhouette in front of him, though, he assumed he was hallucinating on the drink and continued shuffling forward. Feeling sudden resistance against his chest from the tall man's hand, though, he squinted to see his face. When this failed, he tried to shuffle around the obstacle. Yet the tall man easily re-blocked his path. Narrowing his eyes, Dr Weeks ordered in a heavily slurred voice, "Get outta my way—*oof*!"

Dr Weeks' words were violently cut off by the club striking his crown.

Falling forward into the tall man's arms from the force, Dr Weeks was stunned but conscious. Mumbling incoherently, he attempted to regain his footing but was flung backward against the building instead. Fists were repeatedly driven into his stomach, forcing the air from his lungs, before another strike from the club sent him hurtling into oblivion.

* * *

"Have you 'eard from Weeks?" Inspector Conway enquired upon entering the kitchen with his coat and hat from the stand in the hallway.

"No, but there hasn't been a case to assign him to," Miss Trent replied as she emptied the last of the tea into the sink and washed out the pot. "But Miss Hicks has been coming here most days to teach Toby how to read." She dried her hands on a small towel and turned to Inspector Conway with concerned eyes. "She hasn't mentioned Dr Weeks, and I can't ask her about Mr O'Hannigan." She set the towel aside. "Do you know any more about their affair?"

"Nah," Inspector Conway replied with a frown and shake of his head. He put his hat down on the table and pulled on his coat. "Sumin's not right with Weeks. I dunno what it is, but the bloke's been avoidin' me like the bloody plague." He fastened his coat and picked up his hat. "If you see 'im, can you tell 'im I was askin' about 'im?"

Miss Trent offered a reassuring smile. "Of course, I will, John." She crossed the kitchen to unlock the door into the garden. "I might not see him until after his mother leaves, though."

Inspector Conway joined her at the door. "You what?" He stared at her, taken aback. "Weeks' *mum* is in London?"

Miss Trent's eyes twinkled with amusement. "According to Toby she is. He said she surprised Dr Weeks at the railway bar earlier today."

"Blimey." Inspector Conway gave a weak smile. "If she's anythin' like Weeks, all I can say is 'poor bugger.'"

Miss Trent chuckled and opened the door. "Good night, John."

"Good night." Inspector Conway stepped through the door and crossed the garden with a few glances to his left and right. Slipping through the gate at the garden's rear, he entered the service alleyway beyond and headed home under the cover of darkness.

TWELVE

A sudden bang woke Dr Weeks with a jolt. Feeling an explosion of pain in the front and back of his head, the stench of ammonia assaulted him as a damp sensation registered on the side of his face. Forcing his eyes to open a slit, he winced at the daylight coming through a small window. Realising he was lying on something cold and hard, he put his hand down and felt the rough surface of a stone floor against his skin. With a loud, prolonged groan, he dragged himself onto all fours before slowly sitting on his heels. Pulling his feet out from underneath him next, he sat on the floor and felt a wall at his back. With his eyes barely open, still, he looked around and realised he was in a large room with three other men. Upon opening his eyes fully, he saw they were in varying stages of unconsciousness. The air was also poisoned by the combined stench of stale alcohol and bodily odour. A glance to his left revealed a tall, solid iron door with a hatch in its upper third and a second hatch at its foot. He mumbled, "I'm in a damn police cell."

The higher hatch slid back with a loud scraping of metal. The sound sliced through Dr Weeks' senses, causing the agony in his head to intensify. Realising he also had throbbing on the outside of his head, he gingerly touched his crown and felt a large lump. Gingerly touching the right side of his head, he felt a second, smaller lump. The memory of being struck by something flashed through his mind's eye.

"Coffee, doctor?!" a constable called through the hatch with a grin.

Dr Weeks closed and clenched his eyelids whilst bowing his head. "If ya'll shut up!"

The hatch slid back into place, the sound of scraping metal once again assaulting Dr Weeks' senses. Leaning his head back against the cold wall in the hope it might reduce the swelling of the larger lump, he closed his eyes and tried to remember what had happened. He'd been in the *Coach & Horses* drinking. Polly was there. Afterward was a complete blank. He sighed and opened his eyes. Catching another whiff of ammonia, he touched his face and looked at his fingers to find their tips covered in dark urine. Unsure if it was his, he wiped it on the trouser leg of the drunk sleeping nearby.

The thought occurred to him that he might have to appear before the magistrate. If he did, it would happen sooner rather than later, before a court room of curious gawkers and amused policemen. It wouldn't be the first time and undoubtedly wouldn't be the last. Yet, the prospect of being found guilty of public drunkenness, again, didn't worry him. He knew he could afford to pay whatever fine the magistrate issued, thereby avoiding prison, thanks to the allowance his father gave him.

Feelings of paralysis and the walls closing in suddenly struck Dr Weeks as a vision of him with the money pouch at the *Coach & Horses* pub exploded into his mind's eye. His pulse raced, and the sound of his heartbeat thrashed in his ears as he searched his pockets. Finding no sign of the pouch, he desperately sought a memory of Polly taking it home. When his mind came up blank, he released the breath he'd been holding and threw himself forward. Scrambling to his feet, he banged on the door, yelling, "*Hey, you! Get yer ass here now, ya thievin' sonofabitch!*"

The hatch slid back to reveal the constable's glaring face. "I *beg* your pardon?"

"Where is it?" Dr Weeks demanded through rasping breaths.

"I don't know what you're talking about," the constable replied.

Dr Weeks struck the door with the flat of his hand. "*My money, ya bastard!*"

The constable's tone and expression turned cold. "You had nothing except the clothes on your back when you were brought in, Dr Weeks."

Dr Weeks backed away from the door in quick, jerky steps whilst shaking his head in denial. His head spun, and black spots appeared in his vision as his whole body tremored from the adrenaline coursing through his veins. "Nah… yer took it. Yer've got it in yer safe or somewhere."

The constable's expression softened as sympathy entered his eyes and voice. "Constable Richards found you lying in the street drunk, dazed, and confused. You had been struck twice on the head, and all your valuables were missing when he searched you." The constable frowned. "I'm sorry, doctor, but you were robbed."

Dr Weeks' eyes bulged, unable to blink, as he backed further away, this time in small, slow steps. Feeling the wall at his back, he felt the cell closing in on him, again, and an intense weakness in his legs. *All my allowance were in that pouch*, he thought. *Every penny of it.* Clenching his hands into fists and pressing them against the sides of his head, he released a prolonged cry of utter anguish and slid down the wall. Pressing his chin against his chest and drawing his knees in tight, he finally, and uncontrollably, wept.

* * *

"Mr Atteberry is a hardworking and successful gentleman's tailor with his own shop and family to support," Mr Elliott said, addressing the jury. Attired in the black gown and powdered wig of the defence counsel, his pale complexion was lightened further by the latter. His voice and expression were impassioned as he continued his opening argument, "The defence shall prove his innocence beyond reasonable doubt by demonstrating the accusations lodged against him are the product of an ongoing feud with his neighbour and nearest competitor— the alleged victim of the alleged assault—Mr Lucas Quintin."

From his vantage point at the front of the public gallery's balcony, Inspector Lee had a superb view of the court room. Yet, his focus was entirely on Mr Elliott, specifically, his beautiful face, his sharp eyes, and inviting lips. The longer he watched him, the more Inspector Lee contemplated what the eye couldn't see. It was both distracting and invigorating. Also frustrating, because there was little to no chance of him having the opportunity to be so close to the solicitor.

Unfolding his legs to swap them over, he forced his mind to analyse the reports he'd read prior to departing for the Old Bailey. Despite Sergeant Perry being stationed in the front bedroom above the shop opposite the Bow Street Society's house since yesterday afternoon, he'd had little to report. The boy, Toby, had arrived with Miss Hicks in the early evening. She'd then left approximately an hour later, and no further visitors were seen. It was disappointing but not entirely unexpected.

Sergeant Gutman's report had been far more concerning. Having had a verbal update from him last night, in which he'd informed him of Miss Hicks' intimate encounter with a stranger, Inspector Lee had expected this morning's report to be of a scandalous nature. In other words, he'd expected Sergeant Gutman to state he'd witnessed the aftermath of Dr Weeks catching his lover in the arms of this other man. Unfortunately, Sergeant Gutman's report had instead stated not only was Dr Weeks arrested for being drunk in a public place last night, but he was robbed of a considerable amount of money. Such an incident wouldn't bode well for the surgeon's state of mind, a source of great concern for Inspector Lee at the moment. To alleviate the pressure on Dr Weeks, Inspector Lee had sent word to the police station where the surgeon was being held, and requested they release him without charge due to his status as a police informant. The request had been granted, and Dr Weeks was to be released within the hour. Naturally, Sergeant Gutman would follow the surgeon home and report to Inspector Lee any further developments which occurred there.

The only other report of interest was Sergeant Caulfield's. He'd begun his search for Mr Homer Fairburn, Mr Elliott's former clerk, but had discovered no leads thus far. Inspector Lee wasn't surprised by this. He knew it was like looking for the proverbial needle in a haystack, and, besides, it had been less than twenty-four hours since he'd given Sergeant Caulfield the assignment. Nevertheless, his curiosity was piqued by the story. It was the only hint of scandal they'd uncovered in Mr Elliott's life, and Inspector Lee was keen to root out the truth of it.

"Gentlemen of the jury, the defence asks you to look at Mr Atteberry," Mr Elliott said. As he turned to his client in the defendant's dock, he saw Inspector Lee in the balcony. Momentarily taken aback not only by the policeman's unexpected presence but also his smiling face, Mr Elliott stared at him with parted lips for several seconds. Recollecting where he was immediately after, he diverted his gaze to his client and said, "And you will see not a ferocious beast but a gentle, humble man." He turned to the judge. "Thank you, Your Honour." A look of discomfort passed over his face as, upon returning to his seat, he glanced up at Inspector Lee.

Pleased by the effect his presence had had on Mr Elliott, Inspector Lee kept his gaze on the solicitor. Within moments, his thoughts had returned to contemplating what the eye couldn't see. As a consequence, he felt compelled to spend more time with the solicitor and so decided to intercept him the moment the court adjourned for the day.

* * *

Miss Hicks turned over in bed and opened her eyelids a crack. They snapped open when she saw the overcast morning sky through the window, however. Sitting bolt upright, she glanced at the clock on the bedroom's mantel shelf and saw it was almost ten fifteen. *Where's Percy?* she thought. A glance to her left confirmed Mr O'Hannigan's sleeping presence. *Did he come home and find us sleeping?* Feeling a knot forming in her stomach, she slipped out of bed and covered her nakedness with her dressing gown before creeping from the bedroom and into the lounge.

Her immediate reaction was one of panic when she saw Dr Weeks wasn't there. Yet, this feeling subsided as, upon wandering around the room, she found no sign of him having returned at all. In fact, the room appeared as it had when she'd brought Mr O'Hannigan home last night. Relieved, she moved toward the bedroom but stopped as another thought struck her: *If Percy ain't home, where is he?* She went to the window and looked out. There was the usual morning traffic, but no sign of Dr Weeks either on foot or in a hansom cab. *Has he gone to work?* She wondered. *If he has, where'd he sleep last night?* She checked the sofa, but there were no signs of it having been slept on.

"Polly?" Mr O'Hannigan enquired from the bedroom door.

Miss Hicks looked up and felt a twinge of arousal upon seeing his naked body. Growing hot at the same time, she put a hand to her forehand as she tried to focus. "Erm… Percy ain't 'ere." She tidied the cushions on the sofa whilst trying not to glance at him.

"I thought you didn't want him knowin' about us?" Mr O'Hannigan moved behind her and slid his large hands over her hips as she bent over the sofa. "It's a good t'ing he's not here, isn't it?"

Miss Hicks straightened, and the heat in her core intensified as she felt his arousal against her robed behind. Making deep and prolonged eye contact with him over her shoulder as her mind replayed last night's intimacy, she felt a fluttering in her stomach and a tingling between her legs. In a voice at odds with her words, she said, "I… I'm worried."

Mr O'Hannigan put his arm around her whilst moving his face closer to hers. In a soft voice, he enquired, "Are you?"

Miss Hicks' eyelids flickered before closing completely as she breathlessly replied, "Yes."

Mr O'Hannigan captured her lips in a demanding kiss. She released a muffled gasp but nonetheless kissed him deeply in return. Spurred on by her reaction, Mr O'Hannigan broke the kiss to bend her over the sofa. She gasped a second time at the sudden movement but immediately spread her legs and gripped the sofa's arm. A heartbeat later, she felt a shiver of excitement as he lifted her robe and pressed against her.

"What the hell are ya doin'?"

Startled, Miss Hicks looked at the door to the stairwell.

It was Dr Weeks.

THIRTEEN

Time seemed to stop. For several moments, Miss Hicks stared at Dr Weeks, Dr Weeks stared at Miss Hicks, and Mr O'Hannigan glanced between them. Finally, Mr O'Hannigan pulled away from Miss Hicks, prompting her to stand and clumsily cover herself. Whilst he nonchalantly wandered back into the bedroom, she turned worried eyes to Dr Weeks.

Noticing his dishevelled, dirty, and fatigued appearance, she felt even guiltier for what he'd walked in on. It had never been her intention to hurt him. Truth be told, she didn't know what her intention had been. The excitement Mr O'Hannigan had given her was completely different to the excitement she felt with Dr Weeks. It wasn't as if she'd grown tired of the surgeon, far from it. She'd simply wanted her cake and to eat it, too.

Moving cautiously toward him, she quickened her pace upon seeing the lumps on his head. "What happened to you, love?!"

"Get away from me!" Dr Weeks cried in a strangled tone. Stumbling backward at the same time, he lost his balance as his body crumpled in on itself and fell sideways against the doorframe. Leaning there, half-bent over, he gripped the frame with one hand and a fistful of shirt with the other as he gave her a long, agonised look. Tears also saturated his face as he felt a painful tightness in his throat and a constriction in his lungs, making it hard to breathe. Yet, when she averted her gaze, ashamed, he managed to choke out, "*How could ya, darlin'?*"

"I didn't mean—" Miss Hicks stopped when she realised how pathetic she sounded.

"*An accident, were it?!*" Dr Weeks yelled. "*Ya were just happenin' to be bendin' over when he were just happenin' to be passin' with his pisser out?!*"

"*No!*" Miss Hicks cried. "Stop shoutin' at me!"

Dr Weeks hung his head, finding his footing despite the trembling in his legs, and tightly folded his arms and gripped his elbows. Disintegrating into uncontrollable blubbering, he moved away from the doorframe with uneven steps and headed for the stairs.

Miss Hicks ran after him. "Perce, *wait*!"

Dr Weeks threw out his arm, forcing her to rapidly step back. "*I told ya to get the hell away from me!*" When he looked at her, though, his face was bright red and soaked with tears. His features were also contorted into a grimace as pain, the likes of which she'd never seen before, filled his eyes. In a voice weakened by emotion, he pleaded, "Please."

Miss Hicks felt sick to her stomach at the thought of what she'd done to him. Reproaching herself for giving in to temptation, she also longed to go back and change what had happened. Yet, she knew it was too late to change either, which made her feel even worse. Unable to meet his gaze, she bowed her head, and her face dampened with tears. "I'm so sorry, love."

Fresh tears fell down Dr Weeks' face as an intense ache gripped his heart, and an overwhelming sense of betrayal rocked his soul to its core. Between shuttering breaths, he managed to choke out, "Not as sorry as me, darlin'." Tightening his grip upon his elbows, he pressed his arms against his chest and went down the stairs, his breathing repeatedly hitching in his throat as he struggled to suppress his blubbering.

Upon emerging onto St John Street, his mind spun with thoughts of what he'd witnessed and memories of the past as he tried to process what had happened and how. The sound of traffic also became dull, as if his ears were blocked with wax.

"Doctor?" Sergeant Gutman's voice cut through the blockage. The sound of traffic also snapped back to its normal volume, causing Dr Weeks to wince. "Are you all right?"

Dr Weeks' damp, red eyes met Sergeant Gutman's sympathetic ones.

"Let me buy you a drink." Sergeant Gutman took Dr Weeks' elbow to guide him toward the *Coach & Horses* pub.

"Nah, n-not there," Dr Weeks mumbled. "I got some whisky at the Dead Room. Will ya walk with me, Sergeant?"

Sergeant Gutman gave a weak smile. It was only a fifteen-minute walk away, but he suspected the surgeon felt nervous after last night's robbery. "Yeah. Wherever you wanna go. Come on." He put his arm around the surgeon's shoulders.

* * *

Mr Jerome puffed upon a cigar and exhaled the smoke past Miss Hightower's shoulder. "Yow face will stay like that eef the wind changes."

Miss Hightower leant back against the brick wall and sighed. "It will also carry us to the workhouse."

Mr Jerome stood before her. "Will yow stop torkin' like that?" He plucked the cigar from his mouth. "Oy said oy'd look after yow, didn't oy?"

Miss Hightower's eyes lit up as her eyebrows raised, and she leant forward. "You'll tell Miss Ilbert?"

Mr Jerome's head jerked back. He sneered, "*No.*"

"Oh." Miss Hightower lowered her head as she slumped back against the wall.

Mr Jerome glared at her with a tension-filled expression. "Oy was goin' to take yow back to Birmin'ham, but oy'll not now."

Miss Hightower's head shot up; her eyes wide. "No. *Please*, Jack. Take me with you."

"Why should oy?"

Miss Hightower darted her desperate gaze across his face. "Because I love you."

Mr Jerome puffed some more on the cigar and exhaled the smoke against the wall beside her as he studied her expression. "Do yow?"

Miss Hightower swallowed and quietly replied, "Yes."

"Will yow do what oy I want?"

Miss Hightower gave a small nod.

Mr Jerome grinned. Plucking the cigar from his mouth, he held her waist with one hand as he leant in and kissed her demandingly. Releasing her as he pulled away, he gave another grin. "Oy'll think about eet."

* * *

Miss Hicks sat forward on the sofa with her shoulders curled inward and her arms loosely folded. As she stared at the wall with unblinking eyes, she repeatedly pinched her arm to cover her emotional pain with the physical. Yet, nothing could dampen the heaviness in her heart caused by her betrayal of Dr Weeks and nurtured by the memory of his pain. She knew how cruel it had been for him to see her like that. *Like a whore*, she thought. *After all he's done for me.*

She recalled their first meeting. It had been over a year ago at the railway bar. He should've been just another customer, but she was taken by his dark-brown eyes the moment she'd seen them. They held a warmth and gentleness she hadn't expected. When he'd looked at her, she felt like he was seeing a fellow human being and not just another barmaid. Then he'd spoken. She'd never heard a Canadian accent before and so had assumed he was American. When he'd politely corrected her, her interest was piqued, and she'd asked a plethora of questions about Canada and how he'd come to be in London.

He'd answered them all with warmth and enthusiasm and taken a genuine interest in her own upbringing and background. None of which he'd shown disgust or contempt at. They'd talked for hours and, after the bar had closed, he'd walked her home. She'd expected a grope and a cheeky kiss from him. Instead, he'd asked to see her again, and bid her good night with a light kiss on the back of her hand.

When he'd walked away, she was already longing to see him again. This had both surprised and confused her, because she was in an intimate relationship with Miss Trent at the time. Prior to Dr Weeks, she'd only been attracted to women. Looking back at it now, and taking her affair with Mr O'Hannigan into consideration, she realised she was attracted to both. Perhaps she hadn't met the right men in the past? Either way, it didn't matter. She knew she loved Dr Weeks and knew she'd now lost him.

The longing to see him again gripped every fibre of her being. With it was an intense ache to touch, hold, and kiss him. Her mind's eye replayed the painful memory of his reaction upon catching them, and she felt sick to her stomach. The longer the memory went on, the more unbearable it became. Eventually, it was strong enough to drive her to her feet and into the bedroom.

Mr O'Hannigan, who'd been getting dressed in the time since Dr Weeks' departure, looked up from putting on his boots when she entered. Sitting on the edge of the bed, he watched her take a clean dress from the wardrobe and lay it out beside him. It was a dark-blue cotton dress with an impressive bustle, far nicer than anything he'd ever seen her in. Watching her freshen up at the washstand for a time, he put on his other boot and stood. "You're goin' out to find him, I take it?"

"Yes." Miss Hicks retrieved her undergarments from the floor and slipped into them underneath her dressing gown. "You should go, too."

Mr O'Hannigan smirked at her sudden modesty. "You weren't so shy last night, wee girl." His smirk grew into a smile. "Or this mornin'."

Miss Hicks turned away to hide her shame. "That was then, love." She took off her robe and, putting on her corset, looked at him across her shoulder. "Would you?"

Mr O'Hannigan came up behind her and, wrapping the laces around the first couple of hooks, pulled hard to tighten them. In a cold tone, he said, "Not'in's changed for me." He wrapped the laces around the next couple of hooks and pulled hard, again, to tighten them. "If you're now feelin' guilty, I'm sorry. But you weren't feelin' guilty when you bent over for me earlier. It's only your man findin' us that's got you feelin' this way." He wrapped the laces around the next couple of hooks and pulled hard, again, to tighten them.

Miss Hicks grunted softly as her chest was compressed by the corset. The effect it had on her cleavage was what she wanted, however. By both pushing her breasts together and lifting them, whilst also narrowing her waist, she hoped Dr Weeks' desire for her would overcome his feelings of anger and hurt.

"Maybe." She looked up at Mr O'Hannigan but immediately averted her gaze out of guilt. He didn't deserve her contempt or her rejection. This mess was entirely of her own making, after all. Yet, she knew the ache to hold and kiss her Percy wouldn't ease until she'd made amends with him. Between the two of them—Dr Weeks and Mr O'Hannigan—she loved the surgeon and only desired the boxer. It was a shame it had taken Dr Weeks catching her in the midst of committing a scandalous act for her to realise the truth.

Mr O'Hannigan finished tying her corset and, stepping back from her, retrieved his coat from the floor. "Come find me when you know for sure."

Miss Hicks frowned and put her hand on his chest when he headed for the door. "Don't be like that, love." She rested her hand upon his cheek. "I hurt Perce this mornin', and I've got to put it right." She lowered her hand but continued to frown. "I don't know what it means for us, but nothin's makin' much sense at the moment."

Mr O'Hannigan closed the distance between them and put his arms around her. "If 'e loves you, 'e'll come back."

Miss Hicks wondered if he was speaking from experience. He'd been having an affair with Mrs Grosse when they'd met. Not wishing to cause an argument between them, though, she offered a contrived smile.

Mr O'Hannigan pulled away from her and put on his coat. "I'll help you look."

Miss Hicks' eyes widened. "You'll do nothin' of the kind, Noah O'Hannigan! What do you think my Perce'll do if 'e sees you again?"

Mr O'Hannigan shrugged his shoulder. "Not'in' I couldn't handle."

Miss Hicks made an outward sweeping motion with her flattened hands. "*No.*" She met his amused eyes with worried ones of her own. "You'd kill 'im."

Mr O'Hannigan chuckled. "I'll not go near 'im. Don't worry."

Miss Hicks visibly relaxed. "Thanks." Picking up her dress, she slipped it on over her head and fastened the buttons at the back before straightening its skirts. "'E's got enough bumps to be gettin' on with."

She went into the lounge, followed by Mr O'Hannigan, and crossed over to the window where she removed a loose floorboard. With him looking on, she retrieved a small, wooden tea box from the cavity beneath. "I'm hopin' 'e's gone to the pub." She opened the box to reveal a banknote and several coins. Taking the former and stuffing it into her cleavage, she returned the tea box to its hiding place and replaced the board.

"I'll be around if you can't find 'im." Yet, Mr O'Hannigan's gaze was on the loose floorboard.

"Thanks, love." Miss Hicks collected her coat from the sofa.

They descended the stairwell and emerged onto the street together. Not wishing to linger in case Dr Weeks returned, Miss Hicks gave Mr O'Hannigan's arm a gentle squeeze and bid him goodbye. She watched him walk away and turn the corner before departing herself in the opposite direction.

Yet, no sooner had she disappeared, Mr O'Hannigan retraced his steps and returned to Dr Weeks' rooms. Crossing over to the window upon entering the lounge, he looked up St. John Street but saw no sign of either Miss Hicks or the wayward surgeon. Therefore, confident he wouldn't be disturbed, he knelt upon the floor and lifted the loose board. With a quick check of the tea box's contents, he slipped the entire thing into his coat pocket and replaced the board.

He smirked at the thought of Miss Hicks' reaction when she discovered the box missing. "Payment for services rendered, wee girl."

FOURTEEN

Inspector Woolfe blinked a few times to expel the blurriness in his vision. Opening his eyes wide as he focused on the *Gaslight Gazette*'s small print, he noted the number of the page containing the advertisement. To this, he added the edition and date: *Evening. 31st October 1895.*

Prior to leaving Bow Street earlier, he'd agreed with Inspector Conway to make enquiries about Jack Jerome. Specifically, to call upon Madam Mimi at her brothel, and the complainant at the *Royal Opera House* who'd alerted the police about Mr Jerome's blackmail attempt. The visits might lead nowhere, but they'd occupy Inspector Conway long enough for Inspector Woolfe to finish his search of the *Gaslight Gazette*'s archive.

Feeling a tightening in his chest, he took a sip of medicine, grimaced, and took another sip. Despite a cough erupting from his lips anyway, it wasn't remotely near the violent coughing fits which had kept him awake half the night. He set the bottle aside and rubbed his eyes whilst turning the page. When he looked down, again, his attention was immediately drawn to an advertisement in the top-right corner. It read:

CLERK REQUIRED.
Commitment to irregular hours and
utmost discretion essential. Apply in
writing to Smith Brothers c/o
Gaslight Gazette, Fleet Street,
London.

Inspector Woolfe read it again and wondered which business, aside from the police and the Bow Street Society, would require a clerk to work irregular hours. Hospitals and medical practises came to mind, but he suspected those would've enhanced their credibility by providing a doctor's name for applicants to write to. *Smith Brothers* reminded him of the circus and sideshows. "Or an alias," he muttered aloud.

Thus far, he'd been working under the assumption Miss Trent was employed by one person. If this advertisement *was* for the Bow Street Society's clerk position, it would appear she was employed by at least two people. *Unless the entire membership is her employer*, he thought. Sitting back in his chair, he coughed some more. Managing to bring it under control without the medicine's aid, though, he cleared his throat. *If the members employ her, one of them could be the one who hired her*, he thought. *And there's no mysterious employer at all.* He frowned as he noted the page number, edition, and date. It was certainly something to keep in mind, but he wasn't about to abandon his search because of it.

* * *

The door opened, and Madam Mimi's overall countenance brightened upon seeing Inspector Conway standing on the step. Opening the door wide, she followed him with her eyes as he removed his trilby hat and entered the hallway. She kept her gaze upon him as she closed the door and slid the bolt into place. Unlike the morning before, she was fully dressed in a scarlet-red, silk bustle dress with black lace and beaded trim. Her hair was neatly pinned atop her head, and an elaborate black beaded necklace adorned her slender neck. "I wasn't expecting to see you again so soon."

"Is 'e here?" Inspector Conway enquired as he glanced into the adjacent room. It was deserted, had its curtains closed, and the lamps and hearth were unlit.

"Who?"

"Don't play daft," Inspector Conway warned. "Jack Jerome."

Madam Mimi's features tightened. "No. He isn't. He hasn't come back since yesterday either." The tension in her face eased as she ran an admiring gaze over him. "I never got *your* name."

"Detective Inspector John Conway."

"Well, *John*, I was about to have some tea." In a honeyed tone, she added, "Would you like some?"

Inspector Conway wasn't sure her question was entirely about the tea, but, in his experience, it was rare for someone so obviously involved in criminal activity to extend such an invitation to a policeman. Therefore, he knew how important his acceptance could prove to be, especially if she had information. Maintaining an emotionless expression and tone, he replied, "Yeah. Thanks."

Madam Mimi took his hat and coat and hung them on a stand under the stairs. As she led him through the door marked *Private*, he found himself in a moderately sized parlour. Although its curtains were also closed, there was a large fire in the hearth and brightly lit gas lamps upon its walls. A plush two-seater, dark-green sofa was directly before the curtains with a long, low table in front. An elaborately embroidered guard was before the fire, with a large round table a couple of feet away from that. The table was covered by a white lace tablecloth and had four chairs tucked underneath it. In the far-right corner of the room was a piano, whilst a bureau was on the near right. The walls were decorated with an olive-green paper embossed with leaves, and the floor was covered by a deep-pile, dark-green carpet. Paintings depicting the English countryside hung on the walls. A tea set was laid out on the low table.

Sitting on the sofa, Madam Mimi waited until Inspector Conway had joined her before pouring the tea into two cups. Anticipating his question, she explained, "I have tea with a different one of my girls every morning." She passed his cup to him to add his own cream and sugar. Lifting her cup to her lips, she watched him over the rim as she took a delicate sip.

Inspector Conway left his tea untouched. "What do you wanna tell me, then?"

"Tell you?" Madam Mimi put her cup down. "Absolutely nothing."

Inspector Conway looked from her to the tea set and back again. "Why did you invite me in here, if not to tell me sumin'?"

Madam Mimi smiled. "To put you at a disadvantage, clearly."

Inspector Conway narrowed his eyes. "What for?"

"For whatever I want." Madam Mimi straightened the lapel of his suit jacket. "Caleb does what he can to look after me and my girls, but he won't be around forever." She met his gaze. "His ill health will see to that." She reached for his tie to loosen it, but his hand covering hers stopped her. She gave him a disarming smile. "There's no need to be shy, John."

"What do you know about Woolfe's health?" Inspector Conway challenged.

Madam Mimi withdrew her hand. "I know it's bad."

"What else?"

"Nothing you shouldn't already know as his friend."

Inspector Conway was taken aback. "Like what?"

"His cough." She put her hand on his knee. "I don't know any more." She moved her hand to her chest. "With my hand on my heart, I swear it's the truth."

Inspector Conway was suspicious but knew he had no choice but to accept her at her word. For now, at least. "Does Woolfe come here a lot?"

"A couple of times a month."

"Is that all the payment 'e gets?" Inspector Conway didn't believe his friend was corrupt, but the question had to be asked, nonetheless.

Madam Mimi stared at him. "He doesn't get *any* payment. He has to pay for his pleasures like the rest of them."

Inspector Conway furrowed his brow. "But you said 'e looks after you."

"By throwing out the occasional violent customer and asking after the girls' welfare." An edge of irritation entered Madam Mimi's voice. "As you heard yesterday, he doesn't approve of my disciplining the girls."

Inspector Conway was confused, still. "And you want me to do it instead of 'im?"

Madam Mimi smirked. Leaning in close, she replied in a soft voice, "Amongst other things." She gripped his tie and, pulling him toward her, kissed him deeply.

* * *

Miss Hicks bent over with O'Hannigan's filthy hands on her. It was an image Dr Weeks was unable to forget despite the half bottle of whisky he'd drank. Slumped in a chair in his Dead Room, he held the neck of the bottle as it rested on one knee. His puffy, wet, and dull eyes stared into the cavernous, deserted space without seeing it. The lumps on his head also throbbed from the cold, whilst goosebumps had formed on his arms. Yet, he couldn't summon concern for either. In fact, he was unable to see anything in his future beyond loneliness and destitution. Feeling a heaviness in his chest as fresh tears fell, he took a swig of whisky and wiped his runny nose with the back of his shirt sleeve.

"Perce?"

Dr Weeks wearily turned his head toward the doors. He thought he was hallucinating when he saw Miss Hicks standing there. Then he felt elated. Yet, it was fleeting and swiftly followed by anger and a painful tightening in his throat as the image of her bent over erupted into his mind's eye. With his thoughts spinning and building nausea in the pit of his stomach, he turned his head back and took another swig of whisky. In a voice hoarse from sobbing, he ordered, "Get out."

Miss Hicks held her tightly crossed arms against her stomach as she cautiously approached him. With a worried look in her damp eyes, she ran an appraising glance over him. He was, understandably, in a worse state than before. Recalling his pain at catching her with Noah, she recognised it in his eyes now and felt her wretchedness intensify. Questions of how she could've done this to him, how she could've been so selfish and heartless, assaulted her internal hearing. With pain in the back of her throat and a quivering voice, she half-whispered, "Perce… look at me… *please*."

Dr Weeks put the bottle down on the desk but kept hold of it as he rested his other elbow beside it, bowed his head, and gripped a fistful of hair. Within moments, his shoulders quaked, and the sound of deep and erratic breathing filled the air. As Miss Hicks drew closer, she also heard him softly whimpering against the elbow of the bottle-holding hand.

Feeling her heart swell with remorse, she struggled to swallow the lump forming in her throat as she fought to hold back her tears. *You don't deserve sympathy after what you've done*, she internally berated herself. Desperate to resolve the situation at the same time, though, she wracked her mind for a solution, or something to say to ease his suffering. *Nothing you say will make it better*, she realised. *You have to show him.*

Wiping her eyes with her coat's cuff, she crouched beside him and put a gentle hand on his shoulder whilst peering up into his face. "Perce?"

Dr Weeks turned his body away.

Miss Hicks reached around his arm to rest her hand on his cheek. In a soothing voice, she said, "Come on, love."

Dr Weeks suddenly released his hair and, straightening, threw his arm out. "I told ya to get out!"

Miss Hicks gasped as he struck her chest, sending her off balance. Toppling backward, she fortunately managed to grip the desk's edge to break her fall. Stunned and speechless, she stared up at him as he leant down toward her.

"Yer a *damn* filthy *whore*, Polly, and I ain't wantin' anythin' more to do with ya, d'ya hear?" He took the bottle with him as he stood and went to an empty, marble slab in the room's centre. Drinking the remaining whisky, he smashed the bottle by tossing it onto the floor. As he climbed onto the slab and assumed the foetal position, he mumbled in a slurred, hurt-filled voice, "Go back to yer fella."

Trembling and no longer able to hold back her tears, Miss Hicks clambered to her feet and ran from the room. As she ran along the corridor and up the stairs beyond, the door of the storeroom opened, and Sergeant Gutman emerged. Hearing the outside door slam at the top of the stairs, he glanced in its direction before opening the Dead Room's door a crack. He made a decision upon seeing Dr Weeks passed out on the slab. Closing the door, he followed Miss Hicks' route out and headed for the nearest omnibus stop.

* * *

Inspector Conway didn't know how long they'd been kissing for but knew it would have to end soon. Unable to remember the last time he'd been this close to a woman, though, he allowed himself the intimacy for a few more minutes before finally breaking away from her. Red faced and aroused, he cleared his throat and stood. "I ought to go."

"Why?" Madam Mimi stood to block his path. "Because I run a cat house?"

"No," Inspector Conway softly replied. "Because I don't trust myself with you."

"Why is that a problem?" Madam Mimi searched his eyes. "Are you married?"

Inspector Conway released a soft grunt of amusement as he shook his head. "No."

"Then why?"

Inspector Conway's expression and voice turned sombre. "Because I wouldn't be good for you, Mimi."

Madam Mimi adopted a sceptical tone. "And you think the men who come here are?"

Inspector Conway lowered his head and stepped around her. "I'm sorry."

Frustrated and disappointed, Madam Mimi pursed her lips as she watched him go.

* * *

"No." Inspector Woolfe turned the page and scanned the next for any advertisements for clerks by either the Bow Street Society or unnamed companies. Finding none, he repeated his negative aloud and moved onto the classified section of the next edition. Having an identical result, he moved onto the next. As the minutes passed, and the suspect advertisements dried up, he felt his dissatisfaction grow.

When he eventually closed the evening edition of 30th November 1895 having found only one more advertisement, he released a loud sigh. This instigated another cough, however, followed by a full-blown coughing fit. Taking a large swig of medicine, he grimaced and coughed harder. Feeling his face grow hot as he fought to catch his breath, he dragged himself to his feet and staggered from the room.

"*Water*," he wheezed in response to the archive clerk's astounded expression.

"Sit," the latter said as he pulled a chair across. A man in his early fifties, he had thinning light-brown hair, a narrow face, and dark-brown eyes.

Coughing and wheezing, Inspector Woolfe collapsed into the chair.

FIFTEEN

"Thanks." Inspector Woolfe put the empty glass down. Grimacing upon taking another sip of Dr Colbert's medicine, he slipped the bottle into his fur coat's pocket and slid his open notebook toward the archive clerk. "Can you tell me who bought these advertisements?"

The archive clerk read the list and frowned. "It will take a while."

Inspector Woolfe slid a guinea across.

The archive clerk pocketed the coin and gave a half-smile. "I shan't be a moment."

* * *

The cold air battered Inspector Conway's face, chilling it, as the hansom cab weaved through the traffic. With his lips pressed together, his brows pulled in, and his head tilted down, he stared at the doors' top edge whilst absently pulling at his ear. His thoughts were a jumble of things to do before returning to Bow Street and his encounter with Madam Mimi. Although he'd paid the occasional visit to a cat house in the past, he'd not done so in over twenty years. His unerring dedication to his work, coupled with the ungodly hours he'd been in the habit of keeping, had prevented him from considering even a courtship with a woman. Therefore, Madam Mimi's actions had come as a surprise, especially since he didn't consider himself handsome.

Pulling in and slowly releasing a deep breath as he lifted his head, he gazed out at the road. The brief time he'd spent with Madam Mimi had been pleasant and not entirely unwelcome. Yet, allowing it to go further was out of the question. His senior rank and damaged professional reputation aside, a relationship with a brothel madam would bring a new set of problems to his already complicated existence. Concluding the decision to leave had been the right one, he resolved to avoid Madam Mimi and her cat house and focused upon his next task instead.

* * *

The archive clerk set down a large ledger upon his desk and, licking his finger, flipped through its pages. Consulting Inspector Woolfe's notes as well as his own, he stopped at a page and ran his finger down the first column until he came to the desired date. "The 1st of October 1895, Mr Grosvenor paid for the advertisement for a clerk in the evening edition of the 2nd of October."

"Does it give his company?" Inspector Woolfe enquired opposite.

The archive clerk ran his finger along the row. "Grosvenor, Chorley & Green. Lawyers."

Inspector Woolfe gave a grunt of acknowledgement. "And the next one?"

The archive clerk scanned the pages, flipped over to the next, and ran his index finger down the first column until he found the date. "The 11th of October 1895, Mr Jardine of *Jardine & Johnson Ceramics* paid for the advertisement for a clerk in the morning edition of the 12th of October."

Inspector Woolfe shook his head. "Next one."

The archive clerk flipped through several pages before locating the third item on the policeman's list. "Mr Cristoforo Ruggeri paid for the advertisement for a clerk in the evening edition of the 31st of October. He paid for it on the 28th of October. He wanted a clerk to correspond with the English suppliers of his shop."

"What about the other one in the same edition? The one telling applicants to write to the Smith brothers?"

The archive clerk consulted the ledger. "J. Pettifoot paid for the advertisement on the 29th of October."

Inspector Woolfe watched him with expectant eyes. "Not the Smith brothers?"

"No."

141

"Was this 'J. Pettifoot' alone when they placed the advertisement?"

"I haven't the foggiest."

"Is there a company?"

"No."

"But 'J. Pettifoot' is a man?"

"As I said: I haven't the foggiest." The archive clerk turned the ledger around for Inspector Woolfe to read. "All I have is the date—29th of October, the name—J. Pettifoot, and the amount paid—two shillings."

Inspector Woolfe frowned. "Who would've recorded the purchase?"

"Mr Gilbert Berry."

"Where is he? I want to talk to him."

The archive clerk closed the ledger. "Pentonville Prison, the last I heard."

Inspector Woolfe straightened in his seat, causing the chair to creak. "What's he doing there?"

"Serving out his sentence." The archive clerk polished his spectacles with his handkerchief. "There was a rather nasty business last year, and—" He stopped himself and gave a contrived smile. "I'm sure your own archives will tell you all you need to know."

A faint recollection sparked in Inspector Woolfe's mind by those words. *Archives… reports… Fisher's report from the Maxwell murder case*, Inspector Woolfe mused, following his train of thought. *Miss Dexter… she answered an advertisement in… what month was it?* He furrowed his brow as he tried to retrieve the information. Releasing a soft growl when it wasn't forthcoming, he realised he'd have to return to Bow Street to check his files. "Thanks for your help."

* * *

"*Jesus…*" Inspector Conway said softly.

Approaching the prone form of Dr Weeks upon the slab, he was immediately forced back by the strong stench of urine, stale sweat, and alcohol coming from him. Pinching his nose, he covered his mouth with his palm as the foulness in the air penetrated his taste buds. He drew close to his friend again and saw he was unconscious but breathing. Noticing the two lumps on Dr Weeks' head, Inspector Conway considered whether they could be the cause of the surgeon's state. Another look at their bruising told him they weren't fresh, however. Nevertheless, the fact they were present at all worried him. The unkempt and heavily soiled appearance of Dr Weeks' clothes, coupled with his drawn, pallid complexion, and dark stubble, were also causes for alarm. How had his friend deteriorated so dramatically in a day?

"Weeks." Inspector Conway gently shook his shoulder. "*Weeks.*"

Nothing.

Inspector Conway moved away from the slab and halted at the sound of broken glass crunching under foot. He glanced down and saw the remnants of a bottle amidst drops of whisky. Pushing the glass aside with his foot, he searched the Dead Room for something to wake Dr Weeks. A mug of cold coffee on the desk was considered but dismissed as too messy. The surgeon was soiled enough. A scalpel on a trolley was likewise assessed but ruled out as too dangerous and dirty besides. Coming to a tall, wooden cabinet in the rear-left corner of the room, he ran an appraising glance over it. Its top half had solid double doors, whilst a large square shelf rested against its legs. He turned the key in the doors' lock and opened them wide to reveal a set of shelves. They were filled with glass bottles of all shapes, sizes, and colours containing an equally varied assortment of liquids, powders, and crystals. Finding one labelled *smelling salts*, he removed its glass cork and sniffed its contents. Jerking his head back at the strong scent of ammonia, he released a cough and blinked away the tears it had caused. "*Blimey*," he coughed again and thought, *If this don't wake him up, nothing will.*

Holding the bottle at arm's length, he returned to Dr Weeks and considered how best to get the salts' scent into his friend's nostrils. If he was to try whilst Weeks was lying down, he'd likely pour the salts onto his face or worse into his mouth. He grimaced at the thought. Setting the bottle aside on the nearby empty slab, he removed his overcoat and folded it before gently lifting Dr Weeks' head and slipping it underneath to form a pillow. He retrieved the salts and, moving to his friend's side, wafted the bottle under Dr Weeks' nose.

Dr Weeks' face contorted in disgust as he turned his head.

Inspector Conway wafted the bottle under his nose again.

Dr Weeks suddenly lifted his head with a violent gag followed by a cough. His eyes half-opened and narrowed as, with another cough, he pushed his brow down and squinted at his friend. Nausea swept over him the moment he realised who it was. Visions of Miss Hicks with Noah, his father, his mother, and the robbery merged in his mind. The sight of Inspector Conway standing over him threatened to season the noise with memories of Inspector Lee and the envelope. The prospect made him want to run and hide. He rolled onto his side, putting his back to the man who symbolised his guilt and shame.

Inspector Conway watched him with worried eyes. "You all right, mate?"

Dr Weeks gripped the slab's edge as he swung out his legs and pushed himself up into a sitting position. In a voice made rough from his dry throat, he replied, "No. Yer here."

"Charmin'," Inspector Conway mumbled as he recorked the bottle and set it aside.

Dr Weeks stood up from the slab and loosely held its edge as he walked its length. Releasing it to take several unsteady steps toward his desk, he kept his back to Inspector Conway. "Get the hell out, John. I ain't goin' to ask ya twice."

Inspector Conway followed him. "What's the matter with you? Who hit you?"

Feeling like he was about to vomit, Dr Weeks put his hands flat upon his desk and leant over them with his head bowed. At the same time, his breathing turned shallow, and he inwardly repeated, *Go away. Please. Go away.*

Inspector Conway frowned deeply. "Weeks?"

Dr Weeks wanted to run, but his legs felt weak. He wanted to scream, but he could barely catch his breath. The longer Inspector Conway stayed, the worse it became. He wanted him *gone*! With an increasing inability to focus, he felt his instincts take over. He reached underneath a pile of papers and pulled out the scalpel. He straightened, spun around, and thrust the scalpel toward his friend as he cried, "*Get the hell out*!'"

Inspector Conway leapt back, narrowly avoiding the blade. "What the *bloody* 'ell?!"

Dr Weeks advanced upon him, forcing him backward.

Inspector Conway lifted his hands to chest height, his gaze fixed upon the blade.

"Get out," Dr Weeks growled in a low voice.

"Mate—"

"*Get out*!" Dr Weeks yelled, swinging at him with the scalpel.

Inspector Conway ducked and heard the blade strike the door above him. Remaining crouched upon the floor, he looked up at his friend. "I'm goin'."

Dr Weeks' grip tightened on the scalpel's handle as he watched Inspector Conway slowly rise to his feet.

There was a moment's hesitation from the policeman before he finally opened the door and left.

As the door swung shut, Dr Weeks felt nauseous all over again. This time, though, he couldn't control it, and he bent over, vomiting. His stomach cramped repeatedly as he fought to catch his breath against the merciless heaving caused by the taste of bile. Releasing the scalpel, he covered his face with his hands as he dropped to his knees and wept.

SIXTEEN

The East Room at the *Criterion* restaurant in Piccadilly Circus, London, was often chosen by ladies wishing to dine with their friends, male or female, without reproach. Frequented by noteworthy individuals, often before an evening performance at the adjacent theatre, it was both a fashionable and respectable place to dine. The dark-green and gold panels on the walls, gold and red cornices, bronze velvet curtains, yellow-shaded lamps, and exquisite table linen, glass, and silverware also provided opulent surroundings in-keeping with the drama of the stage.

The thoughts in Mr. Thurston's head drowned out the cacophony of conversation from the other diners, however. He'd made another plea to Mr Stone's better nature earlier, but his words had once again fallen upon deaf ears. Furthermore, the stage manager had threatened to tell Miss Ilbert that *he*, Mr Thurston, was the one conspiring with Mr Jerome to blackmail Mr Benton. Such a revelation would not only guarantee his dismissal from the company but would destroy his one and only opportunity to see his play performed.

"You are troubled, Morris."

Mr Thurston looked up from his coffee cup at Miss Kimberly sitting across from him. "Aren't we all?" He bowed his head and, removing his spectacles, took a handkerchief from his pocket to polish them.

"Indeed." Miss Kimberly caught the sparkle of the lenses. This alone made her suspect he didn't wish to look upon her. She could speculate about his reason but decided not to since propriety forbade her from asking him outright. Thus, she'd be condemning herself to a period of lingering curiosity, and she had neither the tolerance nor the inclination to endure such a state at present.

"My heart aches for you the most." Mr Thurston kept his head bowed and put on his spectacles. "You are an old and loyal friend of Mina's." He brought his coffee cup to his lips with both hands. "You do not deserve to be treated in this cold-hearted manner." He took a sip, then another, and mumbled, "I think you ought to speak with her."

"I have."

Mr Thurston's eyes shot up. "What did she say?"

"She intends to see the matter through."

Mr Thurston lifted his head and put his cup down with a small thud. "Surely she does not intend to dismiss *you* if the culprits do not come forward?"

Miss Kimberly's face adopted a pinched expression. "She does." Her flattened lips momentarily faltered as a look of sadness passed through her eyes. "Lily, too."

Mr Thurston was stunned. "But *why*?"

Miss Kimberly gave a weak yet ironic smile. "To protect the theatre."

"There shall be no theatre without people to keep it going."

Miss Kimberly gave another weak yet ironic smile. "She is 'Lily of the Lyceum.' They shall fall over themselves to join her company." She bowed her head as she lifted her cup to her lips. "We can only do what we must to survive."

Mr Thurston envisioned himself walking from theatre to theatre, trying to sell his play, and the doors of each slamming in his face. Miss Ilbert had been enthralled by his work, and now she was about to toss a figurative match upon it. Without realising what he was doing, he said aloud, "If only you were the manager of the *Crescen*t instead of Mina."

Taken aback, Miss Kimberly lowered her cup. "Pardon?"

Mr Thurston's eyes widened as his mind registered his faux pas. "Oh dear." He felt his face warm. "I beg your pardon, Emma. I didn't mean—you would make a wonderful manager, of course, but I didn't mean to presume it was your wish."

Miss Kimberly's features softened. "It's quite all right, Morris." She put down her cup. "Actually, I agree with you."

Mr Thurston straightened in his chair. "You do?"

"The situation *would* be different if I were manager of the *Crescent*," her features fell, "but I'm not."

Mr Thurston put his hand upon hers. "You *are* Mina's closest friend, though. You could tell her this course she is on will only lead to disaster."

Miss Kimberly's eyes turned cold. "She will not listen, and I will not beg her."

Mr Thurston considered telling her the truth about Mr Stone and Mr Jerome. Furthermore, he considered offering to accompany her to Miss Ilbert with the information. Yet, Mr Stone was being just as stubborn, and he knew he would honour his threat of exposing Mr Thurston's part in the scheme. To lose the opportunity to see his play performed was one thing, but to lose Miss Kimberly was quite another. Therefore, he set the idea aside and prayed Miss Ilbert would have a change of heart before the day was through.

* * *

"Mr Snyder usually accompanies me to the bank when I make deposits or withdrawals," Miss Trent said. She sat behind her desk with one hand resting beside her typewriter and the other in her lap. "I'd be happy to do the same with your donation."

Dr Colbert shifted his weight within the infernally uncomfortable chair before her desk. "Thank you, but I haven't decided upon an exact amount." He stiffened his spine, but his hip ached from the hard seat, nonetheless. "If I had the name of the bank, its address, and the name on the account, I could deposit the donation at my leisure." He winced as he transferred his weight from the aching hip to his other. "I shall also gift the Society a new chair."

Miss Trent smiled softly. The unpleasant seat had served her well when dealing with equally unpleasant visitors. They rarely stayed longer than an hour because of it. "That's very generous of you, doctor."

"There is nothing generous about it. I simply can't abide this torture device any longer. I'll even have a chair brought from my own dining room, if you promise to burn this one."

Miss Trent did her best to suppress her amusement as she reassured, "I'll have it replaced as soon as possible."

"*Thank* you." Dr Colbert shifted his weight. "Preferably for one with a cushion."

"I'll see what I can do." Miss Trent wrote down the address of the bank and passed it to him. "The Bow Street Society's account is with the *London & County Banking Company* on Lombard Street in the City of London. Please inform me of the amount once you've made the deposit, as I'll follow up with the bank to ensure it's been safely received into the account."

Dr Colbert neatly folded the address and slipped it into his pocket as he stood. "I shall." His features lifted with a broad smile. "Thank you, again, Miss Trent."

"No. Thank *you*, doctor." Miss Trent stood, prompting him to do the same, and left the room with Dr Colbert following. "Your generosity will allow the Bow Street Society to continue to help those in the greatest need of justice but who also have the smallest amount to spare."

Dr Colbert's smile faded. He hadn't thought of the Society's work in such a way before. Feeling a pang of guilt at his deception, he reminded himself of the fact Miss Trent was endangering as many people as she was helping, and his guilt vanished. "Happy to help," he inwardly added, *the police.* Walking with her to the front door, he put his hat on as she unbolted and opened it. "I shall make the deposit in the next couple of days." He inwardly added, *after I've given the details to Inspectors Woolfe and Lee*. "Good day."

"Good day." Miss Trent watched him as he crossed the porch, descended the steps, and walked away in the direction of Endell Street. Feeling a mixture of pride and satisfaction at the prospect of a substantial donation coming the Society's way, she closed and bolted the door. Recalling she'd left Toby washing the dishes when Dr Colbert had arrived, she headed for the kitchen. "Toby, are you done?!"

As she entered the room, though, she caught Toby standing by the open back door with a look of surprise on his face. Noticing Inspector Conway immediately after, she saw he stood beside Toby, and the latter had his hand on the door's handle. Realising Inspector Conway must've only just arrived, she walked forward with a questioning look. Yet, as she neared, she saw the grey tinge to Inspector Conway's complexion and the haunted look in his eyes. She halted, her mind conjuring all manner of terrible possibilities. "What's happened?"

SEVENTEEN

The rain pummelled the cab's roof as Red-Shirt kicked up the surface water from the road. Tightly holding her coat closed against the inclement weather, Miss Trent went over Inspector Conway's news in her mind for the third time. There were so many questions and painfully few answers. *Why had Dr Weeks reacted so harshly to John's visit? What had changed since Dr Weeks had defended John at his disciplinary board hearing? What had provoked Dr Weeks into threatening one of his oldest and closest friends with a scalpel? Had Dr Weeks' excessive drinking finally caught up with him?*

Once she'd persuaded Inspector Conway to have some brandy to ease his shock, they'd spoken at length about all these things. He'd described how Dr Weeks had avoided him in Inspector Woolfe's office yesterday. Furthermore, how he suspected Dr Weeks had been avoiding him since the boxing match.

She and Inspector Conway agreed something had happened in Dr Weeks' life to cause him to act this way. They'd dismissed the arrival of Dr Weeks' mother as a possible cause, since Inspector Conway had never met the lady. Next, they'd dismissed Inspector Conway's reassignment to Bow Street as another possible cause, since Dr Weeks had played no part in it. They'd finally admitted the most unpleasant of possibilities was the likeliest: Dr Weeks had discovered Miss Hicks' adultery. Although, they couldn't be certain without speaking to the parties concerned. Inspector Conway was adamant—Miss Trent wasn't to approach Dr Weeks. That left Miss Hicks, and Miss Trent was determined to make her talk, provided she hadn't run away with Mr O'Hannigan, of course.

Mr Snyder brought the cab to a slow halt by *R.G. Dunn Pawnbrokers* and glanced at the sky as he felt the rain ease. The dense cloud cover had darkened the afternoon, but the latest encroaching gloom was a sign of the approaching sunset. Wiping the water from the edge of his hat's brim with his hand, he felt the cab tilt as Miss Trent alighted. Once she was standing on the pavement, he enquired, "Want me to come with you?"

Miss Trent offered a reassuring smile. "I'll be fine. Thank you, Sam."

Entering the small hallway, she strode upstairs and knocked on Dr Weeks' door.

"*Perce*?!" Miss Hicks' voice cried from the other side.

A second later, the door opened wide, and the two were face to face.

Miss Hicks stared at her, half-dazed. "Becky…" She darted her gaze to the landing beyond Miss Trent and back again. "Where's Weeks?"

"He was last seen at his Dead Room threatening Inspector Conway with a scalpel."

Miss Hicks laughed weakly in disbelief. When Miss Trent's expression remained grave, though, her own hardened. "Perce wouldn't do that."

"I heard it from Inspector Conway himself."

Miss Hicks gave a brief shake of her head. "But—"

"May I come in? I doubt you'd want the landlord to overhear our conversation."

Miss Hicks glanced at the stairs and stepped aside.

As Miss Trent entered, she noticed the floorboard underneath the window had been removed. "Did you lose an earring?"

"No," Miss Hicks mumbled as she closed the door.

Crossing the room and replacing the floorboard, she kept her eyes downcast whilst moving to the sofa. Only once she was perched upon its edge, her arms folded tightly against her stomach, did she finally look Miss Trent squarely in the face. "Perce was upset when I left him. His mate must of come at a bad time, that's all."

Miss Trent's demeanour cooled. "And why was he upset, Polly?"

Miss Hicks turned her head away and gave a brief shoulder-shrug. "I don't know."

"I think you do." Miss Trent sat on the window ledge opposite. "Noah O'Hannigan."

Miss Hicks' head snapped back to her. "How'd you know about that?"

"You were seen together."

Miss Hicks' face blanched. "When?"

"Last month."

"You *knew* and said nothin'?"

Miss Trent's cold mask faltered. "I was trying to protect Dr Weeks."

Miss Hicks frowned deeply. Unfolding her arms, she wrapped them about herself as she leant forward. After a long pause, she quietly said, "You're right: Perce's upset because of me and Noah." She lowered her head, thereby hiding her face with her hair. "He walked in on us."

Miss Trent released a sound of disgust. "How could you, Polly? After everything he's done for you?"

"I don't know. Noah was strong and exciting and *there*."

"And Dr Weeks wasn't?"

Miss Hicks put her head in her hand. "You're putting words in my mouth."

Miss Trent's features hardened. "I'm simply trying to understand why you've betrayed a man who's been nothing but kind, generous, and gentle with you, and who *you* claim to love."

"I *do* love him!" Miss Hicks glared at her. "It's took me losin' him to see it, but I *do*!" She stood and walked around the sofa, thereby putting her back to her former lover. "Look. I know I was a halfwit for trustin' Noah after what he done to Mrs Grosse." She faced her. "But you don't think it's goin' happen to you, do you?" She paced behind the sofa. "But it has." She gestured to the loose floorboard. "The bloody sonofabitch has scarpered with every penny we had."

Miss Trent felt a heat flush through her body at the news. A vision of Miss Hicks giving Mr O'Hannigan the money also leapt into her mind's eye. With cold eyes and a renewed tightness in her expression, she enquired, "Are you sure it was him?"

"Weeks would've left the box."

"That isn't what I meant."

Miss Hicks stared at her in disbelief. "You think I gave it him?"

"You've given him everything else."

Miss Hicks threw Dr Weeks' specimen jar at her.

As it smashed against the wall beside her, Miss Trent maintained her cool composure. Inwardly, though, she was reminded of the time Miss Hicks had struck her. She realised her former lover's hot-blooded nature could sometimes cause her to resort to violence, especially when things weren't going her way. An uncomfortable thought occurred to her: *Did she hit Dr Weeks, too?* She cooly chided, "I hope you feel better now. You've destroyed his property as well as his heart."

"*No.*" Miss Hicks came around the sofa and sat. "I didn't give Noah the money." Even though she'd repeatedly taken it without Dr Weeks' knowledge in the past. She put her head in her hands and tightly clutched fistfuls of hair. "But you're right: it's about the only thing I've not done with him." Tears slid down her cheeks and onto her skirts. "I've done us in, Becky. I love my Perce like mad, and I've done us in."

Miss Trent studied her in silence. Despite her anger and disgust at Miss Hicks' actions, she could both see and hear her regret and sadness. Knowing it wouldn't be right to leave her alone and therefore vulnerable to harm from either herself, Dr Weeks, or both, Miss Trent stood and picked up Miss Hicks' coat. "Come on."

Miss Hicks looked up, confused. "Huh?"

Miss Trent held the coat out. "You're coming with me."

"What if Perce comes back?" Miss Hicks stood. "He'll think I've run off with Noah."

Miss Trent tore a page from her notebook and gave it to Miss Hicks along with a pencil. "Tell him where you've gone and how sorry you are."

"Sorry's not goin' to make it all right, is it?" Miss Hicks mumbled.

"No, but it's a start."

Miss Hicks hoped it would be, too, as she leant upon the table to write the note. "What if he don't come back?"

"We'll cross that bridge if we come to it."

Miss Hicks folded the note and went into the bedroom to put it on Dr Weeks' pillow. The same pillow Mr O'Hannigan had rested his head upon mere hours earlier. The thought made her feel sick. How could she have been so *stupid*? Hurrying from the room, she pulled on her coat and headed for the door. "I need some air."

Whilst Miss Hicks went downstairs, Miss Trent stayed behind to extinguish the lamps and gather any knives she could find. In doing so, she hoped to prevent Dr Weeks from committing harm to himself or others. Yet, based upon what Inspector Conway had told her, the surgeon needed little provocation in his current state. For someone she, too, considered a close friend, Dr Weeks suddenly seemed like a stranger to her. It saddened her to feel that way, but there was little to be done about it now. Putting the knives into her pocket, she closed the door and left.

* * *

The fortress-like structure of the Sessions House towered overhead like a silent defender of justice as Mr Elliott emerged into the bail dock. A semi-circular brick wall built around the area immediately in front of the courthouse, the bail dock obscured the public's view of the courthouse windows. Its narrow entrance also prevented excitable crowds from flooding the courtroom. Passing through it, he put on his pill-box hat, crossed the yard, and left via the gate to Old Bailey, the street after which the courthouse was named.

The trial had adjourned for the day, and, following a conversation with his client in the prisoners' quarters in the basement, Mr Elliott left feeling optimistic. The case was going well, and he was confident of an acquittal, even at this early stage. Furthermore, he'd been left with ample time to hail a hansom cab and make the journey to Euston Road and Dr Colbert at the A.B.C. Tearooms.

"You were quite remarkable."

Mr Elliott halted upon hearing the familiar voice. Hoping he was mistaken, but knowing he wasn't, he pressed his lips together as he turned to see Inspector Lee standing by a carriage. In his usual monotone, he said, "I was merely doing my duty. If you would excuse me…" He turned to walk away. "I have somewhere else I must be."

"May I ask where?" Inspector Lee enquired.

Mr Elliott halted, again, but kept his back to him this time.

The policeman's presence had been an unwelcome distraction throughout the proceedings. Despite the solicitor's concerted effort to not acknowledge him in any way, Inspector Lee had remained in the public gallery for the duration. Mr Elliott had also seen several notes being passed to Inspector Lee. This had caused Mr Elliott's mind to speculate whether the notes were about him, when he should've been concentrating on the testimony of the witnesses.

"If it's not far, my driver may take you," Inspector Lee added.

Mr Elliott looked back at him. "I'm to be at the A.B.C. Tearooms on Euston Road—"

"Excellent." Inspector Lee smiled. "I'll join you."

"To meet a friend," Mr Elliott finished, his voice audibly colder.

"Really?" Inspector Lee moved closer, obliging Mr Elliott to face him. "I thought you didn't have any of those beyond the Bow Street Society."

"Did your unlawful surveillance tell you such?" Mr Elliott challenged.

Inspector Lee held firm eye contact with him. "Yes."

Mr Elliott attempted to step around him. "This conversation is over."

Inspector Lee stepped into his path, brushing his hand against Mr Elliott's as he did. "We're not obliged to be enemies."

Mr Elliott turned cold eyes on him. "Or friends."

"I would be a powerful friend to have," Inspector Lee lowered his voice. "If you permit yourself to trust me."

Mr Elliott glared at him in silence.

"There are things you ought to know," Inspector Lee continued, keeping his voice low. "About Miss Trent and the Society." He ran a slow, admiring gaze over Mr Elliott's face. "I want to enlighten you, Gregory."

Mr Elliott wasn't entirely certain Inspector Lee's last statement was about Miss Trent or the Bow Street Society. Feeling the policeman's hand brush against his, again, he pulled it away. "Don't touch me."

"I only want to be a friend to you."

"I don't want your 'friendship.'"

Inspector Lee smirked. "Yes. You do." He stepped back to give him some space. "Who are you meeting for tea?"

Mr Elliott remained silent.

Inspector Lee casually inspected his own fingernails. "The undercover detective I have watching you will tell me eventually." He lowered his hand. "If you give me your friend's name, however, I shall stand the detective down for the remainder of the day."

Mr Elliott detested being coerced by anyone, but being coerced by Inspector Lee left a particularly bitter taste in his mouth. Knowing he had no choice but to submit to it if he wanted his privacy, though, he further concluded it was better to have a spy at one's table than at one's window. "Dr Neal Colbert."

"Dr Colbert…" Inspector Lee gently tapped his chin with the handle of his walking cane as he appeared to search his memory. "Ah yes." He pointed the handle at Mr

Elliott. "He was Mr Snyder's second at the boxing match." He lowered the cane. "I'd be delighted to make his acquaintance again." He pointed into the carriage with the cane. "After you."

Mr Elliott's stoic expression momentarily cracked as he peered into the small space. Nevertheless, he climbed inside and sat in the far-right corner with his briefcase at his feet.

Inspector Lee instructed his driver before climbing into the carriage and slamming the door. Taking the near-left corner, he angled his body toward Mr Elliott and cast another admiring gaze over him. Upon feeling the carriage lurch forward, turn, and gradually gain speed as it joined the throng of traffic, he flashed a smile at Mr Elliott. "I was right."

Mr Elliott's hard gaze met Inspector Lee's jovial. "About what, specifically?"

"You don't have any friends beyond the Society."

Tension gripped Mr Elliott's face as he flattened his lips and glared out the window.

As the fading light illuminated his luminous complexion, though, Inspector Lee felt his heart being captivated all over again. *How simple it would be to take his face in my hands,* he thought. *To capture those lips in a kiss.* His mind conjured up other things he could do to him within the privacy of his carriage, and he felt a familiar stirring. Discreetly resting one knee atop the other, he thought of Inspector Woolfe. The thoughts and feelings Mr Elliott had provoked in him were dashed in an instant.

EIGHTEEN

Inspector Woolfe squinted at the advertisements in the *Gaslight Gazette*'s morning edition from Tuesday 6th August 1895. The archive room's dull gaslight made reading difficult, and he was tired besides. Taking a gulp from a glass of water given to him by the archive clerk, he rubbed his face with both hands and sighed.

It hadn't taken him long to locate Detective Inspector Fisher's file on the Maxwell murder case. As he'd suspected, Miss Georgina Dexter had revealed to him the month she'd applied for Bow Street Society membership. It didn't tally with Miss Trent's appointment, but it wouldn't if her employer had recruited the first members.

Inspector Woolfe had been preparing to leave Bow Street when a message came from downstairs, stating Dr Neal Colbert was requesting to see him. Inspector Conway hadn't returned, so Inspector Woolfe felt it was safe enough to hear what the mole had to say.

Dr Colbert walked along the corridor toward Inspector Woolfe with a spring in his step and a glow in his eyes. He extended his hand as he neared and, with a large smile and high colour in his cheeks, said as they shook hands, "I have it, Inspector."

Inspector Woolfe flashed his yellow teeth and guided him into his office.

"Miss Trent gave it me, and I came directly here." Dr Colbert held up a folded piece of paper. "The name and address of the Society's bank and the name on the account."

Inspector Woolfe took it and, as he read it, his features slowly lifted with a smile. "Good work, doctor." He put the paper in the top drawer of his desk and retrieved the bottle of whisky from the bottom. "This calls for a drink."

"Er, no. Thank you," Dr Colbert further declined with a wave of his hand. *"I'm to meet Mr Elliott at the A.B.C. Tearooms at four thirty."*

Inspector Woolfe straightened and studied him with suspicion. *"What for?"*

"To have tea, of course."

Inspector Woolfe narrowed his eyes and put the bottle down with a thud. *"No. Why are you spending time with him? Does the Society have a new case?"*

Dr Colbert furrowed his brow. *"Not to my knowledge."*

Inspector Woolfe poured himself a glass of whisky. *"Then I don't want you to go."*

Dr Colbert stared at him. *"But… Inspector, be reasonable. How am I to gain their trust if I restrict our interactions to cases?"*

Inspector Woolfe gave a soft grunt and drank half the whisky from his glass. Dr Colbert was right, but he still didn't like it. He'd feared Dr Colbert would be seduced by the Society members' charm and intellect, and this seemed to prove it. Rather than rely on mere supposition, though, he decided to take the direct approach. *"You're not coming around to their way of thinking, are you?"*

"Certainly not," *Dr Colbert rebuked, visibly affronted by the suggestion.*

Inspector Woolfe drank the remainder of the whisky and put the glass and bottle away. *"Keep it that way."* *He checked the time on his pocket watch.* *"There won't be time to get what we need if I go to the bank now."* *He locked the top drawer of his desk.* *"I'll go tomorrow."* *He pointed at Dr Colbert.* *"I want to hear what's said at tea, too."*

"Unless something of import is mentioned, I really don't see what—"

"I decide what's important." *Inspector Woolfe put on his coat.* *"I want it tomorrow."*

"Very well." *Dr Colbert sighed.* *"If you insist."*

"I do." Inspector Woolfe cast a glance over his office to ensure he hadn't left anything.

"How is your cough, by the way?" Dr Colbert enquired as they walked to the door.

"The medicine's helping."

"Good. Let me know if you need any more."

Inspector Woolfe grunted before enquiring, "Have you heard the name 'J. Pettifoot' said by any of the Bow Street Society members?"

Dr Colbert looked to their feet as he searched his memory. "Not to my knowledge." Inspector Woolfe opened the door, and Dr Colbert entered the corridor ahead of him. "I'll keep a close ear out for it."

"Thanks."

Attempting to hold back a cough and failing miserably, Inspector Woolfe took a sip of medicine and coughed again. Washing away the foul taste with another gulp of water, he turned the page of the edition and squinted at the next batch of advertisements. Realising this would take a while, he yawned and resisted thoughts of hot stew by an open fire to focus on the task at hand.

* * *

The inclement weather, combined with a need for refreshment on the way to the Euston Square railway station, had brought enough Londoners into the A.B.C. Tearooms to fill them. A handful of tables in the ground-floor shop were also occupied, whilst a queue had formed on the stairs in between. The waitresses, who were always busy, were run off their feet with showing customers to their tables, taking and serving orders, clearing and preparing tables, and accepting payments at the cash till. Their faces were red as they rushed about in all directions, their heels thudding loudly against the floorboards as they went.

Dr Colbert sat at a table in the corner with a window to his left and a wall behind him. The fully lit gas lamp above his head illuminated the space, giving it a cosy feel despite the crowd. Being a loyal patron of the establishment, he was well-versed in its popularity, particularly at teatime. Therefore, he'd taken the precaution of booking his table the previous afternoon.

Whilst waiting for Mr Elliott's imminent arrival, he checked his reflection in the teaspoon's bowl. Smoothing down his hair at the same time, he also wetted his finger and ran it across his eyebrows. Satisfied with their renewed neatness, he returned the spoon to the table and straightened the knot of his tie. Finally, he adjusted his cufflinks and glanced down to reassure himself the remainder of his appearance was in order. There was a fluttery, empty feeling in his stomach as he fixed his bright-eyed gaze upon the door.

When Mr Elliott entered, Dr Colbert felt a rush of adrenaline. The sight of him was enough to send his heart racing. Initially lifting his hand to signal his location, his impatience to be close to the solicitor compelled him to stand a moment later. As their eyes met, Dr Colbert felt the fluttery, empty feeling return to his stomach. He offered a wide grin and watched Mr Elliott cross the room toward him.

"Good afternoon, Gregory. It's so good to see you, again. Please, sit."

"Thank you, Neal." Mr Elliott put his hat down upon the table and unfastened his overcoat. "I invited Detective Inspector Gideon Lee to join us."

Dr Colbert felt a lead weight drop within his chest, and his grin vanished.

"Good afternoon, doctor." Inspector Lee offered his leather-clad hand.

Dr Colbert darted his stunned gaze from Mr Elliott to Inspector Lee and back again.

"I don't believe we've been properly introduced," Inspector Lee added.

"Pardon?" Dr Colbert enquired, taken aback. Realising the policeman's strategy, he felt another rush of adrenaline, this time due to relief. "Yes. I mean, no. We haven't." He forced a smile and shook Inspector Lee's hand. "I'm Dr Neal Colbert, of Bethlehem Hospital. I made Mr Elliott's acquaintance through the Bow Street Society, of which we're both members."

"I suspected as much," Inspector Lee cast a knowing smirk at Mr Elliott.

"I took the liberty of ordering our usual, Gregory," Dr Colbert said as they sat around the table.

Picking up on the subtle allusion to regular meetings between Dr Colbert and Mr Elliott from the former's words, Inspector Lee felt an unexpected flash of anger, followed by unmistakeable jealousy. Since the end of last year, he'd tried to arrange another intimate meeting with the solicitor, but all attempts had come to nought. Yet, Dr Colbert, a thoroughly unattractive and dull man, had enjoyed several such encounters within a month of their becoming acquainted. The fact he was married with two children could've played a part; he wasn't a reminder of Mr Elliott's true self like Inspector Lee was. Furthermore, Dr Colbert was a fellow Bow Streeter, whereas Inspector Lee was Mr Elliott's enemy. Again, Inspector Lee suspected the solicitor's dislike of him was born from his dislike of the feelings he provoked in him. The implication of both these reasons was Dr Colbert's apparently close friendship with the solicitor had no relevance to the friendship Inspector Lee was attempting to build with him.

Feeling his anger and jealousy ease at the reaching of this conclusion, Inspector Lee looked to Mr Elliott whilst addressing Dr Colbert. "The last time Mr Elliott and I were here, we introduced Inspector Conway to the delights of Earl Grey tea. He was not amused."

"We always order Earl Grey," Dr Colbert said. "Unfortunately, being unaware of your joining us, Inspector, I only ordered for two."

"No matter." Inspector Lee gave a polite smile. "I shall order my own." He gained the attention of a passing waitress and placed his order. Once done, he returned his gaze to Mr Elliott. The man appeared even more beautiful in the gaslight. "Do you often take tea together?"

"Whenever our work permits it," Dr Colbert replied. Noticing Inspector Lee's focus was entirely on the solicitor, he felt his own pang of jealousy. He'd hoped to strengthen his friendship with Mr Elliott by spending some time alone with him. Yet, Inspector Lee's intrusion had completely distracted them both. Hoping to at least divert the policeman's attention away from his friend, he enquired, "Were you also in court today, Inspector?"

"Yes." Inspector Lee reluctantly shifted his gaze to Dr Colbert. "In the public gallery."

"Have there been any new patients admitted to the asylum since we last met, Neal?" Mr Elliott enquired, wishing to avoid his friend's awkward questions by changing the subject.

"Fortunately, no," Dr Colbert replied, admiring Mr Elliott's beauty for himself when their gazes met. "And a couple of existing patients are almost ready to be discharged."

"Not to the workhouse, I hope?" Mr Elliott enquired with genuine concern.

"No, to their families," Dr Colbert replied with a flash of a smile.

"Pardon me, sirs," the waitress said as she arrived carrying a tray with their orders. Placing it upon the table once they'd moved back to create the space, she carefully served the three pots of Earl Grey tea, two cream jugs, and two sugar bowls. "Thank you, sirs."

Dr Colbert slipped a pound note into her hand as she passed. "A little something for you, my dear."

The waitress' eyes lit up. "*Thank* you, sir!"

"You shouldn't be so generous, doctor," Inspector Lee chided once she was beyond earshot.

"My generosity guarantees a table whenever I wish it." Dr Colbert poured his tea. "Besides, a little charity goes a long way. Don't you agree, Gregory?"

"Certainly." Mr Elliott turned cold eyes to Inspector Lee. "A small consideration for our fellow man may mean the difference between a life honestly lived and a life of villainy."

"Unless the villains see your monetary gift and decide to rob you of the remainder," Inspector Lee retorted. "Like poor Dr Weeks."

"Dr Weeks?" Dr Colbert enquired, taken aback.

"What do you mean?" Mr Elliott enquired, the concern returning to his voice.

"Dr Weeks was robbed and beaten by two men last night," Inspector Lee explained. "He was found in a state of drunkenness and confusion by a patrolling constable who proceeded to place him under arrest for being drunk in a public place."

Dr Colbert stared at him, stunned. "My God… is he all right?"

"The charges were dropped, and he was released this morning," Inspector Lee replied.

"That isn't what he asked," Mr Elliott challenged.

Inspector Lee smirked. "I know." He poured his own tea. "As far as I'm aware, Dr Weeks is in relatively good health."

Dr Colbert added more sugar than normal into his tea and took a large mouthful. "Thank God for small mercies." He drank some more to further calm his shock.

"Were the men caught?" Mr Elliott enquired.

"Alas, no." Inspector Lee took a sip of tea. "Perhaps, the Bow Street Society could seek them out and bring them to justice."

Mr Elliott's gaze and tone hardened. "This isn't a light-hearted matter."

"I don't recall saying it was," Inspector Lee rebuffed.

Mr Elliott glared at him a moment longer before averting his gaze as he poured his tea. He was already regretting his decision to allow Inspector Lee to join them, but he wasn't about to give him the satisfaction of causing a public scene, either.

* * *

Mr Benton firmly gripped his umbrella against the persistent threat of the wind as he paid the hansom cab driver. Turning upon his heel once the business was concluded, he allowed a young couple to hurry by before striding into the passageway to the *Crecent Theatre's* stage door. Thinking he may have finally rid himself of Mr Jerome and his gang when he reached halfway without seeing any sign of them, he relaxed. His relief was short lived, however, for Mr Jerome intercepted him at the passageway's end.

"Mista Benton, we was wond'rin' when yow was goin' to get 'ere," Mr Jerome said.

Mr Benton came to an abrupt halt, narrowly avoiding a collision with him.

"Do yow have what we want?" Mr Jerome enquired, moving into his personal space.

"Haven't you scoundrels done enough?!" Mr Benton shouted above the din of the rain.

"No." Mr Jerome grinned. "Where's my money?"

Mr Benton glared at him, anger pulsing through his every vein. Yet, it was no longer about him alone. It affected them all, including Mina. Reaching into his coat, he pulled forth several five pound notes. "Take your blasted money." He shoved them against Mr Jerome's chest. "And leave us be."

Mr Jerome caught the notes and carefully counted them. Upon discovering how much was there, he grinned like the cheshire cat. "Good doin' business with yow, Mista Benton." He slipped the notes into his pocket, tipped his hat, and left.

* * *

"There's a question I've never quite been able to fathom the answer to," Inspector Lee began as he dabbed his lips with his napkin. "Perhaps, you gentlemen could assist me?"

Mr Elliott's suspicion was immediately roused.

Yet, Dr Colbert was quick to accept the challenge. "Certainly, Inspector. What is it you wish to know?"

Inspector Lee sat back in his chair and, draping one leg over the other, rested his clasped hands within his lap. In a casual tone, he enquired, "How did two learned men of respectable reputation become involved in a questionable group like the Bow Street Society?"

Mr Elliott scowled. "I've had quite enough of—"

"Please, elaborate, Inspector," Dr Colbert interrupted, casting a sideways glance at Mr Elliott before settling a knowing gaze upon Inspector Lee.

"As I told Mr Elliott earlier: there are things about Miss Trent and the Society you ought to know," Inspector Lee said.

"Which are?" Mr Elliott pressed.

"Miss Trent is employed by someone." Inspector Lee studied Mr Elliott's reaction.

Dr Colbert thought of the 'J. Pettifoot' mentioned by Inspector Woolfe.

"Whose existence she's kept hidden from the Society," Inspector Lee continued.

Mr Elliott's gaze hardened. "You're lying."

"Ask her," Inspector Lee said with a smirk.

"No," Mr Elliott said. "I have implicit faith in her."

"Ask her and prove me wrong," Inspector Lee urged.

"Do you know who the 'someone' is?" Dr Colbert enquired.

"Not at present," Inspector Lee replied.

"For they don't exist," Mr Elliott said in a hard tone.

"Only Miss Trent can tell you for certain," Inspector Lee said.

Mr Elliott's hard gaze bore into him. As much as Mr Elliott was loathe to admit it, he knew Inspector Lee's point was a valid one. Picking up his cup of tea, he exchanged a tense glance with Dr Colbert and took a sip.

* * *

A soft clearing of the throat broke Inspector Woolfe's concentration on the *Gaslight Gazette* edition he was examining. Looking to the door, he saw the archive clerk tapping the glass of his pocket watch to indicate the late hour. A glance at his own told Inspector Woolfe the archives would be closing shortly. He said, "Five more minutes." The clerk pursed his lips but nevertheless left Inspector Woolfe alone to continue his search.

Allowing himself to yawn freely, Inspector Woolfe released several coughs immediately after. Feeling the telltale tightening of his chest, he took a mouthful of medicine and growled at the taste. He was certain he'd never come to like it. The tightening eased, at least, and he turned the page to read the next column of advertisements. Suddenly, his gaze fell on one for membership applications:

MEMBERS REQUIRED FOR NEW PHILANTHROPIC SOCIETY.

Men and women considered. All classes considered. Discretion, empathy, determination, and strong sense of justice essential. Applications to be submitted c/o the Gaslight Gazette, Fleet Street, London.

Inspector Woolfe read the advertisement again to be sure he'd read it correctly. Although it didn't give the name of the Society, his gut instinct told him it was the one. He checked the date and edition: *Monday 19th August 1895, evening edition.* Taking the volume with him as he went into the adjacent room, he put it down before the archive clerk. "Who placed this advertisement for the new philanthropic society?"

"One moment." The archive clerk went to retrieve his ledger.

Inspector Woolfe sat in the chair he'd vacated. Whilst he waited, his thoughts drifted back to hot stew by an open fire, causing his stomach to rumble.

When the archive clerk returned a few minutes later, he carried a ledger open at mid-August 1895. Putting it down for Inspector Woolfe to read, he said, "On Saturday, 17th of August 1895, the advertisement was paid for by one 'J. Pettifoot.'"

Inspector Woolfe picked up and read the ledger. A smile crept across his lips as he made the connection between this advertisement and the one for the clerk. The pieces were coming together. "Thank you, Mr Childs." He slammed the ledger shut and stood as he put it down. "You can go home now."

NINETEEN

"Where *is* he?" Inspector Woolfe muttered under his breath upon returning to his office after yet another fruitless trip downstairs. The sergeant at the front desk hadn't seen hide nor hair of Inspector Conway, still, and no word had been sent either. As Inspector Woolfe crossed over to his window and looked out, his thoughts turned to Miss Trent and the Bow Street Society. Could Inspector Conway be with her? Should he go down there to see? He dismissed the idea with a growl and a softly muttered, "Don't be stupid, Caleb."

His chair creaked in complaint as he sat behind his desk. Taking a pen, ink bottle, and clean sheet of paper, he wrote a brief note requesting to see Chief Inspector Jones the next morning. In addition to fulfilling his obligation to report Inspector Conway's activities to him, Inspector Woolfe also wanted to inform him of his recent discoveries and the next steps he intended to make.

As he folded the note and slipped it into an envelope, he heard the door close at the far end of the corridor, followed by heavy footfalls coming his way. He sealed the envelope and, rising to his feet, crossed the office to put it into his coat on the stand. No sooner had he done so, Inspector Conway walked into view through the open doorway.

"You remembered where the office was, then?" Inspector Woolfe enquired in an ironic tone as he sat behind his desk.

"Don't start, Caleb," Inspector Conway warned. Removing his hat and coat, he hung them on the stand and stood before his friend. "Gimmie some whisky."

"As bad as that?" Nevertheless, Inspector Woolfe poured an inch of whisky into a glass and handed it to him.

"Yeah." Inspector Conway drank it off straight and returned the glass. "Thanks."

Inspector Woolfe put the glass and bottle away whilst watching Inspector Conway sit behind his own desk and push aside a pile of paperwork. "Are you going to tell me about it?" He settled back in his chair. "What happened at Madame Mimi's this morning?"

Inspector Conway felt the back of his neck warm at the memory. Taking a document from the pile, he pretended to read it. "Nothin'."

Inspector Woolfe studied his face as he revealed, "On my first visit, she got me into her parlour, and we done things on her sofa I wouldn't even confess to a priest."

Inspector Conway lowered the document and met his gaze. "You did?"

Inspector Woolfe showed his yellow teeth in a broad smile. "Mimi knows how to please a bloke."

Inspector Conway returned his gaze to the document with a soft clearing of his throat. "If you say so, mate."

Inspector Woolfe's smile faded. "Don't tell me you turned her down?"

Inspector Conway remained silent; his gaze fixed upon the document despite the back of his neck warming further.

Inspector Woolfe rested his folded arms upon his desk and leant forward. "You're not human, John Conway; do you know that?"

Inspector Conway set the document aside and took the next from the pile.

"What about our friend Mr Jerome?" Inspector Woolfe enquired.

Grateful for the change of subject, Inspector Conway glanced at his friend whilst shifting his weight upon his chair. "'E's not been back to Mimi's since 'e scarpered. 'E's not tried blackmailin' the actors at the *Royal Opera House* again, either." He'd paid the theatre a visit prior to returning to the police station. "I've told the manager to let us know if 'e does.

"Sounds simple enough."

"Don't it always?"

171

Inspector Woolfe's tone hardened. "What was the whisky all about, then?"

Inspector Conway stilled. Replaying in his mind what Dr Weeks had done, he felt a mixture of deep concern and sympathy for the surgeon. He'd waited at the Society's house for Miss Trent's return and, when she'd come back with Miss Hicks, he'd heard the whole sorry tale from the horse's mouth, so to speak. He'd wanted to simultaneously toss out and lock away Miss Hicks. Toss her out because she deserved it, but to also lock her away to prevent Dr Weeks from doing something stupid. Therefore, he'd felt relieved when Miss Trent had agreed for Miss Hicks to stay with her. The question of protecting Dr Weeks from himself remained, however.

Putting down the document, Inspector Conway turned sombre eyes to Inspector Woolfe. With an equally grave expression, he said, "Weeks pulled a scalpel on me."

Inspector Woolfe knitted his brow. "By 'pulling a scalpel,' you mean he *threatened* you with it?"

Inspector Conway replied softly, "Yeah."

Inspector Woolfe's frown deepened. "Why? Did he say?"

Inspector Conway sat back in his chair with an audible sigh. "No. Nothin'."

Inspector Woolfe recalled the surgeon's jittery behaviour the day before and wondered if his guilt over the envelope saga had become too much. He couldn't bring it up with Inspector Conway because, by all appearances, he remained ignorant of it, and that was how Inspector Woolfe wanted it to stay. Deciding to raise it with Chief Inspector Jones during his appointment, Inspector Woolfe stood and took their coats from the stand. "Come on." He tossed Inspector Conway's coat onto his desk. "We're going for a pint."

Inspector Conway picked up his coat and put it on. Taking his hat when it was offered, he said, "Thanks, Caleb."

"I don't know what you're thanking me for."
Inspector Woolfe put on his coat. "You're paying."

Inspector Conway softly chuckled, and the two left for the *Bow Street Tavern*.

* * *

Dr Locke thanked Lyons as he held her coat, and she slipped her arms into its sleeves. Fastening its buttons whilst he adjusted its shoulders, she said, "I shall return as soon as I'm able. Dr Weeks' note sounded rather urgent, though, so I may not return until morning. In which case, I shall telephone and instruct Claude to accompany Mr Locke on his walk."

"Yes, ma'am."

"Has Mr Lambert arrived?" Dr Locke checked her reflection in the hallway mirror.

"Yes, ma'am." Lyons opened and held the front door for her.

"Good night, Lyons."

"Good night, ma'am."

Lyons stood in the open doorway and watched her hurriedly descend the steps and climb into the waiting carriage. Exchanging a polite nod of acknowledgement with Mr Lambert, the Lockes' groom and driver, as he closed the carriage door behind their mistress, Lyons stepped back and closed the front door. As he secured its bolt, Mr Lambert returned to his driver's seat and spurred the horses into motion.

On the opposite side of the road, a yellow, glowing dot penetrated the otherwise pitch blackness of the night. Its owner waited until the carriage had turned the corner before approaching the pavement's edge, thereby emerging from the shadows. As they lifted their hand, the dot was revealed to be the tip of a cigarette they proceeded to take a deep pull from. Casting a nervous glance up and down the deserted street, they stepped out into the road and crossed over to the Lockes' residence. Their heart pounded in their chest, and small beads of sweat formed upon their forehead, as they climbed the steps. A glance at the cigarette convinced them to discard it, and they crushed it under their shoe. Running one trembling hand over their matted hair, they knocked on the door with the other.

When Lyons opened it a few moments later, he stilled upon seeing who it was. Forcing the surprise from his features, he greeted in a formal tone, "Good evening, doctor."

"Is Mr Locke at home for visitors?" Dr Weeks enquired.

* * *

"I shan't hear any more of it," Miss Ilbert warned. Standing before her dressing room's mirror, she glared at Mr Benton's reflection in it. He stood behind and to the right of her, whilst Miss Kimberly and Miss Lily were on their knees, smoothing down her costume's skirts. "You defied my wishes by succumbing to his demands, and I shall not stand for it, Luthor."

"If it saved the company from destitution, I would pay a thousand ransoms," Mr Benton said, meeting her glare with his own.

"And each higher than the last," Miss Ilbert pointed out. "You cannot negotiate with blackmailers. Once you have succumbed, they return again and again, increasing the amount, until you have nothing left."

Mr Benton threw up his arms, exasperated. "Listen to reason!"

"This is my theatre." Miss Ilbert turned to him, her hand upon her hip. "And those are my final words on the matter."

Mr Benton's gaze and tone hardened. "You will regret this, Mina." He opened the door. "Mark my words." He strode out and slammed the door behind him, causing it to shake in its frame.

Miss Ilbert turned back to the mirror. "Has anyone come forward yet, Emma?"

"No." Miss Kimberly stood. "I have to fetch something from the office."

Both concerned and irritated by her sudden departure, Miss Ilbert watched her leave.

"Will you really disband the company, Mother?" Miss Lily meekly enquired.

Miss Ilbert pursed her lips together and exhaled loudly through her nose. With regret, she replied, "I see no other option, child."

* * *

Dr Weeks and Mr Locke were silent as Lyons served a glass of brandy to the former and a cup of sweet tea to the latter. Sitting in opposing armchairs on either side of the hearth, they each scrutinised the physical appearance of the other. Their last meeting was several months ago, and both were shocked by the degradation that had occurred in the other during that time.

Once Lyons had left the room, Mr Locke opened his silver cigarette case and held it out to his guest. Dr Weeks took one of the Turkish cigarettes with a muttered thanks and, putting it between his lips, leant forward and allowed his host to ignite its end with a lighter. Settling back within his armchair, Dr Weeks took a deep pull and carefully exhaled the smoke toward the hearth whilst watching Mr Locke light his own cigarette.

"Do you feel more at ease now, doctor?" Mr Locke enquired, resting his elbow upon the arm of his chair to keep the cigarette close to his lips.

Dr Weeks had a mouthful of brandy, a second pull from his cigarette, and nodded.

"Good." The corner of Mr Locke's mouth twitched. "Paying a visit to the heroin-addicted husband and patient of a sober wife, medical doctor, and good friend, with neither her knowledge nor permission, is enough to put a strain on any man."

Dr Weeks was reluctant to dwell on his deception. "Ya admit yer an addict?"

"Of many years. Yes." Mr Locke took a shallow pull from his cigarette. "I have not partaken in the drug in several weeks, however. Alas, my abstinence is more Lynette's doing than my own." A pained look passed through his eyes, and he sombrely added, "She saved my life."

Memories of intimate moments Dr Weeks had shared with Miss Hicks ran through the surgeon's mind, causing him to feel simultaneously sick, aggrieved, and saddened by the loss of the woman he loved. This in turn caused him to feel envious of the Lockes' apparent happiness and guilt at wanting what they had.

There was another dimension to his guilt, too. One caused by the course of action he planned to take without Dr Locke's knowledge or approval. The thought of what he was about to do pressed upon his breast and turned his stomach. Yet, he'd rationalised it into being the only solution to his problem, namely, Inspector Lee holding Dr Weeks' illegitimacy to his head like a gun. The surgeon's life had fallen apart since Inspector Lee had confronted him with the evidence of his shame. If he could somehow steal the evidence back, thereby removing the threat from Inspector Lee, he might be able to piece his life back together.

As if reading his thoughts, Mr Locke said, "But I digress. To what unpalatable reason do I owe this visit?"

Dr Weeks finished his cigarette and, tossing it into the hearth, drank the remainder of his brandy. Sitting forward in his chair, he put the glass down upon the floor at his feet and retrieved a narrow, leather-bound box from the inside pocket of his coat.

Mr Locke's gaze followed it to where Dr Weeks laid it upon the arm of his chair, before flicking back to the surgeon's grave expression.

"I need yer help."

"With?" Mr Locke took another shallow pull from his cigarette.

"Stealin' back my property."

Mr Locke quirked a brow. His movements were calm and measured as he tossed his own cigarette into the hearth and settled back in his chair, however. Resting his elbows upon its arms and steepling his fingers, he studied Dr Weeks' face for several moments whilst contemplating his response. "As invigorating as my past activities were, specifically the errands I carried out on behalf of the Bow Street Society, the present inadequacies of my physical condition and prowess prohibit any chance of successfully executing such an endeavour. Therefore, I am obliged to politely refuse your request, doctor, and recommend you instead seek the assistance of the police, or indeed the Bow Street Society."

"It's the police I need to steal it from," Dr Weeks countered with a scowl. "And I don't want any of the Bow Streeters knowin' 'bout this, d'ya hear?"

"Plainly," Mr Locke replied with a small lift of his chin. "Am I to presume you wish me to scale the walls of New Scotland Yard to rob their vault, or does your dispute lie with an individual policeman?"

Dr Weeks' scowl shifted into a frown. "The second." He briefly averted his gaze as he added, "Inspector Lee."

"And what is it, exactly, he is purported to have stolen from you?"

Dr Weeks narrowed his eyes and glared at him. "There ain't no 'purported' about it; he stole what were rightfully mine, and I want it back."

Mr Locke tried to keep his irritation from his voice but failed. "Yes, but *what* is it?"

Dr Weeks leant further forward, thereby making himself smaller within the armchair, as he reached between his legs to pick up the brandy glass. Tossing back the last few drops in the bottom, he clutched it tightly between his knees and stared into it. In a subdued yet sombre voice, he replied, "Evidence I'm Lord Weeks' bastard son."

Mr Locke recalled the Cosgrove case and the suspicions which had arisen within the Bow Street Society about the possible connection between Lord and Dr Weeks once the identity of their client was known. "I see."

Dr Weeks shook his head. "Nah, ya don't see." His features tightened, and his voice became strained with emotion as he fought to hold back the shame and guilt which threatened to erupt from his breast. "Ya don't know what it's like to be marked all yer life." His grip tightened on the glass. "To be treated like a piece of shit jus' 'cause of who yer parents were."

Mr Locke's voice held a hint of sympathy as he enquired, "You have denied the truth of your parentage to Miss Trent and the other Bow Street Society members, I presume?"

Dr Weeks nodded and wiped the underside of his nose with the back of his hand.

"As well as your peers within the medical profession and the other police officers?"

"Yeah."

Mr Locke picked up his cup of tea and took a small sip. "I see your difficulty."

Dr Weeks wiped his eyes with the heel of his hand as he put the glass back down upon the floor and picked up the narrow, leather-bound box. "I don't expect ya to do it for nothin'." He held the box out to Mr Locke and, as he reached for it, added, "I can get ya more, too."

Mr Locke's hand stilled in midair as his gaze met Dr Weeks'.

"Lynette don't have to know," Dr Weeks added.

Mr Locke took the box and, after setting his cup aside, opened it upon his lap. He felt a tightness form in his chest as he looked upon its contents: a tourniquet, needle, and small vial of heroin.

* * *

There was an unnatural quiet amongst the supers and other performers gathered in the wings. Their eyes were also lacklustre, and the excitement with which they'd anticipated the previous night's performance was absent. Instead, most kept their arms crossed and their gazes downcast. The apparently inevitable dismissal awaiting them after the show weighed heavily on their minds.

Acutely aware of their disquiet, uneasiness and, in some cases, anger, at the situation, Miss Ilbert had remained in her dressing room until the last moment. Walking toward the wings, now, she kept her gaze straight ahead despite the supers and performers parting like the Red Sea around her. Placing herself at the front, she lifted her chin and said, "Our audience deserves the very best from us, still. Do not disappoint them, everyone."

A few murmurs came from those behind her. The rest remained silent.

As the solo flute filled the air with its gentle melody, thereby providing her with her cue, Miss Ilbert moved out onto the stage. Gliding across it with the line of young female dancers following, she spread her arms, and they did the same. With their fingertips almost touching, they curved their line toward the scenery before curving it again to glide back across the stage.

* * *

"Can you believe I was almost halfway there when I noticed I'd forgotten my medical bag?" Dr Locke's voice enquired in the hallway.

Mr Locke and Dr Weeks looked sharply at the door in unison.

"I beg your pardon?" Dr Locke enquired to an unheard statement.

Mr Locke scrambled to close the leatherbound box, but it toppled from his lap, spilling its contents upon the rug at his feet. As he lunged to catch it, he heard the parlour door open and caught Dr Weeks leap to his feet out the corner of his eye.

"What are you doing here?" Dr Locke enquired from Dr Weeks, confused.

As she approached him, though, she saw her husband hastily gathering up the needle, tourniquet, and vial from the rug. She halted abruptly. Staring at him, stunned, she was unable to conjure up anything but blank thoughts for several seconds. She slowly moved her gaze between her husband and Dr Weeks, unable to grasp, let alone believe, what she had inadvertently walked in on. Finally, her mind and senses snapped back into focus as Mr Locke closed the box and passed it back to Dr Weeks.

"Leave my home at once," Dr Locke ordered the latter, her voice quiet with anger.

Dr Weeks stepped forward with a pleading look in his eyes. "I can explain."

"I have already seen *enough*, doctor!" Dr Locke cried. "*Leave* at once, or I shall have you forcibly removed!"

Mr Locke shrank back into his armchair, a sheepish expression upon his face as he kept his head bowed and his eyes downcast.

Dr Weeks attempted to take Dr Locke by the arm, but she pulled it away.

"Do *not* touch me!" Dr Locke cried. "*Claude*!"

"Ya gotta let me explain, Lynette!" Dr Weeks cast a desperate glance back at Mr Locke, but the illusionist remained silent. "I know it were a rotten thin' for me to do, but I ain't got any choice! Lee's got me by the bollocks, and yer husband's the only one who can help me!"

"In return for *heroin*?!" Dr Locke shouted, her face contorted into a fierce glare as she stepped into Dr Weeks' personal space, thereby obliging him to cower away from her. "*You* are the *vilest* creature I have ever had the utter *misfortune* of meeting, Dr Weeks! I hope Inspector Lee *exposes* you as the *filthy, rotten degenerate* you are and *ruins* you!"

Every insult she threw at Dr Weeks felt like a knife to his heart.

Claude entered the room, prompting Dr Locke to shout at Dr Weeks, "Now, *leave*!"

With his shoulders turned inward and his hand tightly clutching the box to his chest, Dr Weeks meekly looked from Dr Locke to Mr Locke and finally to Claude. Feeling his body trembling, his eyes stinging, and his throat constricting, Dr Weeks fled the house with unsteady steps and several stifled sobs.

* * *

The violins joined the flute, and the depth and drama of the musical accompaniment to Miss Ilbert's performance increased. She and the dancers also increased their speed, as the circle which their line formed increasingly tightened until, at the music's crescendo, Miss Ilbert leapt onto the metal plate in the centre of the stage. The tiny lights dotting her crown and costume illuminated white in an instant, and a gasp of awe erupted from the audience. Applause immediately followed, prompting the dancers to gracefully leave via stage right. Miss Ilbert remained standing on the plate, however.

The applause died away, and confused murmurings took its place within the audience. Miss Ilbert was rigid, and her eyes were wide as she stared, unblinkingly, at the chandelier above the auditorium. Soon, the smell of burning flesh drifted across the stage to the orchestra pit, and the ladies in the boxes shrieked in horror as they saw smoke rise from Miss Ilbert.

"*Someone*!" Mr Benton cried as he ran onto the stage. "Extinguish the electricity!"

A second later, Miss Ilbert crumpled to the stage like a rag doll, and a hush fell over all those present. Hurrying over and kneeling beside her, Mr Benton couldn't see any signs of life. With desperation in his voice, he shouted into the auditorium, "*Is there a doctor in the house*?!"

TWENTY

Miss Trent sat away from her desk with her rigid back flush against her chair and her gaze fixed upon Mr Elliott opposite. The solicitor's expression was unreadable, but his words a moment before had told the clerk all she needed to know. In a low, firm voice, she said, "As I made clear to you when you joined, Bow Street Society members are only given the information they need to fulfil their investigative duties. Anything beyond this, including the Society's hierarchy and my wage, is kept strictly confidential."

A hint of surprise entered Mr Elliott's voice. "You're refusing to answer?"

"That *is* my answer."

Mr Elliott kept his eyes locked with hers. "I have a right to know."

Miss Trent lofted an eyebrow. "Do you?"

"Yes."

"Why?"

"To protect my reputation. If I'm to continue my law work, I must have an unblemished character and reputation. Connections, whether direct or indirect, with unsavoury persons may sully one or both of these. Ergo, I have a right to know for whom I'm working."

"I understand and appreciate your concerns, Mr Elliott, but I'm unwilling to break the code governing this Society simply to reassure you. If you're unhappy with my answer, and if you believe your Society membership may harm your professional reputation, I'll readily accept your resignation."

Mr Elliott's lips formed a hard line as Miss Trent maintained a firm expression.

"No," he said after a few moments of intense silence. "It shan't be necessary."

The corner of Miss Trent's mouth lifted. "I'm pleased to hear it." She pulled her chair closer and rested her clasped hands upon her desk. Her tone and expression became sombre as she went on, "I'm disappointed you came here based on Inspector Lee's word alone, though. You know how untrustworthy and manipulative he can be."

"A deceptive man isn't incapable of telling the truth. One may even argue he knows it better than most, for he must be familiar with it to lie about it."

"I agree, but I suspect this was merely another one of Inspector Lee's attempts to sow mistrust between us."

Mr Elliott recalled Inspector Lee had smirked when he'd challenged him to ask Miss Trent about her mysterious employer. Realising the policeman had likely been manipulating him for his own amusement, Mr Elliott felt a wave of embarrassment followed by a pang of guilt. Echoing his own words, he remarked to himself, "His arrogance knows no bounds."

"He'll get his comeuppance eventually." Miss Trent stood, prompting Mr Elliott to do the same. "By the way, have you found out anything about him yet?"

"In truth, I haven't started. The trial I'm presently engaged with is consuming a great deal of my time. I'll begin my search as soon as it's concluded."

They walked from her office to the hallway where he collected his things from the hat stand and put them on. "I'm intrigued to know if there are any skeletons in Inspector Lee's cupboard." She cast a brief glance over him. "Aside from what we already suspect."

"It is more than suspicion on my part."

They walked to the front door.

Miss Trent glanced at the kitchen, but the muffled sounds of Miss Hicks and Toby's voices continued. Lowering her own, she carefully watched Mr Elliott's face as she enquired, "Has something happened?" She lowered her voice further. "Have you and Inspector Lee…?"

Mr Elliott gave a curt shake of his head. "No, but he was at court all day, watching me from the public gallery. He then intercepted me when I left and insisted upon accompanying me to my regular afternoon tea with Dr Colbert. During which he proposed I ask you about your employer."

Miss Trent frowned, concerned about another member being unwittingly dragged into the politics between the Society and the police.

"There is something else." An edge of disgust entered his voice. "During our meeting with him the other day, he brushed his foot against my leg under the table."

"Accidentally?"

"Intentionally."

Miss Trent's frown deepened. "I don't like this shift in behaviour toward you; it's bordering on obsessive." She put a gentle hand upon his arm. "For the time being, I don't want you to be alone with him."

"I would rather put red-hot needles under my fingernails."

Miss Trent smiled. "Please, don't." Her smile faded. "Please, be careful around him?"

"I shall." Mr Elliott left the house and, descending the steps to the street, called back, "Good night, Miss Trent."

"Good night, Mr Elliott." Yet, her worry remained.

* * *

"How long has this been planned for?"

"I beg your pardon?" Mr Locke looked up at his wife as she stood over him, her hands upon her hips. "I had no hand in this."

"Claude." Dr Locke kept her hard gaze upon her husband as the attendant came up beside her. "Search Mr Locke's person."

"Now see here." Mr Locke stood and attempted to approach her, but Claude's firm grip upon his arm stayed him. He cast an angry glance at the attendant in response. "Dr Weeks' visit was as much of a surprise to me as it was to you, Lynette."

"Please, proceed, Claude," Dr Locke cooly instructed.

Claude held Mr Locke firmly by the shoulder and searched his frock coat.

"This is not only humiliating, it is *outrageous*." Mr Locke gripped the armchair's backrest to steady himself. "My word should be enough for you, Lynette."

"Doctor." Claude pulled a vial from Mr Locke's interior pocket and put it into Dr Locke's waiting hand.

Upon examining it, she felt her heart clench at the name on the label: *Heroin*. Suspecting her husband had pocketed it whilst gathering the things from the rug, she held it aloft before his eyes. "*This* is why I can't take you at your word, Percy."

Mr Locke looked from her to the vial and back again. "I was not going to *use* it."

Dr Locke lowered her hand, her eyes glistening with unshed tears. "Of *course* you were. Do you think me a fool?"

"*No*. I know how awful this may appear, but I swear my only intention was to prevent Dr Weeks from using it," Mr Locke insisted.

Claude released Mr Locke at Dr Locke's nod and stepped aside. Dr Locke held the vial aloft a second time as she moved closer to her husband. "Toss it into the fire."

Mr Locke's eyes widened. "I-I beg your pardon?"

Dr Locke held the vial out to him. "If your intention was to protect Dr Weeks from himself, you'll have no difficulty tossing this into the fire. Will you?"

Mr Locke's gaze dropped to the vial. "But the glass shall protect it."

Dr Locke's eyes narrowed. "I *am* a fool." She shoved the vial into his hand and pushed past him. "For thinking you could ever change."

She strode toward the door yet, as she reached for its handle, the sound of smashing glass caused her to halt. Turning her head sharply toward the fire at the same time, she was stunned to see her husband standing before it with empty hands. Slowly clasping her own against her chest as she approached the hearth in a daze, she felt her heartrate

185

quicken when she got close enough to see into the flames. There, amongst the burning coals, were the fragments of the vial and the remnants of its contents.

"I shall do whatever I must to keep you with me," Mr Locke said, softly, at her side.

Dr Locke half-covered her mouth with her hands. Fearing the broken vial was a substitute, she stepped closer to the fire for a closer look. Her breath hitched in her throat when she saw the *Heroin* label amongst the flames. She didn't dare to hope he'd chosen her over the drug, but the evidence was plain to see. Feeling his hand upon the small of her back, she turned her head and saw the ardent love in his eyes. Yet, she'd seen the same so many times before, and each time, he'd broken her heart. On the other hand, he'd never thrown the drug into the fire before. In the depths of her soul, a tiny voice whispered, *Maybe this time it will be different.* She slipped one hand into her husband's and rested her other upon his cheek. In a voice subdued by emotion, she said, "You have." She lowered her hand, "And I hope you will again." As she pulled away and left the room, she softly added, "with all my heart."

* * *

The slow, gentle sound of *Gymnopédie No.3* by French composer Erik Satie drifted along the landing and into the Bow Street Society's hallway. Having heard it upon leaving the kitchen, Miss Hicks had followed it upstairs to the first floor. Seeing the door in the far-right corner was ajar, she crept toward it and realised the music was getting louder as she approached. She eased it open and was met by the sight of Miss Trent playing an upright piano within a modest yet comfortable parlour.

The walls were decorated in two halves with a Daido rail in between. The lower was dark-varnished oak panels, and the upper was mustard-coloured paper covered by a gold, brown, and burgundy floral pattern. Pristine white glass sconces adorned the highly polished brass arms of wall-mounted gas lamps. A plump, burgundy two-seater sofa with a balloon-shaped back was in the middle of the room, facing the fireplace, with an over-stuffed burgundy armchair to the right, facing the window. The piano was against the room's left-hand wall. Beyond the piano, on the same side, thick burgundy velvet curtains covered the window overlooking Bow Street.

Two pairs of bookcases lined the wall to the right of the door with a second door in between. Among the volumes of fiction were *Oliver Twist* by Charles Dickens, *Treasure Island* by R.L. Stevenson, and *The Three Musketeers* by Alexandre Dumas. Non-fiction volumes included *On the Origin of Species* by Charles Darwin, *The Mind in the Face: An Introduction to the Study of Physiognomy* by William McDowall, and *Grammar of Palmistry* by Katharine St. Hill. Copies of theatre programs, *Exchange and Mart*, *Truth*, *Women's Signal* and the *Gaslight Gazette*, were littered about the room. The latest editions of the *Illustrated Police News*, *The Era*, and *The Times* also lay upon the sofa.

The floorboard creaked under Miss Hicks' foot as she entered, causing Miss Trent to cease her playing. The women exchanged startled looks before the clerk enquired, "What are you doing up here?"

"I heard the piano." Miss Hicks closed the door behind her.

"Where's Toby?"

"Washin' the plates from dinner."

"Have you heard from Dr Weeks?" Miss Trent enquired, visibly concerned.

Miss Hicks became subdued. "No. Nothin'."

Miss Trent pulled the lid down over the keys and turned upon the stool to face her. "Would you like me to send Sam to check on him?"

Miss Hicks gave a curt shake of her head and ventured further into the room. "Best to leave 'im be." She ran a slow, appraising gaze over the room. "I didn't know this was up 'ere."

"You wouldn't." Miss Trent stood. "They're my private rooms." She glanced back at the piano. "Playing helps me think, and I've a great deal to think about these days." She crossed over to the armchair and invited Miss Hicks to join her as she sat. Waiting until Miss Hicks had settled herself upon the sofa, Miss Trent continued, "Aside from the situation with Dr Weeks, Inspector Lee has been playing his usual games, and I've not heard a word from Mr Maxwell in America."

"But you can't do sumin' about Mr Maxwell," Miss Hicks pointed out. "And Lee's just being the annoying bugger's he's always been."

"True." Miss Trent studied Miss Hicks a moment. Sensing the same worry in her for Dr Weeks, she reassured, "Try not to worry, Polly. The longer we go without hearing anything about Dr Weeks, the better it is."

Miss Hicks hummed. "I ought to tell his mum what's happened, but he never told me where she's stayin'."

"I'll ask Inspector Conway to find her."

"Thanks." Miss Hicks gave a weak smile. "You and 'im seem close."

"Society business has obliged me to maintain regular contact with him."

"But he ain't at the Yard now, is he?" Miss Hicks enquired, confused.

"No. He was reassigned to Bow Street. But he's one of the few policemen who don't want to see us closed down. He's also an old friend of Dr Weeks'." Miss Trent hoped it would be the end of it but, knowing Miss Hicks as she did, knew it probably wasn't.

"There's not sumin' goin' on between you, then?" Miss Hicks playfully enquired.

Miss Trent lofted an eyebrow. "He's old enough to be my father, Polly."

"He's also the Bulldog," Miss Hicks countered. "A tough 'un who'll look after you."

"I don't need looking after."

"*Every* woman needs looking after, Becky."

"Not this one. Besides, even if I wanted a romance, it certainly wouldn't be with John Conway. We're acquaintances. That's all."

"All I'm sayin' is you could do worse."

Miss Trent cooled. "Forgive me if I don't take relationship advice from an adulteress who's lost her home and both lovers."

Miss Hicks turned her head away. "I deserved that."

Miss Trent immediately felt guilty, and her expression and voice softened. "Maybe, but it's not an excuse for me to be cruel." She joined Miss Hicks on the sofa and put her arm around her. "I appreciate you worrying about me, Polly, but I'm fine. Truly." She smiled. "As for Inspector Conway, he's married to the job. I doubt any woman could coax him away from being a copper."

Miss Hicks lifted her head and smiled, weakly. "Thanks, Becky. For helpin' me and my Perce out."

"It's what the Bow Street Society is here for." Miss Trent stood. "Now, let's see what Toby is doing. He's being suspiciously quiet down there."

Miss Hicks chuckled. "He's probably broken your best china."

Miss Trent playfully rolled her eyes. "Don't tempt fate."

* * *

"Forgive me, I didn't know you were eating," Dr Colbert said.

Standing just inside the door of Inspector Lee's dining room, Dr Colbert watched him arrange his cutlery upon his plate and dab his lips with a napkin.

"Come in, doctor." Inspector Lee dropped his napkin onto his plate, prompting his manservant to gather them up and place them on the sideboard. As the manservant left the room, closing the door behind him, Inspector Lee indicated the vacant chair to the left of him at the head of the table. "Please, make yourself comfortable."

Dr Colbert accepted the invitation and thanked his host when he poured him a small glass of wine. "I have good news, Inspector." He retrieved a note from his coat pocket and set it down before him. With a bounce to his voice and a glow in his eyes, he announced, "The address of the Bow Street Society's bank and the name on its account."

"Excellent!" Inspector Lee cried as he simultaneously put down his wine glass with one hand and plucked up the note with his other. "The *London & County Banking Company*, Lombard Street, City of London," he read aloud. "The Bow Street Society is the name on the account?"

"Yes." Dr Colbert sipped his wine, recognising it as a fine vintage.

"I presume Inspector Woolfe is aware of this and has already called upon the bank."

"He is aware of it, yes. He plans to call upon the bank tomorrow."

Inspector Lee knew if he or one of his men were to be at the bank at the same time as Inspector Woolfe, his former co-conspirator would demand to know why. His alliance with Dr Colbert was too valuable to risk losing again. Therefore, he decided to give Inspector Woolfe space to conduct his investigation undisturbed and unobserved. "Please, keep me informed of what he uncovers there."

"I will." Dr Colbert sipped some more wine. "Do you know a 'J. Pettifoot?'"

Inspector Lee folded the note and slipped it into his jacket. "No. Should I?"

"I thought they might've been the 'someone' you told Mr Elliott about."

Inspector Lee sat forward, intrigued. "What do you know?"

"Only that Inspector Woolfe asked me about the name. He wants me to listen out for it in Bow Street Society meetings and the like."

"Interesting." Inspector Lee sat back in his chair. "I wonder what he has discovered."

"I will endeavour to find out for you," Dr Colbert promised.

"Thank you." His thoughts turned to their mutual friend. "On a similar yet unrelated topic, how long have you and Mr Elliott been taking tea together?"

Dr Colbert set down his wine glass. "A few weeks."

Inspector Lee felt a pang of jealousy. "You're most fortunate. Mr Elliott is a hard man to pin down."

Dr Colbert felt a small sense of triumph. "I've had no difficulty."

Inspector Lee quirked a brow as he wondered if Dr Colbert was speaking of making plans with Mr Elliott, still, or something else entirely. Dismissing the thought as absurd as soon as it had occurred to him, though, he enquired, "When will you be taking tea with him next?"

"Tomorrow." Dr Colbert sipped his wine to hide his disappointment at the prospect of his time with Mr Elliott being intruded upon again.

"May I join you?"

Dr Colbert lowered his glass. "Of course, Inspector." He offered a contrived smile. "I'd be delighted."

Inspector Lee doubted Mr Elliott would be, but he was determined to win the man over. "Thank you." He was already considering means by which he could have Dr Colbert waylaid, thereby allowing him to be alone with Mr Elliott without the solicitor's prior knowledge. "I look forward to it."

TWENTY-ONE

"This should take the chill from your bones." Miss Trent moved away from the hearth where a moderate fire now burned. Wiping the coal dust from her hands using the rag she kept on the mantelshelf for the purpose, she sat and poured some tea for her guest. It was a quarter past nine and raining besides. Consequently, her guest was soaked through, and the Bow Street Society's downstairs parlour was unprepared. Being as well-adjusted to such unexpected visits as she was, though, Miss Trent had supplied her guest with a towel and a fire within minutes of his arrival.

"You're most kind, Miss," the man said, accepting the drink.

Whilst he warmed himself with several large gulps, Miss Trent took the opportunity to garner as much information as she could from his physical appearance. There was a grey tinge to his otherwise fair complexion and dark-brown stubble covered his jaw and upper lip. These, coupled with his sluggish movements and lethargic voice, indicated he'd endured a sleepless night. Contemplating his approximate age next, she determined he was in his mid-thirties but short for his age at only five feet, possibly due to malnourishment in his formative years.

The threadbare appearance of his dark-brown, knee-length cotton overcoat, light-brown trousers, dark-brown waistcoat, and pale-green neckerchief firmly identified him as working class. His cream-coloured shirt and heavy, black leather boots were also well-worn. Callouses on his palms and knuckles alluded to labour intensive employment, possibly as a bricklayer. Yet, the absence of a suntan contradicted this assumption. The remainder of his notable features consisted of drooping, hazel eyes, lank, dark-brown hair, wide nose, and oblong-shaped forehead and jaw.

"I suppose I'd best start from the beginning," the man said, holding the cup on his lap to warm his hands. "My name's Aaron Willis. I'm chief electric man at the *Crescent* Theatre, Strand. Miss Mina Ilbert, the *Crescent*'s Manager, died on stage last night."

"I'm sorry."

"Me, too." Mr Willis' voice rose in both volume and intensity as he added, "Because I've been accused of doing it."

"Of killing Miss Ilbert?" Miss Trent knew it was possible, but her instinct told her it was unlikely. "How did she die?"

"From the electricity in the metal plate she stood on in her dance." Mr Willis' mouth twisted as his expression soured. His grip also tightened upon his cup. "They said it was my fault, and I'd not done what I was supposed to, but I know my business, Miss Trent. I'd done that plate right. Someone else made it wrong."

Miss Trent retrieved her notebook and pencil from the mantelshelf and briefly wrote down what she'd been told thus far. "Who are 'they?'"

"Mr Stone, the stage manager. Mr Thurston, the prompter and super master. Even Miss Kimberly, the business manager said it was my fault." His twisted expression eased a little. "Only Mr Benton, the lead actor, said I ought to be given the benefit of the doubt."

Miss Trent noted the names and occupations. "Were the police sent for?"

"Yeah. The constable who kept order in the theatre for Miss Ilbert went and got a Detective Sergeant Dixon."

Miss Trent noted the name. "What were his thoughts on Miss Ilbert's death?"

"He said it was a tragic accident."

Miss Trent felt relieved the policeman had used his common sense, but the disdain in Mr Willis' voice suggested he thought otherwise as he continued, "And that was that, but how can it be? I've lost my living because of this. I've got a wife and four children to feed, but no theatres will take me on. It's not fair, Miss Trent. All I've done is work to keep my family, and there's been no bad things said about my work until now. The Bow Street Society's my last hope. If you can't help, me and my family will be in the workhouse before the month's out."

Miss Trent topped up his cup with more tea from the pot. "We'll help you, Mr Willis."

Colour flooded Mr Willis' face as his eyes became bright. "Thank you, Miss Trent!" His smile faded, "But," he averted his gaze, "I don't have any money."

"Don't worry," Miss Trent reassured gently. "The Society has a small fund for situations such as these."

Mr Willis' smile returned. "Me and my family thank you."

"Hold onto your gratitude until we've uncovered the truth of the matter, hm?"

Mr Willis nodded and took a large gulp of tea. "I will."

Miss Trent held her pencil poised over her notebook. "I'll need a little more information before I can assign some Society members to your case. Firstly, has Sergeant Dixon continued his investigation into Miss Ilbert's death?"

"No." Mr Willis took another large gulp of tea.

"Secondly, to your knowledge, has a doctor looked at Miss Ilbert's body and given a cause of death?"

Mr Willis set down his cup upon the table. "A surgeon was sent for—a Canadian. But he was shipwrecked before he'd even got to the theatre, so Sergeant Dixon had him sent back."

Miss Trent felt her worry for Dr Weeks rear its ugly head at the news. She pushed it aside, though, by telling herself Dr Weeks had arrived at crime scenes drunk in the past, and Sergeant Dixon was probably overreacting. "Was another doctor sent for?"

"Yeah, but I don't know his name. I know he come from Charing Cross Hospital, because that's where Sergeant Dixon told them to take Miss Ilbert."

Miss Trent noted the name. "Do you think we will encounter any hostility from," she consulted her notes, "Mr Stone, Mr Thurston, Miss Kimberly, Mr Benton, or anyone else at the theatre?"

"Mr Benton, not so much, but the others? Yeah, I'd say so. No one wanted to say it, and no one did when the sergeant was there, but someone did the company a good turn by killing Miss Ilbert."

Miss Trent lofted an eyebrow. "How so?"

"Miss Ilbert was going to dismiss the company after last night's show if them who'd been helping Jack Jerome didn't go and see her."

Miss Trent noted the name. "And who is 'Jack Jerome?'"

"He's the bloke who's been giving Mr Benton the bird when he's not given him the money he's asked for."

Miss Trent searched her memories from her acting days for the term. Recalling it referred to making enough noise to force an actor, or actress, from the stage, she hadn't known it could be used as a form of blackmail. She wondered if Mr Locke had encountered it. He was the most suitably qualified to investigate Miss Ilbert's death. Whether Dr Locke would allow him was another matter. Then again, she was the most suitably qualified after Dr Weeks, and if he was unavailable, she could be assigned alongside her husband. "Miss Ilbert thought someone in the company was helping Mr Jerome?"

"Yeah." Mr Willis picked up his cup. "Mr Jerome knew when Mr Benton was getting to the theatre even when Mr Benton changed his times." He drank the remainder of his tea. "Mr Stone saw Miss Joanna Hightower, the wardrobe mistress' daughter, with Mr Jerome backstage, and he told Miss Ilbert. She was the angriest I've ever seen her. She asked Miss Hightower if she'd been helping Mr Jerome, but she said she hadn't."

"When was this?"

"The other night, before Miss Ilbert told the company what she planned to do after last night's show."

Miss Trent wrote this down. "Thank you, Mr Willis. That will be all for now. We may need to speak to you, again, though, so could I have your address, please?" She transcribed it as he gave it. "If you'd like to continue warming yourself by the fire, I'll send for our driver to take you home."

* * *

Chief Inspector Jones took his time packing tobacco from a humidor into his pipe as he mulled over Inspector Woolfe's discoveries. The latter had just finished his verbal report and was waiting for him to give his thoughts on the matter. Of which there were many, but few he could air, especially to Inspector Woolfe. The possibility one, or more, of his subordinates would make the connection between the Bow Street Society and the *Gaslight Gazette* advertisements had weighed upon Chief Inspector Jones' mind for some time. The possibility they would make the further connection to J. Pettifoot had also been a cause of concern for him. The reality Inspector Woolfe had achieved both these milestones had strengthened his concern but failed to alarm him. Putting his pipe to his lips, he struck a match and ignited the tobacco with several swift puffs before settling back in his chair.

They sat on either side of Chief Inspector Jones' desk in his office at New Scotland Yard. Rain beat a gentle rhythm against the window directly behind Chief Inspector Jones, whilst the echoes of many footsteps and conversations drifted in from the corridor beyond the door.

"What steps have you taken to trace 'J. Pettifoot?'" Chief Inspector Jones enquired.

Inspector Woolfe cleared his throat, coughed, and cleared his throat again. "I've only looked in the *Post Office Directory* so far, sir, with no joy. I'm going to ask the Convict Office to check their records before I go to Lombard Street."

"You suspect 'J. Pettifoot' is a criminal?"

"Maybe. Maybe not. I'm not ruling anything out at the moment, sir."

"As you shouldn't." Chief Inspector Jones puffed upon his pipe, directing the smoke away from Inspector Woolfe. "How did you come by the details of the Society's bank anyway?" Although he knew the answer to his next question, he also knew Inspector Woolfe would expect him to ask it. "Did Miss Trent volunteer the information?"

Inspector Woolfe gave a soft grunt. "She's as impenetrable as the Tower of London."

Chief Inspector Jones smirked; her impenetrability was one of the reasons he could rely upon her. Yet, the question of where the information had come from remained, and he didn't like the possible answer. "How, then? Was it someone else within the Society?"

"No, sir." Inspector Woolfe swiftly added, "I glimpsed a note on her desk."

Chief Inspector Jones deliberately lowered his head to study Inspector Woolfe whilst puffing upon his pipe. "Are you quite certain of that?"

Inspector Woolfe simultaneously averted his gaze, sat back in his chair, and adjusted his coat. "Yes, sir."

Chief Inspector Jones knew he was lying; Miss Trent wouldn't be so careless. Unfortunately, Chief Inspector Jones also knew he'd perpetuated a lie amongst his colleagues that he'd never met Miss Trent. As a result, he couldn't confront Inspector Woolfe about his deception without revealing his own. Deciding to take a different approach, he sat forward and put his pipe on its rest. "You relied upon my discretion and loyalty before, Caleb. You can do so, again, if you later decide you were mistaken."

"Thank you, sir." Given the consequences of Inspector Conway's insubordination, Inspector Woolfe was averse to revealing his own. Sensing Chief Inspector Jones wanted a more substantial answer, he added, "I'll bear it in mind."

Chief Inspector Jones looked him straight in the eye. "Make certain you do."

Inspector Woolfe felt a sudden rush of adrenaline. *Did he know?*

"*Yer devious sonofabitch!*" a familiar voice suddenly roared.

Chief Inspector Jones and Inspector Woolfe exchanged surprised looks.

A man's sharp cry sounded, followed by a cacophony of yelling, male voices.

Chief Inspector Jones and Inspector Woolfe leapt to their feet and ran out the room. They were immediately met by a scene of utter chaos. Inspector Lee leant against a wall, clutching the back of his head, whilst several plain-clothed officers gathered around a poker-wielding Dr Weeks. Each time one of them attempted to get close to him, though, Dr Weeks swung the poker, forcing them back.

Dr Weeks' skin was flushed red and covered in sweat. His nostrils flared as he breathed heavily through uncontrollable sobbing, and his eyes were so wide, the whites around their irises were plainly visible. His grip upon the poker was also so tight, his knuckles had turned white, and his hands shook from the strain. Turning swiftly left and right, darting his eyes from person to person, he yelled, "*Ya don't know what this sonofabitch's done to me! He's ruined my Goddamned life!*"

"*Doctor* Weeks!" Chief Inspector Jones boomed. All eyes turned to him. "What is the meaning of this?!"

"*Ask that piece of shit!*" Dr Weeks pointed to Inspector Lee.

Sergeant Caulfield, who was amongst the officers surrounding the hysterical surgeon, lunged for the poker. Managing to get a firm grip on it, he was momentarily lifted off his feet by Dr Weeks attempting to pull back his makeshift weapon. Regaining his footing, though, Sergeant Caulfield kept a firm grip of the poker with one hand whilst reaching for Dr Weeks' wrist with the other.

"*Ya don't know what this sonofabitch's done to me!*" Dr Weeks screamed into Sergeant Caulfield's face, his own turning bright red.

"He's gone mad!" Inspector Lee cried, moving swiftly away to safety.

Inspector Woolfe glared at him as he went past, disappointed the wound appeared superficial. Reaching Sergeant Caulfield and Dr Weeks, who were still struggling over the poker, Inspector Woolfe wrapped his arms around the latter's waist from behind and squeezed as hard as he could. Dr Weeks' hand reflexively released the poker as he felt the violent expulsion of air from his lungs, temporarily dazing him. Inspector Woolfe instantly seized upon this momentary weakness to lift Dr Weeks off his feet and drag him to a nearby interview room. Taking him inside and tossing him onto the floor, Inspector Woolfe took a backward stride, slammed the door, and locked it before Dr Weeks had scrambled to his feet.

"*Ya don't know! Woolfe, ya damned sonofabitch! Ya don't know!*" Dr Weeks screamed, sobbing uncontrollably, as he kicked and punched the door.

Sergeant Caulfield and the other officers looked on in shocked silence.

Red faced and out of breath, Inspector Woolfe succumbed to a coughing fit as he walked away. Taking the remainder of Dr Colbert's medicine, he growled, "No one lets him out unless *I* say so." Returning to Chief Inspector Jones and Inspector Lee by the door to the former's office, Inspector Woolfe coughed, cleared his throat, and explained, "He's locked in the interview room, sir."

"It shan't contain him for long if he carries on like he is," Chief Inspector Jones remarked with a frown. Looking down the corridor, he saw Sergeant Caulfield lingering by the interview room. "Sergeant!"

"Yes, sir?" Sergeant Caulfield enquired, startled at being suddenly addressed.

"Stand guard at the door," Chief Inspector Jones instructed.

Sergeant Caulfield gave a curt nod. "Yes, sir."

"I want to speak to you in my office," Chief Inspector ordered Inspector Lee. "*Now*."

TWENTY-TWO

"What just happened, Gideon?" Chief Inspector Jones demanded, striding swiftly into his office and turning to Inspector Lee as the latter closed the door.

"Dr Weeks struck me from behind with a poker," Inspector Lee cooly replied.

"That much is as plain as the nose on your face. I want to know *why*."

Inspector Lee gingerly touched the lump forming upon his crown. "He's gone mad."

Chief Inspector Jones' hard gaze bore into him. "He accused you of ruining his life. Why?"

Inspector Lee lowered his hand. "I don't know. He's clearly lost all rational thought."

"That is your explanation?"

"It's the only explanation," Inspector Lee curtly replied. "Sir."

Chief Inspector Jones recalled Inspector Woolfe's words: *Whatever Inspector Lee has on him, it's bad enough to make Dr Weeks want to throw himself on his sword, instead of letting whatever it is come out. Dr Weeks' willingness to make a statement putting all the blame at his own door also says two things to me. First, he wants to protect Conway, his mate. Second, he wants to protect Inspector Lee. The only reason he'd want to do that is to stop Inspector Lee from exposing whatever it is he's got on him.*

If Inspector Lee was blackmailing Dr Weeks as Inspector Woolfe suspected, it would be a strong motive for assault. Yet, the circumstances which had led Inspector Woolfe to air his suspicions had occurred almost a month ago. Whilst it was possible Dr Weeks had stewed in anger until it boiled over, Chief Inspector Jones' instinct told him there was more to it. Despite accusing Inspector Lee of 'ruining' his life, Dr Weeks hadn't mentioned the how or why. Therefore, if Inspector Lee was indeed his blackmailer, Dr Weeks had demonstrated considerable restraint whilst in a state of great hysteria. A possibility whose unlikelihood decreased when one considered Dr Weeks' prior efforts to keep his secret hidden.

"The Mob Squad detectives have had the Bow Street Society's members under surveillance for some time now, including Dr Weeks in recent days," Chief Inspector Jones began, recalling the daily reports he'd received. "What have they discovered about his activities and relationships?"

"Two days ago, Dr Weeks' mother, Evangelina Breckenridge, was observed surprising her son at the underground railway bar where Dr Weeks' common-law wife, Miss Polly Hicks, is employed as a barmaid," Inspector Lee replied. "Later, Dr Weeks and his mother were observed calling upon a solicitor by the name of Mr Fry. The visit was noteworthy because it was held at Mr Fry's offices after closing time."

"What was the purpose of their meeting?"

"We don't know, sir. Sergeant Gutman was obliged to wait outside."

"Where is Mrs Breckenridge now?"

Inspector Lee decided not to tell him 'Mrs' Breckenridge was actually a 'Miss.' "She's staying at the hotel on Henrietta Street, but we suspect she plans to return to Canada in the coming days."

Chief Inspector Jones furrowed his brow. He would like to speak to her before she left, if only to hear her assessment of her son's recent demeanour. Making a mental note to have her fetched, he turned his attention to the other woman in Dr Weeks' life. "What is the health of Dr Weeks' relationship with Miss Hicks?"

"If it was a person, it would be taking its last breath, sir," Inspector Lee replied, hiding his amusement beneath a mask of contrived sombreness.

Chief Inspector Jones was surprised by this as he'd thought Dr Weeks and Miss Hicks were happy together.

After all, she'd ended her affair with Miss Trent to be with him. "How so?"

"To put it delicately, sir: Dr Weeks caught her in the arms of another man."

Chief Inspector Jones was taken aback. "Which man?"

"Mr Noah O'Hannigan, sir."

Chief Inspector Jones was shocked. "The same one who…?"

"Yes. The same one who was having an affair with Mrs Grosse."

Chief Inspector Jones turned away and ran his thumb and forefinger over the ends of his moustache as he sat behind his desk. Resting his hands upon the arms of his chair, he took a few moments to digest the revelations. Walking in on one's paramour in the arms of another man, especially a man with Noah O'Hannigan's reputation, was enough to send most men into an emotional, downward spiral. Therefore, Inspector Lee's assault could've been a simple case of him being in the wrong place at the wrong time.

"I received a note from Detective Sergeant Keith Dixon of C Division on Vine Street in Piccadilly," Chief Inspector Jones began, meeting Inspector Lee's gaze. "He was obliged to dismiss Dr Weeks from the scene of an unexpected death at the *Crescent Theatre* last night due to him being so inebriated, he could barely stand. Miss Hicks' betrayal would've almost certainly been a reason for him to drink more heavily than usual."

Inspector Lee knew Sergeant Dixon had indirectly admitted to insubordination with his note, since Chief Inspector Jones' order forbidding all officers from summoning Dr Weeks to crime scenes and the like still stood. Yet, Inspector Lee also knew this fact wouldn't have gone unnoticed by Chief Inspector Jones. Furthermore, Chief Inspector Jones would've suitably reprimanded Sergeant Dixon for his indiscretion. Therefore, he left his observations unsaid.

Suddenly, a diabolical idea struck him. Feeling a flash of delight at the same time, he couldn't help but smile at his own genius. Realising how inappropriate the smile would appear to his senior officer, though, he pursed and downturned his lips a heartbeat later. With contrived weight to his voice, he enquired, "May I speak freely, sir?"

"You may."

"Dr Weeks' considerable alcohol consumption is the thing of legend within the police. Such prolonged abuse of one's body cannot be good. Dr Weeks was also assaulted and robbed the night of the visit to Mr Fry. A patrolling constable found him hurt and dazed in the street. Believing him to be drunk, the constable arrested him. He was released the next morning without charge. I believe this, coupled with the mysterious visit to the solicitor's office, the surprise visit by his mother, and Miss Hicks' betrayal, has pushed his mind to breaking point." Inspector Lee paused for dramatic effect. "In basic terms, sir, I believe Dr Weeks has been driven insane by his drinking and must be hospitalised."

Although reluctant to admit it, Chief Inspector Jones saw the logic behind Inspector Lee's conclusion. The thought of sending Dr Weeks anywhere against his will, let alone an asylum, both sickened and troubled him. He would have to gather more information before he could even consider taking such a drastic course of action.

"Thank you, Gideon," Chief Inspector Jones said in a low, sombre voice. "You may return to your duties."

"With all due respect, sir, I think I shall call upon a doctor first." Inspector Lee smiled freely, revelling in the impact his words had had on his senior officer.

Already considering his next step, Chief Inspector Jones hadn't heard him at first. "Hm? Yes. Yes, of course. Do so." He reached for the pen in his inkwell to write an order for Dr Weeks' mother to be brought to him within the hour. "And send Inspector Woolfe in."

"Yes, sir."

* * *

"I don't hear anythin'," Toby said in a softened voice whilst tilting his body sideways toward the door and cupping his ear. Squinting at the same time, he strained to hear any hint of a voice or footstep.

"Come away from there." Miss Trent pulled him back by the arm.

The waiting room of Dr Locke's medical practice was as disused as the last time the clerk had visited. The natural light pouring in through the windows highlighted the dust on the floor, mantel shelf, and picture frames. The wall-mounted gas lamps were unlit, and the hearth was empty of coal or wood. The few chairs were also covered in dust sheets. Miss Trent suspected if anyone other than her and Toby had been calling upon the Lockes, they probably would've been turned away.

"I was just listenin'," Toby mumbled, shoving his hands into his coat pockets.

Miss Trent placed a gentle hand on his shoulder and gave him a reassuring smile. "I know, but things are done differently by the rich."

"Only 'cause they've never done a day's work."

"And I expect you to be on your best behaviour," Miss Trent warned. "The Lockes are my friends, regardless of their wealth. *Don't* embarrass me."

"I won't, promise," Toby mumbled, giving her a sheepish look.

The door opened, and Lyons entered. "The master and mistress shall see you now."

Miss Trent straightened Toby's tie. "Take your hands out of your pockets."

Toby did as he was told.

Leaving the waiting room, Miss Trent followed Lyons to the parlour with Toby behind her. She lifted her arm to bar his way as they stopped outside the parlour door to be announced. Upon being invited to enter by Lyons, she cast Toby a final warning glance before striding into the room.

She halted the instant she saw Mr Locke. His thin and frail appearance made him almost unrecognisable compared to the man she'd seen several months ago. Although he had stood to greet them, he was leaning upon a walking cane and gripping Dr Locke at his side. As the numbness of her initial shock subsided, Miss Trent felt a heavy ache enter her heart. She couldn't look away, but felt her sadness and pity intensify with every moment her gaze lingered upon him. Realising her shock and silence could be construed as rude by her friends, she swallowed against the tightening of her throat and tried to calm her emotions. "Mr Locke, you look… well."

"And you look as if you have seen a corpse," Mr Locke said with a wry smile.

"I was merely taken aback by your appearance," Miss Trent rebutted, moving further into the room.

"Believe me, he looks better than he did," Dr Locke said.

"Thank you, Lyons," Mr Locke said.

Lyons gave a shallow bow and left the room.

"Please, sit." Mr Locke indicated the sofa whilst lowering himself back into his armchair with Dr Locke's assistance.

"And who is this young man?" Dr Locke enquired as she took the armchair opposite her husband's, whilst Miss Trent and Toby sat on the sofa.

Toby spat into his palm and held out his hand. "Lord Toby Grenville the Third, Esquire, but you can call me Toby."

Dr Locke looked at the hand in disgust.

Miss Trent rolled her eyes. "I told you not to embarrass me."

Mr Locke smiled broadly and shook Toby's damp hand. "A pleasure to make your acquaintance, your lordship. Although, a word from the wise." He leant forward, prompting Toby to do the same. Lowering his voice, he continued, "A gentleman does not offer his hand to a lady he is neither acquainted with nor engaged to." He gave a knowing look and settled back in his chair. From Miss Trent, he enquired, "A friend of yours?"

"An adopted younger brother," Miss Trent replied. "He was the Pot Boy at the *Key & Lion*. He lost his position and home when Mr Sparrow was arrested for murder. I didn't want Toby to be sent to the workhouse, so I let him stay at the Society's house. He helps me with the cleaning and brings in a wage from his work at the underground railway bar."

"I also keep the wrong 'uns away when Mr Snyder ain't there." Toby gave a firm nod.

"I am glad to hear it," Mr Locke said.

Lyons returned with a glass of brandy and gave it to Miss Trent.

"Your note stated you had an urgent matter you wished to discuss with us," Dr Locke said once the butler had left.

Miss Trent took a sip. "I do." She set the glass down. "The Bow Street Society has been commissioned to investigate the death of Miss Mina Ilbert, manager of the *Crescent Theatre*, Strand."

"The Lily of the Lyceum is *dead*?" Mr Locke was stunned. "When? How?"

"Last night," Miss Trent replied. "During her performance. The details aren't fully established yet. Which is why we need your help. Both of you."

"You wish to assign us to the case?" Mr Locke enquired.

"Out of the question," Dr Locke stated, firmly. "You can see the poor state Percy's health is in. He isn't strong enough to undertake an investigation." Her thoughts went to the article in *The Era* newspaper. "Especially not one within the theatre."

Mr Locke lifted his hand. "Wait a moment, Lynette. You said yourself I am better than I was. I have also been making great progress with increasing my stamina on my nightly walks. A Bow Street Society investigation would serve to increase my physical activity and restore a further aspect of normalcy to my life. Both of which would support a faster recovery, do you not agree?"

"You've barely ventured more than a mile from this house in the past few months," Dr Locke reminded him, her voice and eyes filled with concern. "As much as additional physical activity could support your recovery, it could also hinder it. Then there's the question of your reputation. Your fellow actors haven't seen hide nor hair of you since last year. You saw how shocked Miss Trent was when she saw you, and she's one of your oldest and dearest friends. How do you think the wider world is going to react?"

"Unfavourably, I wager," Mr Locke replied, gravely.

"Then you understand my concern?" Dr Locke enquired, sadly.

"I do, but I also know I cannot live like a hermit for the remainder of my days," Mr Locke replied. "It is true they have not seen me, but I am certain they will accept my explanation of prolonged ill health when I give it." He took Dr Locke's hand. "Lynette, my darling. I appreciate all you have done for me, and continue to do, but I feel accepting the assignment to the Bow Street Society's case would help me considerably."

"I'd like to assign you, too, doctor," Miss Trent reminded her.

The clerk's thoughts turned to the events of this morning. After Mr Snyder had returned from taking Mr Willis home, he'd driven Miss Trent to Dr Weeks' rooms and the Dead Room. The surgeon hadn't been at either. Yet, she'd found several empty bottles on and around the sofa, and noticed the poker was missing from the fireplace, at his rooms. Both observations had filled her with a mixture of concern and dread.

"Dr Weeks is currently unavailable," Miss Trent continued, noting the cooling of Dr Locke's gaze at the mention of their mutual friend. "Therefore, I need your medical expertise to help the Society uncover the truth behind Miss Ilbert's death."

"It would also allow you to keep an eye on me," Mr Locke said with a wry smile.

"Claude would accompany you at all times," Dr Locke firmly corrected.

Mr Locke's smile vanished. Averting his gaze, he said, softly, "Of course."

"Very well, Miss Trent," Dr Locke said. "We accept the assignment."

Miss Trent cast a concerned glance between them but decided against prying into their private affairs. Instead, she took out her notebook, turned to the relevant page, and explained, "Our client is Mr Aaron Willis. He was the chief electric man at the *Crescent Theatre*. He was dismissed this morning after being accused of causing Miss Ilbert's death through negligence. Detective Sergeant Dixon was summoned to investigate but ruled Miss Ilbert's death as a tragic accident. As far as Mr Willis was aware, Miss Ilbert's body was taken to Charing Cross Hospital. He didn't know the name of the examining surgeon, though."

"I shall visit the hospital this morning and find out," Dr Locke said.

"Thank you," Miss Trent said. "In the meantime, I'll assign the other members and arrange for you all to meet at the *Crescent Theatre* this afternoon."

"What am I doin'?" Toby enquired with hopeful eyes.

"Coming home with me," Miss Trent said.

Toby's face fell.

* * *

The chair creaked loudly in complaint as Inspector Woolfe shifted his weight from one side to the other. Switching to the other elbow as well, he leant it upon the arm whilst repeatedly pinching his lower lip. At the same time, he clenched and unclenched his other hand around his coat's lapel, scrunching it into a ball and releasing it. Although his eyes were fixed upon Chief Inspector Jones, his gaze had turned inward as his mind tried to make sense of what he'd been told.

"What are your thoughts on the matter, Caleb?"

Inspector Woolfe tightly pinched his lower lip, hoping the pain would snap his garbled mind into focus. Unfortunately, he only succeeded in bringing thoughts of Inspector Conway into the mix. The incident with the scalpel was undoubtedly significant in light of Dr Weeks' assault of Inspector Lee. Inspector Woolfe knew it was his duty to disclose it to his senior officer, but his loyalty to Inspector Conway had kept him silent.

Curious by Inspector Woolfe's stillness following the question, Chief Inspector Jones leant forward in his chair. "If you know something further, I want to hear it."

Inspector Woolfe released his lip and dropped his hand into his lap. Lowering his head and dropping his gaze to the desk's edge, he cleared his throat, coughed, and mumbled, "I don't know anything more, sir."

"Say it again, but with more conviction this time," Chief Inspector Jones challenged. "I dislike being kept in the dark, but I detest being lied to." He watched the hands of his pocket watch. "You have precisely ten seconds to tell me what you know before I suspend you for insubordination."

Inspector Woolfe clenched his hand into a fist upon his lap and growled, "I *can't*, sir."

"Five seconds."

Inspector Woolfe grimaced as, with a low, curt shake of his head, he blurted out, "Weeks pulled a scalpel on John."

"When?"

Inspector Woolfe bowed his head and quietly replied, "Yesterday."

"Was anyone hurt?"

Inspector Woolfe gave another curt shake of his head.

"Do you agree with Inspector Lee's conclusion?"

"I don't agree with anything the bastard says," Inspector Woolfe muttered.

Chief Inspector Jones narrowed his eyes. "Remember who you are speaking to."

"Sorry, sir," Inspector Woolfe mumbled half-heartedly. "But I don't."

Chief Inspector Jones flattened his lips and, filling his lungs, exhaled loudly through his nose. "Do you agree Dr Weeks has been driven insane by his drinking?"

"No."

"Because it was Inspector Lee who suggested it?"

"Yes."

The corners of Chief Inspector Jones' eyes and lips tightened. "Remove Inspector Lee from the equation and consider your answer in light of what we know. On that basis, do you believe Dr Weeks has been driven insane by his drinking?"

Inspector Woolfe frowned. "It's possible." He lifted his eyes to meet Chief Inspector Jones'. "But I don't believe it." As his senior officer parted his lips to argue further, Inspector Woolfe cut him off. "If Dr Weeks is insane, I'm a Duke."

Realising he couldn't persuade Inspector Woolfe otherwise, Chief Inspector Jones settled back in his chair with a soft exhale. "Well, it doesn't matter what you or I think. I've submitted an urgent application for a Reception Order to the magistrate. The two doctors he asks to assess Dr Weeks will form their own unbiased opinions on his state of mind."

Inspector Woolfe's bushy eyebrows lifted in unison. "You're getting him certified?"

"I'm having him assessed. Whether a Certificate of Insanity is issued depends upon the doctors' findings. In the meantime, I've arranged for Dr Weeks' mother to be brought to me to talk about her son."

Inspector Woolfe grimaced at the thought of Dr Weeks being put away in an asylum. He knew Inspector Conway would be equally appalled, if not more so. He and Dr Weeks had been friends for years. "I don't like it, sir."

"Neither do I," Chief Inspector Jones admitted with regret. "But sometimes we must take unsavoury action to ensure the best outcome."

Conceding he agreed with that much at least, Inspector Woolfe gave a small nod. "What should I tell Inspector Conway, sir?"

"Tell him of the assault and that I require his assistance with Dr Weeks."

Inspector Woolfe sat bolt upright. "You mean send him *here*, sir?"

"At once."

Inspector Woolfe stared at him. "But the Bow Street Society, sir. The bank."

"They'll have to wait for the time being. I want Inspector Conway here as soon as possible. If Dr Weeks becomes violent again, John may be the only one capable of calming him down."

Inspector Woolfe grimaced again but nonetheless muttered his agreement and left.

TWENTY-THREE

"Tell him of the assault and that I require his assistance with Dr Weeks." Chief Inspector Jones' words resonated in Inspector Woolfe's ears as he alighted from the hansom cab, thereby relieving the pressure on its axis. Instructing the driver to wait for him, he climbed the steps two at a time and strode into Bow Street police station. Seeing the fierce determination in his senior officer's eyes, the desk sergeant immediately lifted the hatch and stepped aside.

"Is Inspector Conway here?" Inspector Woolfe demanded as he passed through.

"In your office, sir," the sergeant replied.

Inspector Woolfe strode down the corridor, obliging the clerks coming from the opposite direction to step aside, and flung open the stairwell's door. Climbing them within a matter of seconds, despite the burning in his lungs and the sweat on his brow, he strode down the second corridor and into his office. Spotting Inspector Conway behind his desk, he wheezed, "Dr Weeks has just attacked Lee. Jones wants you at the Yard. Now." He immediately left the office, striding back the way he'd came.

"*Oi!*" Inspector Conway yelled, leaping to his feet and grabbing his coat and hat as he ran after his friend. Rushing into the corridor, he stopped when he saw Inspector Woolfe by the stairwell door. "What do you mean Weeks attacked Lee?!"

"He hit him with a poker." Inspector Woolfe wiped his brow with his coat sleeve.

"Where are you goin'?!"

"I've got somewhere to be." Inspector Woolfe entered the stairwell and returned downstairs. He knew Inspector Conway had a lot of questions, but he also knew he wasn't in a position to answer them. Therefore, it had been better to get in, deliver the news, and get out. Leaving the station, his hot face gained some relief from the cold air. Climbing back into the hansom cab, thereby restoring the pressure on its axis, he saw Inspector Conway emerge onto the station's steps. As he approached, Inspector Woolfe knocked on the cab's roof and instructed, "Lombard Street, please, mate."

"Caleb!" Inspector Conway called when the cab lurched forward. By the time he'd run down the steps, across the pavement, and into the road, though, the cab was well on its way.

* * *

The Charing Cross Hospital on Agar Street, West Strand, was a stone's throw from the *Crescent Theatre*. Founded in 1820, it had a well-established and respected reputation within London's medical profession. Thus, Dr Locke had heard its name mentioned on innumerable occasions. She approved of its policy to automatically accept in-patients in cases of emergency and was intrigued by its electrical department.

Following a humiliating conversation with an attendant in which she was obliged to prove she was a qualified medical doctor (her certificate was permanently kept in her bag for this purpose), she was led to Dr Jonathan Caden's office. Fortunately, he didn't share his subordinate's low opinion of women and greeted Dr Locke with warmth and respect.

In his mid-sixties, he was approximately five feet ten inches tall with receding hair, impeccable beard, and neat moustache, all of which were a brilliant white. His dark-blue eyes gazed at Dr Locke through brass-rimmed spectacles as they sat on opposite sides of his desk. His attire consisted of a knee-length black overcoat, waistcoat, trousers, and black tie. The corners of his white shirt's starched collar were bent over to form triangles, whilst a silver tie pin caught the daylight from the window as he moved.

"Tragic, very tragic," Dr Caden said as he retrieved a folder from the pile and put it before Dr Locke. "The police concluded it was an accident, so I see no harm in allowing you and the Bow Street Society to see Miss Ilbert's postmortem report. An admirable group, by the way."

"I shall pass on your compliments." Dr Locke opened the folder. "I understand you were called upon to examine Miss Ilbert's body after the police dismissed the first surgeon?"

Dr Caden hummed. "Indeed." He pushed his brows together and down. "I don't usually indulge in sullying the names of my fellow doctors, but Dr Weeks stumbling from the *Crescent Theatre* was observed by all present." His brows relaxed as he considered what he knew of Dr Weeks' professional reputation. "Quite a shame really. He seemed to have such promise."

"Addiction can ruin the most accomplished of men," Dr Locke muttered.

"Hm?"

"Never mind." Dr Locke scanned the report. "The cause of death was electrocution?"

Dr Caden polished his spectacles with his handkerchief. "Yes. The entire company and an auditorium of people witnessed her step onto a metal plate and become as rigid as a statue. Seconds later, smoke was seen rising from her body. She collapsed only when the electricity was extinguished." He replaced his spectacles. "The only signs of electrocution I found upon her body were scorching of the tissue on the soles of both feet."

"She was barefooted?"

"No, but there were metal plates on the soles of her shoes. They were necessary for the effect to occur, or so I was told."

"The 'effect?'"

Dr Caden gave a small dismissive movement of his hand. "I haven't the faintest idea. As I say, though, the strength of the electricity passing through her was sufficient to cause the scorching."

Dr Locke made a mental note. "In your opinion, was Miss Ilbert's death an accident?"

Dr Caden considered his answer. "There are forces in this world we do not understand and, some may argue, should not. Our discovery of electricity has both enlightened and endangered us. Its potential is not yet fully understood, and yet there are those who wish to see it in every home in the country. Miss Ilbert's death demonstrates how little we understand despite humanity's arrogance. Do I think her death was accidental? It's possible, and it's the theory the police subscribe to. Do I think she murdered herself with electricity? It's possible, but I have never heard of such a thing. Do I think she died by another's hand? It's possible, as most people were distracted by the pantomime. I cannot say with certainly which possibility applies, however. Even the physician in our electricity department here could not provide me with a conclusive answer."

"Thank you, Dr Caden. You've been very helpful." Dr Locke held up the report. "May I borrow this to show my fellow Society members? I'll return it as soon as the case is concluded."

"By all means." Dr Caden stood as she did. "Would you give Dr Weeks my best when you see him?"

Dr Locke hoped she never would. Nevertheless, she gave a contrived smile and replied, "Certainly, doctor."

* * *

"Come in!" Chief Inspector Jones called in response to the knock on his door.

Sergeant Gutman entered. "Dr Weeks' mother—" He grunted as he was shoved aside.

"Evangelina Breckenridge," Miss Breckenridge announced, striding into the room.

"Chief Inspector Richard Jones." He looked to Sergeant Gutman. "Thank you."

"What's this all about, son?" Miss Breckenridge demanded once they were alone. "I were in the foyer of my hotel waitin' for my cab to the station when yer boy come up and told me I were needed at Scotland Yard."

"Would you like to sit?"

"No. I've got a boat to catch. What's this all about?"

"You're returning to Canada?"

"Either yer deaf or plain dumb, son. I ain't goin' to ask ya a third time."

Chief Inspector Jones gave a polite smile. "My apologies. It's a habit of mine to want to be answered before answering." His expression turned grave. "Your son has been detained following an assault. He struck one of my officers with a poker. Fortunately, the injury was only minor, but your son was in a state of great distress at the time."

"Yer officer must of said somethin' to make him mad."

"I've spoken to the officer, and he told me there was no provocation."

Miss Breckenridge put her hand on her hip. "There's always got to be provocation for my Percival to attack someone. He ain't a fighter. Hell, he only become a surgeon 'cause he were too scared to fight in the militia."

Chief Inspector Jones had a vague memory of Inspector Conway telling him the story of how Dr Weeks had entered his profession, but he couldn't recall the details at present. "When was the last time you saw your son?"

"Two nights ago."

"When you had a meeting with Mr Fry, the solicitor?"

Miss Breckenridge's features tightened. "How d'ya know about that?"

"Your son is a member of the Bow Street Society and, as such, has been under surveillance by our undercover detectives." Chief Inspector Jones perched on the edge of his desk. "Are you aware your son was beaten and robbed the same night?"

217

"No, I ain't." Miss Breckenridge closed the distance. "If one of yer boys were watchin', why didn't they help him?"

"We didn't want him to know he was under surveillance."

Worry entered Miss Breckenridge's face and eyes. "Were he badly hurt?"

"He has a couple of lumps on his head, but I think his inebriated state deadened the pain." Chief Inspector Jones stood and indicated the low-backed, brown leather Chesterfield sofa before the fire. "Please, come and sit down."

Miss Breckenridge followed and sat on the opposite end of the sofa to him. "Yer boy my Percival hit, were it the same one who were watchin' him when he were robbed?"

"No." Chief Inspector Jones softened his voice. "I'm deeply concerned for Dr Weeks. I fear the assault on my officer is a symptom of a deeper problem. Namely, insanity brought on by excessive and prolonged alcohol consumption."

Miss Breckenridge looked at him sharply. "Beggin' ya pardon?" She scowled. "Percival ain't insane."

"I've submitted an urgent request for a Reception Order to a magistrate. He will ask two doctors to assess Dr Weeks. If they deem him to be unwell in mind, they will issue a Certificate of Insanity, and he will be admitted to an asylum."

Miss Breckenridge stood. "Over my dead body!"

Chief Inspector Jones also stood. "Given your son's uncharacteristic and violent behaviour this morning, and on another occasion, I was obliged to act under my authority as a policeman to protect him from himself. Believe me, if there was any other way, I would take it."

Miss Breckenridge looked pale. "And if he ain't mad? What then?"

Chief Inspector Jones frowned. "He may be tried for assault."

Miss Breckenridge lowered herself onto the sofa. "Does his woman know?"

"No. She'll be informed once his fate is known."

"I can't believe it," Miss Breckenridge said, her voice strained by emotion.

"Would you like a brandy?"

"No, I'm all right." Miss Breckenridge glanced at her dainty pocket watch. "'Sides, I've got a boat to catch."

Chief Inspector Jones furrowed his brow. "You still intend to leave for Canada?"

"I've got no choice, son. I'm in *Much Ado About Nothin'* come Friday in Toronto." She put her hand on his. "Tell my Percival I love him, will ya? And… to get better soon."

Chief Inspector Jones deeply disapproved of Miss Breckenridge's decision to leave the country despite her son's condition. The knowledge it wasn't his place to persuade her to stay offered him little comfort. Yet, aside from this, her leaving also meant this was his last opportunity to get the information from her. "May I ask you a couple of personal questions?"

"Sure."

"What was the purpose of you and Dr Weeks' meeting with Mr Fry?"

"Oh that." Miss Breckenridge gave a weak smile. "We were jus' talkin' about some property I've been wantin' to buy here in London. Turned out I ain't got enough money, though. What's yer other question?"

Chief Inspector Jones considered how to put it tactfully. "Why doesn't Dr Weeks share your surname?"

Taken off guard by the indirect enquiry into Dr Weeks' parentage, Miss Breckenridge turned her head toward the fire to buy some time. Searching her mind for a way of avoiding answering the question, she soon felt the weight of Chief Inspector Jones' gaze upon her. Admitting the truth wasn't an option. She relied upon her allowance to survive, and she couldn't be sure news of her indiscretion wouldn't get back to Lord Weeks.

219

"He does," Miss Breckenridge said, her gaze fixed upon the fire.

Chief Inspector Jones furrowed his brow, confused. "He does?"

This 'ere's for the best, Miss Breckenridge thought. *There ain't any other way.* "He made up a story to tell folks, about how he's the bastard son of an English lord who never wanted him, just so he wouldn't have to admit his real father were an out-of-work actor and drunk," she lied, her words spewing out like verbal diarrhoea. "Breckenridge were his father's name, but we never married." Realising she was trembling from the rush of adrenaline caused by her wilful deceit, she quietly said, "Reckon I'll have some brandy now."

Chief Inspector Jones gave her a sympathetic smile and stood to pour her a small measure.

Miss Breckenridge wanted a hole to swallow her up. Feeling a thickness in her throat, she glanced at the door and considered running away. She realised it would raise more questions, though, and she'd be detained for longer as a result.

"Here," Chief Inspector Jones held out the glass.

"Thank you." Miss Breckenridge took it from him and drank half the brandy. *This 'ere's for the best*, she reminded herself. *'Sides, Percival's better off in an asylum than a jail.* She felt her guilt ease at the realisation. Her Percival *would* be better off in an asylum. He was too delicate and too cowardly to survive in an overcrowded, squalid jail. She drank the remaining brandy and returned the glass to Chief Inspector Jones. "D'ya need me for anythin' else, son?"

"If you could leave your address in Canada with Sergeant Gutman, I'll write to you about your son's ongoing condition and treatment."

Miss Breckenridge stood, prompting Chief Inspector Jones to do the same. "We're obliged to ya, Chief Inspector." She walked with him to the door. "If yer ever in Toronto, ya'll come visit me, d'ya hear?"

Chief Inspector Jones smiled softly. "I'd love to." He held the door open for her. "Goodbye."

"Goodbye." Miss Breckenridge left the office but halted when she heard the door close. Swiftly filling her lungs, she closed her eyes and slowly exhaled through her nose. *Forgive me, Percival.*

She walked away.

TWENTY-FOUR

Twenty minutes. I've been in this bloody queue for twenty bloody minutes, Inspector Woolfe inwardly fumed whilst glaring at the clerk behind the counter. *A snail can move faster than this bloke*. Seeing the clerk bid farewell to his customer, Inspector Woolfe watched as the next man in the queue moved forward and explained the purpose of his visit to the *London & County Banking Company*. Although it meant Inspector Woolfe would be seen next, it didn't guarantee he wouldn't be waiting for *another* twenty minutes.

Hearing a throat being cleared close by, Inspector Woolfe turned and lowered his head to meet the gaze of a thin man with steely eyes and chiselled features. The man's tailored suit and general air of superiority denoted him as a senior bank employee. "Excuse me," he said, his lips barely moving. "Vagrants are not permitted in the *London & County Bank*. I must ask you to leave."

"I'm not a vagrant," Inspector Woolfe said.

"With your coat and," the man sniffed the air, "*odour*, what else could you be?"

Inspector Woolfe shoved his warrant card into the man's face, obliging him to lean his head back to read it. "Detective Inspector Caleb Woolfe of the Metropolitan Police."

"The *police*?" the man enquired in a half-whisper.

Inspector Woolfe put his warrant card away. "I've been waiting for twenty minutes to talk to someone about the Bow Street Society, and I'm losing my patience."

The man pursed and rolled his lips as he darted his eyes to the curious onlookers nearby. Returning his gaze to Inspector Woolfe, he appeared to make a decision as, with an attempted smile that ended in a grimace, he indicated a vacant position at the counter. "Right this way, Inspector." He moved behind whilst Inspector Woolfe stood in front. "Let it not be said the *London & County Banking*

Company does not play its part in maintaining law and order." The man rested his clasped hands upon the counter. "What would you like to know?"

"Who opened the Bow Street Society's bank account and when."

The man gave a condescending smile. "That is a rather simple one to answer for it was *I* who oversaw its opening." He pushed back his shoulders and held the lapels of his suit jacket. "I am but one of a handful of senior clerks permitted to oversee the opening of accounts of such a size."

Inspector Woolfe glared at him. "*Who* opened it and *when*?"

The man dropped his hands and returned the glare. "Mr Calvin in November 1895."

Inspector Woolfe searched his memory until he located the name. *Mr Calvin is the name of the Society's solicitor*, he realised. "Did he give another name?"

"Miss Trent," the man replied. "She is the account holder, alongside Mr Calvin."

Realising the 'J. Pettifoot' who placed the advertisements could be Mr Calvin using a pseudonym, Inspector Woolfe wondered why he hadn't done the same when opening the bank account. The visit to *Derby's Stationer's* on Endell Street sprang into his mind. Mr Derby had told him Mr Calvin had not only acted on Miss Trent's behalf in the initial negotiations of leasing the office above his shop but had also provided a character reference for her. Within this scenario, Mr Calvin was acting as the Bow Street Society's solicitor. It was possible he had been acting in the same capacity when he'd assisted Miss Trent in opening the bank account.

Yet, he might've been acting in his capacity as the Bow Street Society's founder when he placed the advertisements in the *Gaslight Gazette*. As such, he would've been stepping outside the regular duties of a respected solicitor. In short, the pseudonym of 'J. Pettifoot' would've served to conceal his identity and thus protect his professional position and reputation.

"I want the names of all borrowers and depositors connected to the Bow Street Society's account," Inspector Woolfe instructed.

"I'll need some time," the man warned.

"I'll be back in the morning," Inspector Woolfe said, leaving before the man could argue. Once outside, he filled his lungs and coughed as he exhaled. Reaching into his coat pocket, he frowned when he remembered he'd finished the medicine. He considered visiting Dr Colbert for more but set the idea aside as nonurgent. Instead, he headed to the nearest omnibus stop to return to Bow Street. He'd remembered Inspector Lee had called upon Mr Calvin last November, and he was almost certain he'd given him the address of Mr Calvin's office. If he had, it would be in his desk. The sooner he found it, the sooner he could question Mr Calvin and, with any luck, expose 'J. Pettifoot.'

* * *

"Mr *Locke*! How *wonderful* it is to see you again!" Mr Bertram Heath exclaimed as he met the illusionist on the pavement outside the *Crescent Theatre*.

In his mid-twenties, Mr Heath was five feet three inches tall with a slender build. His dark-brown, knee-length overcoat swamped his frame, thereby largely concealing the remainder of his attire. This consisted of a light-brown suit, waistcoat, and tie, and a white shirt with starched Eton collar. His short, light-brown hair, gleaming green eyes, and unblemished complexion gave him a misleading, boyish appearance.

"My *word*, you have been in the wars, haven't you?" Mr Heath observed upon taking in Mr Locke's frail appearance. "It must be almost four months since we last met. It was the case in Birmingham, wasn't it?" Smiling broadly, he looked to Claude at Mr Locke's side. "You should've seen how Mr Locke dealt with a *fierce* policeman there. Now, what was his name? Martin? No. Morton? No, that wasn't it, either. Ah, yes! Matthew! Detective Inspector Matthew Rupert Peter Donahue. The man they called the Ripper, would you believe!"

"Pardon me, we haven't met," another man said, extending his hand to Mr Heath as he approached the group. "I'm Dr Neal Colbert of Bethlehem Hospital and the Bow Street Society."

"Mr Bertram Heath, architect." He vigorously shook Dr Colbert's hand. "And Bow Street Society member, of course. It's a pleasure to meet you, doctor. Have you met Mr Percival Locke?"

"No." Dr Colbert extended his hand to him. "I'm delighted to meet you, Mr Locke. I've seen you perform at the *Paddington Palladium* many times."

"Thank you, doctor." Mr Locke shook his hand. "This is my manservant, Claude."

Recognition flashed through Dr Colbert's eyes. He was almost certain Claude was a former Bethlehem Hospital attendant. Reluctant to cause problems between himself and Mr Locke, he chose not to air his suspicions.

"Forgive me, doctor, but are you not an inappropriate choice to assist with the investigation into Miss Ilbert's death?" Mr Locke enquired. "After all, your mere presence insinuates a suspicion Miss Ilbert's mind was unsound prior to her demise when, in reality, nothing of the kind has been put forth by any individual connected to the case. At least, thus far."

"I was assigned for my knowledge of physiognomy," Dr Colbert calmly explained.

"Is physiognomy not a pseudoscience?" Mr Locke enquired.

"To some," Dr Colbert replied.

"But not to you?" Mr Locke enquired.

"Physiognomy isn't an accepted science by any stretch of the imagination, nor is it recognised as a viable form of philosophy," Dr Colbert replied. "Nevertheless, I am fascinated by the application of physiognomy's principles to my patients to test the accuracy—or lack thereof—of its claims."

"It sounds complicated," Mr Heath cheerily observed. "I prefer bricks and mortar."

"Miss Trent wishes you to apply the principles of physiognomy to the friends and associates of Miss Ilbert?" Mr Locke enquired with a hint of cynicism.

"She wishes me to try, yes," Dr Colbert replied. "Shall we go inside?"

The corner of Mr Locke's mouth lifted at Dr Colbert's polite halting of their debate. "Certainly, doctor. After you."

Dr Colbert glanced at the others and entered the theatre's foyer. Expecting it to be empty, he abruptly halted when he found a middle-aged man standing in its centre, awaiting their arrival. Parting his lips to explain his presence, the man coming toward him with his arms outstretched prevented Dr Colbert from doing so. Unsure how to react, Dr Colbert pursed his lips and stood his ground. When the man strode past him as if he wasn't there, Dr Colbert felt his unease turn into embarrassment.

"The Great Locke as I live and breathe!" the man exclaimed, patting Mr Locke on the back and shaking his hand. "We thought you were dead, old man."

"The Grim Reaper has not caught up with me yet," Mr Locke said with a smile.

"Are you considering a new venture?" the man enquired.

"No, I am here in my capacity as a member of the Bow Street Society," Mr Locke replied. "This is my manservant, Claude, and these are my associates and fellow Bow Street Society members, Dr Neal Colbert, an expert in physiognomy, and Mr Bertram Heath, an architect." He half-turned toward the others. "This is Mr Luthor Ellis Benton, an actor of the finest calibre."

"Mr Willis warned me of the Society's arrival, but he never mentioned the Great Locke," Mr Benton beamed.

"Is this a private party or can anyone join?" another man enquired with obvious irritability from a set of double doors on the foyer's opposite side.

"Mr Locke, Mr Heath, and Dr Colbert, allow me to introduce Mr Ronald Stone, our stage manager," Mr Benton said. "Mr Stone, this is Mr Percival Locke, Mr Betram Heath, and Dr Neal Colbert of the Bow Street Society. They are here to investigate Mina's death."

Mr Stone entered the foyer proper. "At whose request?"

"Your former chief electric man's," Mr Locke replied.

"And my own," Mr Benton interjected.

"May I help you, gentlemen?" a woman's voice enquired.

"Miss Kimberly, this is—" Mr Benton began.

"I know who they are, thank you. I overheard your introductions as I was walking from the office." Miss Kimberly turned her attention to the Bow Streeters. "I'm Miss Emmaline Kimberly, the *Crescent*'s business manager." Her gaze softened as it rested upon the illusionist. "Mr Locke, it is good to see you, again."

"As it is you," Mr Locke said.

"They're here to investigate Mina's death," Mr Stone said, folding his arms.

"I'm afraid you've wasted your time, gentlemen," Miss Kimberly said. "The police have already ruled dear Mina's death a tragic accident."

"With all due respect, Miss Kimberly, your former chief electric man thinks otherwise," Mr Locke said. "And I for one am willing to bow to his superior knowledge on the matter."

"I'm not standing for this," Mr Stone muttered, heading for the entrance.

"Where are you going, Ronnie?" Mr Benton enquired through a sigh.

"To fetch Sergeant Dixon." Mr Stone looked back at the others, his hand on the door. "He'll soon put a stop to this wanton intrusion."

"You'll have to forgive my associate," Mr Benton said after Mr Stone had left. "I presume you wish to see where it happened?"

"Please," Mr Locke replied.

Miss Kimberly indicated the double doors. "This way, gentlemen."

* * *

Thunder rumbled overhead, and rain beat against the windows as Chief Inspector Jones walked down the corridor toward the interview room. The inclement weather had caused the day to darken, and he inwardly observed how well it reflected the mood. Despite several officers moving around the building, their demeanours were sombre and subdued. Word of the attack had spread swiftly through the Yard, with most being shocked and dumbfounded by the surgeon's behaviour.

Noticing his senior officer's approach, Sergeant Caulfield moved forward to meet him. "He went quiet a few minutes ago, sir."

"Do you have your handcuffs, Sergeant?"

"Yes, sir." Sergeant Caulfield slipped his hand into his jacket pocket.

"Then follow my lead." Chief Inspector Jones went over to the door and, putting his ear to the wood, listened intently. When he heard nothing, he turned the key with a soft click and eased the door open an inch.

He held his breath.

The gloom beyond was so thick, it was almost impossible to see. Allowing his eyes to adjust, he eased the door open a little more and scanned the room. His gaze landed on a figure sitting upon the floor in the far-right corner with their knees pulled up to their chest and their arms wrapped around their legs.

"Dr Weeks, Sergeant Caulfield and I are coming in."

The figure remained still.

Chief Inspector Jones motioned to Sergeant Caulfield to follow. "Lock it behind you." He softly instructed once they were in the room.

Sergeant Caulfield locked the door and passed the key to Chief Inspector Jones.

"Doctor?" Chief Inspector Jones moved forward. Immediately his nostrils were assaulted by the mixed stale stenches of alcohol, sweat, and urine. Swallowing against his gag reflex, he breathed through his nose and stood a few feet from Dr Weeks. "Percy?"

Dr Weeks lifted his head to reveal smooth, expressionless features, tear-soaked cheeks, and large bags beneath his heavily bloodshot eyes. There was a dark look to them he'd never observed in the surgeon before. It was as if someone had erased the happiness from every fibre of his being.

Chief Inspector Jones crouched so they were eye to eye. Dr Weeks lowered his head in time with the movement but remained silent. It wasn't until he was closer, did Chief Inspector Jones notice the slight bobbing of Dr Weeks' right foot.

"Do you know where you are?" Chief Inspector Jones softly enquired.

Dr Weeks gave a slow nod.

"Where?" Chief Inspector Jones encouraged.

"An interview room at the Yard." Dr Weeks' voice was hoarse. "Did I kill the sonofabitch?"

Chief Inspector Jones frowned. "No."

Dr Weeks turned his head and muttered into the air, "Damn Woolfe."

"Why did you assault Inspector Lee?" Chief Inspector Jones enquired.

Dr Weeks pressed his lips firmly together and gave a hard, obvious swallow.

"Why did you say he'd ruined your life?" Chief Inspector Jones probed further.

The tapping of Dr Weeks' foot increased as he pressed his forehead against his knees. Running his fingers over his scalp, he curled them against his crown, clutching the hair with tight fists. Hard, wet sniffs also interspersed his loud, shuddering breaths.

"We only want to help you," Chief Inspector Jones said.

Dr Weeks didn't respond.

"Leave us, Sergeant," Chief Inspector Jones ordered.

"But sir—" Sergeant Caulfield began, alarmed.

"I said, 'leave us,'" Chief Inspector Jones insisted, holding out the key. "Stay by the door. I'll knock when I'm ready."

Sergeant Caulfield hesitated but took the key and left.

"Nothing you say will go beyond this room," Chief Inspector Jones said when he heard the click of the lock.

Dr Weeks didn't respond.

Frowning deeply, Chief Inspector Jones knew he was running out of both time and options to prevent Dr Weeks from being committed. Wanting to get *any* response from the surgeon, he steeled himself and said, "I know about the envelope of money in John's house."

Dr Weeks held his breath.

"I read your statement confessing to putting it there," Chief Inspector Jones went on.

Dr Weeks' shoulders shook as quiet, muffled crying sounded from behind his knees.

"Why did you confess, Percy?" Chief Inspector Jones gently enquired.

Dr Weeks' crying turned to sobbing.

"You're John's friend. You wouldn't do anything to hurt him."

"Stop. *Please.*" Dr Weeks begged.

"Talk to me, Percy. Tell me what happened."

"I *can't*," Dr Weeks whispered.

"You can."

"*Leave me alone*, damn you."

"Why did you confess to putting the money in John's house?"

"I said '*leave me alone*!'" Dr Weeks suddenly lunged forward, shoving Chief Inspector Jones off balance. A loud thud sounded as his head struck the table's edge behind him. Grunting at the same time, Chief Inspector Jones fell sideways immediately after. Fearing Dr Weeks may attempt to finish the job, he rolled onto his back and threw up his arms to defend himself. He felt only air, however. Searching the gloom for his assailant, he saw Dr Weeks had returned to sitting in the corner with his legs against his chest and his forehead pressed against his knees.

His uncontrollable sobbing filled the room as light suddenly poured in from the corridor, and Sergeant Caulfield rushed to Chief Inspector Jones' side. "Are you all right, sir?!"

"I'm fine, Sergeant." Chief Inspector Jones allowed him to help him to his feet. "I just lost my balance." He straightened his jacket. "I'm not as spry as I once was."

They looked at Dr Weeks' shaking, sobbing form.

"Did he say anything, sir?" Sergeant Caulfield quietly enquired.

"No." Chief Inspector Jones felt the weight of sadness creep into his soul. "I'm afraid there's nothing more we can do for him now."

TWENTY-FIVE

"May I have a chair, please?" Mr Locke leant his weight upon his walking cane.

Mr Benton at once retrieved a stool from the wings and put it beside the illusionist.

"Thank you." Mr Locke lowered himself onto the stool, using his cane for balance. A relieved look passed over his face the moment he sat.

Meanwhile, Mr Heath was crawling around the metal plate embedded in the stage. Dr Colbert, who had been momentarily distracted by Mr Locke's request, watched the architect with a mixture of intrigue and confusion.

When Mr Heath ran his hand over the gap between the plate and floorboards, Miss Kimberly tilted her head to the side and enquired, "May I know what you're looking for, precisely?"

"Any wires which shouldn't be here." Mr Heath traced the plate's remaining edges. "I can't find any on this side." He clambered to his feet and patted the dust from his trousers. "I see the lights are the new carbon-filament bulbs." He pointed to the auditorium's gigantic chandelier. "The Savoy Theatre was the first to be entirely lit by electricity in 1881—but I'm sure you knew that."

"Yes," Miss Kimberly and Mr Locke replied in unison.

"Where is the electricity generated?" Mr Heath turned to Miss Kimberly. "As I understand it, several theatres rely upon steam-engines and dynamo. If the *Crescent* does the same, is the engine inside or outside? Unless you've changed to a supply from an electricity company?"

Miss Kimberly folded her arms and cast a sideways glance at Mr Locke. "Forgive me for not answering."

"Don't you know?" Mr Heath enquired.

"I do," Miss Kimberly replied.

"May I ask why I'm prohibited from knowing?" Mr Heath gave a weak smile. "Granted, theatres are not my usual fare, but I consulted several of my peers who have considerable knowledge and experience in this architectural field when I received Miss Trent's request. Otherwise, I wouldn't have known as much as I do, but I still don't know enough about *this* theatre to create a complete picture of its architectural features to inform our investigation."

"I'm sorry, it's simply not possible," Miss Kimberly said.

Mr Heath's shoulders slumped.

"Miss Kimberly fears the exposure of how the theatre generates its power, and the other practises and processes which are employed to keep it operating at a fundamental level, would make it vulnerable to the competition," Mr Locke explained. "Superficially, she is right to be wary. I am, after all, a fellow theatre manager and owner. However, I give my word as a gentleman I shan't knowingly replicate at the *Paddington Palladium* what I see and hear here." Mr Locke lifted his chin. "I am also willing to sign an agreement to that effect, thereby making myself accountable to the law should I consciously break its terms."

Mr Heath looked to Miss Kimberly with hopeful eyes.

"Very well. I shall have an agreement drawn up before you leave," Miss Kimberly said. "And I shall answer your questions, Mr Heath, but only if Mr Locke abides by the terms of our agreement from this moment on."

"I shall," Mr Locke said.

"Are you witness to this?" Miss Kimberly enquired from Mr Benton.

"I am," Mr Benton replied.

"*Marvellous*!" Mr Heath put his hands together.

"Then it is settled," Mr Locke said. "But, for the record, Miss Kimberly, I am already familiar with the theatrical effect whereby an electrical charge from a battery is used to illuminate one's costume."

"You are?" Miss Kimberly enquired.

"Yes, I considered employing it at the *Paddington Palladium*," Mr Locke replied. "If executed as designed, it should pose no threat to life. Clearly, the battery has been substituted for a far stronger electrical current."

"Therefore, I must know how the theatre generates its electricity," Mr Heath added.

"The *Crescent* receives it from an external company," Miss Kimberly explained. "Its gaslight system has also been maintained in case the electric lighting fails."

"And how much candlepower does the electric lighting give?" Mr Heath enquired.

"That I truly don't know," Miss Kimberly replied. "But Mr Willis would."

"May I see the underside of the metal plate?" Mr Heath enquired.

"Perhaps we ought to wait for Mr Stone?" Mr Benton suggested.

"I'm still the business manager here," Miss Kimberly firmly reminded him. "Escort Mr Heath below stage."

"Of course." Mr Benton furrowed his brow. "If you'll walk this way, Mr Heath?"

"If you would wait a moment," Mr Locke said, thereby halting the actor and architect. "I see there is a trap in the stage." He pointed with his cane to a set of wooden doors located a few feet from the metal plate. "If you were to open them, we would be able to hear Mr Heath's findings as he gives them."

Mr Benton met Miss Kimberly's gaze.

"Open the trap," the latter instructed.

"Thank you," Mr Locke said.

Mr Heath grinned as he followed Mr Benton into the wings.

"The theatre seems deserted," Dr Colbert observed.

"It is closed as a mark of respect for Miss Ilbert," Mr Locke said. "Correct?"

"Yes," Miss Kimberly confirmed. "It was only supposed to be Mr Stone and I today. Mr Benton's arrival was quite unexpected. As was yours." She cast an appraising glance over Mr Locke. "Rumours about your whereabouts have been rife."

"I have been ill these past few months, but I am recovering now," Mr Locke stated.

Dr Colbert cast a sideways glance at Claude and wondered if Mr Locke's illness was in his mind or his body.

The doors into the foyer opened, and Mr Stone strode in.

Following him was a man in a dark-blue, double-breasted cotton overcoat, black trousers, and a dark-blue trilby hat sat at an angle upon his head. His short, dark-brown hair and moustache were immaculate, and his fair complexion was unblemished but pink from the cold. A light-blue handkerchief protruded from his overcoat's breast pocket, tan-coloured leather gloves adorned his hands, and a plain ebony cane swung casually at his side. Approximately five feet nine inches tall, he had a slender build and appeared to be in his late thirties.

"Detective Sergeant Keith Dixon of the Metropolitan Police, I presume?" Mr Locke enquired as the unknown man climbed the steps to the stage with Mr Stone.

"Yes, from Vine Street, Piccadilly," Sergeant Dixon replied in a thinly veiled East End of London accent. "Mr Percy Locke, I presume?"

"Yes," Mr Locke replied. "Please pardon my not getting up."

They shook hands.

"This is my manservant, Claude, and my fellow Bow Street Society member, Dr Neal Colbert," Mr Locke introduced. "Another of our members, Mr Bertram Heath, is with Mr Benton below stage."

Mr Stone glared at him. "What's he doing there?"

"Examining the metal plate's mechanism," Mr Locke replied.

Mr Stone moved toward the wings, but Mr Locke lifted his cane to bar his path.

"Get out of my way." Mr Stone pushed the cane aside.

"I am merely attempting to save both your time and energy," Mr Locke said.

"What do you mean?" Mr Stone demanded.

The trap's doors opened with a dull thud.

"Can you hear me, Mr Locke?!" Mr Heath called from below.

"Clearly, Mr Heath!" Mr Locke replied.

"*Excellent*!" Mr Heath said in delight. In a quieter voice, he observed, "My, this is a rather complicated contraption, isn't it? All these ropes and pulleys. What does it do?"

"Lift a performer onto the stage using the strength of four men," Mr Locke replied before Mr Benton could.

"My *word*..." Mr Heath said.

"Do not allow yourself to be distracted, Mr Heath," Mr Locke gently warned.

"Right!" Mr Heath agreed. "Going to the plate now!"

"Mr Stone said the Bow Street Society was meddling," Sergeant Dixon said.

"We have been commissioned by Mr Willis, the *Crescent*'s former chief electric man, to investigate Miss Ilbert's death and prove him innocent of negligence," Mr Locke explained. "He informed our clerk Miss Ilbert's death was ruled a tragic accident by the police."

"Because it was," Miss Kimberly interjected.

"The Bow Street Society is wasting its time," Sergeant Dixon stated.

"My good man, time spent investigating a suspected miscarriage of justice is always time well spent," Mr Locke said.

Dr Colbert admired the illusionist's tenacity.

"If, at our investigation's end, we reach the same conclusion as you, so be it," Mr Locke continued. "But we would have fulfilled our obligation to our client. I trust the police have no objection to our looking into the matter?"

"We find the whole Bow Street Society objectionable," Sergeant Dixon wryly replied. "But no. As far as Miss Ilbert's death is concerned, we consider the matter closed."

"I expect you still wish to be informed if we uncover evidence suggesting otherwise?" Mr Locke enquired.

"That goes without saying," Sergeant Dixon replied.

"Of course, it would not be the first time the Bow Street Society has succeeded where the Metropolitan Police has failed," Mr Locke observed in a nonchalant tone.

Sergeant Dixon's voice hardened. "But it could be the first time the Bow Street Society has failed where the police have succeeded."

"Touché," Mr Locke conceded.

"We'll communicate with you often, Sergeant," Dr Colbert said. "The Bow Street Society isn't interested in a conflict with the police. Is it, Mr Locke?"

"Only if the police are uninterested in a conflict with us," Mr Locke replied.

"We have more important things to do," Sergeant Dixon said.

"How odd," Mr Heath remarked, drawing their attention to the trap.

Mr Locke leant upon his walking cane as he stood and approached the hole. "What have you discovered, Mr Heath?"

Sergeant Dixon, Dr Colbert, Mr Stone, and Miss Kimberly joined the illusionist at the trap, whilst Claude remained by the stool.

"I've found the battery you mentioned, Mr Locke. It's on a shelf beside the plate," Mr Heath replied. "But its wires are hanging loose."

"There should be another wire," Sergeant Dixon said.

"Ah yes, so there is," Mr Heath said. "It's connecting the plate to the fixture for the lightbulb, though."

"We found the same," Sergeant Dixon said. "The wires are so close together; Mr Willis obviously connected the wrong one by mistake."

"But this wire doesn't appear to be part of the lighting system," Mr Heath said.

"It doesn't?" Sergeant Dixon crouched and peered into the gloom.

"No. One end is connected to the plate, and the other is hooked into the fixture where the lightbulb ought to be," Mr Heath explained.

Miss Kimberly wrapped her arms about herself and moved away from the hole. Mr Stone had also grown still.

"Would such an alteration require an electric man's expertise?" Mr Locke enquired.

"I don't believe so," Mr Heath replied. "It's rather a simple change. Mr Benton, if you would be so kind as to confirm the switch for the electric light is in the off position, I'll remove the wire so there aren't any more nasty accidents."

Sergeant Dixon stood and, rubbing his chin, stared into the hole.

"Miss Ilbert was murdered after all, then," Dr Colbert said in a subdued voice.

"Not necessarily." Mr Locke returned to his stool.

"But if the plate was wired to the lightbulb fixture, the electricity could've only been applied when the lightbulb's switch was flipped," Dr Colbert observed. "Someone had to flip it. Why not a murderer?"

"It could have been as Sergeant Dixon surmised: Mr Willis failed to notice the wire he was connecting to the plate was a wayward one from the lighting system. Anyone could have flipped the switch under the mistaken assumption they were turning on the lightbulb."

"Most people would've noticed the room remained dark, though," Dr Colbert said.

"Not if they flipped the switch in passing," Sergeant Dixon said.

"Did any performers step onto the plate prior to Miss Ilbert?" Mr Locke enquired.

"I don't know," Miss Kimberly replied. "Possibly."

"If they did, they were clearly unharmed," Mr Locke mused aloud. "Which gives credence to your hypothesis, doctor, about the flipping of the switch."

"What do you think, Sergeant?" Dr Colbert enquired.

Sergeant Dixon moved slowly away from the hole, his eyes upon the stage as he knitted his brow. "I think the switch could've still been accidentally flipped, just at the worst possible time. A simple case of mere coincidence. There's no physical evidence to say this was deliberate." He lifted his head to meet Dr Colbert's gaze. "As much as I feel sorry for him, I still think Mr Willis rewired the plate wrong."

"An opinion you are entitled to," Mr Locke said.

"You shan't be continuing your investigation?" Miss Kimberly quietly enquired from the policeman.

"Not for the moment," Sergeant Dixon replied.

"But the Bow Street Society shall," Mr Locke interjected.

"You don't have to answer their questions or let them see anyone or anything they want," Sergeant Dixon told Miss Kimberly and Mr Stone. "They're not with the police. If they become a nuisance, let us know at Vine Street, and we'll have a word with their Miss Trent."

"All right," Mr Stone said.

"Good day." Sergeant Dixon tapped his hat's brim and left the stage.

"A naïve fellow," Mr Locke softly remarked as he watched Sergeant Dixon retrace his steps to the foyer doors which opened the moment he reached them. Obliged to step aside to allow Dr Locke to enter, Sergeant Dixon tapped his hat's brim when she politely thanked him and slipped into the foyer behind her as she moved toward the stage.

"Darling!" Mr Locke exclaimed with delight.

Dr Locke felt the weight return to her heart when she saw him seated upon a stool.

"What have you discovered?" Mr Locke enquired.

* * *

"I don't get it; Weeks' always been a lush; why's now any different?" Inspector Conway demanded, pacing before Chief Inspector Jones who sat behind his desk. "Yeah, 'e's been off, but we all have since the fight," Inspector Conway went on. "Findin' out about what his old lady's been up to wouldn't of done him any favours, either. The bloke's got a right to be upset, hasn't 'e?"

"He threatened you with a scalpel and struck Gideon with a poker, John," Chief Inspector Jones pointed out. "You didn't see him. He was hysterical."

"Nah, 'e never meant to hurt me." Inspector Conway curtly shook his head. "And if 'e's hit Lee, 'e'll have had a bloody good reason to."

Chief Inspector Jones kept his expression stoic. He'd told Inspector Conway everything, except the envelope of money and Dr Weeks' alleged part it.

"'E's not mad, Richard."

"That is for the doctors to decide."

Inspector Conway suddenly slammed his fists down upon the desk. "I'm not gonna let you haul 'im off to Bedlam!"

Chief Inspector Jones stood. "I have no choice, John!" His features and voice softened. "I have no choice."

"Give 'im a bit more time, yeah?" Inspector Conway pleaded. "'E'll be fine once 'e sobers up."

"The request for a Reception Order has already been made."

Inspector Conway glanced at the door as a pained expression fell upon his face. "But it's Weeks."

"I know," Chief Inspector Jones said, softly. "Which makes this much harder." He moved around the desk and approached his friend. "I need your help, John."

"No." Inspector Conway turned his back and walked away.

"He needs medical help," Chief Inspector Jones insisted.

Inspector Conway halted and, in a voice made rougher by its softness, said, "Don't ask me to do this, Richard." He faced him with sorrow-filled eyes. "I'll do anythin' else but not this." His voice cracked as he added, "'E's my mate."

Chief Inspector Jones' lips pressed tightly together in a grimace as his shoulders slumped slightly in disappointment. Nevertheless, his friend's pain-fuelled reluctance was enough to make him abandon any further attempt to procure his assistance. He gripped his shoulder. "It's all right, John. I'll carry the burden for the both of us."

The fleeting relief failed to dent Inspector Conway's sombre expression. "Thanks."

Chief Inspector Jones released his shoulder, only to put his arm around it and lean in close. "I think it's best if we keep this from Rebecca. At least until we know the final diagnosis."

"Yeah." Inspector Conway knew she'd be as conflicted about this as him.

TWENTY-SIX

Inspector Woolfe sat stiffly, his hands tucked into his armpits, as he glared at Mr Calvin's office door. Hung on the wall behind him, directly above his head, was a clock in a wooden casing. Its ticking provided an annoyingly loud accompaniment to his wait, preventing him from finding solace within his mind. Each time he tried to concentrate on the reason for his visit, a tick disrupted the thought like a pebble tossed into water. When the clock chimed, and a small, wooden bird was thrust outward to "cuckoo" repeatedly, Inspector Woolfe stood and crossed over to the window.

The ground floor waiting room had three chairs lining the wall, a hat stand, and a brass vase for umbrellas and walking canes. Rectangular in shape, it only had enough floorspace for three or four people to stand comfortably. The window overlooked a cobbled courtyard with a vaulted, arched gateway on its far side. Beyond the gateway was the street the hansom cab had brought him to.

Finding the courtyard apparently deserted, Inspector Woolfe walked the length of the room to the outer door, stopped, and muttered a curse under his breath. A glance at the clock told him he'd been waiting for almost forty minutes. He muttered another curse and returned to his seat. Although he'd expected to wait—he'd arrived without an appointment—he hadn't expected to wait this long. It was bordering on infuriating.

The sound of a door opening made him look up. When he saw Mr Calvin, he stood and crossed the room to greet him. Inspector Woolfe made a point of not extending his hand to him as he growled, "About time."

"My apologies for the long wait, Inspector, but it was necessary to allow the arrival of another," Mr Calvin explained in a light, unassuming tone.

In his mid-forties, Mr Calvin had high cheekbones and a defined jawline. Approximately five feet eight inches tall, he had a broad yet angular frame. His attire consisted of a cream shirt under a forest-green suit with matching waistcoat and tie. The splendid fit of his clothes suggested they were tailor made. This, coupled with the lawyer's gold cufflinks and watch chain, reminded Inspector Woolfe of Inspector Lee.

"Another?" Inspector Woolfe enquired. "Who?"

"Me."

Turning his head, Inspector Woolfe saw Miss Trent stood in the outer doorway.

Her body was largely hidden by an ankle-length, dark-brown fur coat in perfect condition. Her youthful face and immaculate hair remained exposed, however. Running his gaze over her corkscrew ringlets, plump lips, and slender neck, Inspector Woolfe felt desire replace his annoyance as he imagined what was concealed beneath her coat.

"Good afternoon, Inspector." Miss Trent entered the room proper. "Mr Calvin."

Inspector Woolfe stepped back to give her room and, clearing his throat, coughed, and said, "Good afternoon."

"If you'd both like to step into my office," Mr Calvin invited as he moved aside.

"Ladies first," Inspector Woolfe said, indicating with his hand.

"Thank you." Miss Trent walked into the office ahead of him and sat in one of two winged-back chairs stood before Mr Calvin's desk.

Deciding he needed to pay a visit to Madam Mimi's later, Inspector Woolfe pushed aside his unholy thoughts and feelings about the clerk and strode into the office. Sitting in the other chair, he was grateful to find it not only had the room to house his larger frame but was gentler on his hips than the waiting room's chair.

"We all know one another so we can forego the formalities." Mr Calvin closed the door and sat behind his desk. "As your visit concerns the Bow Street Society, Inspector, I thought it pertinent to have its clerk here. I was confident you wouldn't object to such an arrangement so I chose to save time by telephoning Miss Trent immediately after you informed me of the purpose of your visit."

"How considerate of you," Inspector Woolfe mumbled.

"Even if you had objected, I still would've come," Miss Trent said. "I and the Bow Street Society have a right to know what's being discussed about us."

"What is being discussed, Miss Trent, is the Society's bank account at the *London & County Banking Company*," Mr Calvin said. "A bank employee informed the inspector you and I are the co-holders of the account."

"What did you hope to discover by prying into the Society's financial affairs?" Miss Trent fixed Inspector Woolfe with a hard gaze.

"Your employer's name." Inspector Woolfe returned the gaze in kind.

"The Bow Street Society is my employer," Miss Trent stated unequivocally.

"We know you're paid a regular wage by someone," Inspector Woolfe challenged.

"The Bow Street Society is my employer," Miss Trent repeated.

"Are you her employer?" Inspector Woolfe enquired from Mr Calvin.

"Certainly not," Mr Calvin replied as unequivocally as Miss Trent.

"Who's J. Pettifoot?" Inspector Woolfe looked between them.

"I haven't the foggiest idea," Mr Calvin replied.

Miss Trent took a moment longer, however. "Neither do I."

Inspector Woolfe scrutinised her face. "Don't you?"

"No," Miss Trent replied without delay this time.

"I don't believe you," Inspector Woolfe said.

"Then it is a cross you must bear," Miss Trent dismissed. "Was there anything else you wanted to discuss, Caleb?"

Inspector Woolfe scowled at the use of his first name. "No. *Rebecca*."

"In that case, our meeting has come to an end." Miss Trent stood, prompting the men to do the same. "If you have any further questions about either the Bow Street Society or myself, Inspector, please come directly to me in future. I've tolerated your and Inspector Lee's behaviour so far—"

"I'm not working with that arrogant bast—" Inspector Woolfe angrily interrupted.

"*Inspector*!" Mr Calvin cried. "May I remind you there's a *lady* present?"

"I've heard worse from Dr Weeks," Miss Trent reassured the lawyer.

The Canadian's name forced Inspector Woolfe to avert his gaze.

"As I was saying: my patience and tolerance can only go so far, Inspector," Miss Trent continued. "I *will* submit a complaint to the assistant commissioner if this carries on."

Inspector Woolfe looked her square in the eye. "I'm only doing my job. You're the one putting innocent people in danger."

Miss Trent's features tightened. "I don't have time to debate this with you, again. Mr Snyder is waiting for me. Good afternoon, Inspector, Mr Calvin."

Inspector Woolfe stepped forward as she turned to leave, causing her to halt. "Could he drive me back to Bow Street, too?" He detested having to ask her for any favours, but his travels across London had left him short of money.

Miss Trent felt tempted to refuse, but her determination to be the better person overrode such pettiness. "Only if you promise not to interrogate me along the way."

Inspector Woolfe's glare returned, but he knew he had no choice. "*Fine*."

"Good." Miss Trent smiled. "Sam will stop on Endell Street to avoid embarrassment."

Inspector Woolfe was grateful for her consideration of his professional reputation, but this gratitude only annoyed him further. With a softly muttered, "Thanks," he followed her to the Society's waiting cab.

* * *

"How are you feeling, Mr Benton?" Dr Colbert enquired as he closed the stage door ajar.

"Better. Thank you." Mr Benton breathed in the alleyway's cold air and, closing his eyes, slowly exhaled. Standing to the right of the door, he had his back against the theatre.

"May I join you? It's rather stuffy inside."

"Be my guest."

Dr Colbert crossed the alleyway and stood with his back against the wall there, ensuring he was opposite the actor. Taking the opportunity to study his face, he saw Mr Benton's high forehead was an illusion created by his receding hairline. The actor's moustache wasn't as follicle free, however, as it covered his lips and most of his chin. The narrow lines of his otherwise thick eyebrows accentuated the angular nature of Mr Benton's brow. The shape of his brown eyes was akin to an oval, and his nose had a narrow bridge but a wide tip.

Applying the principles of physiognomy to Mr Benton's face next, Dr Colbert noted the hooked tip of Mr Benton's nose, and the shape of his eyes were similar to the characteristics seen in someone gripped by vice. It was difficult to determine the height of Mr Benton's forehead, but Dr Colbert was certain it was different to the forehead physiognomy attributed to great intelligence. In short, Mr Benton was a villain of the stupidest sort, if physiognomy was to be believed. Yet, Dr Colbert had watched many plays, and it was a rare thing indeed for him to be left unimpressed by an actor's ability to not only memorise his lines but also deliver them in a naturalistic way. Such skills, in his humble opinion, demanded a degree of intelligence far higher than a common thief's. Therefore, on this occasion, he set the findings of physiognomy aside in favour of his experienced instincts and honed logic.

"I'd suspected the cause of Mina's death, I recognised it as soon as I saw it, but to hear Dr Locke confirm it… A part of me died and became lost forever." Mr Benton's voice lacked strength, whilst his vacant eyes looked through Dr Colbert as if he weren't there.

"Was Miss Ilbert very dear to you?"

"She was my heart." Mr Benton put his hands in his pockets and, turning his shoulders inward, held his elbows tight against his sides. "Countless times, I proposed to her, and countless times, she politely declined, but my adoration only grew stronger." He looked skyward. "She would scold me for being so sentimental."

"I'm sorry for your loss." The words sounded empty, but Dr Colbert didn't know what else to say.

"It's our loss. Mina is gone and, with her, the *Crescent*'s soul."

"You said you'd recognised the signs of electrocution. How?"

"A good friend of mine, an actor, foolishly gripped some electrical wiring. I witnessed him die before my eyes, too."

"Were you with Miss Ilbert on stage when she stepped onto the plate?"

"No, I was in the wings, waiting for my cue." Mr Benton grimaced. "When I saw what was happening, I ran onto the stage and yelled for the electricity to be extinguished."

"Mr Willis told the Society about Miss Ilbert's ultimatum," Dr Colbert ventured with caution, recalling the letter of assignment he'd received from Miss Trent.

"She hoped the bad apples could be found before the rest of the barrel spoiled." Mr Benton's expression and voice turned grave. "When she gave her ultimatum, she sealed her own fate as much as the *Crescent*'s. I'm certain of it." He bowed his head. "I tried to dissuade her but… her mind was made up, and there was no changing it."

"Did either you or Miss Ilbert have any idea who the bad apples were?"

"Erm." Mr Benton released a loud sigh and lifted his head. "Miss Joanna's name was mentioned, the daughter of the *Crescent*'s wardrobe mistress. Mr Stone had seen her backstage with the rogue who was blackmailing me: Jack Jerome." He gave a curt shake of his head. "I can't see her risking her own position, as well as her mother's, by helping him."

"What was Miss Ilbert's opinion?"

"She gave Miss Joanna the benefit of the doubt but promised her and her mother they would be dismissed if she discovered Miss Joanna had lied to her about telling Mr Jerome when I was due to arrive at the theatre," Mr Benton said, the gravity easing from his features.

"Did you witness her saying such?"

"No. I was backstage, feeling rather unsteady following the ordeal of being yelled off the stage by my audience." Mr Benton met his gaze. "One does not have to wait long for news to travel in a theatre, doctor. Miss Kimberly and Mr Stone were present when Miss Ilbert confronted Miss Joanna in her mother's presence. I wager it was Mr Stone who spread the salacious details amongst the company."

"Has anyone come forward since Miss Ilbert's death?"

"No, and nor do I expect them to." Mr Benton moved away from the wall. "When Mina was alive, everyone faced almost certain destitution. Now she's dead, there's a chance the theatre and its company could be saved. Only a fool would jeopardise their future by confessing to the blackmail after the fact, even if they were innocent of Mina's murder."

"We haven't proven it was murder," Dr Colbert firmly reminded him.

"Not yet." Mr Benton opened the stage door. "But you will."

After Mr Benton had gone inside, Dr Colbert quickly wrote down the salient points of their conversation whilst they were fresh in his mind. His excitement as he did both intrigued and surprised him. He wondered if every Bow Street Society member felt the same when interviewing possible witnesses and suspects. If they did, it could be one of the reasons they involved themselves in the otherwise questionable and, frankly dangerous, endeavour of a semi-criminal investigation. Realising it was now a reason for him doing the same, he inwardly scolded himself. *Remember why you became a member in the first place, Neal,* he thought. Yet, even as these words passed through his mind, he pictured another reason for his continued Bow Street Society membership: Mr Elliott. *Focus*, he inwardly ordered, putting his notebook away and returning inside to find the others.

* * *

Mr Locke took a moment to savour his surroundings. Alas, it wasn't the *Paddington Palladium*'s auditorium, but the sense of home was in his heart, nonetheless. Performing seemingly impossible feats to the astonishment of his adoring audience was a thrill he greatly missed.

The sound of another sitting in the stalls' front row pulled him from his thoughts. Looking to his left, he saw Mr Stone sitting three seats along. Mr Heath wandered about backstage, marvelling at the various pulleys and mechanisms, while Miss Kimberly had taken Dr Locke to Miss Ilbert's dressing room. Mr Locke had seen Dr Colbert following Mr Benton outside; the news from the surgeon at Charing Cross Hospital had shocked the actor. Finally, Mr Locke had sent Claude to notify his driver they would be leaving soon. Therefore, for all intents and purposes, Mr Locke and Mr Stone were alone.

Using his cane to steady himself, Mr Locke moved to the seat beside Mr Stone's. Offering him a Turkish cigarette from his silver case, Mr Locke was a little offended when he refused. These cigarettes weren't cheap.

"Stray ash from a cigarette can cause a fire," Mr Stone said. "I would've thought you more than anyone would know that, being a theatre owner yourself."

"I do." Mr Locke put his cigarette case away. "But I also do not make a habit of smoking without an ashtray nearby." He flicked open his cane's silver handle to reveal a hidden ashtray.

Mr Stone smirked. "I should've expected no less from a magician."

"Illusionist, if you please." Mr Locke closed the handle. "How long have you been stage manager at the *Crescent*?"

"A few years."

"Have you always been a stage manager?"

"You ask a lot of questions."

"Thus far, I have only asked two. I hardly think it 'a lot,' but I will admit I am only getting started." Mr Locke smiled. "Truth be told, I do recall reading the name 'Ronald Stone' in *The Era*. It was in connection with a tragic theatre fire some years ago. You would not happen to be the same Ronald Stone, would you?"

Mr Stone's eyes narrowed. "I don't have to answer that."

"No, but it would be wise if you did."

"Why?"

"Because it is better to answer the questions of a fellow thespian than an uncouth policeman. Did you become stage manager here because of the fire?"

"Yes," Mr Stone replied through semi-gritted teeth.

"Miss Ilbert rather did you a favour, then, did she not?"

Mr Stone exhaled loudly through his nose and replied with disgust, "*Yes*."

"A favour you have despised ever since by the sounds of it."

"I don't like working for someone else, especially not an arrogant, incompetent, and decrepit actress."

"Are you a bachelor by any chance?"

"Yes." Mr Stone's eyes narrowed. "Why do you ask?"

Mr Locke smiled. "No reason."

"I wasn't Mina's fancy man, if that's what you're insinuating."

One must be fancy to be a lady's fancy man, Mr Locke inwardly remarked. Aloud, he enquired, "You are not romantically involved with anyone in the theatre? Miss Kimberly, perhaps?"

"No!" Mr Stone scoffed. "I like women with a bit more fire in the belly." He shook his head. "Mr Thurston's the one who's been following Emmaline around like a love-sick puppy."

Mr Locke recalled Miss Trent's briefing. "The prompter and super master?"

"Yes. But if you want to know who was romantically involved with Mina, I suggest you look at Mr Benton. He's proposed to her more times than I've had hot dinners."

"Thank you, I shall do so." Mr Locke suspected Dr Colbert had already discovered the fact, however. *A doctor of the mind must be very adept at uncovering one's secrets*, he thought. "Who amongst the company disliked Miss Ilbert?"

"Everyone," Mr Stone scoffed.

"Come now, even the Devil has his followers," Mr Locke pointed out.

"Not Mina. She made sure everyone hated her when she threatened to dismiss them."

"Ah yes." Mr Locke lifted his chin. "The ultimatum. As stage manager, you must see and hear a great deal of what occurs both backstage and in front. What are your thoughts on the matter?"

"I don't have any." Mr Stone averted his gaze. "Except she was a fool for thinking threats would work against anyone."

"They would not work against you?"

Mr Stone looked him square in the eyes. "Never."

Mr Locke offered a polite smile in spite of his suspicion Mr Stone had given away more than he had intended with his statement. "Do you have any suspicions as to who may have assisted Mr Jerome in his scheme?"

Mr Stone smirked. "I saw Joanna Hightower talking with him backstage."

"And who is she?"

"The daughter of the wardrobe mistress." Mr Stone's smile grew, but he immediately suppressed it. "I told Mina what I'd seen. She shouted at Joanna who ran off in tears."

"Do you have an address for Miss Hightower?"

"It will probably be written down somewhere in the office, but she's due to come back to work when the theatre reopens tomorrow."

"Aside from Miss Hightower and those threatened with destitution, who else had a reason to harm Miss Ilbert?"

Mr Stone smirked. "Mr Stanley Akers."

"Who is he?"

Mr Stone's smirk grew into a smile. "The chief scene painter for the *Crescent* and a few others. He and Mina argued about the new electric lighting at the scenery rehearsal. He demanded she remove it, and she refused."

"Why did he want it removed?"

"Mr Akers thinks himself an 'artist,'" Mr Stone sardonically replied. "He told Mina the brighter electric light was doing the 'art' of his scenery a disservice."

"I presume, due to you bringing up his name, Mr Akers did not resolve his disagreement with Miss Ilbert?"

"No. She ended the discussion by telling him they would discuss it further in the morning."

"And did they?"

"I don't know."

"Mina receives a fresh bouquet from Mr Benton every week," Miss Kimberly informed Dr Locke as they emerged from the wings. "He also gifted the photograph to her."

"Miss Kimberly, how fortuitous for you to arrive at this moment," Mr Locke called. "I was about to enquire from Mr Stone who assumes control of the *Crescent* following Miss Ilbert's passing."

"That would be me, Mr Locke," Miss Kimberly said, clasping her hands against her skirts as she walked to the stage's edge with Dr Locke at her side.

Mr Stone was on his feet in an instant. "Who says?!"

"Mina, Ronald," Miss Kimberly calmly replied. "She and I had a written agreement."

"*What* agreement?!" Mr Stone spat.

"I shall bring it with me tomorrow," Miss Kimberly replied. "You may see it, along with the Bow Street Society."

Mr Stone glared at her. "There's going to be a new manager, Emma, but it's *not* going to be *you*!" He strode toward the foyer doors only to pause upon reaching them to add, "Just you wait and see!"

The thud of the door striking the wall as he flung it open reverberated around the auditorium.

"Please, forgive Mr Stone's rude behaviour," Miss Kimberly said, addressing both Lockes. "He's upset by Mina's death, as are we all." She looked to Dr Locke. "If you'll come this way, doctor, I'll show you Mina's office next."

"Thank you," Dr Locke said.

"Pardon me, Miss Kimberly." Mr Locke raised his hand. "If you are going to the office, may I have a copy of Miss Hightower's address, please?"

Miss Kimberly's features tightened. "No. You may not. You may speak with her, and the others, tomorrow when the theatre reopens. This way, doctor."

Dr Locke exchanged a knowing glance with Mr Locke as she followed Miss Kimberly offstage.

253

TWENTY-SEVEN

Chief Inspector Jones sat behind his desk, his arms resting upon those of his chair. He stared at the door as his mind's eye conjured up Dr Weeks in the interview room. The knowledge he now possessed felt like a lead weight upon his heart, despite making his course of action clear. He lit his pipe and, taking several deep puffs, considered his approach. He was keen for it to happen peacefully and without incident. Yet, he knew the news would be, understandably, difficult to take.

Knocking broke through his thoughts.

"Come in," he half-heartedly called but sat bolt upright when his visitor entered. "John? What are you doing here?"

"I couldn't keep away," Inspector Conway admitted. "Have the doctors been?"

"Yes."

Inspector Conway approached the desk. "What did they say?"

There was a grim twist to Chief Inspector Jones' mouth as he sat forward and rested his elbows upon the desk. He met his old friend's worried gaze with a serious one. "They've certified him insane."

Inspector Conway sat limply in the chair before the desk, his unblinking eyes fixed upon Chief Inspector Jones. His thoughts swirled, causing him to feel light-headed. Leaning forward, he put his elbows upon his knees and held his tightly clasped hands against his mouth. As he contemplated the implications of the doctors' decision, he felt a tightening of his stomach, followed by a wave of nausea. "I don't believe it."

"It's certainly a hard pill to swallow."

"No." Inspector Conway stood, allowing his arms to hang loosely at his sides. "I don't believe 'e's insane."

"*Two* doctors have issued the certificate, following a detailed assessment."

"They're wrong." Inspector Conway paced, repeatedly shaking his head.

Chief Inspector Jones set aside his pipe. "John, I know this is difficult for you—"

"Too right it's bloody difficult!" Inspector Conway approached the desk. "What have they said 'e's got?"

"Chronic Alcoholic Insanity. They've based their diagnosis upon his current condition, as well as his admissions concerning his daily alcohol consumption and frequent inebriation."

Inspector Conway opened and closed his lips when he tried to think of a counter argument but couldn't. Everything he knew about Dr Weeks supported the diagnosis.

"I'm sorry it's had to come to this, John," Chief Inspector Jones' expression was grave. "The doctors have issued their Certificates of Insanity to the magistrate who, in turn, has issued the Reception Order legally permitting Dr Weeks to be admitted to Bethlehem Hospital."

"When?"

"Today."

"I don't believe it…" Inspector Conway sat in a daze.

Chief Inspector Jones filled a glass with some brandy and placed it before his friend. "Believe me, John, no one more than I wanted a better outcome for Dr Weeks. Yet, it isn't, and now we have a duty to do what is right for him, and not ourselves."

Inspector Conway drank half the brandy, but it didn't touch his growing nausea. "I don't know if I can." He held the glass tightly upon his lap, his head bowed. "It would be like betraying 'im."

"Dr Weeks is a very sick and dangerous man. It was either Bethlehem Hospital or Newgate. I'm sure you'd agree the former is the better option for him."

Inspector Conway didn't want Dr Weeks to be admitted either but understood the dilemma Chief Inspector Jones had faced. "Yeah… it is," He drank the remaining brandy and set the glass aside upon the desk.

"You think the doctors at Bedlam can make 'im better, though?"

"I think they ought to be given the chance."

"With all due respect, Richard, that's not what I asked."

Chief Inspector Jones' voice softened. "I don't know if they can, but they certainly can't if he isn't admitted."

Inspector Conway wasn't convinced the doctors could do Dr Weeks any good at all but, alas, he was unable to think of a better solution. Feeling his nausea intensify at the thought of dragging Dr Weeks off to Bedlam against his will, he pushed the empty glass toward Chief Inspector Jones. "I want another before we do this."

"'We?'"

Inspector Conway gave a curt nod. "I don't want strangers takin' 'im, or you gettin' hurt tryin' to take 'im on your own."

"You don't have to if you don't want to, John. Sergeant Caulfield can assist me."

"I don't want to," Inspector Conway quietly admitted. "But I'm gonna. Like you said: we've got a duty to do what's right for 'im, not us."

"Yes, we do. Thank you."

"Don't. It's not sumin' I ought to be thanked for."

Seeing the pain in his friend's eyes, Chief Inspector Jones poured some more brandy into his glass. "Quite. I'm sorry." He poured some brandy into a second glass for himself. "Word has already been sent to the resident physician at Bethlehem Hospital, notifying him of the imminent arrival of a new patient."

They knew it would be one of the hardest things they'd ever have to do, but at least they'd still have the other's support once it was done. Falling silent as they drank their brandy, they mentally prepared themselves for the task ahead.

* * *

Claude held the door open as Mr Locke emerged from the *Crescent Theatre*, his arm intertwined with Dr Locke's. Yet, it was he who leant upon her whilst taking small, laboured steps onto the Strand's pavement. His face was also flushed, and droplets of sweat had formed upon his forehead. Therefore, he was grateful for the cold breeze brushing against his face. Seeing his driver and carriage, he crossed over to it and turned to Dr Colbert and Mr Heath who had followed them outside. "Well, everyone, we have had a splendid but, more importantly, intriguing start to our investigation. We should return to Bow Street and discuss our findings in more detail."

"Shall we reconvene at seven o'clock?" Dr Locke looked to her fellow Bow Streeters.

"Actually, darling, I rather thought we could go now," Mr Locke replied.

"As your doctor, I insist you rest a while first," Dr Locke stated. "Gentlemen?"

"Seven o'clock is convenient for me," Mr Heath replied.

"Excuse me." A gentleman with dark-brown hair touched with silver, large nose, angular cheekbones, and squared jaw entered the group. Red faced and short of breath, his hazel eyes immediately sought out Dr Colbert. "Pardon my intrusion, doctor, but your presence is required at the hospital."

"Dr McWilliams," Mr Locke said. "A pleasure to make your acquaintance again."

Dr McWilliams blinked as if noticing the illusionist for the first time. "Mr Locke… yes, and yours."

"May I introduce my esteemed colleague: Dr Charles McWilliams. Charles, this is Mr Bertram Heath and Dr Lynette Locke from the Bow Street Society. You already know Mr Locke from… the unpleasant business last year."

"How is Dr Devereux?" Mr Locke enquired.

"Well. Thank you." Dr McWilliams moved closer to Dr Colbert and lowered his voice. "I have a cab waiting around the corner, Neal."

Dr Colbert turned to the others with an apologetic smile. "You will have to excuse me, I'm afraid."

"It is nothing serious, I hope?" Mr Locke enquired.

"All matters pertaining to Bethlehem Hospital are serious, Mr Locke," Dr McWilliams replied.

"All of which we are more than capable of dealing with," Dr Colbert said. "Goodbye."

"Dr McWilliams has not lost his penchant for melodrama, I see," Mr Locker remarked as he watched him and Dr Colbert hurry away.

* * *

"I've brought a peace offering." Chief Inspector Jones set down the glass beside Dr Weeks' elbow.

The surgeon sat in the middle of the interview room with his elbows on the table and his head in his hands. At the scent of the alcohol, he lifted his head to reveal a haggard, drawn face. His bloodshot eyes were also damp as his hands reached for the glass. Holding it as tightly as if it were the Holy Grail, he drank the brandy in a few swallows. Afterward, he put the glass down with a thud, closed his eyes, and released a guttural sigh. "That's some *damn* fine brandy."

"I'm pleased you approve." Yet, Chief Inspector Jones suspected Dr Weeks would've said the same about the cheapest gin at present. After all, it had been several hours since the assault and not a drop of alcohol had passed the surgeon's lips during that time. "May I sit?"

"Sure." Dr Weeks scraped the inside of the glass with his finger and sucked off the minute traces of brandy he'd salvaged.

Momentarily taken aback by the act, Chief Inspector Jones swiftly gathered himself and sat on the table's opposite side. "We've known each other for quite some time, haven't we, doctor?"

"Nearly three years." Dr Weeks scraped some more brandy from the inside of the glass and sucked it from his finger. "D'ya have any more brandy?"

Chief Inspector Jones had considered bringing the bottle but decided against it. "No."

"When am I goin' to be let go so I can get a proper drink, then?" Dr Weeks lifted the glass, sniffed it, and studied its now dry interior. Conceding he'd drunk every last drop, he set the glass down before Chief Inspector Jones. "Ya'll goin' to have to drive me 'ome, though. I ain't got two pennies to rub together."

Chief Inspector Jones watched Dr Weeks intently whilst he said in a sombre tone, "You'll be leaving soon, doctor, but not to return home."

"What d'ya mean?"

"Those two men who spoke to you earlier. Do you know who they were?"

"They said they were doctors."

"What did they talk to you about?"

"What did they talk to me about?"

"Yes, what did they ask you?"

"They, uh." Dr Weeks turned his head away and downward as he rested a bent arm upon the table and rubbed his opposite temple. "They asked how much I drink."

"What did you say?"

Dr Weeks allowed his free hand to drop to his lap and, lifting his head, looked everywhere but into Chief Inspector Jones' eyes. "I said I enjoyed a good drink."

"They told me you admitted to drinking excessive amounts of alcohol on a daily basis."

Dr Weeks gave a one-sided shoulder shrug. "It keeps my hands steady."

Chief Inspector Jones had heard all he needed. "Doctor Weeks—Percy—the doctors have diagnosed you with Chronic Alcoholic Insanity."

Dr Weeks looked sharply at Chief Inspector Jones. "Ya ain't serious?"

"I'm afraid I am."

Dr Weeks stared at him, stunned, before suddenly leaping to his feet. The sudden movement caused his chair to topple backward and strike the floor with a loud thud. The door immediately opened, and Inspector Conway entered. Halting upon seeing Dr Weeks on his feet and Chief Inspector Jones sitting, unharmed, at the table, Inspector Conway looked to the latter for instruction.

"Come in, John," Chief Inspector Jones said, his gaze fixed upon Dr Weeks.

Inspector Conway closed and locked the door and ventured further into the room.

"What the hell is this?" Dr Weeks enquired, a mixture of fear and anger in his eyes and voice as he darted his gaze between the two of them.

"John and I are going to escort you to Bethlehem Hospital, Percy."

"*Bedlam*?!" Dr Weeks cried. Rapidly shaking his head, he took several steps back. "Nah. I ain't goin' to that torture chamber."

Chief Inspector Jones stood. "You don't have a choice. The doctors have issued their Certificates of Insanity, and the Reception Order has been issued by the magistrate. You are effectively a patient of Bethlehem Hospital from this moment on, and the resident physician is expecting your arrival before the day is through."

Dr Weeks' face blanched. "N-Nah. This… this ain't happenin'."

"Come on, mate," Inspector Conway said softly as he cautiously approached. "We aren't gonna let anythin' happen to you."

Dr Weeks took a backward step the closer Inspector Conway came. "Ya don't understand, John. Places like Bedlam… ya get more *insane* the longer yer in 'em!"

"We only want to help you, Percy," Chief Inspector Jones insisted.

"And so do the doctors." Inspector Conway reached into his jacket pocket and pulled out a set of handcuffs. "I don't want to use these, but I will if I have to."

Dr Weeks continued to retreat until he felt the wall at his back. "I *ain't* mad!"

Inspector Conway continued to close the distance between them. "I know you're not, mate. The doctors just want to make sure, too."

Dr Weeks shook his head. "I *ain't* goin'!"

He suddenly lunged forward, attempting to push Inspector Conway aside. The former boxer easily stepped aside, though, and gripped Dr Weeks' arm. He pulled him back against the wall, and Dr Weeks gasped as the air was knocked out of him. Taking advantage of his daze, Inspector Conway turned him around and snapped the first handcuff onto his wrist. Pinning Dr Weeks' wrists against the small of his back, Inspector Conway secured them with the second handcuff. Tightly gripping Dr Weeks' lower arms, despite the pain throbbing through his chest from his broken ribs, Inspector Conway repeatedly told himself this was the right thing to do.

"Conway, *please*!" Dr Weeks pleaded, struggling desperately against his friend's iron-like grip. "*Don't* send me there, *please*!"

"I'm sorry, mate," Inspector Conway's pained voice said softly into his ear. "I have to."

"I'll have the black maria brought around to the rear entrance," Chief Inspector Jones said as he left, not wishing Dr Weeks to suffer the humiliation of being dragged through the corridors of New Scotland Yard.

"Now's our chance. Take these off me, and I'll get away before he's back."

Inspector Conway tightened his grip with a wince.

"John, listen to me." Dr Weeks tried to look over his shoulder, his face wet with tears.

"*Quiet*," Inspector Conway growled, his grip tightening further.

"John, *please*."

"I *said* be *quiet*!" Inspector Conway put his weight upon Dr Weeks' arms.

Dr Weeks felt his body turn cold as he realised it was futile. His mind conjured wild imaginings of what life at Bedlam would be like, and fresh tears slipped down his cheeks. "… John…" His face crumpled, and a loud sob escaped his lips. "John, *please*."

Inspector Conway rested his forehead between Dr Weeks' shoulder blades as his heart clenched with each of his friend's pitiful sobs. Yet, his grip held firm until, finally, it was time to leave.

TWENTY-EIGHT

"I'm a guest of Dr Colbert," Mr Elliott informed the waitress. The A.B.C. Tearooms beyond were full. Consequently, the cacophony of conversation made it difficult for the solicitor to be heard.

"Begging your pardon, sir?" the waitress enquired over the din.

Mr Elliott raised his voice. "I'm a guest of Dr Colbert's. He's reserved a table."

The waitress also raised her voice. "Yes, sir. This way, sir."

Mr Elliott followed the waitress through the jumbled sea of tables to the one he, Dr Colbert, and Inspector Lee had occupied yesterday. Expecting to find it unoccupied today, Mr Elliott slowed when he saw the policeman rise to his feet. Casting his mind back to Dr Colbert's invitation, he couldn't recall seeing Inspector Lee's name.

"This is the wrong table," Mr Elliott informed the waitress.

"It's the one Dr Colbert reserved, sir," the waitress said.

"Then where is he?" Mr Elliott demanded.

"He hasn't arrived," Inspector Lee replied. If Chief Inspector Jones had acted upon his suggestion of hospitalising Dr Weeks, it was unlikely Dr Colbert would join them at all.

"I haven't had word of him running late," Mr Elliott stated.

"He's probably delayed by traffic," Inspector Lee indicated the vacant seat beside his. "Would you care to join me?"

"Not particularly."

"How long is the wait for a table?" Inspector Lee enquired from the waitress.

"About thirty minutes, sir," the waitress replied.

"Are you certain you wouldn't care to join me, Mr Elliott?" Inspector Lee enquired.

Mr Elliott knew he couldn't leave before Dr Colbert's arrival without appearing rude. Furthermore, he didn't want to wait thirty minutes for a table. Pulling out the chair opposite Inspector Lee, he sat without meeting his gaze.

"Would you like your usual?" Inspector Lee enquired, returning to his seat.

Mr Elliott glared at him. "I'd like—" He cut himself short when he remembered the waitress was patiently waiting for their order. "Yes. A pot of Earl Gray tea for one."

"For two, please," Inspector Lee corrected.

"For *one*. Please." Mr Elliott insisted.

"I see you're as stubborn as ever." Inspector Lee gave a contrived smile. "Two pots of Earl Gray tea, please."

"Yes, sir." The waitress curtsied and hurried away.

"You're looking well," Inspector Lee complimented the solicitor.

Mr Elliott had noticed Inspector Lee's small head wound. His professional curiosity urged him to enquire after its cause. Yet, he knew Inspector Lee would likely misinterpret it as concern derived from affection, neither of which Mr Elliott felt for the policeman.

"Why are you here?" Mr Elliott demanded. "Where is Dr Colbert?"

"I haven't the faintest idea," Inspector Lee replied with mock ignorance. "But I was invited the same as you were."

Mr Elliott's eyes hardened. "You didn't have to accept."

"And waste a rare opportunity to spend time with you? I think not."

"Why can't you leave me alone?"

Inspector Lee sat back in his chair and lit a cigarette, whilst he carefully considered his reply. His true feelings couldn't be uttered in a busy tearoom. He didn't want to portray himself as a cold-hearted policeman doggedly pursuing his prey, either. Therefore, he settled upon the middle ground. "Circumstances have made it necessary."

Mr Elliott suspected it was emotions rather than circumstances which drove the policeman, but he decided to humour him, nonetheless. "Which circumstances?"

Inspector Lee exhaled the smoke away from Mr Elliott, took another pull from his cigarette, and exhaled the smoke, again. "The Bow Street Society involving itself in my case, for one. My becoming the head of the Mob Squad, for two. The determination shown by you, Miss Trent, and the other Bow Street Society members to meddle in police investigations, for three. My sworn duty to uphold the law and protect the reputation of the police, for four."

"You may exclude point four," Mr Elliott said. "We both know you act in your own interests before others'. Your deception and blackmail over the *Gaslight Gazette*'s article on the Cosgrove case proved it."

Inspector Lee tapped the excess ash from the end of his cigarette into a nearby ashtray. "And Miss Trent and the Bow Street Society doesn't?"

"We act in our clients' interests first and foremost."

The corner of Inspector Lee's mouth lifted. "Miss Trent's reputation is interchangeable with the Bow Street Society's. If she is proven deceitful so, too, is the Society. As you and I know, reputation is essential to one's professional survival. Ergo, Miss Trent's priority will always be to protect her reputation as well as the Bow Street Society's."

Mr Elliott inwardly conceded the strength of Inspector Lee's logic, albeit reluctantly.

"Just as my priority is always to protect my reputation as well as the police's." Inspector Lee took another pull from his cigarette. "I didn't want to blackmail you and the Society into keeping your silence over who solved the Cosgrove case, but you gave me no choice. Like Miss Trent and the Bow Street Society, my reputation is interchangeable with the Metropolitan Police. I couldn't allow the journalistic press to portray me as incompetent, as it would've also portrayed the police service as the same."

"If the police were more transparent in their investigations and cooperated fully with the Bow Street Society, its reputation, and yours, would be improved in the public consciousness," Mr Elliott pointed out. Although he had agreed with Inspector Lee's logic thus far, he was still taking it with a pinch of salt simply because it was Inspector Lee making the argument.

"True, but one cannot always control what is written," Inspector Lee extinguished his cigarette. "The Bow Street Society, on the other hand, can. You have Mr Maxwell, a journalist, amongst your members. In this aspect, the Society has a considerable advantage over the police."

"If your actions and motives are noble, the gentlemen of the press are likelier to portray you as such," Mr Elliott stated.

"Alas, my profession often condemns me before I've had an opportunity to explain myself. Such is the tendency of the press," Inspector Lee said with a hint of sadness. "I will admit I want to bring about the end of the Bow Street Society, but only to ensure my own survival." A wry smile crept across his lips. "In the same way you harbour a secret desire to bring about my end to ensure your survival."

Mr Elliott's features visibly tensed. "I harbour nothing of the sort."

Inspector Lee's smile grew. "I'm glad to hear it."

Mr Elliott's lips formed a hard line. He'd not only been tricked into making his admission, but he couldn't retract his statement without casting himself in a negative light. With clear tension in his voice, he demanded, "What is your point, Inspector?"

Inspector Lee sat forward and looked him straight in the eye. "None of what I've done against you, or the Society, has been a personal attack. Each victory the

Society has over the police makes my life more difficult. All I'm doing is trying to limit the damage."

"Excuse me, sirs." The waitress placed two large teapots, two cream jugs, and a sugar bowl upon the table.

Mr Elliott dropped a sovereign into her hand. "For your trouble."

"*Thank* you, sir!" the waitress exclaimed in delight, pocketing the coin.

"You've acquired some bad habits from Dr Colbert, I see," Inspector Lee remarked once the waitress had left them.

Mr Elliott poured his tea. "And you haven't acquired enough."

"Touché." Inspector Lee sat back in his chair and, pouring his tea, waited until Mr Elliott had taken a sip of his before adding, "Perhaps you ought to teach me."

Mr Elliott breathed in sharply, inhaling some tea as a result. Coughing violently, he picked up the napkin and pressed it to his lips whilst trying to catch his breath.

Meanwhile, Inspector Lee sipped his tea, smirking in triumph.

* * *

Dr Colbert consulted his pocket watch and made a small noise in his throat upon seeing the time. He imagined Mr Elliott doing the same as he waited for him at the A.B.C. Tearooms and selfishly hoped he was alone. Scrubbing a hand over his face, Dr Colbert knew he had to send word to the solicitor but didn't want to. Calculating how long it would take to process the new patient once they'd arrived, though, he concluded it would be nearing the tearooms' closing time. Releasing a heavy sigh, he left his office and sought out Dr McWilliams.

"Charles, could you carry out a small errand for me?" Dr Colbert softly enquired upon finding him in the male patient gallery. "I've arranged to meet a friend of mine at the A.B.C. Tearooms, but I'm going to be unable to attend.

Could you go there, offer my apologies, and inform him I'll be in touch to rearrange?"

"Of course," Dr McWilliams replied as they left the gallery. "What is his name?"

"Mr Gregory Elliott." Dr Colbert firmly shook Dr McWilliams' hand. "Thank you."

"A black maria has arrived, Dr Colbert," Mr Corwin, the head attendant, said upon approaching them. "A Chief Inspector Jones is also waiting for you in the foyer."

Dr Colbert did a double take upon recognising the name. "Chief Inspector Jones?" He immediately made his way to the foyer and halted when he saw the same officer he'd met during the boxing match last December. Casting a glance around the foyer, he found the policeman was unaccompanied. "Chief Inspector Jones?"

"Yes." Chief Inspector Jones extended his hand. "It's a pleasure to meet you, again, doctor. I'm only sorry it's not under better circumstances."

Dr Colbert firmly shook his hand. "Forgive my confusion, Inspector, but I'm expecting a new patient, and, for a moment, I thought you were they."

Chief Inspector Jones' expression turned grave. "No, but I've brought him." He half-turned and indicated the main door. "He's in the black maria outside." He momentarily bowed his head as he faced Dr Colbert, again. "I'm afraid he's not a stranger to you, doctor."

Dr Colbert steeled himself. "Who is he?"

"Dr Percy Weeks."

Dr Colbert felt his blood run cold as his worse fears were realised. "Take me to him."

Chief Inspector Jones led him outside to where the black maria, driven by a uniformed police constable, was waiting at the bottom of the steps. Standing beside its rear door was Inspector Conway with a haunted look in his eyes. In a subdued tone, Chief Inspector Jones informed Dr Colbert, "Unfortunately, it was necessary for us to handcuff him."

"I *beg* your pardon," Dr Colbert scolded. "He is *unwell*, not a *criminal*." He strode over to the rear door. "Open this at once."

Inspector Conway looked to Chief Inspector Jones, who gave a subtle nod. When the former pulled back the bolt and swung open the door, though, the strong stench of stale sweat, alcohol, and urine instantly assaulted Dr Colbert's nose. Covering it with his handkerchief as his face contorted in disgust, he climbed inside and found a line of doors. The smell seemed to be coming from the first. Taking a step back, he looked between it and Inspector Conway. "And this one, please."

"'E might try and scarper," Inspector Conway said as he climbed inside.

"Probably, but we shall be ready for him," Dr Colbert said.

Inspector Conway pulled the outer door closed before unlocking and opening the inner. Contrary to his suspicions, though, Dr Weeks remained sitting on the narrow bench within, his head bowed.

"Please, fetch my head attendant, Mr Corwin," Dr Colbert instructed.

"You want me to leave you alone with 'im?" Inspector Conway was taken aback.

"He's handcuffed and wedged into a tiny cell," Dr Colbert dryly replied.

Inspector Conway frowned deeply but left to fulfil the request, nonetheless.

Closing the outer door after him, Dr Colbert returned to the cell and knelt before Dr Weeks. Looking up into his face, he said in a gentle voice, "I'm truly sorry it has come to this, but you have my word as a fellow doctor I shall do my utmost to make your time at Bethlehem Hospital as short and as comfortable as possible."

"I shouldn't be here," Dr Weeks said in a pitiful voice.

Dr Colbert's eyes and voice were sympathetic as he stated, "Yes. You should."

* * *

"By the way," Inspector Lee began. "Did you ask Miss Trent about her mysterious employer?"

"Yes," Mr Elliott curtly replied as he topped up the tea in his cup.

"May I know her answer?"

"No." Mr Elliott set down his teapot.

Inspector Lee watched him intently. "She didn't give one?"

"She did."

"Was it a denial, or did she simply refuse to give a name?"

"She thought it was another attempt to sow mistrust between us."

"She wouldn't answer you," Inspector Lee said, projecting his voice as he settled back in his chair with exaggerated casualness. "How amusing."

"Whether she has an employer, and whoever they are if she does, is none of my business," Mr Elliott stated.

"Come now, Gregory. You're far too intelligent to ignore such an important aspect of your work. What if her employer belongs to the criminal underworld?"

"She wouldn't involve herself in such circles."

"And yet, she involves herself in murders, robberies, and blackmail."

"Mr Elliott?" an unfamiliar voice enquired from behind him.

Mr Elliott twisted in his chair to look up at the newcomer. "I'm he."

"I'm Dr Charles McWilliams, sir," the man said. "I've a message from Dr Colbert. Unfortunately, he is unable to have tea with you and offers his apologies. Furthermore, he will be in touch soon to rearrange."

Mr Elliott stood and faced Dr McWilliams. "It's nothing serious, I hope?"

"No, sir," Dr McWilliams replied. "Only a new patient being admitted."

Mr Elliott frowned and glanced back at Inspector Lee. "Thank you, doctor. Please, tell Dr Colbert I understand and accept his apologies."

"Yes, sir." Dr McWilliams gave a small nod and bid them goodbye.

"Shall we depart?" Inspector Lee enquired.

"Pardon?" Mr Elliott enquired in return. When he looked to the policeman, he was already upon his feet and pulling on his coat. Initially taken aback, he realised their staying put would be pointless now that Dr Colbert wasn't coming. "Yes. I have some work to do to prepare for tomorrow's hearing."

"May I drive you home?"

Mr Elliott looked to the window. It had stopped raining, but it was also dark outside. The solicitor knew better than to walk London's streets at night. "Yes. Thank you."

"I don't like this shift in behaviour toward you; it's bordering on obsessive. For the time being, I don't want you to be alone with him." Miss Trent's voice echoed in his mind, reminding him of the risks. It was swiftly followed by the memories of Inspector Lee's foot brushing against his calf, and the policeman's general inability to keep his hands to himself.

"After you," Inspector Lee invited, indicating the way ahead.

Mr Elliott recalled the carriage ride they'd shared from the Old Bailey to the tearooms yesterday. It had passed without incident, and Mr Elliott was confident this one would, too. After all, Inspector Lee's driver would be within earshot of their conversation the entire time. Feeling his concern ease at this conclusion, he made his way through the tearoom, down the stairs, through the shop, and onto Euston Road.

By the time he stood on the pavement, he had already convinced himself the carriage ride would be the perfect opportunity to garner further information about Inspector Lee's personal life. Information he could base his own enquiries upon. *"I'm sure Inspector Lee has plenty of secrets of his own."* Miss Trent's voice echoed in his mind.

"Here's my driver now." Inspector Lee stepped forward and held his walking cane aloft. Lowering it, again, as the carriage drew near, he stepped back and waited for it to come to a complete halt before holding the door open for the solicitor.

"Doesn't the driver need my address?" Mr Elliott cynically enquired.

"I'll pass it to him." At Mr Elliott's questioning look, Inspector Lee added, "It was in my detective's report."

"Another violation of my privacy."

"But a necessary one," Inspector Lee said, alluding to their earlier conversation.

"I wish to be taken straight home," Mr Elliott ordered as he climbed into the carriage.

"And you will," Inspector Lee said. Yet, as he approached his driver, he added under his breath, "Eventually."

TWENTY-NINE

"Nah," Dr Weeks said, leaning back and pressing his feet against the floor, as Inspector Conway and Mr Corwin tried to pull him into the room by the arms. "I *ain't* stayin' *here*!"

"Come on, mate," Inspector Conway urged, easing the force he was applying to Dr Weeks' arm long enough for the surgeon to relax. Taking immediate advantage of this, Inspector Conway gave Dr Weeks' arm a firm tug, thereby momentarily pulling him off his feet. Compelled to walk forward to regain his balance, Dr Weeks entered the room.

"I'll fetch him after I've spoken to the chief inspector," Dr Colbert said, closing and locking the door.

"Over there, please, Inspector," Mr Corwin instructed, indicating the middle of the small room with a sideways nod.

Aside from a tread-worn, brown rug, the space was empty. Around its edges, placed against the walls, were a modest bureau, hat stand, two high-backed wooden chairs, and a table. Upon the table was a large, ceramic bowl with matching jug, an old rag, comb, notepaper, and pencils. The walls were adorned with a light-brown paper with a thin, dark-brown stripe. The frosted glass shades and brass arms of the wall-mounted gas lamps were polished to a shine.

Dr Weeks leant back again, and Inspector Conway and Mr Corwin grunted as they pulled him across the room. When the latter released him, the former turned him around, gripped his shoulders, and forcibly sat him on a chair.

"Don't move," Inspector Conway warned through the pain in his ribs, pointing at him.

Dr Weeks felt like his stomach rolling as he lowered his gaze to Inspector Conway's feet. He'd tried to flee after leaving the black maria, but Inspector Conway had easily overpowered him. His mind whirled with thoughts of escaping, the stories he'd heard about asylums, and everything which had happened in the past two days. He wanted to become invisible, to hide. *Maybe Colbert will convince Jones I ain't insane after all*, he thought, but the memory of Dr Colbert's words to him in the Maria put paid to the notion. Feeling an ache in the back of his throat and a sour taste in his mouth, he tried to swallow, but his gullet was bone dry. Rubbing his wrist where the handcuff had been, he mumbled, "I need a drink."

"No. You don't." Inspector Conway sat beside him.

"I *need* a *drink*." Dr Weeks' rubbed his wrist harder and bobbed his leg.

"No more of that for you, I'm afraid," Mr Corwin said.

Dr Weeks' head shot up, and he stared at him, wide eyed. "What d'ya mean?"

"Doctor's orders," Mr Corwin replied. "Now, to examine you."

"Ya'll ain't comin' near me 'til I get a goddamned *drink*!" Dr Weeks bellowed.

"Calm down," Inspector Conway urged.

"I *am* calm!" Dr Weeks cast a glare at him before turning hard eyes to Mr Corwin. "Ya'll don't understand. I get *sick* if I don't have a drink. All I need is a small glass of brandy, or somethin'. Ya'll have got that, right?"

Mr Corwin exchanged concerned glances with Inspector Conway. "I'll ask Dr Colbert when I've completed the examination."

Inspector Conway turned his head away. He knew neither Mr Corwin or Dr Colbert would be giving his friend alcohol anytime soon, and he was dreading the moment Dr Weeks came to the same realisation.

"Thanks," Dr Weeks said, a hint of gratitude in his voice.

Mr Corwin stood beside Dr Weeks and examined the lumps on his head with the lightest of touches. Going over to the table, he wrote down the injury on the notepaper, before continuing with the examination. Returning to the notepaper and recording his observations several times, he also asked Dr Weeks to remove his jacket and roll up his shirt sleeves, which he did. The findings from the subsequent examination of his arms were added to the notepaper. Dr Weeks' possessions were also removed from his jacket and placed in a small papier-mâché box.

The door was unlocked from the other side, and a man in his mid-forties entered. Attired in a uniform similar to Mr Corwin, he had light-brown hair, large brown eyes, and a strong jaw. He relocked the door and exchanged a few hushed words with Mr Corwin, who appeared to be outlining his findings. Finally, he extended his hand to Inspector Conway.

"Good evening, Inspector. I'm Mr Shayne, the steward," the man introduced in a warm tone. "Once Mr Corwin has finished the list, I'm going to need you to sign to confirm the sums of money and other property we've taken from Mr Weeks for safekeeping."

"*Doctor* Weeks," Dr Weeks corrected, but Mr Shayne appeared to have not heard.

"Safekeepin'?" Inspector Conway didn't like the sound of that.

"Yes, it's kept in my custody until Mr Weeks' release," Mr Shayne explained. "Don't worry. It's all recorded in our book, and the book is laid before the Bethlehem Sub-Committee at every meeting. Nothing will go astray."

"Inspector?" Mr Corwin held out a pencil.

Inspector Conway frowned as he went over to the table and read the list of Dr Weeks' meagre possessions. There was a box of matches, two cigarettes, and an empty gin bottle, but no coins. The pocket watch, handkerchief, and hip flask he was accustomed to seeing in the surgeon's possession were also missing. Taking the pencil, he signed where Mr Corwin indicated and passed the pencil to Mr Shayne who added his countersignature.

"What's gonna happen to 'im now?" Inspector Conway quietly enquired.

"Mr Corwin will submit his findings to Dr Colbert who'll immediately examine the injuries listed," Mr Shayne replied.

Inspector Conway furrowed his brow. "What was all this about, then?"

"*Bethlehem Hospital Rules & Orders* dictate all patients are examined upon arrival for injury," Mr Shayne explained. "These are recorded, so the hospital cannot be held liable if they're discovered later."

"Dr Colbert is with Chief Inspector Jones," Mr Corwin informed Mr Shayne. "I'll type up my notes while we're waiting."

"Good man," Mr Shayne complimented.

"Get me my drink!" Dr Weeks called after Mr Corwin as he left and locked the door.

"How long do you think 'e's gonna be here for?" Inspector Conway quietly enquired from Mr Shayne with concern etched upon his face.

"One can never really say for certain," Mr Shayne quietly replied. "I've known patients with alcoholic insanity recover within two months, and others have been here for years."

Dr Weeks stood and, tucking his hands under his arms, paced the room. His stomach continued to feel like it was rolling, making him feel nauseous. A stabbing pain had also started in the side of his head, adding to his irritability and agitation. His earlier thoughts of escape had been replaced by thoughts of alcohol—*any* alcohol—and he wondered how long it took to pour him a drink. Feeling his shirt collar become damp from sweat, he tugged at it with a finger and undid the top button.

Watching Dr Weeks from across the room, Inspector Conway felt like his friend was disintegrating before his eyes. Although Chief Inspector Jones had assured him admitting Dr Weeks was the right thing to do, he hadn't agreed with him until now.

* * *

Four small Davey lamps hung in the corners of the carriage, casting out their candlelight to illuminate the interior. Within their yellow glow, Mr Elliott's fair complexion resembled smooth porcelain even more. The red of his lips also appeared darker, giving him an overall unworldly appearance. Inspector Lee admired every inch of his face, but his gaze continually drifted back to those lips. Opening his legs slightly, he drew small circles upon his knee with his finger as he continued to stare at the solicitor.

"Why did you instruct your driver to prolong our journey?" Mr Elliott enquired.

Inspector Lee had kept his voice low to avoid being overheard when he'd issued the instruction to his driver. "What makes you think I did?"

"We've been travelling for almost twenty-five minutes without encountering any notable congestion on the roads." Mr Elliott turned cold eyes upon him. "Under such conditions, the journey should take only fifteen minutes."

"You're a very astute man." Inspector Lee closed his legs and, sitting forward, lowered his voice. "Therefore, you must have sensed the truth of it by now." He rested his hand upon Mr Elliott's knee. When the solicitor didn't pull away, he looked him in the eyes and slid his hand down the inside of his knee. "You have bewitched me, Gregory, and I can't resist any longer."

Mr Elliott gripped Inspector Lee's wrist and, lifting his hand from his leg, pushed it toward him. "I didn't give you permission to touch me, Gideon."

Inspector Lee withdrew his hand but leant in closer. In a voice barely above a whisper, he enquired, "Are you afraid you might enjoy it?"

"I'm not afraid of an impossibility."

"Because you're not attracted to men?"

"Because I'm not attracted to *you*."

Inspector Lee's eyes momentarily widened before narrowing. "You're lying."

"I never lie."

Inspector Lee's jaw visibly clenched before he said in a terse tone, "You're reluctant to admit your true feelings. I understand. What we are is not only condemned by society but is also highly illegal. You have your reputation, and therefore your livelihood, to protect, as do I. Here, with me, in this moment, you may speak freely, you may *act* freely, without fear of consequence or reproach."

"You've proven yourself untrustworthy on several occasions, Gideon, this carriage ride included. But even if you hadn't, I can't act on feelings which don't exist."

Inspector Lee sent Mr Elliott a long, pained look before sitting back against the seat and turning his head toward the window. His mind replayed the dinner they'd shared and their interaction outside Mr Calvin's office. The hints of Mr Elliott harbouring an attraction toward him were there, he was certain of it. He knew his handling of the Cosgrove case had coloured Mr Elliott's perception of him, but he hadn't realised it was to this extent. "But they did exist."

"Pardon?"

"You were attracted to me before. You will be again."

"I promise you. I shan't."

The corner of Inspector Lee's mouth twitched when Mr Elliott didn't refute the first part of his statement. "Perhaps." He used his cane to knock on the ceiling. "To Mr Elliott's lodgings!"

Mr Elliott turned his head toward the window. Staying like this for the remainder of the journey, he felt the weight of Inspector Lee's gaze on him the entire time. His mind also replayed their past interactions. Their professional relationship had deteriorated since the Cosgrove case, but had he felt attracted to him before? Hindsight suggested he had. His contempt for Inspector Lee, born from the policeman's dishonest, arrogant, and self-serving actions in recent months, certainly hid any desire he had for him, however.

He'd agreed with Miss Trent to uncover Inspector Lee's secrets. The policeman's confession about his homosexuality, and his feelings for him, were undoubtedly secrets he wanted to keep hidden. Inspector Lee's wishes aside, though, Mr Elliott knew he could never remove a man's respectability and liberty by exposing such things. He held himself to strict, high standards, and not even Miss Trent or the Bow Street Society could convince him to act otherwise.

When the carriage eventually slowed and came to a stop, Mr Elliott stuck his head out the window and immediately recognised his lodgings. He lifted the door's external handle and, withdrawing inside, pushed the door wide. He filled his lungs with the cold night air as he stepped down onto the pavement and, closing the door, exhaled loudly. It felt as if he were being released from a prison ship. He couldn't bring himself to bid Inspector Lee a good night, as it had been far from it. Instead, he turned his back on the carriage and strode inside.

Inspector Lee briefly considered following him but knew it would do him no good. Winning back Mr Elliott's affection would take time. Fortunately, he was a patient man.

THIRTY

There was an unmistakably tense atmosphere in the Bow Street Society's meeting room tonight. Sitting at the head of the table, Miss Trent went over in her mind the members' account of their last moments with Dr Colbert. Dr McWilliams had told him his presence was required at the asylum. It was an innocuous request by all appearances. Yet, no one had heard from Dr Colbert since. She suspected her pessimism was getting the better of her when she imagined Dr Colbert being assaulted by a patient. The tragic events of last year with Mr Maxwell had heightened her sensitivity to such things. Nevertheless, she doubted her concern would ease until she'd heard from Dr Colbert.

Miss Hicks, who'd barely eaten anything all day, had her chair pulled back from the table and close to the open door. Sitting sideways, she had an arm upon the backrest and another across her stomach. With her focus turned inward and her eyes glazed over, she stared into the hallway. No one had heard from Dr Weeks either. Miss Trent knew her pessimism about his situation was justified, but it was the prolonged wait for news which threatened to get the better of them both. Miss Hicks more so, since her feelings of guilt were all consuming.

On Miss Trent's left, Dr Locke tapped her pencil against her open notebook whilst intermittently checking the time on her dainty pocket watch. Her lips formed a harsher line with each moment that passed without the meeting's commencement. When she and Mr Locke had arrived, she'd been swift to take Miss Trent aside and warn her of his fatigued state. She'd also expressed her intention to withdraw him from the case if she thought his recovery was being compromised.

Miss Trent was offended; she had no intention of hindering his progress. Yet, upon reflection, she knew Dr Locke was only acting out of love for her husband. Given what they'd endured through his addiction, Miss Trent was relieved to know there was still some love left between them. She'd managed to appease Dr Locke by promising to take her medical advice into consideration when assigning tasks to her husband.

If Mr Locke had overheard the conversation, he'd shown no sign of it. Instead, he'd shuffled into the meeting room and occupied the seat closest to the fire. Toby had joined him soon after, and Mr Locke couldn't resist showing him a magic trick. Toby watched, entranced, as Mr Locke placed a small, paper ball into his left palm, closed his hands into fists, and opened them again to reveal they were empty. Closing his hands into fists a second time, he re-opened them to reveal the ball upon his right palm. Toby's eyes widened. Closing his hands into fists a third time, Mr Locke waved them in front of Toby's eyes before opening them again to reveal the ball had returned to his left palm.

"*Cor*!" Toby plucked up the ball to inspect it. "Can you show me 'ow to do that?"

"Certainly," Mr Locke smiled.

"Another time," Dr Locke curtly interjected.

Toby's face fell.

"This shortbread is absolutely *delicious*," Mr Heath remarked. "Doctor, you *must* try some!" He offered her the plate.

"No. Thank you." Dr Locke consulted her pocket watch. "Time is moving on."

"I'll have some!" Toby raised his hand.

"You've had two pieces already," Miss Trent reminded him.

"He's a growing boy," Mr Heath took the plate over, and Toby helped himself to the largest piece. Mr Locke took two but slipped the second to Toby beneath the table.

Mr Heath gave a wink to Miss Trent as he returned to his seat.

Miss Trent had guessed he was trying to ease the tension in the room and gave him an appreciative smile.

"Dr Locke is right; the evening grows short, and we've much to discuss." She turned knowing eyes to Toby. "There's a pile of unwashed dishes in the sink."

"Can't I stay and watch?" Toby enquired.

Miss Trent lowered her chin and lifted her brows in silent warning.

"I'm goin'," Toby said through a sigh and headed off to the kitchen.

"If I may begin?" Dr Locke enquired.

"Be my guest," Miss Trent replied.

Dr Locke's medical bag was on the chair beside her. Retrieving a folder from it, she had a sip of tea and began, "Dr Jonathan Caden conducted Miss Ilbert's postmortem at Charing Cross Hospital. He spoke highly of the Bow Street Society." She omitted his unfavourable speech about Dr Weeks; she found the mere thought of the surgeon repugnant. Opening the folder, she summarised the report within. "His initial examination found deep burns on the soles of her feet, but no additional wounds or signs of disease. He concluded the burns were likely the entry point of the electricity.

"His internal examination revealed severe tissue damage to her feet and lower legs. He concluded this was likely caused by the electricity travelling through her limbs. Both of Miss Ilbert's fibulas were fractured, along with six of her ribs. At first, Dr Caden was puzzled by these fractures, as Miss Ilbert hadn't fallen from a height or suffered any impact. Acting on the basis Miss Ilbert had been electrocuted, Dr Caden sought advice from the physician in Charing Cross Hospital's Electricity Department, who explained patients' muscles commonly contracted when electricity was applied. Between them, they concluded the fractures in Miss Ilbert's fibulas and ribs were caused by a considerable muscle contraction caused, in turn, by the high level of electrical current coursing through her body." Dr Locke closed the folder and addressed Miss Trent. "Dr Caden recorded Miss

Ilbert's cause of death as sudden heart failure caused by a high level of electrical current."

"Theatrical devices and the like don't usually fall within the sphere of my expertise, as you know, Miss Trent," Mr Heath began. "Mr Locke will tell you; I became utterly distracted by a platform capable of lifting a performer to the stage, from *beneath*, using *only* the strength of four men and miles, and I mean *miles*, of rope and pulleys. Why—"

Miss Trent softly cleared her throat.

Mr Heath momentarily bowed his head and lifted his hand. "Yes, back to my original point." He put his notebook in the middle of the table. "Imagine the table is the stage and this," he tapped his notebook, "is the metal plate. Now, Mr Locke has a greater knowledge of *precisely* how it ought to work more than I, but the *basic* principle is a small number of volts are created by a battery on a shelf concealed beneath the stage." He moved the cream jug into position. "Wires connect the battery to the plate to create an electrical circuit. When Miss Ilbert stepped onto the plate, the metal plates on the soles of her shoes would've completed the circuit. The minor electrical current was supposed to illuminate small lights sewn into her costume. Am I correct so far, Mr Locke?"

"You are," Mr Locke replied.

"*Marvelous*!" Mr Heath rubbed his hands together. "Now, located close to the concealed shelf is a fixture for a lightbulb." He moved the sugar bowl into position. "There was no lightbulb, but there *were* wires!" He tapped the side of the sugar bowl. "Leading from this, the lightbulb fixture," he tapped the notebook, "to *this*, the metal plate, and *not* from the metal plate to this," he tapped the side of the cream jug, "the battery." He looked to Miss Trent. "The *Crescent*'s electricity is supplied by an external company. The number of volts travelling into poor Miss Ilbert would've been considerable!" He sat back in his chair. "One can't conceive the pain she must've felt."

"But is it a case of intentional murder, or an accident caused by negligence and incompetence?" Miss Trent enquired.

"I'm going to see if Toby wants a hand," Miss Hicks muttered as she left the room.

Dr Locke's shoulders visibly relaxed when she heard the barmaid enter the kitchen.

"There were wires hanging loose from the plate in addition to those I've described," Mr Heath said, addressing Miss Trent. "Which, unfortunately, does suggest Mr Willis attached the wayward wires from the lighting system in error."

"Mr Willis was adamant he knew what he was doing with the plate and had prepared it accordingly, but we only have his word," Miss Trent said.

"Those who are employed backstage have been known to change theatres frequently over the course of their working lives," Mr Locke said. "I shall instruct Mr Natan Cokes, my business manager, to discuss Mr Willis with the electric men at the *Paddington Palladium*. They may have heard of him and may be able to provide anecdotal evidence either in support or contradiction of Mr Willis' account of himself."

"Thank you," Miss Trent said.

"Dr Colbert made a valid point about the lightbulb fixture which *could* balance the scales in favour of murder," Mr Heath said, consulting his notes. "To apply the electrical current to the metal plate, one had to flip the switch. One had to flip it again to remove it."

"Miss Kimberly was also uncertain whether other performers had stepped onto the plate prior to Miss Ilbert," Mr Locke said. "The flipping of the switch could have been deliberate, or it could have been a tragic coincidence. Either way, I propose we do not remove our client from our list of suspects at this time."

"Agreed," Dr Locke said.

Miss Trent noted Mr Willis' status against his name on a typed list. She turned the list around and put it in the table's centre. "Here are the names given by Mr Willis. Which of them should we consider suspects in your opinion?"

Mr Locke sat forward to skim-read the names. "Mr Ronald Stone is a foul human being who despised being managed by women. Miss Ilbert showed him great kindness by providing him with employment as stage manager at her theatre when his was destroyed by fire. Despite this, he harboured a bitterness toward her that could have led him to murder her, thereby 'freeing' himself from the chains of obligation she had imposed upon him. If he had perceived the arrangement in such a manner, of course."

"I would say so," Dr Locke said. "He was furious when Miss Kimberly said she'd signed a written agreement with Miss Ilbert granting her the authority to assume control of the theatre's management in the event of Miss Ilbert's death. He warned her there would be a new manager, but it wouldn't be her."

"Do you think Miss Kimberly could be in danger from him?" Miss Trent enquired.

The Lockes looked to one another.

"Although possible, I believe it improbable," Mr Locke replied.

"She's bringing the signed agreement to the theatre in the morning," Dr Locke added.

"Please request a typed copy of it, if you can," Miss Trent said. "I'd like Mr Elliott to read it and give his professional opinion."

"May I ask the reason for Mr Elliott's absence this evening?" Mr Locke enquired.

"He's in the middle of a trial at the Old Bailey," Miss Trent replied. "It's left him with little time to spare." She noted Mr Stone's status against his name on the list. "Do you all agree the written agreement gives Miss Kimberly a motive for Miss Ilbert's murder?"

"Signing an agreement to assume control of the theatre's management is one thing," Mr Locke began.

"Assuming responsibility for the lease agreement with the building's owner is quite another. Was there a copy of the lease in Miss Ilbert's office, darling?"

Dr Locke consulted her notes. "Yes."

"Fortunately, I own the *Paddington Palladium's* building and the land upon which it stands," Mr Locke said. "The vast majority of theatre managers are obliged to lease their theatre buildings from their owners, however. If Miss Kimberly intends to assume the management of the *Crescent*, she must also assume responsibility for the lease. In which case, new negotiations between her and the building's owner would have to take place. When Mr Elliott is available, it may be wise for him to request to see the existing lease and speak with the building's owner direct."

Miss Trent noted the suggestion.

"Miss Kimberly confirmed Miss Ilbert had given the entire company an ultimatum," Dr Locke said.

"Mr Stone told me the same," Mr Locke interjected.

"It alone gives every member of the company a motive," Dr Locke added.

"Mr Stone thought Miss Ilbert a fool for thinking her threat would scare the perpetrators into confessing," Mr Locke said. "I enquired if they would scare him. He looked me directly in the eye and said 'Never.' I could not help but suspect he was hinting the threat had directly applied to him, and he had not been the faintest bit frightened by it. Naturally, I enquired if he suspected who could have assisted Mr Jerome in his scheme. He volunteered Miss Joanna Hightower, the daughter of the *Crescent*'s wardrobe mistress. He said he had seen her speaking with Mr Jerome backstage. Furthermore, he had told Miss Ilbert of what he had seen, and she had confronted Miss Hightower, causing her to run away in tears. I requested Miss Hightower's address from Miss Kimberly but was bluntly refused. She did say we could speak with Miss Hightower, and the others, come tomorrow when the theatre reopens following its obligatory day of mourning."

"Miss Kimberly briefly spoke of Mr Jerome," Dr Locke said. "She said she has never met him and expressed disappointment over Miss Ilbert's determination to see her threat to the company through. I got the distinct impression she didn't want to speak of the matter in any great detail."

"It would be useful if we could speak to Mr Jerome direct," Mr Locke mused aloud. "If Sergeant Dixon accompanies us, Mr Jerome may be likelier to surrender the name, or names, of his accomplices. Miss Hightower may be able to tell us where he can be found."

"I shall speak with her tomorrow," Dr Locke volunteered.

"What are your thoughts on Mr Benton?" Miss Trent enquired.

"Mr Benton is the unlikeliest murderer, in my opinion," Mr Locke said. "Dr Colbert spoke to him alone, and I would not presume to speak for my fellow Bow Street Society member, but I have known of Mr Benton's reputation for many years. He is an actor of the highest calibre, and a gentleman besides. He was also the only person at the theatre today who vehemently defended Mr Willis as a capable and experienced electric man."

"There was a photograph of Mr Benton in Miss Ilbert's dressing room," Dr Locke said. "He was wearing formal attire, rather than a theatrical costume, suggesting it wasn't a promotional postcard." Dr Locke consulted her notebook. "There was also a bouquet of red roses. Miss Kimberly said Mr Benton bought Miss Ilbert a fresh bouquet every week, and he'd proposed to Miss Ilbert on several occasions."

"Mr Stone said the same," Mr Locke interjected.

"What of Mr Morris Thurston, the prompter and super master?" Miss Trent enquired.

"According to Mr Stone, Mr Thurston harbours a romantic interest in Miss Kimberly," Mr Locke replied.

"She expressed little emotion when she spoke of him, however," Dr Locke added.

"Could she have been hiding her feelings for him?" Miss Trent enquired.

"Perhaps, it's difficult to say," Dr Locke replied. "The dramatic script for Mr Thurston's play about the red barn mystery was on Miss Ilbert's desk in the office she shared with Miss Kimberly. She said Miss Ilbert had not only read Mr Thurston's play a day or so prior to her death but had loved it enough to put it in the theatre's program. She'd planned to commence preparations immediately so the play could be performed as soon as the pantomime's run ended."

"Given the small amount of time between Miss Ilbert reading the play and her death, I presume she had not yet received permission to have it performed on stage?" Mr Locke enquired.

"No," Dr Locke replied. "Miss Kimberly said Miss Ilbert intended to submit it this week."

"Pardon me, but I'm a little lost," Mr Heath said. "From whom did she have to get permission?"

"The Lord Chamberlain of Her Majesty's Household," Mr Locke replied.

"Does he enjoy the theatre *that* much?" Mr Heath enquired, taken aback.

Mr Locke smiled. "No. Under the Act for Regulating Theatres from 1843, it is a requirement for all masters or managers of theatres to submit the whole of a play, or any additions made to an existing play, such as new acts, scenes, or parts, to the Lord Chamberlain at least seven days prior to the date when said masters or managers intend to perform the play on stage. A fee for the examination of the play, usually two guineas, must also be paid at this time. The Lord Chamberlain will only grant permission to the masters and managers of the theatre to perform the play if he believes it preserves good manners, decorum, and peace of the public. It is a rather tedious process one must endure, and it is terribly frustrating to the artistic soul for, quite often, one must rewrite a play, scene, act, or part, and resubmit it for examination so one may perform it. The fee must also be paid each time. Thus, many managers will only consider a play if it is similar to one the Lord Chamberlain has previously approved. Although even then there is no guarantee permission for the new play will be granted."

"Miss Kimberly said Miss Ilbert had asked Mr Thurston to implement some rewrites to his play, but she didn't know if he had," Dr Locke said.

"It is a small possibility, but Mr Thurston could have removed Miss Ilbert to prevent the rewrites and thereby gain permission from the Lord Chamberlain for his original play through a request made by Miss Kimberly—if she assumes responsibility for the theatre's lease and management, of course," Mr Locke mused aloud.

"It wouldn't be entirely beyond the realm of possibility given how passionate people in the theatre business can be," Dr Locke said.

"When I asked Mr Stone who else could have wanted Miss Ilbert dead, he volunteered the name of the *Crescent*'s chief scene painter, Mr Stanley Akers," Mr Locke said. "Mr Stone alleged Mr Akers and Miss Ilbert argued about the brighter electric light at the scenery rehearsal. Mr Akers felt it was doing a disservice to his art."

"Do you think Mr Stone's allegation is a credible one?" Miss Trent enquired.

"Yes," Mr Locke replied. "The introduction of electrical lighting has been widely condemned by scenery painters. At least, according to the journalists of *The Era*."

"Another person of note is Father Ananias Mullins," Dr Locke said. "A resident clergyman at Hampstead Public School, he called upon Miss Ilbert at the theatre on the day prior to her death. He accused her of corrupting the boys at the school and used some rather unpleasant language whilst addressing her." Dr Locke consulted her notes. "I found a recent letter of complaint, signed by him, amongst

Miss Ilbert's papers. It was then Miss Kimberly told me of their meeting. She also showed me several love letters, all of an innocent nature, which Miss Ilbert had received from the older boys at Hampstead Public School. Granville Norton appeared to be the most prolific author amongst them."

"What else did you find in Miss Ilbert's office?" Miss Trent enquired.

"Aside from the lease agreement and letters, there were the usual documents and records associated with managing a theatre," Dr Locke replied.

"Which are?" Mr Heath enquired, intrigued.

"Ledgers for the theatre's accounts, Miss Ilbert's rental agreement with the caterers, her contract with Mr Akers, and employee records which included details of wages."

"Did anything in those documents arouse your suspicions?" Miss Trent enquired.

"No," Dr Locke replied. "I've recently become more involved in the management of the *Paddington Palladium*. Nothing I saw in the *Crescent*'s records seemed amiss by comparison."

"Thank you," Miss Trent noted this. "Please, continue."

"Other items I found were the usual promotional postcards depicting Miss Ilbert in costume, recent and past editions of *The Era* newspaper, a few telegrams from hopeful actors and actresses seeking employment, and programs for the pantomime and past plays at the *Crescent*," Dr Locke said. "Miss Ilbert's appointment diary was also on her desk. Within it, I found a technical rehearsal with Mr Akers scheduled for the night prior to Miss Ilbert's death. When I enquired after Mr Akers' name with Miss Kimberly, she made the same allegation against him as Mr Stone. She claimed to have witnessed the argument firsthand, however."

Miss Trent recorded the information in her notebook. "We have several points of interest which require further investigation. First, Miss Kimberly's written agreement with Miss Ilbert and the implications it may have on the building's lease agreement. Second, Mr Thurston's ambitions for his play. Third, Akers' argument with Miss Ilbert. Fourth, Father Ananias' confrontation of Miss Ilbert. Fifth, the ardent young admirer, Granville Norton. Sixth, Dr Colbert's account of his conversation with Mr Benton. Seventh, Miss Hightower's possible connection with Mr Jerome, and eighth, Mr Jerome's whereabouts."

"Mr Heath and I shall speak with Mr Thurston at the theatre in the morning," Mr Locke said.

"I shall be *wherever* you need me, Mr Locke!" Mr Heath exclaimed.

Dr Locke pursed her lips as her husband omitted Claude from his statement. She hoped it was an unintentional slip caused by the assumption Claude would be with him regardless.

"Dr Locke, you will be accompanying them?" Miss Trent enquired.

"Yes; to speak with Miss Kimberly and Miss Hightower separately." Dr Locke looked at her husband and added, "Claude will also be with us."

"Yes, darling," Mr Locke agreed with the hint of a sigh.

"I will assign Mr Verity to the case in the morning and ask him to speak with Father Ananias and Greville Norton at Hampstead Public School in the afternoon," Miss Trent said. "Dr Locke, could you accompany him?"

"What will Percy and Mr Heath be doing?" Dr Locke enquired.

"I propose we call upon Mr Akers," Mr Locke replied. "Claude, Mr Heath, and I."

The tension eased from Dr Locke's face. "In that case, I'd be delighted, Miss Trent."

"We shall also call upon Mr Cokes," Mr Locke said.

"*I* will call upon him, darling," Dr Locke said.

Mr Locke parted his lips to protest. A glance at the others convinced him to close them, again, however. It wasn't a conversation he wanted to have in public.

"Let me know as soon as Miss Hightower reveals Mr Jerome's whereabouts," Miss Trent said. "I don't want anyone putting themselves into unnecessary danger by confronting him without the police."

"Of course," Dr Locke said.

"Thank you," Miss Trent said. "This meeting is now at an end."

As Dr Locke put her notebook and folder into her medical bag, Mr Heath drained his tea and slipped his notebook into his suit jacket. Meanwhile, Mr Locke warmed himself by the fire to guard against the carriage ride home.

A knock sounded upon the front door, prompting Miss Trent to leave the room.

In the end, the meeting had only lasted around forty minutes. Fewer members equalled less discussion, which meant Miss Trent could look forward to a relaxing evening by the fire.

Smoothing her skirts and hair, she slid back the bolt and pulled open the door.

She stilled the moment she saw her visitor.

"Evenin', Miss Trent." Inspector Conway removed his hat. "Can I come in?"

THIRTY-ONE

Dr Weeks unfastened another two buttons of his shirt and used its cuff to wipe the sweat from his face and brow. The craving for alcohol had intensified when Inspector Conway left; it was like the only chance Dr Weeks had of getting to a pub left, too. The stabbing pain in his head's side had also evolved into a hammer pounding the inside of his skull. Wincing as the gaslight hurt his eyes, he clenched them shut and sat forward, his elbows upon his knees.

He imagined an overflowing pint of beer and licked his lips. Swallowing, he coughed when the sides of his bone-dry gullet stuck together. He wanted Dr Colbert to fetch him from the examination room but also leave him for as long as possible.

"I need a drink," he mumbled.

"No. You don't…"

"Get the hell out, John. I ain't gonna ask ya twice." His friend's stunned expression was ingrained in his memory, like blood soaked into wood.

"*You wouldn't betray Conway,*" Inspector Woolfe had said, but he was wrong. Dr Weeks had given Inspector Lee the envelope to implicate Inspector Conway in corruption and attacked Inspector Conway with a scalpel. *And for what?* He asked himself. *To save myself.*

"And you certainly don't want the world to know that you were conceived as a result of a scandalous liaison between an errant actress and married aristocrat."

Dr Weeks held his elbows against his sides and, lifting his feet onto their tiptoes, covered his eyes with his hands. *All I've done is damn myself*, he thought, wishing he could go back and change what had happened with Inspector Conway, with everything. *I'm so stupid*, he scolded. *A stupid and weak coward.*

"Bastard son, who should be grateful for what he receives." The words brought tears to Dr Weeks' eyes—

not because they were cruel, but because he knew they were more meaningful than Mr Fry had intended. "I'm just a bastard, plain and simple," Dr Weeks softly lamented as his mind replayed the moment when he'd offered Mr Locke heroin.

"Your parentage certainly explains much of your behaviour."

Resting his palms against his brows, he stared at the floor. He took small comfort from the knowledge Inspector Lee couldn't manipulate him here. *The damage's already been done*, he thought, replaying in his mind the moment when he'd struck Inspector Lee with the poker. He'd spent hours drinking to muster up the courage to expel the devious sonofabitch from his life forever. That's how he'd justified it to himself, anyway. He'd failed, and not only was he feeling wretched for attempting to murder someone, but he was also fairly sure Inspector Lee had had a hand in getting him admitted to Bedlam.

"Don't play games with me, Doctor. You shan't win." Inspector Lee had given him the warning in the stinking toilets at the boxing match, but he hadn't listened. *And now I've damned myself*, he realised.

"Am I s'pposed to 'weather the storm,' too?"

He lifted his head and lowered his hands, only to see they were trembling. Resting his hands upon his thighs to steady them, he felt sick when the trembling continued. They hadn't been this bad in over a year. Back then, he'd tried to come off the drink by stopping his intake dead. By midday, he'd felt like death warmed up, and by the evening, his hands trembled like an eighty-year-old's. He'd gone to the railway bar on his way home and met Polly for the first time.

She'd mistaken him for an American but had shown genuine enthusiasm about, and interest in, his home country and how he'd come to be in London. *She'd been interested, and all I wanted were a drink*, he thought, remembering how he'd kept her talking simply to ensure a swift service. He'd walked her home and charmed her with a kiss to the back of her hand because he'd realised having a barmaid for a lover would keep him well-supplied with alcohol.

It wasn't until he'd walked in on her with Noah O'Hannigan and felt the debilitating pain of betrayal, he knew he loved her. Yet, he'd hated her, too. In those moments, and for a day afterward, at least. He couldn't fathom how she could hurt him so badly, how she could part her legs so easily, for a man she barely knew. Looking back now to when they'd first met, though, he realised he'd found it just as easy to charm and seduce her. He'd been selfish then, and he was being selfish now. He felt his heart clench with guilt as his mind replayed the moment in the Dead Room when he'd pushed her.

"I'm just a bastard… plain and simple," he muttered. *And I deserve all I get.*

* * *

The Bow Street Society's parlour felt cavernous to Inspector Conway as he waited for Miss Trent and Miss Hicks to join him. Standing by the window, he watched Mr Locke's slow descent down the steps to the street. The illusionist leant heavily upon his walking cane and wife's arm respectively. When he turned his face toward the light of the streetlamp, the severe angles of its features were illuminated. It was the first time Inspector Conway had seen him in months. Under normal circumstances Inspector Conway might've pitied him, but the events of the day had left him mentally exhausted and emotionally numb.

He watched Dr Locke climb into the carriage first, followed by her husband. Mr Heath kept Miss Trent talking on the porch for several minutes until the clerk politely, but firmly, reminded him she had a guest to attend to. Mr Heath expressed his sincere apologies and hurried down the steps and along the street.

Inspector Conway turned to the empty parlour when he heard the front door close.

Miss Trent and Miss Hicks entered the room a few moments later.

"Evenin', ladies." Inspector Conway's voice was devoid of emotion.

Miss Trent cast an appraising glance over him; his tie was crooked, the lapels of his suit jacket were crumpled, and his hair and beard were unkempt. There was a grey tinge to his smooth, expressionless features, and an intensely serious look to his eyes. What struck her the most, though, was his unnatural stillness.

"Please, sit, Inspector." Miss Trent indicated the far end of the sofa whilst Miss Hicks sat on the other.

"Thanks." Inspector Conway crossed the room at a sedate pace. He looked to Miss Trent and waited until she sat in the armchair before sitting himself. With an already marked space between him and Miss Hicks, he sat at an angle to face them both, thereby increasing it further. "I won't stay long."

Miss Trent was perched on the armchair's edge, her spine rigid and her hands clasped in her lap. She fixed Inspector Conway with an unblinking gaze as she waited for bad news. Everything about him—his mannerisms, his voice, his face—filled her with an unforgiving sense of impending doom.

In contrast, Miss Hicks had turned to sit in the sofa's corner but leant toward Inspector Conway. With one hand gripping the sofa's arm and the other clutching her stomach, she watched Inspector Conway with wide, hopeful eyes. "Have you come 'bout my Percy? Is he all right?"

Miss Trent lifted her chin and held her breath, fearing the worst.

"Yeah… and no," Inspector Conway replied.

Miss Hicks slowly straightened as the colour visibly drained from her face. "Is 'e…?"

"No," Inspector Conway replied.

Miss Hicks felt an unexpected release of tension in her body, and her head drooped forward. Easing her grip upon the sofa's arm and her stomach, she kept her head bowed as she let out a huge breath. Quietly, she said, "*Thank God.*"

Miss Trent didn't share her relief, however. "But he isn't all right."

There was sadness in Inspector Conway's eyes when he met the clerk's gaze. "No."

Miss Hicks turned her head sideways to glare at him with accusing eyes. "What've you done to 'im?"

Inspector Conway returned her glare. "*Nothin'*."

Miss Hicks sat bolt upright. "You must've done sumin'."

"Let him speak, Polly," Miss Trent gently warned. "Please, continue, Inspector."

The emotionless mask dissolved from Inspector Conway's face. In its place were slackened features and a look of deep sorrow in his eyes. When he spoke again, his voice was subdued by emotion. "Today… me and the chief inspector… we took Weeks to Bethlehem Hospital." He took a moment to steady his emotions. "'E's been admitted."

Miss Trent felt her stomach somersault.

"You *what*?" Miss Hicks stared at him, stunned. "What *for*?"

"Alcoholic insanity," Inspector Conway replied.

"'E's in Bedlam 'cause 'e likes a few *drinks*?!" Miss Hicks cried, leaping to her feet.

"It's more than a few," Inspector Conway retorted, looking up at her.

"You *bastard*!" Miss Hicks struck him across the face. "You was meant to be 'is mate!" She covered her mouth with her hand and ran, sobbing, from the room.

Miss Trent watched her go but remained seated. When she looked to Inspector Conway, she saw he still had his face turned away. She stood and closed the door before going to the bookcase and pouring a small measure of brandy into a glass. Inspector Conway lifted his head as she approached with it, thereby revealing his red face and sorrowful eyes.

"Drink this." Miss Trent pressed the glass into his hand.

"Thanks." Inspector Conway drank the brandy in one swallow and put the glass down on the low table before the fire.

"You and Richard wouldn't have Dr Weeks admitted to Bedlam for mere drunkenness," Miss Trent began once she'd returned to her armchair. "Otherwise, he would've been admitted a hundred times over. Something else has happened. What is it?"

Inspector Conway lowered his gaze as his expression turned grave. "'E hit Lee."

Miss Trent lofted an eyebrow. "For a particular reason, or because he felt like removing the smug, self-satisfied look from Inspector Lee's face?"

Inspector Conway smiled weakly. "I've wanted to do that a few times myself." His smile quickly faded. "We don't know. Weeks was yellin' sumin' about Lee ruinin' his life. I wasn't there. Woolfe come to Bow Street and told me what had happened, said the chief inspector wanted me back at the Yard." He shook and bowed his head. "Weeks was locked in an interview room when I got there. Richard had already done the request to the beak for a reception order." He rested his elbow upon his knee and rubbed his eyes with the same hand. "The doctors who come and looked 'im over said it was alcoholic insanity."

"And you and Richard took him to Bedlam yourselves."

Inspector Conway gave a curt nod. "Yeah. Handcuffed. In a maria."

Miss Trent stood and picked up his glass. Refilling it from the bottle on the bookcase, she pressed it into his hand again and sat beside him on the sofa. "I'm sorry you had to do that, John." She rested a gentle hand on his arm. "You look exhausted. Get yourself home, have something to eat, and get some sleep. There's nothing more you can do for him tonight."

Inspector Conway glanced at the door. "What about Miss Hicks?"

"I'll look after her." Miss Trent gently squeezed his arm. "You did the right thing."

"Did I?" Inspector Conway drank the brandy in one swallow. "Don't feel like it."

"Dr Weeks' drinking has become more and more excessive in recent months," Miss Trent gently reminded him. "Not to mention the incident with you and the scalpel *and* the business with Polly. Bedlam's probably the best place for him at the moment."

Inspector Conway stared into the fire. "Yeah… maybe." His mind replayed the last time he'd seen the surgeon, reminding him of the conclusion he'd reached then.

"How is Dr Weeks' mother?"

Inspector Conway frowned. He'd forgotten about her. "I dunno."

"Does she know he's been admitted to Bedlam?"

"Richard told her before she went back to Canada."

Miss Trent momentarily lifted her brows and ironically remarked, "Charming." She imagined Dr Weeks' likely reaction to the news. "Who needs enemies with a mum like her?"

"Richard said 'e was gonna write her with news about Weeks."

"She's not abandoned him completely, then," Miss Trent dryly remarked.

"Folk take things in different ways." He put the glass down and stood, prompting Miss Trent to do the same.

"You're too generous, John."
"Yeah. Maybe."

* * *

"Dr Weeks?"

Sitting in the examination room with his hands tucked under his arms, Dr Weeks lifted his head and was surprised to see Dr Colbert standing over him. He'd either been so lost in his thoughts, he'd not heard him enter, or Dr Colbert had crept in to observe the natural behaviour of his newest patient. It was actually a little of both. Dr Weeks' movements were sluggish as he looked from Dr Colbert to the door and back again. "How long've ya been here?"

"A little while." Dr Colbert set the other chair down opposite Dr Weeks' and put his notebook and pencil on it. "I'd like to examine you, if I may?"

"I thought that's what the other fella were doin'?"

"He was, and he presented his findings to me. As the hospital's resident physician, it's my responsibility to immediately examine the injuries he noted in his report. I also wish to examine you for other injuries or symptoms." Dr Colbert held his open hands at chest height in readiness. "May I?"

"Will ya do it anyway if I say no?"

"Yes, but you are a fellow doctor and, as such, you are entitled to a level of respect far greater than that reserved for my usual patients."

Dr Weeks squinted, unsure if he could trust his word. He recalled the encounters he'd had with Dr Colbert during the Grosse murder case and couldn't think of a time when he'd felt threatened by him. On the contrary, Dr Colbert had tried to protect him from Mr Skinner's bribery. Deciding Dr Colbert was trustworthy, at least for now, he unfolded his arms and rested his hands in his lap. "Go ahead."

Dr Colbert smiled softly. "Thank you." He lightly traced the lumps on Dr Weeks' head with his fingers. They were swollen but not enough to be a cause for concern. He applied a small amount of pressure as he enquired, "Does this hurt?"

"A little."

"What happened to cause these lumps?" Dr Colbert knew the answer, for Chief Inspector Jones had told him during their discussion. He wanted to see if Dr Weeks would be equally as honest with him, however.

"I were robbed." Dr Weeks downcast his eyes. "The sonsofbitches took every penny I had."

Dr Colbert lifted Dr Weeks' eyelids with his thumb and inspected his pupils. Finding they were medium in size, he wrote the observation in his notebook. "Penniless surgeons aren't common within these walls." He lifted Dr Weeks' eyelids again and, finding the whites of his eyes were bloodshot, noted the observation in the same manner as before. "When was the last time you had some sleep?"

"Last night, I think."

"Don't you remember?"

"The last few days're a blur," Dr Weeks mumbled.

Dr Colbert held the back of his hand against Dr Weeks' forehead and hummed. "You're showing signs of a fever." He picked up his notebook and sat in its place. Noting his latest observations, he left the notebook open upon his lap and cupped Dr Weeks' right hand in his.

He studied the tremble in Dr Weeks' hand for several moments and found it was subtle in the palm but notable in the fingertips. Overall, the jolting motions weren't as severe as those he'd observed in other alcoholic insanity patients, but it was still early days for the surgeon. "How much alcohol do you drink in a day?" Dr Colbert looked him in the eye. "Be honest."

Dr Weeks searched his memory but couldn't pin down a number. "I ain't sure."

"Do you have alcohol when you first wake up?"

"If it's there."

"Is it usually there?" Dr Colbert noted his observations and Dr Weeks' answers.

Dr Weeks read the upside-down writing and felt reassured by its unbiased and factual tone. "Yeah."

"How is your appetite?"

"I ain't got one."

"Do you feel nauseous?"

"Yeah, like I've got a damned milk churn for a stomach."

Dr Colbert noted his answers. "How does your head feel?"

"Right now, there's a hammer tryin' to break through my skull."

Dr Colbert noted his answer, hummed, and closed his notebook. With his hand resting upon its outer cover, he turned his attention inward as he carefully considered his diagnosis. Finally, he set the notebook aside and looked Dr Weeks in the eye. This time, though, the gravity in his eyes was also in his voice. "Based upon my observations and our discussion, I must also diagnose you with chronic alcoholic insanity, doctor."

Despite knowing, deep down, this would be the inevitable outcome, Dr Weeks still felt his blood run cold. This was swiftly followed by an intense heat sweeping through his body, causing his insides to feel like they were quivering. Feeling his chest tightening and his breathing accelerate at the same time, he struggled to form any thoughts beyond being locked away in a dank cell and forgotten about. He held his stomach and bent forward slightly as he fought to regain control of his breathing.

Meanwhile, Dr Colbert watched Dr Weeks' reaction closely and continued, "Your £100 bond has been paid by your poor union, so I will be submitting your petition to the hospital's Sub-Committee of the Court of Governors at their next meeting on Wednesday with the recommendation you be admitted as a curable, poor lunatic."

"I *ain't* insane… I *can't* be," Dr Weeks breathed. He dug his fingers into his hair and, resting his elbows upon his knees, bowed his head. Taking deep breaths, he finally managed to bring his breathing back under control, but his mind continued to spin. "I *don't* want to be here… I *can't* be here… I *ain't* insane."

"You're not insane in the same way a man who suffers delusions or hallucinations is," Dr Colbert conceded. "But you are unwell and have been for quite some time by all accounts."

Wanting to hide himself away, Dr Weeks closed his eyes to block out the reality of his surroundings. This wish was quickly replaced by an intense desire to block everything out; the past few days, what had been said, the diagnosis—all of it. Only one thing could give him oblivion, though, and he craved it more than his liberty. In a pitiful voice, he said, "*I need a drink.*"

"I know." Dr Colbert put his hand upon Dr Weeks' shoulder. "I give you my word I'll do all I can to free you from this curse. In return, you must give me time and your cooperation, Percy. Will you give those to me?"

"I *can't… please… one* drink." Dr Weeks' voice was strained. "Let me forget."

Dr Colbert withdrew his hand and frowned deeply. "I'm afraid I can't do that."

Dr Weeks released a sob, and his shoulders shook as he silently broke down.

Dr Colbert stood and, picking up his notebook and pencil, looked back at Dr Weeks' quaking form. He watched until Dr Weeks' state deteriorated, and his sobbing filled the room. At which point, he opened the door and addressed Mr Cowen and Mr Shayne standing on the other side. "Leave him be for another five minutes, then put him into the cold bath."

"Yes, doctor." Mr Shayne stepped aside as Dr Colbert joined them in the corridor.

"I'll complete my inspection of him there." Dr Colbert closed and locked the door and gave the key to Mr Shayne. "You'll then escort him to his room and restrain him whilst I give him a dose of sulphanol."

"Yes, doctor," Mr Shayne repeated.

As Dr Colbert walked away, he visualized the different scenarios which could unfold in the coming hour. He knew it was necessary to put Dr Weeks on the road to recovery, but the distress such treatment invariably caused his patients in the beginning was an unpleasant side of his work he'd never become accustomed to. He doubted he ever would.

THIRTY-TWO

"Get *lost*, Toby!" Miss Hicks yelled.

Miss Trent entered the kitchen in time to see Miss Hicks push the sixteen-year-old. Toby stumbled backward, landing against the back door with a thud and rattle of hinges. Miss Trent immediately strode over to the pair; her chin lifted and an obvious tightness in her eyes and face. She put her arm around Toby's shoulders and guided him into a chair at the table. Her eyes and expression softened momentarily as she enquired, "Are you hurt?"

"No." Toby gave a small smile. "Thanks."

Miss Trent returned his smile. "I'll make us some hot cocoa."

Miss Hicks stood with her back against the window and her head in her hand.

Miss Trent filled a pan with milk and put it on the stove's hob to warm.

"It's bad enough you hit the inspector when he was only trying to help," Miss Trent began, addressing Miss Hicks in a low, hard tone. "But Toby's a mere *boy*, Polly." She turned cold eyes upon her. "I won't tolerate you hurting him."

"You hit the bulldog?" Toby looked at Miss Hicks, wide eyed. "*Cor*! You're brave, ain't you?"

"And what about me, Becky, aye?" Miss Hicks' face was red.

Miss Trent watched the bottom of the pan for bubbles. "What about you?"

Miss Hicks went over to her. "I've just been told my bloke's in the madhouse."

"Your mate the lush?" Toby interjected.

Miss Hicks glared at him. "I wasn't talkin' to *you*."

"Don't speak to him like that," Miss Trent warned.

Miss Hicks looked at her sharply. "He's bargin' in on sumin' that's got nothin' to do with him."

Miss Trent put her hand on her hip as she faced her. "What do you expect, Polly? Sympathy? A shoulder to cry on? You'll get neither from me."

Taken aback, Miss Hicks watched Miss Trent add the cocoa to the warm milk. "My Perce is in Bedlam and—"

"*Your* Perce?" Miss Trent stirred the warm milk to dissolve the cocoa. "He wasn't 'your Perce' when you had Noah O'Hannigan between your legs. He was just the man who put a roof over your head, clothes on your back, and food in your belly."

"I *love* him," Miss Hicks insisted.

"As you've told me before," Miss Trent said. "But you didn't love him enough to stay faithful to him, did you? And now, your selfishness has driven him to madness."

Miss Hicks blinked. "*I* didn't put him in *Bedlam*!"

"No, but you did your part in convincing him to drink his way there." Miss Trent poured the cocoa into two mugs and set the pan aside. Serving Toby his drink, she returned to Miss Hicks at the stove. "I'm going to ask Sam to collect Dr Weeks' belongings from St. John Street in the morning and bring them here. Dr Weeks will have the remnants of his former life and somewhere to live once he's released, at least. You may have your belongings brought here, too, if you want. You may stay here until you've made alternative arrangements, but then I want you gone."

Miss Hicks stared at her, stunned. "But where will I go? What will I do?"

"At this precise moment, Polly, I don't care," Miss Trent replied. "The only reason I'm not throwing you out tonight is because the principles of the Bow Street Society don't allow it." She took her cocoa with her as she left the room. "Toby, will you help me tidy the meeting room, please?"

"Yes, Miss Trent." Toby picked up his mug and followed her out.

* * *

The echo of a door closing spurred Sergeant Jude Perry to push the curtain aside and peer out at the Bow Street Society's house opposite. Seeing a figure emerge, he watched them descend the steps. When they moved into the weak gaslight of the streetlamp, he recognised Inspector Conway at once.

In his early thirties, Sergeant Perry had served as an undercover Mob Squad detective for five years. He had a round face, short, dark-brown hair with no parting, hazel eyes, and a double chin. Approximately five feet eight inches tall, he was on the stocky side with broad shoulders and a large belly. Given his current assignment, he had opted for comfort over style. Therefore, his attire consisted of a loose-fitting white shirt, dark-brown trousers, and a thick, dark-brown, knee-length coat.

His gaze followed Inspector Conway to the police station. Checking his pocket watch, he noted down the time and a brief description of what he'd seen. Compared to the rest of his surveillance thus far, tonight had been the busiest he'd seen the Bow Street Society's house. It had certainly made the time pass quickly, and Inspector Lee would be pleased with his report, besides.

Meanwhile, Inspector Conway had greeted the desk sergeant with a nod and made his way upstairs. When he reached his office, Chief Inspector Jones and Inspector Woolfe were waiting for him. Looking at him in unison, it was the former who spoke first. "How was the news received?"

"Miss Hicks took it badly." Inspector Conway's cheek still stung a little.

"I suspected she might," Chief Inspector Jones said.

"And Miss Trent?" Inspector Woolfe enquired.

Inspector Conway hung up his hat and coat. "She was shocked but understood why we done it." He sat at his desk.

"An unfortunate business all around," Chief Inspector Jones observed.

"But one that's been brewing for a while," Inspector Woolfe said. "Weeks hasn't been right since before Christmas."

"What I don't get is Weeks tellin' Lee 'e'd 'ruined' his life," Inspector Conway said. "What was that about?"

Chief Inspector Jones and Inspector Woolfe exchanged glances. The former had described his earlier conversation with Inspector Conway to the latter. Specifically, his omission of the business with the envelope.

"Dr Weeks is unwell," Chief Inspector Jones replied. "One can't take everything he says seriously."

"I suppose not." Inspector Conway lit a cigarette.

Inspector Woolfe was keen to change the subject. "Did Miss Trent mention our meeting?"

Inspector Conway's head was downturned as he took some pulls from his cigarette. Encounters between Inspector Woolfe and Miss Trent made him nervous, particularly those he wasn't present for. "No. What was it about?"

"She and Mr Calvin, her solicitor, didn't like me asking questions about the Society's account at the bank," Inspector Woolfe replied. "I was meant to be meeting Mr Calvin alone but, unbeknownst to me, he'd summoned her into it, too."

Inspector Conway lifted his gaze to Chief Inspector Jones who remained stoic.

"She asked what I hoped to gain by prying into the Society's financial affairs," Inspector Woolfe continued. "I told her I wanted to find out the name of her employer."

Inspector Conway's gaze slid to Inspector Woolfe. "And what did she say?"

"The Bow Street Society is her employer," Inspector Woolfe replied.

"Which is true, on the face of it," Chief Inspector Jones remarked.

Inspector Woolfe grunted his acknowledgement, only for it to bring on a coughing fit. Sitting back in his chair as he repeatedly coughed, he took a large mouthful of cold tea, cleared his throat, and coughed again.

"I hope you've seen a doctor, Caleb," Chief Inspector Jones remarked, concerned.

"It's getting better." Inspector Woolfe sat forward in his chair and rested his folded arms upon the desk. "As I was saying: I asked Mr Calvin if he was her employer, and he denied it."

"Do you believe him?" Chief Inspector Jones enquired.

Inspector Conway downturned his head and took another pull from his cigarette.

"I don't know," Inspector Woolfe replied. "I've not got any evidence either way."

"Have you made any progress locating 'J. Pettifoot?'" Chief Inspector Jones enquired.

Inspector Conway lifted his head sharply and looked between them. "J. Pettifoot?"

"Inspector Woolfe discovered they were the one who placed the advertisements in the *Gaslight Gazette* seeking a clerk and members for the Bow Street Society," Chief Inspector Jones explained, a warning look in his eyes as he fixed his gaze upon Inspector Conway.

"Do you know them, John?" Inspector Woolfe enquired.

Inspector Conway darted his gaze to Inspector Woolfe. "No." He despised lying to his friend, but it was a necessary evil. "Should I?"

"I thought you might've heard it at the Society's house," Inspector Woolfe replied.

"I didn't," Inspector Conway crushed out his cigarette. "I never met all the members."

"I think 'J. Pettifoot' is Miss Trent's employer," Inspector Woolfe said. "So, I asked her and Mr Calvin about it at our meeting."

309

"What did they say?" Chief Inspector Jones enquired in a calm, even tone.

"He said he didn't know them," Inspector Woolfe replied. "She hesitated, then agreed with Mr Calvin."

"I imagine Miss Trent meets many people as clerk of the Bow Street Society," Chief Inspector Jones said. "I wager the pause you perceived as hesitation was merely her searching her memory."

"Maybe," Inspector Woolfe conceded, his eyebrows pushed together in a frown.

"What if 'J. Pettifoot' is an alias?" Inspector Conway enquired. "Mr Calvin and Miss Trent might know them under another name."

Inspector Woolfe rubbed his face. "I thought of that." He lowered his hand, "But, without a photograph of 'J. Pettifoot,' I can't check with them." He sat back in his chair, causing it to creak. "I've asked the bank to prepare a list of all depositors and borrowers for me to collect tomorrow. I'm hoping to see J. Pettifoot's full name on it. If they've also got an account at the bank, I'll be able to get their address, too."

"Given the hostility received from Miss Trent and Mr Calvin, I rather suspect the latter has instructed the bank to withhold the information from us," Chief Inspector Jones said. "If he has, the visit may prove fruitless."

"He might've told the bank not to give us the list, but the bank might decide to go against his wishes on the basis it's us, the police, who are asking," Inspector Woolfe pointed out.

"A reasonable assumption," Chief Inspector Jones conceded. His gaze slid to Inspector Conway. "I'd like John to go with you. He may recognise some of the names."

Inspector Conway knew Chief Inspector Jones' motives for making such a suggestion extended beyond simple policework; he was making him a mole in Inspector Woolfe's investigation. The idea of spying on his friend was an uncomfortable one, despite it being for the greater good.

"Whatever you say, sir," Inspector Woolfe said.

"What if the bank don't have any record of a 'J. Pettifoot?'" Inspector Conway enquired.

"Then we'll at least know for sure," Inspector Woolfe replied.

Inspector Conway sat back in his chair. He couldn't fault his friend's logic. "Okay," he exhaled, loudly. "What time?"

"First thing," Inspector Woolfe replied. "We'll meet here."

Inspector Conway looked to Chief Inspector Jones with a mixture of worry and irritation. "Do you want us to report what we find as soon as we find it?"

"Please," Chief Inspector Jones replied.

Inspector Conway reached for an unrelated file. "We'll see you tomorrow, then."

Chief Inspector Jones stood, prompting Inspector Woolfe to do the same. "Well, gentlemen, my supper will be on the table." He retrieved his hat, coat, and scarf from the stand. "Good night."

"Good night, sir," Inspector Woolfe said and waited until Chief Inspector Jones had left before sitting. Looking across at Inspector Conway, he saw him reading the file with a slight grimace. "You don't have to come with me if you don't want to."

"I said I would."

"So, why have you got a face like a slapped arse?"

Inspector Conway stood and tossed the file onto his desk.

"Where are you going?" Inspector Woolfe demanded.

"*Home*." Inspector Conway retrieved his hat and coat as he left.

* * *

The sound of tiny bells rang out from the ornate mantel clock as it struck ten o'clock. Standing before the fire in a dark-plum, ankle-length velvet dressing gown with silk lapels, Inspector Lee sipped from a glass of red wine. As well as himself, the reflection in the large mirror hung on the chimney breast revealed the dark-wood, four-poster bed, side tables, and blanket box of the guest room behind him. The burgundy, damask curtains which hung from three sides of the bed were untied from their posts but open. The remainder of the décor was modest compared to the rest of the house: burgundy wallpaper with a dark-brown floral print, exposed floorboards covered with a dark stain, and two wall-mounted gas lamps. The last were unlit, thereby making the fire the only source of light.

"Yes?" Inspector Lee called in answer to a knock.

The door opened, and his manservant entered. "Your guest has arrived, sir."

"Send him up."

"Yes, sir."

As his manservant left and closed the door, Inspector Lee set his glass of wine down upon the mantel shelf and opened the blanket box. From it, he took a small bottle of olive oil and clean rag which he put on the right-hand table. Next, he closed the curtains on all but one side of the bed, namely the one facing the door. Returning to the fireplace, he picked up his wine as another knock reached his ears.

"Come in," Inspector Lee called.

A dark-haired man in his early twenties with a slender face, delicate nose, and naturally rose-pink lips entered. He wore a faded, dark-blue waistcoat with matching cravat, black trousers, and an off-white long-sleeved shirt.

"Good evening, Stephen." Inspector Lee smiled. "Please, lock the door and come over here."

Stephen did as he was instructed and joined Inspector Lee at the fireplace. "Your usual, sir?"

"Yes." Inspector Lee ran an appraising gaze over Stephen's feminine-looking features. They weren't of Mr

Elliott's beauty, but they were close enough. He felt a stirring of desire as he envisioned the night ahead. "Most definitely."

THIRTY-THREE

Dr Colbert closed his eyes and plunged into the abyss of sleep, only to awaken with a jolt when his head fell forward. He lifted his eyebrows, opened his eyelids wide, and pushed his eyeballs forward, until the compulsion to sleep subsided. Moving in the hard-backed chair, he winced at the painful stiffness in his shoulders and lower back. He had barely moved in the past nine hours. This, coupled with the absence of a blanket or fire, meant he was chilled to the bone.

Yet, his wellbeing and comfort were only fleeting concerns. The moment his sleep-deprived mind could focus, again, he stood and removed the damp cloth from Dr Weeks' forehead to hold the back of his hand against the latter. Despite last night's cold bath, the surgeon's fever had continued. He lay, shivering and trembling, on a bed beneath a tall window overlooking the grounds. The room they were in was one of many which formed Bethlehem Hospital's ground floor male patient gallery.

Dr Colbert retrieved his stethoscope from underneath his chair and, putting the earpieces in, placed the bell-shaped end over Dr Weeks' heart and listened. The heartrate was raised but not as severely as it had been around one o'clock this morning. Dr Colbert moved the stethoscope over Dr Weeks' lungs. His breathing remained shallow and quick, but there was no gargling or hint of fluid or obstruction.

Dr Colbert put his stethoscope on his chair and dipped the cloth into a bowl of water on a small table in the corner. Fortunately, the water had remained cold despite standing all night. Returning to Dr Weeks, he folded the cloth and wiped Dr Weeks' face before laying it across his forehead.

Dr Colbert looked over his shoulder as he heard the door open behind him.

"How is he?" Dr McWilliams enquired, joining his colleague at Dr Weeks' bedside.

Dr Colbert furrowed brow. "In the grip of a fever, still."

"The cold bath did not help?"

"No." Dr Colbert lifted Dr Weeks' eyelids to examine his pupils. Finding them to be normal in appearance, he straightened and checked his pocket watch. "I gave him a full dose of sulphanol after the bath and a half dose an hour ago." He put his pocket watch away. "I've found no hint of an infection on his person or in his lungs. My examination for symptoms of general paralysis of the insane also turned up nought." He tightened the knot of his tie, straightened his waistcoat, and smoothed down the lapels of his jacket. "All signs point to his alcohol dependency being the cause of his fever."

"I am inclined to agree with you." Dr McWilliams ran an appraising gaze over Dr Weeks' prone form lying atop the blankets. The surgeon's soiled clothes had been thrown away and replaced with a simple man's knee-length nightshirt. "He has survived the first night, though. His constitution must be a strong one."

Dr Colbert hummed. "You know as well as I, Charles, the first couple of days are the most crucial, and the most dangerous, when treating those with alcoholic insanity. Their bodies need alcohol as much as they need air. Removing it can either suffocate them or set them free." His expression turned grave. "I'm praying it's the latter case for Dr Weeks."

"You are doing your best, and that is all anyone can ask of you." Dr McWilliams cast a worried glance over Dr Colbert. "Have you sat with him all night?"

"Yes." Dr Colbert lowered his head and rubbed his eyes. "I knew I wouldn't be able to rest if I went home."

"You should try to get some sleep, Neal," Dr McWilliams urged. "I shall send for you if his condition worsens."

Dr Colbert scrutinised Dr Weeks' shivering and trembling form as he fought against overwhelming exhaustion and an overwhelming desire to keep watch over his patient. Yet, Dr Weeks was more than a patient to him; he was a fellow doctor, a man whose impressive intellect required saving. Most importantly, though, he was someone he knew personally, and this, above all else, bore in him a sense of duty far stronger than what he felt for his other patients.

"Thank you, Charles," Dr Colbert sat. "But I want to stay."

Dr McWilliams softly exhaled. "As you wish." He offered a small smile as he headed for the door. "I shall have some coffee brought to you instead."

Dr Colbert twisted in his chair to look at him. "Some food wouldn't go amiss, either."

Dr McWilliams' smile grew. "Consider it done."

* * *

Despite being in Miss Mina Ilbert's office only twenty-four hours prior, Dr Locke noticed a marked difference in it today. Two large packing crates filled with books, theatre programs, and photographs sat beside the now bare bookcases. The desk had also been cleared of all scripts, documents, and notepaper. The most notable change, though, was the absence of Miss Kimberly's desk. The lady herself was sat behind Miss Ilbert's desk with the theatre's account ledger closed before her.

Having completed her appraisal of her surroundings, Dr Locke enquired, "Yesterday, you said you would bring the written agreement in for us to see. Did you?"

Miss Kimberly took a single page document from underneath the account ledger and passed it to Dr Locke. It read:

> I, the undersigned, hereby grant Emmaline Kimberly full and indefinite administrative

and legal authority over the management of the *Crescent Theatre*, Strand, London, in the event of my passing by natural or accidental cause(s).

 Signed: *Mina Ilbert,*
6ᵗʰ November 1896.

I, the undersigned, hereby accept full and indefinite administrative and legal authority over the management of the *Crescent Theatre*, Strand, London, in the event of Mina Ilbert's passing by natural or accidental cause(s).

 Signed: *Emmaline Kimberly,*
6ᵗʰ November 1896.

"It refers only to Miss Ilbert dying by natural or accidental causes. Was another agreement in place in the event of murder or suicide?" Dr Locke enquired.

"No, but Mina wouldn't commit suicide."

"Was she religious?"

"She thought too highly of herself to contemplate such things."

Dr Locke lofted an eyebrow. "That's a rather callous remark to make about someone you claim was a dear friend."

"She was." Miss Kimberly's features tightened. "To be perfectly honest with you, doctor, I'm angry with her and her foolish ultimatum. She should've never given it. This theatre company was like a family to her. One doesn't disown one's family merely for the sake of one's pride."

"I presume Miss Ilbert included her daughter in her threat of dismissal?"

"She threatened to dismiss Miss Lily if the conspirators didn't come forward, yes," Miss Kimberly replied. "It was utterly unfair and heartless of Mina."

"She was trying to protect her theatre," Dr Locke pointed out, reminded of her own struggles to preserve the *Paddington Palladium* for her husband.

His silence during the carriage ride to call upon Mr Cokes had spoken volumes. She knew he disagreed with her prohibiting him from entering his own theatre, but he wasn't ready. Everyone at the *Paddington Palladium* remembered him as a handsome, suave, and healthy gentlemen. She didn't want to shatter the illusion by allowing them to see him as the gaunt, tired, and weakened heroin addict he'd become, albeit a recovering one.

"And dismissing the entire company would've guaranteed its end," Miss Kimberly rebuffed, pulling Dr Locke from her thoughts.

Taking a moment to regain her focus, Dr Locke concluded winning the argument was both unnecessary and irrelevant. She'd gained further insight into the reasons behind Miss Kimberly's attitude and behaviour which was sufficient for now. "Perhaps. May I have a typed copy of this?" She raised the agreement. "We'd like Mr Gregory Elliott, a solicitor and Bow Street Society member, to read it and give his professional opinion."

Miss Kimberly darted her eyes from Dr Locke's face to the agreement and back again. "Do you think it's a forgery?"

Dr Locke tilted her head to the side as she replied in a casual tone, "Some people may say the revelation of its existence coming so soon after Miss Ilbert's death is convenient, but the Bow Street Society tends to keep an open mind until all the evidence is gathered."

"People like Ronald Stone, you mean."

"He was clearly displeased when you informed him of its existence. Has he seen it?"

"No. He didn't come in this morning." Miss Kimberly gave a slight lift of her chin. "If he thinks he can break the agreement by hiring the Society's solicitor to invalidate it, he's gravely mistaken."

Dr Locke put the agreement down. "The request for a typed copy came from Miss Rebecca Trent, the Society's clerk. As far as I'm aware, Mr Stone isn't a client of ours."

"If your Mr Elliott wishes to read it, he will have to do so in my presence."

"Don't you think you are being unnecessarily overcautious?"

"The agreement ensures my position at this theatre and therefore my future income. As a woman, you'll understand, I'm sure."

"I do, but as someone who has recently gained insight into a theatre's management, I also know your agreement with Miss Ilbert is meaningless without the building owner allowing you to assume responsibility for the lease."

"Actually, doctor, he has already seen the agreement. Furthermore, he has agreed to amend the lease to remove Mina's name and add mine," Miss Kimberly said with a hint of triumph.

"And if Mr Elliott also wishes to read the amended lease and speak with the building owner, he will have to do so in your presence, I presume?"

"Yes."

Based upon her own experience, Dr Locke felt Miss Kimberly's paranoia went beyond a woman's fundamental desire to avoid being deceived by the patriarchy. Consequently, Dr Locke concluded Miss Kimberly's stubborn and untrusting behaviour must've arisen from a betrayal in her past. What the betrayal was, and who committed it remained to be seen, but Dr Locke sensed it was worth investigating further. Realising she couldn't gain any further ground on the matter for the moment, though, she turned her attention to her visit's second objective. "I'd like to speak with Miss Joanna Hightower, if I may?"

"You can't. She was too upset to come in this morning."

"Were those her words?"

"Her mother's, Mrs Naomi Hightower, our chief wardrobe mistress."

"Mr Stone told Mr Locke he'd seen Miss Joanna backstage with Jack Jerome prior to Miss Ilbert's death. Mr Stone also admitted to telling Miss Ilbert of it."

"Mr Stone delights in causing chaos." Miss Kimberly had a sharp edge to her voice.

"We'd like to locate Mr Jerome, and we believe Miss Joanna may be able to help us."

"I doubt it."

"All the same, we'd like to try. May I have the Hightower's address?"

Miss Kimberly didn't move as her hard gaze bore into Dr Locke. Suddenly, she averted her gaze, and her entire body and face relaxed.

"Very well," she replied through a soft sigh. She took an address book from her desk and flipped through its pages until she found the Hightowers' entry. "They reside in rooms at 72, Great Queen Street."

Dr Locke wrote the address in her notebook. "Thank you." She stood, prompting Miss Kimberly to do the same. "Where can I find you if I have any further questions?"

"I'll be here." Miss Kimberly indicated the ledger. "Going through the books."

"Do you intend to continue with Miss Ilbert's planned program?"

"For the time being."

"You've sent Mr Thurston's play to the Lord Chamberlain for examination, then?"

"Not yet, but I will. Tomorrow. Now, if you'll excuse me." Miss Kimberly sat.

"Of course." Dr Locke offered a contrived smile and left.

* * *

"I am afraid Dr Colbert is currently unavailable," Dr McWilliams said.

"But I want to see my Percy!" Miss Hicks exclaimed, advancing upon him.

"Calm down," Miss Trent ordered, stepping between them.

Miss Hicks folded her arms in an exaggerated gesture.

Miss Trent turned to Dr McWilliams. "We understand Dr Colbert has other patients to look after, but we only want to take a few minutes of his time to discuss our friend Dr Weeks."

"It is your friend who is preventing Dr Colbert from speaking to you," Dr McWilliams said.

"What do you mean?" Miss Hicks glared at him across Miss Trent's shoulder.

"Dr Weeks is seriously ill," Dr McWilliams replied. "Dr Colbert has kept watch over him all through the night." He indicated the two chairs before Dr Colbert's desk as he moved behind it. "Please, sit down, and I will explain."

"I'll stand. Thanks," Miss Hicks rebuffed.

"*Polly*," Miss Trent warned as she stood by one of the chairs.

Miss Hicks exhaled loudly through her nose and sat in the other chair.

Miss Trent sat and, once Dr McWilliams was seated, enquired, "Is Dr Weeks' condition life-threatening?"

Dr McWilliams' expression turned grave. "It can be." He put his back flush against his chair, thereby maintaining the greatest degree of space between them. "Patients with alcoholic insanity have been known to experience fits in the first few days of abstinence. These fits have sometimes proven fatal.

"I see," Miss Trent said quietly.

"Has my Percy had one of these 'fit' things?" Miss Hicks enquired.

"Not yet," Dr McWilliams replied. "And the longer he goes without experiencing one, the more hopeful we shall be he will not experience one in the future. Currently, he is in the grip of a fever and unable to speak."

"Can I see 'im?" Miss Hicks enquired, her voice subdued by emotion.

"I am afraid not," Dr McWilliams replied. "These first few days are critical and so, the focus must be entirely on getting Dr Weeks into a stable condition. We shall contact you if the situation changes."

"Thank you, doctor." Miss Trent stood. Looking to Miss Hicks, she saw her eyes were glazed over, and she was staring into an invisible horizon. She slipped her arm under Miss Hicks' and gently guided her to her feet. "Come on, Polly. There's nothing more we can do here."

Miss Hicks, seemingly in a trance, allowed Miss Trent to guide her to the door where she suddenly stopped and looked back at Dr McWilliams. "Will you tell 'im I love 'im?"

"I will," Dr McWilliams replied. "Look after yourselves. Dr Weeks is going to need your strength if he is going to fully recover."

"Please, tell Dr Colbert I also wish to speak to him about Bow Street Society business," Miss Trent said. At Dr McWilliams' agreement, she guided Miss Hicks to where Mr Snyder was waiting with the cab.

THIRTY-FOUR

The sounds of jumbled conversations, interspersed with occasional laughter, filled the *Crescent*'s stage as the costumed supers waited to rehearse. In the left wing, Mr Thurston sat behind a small, slanted desk and awkwardly collated loose sheets of paper into a pile by the light of a kerosene lamp. With a tremor to his voice, he said, "I don't know what you want me to say. Mina's death was a tragic accident. To make it into anything more is crude and tasteless."

"Not if it is the truth," Mr Locke said. He and Mr Heath sat on stools perpendicular to the desk.

Mr Thurston pursed his lips and expelled a short, sharp burst of air through his nose as he noticed he'd placed the sheets in the wrong order.

Peering over Mr Thurston's arm, Mr Locke saw the sheets were the typed, annotated pages of the pantomime's script.

"I really don't have time for this," Mr Thurston said in a higher pitch. There was also an audible tension to his voice, and the tremor had worsened. "I must rehearse the revised choreography with the supers, instruct and rehearse Miss Lily so she may assume Mina's part during this evening's performance, and prepare for a meeting with Emmaline about my play."

"The red barn mystery, was it not?" Mr Locke enquired.

"Yes." Mr Thurston tapped the pile against the desk to straighten the pages. "Emmaline has agreed to continue with its production."

"How very fortunate for you," Mr Locke observed.

"Which is *precisely* my point." Mr Thurston dropped a page onto the floor but immediately leant down to pick it up. "Mina's death risked my losing the first opportunity I've had to see my work on stage." He tapped the pile several times against the desk, far more than was necessary. "I didn't murder her. *No one* here did."

"My good man," Mr Locke began with a contrived smile. "Everyone in this company had a motive for removing Miss Mina Ilbert from the mortal coil. Her ultimatum, and the consequences it spelt, *is* the motive. From an unbiased perspective, there are further motives which must also be considered. For example, Miss Lily assuming the part played by her late mother so soon after her death. One must question whether she had grown weary of standing in her mother's shadow and murdered her to step into the spotlight."

"Now, see *here*—!" Mr Thurston began, glaring at him.

"And there is also your second motive," Mr Locke interrupted.

"I *didn't* murder her," Mr Thurston insisted.

"Would I be correct in stating you are fond of Miss Kimberly?" Mr Locke enquired.

Mr Thurston stilled. "I think… highly of her, y-yes."

"Does she reciprocate your fondness?" Mr Locke enquired.

Mr Thurston continued tidying the pile. "I'd prefer *not* to discuss this."

"It is your right to refuse to answer, Mr Thurston," Mr Locke said. "However, you must acknowledge the answers you have given do not paint a favourable picture for yourself or Miss Kimberly. It is true Miss Ilbert intended to put your play into production as soon as the pantomime's run was complete. Yet, it is also true Miss Kimberly has agreed to the same. When one considers the potential fondness between you and Miss Kimberly, one can swiftly see how it negates your claim you had no additional motive for removing Miss Ilbert. Without her, you and Miss Kimberly are at liberty to create a production of your play true to your vision, and not Miss Ilbert's, as it would have been had she lived."

"That's a *lie*!" Mr Thurston shouted.

The din of conversations and laughter abruptly ceased as the supers' attention was instantly drawn to Mr Thurston. Noticing their stares, he felt his cheeks warm.

"One can only lie if the truth is known," Mr Locke said. "At present, it is not."

"I know it's unpleasant, Mr Thurston. Personally, I detest asking these sorts of questions," Mr Heath said. "But we only ask them because we must. If Miss Mina *was* murdered—and I'm not suggesting for one moment she undoubtedly was—it's the duty of us all to identify her murderer and bring them to justice. Similarly, if Miss Mina was *not* murdered—and, again, I'm not suggesting she undoubtedly *wasn't*—it's our duty to remove the cloud of suspicion from the innocents involved." He took out a brown paper bag and offered it to Mr Thurston. "Cherry drop?"

"Thank you." Mr Thurston stuck his hand into the bag and, taking a couple, popped one into his mouth. He sucked on it as he gathered his thoughts and calmed his emotions. After a few moments, he apologised and explained in a subdued tone, "Things have been a little fraught for me recently."

Mr Locke noted the word choice. "Could you elaborate?"

Mr Thurston sat forward and, resting his elbows upon the script, toyed with the top corner of the first page. "The business with Mr Jerome, the ultimatum." He sucked the cherry drop some more and visibly swallowed. "I wish he'd never come here."

"If he returns prior to this evening's performance, please send word to Miss Rebecca Trent at the Bow Street Society," Mr Locke said. "We are keen to speak with him."

"Why? What could he tell you of Mina's death?" The tremor had returned to Mr Thurston's voice.

"His behaviour was the catalyst for Miss Ilbert's ultimatum," Mr Locke replied. "If our supposition is correct, and he was romantically involved with Miss Joanna Hightower, he may have coerced her into assisting him in orchestrating Miss Ilbert's demise. To either ensure he could continue to blackmail Mr Benton or to protect Miss Hightower from destitution, or both."

"He is a common blackmailer, not a murderer," Mr Thurston said, taken aback.

"Forgive me, I was unaware you knew him," Mr Locke sardonically retorted.

"I don't," Mr Thurston said in a higher pitch.

"Yet, you are certain he is not a murderer?" Mr Locke gently challenged.

Mr Thurston swallowed the remnants of the cherry drop. "I interrupted him when he was threatening Mr Benton at the stage door. He could've murdered Mr Benton then but didn't."

"Because you interrupted him," Mr Locke pointed out.

"Because he wanted Mr Benton's money, not his corpse," Mr Thurston snapped.

Mr Locke altered his approach. "You were arriving when you interrupted them?"

"No, I heard a commotion and opened the door to find Mr Jerome threatening Mr Benton," Mr Thurston replied.

Mr Locke glanced in the direction of the stage door. "You heard it from here?"

Mr Thurston put his hands in his lap and picked at his thumbnail. "No."

From experience at his own theatre, Mr Locke knew there were few reasons for a super master and prompter to be loitering around a stage door. Contemplating the layout of the *Crescent*'s backstage area, though, he conceded Mr Thurston could've been on his way to or from the dressing rooms or wardrobe department.

"Thank you, Mr Thurston." Mr Locke offered a disarming smile. "Two final questions, then we will allow you to resume your work."

Mr Thurston darted his gaze between them. "What are they?"

"First, did you implement the changes to your play which Miss Ilbert requested? Second, have you or Miss Kimberly submitted the play to the Lord Chamberlain for examination?"

"The answer to both is no." Mr Thurston picked up the script and stood.

"Why?" Mr Locke enquired.

"That is three questions," Mr Thurston pointed out.

"Forgive me, my mathematics is a little askew," Mr Locke wryly retorted. "Why did you not implement the changes?"

"I hadn't the time," Mr Thurston replied.

Mr Locke was struck by the contradiction between Mr Thurston's explanations but chose to hold his tongue on the matter. "Where might we find Mr Stone?"

"I don't know." Mr Thurston side-stepped past the Bow Streeters and muttered, "He's always disappearing these days."

Mr Locke watched him walk away, noting the two occasions he glanced back over his shoulder at them. Seeing his wife cross the stage from the auditorium's stairs, he glanced around for Claude. Finding him talking to a workman, he loudly cleared his throat to get his attention. When Claude looked his way, Mr Locke subtly gestured him over and pointed to the approaching Dr Locke.

"Miss Hightower is unwell at home," Dr Locke said once she'd reached them. "Miss Kimberly gave me her address, so I'm going there now."

"Would you like me to accompany you, darling?" Mr Locke enquired.

"No; I think Miss Hightower is likelier to open up if I'm alone," Dr Locke replied. "How are you feeling?" She cast a concerned glance over him.

"A little fatigued, but I am coping well," Mr Locke reassured.

"Perhaps Claude should take you home to rest," Dr Locke said.

A hint of a grimace touched Mr Locke's lips. "That shan't be necessary."

"I'll keep a close eye on him, doctor," Mr Heath added.

Dr Locke had been about to argue but felt reassured by the architect's words. "Thank you, Bertram." She looked to her husband. "I'll meet you at Bow Street later."

"I owe you a favour, old man," Mr Locke quietly said as Dr Locke walked away.

"Two free tickets to your triumphant return at the *Paddington Palladium* will suffice," Mr Heath said with a playful twinkle in his eyes.

Mr Locke smiled as they shook hands. "Consider it done."

* * *

Mr Sheldon Shepherd, senior partner of the *London & County Banking Company*, was in his late-forties and approximately five feet eight inches tall. Lean in build, he wore a tailored black frockcoat over matching trousers, plain dark-blue waistcoat, dark-blue tie, and white shirt with a starched collar. His broad chin hid his neck as his thick dark-brown eyebrows hid the top of his large, pale-green eyes. When he spoke, his voice had a naturally commanding tone to it. "What is the police's interest in the Bow Street Society's bank account?"

"We want a list of all its depositors and borrowers," Inspector Woolfe replied.

Mr Shephard's office had a high ceiling with an ornate plaster rose around the highly polished, unlit chandelier. Dark oak panels covered the walls, and a dark-green, thick-piled carpet covered the floor. The desk behind which Mr Shephard sat had been altered to stand taller than usual. The same alteration had also been made to his wing-backed leather chair. Similarly, the chairs in which Inspectors Woolfe and Conway sat had been altered to stand shorter than usual. The resulting effect was Mr

Shephard was held aloft as a metaphorical king, whilst his subjects were perpetually reminded of their lowly status.

"Mr Calvin has instructed the bank to refuse your request on privacy grounds," Mr Shephard replied. "Unless you have a persuasive counterargument, the bank will honour his wishes."

"Despite the request coming from the police?" Inspector Woolfe enquired.

"The only reputation of value within these walls is the bank's," Mr Shepherd replied.

"Miss Trent is putting the lives of ordinary people in danger," Inspector Woolfe said.

"That is your view, and you are entitled to it," Mr Shepherd dismissed.

Inspector Woolfe spoke over him, "A Society member was shot."

Mr Shepherd's head jerked back. "Shot?" He momentarily turned his head away. "Was it fatal?"

Inspector Woolfe adopted a challenging tone. *"No*, but that isn't the point."

"Did Miss Trent fire the shot?" Mr Shepherd enquired.

"No," Inspector Woolfe replied.

"Do you have *any* evidence Miss Trent is engaged in criminal activity?" Mr Shepherd enquired.

Spots of colour entered Inspector Woolfe's cheeks as his features tightened. "*No*, that's why I want the *list*—to investigate the backgrounds and reputations of the depositors and borrowers."

Mr Shepherd held his chair's armrests. "Inspector." He stood and nodded to Inspector Conway, "Inspectors." He walked around his desk to stand beside them. "The bank cannot disregard the wishes of a valued account holder without evidence or justification more substantial than your word." He indicated the door. "I'm sorry I couldn't be of more assistance."

Inspector Woolfe's shoulders slumped, and his lips pressed into a tight grimace, as he stood to tower over the banker. "You can't give us any help?"

"I'm afraid not," Mr Shepherd replied with an apologetic smile.

"What if we just asked questions?" Inspector Woolfe enquired.

"Questions?" Mr Shepherd enquired in return.

"About what's on the list," Inspector Woolfe replied.

Inspector Conway stood between them. To Inspector Woolfe, he said, "'E's already said 'e can't help us, mate."

"What sort of questions?" Mr Shepherd enquired.

Inspector Conway half-turned as he and Inspector Woolfe looked to the banker.

"If a particular name is listed, who deposits the most, who borrows the most, and so on," Inspector Woolfe replied.

"That's the same as 'im givin' us the list," Inspector Conway warned.

"No, it isn't," Inspector Woolfe snapped. Addressing Mr Shepherd, he continued, "You don't have to answer my questions or give more information than you want to. All I'm asking is you give us a few crumbs at least."

Inspector Conway frowned as he studied Mr Shepherd's face. He had no idea whether 'J. Pettifoot' had a connection to the Bow Street Society's account, but even if they didn't, Inspector Conway felt like a cad, still. There was no way he could be honest with Inspector Woolfe without endangering the positions of himself and others. Yet, it wasn't fair for this circumstance to be taken advantage of to manipulate him.

"You put forth an intriguing proposition, Inspector." Mr Shepherd's voice was softer. "Technically speaking, the bank would still be honouring Mr Calvin's wishes as his instruction was only to withhold the list. Very well," He indicated for them to be seated as he returned behind his desk to do the same. "I have the list here." He pulled across a file and, opening it, held it upright with its pages facing toward him. "What is your first question?"

"Thank you, Mr Shepherd!" Inspector Woolfe said, taking his seat again. "It's much appreciated." He took out his notebook and turned to a blank page. "First: Is a 'J. Pettifoot' listed as either a depositor or a borrower or both?"

Inspector Conway sat low in his chair and, resting his elbow upon its armrest, rubbed the underside of his chin as he stared at the file. His mind was throwing up all possible answers to Inspector Woolfe's question, and all possible approaches he could use to deter his friend from pursuing them further. He had no confidence in the success of any of them, since Inspector Woolfe shared his stubbornness.

Inspector Conway and Inspector Woolfe waited with bated breath as Mr Shepherd read the list.

"'J. Pettifoot' isn't listed," Mr Shepherd finally revealed.

Inspector Conway covered his mouth with his hand as he inwardly thanked God.

Inspector Woolfe did a double take. "What, not at all?"

"They aren't listed, Inspector," Mr Shepherd replied in a firmer tone.

Inspector Woolfe sat back in his chair with a heavy sigh and frustrated shake of his head. "Are there any Pettifoots listed?"

"No," Mr Shepherd replied.

Inspector Woolfe released another heavy sigh and, turning his head away, muttered, "I don't believe this."

Inspector Conway sat up straight and rested his hands in his lap. *Jones knew we'd find nothing*, he thought. The realisation made him feel angry, reassured, and guilty in equal measure. Shifting in his chair to face Inspector Woolfe, he enquired, "Do you still want to ask the other questions?"

Inspector Woolfe turned a stony expression to his friend. "I've not gone through all this for nothing." He looked to Mr Shepherd. "Who regularly puts money into the account?"

"Aside from Miss Trent?" Mr Shepherd enquired. At Inspector Woolfe's nod, he read the list again and replied, "Mr Percival Locke, Lady Katheryne Owston, Mr Gregory Elliott. They make monthly deposits into the account. On a more sporadic basis are Mr Joseph Maxwell, Mr Bertram Heath, Dr Rupert Alexander, and Mr Virgil Verity."

Inspector Woolfe noted the names. "Out of the monthly depositors, who deposits the most money?"

"Mr Locke," Mr Shepherd replied. "I draw the line at naming the amount, however."

"We don't need it for the time being." Inspector Woolfe put an asterisk next to Mr Locke's name. "Who regularly takes money out of the account?"

"Miss Trent and Mr Calvin are the only ones with the authority to make withdrawals," Mr Shepherd replied. "Mr Calvin rarely exercises his, however."

Inspector Woolfe noted this down. "Is there a set amount Miss Trent withdraws either monthly or weekly?"

Mr Shepherd read the amounts listed and shook his head. "No. The withdrawals vary in amount and regularity."

Inspector Woolfe leant forward. "There's nothing which looks like it could be her wages?"

Mr Shepherd read the list again. "Unless her wage amount fluctuates, it doesn't appear to be included in her withdrawals."

Inspector Woolfe frowned deeply, his eyebrows furrowed as he noted this down and mumbled to himself, "Which means she's getting paid some other way." He closed his notebook and slipped it into his pocket. "Thank you, Mr Shepherd." He stood and offered his hand. "You've been very helpful."

"Good." Mr Shepherd stood and shook Inspector Woolfe's hand. "I'm glad we were able to reach a suitable compromise." He shook Inspector Conway's hand. "Is there something else I may help you with?"

Inspector Woolfe smiled broadly, exposing his yellowed teeth. "Yeah; can you tell us if 'J. Pettifoot' has their own account here?"

Inspector Conway felt the pressure of apprehension return to his chest.

"Certainly. If you'd like to wait here, Inspectors, I'll ask one of our clerks to check for you," Mr Shepherd replied, returning the smile.

* * *

"Joanna isn't up to visitors," Mrs Hightower said. "She's frightfully tired. She cried herself to sleep last night, poor love." She gave a nervous smile. "She's too wrought by grief to speak to anyone, let alone a stranger." She pushed her hair behind her ears as she crossed the lounge and plumped a pillow from the sofa. "Maybe tomorrow, hm?" She put the pillow down and started on the next. "Actually, maybe the day after would be better." She put the second pillow down and put her hand on her hip. "Dear me, what day is it?" She held up the same hand. "No, I remember now." She continued her plumping. "Visit again in two or three days. We'll be back at the theatre, and everything will be as it should be."

Dr Locke watched the flustered Mrs Hightower closely.

The Hightowers' rooms on Great Queen Street were on the second floor of a respectable-looking townhouse. They comprised of the previously mentioned lounge, a small kitchen, and two bedrooms. The doors into the kitchen and one of the bedrooms were open. Through the latter, Dr Locke could see a neatly made double bed, presumably belonging to Mr and Mrs Hightower. If so, the second bedroom was Joanna's.

"As I said when I arrived, I'm a fully qualified medical doctor, Mrs Hightower," Dr Locke said. "If I could speak to and examine your daughter—"

"She isn't sick," Mrs Hightower curtly interrupted. "Only upset."

"I can prescribe a sleeping draught, but I need to examine her first."

Mrs Hightower stepped back from the sofa. "*Which* pillows *haven't* I plumped?"

"Mrs Hightower—"

Mrs Hightower turned fierce eyes upon her. "*Please*, doctor! *Stop* trying to *interfere*! *Me* and *Derek* don't *need* your help or anyone else's!" She abruptly turned her back and clapped her hands over her mouth.

Dr Locke's eyes turned cold as her mouth formed a hard line. Calmly rising to her feet, she strode over to Joanna's bedroom.

Mrs Hightower bolted after her. "*No*! You *mustn't*!"

Dr Locke turned the knob and pushed open the door.

The bedroom was empty.

Dr Locke lofted her eyebrow and looked to Mrs Hightower for an explanation. Yet, Mrs Hightower's face paled, and her lips trembled as she stared into the empty room. Realising she wouldn't get a response soon, Dr Locke entered the room and noted the absence of basic toiletries on the washstand. Specifically soap, flannel, and hairbrush. She opened the nearby drawers and found them to be empty. An inspection of the bed also confirmed it hadn't been slept in.

Dr Locke approached Mrs Hightower. "When did she leave?"

Mrs Hightower's damp eyes slid to Dr Locke. "The night Miss Ilbert died."

Dr Locke cast a final glance over the empty room and frowned. This didn't bode well for Joanna.

THIRTY-FIVE

Entering New Scotland Yard felt like taking a shot to the heart to Inspector Conway. Once a sanctuary from the violence and depravity he routinely encountered in his work, the building had become a hostile and forbidden territory. He'd never felt more of a pariah than when his fellow officers, many of whom he'd once considered friends, looked or walked away upon seeing him. He was certain escorting Dr Weeks to the black maria had tarnished his already fragile reputation further, despite Chief Inspector Jones also being present. To some, it was impossible to give the benefit of the doubt to the previously guilty. To these officers, he was no different to the villains they'd sent to Newgate.

He'd soon learnt keeping his head down and avoiding eye contact made the occasional, but necessary, visit bearable. Following this rule, he walked along the corridor to Chief Inspector Jones' office and knocked. In the few seconds it took his senior officer to bid him enter, he felt the glares at his back as keenly as if they were knives. He was relieved when he finally went inside.

Chief Inspector Jones sat at his desk with several documents and files spread out before him. Lifting his head, he looked from Inspector Conway to the door and back again. "Where is Inspector Woolfe?"

"Doctor's appointment."

Chief Inspector Jones held a document out to Inspector Conway. "This morning's report from Inspector Lee about the Mob Squad's ongoing surveillance into the Bow Street Society."

Inspector Conway took the document and immediately spotted his name. Reading the passage in full, he passed the document back. "I was tellin' Miss Trent and Miss Hicks about Weeks."

"Yes, and I will speak to Inspector Lee to clear up the matter, but this incident serves as a reminder of how closely the Bow Street Society is being scrutinised."

"I never forgot."

Chief Inspector Jones gave a slight frown. "Neither had I, but I may have underestimated the resources Inspector Lee is pouring into these surveillance activities of his." He set the document aside and invited Inspector Conway to sit. "Speaking of which, I know you weren't happy about accompanying Inspector Woolfe to the bank."

"I don't like spyin' on my mates."

"That isn't why I sent you, John."

Inspector Conway was taken aback. "It wasn't?"

"No."

"What was it for, then?"

"I strongly suspected Mr Calvin would instruct the bank to refuse Inspector Woolfe's request, but it was imperative he be shown the list regardless. By sending two detective inspectors instead of one, I hoped the bank would recognise the seriousness of the request and grant it."

"'Imperative' because you wanted Caleb to find out there's no record of J. Pettifoot at the bank?" Inspector Conway sardonically enquired. "You could of let me in on the secret."

"There was no time." Chief Inspector Jones' tone and demeanour held an openness which convinced Inspector Conway of his sincerity. "What else did you discover from the list?"

"We never got to see the list." Inspector Conway settled back in his chair. "Mr Shepherd, a senior partner at the bank, would only agree to answerin' questions about it." He scratched his cheek. "'E told us Mr Locke deposits the most money, and 'e, and some others, put money in often. 'E also told us only Miss Trent and Mr Calvin can take money out."

"A condition I requested be put in place when she and Mr Calvin opened the account," Chief Inspector Jones thought aloud. "Anything else?"

"Miss Trent don't take her wages from the account, but only Caleb was in the dark about that before today." Inspector Conway rubbed and stretched his neck. "Caleb said 'e'd send you a full report." He lowered his hand. "'E still wants to find J. Pettifoot, but 'e didn't say how 'e was gonna go about it."

Chief Inspector Jones settled back in his chair and stroked his moustache as he analysed the situation in his mind. Eventually, he sat forward, again, and said in a definitive tone, "Make sure he sends me reports about the visit to the bank and whatever else he uncovers about the Bow Street Society. Between those reports and Inspector Lee's, I'll be able to keep a firm grip on where their respective investigations are at."

"They're not gonna give up, Richard," Inspector Conway gently warned.

"And nor do I expect them to, for they wouldn't have come as far as they have in their careers if they weren't doggedly determined policemen. Nevertheless, determination doesn't always guarantee results. Lines of inquiry can lead nowhere, and cases can quickly reach a dead end. When both eventually happen in Inspectors Woolfe and Lee's Bow Street Society investigations, they'll have little evidence upon which to argue an extension of the authority delegated to them to pursue the matter. Then, finally, the threat they pose to us all will be removed."

Inspector Conway gave a weak smile. "You make it sound so simple."

"It is, but only if fate, luck, God, and any other deity and superstition you'd care to name is on our side." Chief Inspector Jones' expression was sombre. "Which they have been—so far. We both know how quickly and unexpectedly it can change."

Inspector Conway lowered his head as he thought of Dr Weeks. "Yeah. We do."

* * *

Noah naked in the bedroom doorway. Her bent over the sofa wearing only a robe. His firmness against her behind. His hand slipping into her robe and his fingers playing with her nipple. The feel of him inside her, Miss Hicks took in a deep, shuddering breath at the memory. Standing in the lounge of Dr Weeks' rooms, she looked around at the many boxes and piled possessions which littered the furniture and floor. *Percy stood in the doorway. The hurt on his face. The pain in his voice*, she felt her heart clench in grief and guilt.

"Are you okay, lass?" Mr Snyder's voice enquired, pulling her from her thoughts.

"Not really." Miss Hicks offered him a feeble smile. "But I'll survive."

Mr Snyder was loading a hired horsedrawn van with Miss Hicks and Dr Weeks' smaller possessions and had come back inside for another batch to take downstairs.

"Miss Trent don't mean it when she says she wants you out, you know." Mr Snyder picked up a box.

"Don't she?" Miss Hicks enquired, sadly.

"No. It's just her anger talkin'." Mr Snyder gave a reassuring smile. "Give her time, and she'll come 'round." He carried the box to the door. "The van's full after this one, so I'll take it to Bow Street, unload it, and come back."

"Thank you, Sam." Miss Hicks gestured to the chaos. "I'll keep sorting this lot."

"Right-o." Mr Snyder carried the box downstairs and, a few moments later, Miss Hicks heard him geeing up the horses outside. Going to the window, she watched him drive the van up the street and around the corner.

"Alone at last," a familiar voice said.

Miss Hicks stilled when she turned and saw Noah O'Hannigan leaning sideways against the doorframe. She stared at him for several moments, wondering if he was an hallucination and how he could have the audacity to come back if he wasn't.

"Ain't you goin' to say somet'ing?"

Miss Hicks slowly walked over to him and suddenly slapped him across the face. "You robbed me, you bastard!"

Mr O'Hannigan kept his head half-turned as he held his cheek and looked sideways at her.

"And left me to face my Perce's pain and hatred alone!" Miss Hicks' eyes were damp. "Now he's in Bedlam, and I've got to move in with Becky at Bow Street, but only until I find sumin' else because she's as disgusted with me as I am!" She slapped his chest. "Where've you *been*, Noah?!"

Mr O'Hannigan let her get a few slaps in before gripping her shoulders and pushing her back against the wall. Pressing his body against hers, he released her shoulders to slide his arms around her waist. "Here and there. T'inkin' about you."

Miss Hicks put her hands on his chest. "I'm *done* with you, do you hear?!"

Mr O'Hannigan grinned. "Are you sure?"

"Yes." Miss Hicks felt her resolve weakening the longer she looked into his eyes.

Mr O'Hannigan lifted her into his arms and, carrying her over to the sofa, laid her down upon it. Standing over her as he loosened and removed his belt, he lay over her as he dropped the belt onto the floor. Miss Hicks' breath hitched in her throat as she felt him against her. When his lips met hers, she closed her eyes, and the last of her resolve vanished in the heat of lust and excitement. Returning his deep and passionate kiss, she broke it to whisper, "I want you, Noah, but I don't love you."

"Good enough for me." Mr O'Hannigan grinned, unfastening his trousers.

She knew it was wrong. She knew it was heartless of her to take him back when her poor Perce was going through goodness knows what in Bedlam, but a part of her had missed the intimacy Noah had given her. Her body had missed him, too.

* * *

"I hope this is important, Inspector," Dr Colbert declared upon entering his office.

Inspector Woolfe noted Dr Colbert's dishevelled clothes, dark circles under his eyes, and grey tinge to his complexion. There was also visible tension in Dr Colbert's neck, shoulders, and arms as he strode over to his desk, stopped, turned to Inspector Woolfe, and closed the distance between them.

"Because I've left the bedside of a very sick man to be here," Dr Colbert added.

"I won't keep you longer than I have to, doctor." Inspector Woolfe coughed, cleared his throat, and coughed again. "I need your help."

Dr Colbert strode past him toward the door. "If you're here for more medicine, speak to my colleague, Dr McWilliams."

Inspector Woolfe reached the door in a couple of strides and stood before it, thereby blocking Dr Colbert's retreat. "I'm not. I need you to search Miss Trent's office."

"I beg your pardon?" Dr Colbert momentarily stared at him, dumbfounded, before his features twisted into a scowl, and he threw his arm out to point beyond Inspector Woolfe. "I have a patient in my care who could *die* at any moment, and you want me to *abandon* him to carry out an errand you could do yourself?"

Inspector Woolfe narrowed his eyes. "You know I can't get near, and I didn't say you had to do it now, did I?"

Dr Colbert's head slowly swivelled as he glanced around. Turning and walking away from Inspector Woolfe, he put one hand on his hip whilst the other dry-washed his face. Releasing a heavy sigh, he turned his head sideways to address him over his shoulder. "What would you like me to search for?"

"J. Pettifoot's address."

Dr Colbert turned to face him. "Were you unsuccessful at the bank?"

"They had no record of J. Pettifoot."

"Perhaps they have no connection to the Bow Street Society?"

"They put the advertisements in the *Gaslight Gazette* for the Society's clerk and membership applications."

"Isn't it possible J. Pettifoot paid for the advertisement as a favour to Miss Trent's employer?"

Inspector Woolfe furrowed his brow. "Yeah, but I'm not convinced."

"If I were caught searching Miss Trent's office, I would risk losing my membership."

"You won't get caught."

"I don't see how I couldn't be, especially if Miss Trent is at home."

"I'm going to help you."

Dr Colbert's brows lofted in unison. "How?"

"I want you to go there and ask her to add a second address to your record so she can contact you if you're not in London. Do you have an address like that you can use?"

Dr Colbert slid the fingers of his right hand into his hair and held his head. "Yes, my sister's house in Devon, I suppose. We sometimes holiday there."

Inspector Woolfe gave a subtle nod. "You've got to insist she writes it on the record when you're there. Tell her you don't want your sister's address on a scrap of paper, or in a notebook."

Dr Colbert squinted as his tired mind fought to memorise what he was being told.

"I'll visit the Society ten minutes or so after you've arrived. Hopefully, she'll have unlocked the filing cabinet by then, and I can keep her talking in the hallway whilst you search the drawers for Pettifoot's address."

"And what should I do with the address if I find it?"

"Memorise it and put the file back *exactly* where you found it."

Dr Colbert dry washed his face again, this time with both hands. Afterward, he allowed his arms to fall with a slap of his hands against his sides. "I'll do as you ask." He returned to the door. "I'll send word when I'm available."

"Thank you, doctor."

"You're welcome, Inspector." Dr Colbert opened the door.

"Give my best to Dr Weeks, will you?"

Dr Colbert gave a soft smile which failed to reach his eyes. "I will. Goodbye."

* * *

"This can't happen again." Miss Hicks hurriedly straightened her clothes.

"But it will," Mr O'Hannigan fastened his trousers and put on his belt. "You know it, and I know it."

"Noah, I—" Miss Hicks looked sharply to the window as she heard the wheels of the van against the cobblestones. "Mr Snyder's back!" She pulled Mr O'Hannigan to his feet and pushed him toward the door. "Use the back way."

"I'll see you tonight, lass." Mr O'Hannigan stole a kiss.

"Remember: the back of the Society's house," Miss Hicks reminded him.

"I'll be there." Mr O'Hannigan grinned and hurried downstairs and out of sight.

Miss Hicks was already wishing it was tonight when she straightened the cushions on the sofa and checked for any telltale stains or marks. Finding none, she knelt beside a box and pretended to be going through its contents as she heard the door to the street open and close.

"Only me!" Mr Snyder called, appearing in the doorway a few moments later. Upon seeing little progress, he observed with an amused twinkle in his eyes, "You're just like my Louise when she's sortin' the 'ouse. She starts, wantin' to break eggs with sticks, but a photograph or a book or some jewellery gets her thinkin' about happy memories and, before you know it, an 'our's gone, and she's done nothin'." He chuckled softly. "Mind you, none of the family likes gettin' rid."

Miss Hicks offered a feeble smile. "Neither does Percy." She stood. "But you sayin' about jewellery's reminded me I've got a box of it in the bedroom." She went into the bedroom, relieved to be out of Mr Snyder's sight. Her guilty conscience had her convinced he could see or smell the adultery on her. Releasing a soft exhale, she cast a glance over the bed. Her mind immediately conjured up the last night she'd spent in it with Noah. She gave a swift shake of her head to dismiss the lust-fuelled thoughts and approached her dressing table.

The moment she picked up her jewellery box and opened it, though, all erotic thoughts vanished. Where there used to be a pile of gold, silver, and pearl necklaces, chokers, and bracelets was an empty compartment. Pulling out the drawer reserved for the rings, she found this had also been pilfered, too. She remembered the box Noah had stolen money from and felt sick. *He come back and stole my jewellery*, she thought. Her blood ran cold as another realisation hit her: *And he come back today to steal more.*

She sat on the bed, the empty jewellery box in her hands, and cried.

THIRTY-SIX

The chapel at Hampstead Public School dated back to medieval times, at Mr Virgil Verity's educated guess. Its stained-glass windows, rendered dull by the overcast sky, depicted the Holy Mother, Jesus Christ, and other biblical imagery. The brass candelabras mounted upon the stone pillars lining the chapel's north and south aisles provided a good amount of light, but only the illusion of warmth. Sitting on the front lefthand pew before the altar, Mr Verity felt the cold at his back as the wind howled beneath the chapel's heavy oak doors.

Soon to be entering his sixty-first year, Mr Verity had a head of thick silver hair and an off-white beard and moustache which were equally voluminous. Yet, his once smooth and pink complexion had turned grey and wrinkled over the years. His spine had also weakened, causing him to bend as he walked and slouched as he sat. Like many his age, he also suffered from arthritic joints, particularly in his fingers and wrists. His attire consisted of an ankle-length black woollen overcoat, dark-blue woollen scarf, and fitted black leather gloves.

"Following two cups of tea and thirty minutes of persuasion, Mrs Hightower finally admitted her daughter had run away with Mr Jack Jerome, possibly to Birmingham," Dr Locke said. Sitting beside Mr Verity, she'd also guarded against the cold with a dark-burgundy, ankle-length coat and dark-brown leather gloves. "Mrs Hightower and her husband discovered their daughter's bedroom was empty the morning after Miss Ilbert's death."

"Was there a note?" Mr Verity enquired in a strong northeast of England accent.

Dr Locke gave him an envelope from her coat pocket.

Removing and unfolding the note, Mr Verity read:

Darling Mother and Father,

> Jack and I are madly in love but know you do not approve, so we have run away to be together. Underneath it all, he is a good man, and we hope, one day, you will be happy for us. Until then, please do not try to find us. I will write from time to time to let you know how I am doing but, for now, this is goodbye.
> My love always, Joanna.

"Love." Mr Verity returned the note to Dr Locke. "It makes fools of us all."

"Indeed." Dr Locke thought of the night her husband slipped into her bedroom after breaking into her parents' house. They would've thought her foolish for embracing the handsome criminal and would probably think her foolish now for enduring his addiction.

Hearing the door open, Mr Verity and Dr Locke looked over their shoulders in unison and felt a blast of cold air against their faces. Seeing a figure enter and hearing the door close immediately after, they watched the newcomer walk forward into the candlelight.

He was an adult male in his early sixties with salt-and-pepper bushy whiskers, receding, wavy hair of the same colour, and cheeks reddened by the cold. He wore a black cassock with white collar underneath an ankle-length black coat and scuffed shoes. The heels of which tapped loudly against the flagstones as he strode down the nave's central aisle toward the Bow Streeters.

"Good afternoon, Mr Verity, Dr Locke. I'm Reverend Ananias Mullins," the clergyman said as he reached them. "I understand from Mr Rogers you have a few questions for me."

Mr Verity recalled Mr Jeconiah Rogers, the school's headmaster, from his last visit when he and Miss Dexter had checked on the welfare of Mr Dominic Waller. Wondering how the man was, Mr Verity decided to enquire after him at the Bow Streeters' meeting with Mr Rogers later today. For now, though, he turned his attention to the matter at hand. "The Bow Street Society is working on behalf of Mr Aaron Willis, the former chief electric man at the *Crescent Theatre* on the Strand. Miss Mina Ilbert, the theatre's manager, died the other night."

"Yes. I heard," Reverend Ananias said in a cool tone. "The news swept through the school like cholera."

"You wrote a letter of complaint, accusing Miss Ilbert of corrupting the boys at the school," Dr Locke said. "And called upon her at the theatre to accuse her of the same."

Reverend Ananias lifted his chin. "I stand by my words."

"You called her a 'vile harlot' before witnesses," Dr Locke pointed out.

"An appropriate form of address for one like her," Reverend Ananias said.

Dr Locke's eyes hardened. "She was an actress, Reverend; a hard-working and dedicated practitioner of the arts who delighted audiences through her performances. She was utterly undeserving of your contempt and abuse."

"For the lips of a harlot are like a honeycomb dropping, and her throat is smoother than oil," Reverend Ananias quoted, projecting his voice. "*All* actresses are harlots, doctor, for *all* actresses speak through honeycomb lips. She, like many a harlot before her, has met an end as bitter as wormwood, and as sharp as a two-edged sword. She shall be judged, and she shall be found to be *wicked*, and God will by no means clear the guilty, as he that committeth sin is of the devil; for the devil sinneth from the beginning. If we confess our sins, He is faithful and just to forgive us our sins, and to cleanse us from all unrighteousness. *She* not only refused to confess her sins but continued to deceive and corrupt others to hide her wickedness. There is no hiding from God, doctor. It's my belief her death, and specifically its violent nature, was His way of removing the devil from the innocent hearts and minds of these young men."

"For if you forgive other people when they sin against you, your heavenly Father will also forgive you. But if you do not forgive others their sins, your Father will not forgive your sins," Mr Verity quoted, drawing Reverend Ananias' attention to him. "And if we say that we have no sin, we deceive ourselves, and the truth is not in us."

Humbled, Reverend Ananias gave a small nod. "You know the Bible well, sir."

"I was going to follow my Da into the church but took up the chalk instead," Mr Verity explained. "It's commendable; you wanting to protect these bairns, but Miss Ilbert didn't commit the sin you've accused her of."

"Your capacity to forgive is commendable, sir," Reverend Ananias said. "But as I said before: I stand by my words."

"Did you murder her?" Dr Locked coldly enquired.

"No," Reverend Ananias firmly replied.

"Not even to 'remove the devil from the innocent hearts and minds' of the young men at this school?" Dr Locke challenged.

"Unlike Miss Ilbert, I obey the Ten Commandments," Reverend Ananias dismissed.

"And yet, you have borne false witness against your neighbour," Dr Locke retorted. "Good day, Reverend."

* * *

"Mina Ilbert was a typical theatre manager; she knew what she wanted, and she wanted it yesterday," Mr Stanley Akers said as he exchanged one paintbrush for another.

In his early fifties, he was approximately five feet eleven inches tall, square-shouldered, and leanly built. Half-moon shaped brown eyes complemented his neat, dark-brown moustache, curved eyebrows, and combed hair. His attire consisted of a white shirt with the sleeves rolled up to his elbows, dark-brown trousers and waistcoat, and green tie under a paint-stained cotton apron tied around his neck and waist.

"Up a few inches!" Mr Akers called.

A moment later, the scenery he was working on lifted the desired amount. Painted upon canvas attached to a vertical wooden frame approximately forty feet wide and twenty-five feet high, the scenery was lifted and lowered through a cut in the floor using an elaborate rope-and-pulley system. The system was operated by a small army of Mr Akers' assistants beneath the raised platform upon which he, Mr Heath, Mr Locke, and Claude stood. This entire apparatus, coupled with innumerable work benches for the construction and decoration of three-dimensional scenery elements, meant Mr Akers' studio had to be housed within a former warehouse.

"I admired her tenacity," Mr Akers continued as he leant in close to the canvas and touched up the shadow under a branch. "There are not many women theatre managers."

Feeling fatigued, Mr Locke put half his weight upon his walking cane, and the other half against Claude who he discreetly leant against. "Mr Ronald Stone informed me you had argued with Miss Ilbert during a technical rehearsal the night prior to her death."

"We had a disagreement; she'd introduced electrical lighting into the auditorium, and it proved unflattering to my art." Mr Akers walked along the platform to touch up another part of the woodland scene. "Previously, I could leave a piece of scenery hanging for months at a time, and no one would be any the wiser, because the gas light hid most of the wear and tear. The so-called 'modern' lighting shows up every scratch, every tear, and every patch of faded colour, however."

"I have read of its unpopularity amongst scenery painters," Mr Locke said. "As chief scene painter at the *Crescent*, and numerous other West End theatres, your opinion must have carried some weight with Miss Ilbert."

"It did." Mr Akers returned to his previous spot. "Lower it a few inches!"

A moment later, the canvas lowered the desired amount.

"I knew Mina would come around to my way of thinking, so I delayed painting the new scene," Mr Akers went on, addressing Mr Locke.

"And did she?" Mr Locke enquired.

"No." Mr Akers switched paintbrushes and paint. "She proposed a compromise: dimmers."

"'Dimmers?'" Mr Locke repeated.

"They are devices which introduce resistance into an electrical circuit to allow lighting levels to be varied," Mr Heath explained.

"Thank you," Mr Locke said.

"You are *most* welcome," Mr Heath said.

"Mina proposed dimmers to allow the electrical lighting to be altered to six different levels," Mr Akers said as he added another coat of paint to the trunk of a large oak tree. "I was initially sceptical about their effectiveness but was persuaded when I saw them in operation at another theatre."

"Mr Akers, would it be possible for me to observe how the mechanism works from underneath the platform?" Mr Heath enquired, his eyes bright with excitement.

"Yes but don't obstruct or interfere with my assistants' work," Mr Akers replied.

"I shan't!" Mr Heath practically bounded down the steps. "You have my word!"

"Were you at the *Crescent* when Miss Ilbert died?" Mr Locke enquired.

"No, I was at the *Royal Opera House* overseeing the scenery changeover," Mr Akers replied. He took a few backward steps, cast an appraising glance over the scene, and walked to its far end to add another coat of paint to a second oak tree. "I heard of her death from Miss Kimberly the next morning. I was scheduled to have another technical rehearsal with Mina in the evening but, naturally, it was cancelled and rescheduled for tonight." He switched to a different paintbrush and paint. "Up a foot!"

The canvas swiftly lifted the desired amount, and Mr Akers painted daffodils into the scene's grass. "I was surprised when Miss Kimberly said she was the new manager."

"Why?" Mr Locke enquired.

"Mr Stone told me the *Crescent* would soon be under new management, but I assumed he was referring to himself," Mr Akers replied.

Mr Locke shifted his weight from one foot to the other as they started to ache. "When did he tell you this?"

Mr Akers withdrew the paintbrush from the canvas and, lowering his head, fell silent as he searched his memory. "Let me see now…" He went through in his mind his schedule for the past few days. "It was after the technical rehearsal." He lifted his head and met Mr Locke's gaze. "You know, I hadn't connected the two until now." He continued painting, "The mind works in mysterious ways, doesn't it?"

"It certainly does." Mr Locke watched Mr Akers closely as he enquired, "Were you aware Miss Ilbert was electrocuted because the metal plate she stood upon during her performance was connected to the mains electricity supply and not a battery as intended?"

Mr Akers stood bolt upright. "No." He gave a slight grimace. "That's horrific."

"As chief scene painter, did you have access to the battery?"

"Yes, but you don't think *I* had anything to do with it, do you?" He tossed his paintbrush into the pot. "Mina and I disagreed about the lighting, but I wouldn't have *murdered* her over it." He retrieved his paintbrush. "Aside from the idea being absolutely abhorrent to me, it would've been very bad for business."

THIRTY-SEVEN

Inspector Lee stroked his arm and imagined it was Mr Elliott's as he watched the solicitor cross-examine Mr Paul Quinton, the brother of the alleged assault victim, Mr Lucas Quinton. Sitting in the front row of the court room's public gallery balcony, Inspector Lee was disappointed he couldn't get any closer. The memory of being so close to Mr Elliott in the carriage and being pushed away, aroused and hurt him in equal measure. He'd known Mr Elliott's affection couldn't be bought as easily as Stephen's, but he'd hoped Mr Elliott would've been honest with himself. There was an unmistakeable energy between them; he'd felt it every time he was allowed to be close, but Mr Elliott had stubbornly denied it. Clearly, the desire to protect his reputation was greater than his carnal one, which was a shame.

"You were in the back parlour when Mr Atteberry allegedly assaulted Mr Lucas Quinton in Mr Quinton's shop, correct?" Mr Elliott enquired.

"Yes," Mr Paul Quinton replied.

"Was the door between the back parlour and the shop open or closed?"

"Sorry?"

"Was the door between the back parlour and the shop open or closed?"

"Objection, Your Honour," the prosecutor said, addressing the judge as he stood. "What is the relevance of this question?"

"I'm merely trying to establish how much the witness could hear of the alleged assault, Your Honour," Mr Elliott explained.

"I'll allow it," the judge ruled. "Please, answer the question, Mr Quinton."

Mr Paul Quinton glanced at his brother in the public gallery.

"Mr Quinton," the judge urged.

"Closed," Mr Paul Quinton said. "It-it was closed."

"What did you hear?" Mr Elliott enquired.

"I heard Mr Atteberry threaten my brother."

"Anything else?"

"I heard my brother yell for help."

"What did you do when you heard his yell for help?"

"I went into the shop and found him lying on the floor."

"Did you see Mr Atteberry in the shop?"

Mr Paul Quinton glanced at his brother in the public gallery again. "Y-yes."

"Whereabouts in the shop was Mr Atteberry?" Mr Elliott enquired.

"He... he was standing over my brother."

Mr Elliott retrieved a typed document from his table. "According to your sworn, written statement, Mr Quinton, you saw Mr Atteberry run out of the shop as you entered it from the back parlour."

"Y-yes, that's right," Mr Paul Quinton said. "He run out when he saw me. A-after I saw him standing over my brother."

"According to the testimony of Mr Atteberry's apprentice, Master Joshua Banks, already heard by this court, Mr Atteberry was out of his shop for only three minutes," Mr Elliott said. "Furthermore, Master Banks witnessed your brother follow Mr Atteberry into Mr Atteberry's shop immediately after Mr Atteberry had left your brother's. How then could you have witnessed Mr Atteberry standing over your brother lying on the floor of his shop immediately after the alleged assault took place?"

"Banks is lying," Mr Paul Quinton replied.

"Are you close to your brother?"

"Yes, I'd say so."

"Are you loyal to your brother?"

"Very."

"No further questions, Your Honour." Mr Elliott returned to his seat.

Inspector Lee considered his plan of action. He needed to get Mr Elliott alone again but doubted the solicitor would agree to another carriage ride. Realising Mr Elliott was probably unaware of Dr Weeks' admission to Bedlam due to the solicitor being preoccupied with the court case, Inspector Lee smiled. Mr Elliott's reaction was always predictable when it came to the Bow Street Society and its members.

* * *

Mr Jeconiah Rogers was older than Mr Verity by seven years, but his posture was perfect by comparison. Unlike Mr Verity, though, his curly, light-grey hair and sideburns were thinning, and his grey skin appeared to be stretched over his skull. His blue eyes also appeared small within their deep-set sockets, and his thin lips held a perpetual sneer even when at rest. His attire consisted of a white shirt under a dark-grey suit, waistcoat, and tie. Worn over everything was a black robe denoting his elevated position.

"Whilst there can be no doubt Reverend Ananias is fanatical and uncompromising in his faith, he also can't be seriously considered as a murderer for the same reason," Mr Rogers said. "The sanctity of his immortal soul is, above all else, the most important thing to him."

"Do you share his beliefs about Miss Ilbert?" Dr Locke enquired.

"Of course," Mr Rogers replied. "But I'm also a pragmatist. As the saying goes: sunt pueri pueri, pueri puerilia tractant."

"Boys are boys, and boys will act like boys," Mr Verity translated the Latin aloud.

"If they want to become besotted with an 'actress,' they will, and there's little to be done about it," Mr Rogers continued. "Aside from punishing the indiscretions brought about by such an obsession, such as leaving school grounds when prohibited from doing so."

Mr Verity flinched as he recalled dealing out such 'punishments.' He despised the use of the cane when he was a schoolmaster and avoided it as much as possible. Unfortunately, there had been the rare occasion when a pupil's indiscretion had been so public, he'd had no choice but to cane him or risk being dismissed from his position. In those incidences, he'd dealt only one or two blows, but he was ashamed of each one to this day.

"How is Mr Waller, by the way?" Mr Verity enquired.

"Doing rather well, I hear," Mr Rogers replied. "He is now living with an uncle somewhere on the coast."

"Good," Mr Verity said, genuinely pleased.

The office which Mr Verity, Dr Locke, and Mr Rogers were in was of a considerable size with a vaulted stone ceiling and dark-oak panelling covering its walls. On the left-hand side of the room was an impressive stone fireplace with a traditional log fire burning within it. The portrait of a benevolent-looking middle-aged man in black robes hung from its wide chimney breast. On the right-hand side of the room were several bookcases and a grandfather clock. Opposite the only door was a pair of dual-latticed arched windows with Mr Rogers' desk in front. The Bow Streeters stood on one side of the fireplace whilst Mr Rogers was on the other.

A knock sounded as a natural silence descended between the trio.

"There's Master Norton now," Mr Rogers said. "*Enter*!"

A boy with short, dark-brown hair parted at the side and hazel eyes sheepishly entered. Approximately four feet nine inches tall, he was lean in build and was attired in the school's uniform. This consisted of light-grey trousers, black tailcoat, double-breasted waistcoat, and tie, and white shirt with starched Eton collar.

"Come here, boy." Mr Rogers pointed to the rug before the fire.

The boy kept his head low as he crossed the room and stood between Mr Rogers, Mr Verity, and Dr Locke.

"What is this?" Mr Rogers pointed to a black armband the boy was wearing.

"An armband, sir," the boy replied.

"Do not be insolent," Mr Rogers warned. "Why are you wearing it?"

"Out of respect for Miss Ilbert, sir," the boy replied.

"Do not be ridiculous. Remove it at once," Mr Rogers ordered.

"But everyone is wearing one, sir," the boy insisted.

"Do *not* be insolent, *boy*," Mr Rogers warned.

"Yes, sir…" The boy removed the armband and put it into his pocket.

"This is Mr Verity and Dr Locke from the Bow Street Society." Mr Rogers indicated the Bow Streeters. "They are going to ask you some questions, and you are to answer them truthfully and in full. Do you understand?"

"Yes, sir," the boy mumbled.

"Granville," Dr Locke began. "May I call you Granville?"

Master Norton nodded. "Yes, doctor."

"Granville." Dr Locke offered him a reassuring smile. "We found several letters, written by you, amongst Miss Ilbert's possessions. Were you very fond of her?"

Master Norton gave a worried, sideways glance at Mr Rogers. "I loved her, doctor."

"Bah!" Mr Rogers exclaimed.

"He is only following your instructions," Dr Locke pointed out. "Telling the truth."

Mr Rogers pursed his lips, unamused.

"Please, continue, Granville," Dr Locke encouraged.

"I loved her, but she didn't ever say she loved me," Master Norton said. "I didn't mind, though, because I knew she loved someone else, and all I wanted was for her to be happy, and he made her happy."

"Who?" Mr Verity interjected.

"Mr Benton, sir," Master Norton replied. "I overheard him proposing to her again. She said no, but she always said no. I think she was testing him, sir, which is a good idea in the theatre business because you never know what someone wants, do you?"

"No, you don't," Dr Locke replied.

Master Norton's eyes widened. "Wait a minute. 'Locke.' You're not married to the Great Locke, are you?"

"I am," Dr Locke replied.

Master Norton's eyes widened further. "*Really*?!"

"Focus, boy," Mr Rogers warned.

"But-but, sir, the *Great Locke*, sir!" Master Norton excitedly cried.

"I'm familiar with his work," Mr Rogers said. "But we are not discussing him."

"Oh… no… sorry, sir," Master Norton said, sheepishly lowering his head.

"He'll be delighted to hear you think so highly of him," Dr Locke reassured.

Master Norton's head shot up, and he smiled from ear to ear.

"You said you overheard Mr Benton and Miss Ilbert talking. Do you often sneak into the theatre?" Mr Verity enquired.

Master Norton's smile vanished, and he turned sheepish again. "Yes, sir."

"You could be arrested for that, boy," Mr Rogers said.

"I didn't mean any harm by it, sir," Master Norton insisted. "I just wanted to see Miss Ilbert, talk to her about my letters. Mostly I'd hide and watch everyone working backstage, though. It's very interesting, sir."

"Eavesdropping is highly disrespectful, boy," Mr Rogers warned. "I hope you do not eavesdrop around the school."

Master Norton cast a sideways glance at Dr Locke and replied without conviction, "No, sir."

Mr Rogers hummed, unconvinced, and made a mental note to keep a closer eye on Master Norton from hence forth.

"Was there anybody at the theatre who wanted Miss Ilbert dead?" Mr Verity enquired.

"No, sir. Everyone loved her," Master Norton swiftly replied.

Recalling the alleged argument between Miss Ilbert and Mr Akers, Dr Locke enquired, "Did you witness any trouble at the theatre, Granville?"

Master Norton stepped forward and excitedly replied, "I saw Miss Ilbert giving a young woman a good talking to, and a man threatening Mr Benton at the stage door."

"Do you know the names of the young woman and man?" Dr Locke enquired.

"No, doctor. I think the young woman works at the theatre, though. The man had a strange accent; I'd never heard anything like it in my life. It was like yours, sir," he looked to Mr Verity, "but different."

"What did the man say to Mr Benton?" Dr Locke enquired.

"I think the strange-sounding man wanted money from Mr Benton, but Mr Benton refused, and the strange-sounding man *punched* Mr Benton in the jaw!" Master Norton exclaimed.

Dr Locke's eyes widened a fraction at the sudden noise.

"Then I… I ran away," Master Norton quietly admitted. "I was too frightened to stay."

"Let this be a warning to you about eavesdropping, boy," Mr Rogers said. "Rarely is it a good thing."

Master Norton mumbled, "Yes, sir."

* * *

"My commiserations."

Mr Elliott halted when he heard Inspector Lee's voice behind him.

"I fully expected you to win."

Mr Elliott stole himself before facing him. "I have somewhere to be, Inspector."

Inspector Lee stepped aside to allow a group of public gallery spectators to pass them. Standing on the pavement outside the Old Bailey, Inspector Lee was conscious of the dark clouds overheard which threatened an imminent downpour. He wasn't about to abandon this opportunity, however. "I know you put little value in my opinion but, as a police officer, I believe your client was innocent, and Mr Quinton and his brother colluded to remove their nearest and greatest competitor."

"I shan't discuss this with you." Mr Elliott turned to walk away. "Good day."

"Have you heard?"

Mr Elliott halted, again. He knew it was a ploy to keep him there, but his curiosity nonetheless got the better of him. "Have I heard what?"

"Dr Weeks has been admitted to Bedlam, suffering from alcoholic insanity."

Mr Elliott turned to face him. "Under whose authority?"

"Detective Chief Inspector Richard Jones instigated the process." Inspector Lee moved closer and lowered his voice. "My driver can take us to New Scotland Yard."

Mr Elliott's suspicions were immediately aroused. "And there's the truth of it."

"I don't know what you mean," Inspector Lee said in mock indignation.

Mr Elliott lowered his voice. "You're so desperate to get me alone again, you'll resort to libelling an innocent man."

Inspector Lee moved in closer. "It's true I want to be alone with you."

Mr Elliott took a step back.

"But what I said about Dr Weeks is true," Inspector Lee added.

Mr Elliott recalled Inspector Lee's closeness and words in the carriage and imagined the same happening again if he agreed to be driven to New Scotland Yard. His stomach clenched at the thought, but only because he felt the attraction despite his better judgement. He despised Inspector Lee's behaviour and was staunchly against everything he represented, but the pull was there, nonetheless. Conflicting thoughts and emotions were just some of the reasons he'd chosen a life of self-imposed celibacy.

"Ask Miss Trent," Inspector Lee continued. "Inspector Conway called upon her and Miss Hicks to give them the news."

Mr Elliott kept his expression stoic despite his inner turmoil. "If you're lying—"

"May you and God strike me down." Inspector Lee smirked.

Mr Elliott's gaze cooled. "I'll encourage Dr Weeks to sue you."

"You'll have to get him sober first." Inspector Lee's smile grew as he walked away.

Mr Elliott glared after him and thought, *Unbelievable.*

THIRTY-EIGHT

Laughter and hushed conversations drifted into the hallway where Inspector Conway waited by the front door. Glancing at his pocket watch, he realised he'd been standing there for almost twenty minutes. He began to sigh but cut himself off when he heard another burst of laughter coming from the other room. He darted his gaze to the open doorway, but no one had emerged. Allowing himself a proper sigh, he crossed the hallway, peered up the stairs, and returned to the front door. When he was halfway there, though, the sound of a door opening to his right caused him to stop and turn his head in its direction.

"Well, well, well." A relaxed smile crossed Madame Mimi's face. "Hello, John."

"Mimi." Inspector Conway cleared his throat and walked the remaining distance to the front door.

"Come now, you can do better than that." Madame Mimi sashayed over to him.

Inspector Conway looked everywhere but her. "I'm not here for company."

Madame Mimi rested a hand upon her hip. "Not even mine?"

Inspector Conway felt the back of his neck grow hot. "No. I'm waitin' for Caleb." He forced himself to look at her. She was wearing a low-cut green satin bustle dress which accentuated her already large bust and slim waist. He kept his gaze fixed upon hers.

Madame Mimi stroked his arm. "You can wait for him in my parlour, if you'd like?"

Inspector Conway felt the warmth creep onto his face. "I'll wait here. Thanks."

"You should let yourself relax and enjoy yourself from time to time, John. After all, all work and no play makes John a dull boy." Madame Mimi pulled away and sashayed across the hallway. Upon reaching the door into her parlour, she rested her hand on its frame and looked back over her shoulder at him. "You know where I am if you change your mind."

"Yeah. Thanks."

When the door closed behind her, Inspector Conway wiped his forehead with the back of his sleeve and shot a hard glance up the stairs as he paced. Muttering under his breath about wanting to get out of there as soon as possible, he cursed Woolfe a few times and checked his pocket watch, again.

Eventually, he heard heavy footfalls on the stairs and looked up to see his friend descend. Striding forward to meet him at the stairs' foot, he growled, "About time, mate." He lowered his voice. "How long does it take to get some bloody information?"

"You don't pay for a woman to just talk to you, mate," Inspector Woolfe replied.

The vision Inspector Conway's mind conjured up was enough to put him off his supper. Sensing the threat of Madame Mimi's return as keenly, he strode back to the front door and went outside. The cold night air cooled his red face and cleared the fog of desire from his senses. Madame Mimi affected him in a way that made him feel vulnerable. He didn't like it.

Inspector Woolfe joined him outside and was immediately gripped by a coughing fit.

They'd briefly discussed Inspector Woolfe's doctor appointment during the cab ride from Bow Street. As Inspector Conway had anticipated, though, Inspector Woolfe kept his explanation brief, saying only he'd been prescribed more medication. He'd also swiftly changed the subject by enquiring after Inspector Conway's meeting with Chief Inspector Jones. Acting in kind, Inspector Conway had kept his explanation brief, saying only their senior officer was disappointed by the lack of progress they'd made at the bank. To which Inspector Woolfe had cryptically replied he had "many other avenues to try" in his search for the elusive J. Pettifoot.

Waiting for the coughing fit to subside, Inspector Conway enquired, "Did she have sumin' to say after all that, then?"

"Yeah." Inspector Woolfe halved his stride so Inspector Conway could keep in step beside him as they walked to the entrance of the dead-end street. "Jerome's scarpered to Birmingham with a young woman called Joanna Hightower."

"How did Colette know her name?"

"Jerome told her this morning," Inspector Woolfe replied.

After spending the night, Inspector Conway thought.

"He also said trouble at the *Crescent Theatre* was the reason for them leaving London," Inspector Woolfe added. "When we get back, I'll send word to C Division to see if they can tell us anything."

Inspector Conway stopped at the entrance of the dead-end street and glanced at his pocket watch. They'd agreed with the hansom cab driver to pick them up around now. "When we've got their answer, I'll get a train up there and have a word with the Birmingham City Police."

Inspector Woolfe nodded. It would keep his friend out of trouble with the Bow Street Society, at least. "And I'll ask the superintendent to wire them for a local's help." As their cab arrived, he hoped the Birmingham City Police welcomed Inspector Conway as warmly as the Kent County Constabulary had welcomed him.

* * *

Miss Trent stood amongst the boxes and piles of Dr Weeks' possessions which Mr Snyder had put into a second-floor bedroom. With her was Dr Peter Holmwood, a man in his early sixties with short, neatly combed white hair and moustache. Approximately five feet eleven inches tall and leanly built, he wore the conservative attire of a black frock coat and trousers, dark-green waistcoat and tie, and white shirt with starched collar.

His warm-brown eyes looked through a pair of brass-rimmed spectacles at a framed black and white photograph. In it was a posed group of men standing and sitting in front of a tent. Some of the men held rifles whilst others had their arms folded.

Dr Holmwood tapped the face of a man standing at the back of the group. "This is me." He tapped the face of a much younger man standing beside him. "And this is Dr Weeks. He was only eighteen at the time." He gave a small shake of his head. "The moment I laid eyes on him, I knew he wasn't cut from the same cloth as the others in the Canadian militia." He softly chuckled. "Frightened of his own shadow doesn't begin to describe him." He passed the photograph to Miss Trent. "He drank, even back then, but we all did. An occasional spot of brandy kept the cold out, and the harder stuff was usually the only thing we had on hand to render the patient unconscious for amputations."

"Dr Weeks has drunk for as long as I've known him." Miss Trent put the photograph into a nearby box. "I hadn't noticed how bad his drinking had become, though."

"None of us had," Dr Holmwood said. "I spoke to those he works alongside in the dead room, and they were as surprised as I was to hear of his admission to Bedlam." His features drooped. "It's an absolute shame."

"Will the hospital board keep his position open for him?"

Dr Holmwood took off his spectacles and used his handkerchief to polish their lenses. "Yes. We discussed his situation at length, and we were all in agreement he should be permitted to return once he's recovered." He put his handkerchief away and his spectacles on, "How much of his former work he will be physically capable of doing remains to be seen, however."

Miss Trent pushed her eyebrows together in a frown. "What do you mean?"

"Those suffering from alcoholic insanity usually have tremors in the hands. It makes performing operations on live patients nigh-on impossible." He held up his crooked fingers. "I myself have been obliged to abandon surgery due to my arthritis." He lowered his hands. "Tremors may not prove as problematic during postmortems, however."

Miss Trent's heart ached at the thought of Dr Weeks being unable to do what he was brilliant at despite recovering from the illness that had crippled him. "I hope so."

"*Cor*!" Toby's excited exclamation instantly drew Miss Trent and Dr Holmwood's attention to him as he held up a small specimen jar containing a human kidney. "What's this?"

"A kidney, my boy." Dr Holmwood gently took the jar from him.

"What's Dr Weeks doin' with it?" Toby's eyes widened. "Did he do someone in?"

Dr Holmwood chuckled softly. "No; it will be a specimen he took from a corpse who'd died from kidney disease," Dr Holmwood pointed to different parts of the kidney. "You can see the damage the disease has wrought here and here."

Miss Trent put a hand on her hip and enquired from Toby in a firm tone, "Is the meeting room ready for tonight's meeting?"

"Yeah." Toby reached for another specimen jar.

Miss Trent picked it up first, however. "These don't belong to you."

"I was only lookin'," Toby countered.

"I'm sure Dr Weeks would enjoy showing you, if he were here," Dr Holmwood said.

"We're going to Sam's for supper after the meeting," Miss Trent informed Toby. "Please, change your clothes and wash your face."

Toby reluctantly left the room, his hands in his pockets.

"His curiosity ought to be nurtured," Dr Holmwood gently advised.

"Believe me, it is," Miss Trent reassured, thinking how there was rarely a dull moment for Toby living in the

Bow Street Society's house. "Thank you, doctor. I know Dr Weeks will appreciate your support as much as I do."

"You're most welcome, Miss Trent," Dr Holmwood said. "Please, do let me know if there's anything else I can do to help. Dr Weeks was one of my best students; I'd hate to see his talent wasted."

"Me, too." Miss Trent led him downstairs to the front door. "Good night, doctor."

"Good night." Dr Holmwood left the house and descended the steps to the street.

Hearing the kitchen door open as she closed the front, Miss Trent looked back and saw Miss Hicks coming past the stairs. The barmaid had her head down whilst she simultaneously smoothed down her skirts and blew out her cheeks. Releasing the air as a soft sigh when she reached the foot of the stairs, she tilted her head sideways, closed her eyes, and rubbed the middle of her forehead whilst turning the corner and ascending the first few steps.

"Polly?" Miss Trent called.

Miss Hicks spun around.

"Are you all right?" Miss Trent enquired, walking toward her.

Miss Hicks gripped the handrail and wrapped her other arm around her middle. "Yes."

"The meeting will be starting soon."

Miss Hicks glanced at the meeting room door. "I wasn't goin' to come."

Miss Trent stood at the bottom of the stairs and looked up at her. "Why not?"

Miss Hicks forced a smile. "Well, I've not done anythin', have I?" She toyed with a blond curl. "I'd only put people off."

Concern entered Miss Trent's eyes. Miss Hicks had been quiet since she'd returned from St. John Street. Mr Snyder had also taken Miss Trent aside and said he'd overheard Miss Hicks crying whilst they were there. She knew how difficult she was finding not being able to see Dr Weeks, and she was only a friend. She also knew Miss

Hicks and so could well imagine how heartbroken she was about it. Granted, it still hurt whenever she thought of Miss Hicks leaving her for the Canadian, but it hurt more when she thought of how close Miss Hicks had come to throwing it all away. As strange as it might sound, Miss Trent had taken solace in the knowledge Miss Hicks was happy with Dr Weeks. Like her sacrifice had been worth it.

"I'm taking Toby to Sam's for supper afterward," Miss Trent said.

Miss Hicks' expression perked up. "You are?"

"You're welcome to come," Miss Trent replied. "The change of scenery might do you some good."

Miss Hicks shook her head, but her smile was genuine this time. "No. Thanks. I'm tired." She lifted her hand to indicate the upstairs. "I'm just goin' to go to bed."

"It's only seven o'clock."

"I've a book I'm readin'," Miss Hicks lied. "Night."

Miss Trent parted her lips to question Miss Hicks further, but she was already heading upstairs, and there was a knock on the door besides. Pursing her lips into a frown, Miss Trent went to answer the front door and admit the first of the Bow Streeters for the meeting.

THIRTY-NINE

Miss Trent stood at the head of the table and arranged her things whilst the others poured themselves a cup of tea and settled into their seats. Taking her own, Miss Trent consulted her personal agenda for the meeting and put her pocket watch beside it. She cleared her throat and waited for the conversations to fade.

"Good evening, everyone," she greeted once it was quiet. "I have two items of business before we begin the meeting proper. First, I'd like to introduce the members who are sharing a case for the first time." Whilst indicating Mr Heath, she looked to Mr Verity sitting at the foot of the table. "This is Mr Bertram Heath, an architect." Whilst indicating Mr Verity, she looked to Mr Heath sitting to her right. "This is Mr Virgil Verity, a retired schoolmaster and spiritualist."

Mr Verity gripped his walking cane but abandoned his intention to stand when he saw Mr Heath rise and walk toward him instead. "Good to meet you, Mr Heath."

"And you, sir," Mr Heath said as they shook hands. "My word, I've never heard an accent like yours before."

"It's from County Durham, lad," Mr Verity explained. "Northeast of England."

"Ahh." Mr Heath gave a small lift of his chin. "It's very interesting on the ear."

Mr Verity chuckled. "It's never been called that before."

"Clearly, some have no appreciation for the wonderful accents which can be found across England's green land," Mr Heath said.

"Gentlemen?" Miss Trent gently interrupted.

"Oh! My apologies, Miss Trent," Mr Heath hurried back to his seat.

"Thank you." Miss Trent referred to her agenda. "The second item of business is to inform you Dr Colbert has withdrawn from the case due to reasons which I'll give at the end of the meeting."

"But we still don't have his account of his conversation with Mr Luthor Ellis Benton," Dr Locke pointed out. "We need to know what was said."

"Dr Charles McWilliams, Dr Colbert's colleague, delivered the account this afternoon," Miss Trent said. "I've put it on the agenda to discuss."

"McWilliams… McWilliams… wasn't he a Bow Street Society client once upon a time?" Mr Verity enquired.

"Yes; the disappearance of Dr Westley Devereux," Mr Locke replied.

"Aye, I remember now," Mr Verity said. "It was a canny little case."

"Is Dr Weeks a reason for Dr Colbert's withdrawal?" Mr Elliott enquired.

Dr Locke downcast her gaze and bowed her head at the mention of Dr Weeks.

"I will give Dr Colbert's reasons at the end of the meeting," Miss Trent replied.

Mr Locke's gaze slid to his wife and remained there as he enquired from Mr Elliott, "Why would Dr Weeks be a reason for Dr Colbert withdrawing from the case?"

"I heard some concerning news about Dr Weeks this afternoon and thought it could be connected," Mr Elliott replied.

"Did you not hear what I said, Mr Locke, or did you simply choose to ignore it?" Miss Trent challenged. "Mr Elliott, please refrain from discussing this any further. I'll answer your questions at the end of the meeting, which is why I chose to put it there in the first place."

"Forgive me," Mr Locke said in an apologetic tone. "I am rather tired."

Dr Locke sharply lifted and turned her head to look at him. "You are?"

Mr Locke gave her hand a gentle squeeze. "I am fine, Lynette." He offered a weak smile. "Alas, I may have to forego tonight's walk."

Dr Locke cast an appraising glance over him and cooly stated, "We'll discuss it later."

Mr Locke's smile faded, and he withdrew his hand as Dr Locke turned to the others.

Meanwhile, Mr Elliott cooly replied to Miss Trent, "If you insist."

"I do," Miss Trent said. "There is a logic to my agendas, Mr Elliott, even if you can neither grasp nor agree with it." She suspected who had given him the news, but it could wait until the meeting's end. "Speaking of which, Dr Colbert's account of his conversation with Mr Luthor Ellis Benton is the first agenda item. I'm aware you are coming into this after the fact, Mr Elliott, Mr Verity, but I'd still like you to give your opinion." She picked up a pile of typed documents and, taking the topmost one for herself, handed the rest to Mr Heath. "Please, take one and pass it on." When the architect had obeyed, and the pile was making its way around the table, she left the room to check on Toby and allow the others to read the account.

Mr Locke read the initial few sentences at least three times, but his fatigued mind struggled to remain focused and was barely able to retain any of the details. Therefore, abandoning the task as soon as he'd begun, he looked across the table at Mr Elliott and considered probing him further about Dr Weeks, whilst Miss Trent was out the room. Sliding his gaze to his wife, he doubted she'd appreciate being reminded of what Dr Weeks had done. Mr Locke himself didn't want the Bow Street Society discussing his private business, either. Consequently, he decided to stay silent and held Dr Colbert's account under the pretence of reading it. Yet, a part of him remained curious about what news Mr Elliott had heard about Dr Weeks, if only because he felt sorry for the Canadian and the trouble caused by the man who had stolen from him.

Miss Trent entered a few moments later and returned to her seat. "What are your thoughts?"

"I believe Mr Benton was honest in what he told Dr Colbert, but he also omitted an important detail from his recounting of the confrontation with Mr Jerome," Dr Locke replied. "Master Granville Norton witnessed a portion of it and said Mr Jerome struck Mr Benton, but there's no mention of this in Dr Colbert's account."

"Master Norton could've misinterpreted what he saw, Dr Colbert could've forgotten to include the assault in his account, or, as you say, Mr Benton could've intentionally omitted it," Mr Elliott said. "The question over its omission must be answered, though, and given Dr Colbert's withdrawal from the case, the only person who can do that is Mr Benton. Mr Locke, have you encountered Mr Benton during your theatrical career?"

"Yes; he is an actor of the highest calibre," Mr Locke replied. "I shall speak to him."

Mr Elliott noted the action.

"What else did Master Norton say?" Miss Trent enquired.

"The bairn sneaks into the *Crescent* and hides from time to time," Mr Verity replied. "To talk to Miss Ilbert about his letters and to watch folk working."

"Which technically gives him access to the metal plate," Mr Elliott mused aloud.

"I hardly think a child is capable of committing cold-blooded murder," Dr Locke said.

"It's rare, but it has been known to happen," Mr Elliott countered.

Mr Heath tapped his chin. "Rewire the plate, though?" He hummed, "I don't know."

"Did Master Norton witness anything unusual during his visits?" Mr Locke enquired.

"Miss Ilbert confronting Miss Hightower about her possible collusion with Mr Jerome, and Miss Hightower becoming upset about it," Dr Locke said. "He also overheard Mr Benton proposing to Miss Ilbert and Miss Ilbert turning him down."

"Did Master Norton overhear Mr Benton's reaction?" Mr Elliott enquired.

"If he did, he didn't say," Dr Locke replied. "What he did say was he thought Miss Ilbert loved Mr Benton and was testing him because one doesn't always know what someone wants in the theatre business."

"The bairn said Mr Benton was proposing to Miss Ilbert again, and she always said no," Mr Verity interjected.

Mr Elliott referred to Dr Colbert's account and read aloud, "'She was my heart. Countless times, I proposed to her, and countless times, she politely declined, but my adoration only grew stronger.' Those were Mr Benton's words to Dr Colbert on the matter." Mr Elliott put down the document. "We only have Mr Benton's word, however."

He picked up his pencil and gently tapped his notebook with it as he considered Miss Ilbert and Mr Benton. "Aside from testing Mr Benton, Miss Ilbert could've turned down his proposal for the simple reason she was already married."

"But no one at the theatre disclosed Miss Ilbert had a husband," Dr Locke pointed out.

"They might not know." Mr Elliott laid down his pencil. "Mr Benton clearly doesn't, or he wouldn't have repeatedly proposed to her. I could search the records at Somerset House, but, without the name of the groom, location, or even a date, I'd struggle to find the marriage."

"Miss Ilbert was known as the Lily of the Lyceum in her younger days," Mr Locke said. "If one as famous as she were indeed married, I would expect *The Era* newspaper to include an announcement at the very least. I propose a visit to their office, and the *Gaslight Gazette*'s, to conduct a search of the archives."

"Agreed," Dr Locke said. "I shall visit both offices tomorrow afternoon."

Mr Locke's expression cooled, but he knew it would be futile to argue with her.

"Request Mr Baldwin's assistance at the *Gaslight Gazette*," Miss Trent suggested.

"Very well," Dr Locke noted the arrangement.

"It's worth noting, under the Married Women's Property Act of 1882, Miss Ilbert would've retained the *Crescent*'s lease as her own property, in the same manner as if she were a *feme solo*, without the intervention of a trustee," Mr Elliott explained. "Therefore, she wouldn't have been obliged to transfer the lease to her husband, if she were indeed already married, or if she married Mr Benton."

"Pardon me, but what is a 'feme solo?'" Mr Heath enquired.

"It means 'single woman' and refers to any woman who has never been married, or who has been divorced, widowed, or had her legal subordination to her husband invalidated by a judicial decision," Mr Elliott replied.

"Ah, I see." Mr Heath gave a small nod. "Thank you."

"Returning to the matter of Mr Benton," Mr Elliott continued. "I'm certain you'll get to the truth of it when you speak to him, Mr Locke, but another possibility relating to the punch and the ultimatum has just occurred to me." He picked up Dr Colbert's account. "When Dr Colbert asked Mr Benton if anyone had come forward with information about the blackmail following Miss Ilbert's death, Mr Benton said, 'No, and nor do I expect them to. When Mina was alive, everyone was facing almost certain destitution. Now she's dead, there's a chance the theatre and its company could be saved. Only a fool would jeopardise their future by confessing to the blackmail after the fact, even if they were innocent of Mina's murder.'" Mr Elliott lowered the document and looked at the others. "What if Mr Benton was party to his own blackmailing?"

"He falsified the entire scheme with Mr Jerome, you mean?" Mr Locke enquired.

"Yes; he may have loved Miss Ilbert but could've also grown tired of her repeated rejections," Mr Elliott said. "He could've concocted the scheme with Mr Jerome to hurt Miss Ilbert by damaging the reputation of the very thing she cared most about: the *Crescent Theatre*. When she gave the ultimatum, he," he picked up Dr Colbert's account and read aloud, "'tried to dissuade her, but her mind was made up, and there was no changing it.' Also, here, he states, 'When she gave her ultimatum, she was sealing her own fate as much as the *Crescent*'s. I'm certain of it.'"

"The words of a man concerned about the woman he loved," Dr Locke said.

"Or the words of a man who decided murdering the woman he loved was the only way to protect himself and his only means of income: the theatre," Mr Elliott countered.

"According to Dr Colbert's account, Mr Benton was in the wings when Miss Ilbert was electrocuted," Dr Locke reminded him. "He couldn't have possibly flipped the switch."

"If one assumes the switch was flipped at the precise moment Miss Ilbert stepped onto the plate," Mr Elliott said. "It could've been flipped moments earlier."

"Which would've risked electrocuting a different performer," Dr Locke countered. "If I were determined to murder Miss Ilbert, I'd have made sure I murdered Miss Ilbert."

"True," Mr Elliott conceded. "Let us consider another scenario, then. If Mr Benton had concocted the blackmailing scheme with Mr Jerome, do you agree it's possible he coerced Mr Jerome into flipping the switch at the precise moment Miss Ilbert stepped onto the metal plate? Thereby providing himself with a perfect alibi?"

"Yes, of course," Dr Locke curtly replied.

"Even my charm could not persuade Mr Benton to put his head into the hangman's noose," Mr Locke said with a wry smile. "If we are to prove any of your theories, Mr Elliott, we must have the testimony of Mr Jerome."

Mr Elliott referred to Dr Colbert's account. "Miss Joanna Hightower was seen backstage with Mr Jerome. Could she tell us his whereabouts?"

"She and Mr Jerome have run away." Dr Locke passed Miss Hightower's note to Mr Elliott. "Her mother and father suspect they've travelled to Birmingham."

"The bairn, Master Norton, said Mr Jerome's voice was strange; like mine but different," Mr Verity said. "The West Midlands and northeastern accents are similar in some ways."

Mr Elliott passed Miss Hightower's note to Mr Heath. "We've previously placed newspaper advertisements to encourage people to contact us, but I doubt such an exercise would bear fruit in this instance. If Mr Jerome is involved in the blackmailing scheme, and possibly Miss Ilbert's murder, and Miss Hightower knows he's involved, neither of them are going to come forward for fear of being arrested by the police." Mr Elliott picked up his pencil and held both ends whilst resting his elbows upon the table. "I propose we travel to Birmingham and enlist the assistance of the Birmingham City Police."

"I have two caveats which I would like to add to your proposal," Mr Locke said.

Mr Elliott lowered the pencil. "Which are?"

"Firstly, we must also question Mr Jerome about Mr Morris Thurston's potential involvement in the blackmailing scheme, and Miss Ilbert's death, if we are successful in locating him," Mr Locke replied.

Mr Elliott poised his pencil over his notebook. "Please, elaborate."

"Mr Thurston claimed to be passing by the stage door when he overheard the argument between Mr Benton and Mr Jerome and intervened," Mr Locke said. "A super master and prompter have little reason to be loitering around a stage door. Whilst I concede it is possible Mr Thurston was returning from the dressing rooms or wardrobe department when he overheard the argument, his nervous demeanour nevertheless roused my suspicions.

"Furthermore, he defended Mr Jerome. He said he was just a blackmailer and not a murderer. I sarcastically remarked I had not realised Mr Thurston knew Mr Jerome, to which he said he did not.

"Lastly, he became most upset when I suggested he and Miss Kimberly could have murdered Miss Ilbert to ensure their vision of Mr Thurston's play would be performed and not Miss Ilbert's. In short, Mr Thurston may have also been involved in the blackmailing scheme and murdered Miss Ilbert not only to protect himself and the theatre, but also the opportunity to see his play performed in the way he had always envisioned it. As super master and prompter, he also had unrestricted access to the area below stage."

Mr Elliott considered the argument. "It seems logical to me. What is your second caveat?"

"Be wary of Detective Inspector Matthew Rupert Peter Donahue. Otherwise known as 'The Ripper,'" Mr Locke replied. "He was far from pleased about a group of southern civilian detectives interfering with his work when Mr Heath, Lynette, and I assisted the Birmingham Bow Street Society with a case of theirs last year."

"He may be displeased by our interference but, as a policeman, he can't argue with the letter of the law," Mr Elliott said.

The corner of Mr Locke's mouth lifted. "May I assume you are putting yourself forward for the assignment?"

"You may," Mr Elliott replied.

"With Mr Snyder," Miss Trent said. "We don't know how volatile Mr Jerome can be. If Inspector Donahue is also as confrontational as you say he is, Mr Locke, Mr Snyder is tough enough to defend both himself and Mr Elliott."

"I don't intend to allow our conversations with Inspector Donahue to descend into fisticuffs, but I appreciate the need to err on the side of caution," Mr Elliott said.

"Good," Miss Trent said. "I'll check the timetable and tell Sam when to meet you at Euston railway station tomorrow. I'll send word to you in the morning."

"I'll keep an eye out for your message," Mr Elliott noted the arrangement.

FORTY

"So far, we've been discussing Miss Ilbert's death as if it were murder, but the question was unanswered at the end of our last meeting," Miss Trent said. "Mr Locke, have you heard from your business manager at the *Paddington Palladium*?"

Mr Locke parted his lips, but it was Dr Locke who replied, "We came home to his letter this afternoon." Mr Locke frowned and sipped his sweet, black tea, whilst his wife took Mr Cokes' letter from her notebook and summarised its contents for the others. "Mr Aaron Willis has never worked at the *Paddington Palladium*, but several of our electric men and carpenters have worked with him at other theatres in the past. In their opinions, his expertise as an electric man was never in question. Some of our electric men also gave anecdotal evidence of occasions when Mr Willis was loaned to other theatres to advise on their plans to introduce electrical lighting in their auditoriums."

"They don't believe he would've connected the metal plate to the main supply of electricity in error?" Miss Trent made a point of addressing Mr Locke again.

"No," Mr Locke replied. "They consider him an upstanding electric man."

"We mustn't forget Mr Willis' employment at the *Crescent Theatre* was also threatened by Miss Ilbert's ultimatum," Mr Elliott pointed out.

Mr Locke shifted in his chair as his joints ached. "I and, undoubtedly, countless other theatre owners and managers would have had no reason to decline Mr Willis' application if Miss Ilbert had followed through with her threat. An electric man confident in his own ability would have known that. As it is, Mr Willis cannot secure further employment whilst the cloud of alleged negligence hangs over him. Also, we must not forget he was the only one from the *Crescent Theatre* who contacted the Bow Street Society to request we investigate."

"It wouldn't be the first time our client's credibility was cast into doubt," Mr Elliott reminded him.

"True, but only a foolish man would commission a group of civilian detectives to prove his employer was murdered when the police had ruled her death an accident if he himself were guilty of committing the crime," Mr Locke said.

"Or he is an intelligent man with no confidence in our abilities who hired us to prove Miss Ilbert died by her own hand," Mr Elliott countered.

"He would have had no realistic chance in succeeding, since Miss Kimberly admitted Miss Ilbert thought too highly of herself to take her own life," Mr Locke said.

"One can never be certain of what is in a person's mind, especially those closest to us," Mr Elliott pointed out.

"I agree." Dr Locke looked to her husband.

Mr Locke felt himself warm under his wife's gaze but kept his own fixed upon Mr Elliott. "I trust the judgement of my carpenters." His tone and expression turned sombre. "Yet the switch to the lightbulb fixture had to be flipped to apply the electrical current to the metal plate. If the wires were altered deliberately, it would be reasonable to assume the switch was flipped deliberately, too. I am satisfied in my own mind Mr Willis did not erroneously rewire the metal plate to the main electricity supply. I concede it does not eliminate him as the one who rewired the plate and flipped the switch deliberately, however."

"Agreed," Mr Elliott stated.

"The next item on the agenda is Reverend Ananias Mullins," Miss Trent said, deciding to move the discussion along. "Dr Locke, Mr Verity, what did you discover from your conversation with him?"

"He is a bigoted zealot who openly condemned Miss Ilbert simply because she was an actress," Dr Locke replied. "He condemned all actresses as harlots and insisted Miss Ilbert had corrupted the boys at the school." She referred to her notes. "Master Norton admitted he loved Miss Ilbert but also admitted she'd never said the same to him. When he arrived for our discussion in the headmaster's office, Master Norton was also wearing a black armband out of respect for Miss Ilbert. Mr Rogers insisted he remove it, and he did." Dr Locke glanced around the table. "My point is Reverend Ananias was partially correct as far as his accusation of Miss Ilbert corrupting the boys was concerned as, according to Master Norton, 'everyone' at the school is wearing a mourning armband. Yet, many people are enamoured by the Great Locke, and Percy regularly receives letters from admirers." Her tone cooled as she quietly remarked, "Not all of them are welcome, of course." At her natural volume, she added, "But it happens."

Mr Locke kept his gaze downcast as he sipped his tea.

Miss Trent, aware of the liaisons Mr Locke had enjoyed with some of the adult female admirers who had written to him over the years, diverted the discussion back to Reverend Ananias. "Could the reverend have murdered Miss Ilbert in your opinion?"

"He certainly wanted her 'influence' removed, but he denied murdering her because it would've broken the commandment," Dr Locke replied.

"Mr Rogers thought the same about Miss Ilbert as Reverend Ananias," Mr Verity said. "But he also thought the reverend wouldn't of damned his soul by murdering her." He scratched his cheek. "Reverend Ananias is a bigoted zealot." He smiled. "I surprised him when I quoted the Bible back." His expression became serious. "But he didn't murder Miss Ilbert."

"I must agree in spite of my hatred for the man," Dr Locke said.

"Did Reverend Ananias have access to the metal plate at all?" Mr Elliott enquired.

"No, he confronted Miss Ilbert in the theatre's foyer," Dr Locke replied.

"Therefore, we are eliminating him and Master Norton as suspects?" Mr Elliott enquired, glancing around the table.

"I think so," Mr Locke replied.

Mr Verity and Dr Locke nodded their agreement.

Miss Trent took out her typed list of names and put a line through Reverend Ananias and Master Norton's. Putting the list in the table's centre, she referred to her personal agenda and said, "The next item is Mr Stanley Akers, the chief scene painter at the *Crescent*. Mr Locke, Mr Heath, you called upon him at his studio, correct?"

"We *did*!" Mr Heath put his hands flat upon the table and leant forward, his eyes bright with excitement. "*Miss* Trent, you should've *seen* how he paints the scenery!" He gesticulated with his hands as he continued, "There was a platform *so* tall, we had to use *stairs* to reach it and *underneath*! Why, it was *astounding*! Ropes, pulleys, and a *host* of assistants lifted and lowered the canvas through a slot in the platform and—"

"There is a great deal about the mechanics of theatrical work which astounds Mr Heath," Mr Locke gently derided with a playful twinkle in his eyes.

Mr Heath sat back in his chair. "I appreciate the ingenuity of engineering."

"What did you discuss?" Mr Elliott enquired from Mr Locke and Mr Heath both.

Mr Locke took a cigarette from his silver case and, snapping the latter shut, tapped the former against its outside. "Mr Stone's allegation Mr Akers and Miss Ilbert argued during a technical rehearsal." He put the cigarette between his lips and lit it with a match. Taking a small pull from it, he exhaled the smoke over his shoulder and rested the heel of his hand upon the table's edge. "Mr Akers claimed it was a disagreement over Miss Ilbert's use of electrical lighting. He alleged the greater illumination it provides highlights every scratch, every tear, and every patch of faded colour present on the scenery." Mr Locke took another small pull from his cigarette and, exhaling the smoke over his shoulder, tapped off the excess ash into the ashtray. "He admitted to not commencing work on Miss Ilbert's new scenery because he hoped she would come around to his way of thinking. She did not. Instead, she proposed a compromise: dimmers."

"Dimmers?" Mr Elliott enquired, confused.

Mr Heath briefly explained the concept and how they worked.

"And Mr Akers was satisfied with those?" Mr Elliott enquired.

"He claimed to be initially sceptical about their effectiveness but was persuaded when he saw them in operation at another theatre," Mr Locke replied. "In my opinion, Mr Akers is a passionate artiste, but he is not a murderer. He was also supervising the scenery changeover at the *Royal Opera House* when Miss Ilbert died, a fact I confirmed with the *Royal Opera House*'s manager prior to attending this meeting."

"You were able to gain access to the *Royal Opera House*'s manager without an appointment?" Mr Elliott enquired with a loft of his brow.

"The theatre business is rather incestuous in that regard," Mr Locke replied.

"Mr Akers couldn't of flipped the switch if he weren't there," Mr Verity observed.

"Unless he had an accomplice," Mr Elliott pointed out. "An assistant, perhaps?"

"Miss Ilbert's ultimatum did not apply to either Mr Akers or his assistants as his studio supplies and maintains scenery for a multitude of West End theatres," Mr Locke replied. "Consequently, they had no motive for wishing her dead."

Miss Trent put a line through Mr Akers' name on the typed list and referred to her agenda. "Mr Ronald Stone is the next item of discussion."

"According to Miss Kimberly, he didn't come into the theatre today," Dr Locke said.

"Mr Thurston made a passing comment to that effect at the end of our conversation," Mr Locke said. "You wrote it down, did you not, Mr Heath?"

"Hm? Oh, yes." Mr Heath consulted his notebook. "Here it is: 'He's always disappearing these days.'"

"It suggests he has been elusive on multiple occasions recently," Mr Elliott observed.

"Indeed," Mr Locke agreed. "One of which may have been to flip the switch to cause Miss Ilbert's death." He took a final pull from his cigarette and, exhaling the smoke, crushed it out in the ashtray. "Mr Akers also told me of an occasion when Mr Stone had said the *Crescent Theatre* would soon be under new management. Mr Akers assumed Mr Stone was referring to himself, so he was surprised when Miss Kimberly assumed the manager's position."

"I'll have a word with the lad," Mr Verity said. "He might talk to someone new."

Miss Trent noted the action. "Miss Emmaline Kimberly, specifically the agreement she had with Miss Ilbert. Dr Locke, did you get a typed copy of it from her?"

"No," Dr Locke replied. "She allowed me to see it, and I transcribed it from memory, but she insisted Mr Elliott would have to read it in her presence." She turned to the relevant page in her notebook and passed it to the solicitor. "As you will see, the agreement only has value if Miss Ilbert dies from natural or accidental causes. It certainly gives Miss Kimberly a reason to stage Miss Ilbert's death to make it appear accidental, in addition to the motives we've already discussed."

"The agreement was signed by both parties?" Mr Elliott returned the notebook.

"Yes," Dr Locke replied.

"I'll need to see samples of Miss Ilbert's and Miss Kimberly's known signatures to compare to those on the agreement to confirm its authenticity," Mr Elliott said. "Did Miss Ilbert lease the building?"

"Yes, and Miss Kimberly claims the building's owner is arranging for the lease to be amended in light of this agreement," Dr Locke replied. "Again, if you wish to see the existing and new leases, and speak to the building's owner, Mr Elliott, you will have to do so in Miss Kimberly's presence."

"And I shall as soon as I've returned from Birmingham," Mr Elliott said.

"In the meantime, I'd like to speak to Miss Lily Ilbert, Miss Mina Ilbert's daughter," Dr Locke said, addressing Miss Trent. "She wasn't immune to the ultimatum and, like Mr Thurston and Mr Stone, had unrestricted access to the metal plate."

"She is also to assume her mother's part in the pantomime," Mr Locke interjected.

"Visit the *Crescent* in the morning with Mr Locke and Mr Verity and see if you can speak to her alone," Miss Trent informed Dr Locke.

"And me?" Mr Heath enquired.

"You may accompany me," Mr Locke offered.

"*Excellent.*" Mr Heath grinned.

"Is the agenda concluded?" Dr Locke enquired.

"Yes, apart from Dr Colbert's withdrawal from the case," Miss Trent replied.

"Does it concern Dr Weeks?" Dr Locke enquired.

Miss Trent glanced at Mr Elliott. "Yes."

"Then Percy and I shall take our leave." Dr Locke stood and gathered her things.

"Darling," Mr Locke gently discouraged, but his wife ignored him.

Miss Trent's head jerked back slightly. "You don't want to hear what I have to say?"

"Not particularly." Dr Locke gripped her husband's arm and pulled him to his feet. "Percy is tired, and I'm uninterested in whatever trouble Dr Weeks has gotten himself into."

Miss Trent stared at her, stunned. "You might not feel the same way once I—"

383

"I would, I can assure you." Dr Locke interlinked her arm with Mr Locke's.

"I prefer to stay," Mr Locke said.

"You need rest," Dr Locke ordered.

Mr Locke looked apologetically at Miss Trent but permitted his wife to lead him out.

"My goodness," Mr Heath quietly remarked once the door had closed behind them. "What has the poor fellow done to Dr Locke to make her so cold toward him?"

"I don't know," Miss Trent replied.

"To spare us from any needless discussion, the news I heard was Dr Weeks has been admitted to Bethlehem Hospital suffering from alcoholic insanity," Mr Elliott said, addressing Miss Trent. "Dr Colbert is the resident physician at the same institution. Has he withdrawn from the case to care for Dr Weeks?"

Miss Trent's expression turned grave. "Yes. I'm afraid so."

"I'd hoped my source was lying," Mr Elliott said in a sombre tone.

Miss Trent lifted her chin as her earlier suspicions were confirmed. "Inspector Lee?"

"Yes; he intercepted me outside the Old Bailey this afternoon," Mr Elliott replied.

Miss Trent gathered up her agenda and the typed list of suspects. "Dr Weeks assaulted Inspector Lee in the corridor at New Scotland Yard. It obliged Detective Chief Inspector Richard Jones to begin proceedings to have Dr Weeks medically assessed and eventually admitted to the asylum." Miss Trent stood and collected in the copies of Dr Colbert's account. "There were other incidents which contributed to Detective Chief Inspector Jones' decision, but the assault was the final nail in the proverbial coffin." She put the pile on the table and folded her arms. "Miss Hicks has taken the news badly, as I'm sure you can imagine." She returned to her seat. "I know Dr Weeks would appreciate your discretion in this matter, gentlemen."

"He has it," Mr Elliott said. "As do you."

"Poor Dr Weeks," Mr Heath said, sadly. "I'll do whatever I can to help."

"Me, too," Mr Verity added.

Miss Trent gave a genuinely appreciative smile. "Thank you."

FORTY-ONE

The service alleyway running perpendicular to the Bow Street Society's house was shrouded in darkness when Inspector Conway entered it. He'd left Inspector Woolfe back at the police station, informing him he was going home. Yet, he needed to speak with Miss Trent about a whole host of things first, not least 'J. Pettifoot.' As he walked down the alleyway, though, he heard whispered voices and realised they were coming from the Society's back gate. Crossing to the alleyway's opposite side, he crept forward and stopped a couple of metres away to listen.

"I want a word with you, Noah O'Hannigan," Miss Hicks whispered. "Where's my jewellery?"

"I sold it," Mr O'Hannigan replied in a whisper.

"You *what*?!" Miss Hicks cried.

"A man's got to eat," Mr O'Hannigan replied, his voice closer to its normal volume.

"It wasn't *yours* to *sell*," Miss Hicks whispered sharply. "Just as the *money* wasn't *yours* to take."

"You ain't mad, wee girl," Mr O'Hannigan said. "Not after what I gave you."

"I *am* mad with you, Noah. Very, uh, mad."

Inspector Conway heard the sound of kissing through the darkness.

"Can I come in?" Mr O'Hannigan enquired.

"Don't be daft!" Miss Hicks chastised.

"You said yourself she ain't home," Mr O'Hannigan said.

"Becky would toss me out *tonight* if she caught us!" Miss Hicks said.

"But she ain't goin' to catch us," Mr O'Hannigan said.

Inspector Conway heard more kissing, followed by footsteps, and the creak of the gate's hinges. Rubbing his hand over his face, he released a soft sigh and considered what he should do.

* * *

Mr Elliott alighted from the hansom cab and paid its driver. It was almost ten o'clock, and the warmth of his fireside and comfort of his bed were calling to him. The verdict, Dr Weeks, and his conflicting thoughts and emotions about Inspector Lee all weighed heavily upon his fatigued mind. Deciding to set them aside for the remainder of the night, he took out his latch key and approached his lodgings.

"Good evening."

Mr Elliott halted and saw Inspector Lee walking toward him. A glance into the street confirmed it was deserted, thus begging the obvious question. "Where did you come from?"

"My carriage and driver are around the corner."

Mr Elliott glanced up and down the street. "And your spies?"

"I've ordered them to cease their surveillance of you as of this afternoon."

"Why are your carriage and driver around the corner, then?"

"I didn't think you'd stop if you knew I was waiting for you."

"Shouldn't the same thought also give you cause not to wait for me?"

"Yes." Inspector Lee moved closer. "But I find it difficult to stay away."

Mr Elliott's posture stiffened. "Don't expect me to invite you in."

"Don't you trust yourself to be alone with me?" Inspector Lee gave a wry smile.

Mr Elliott's features tightened, and he strode to his front door. "Good night, Gideon."

"What did she say?" Inspector Lee called after him.

Mr Elliott closed his eyes in exasperation, his back to the policeman.

"Miss Trent? When you asked her about Dr Weeks?"

Mr Elliott turned to face him and replied in a hard tone, "She confirmed it."

Inspector Lee closed the distance between them. "You seem disappointed."

"She also said he'd struck you, making me wonder what you'd done to provoke him."

"Nothing whatsoever. The man is sick in mind."

"And you've proven yourself to be untrustworthy on multiple occasions, so forgive me if I don't believe you on this."

Inspector Lee moved closer still. "I can be trustworthy, Gregory." He ran an appraising glance over Mr Elliott. "When it matters."

"I have my serious doubts."

Inspector Lee's gaze and voice softened as he looked to Mr Elliott's lips and said, "All I need is an opportunity to prove it to you."

"I don't want anything from you."

The corner of Inspector Lee's mouth twitched. "I think you do."

He leant in and gave Mr Elliott's lips the lightest of kisses. Meeting the solicitor's intense gaze, he held it for a prolonged moment before leaning in again. This time, the kiss was harder, and the tip of Inspector Lee's tongue pressed against Mr Elliott's lips. There was resistance at first, then they parted, and Inspector Lee tasted the solicitor for the first time. Feeling a shiver course through him, he closed his eyes and held the back of Mr Elliott's head as they shared a passionate kiss. After only a few moments, though, the kiss was broken, and he was pushed away.

"No," Mr Elliott breathlessly said, holding the back of his hand against his mouth. "I can't. Please," he turned and unlocked the door, "leave me alone."

"Gregory—" Inspector Lee began, stepping forward. His words were cut off by the closing of the door, however. Taking an immediate backward step to prevent a collision with the wood, he glanced around in the hope of seeing Mr Elliott at a nearby window. Seeing neither hide nor hair of him, though, he took several more backward steps and looked up at the window belonging to Mr Elliott's rooms. Seeing no sign of him there either, Inspector Lee frowned. Yet, the taste of the solicitor remained fresh in his mouth. Feeling his heart swell with delight at the realisation, he licked his lips and walked back to his carriage.

* * *

"Would you like some cocoa?" Miss Trent enquired as she removed her coat and hung it on the hatstand. At Toby's nod, she indicated the parlour. "Settle down in front of the fire, and I'll bring you some." As the lad headed into the other room, she glanced up the stairs and wondered if Miss Hicks was asleep. Deciding not to disturb her in case she was, Miss Trent entered the kitchen but halted when she saw Inspector Conway at the window. Striding over to the back door and letting him in, she felt the cold coming off him despite the warmth of the stove. "John?" She touched his arm. "You're freezing."

"Never mind that." Inspector Conway removed his hat. "Where's Miss Hicks?"

"Upstairs, asleep, I think," Miss Trent replied.

"No, she ain't." Inspector Conway strode past her, heading for the hallway.

"Wait a minute." Miss Trent blocked his path. "What do you mean? She isn't asleep, or she isn't upstairs?"

"She's upstairs all right," Inspector Conway replied, "With bloody Noah O'Hannigan."

Miss Trent's head jerked back. "I beg your pardon?"

"I come by earlier. I didn't know you was out, and I heard them in the alleyway," Inspector Conway replied. "They was kissin', then they come in here."

Miss Trent's eyes widened.

Inspector Conway tried to step around her. "Weeks' rottin' in Bedlam and she's—"

"Stop!" Miss Trent blocked his path, again, and put her hand on his chest. "If you heard them come inside, why did you wait until now to intervene?"

Inspector Conway looked at her. "I wanted you here, didn't I?"

"To do what, precisely?" Miss Trent enquired with a lift of her eyebrows.

"I don't know." Inspector Conway glanced at the kitchen door. "Toss them out?"

Miss Trent put her hand on her hip. "How is throwing Miss Hicks onto the streets, naked and penniless, going to help Dr Weeks?"

Inspector Conway frowned. "It won't. But it still not right."

"I agree." Miss Trent took him by the arm and guided him to the table. "Sit down." She prepared a mug of tea and put it in front of him. "Drink this." She smoothed down her skirts and prepared Toby's cocoa in a pan on the stove's top. "Polly will have to sneak Mr O'Hannigan out of the house eventually and, when she does, I'll be waiting. Besides, confronting her now would only let her know you're here, and she's already asked me if there's something going on between us."

Inspector Conway blinked. "She what?" He wrapped his numb hands around the mug and, lifting it to his lips, gave a small shake of his head. "Girl needs her head lookin' at." He blew away the steam and took a sip. "Don't know what Weeks bloody sees in her."

Probably the same thing I saw in her once, Miss Trent thought. Stirring the cocoa into the warmed milk until it dissolved, she poured it into a mug and took it to Toby. Returning a few moments later, she poured some cocoa for herself and joined Inspector Conway at the table. "You didn't come here to confront an adulteress and her lover." She took a sip of cocoa. "Have you heard something about Dr Weeks?"

"No." Inspector Conway had another sip of tea. "Caleb told me about the meetin' you had with 'im and

Calvin." He held the mug with both hands as he looked across the table at her. "Me and Caleb went to the bank after and couldn't find anythin' about J. Pettifoot from them, but Richard knew we wouldn't. 'E's playin' a bloody dangerous game, Rebecca."

"As are we all," Miss Trent reminded him. "I know J. Pettifoot is serving their purpose, but it makes me feel uncomfortable knowing how much Inspector Woolfe is investigating them, me, and the Society's affairs."

"Lee, too." Inspector Conway took a mouthful of tea this time. "'E's got a bloke watchin' the house from across the road."

Miss Trent released a soft sigh as she tilted her head to the side and rubbed her temple. "It's not surprising, but it's still infuriating." She lowered her hand. "Inspector Lee's men are also watching me and the Society's members."

"Yeah, it's why Richard's not been able to meet you."

"I know." Miss Trent picked up her mug of cocoa. "I'll have a progress report ready for him soon." She took a sip of cocoa. "How's your ribs?"

Inspector Conway glanced down. "Hurtin', but I'll be okay."

Miss Trent put a gentle hand on his arm. "I'll talk to Polly; try to make her see some sense." She withdrew her hand. "I can't believe she'd be so stupid as to take Mr O'Hannigan back after finding out about Dr Weeks."

"And knowin' O'Hannigan's thieved off her," Inspector Conway said. At Miss Trent's questioning look, he explained, "I heard her ask 'im about some money and jewellery she thought 'e'd taken.

Miss Trent frowned. "I knew about the money but not the jewellery." Suddenly, Mr Snyder's account of overhearing Miss Hicks crying had an entirely different meaning.

"If she ends it but 'e don't walk away, let me know, and I'll sort 'im out," Inspector Conway said.

Miss Trent lofted an eyebrow. "Thank you, John, but I'd prefer not to put you at risk of being arrested for assault."

"Nah, a bloke like O'Hannigan wouldn't peach, not for sumin' like that. 'E'd never live it down." Inspector Conway drank the remainder of his tea.

"*Shh.*" Miss Trent put her finger to her lips and whispered, "I hear something."

Inspector Conway listened.

"Someone's coming downstairs." Miss Trent stood and opened the pantry door. "Hide in here."

Inspector Conway stood and, going into the pantry, closed the door behind him.

Miss Trent stood between the doors leading into the hallway and listened.

"She's in the parlour with Toby," Miss Hicks said quietly beyond the right-hand door.

"I ain't creepin' 'round like this next time, wee lass," Mr O'Hannigan quietly replied.

The right-hand door opened, and Miss Hicks entered. "You won't have to."

Miss Hicks froze when she looked back and saw Miss Trent.

"Why not?" Mr O'Hannigan enquired as he entered. Seeing the colour drain from Miss Hicks' face, he followed her line of sight.

"Because, Mr O'Hannigan, there shan't be a 'next time,'" Miss Trent replied.

"Becky, I…" Miss Hicks began, her voice trailing off when she realised how pathetic she sounded. "Don't toss me out."

"I'm not going to," Miss Trent reassured. "If Mr O'Hannigan leaves immediately."

Mr O'Hannigan grinned. "I was goin' anyway." He rested his hands on Miss Hicks' hips and, making a point of kissing her deeply, sauntered through the back door and across the yard.

Miss Hicks wiped her mouth and sheepishly said, "I'm sorry, Becky."

"Who for?" Miss Trent cooly enquired. "Yourself for getting caught, me for having an adulteress carrying on an affair under my roof, or the Bow Street Society, whose reputation you've almost ruined with a scandal? Because your sorrow *certainly* isn't for Dr Weeks."

"That's not fair," Miss Hicks said without conviction.

"Isn't it?" Miss Trent entered Miss Hicks' personal space. "Mr O'Hannigan is never to come into this house again. Do you understand?"

Miss Hicks gave a small nod.

"Because if he does, you *will* be leaving with him," Miss Trent added.

Miss Hicks lifted her chin. "Maybe I'll leave with him anyway."

"If you do, you're more naïve and foolish than I thought you were."

"He cares about me."

"Noah O'Hannigan only cares about one person: Noah O'Hannigan."

"He come back for me, didn't he?"

"He came back for your *money*. Actually, he came back for *Dr Weeks'* money."

Miss Hicks folded her arms. "You don't know anythin' about survivin', Becky. You sit here in your big house with your fancy furniture and don't know what others do to make ends meet."

Miss Trent stared at her. "How can you stand there and justify your betrayal of Dr Weeks as 'survival?' *I* have provided a roof over your head, food, and warmth, *and* arranged for your worldly possessions to be brought here at no cost to you. Your 'survival' doesn't rely on you putting Noah O'Hannigan between your legs!"

"But your 'charity' ain't forever, is it? And my Perce can't look after me. Noah's the only choice I've got." Miss Hicks glanced over Miss Trent. "Unless you want me to stay forever, Becky?"

Miss Trent's gaze hardened. "Don't try to put the blame on me, Polly. This entire situation is the bed you've made for yourself, so either lie in it or get yourself a new bed."

"I have." Miss Hicks walked past her. "I've got Noah's." She left the room.

Miss Trent shook her head in disbelief and opened the pantry door.

"She's got more front than Brighton," Inspector Conway remarked as he emerged.

"Than Brighton and Blackpool combined," Miss Trent added.

"I'll let you know if I hear sumin' about Weeks."

"Thanks." Miss Trent smiled softly and locked the back door after he'd left.

FORTY-TWO

The grandfather clock struck seven thirty, its chimes echoing in the Bow Street Society's dark hallway. Upstairs, Miss Hicks and Toby slept soundly in their respective rooms, oblivious to the knocking at the front door. After several minutes of trying, the visitor abandoned the endeavour and turned toward the deserted street with a decision to make. Yet, as they considered their next move, the rattle of wheels across cobblestones sounded in the distance, pulling them from their thoughts. They walked to the porch's edge and, peering through the gloom, saw a dog cart approaching from Endell Street.

Their heart leapt when they saw Miss Trent driving but fell again when they saw Mr Snyder beside her. The visitor contemplated leaving but realised the clerk and cabman had probably seen their carriage already. Nevertheless, they retreated into the shadows to avoid an awkward conversation with Mr Snyder and waited as Miss Trent alighted from the dog cart and bid him goodbye.

When he'd driven away, and Miss Trent had begun to ascend the steps, Dr Locke moved into the light and waited for the clerk to notice her. When she did, it was with an emotionless expression and gentle halt on the third step, thus confirming Dr Locke's earlier suspicion about her carriage.

"I must speak to you at once," Dr Locke said.

"Of course." Miss Trent was troubled by Dr Locke's presence at such an early hour. Swiftly climbing the remaining stairs, she released a mechanism hidden behind a panel in the front door to open it and invited Dr Locke inside. "Has something happened to Percy?"

"No, he was asleep when I left." As she entered, Dr Locke inwardly scolded herself for not realising the early morning visit would in itself be a cause for alarm to the clerk. "It's about Dr Weeks." Her voice adopted an urgent tone, "I must know what the news is."

"Come into the kitchen where it's warmer—"

"No," Dr Locke snapped. Turning away sharply at the same time, she paced between the front door and stairs. "I've laid awake half the night thinking about what could've happened to him." A tremor entered her voice as she continued, "He is a foul-mouthed, ill-mannered, narcissistic, and utterly disgusting excuse of a man but also a brilliant surgeon who has supported and encouraged me in spite of misogynistic conventions dictating he do otherwise." She turned to Miss Trent. "I loathe him because of what he has done, but I also worry about him because he is my friend, which makes me loathe him even more." She swiftly closed the distance between them. "Is he ill? Is he dead? I must know."

Miss Trent was a little taken aback by Dr Locke's conflicting statements. Seeing the intense worry in Dr Locke's eyes, though, Miss Trent put an arm around her and gently guided her to sit on the stairs. Sitting beside her, she held her hands and said in a neutral tone, "He isn't dead, but he is ill. Two nights ago, he was admitted to Bethlehem Hospital after being formally diagnosed with alcoholic insanity."

Dr Locke's head dropped. Closing her eyes, she softly admitted, "I knew it." She held Miss Trent's hands in return as she felt her heart grow heavy. "His drinking… he is as crippled by addiction as my husband. I witnessed it but chose not to see it." Her eyes glistened with unshed tears as she raised her head. "I couldn't cope with the burden of his addiction, as well as Percy's. I turned my back on him, Rebecca."

Miss Trent put a hand on Dr Locke's shoulder. "No one expected you to take on Dr Weeks' problems. I certainly didn't."

"But I should've. I'm a doctor and his friend besides. It didn't have to come to him being put into an asylum. Do you have any idea what it is like in such places?"

"Dr Colbert is the resident physician at Bethlehem Hospital and is personally overseeing Dr Weeks' care,"

Miss Trent gently reassured. "Hence his reason for withdrawing from the investigation."

"Thank you, but it brings me little comfort. You see." Dr Locke bowed her head. "Something happened recently that should've shown me how unwell he was. Instead, I allowed myself to think the worst of him. Now, I fear my cruelty might have contributed to him being admitted."

Miss Trent felt the same feeling of dread creep into her heart she'd felt when waiting for Inspector Conway to break the news. Until recently, she could've sworn under oath what Dr Weeks was and wasn't capable of. Unfortunately, nothing was beyond possibility anymore. Therefore, it was with some trepidation she enquired, "What happened, Lynette? What did Dr Weeks do?"

Dr Locke swallowed. "A few nights ago, he asked to meet me at the Dead Room."

Miss Trent darted her gaze to Dr Locke's face and wrists but saw no bruises.

"I was halfway there when I noticed I'd forgotten my medical bag," Dr Locke continued. "Mr Lambert drove me back home, but when I arrived, Lyons informed me Dr Weeks was with Percy. I entered the room and asked Dr Weeks what he was doing there." She grimaced. "I saw Percy on the rug by the fire… picking up a needle, tourniquet, and vial… of heroin." She lifted her hand and rested her forehead against her palm. "Dr Weeks had *offered* Percy *heroin*." She closed her eyes, causing tears to slide down her cheeks. "I couldn't believe what I was seeing. I couldn't *grasp* what I was seeing. Then everything seemed to shift back into focus, and I was angry. I-I was hurt as well, but I was so very, *very* angry, Rebecca. I said some truly terrible things to him, *cruel* things, and made him leave. That was the last time I saw him." She lowered her hand. "How could what I said not have contributed to his admission to the hospital?"

"Because the incident with you and Mr Locke wasn't the only thing to happen to Dr Weeks in the past few days," Miss Trent replied. "You'll understand why I can't divulge any further details, but please know you aren't responsible for his current situation, Lynette."

"Truly?" Dr Locke's eyes were initially hopeful but swiftly turned sad. "It is worse than I'd feared, then." She slowly turned her head to stare into an invisible horizon. "I abandoned him at his greatest hour of need."

"You reacted as anyone would've. Dr Weeks tried to give Mr Locke the very drug you've been trying to wean him off." Even as she spoke, Miss Trent wondered what had driven Dr Weeks to do it. Yet, the memory of Inspector Conway's haunted look after the incident with the scalpel reminded her Dr Weeks had been far from himself lately. "Regardless of Dr Weeks' illness, he shouldn't have done such a horrible thing." Miss Trent held up Dr Locke's hands and gave them a gentle squeeze. "You should come with me when he's allowed visitors. I'm sure he'd like to see you."

"He probably hates me," Dr Locke said, sadly.

"He probably hates himself," Miss Trent corrected in a sombre tone. "You, better than anyone, understands the damage an addiction does to a person, because you've witnessed it firsthand in Percy. Dr Weeks would appreciate your support, and your friendship."

"I hope you're right."

"Of course I'm right." Miss Trent's expression softened. "I wouldn't be the clerk of the Bow Street Society if I had a tendency to be wrong, would I?"

Dr Locke smiled. "No, I suppose you wouldn't."

* * *

"Good morning, Gregory."

Mr Elliott glanced past Inspector Lee at the deserted landing. "How did you get in?"

"I told your neighbour I was your uncle. May I come in?"

"No." Mr Elliott closed the door, but Inspector Lee blocked it with his foot.

"We must talk about last night." Inspector Lee lowered his voice. "We kissed."

"I don't recall that," Mr Elliott stated, coldly. "Please, remove your foot."

"You deny it?"

"Unequivocally."

Inspector Lee lifted his chin as he carefully considered his options. "Then you have no reason to decline my dinner invitation."

"I have every reason."

Inspector Lee moved closer. "I only want to talk to you, Gregory."

"But I don't want to talk to you."

"Why are you being like this?" He reached to caress Mr Elliott's face.

Mr Elliott moved his head beyond reach. "Last night was a mistake."

Inspector Lee tilted his head. "You acknowledge it happened, then?"

"Leave me alone." Mr Elliott kicked away Inspector Lee's foot and closed the door.

Inspector Lee smirked and, whistling softly, descended the stairs.

Listening with his back against the door, Mr Elliott put his head in his hands.

* * *

Dr Weeks' damp hands struggled to gain a grip on the rough stone, whilst his feet slipped, and his legs gave way beneath him. Calling upon every ounce of his strength, he dug his fingernails into the stone and pulled himself up onto the ledge. It was dark; he could barely see his hand in front of his face. He reached out and felt the harsh, angular edge of a step. Reaching higher, he felt another step and another. Slowly, he crawled up them, his body feeling like it was surrounded by thick mud.

Suddenly, his hand touched a foot, and he looked up to see a dark figure standing over him. He couldn't see their face, but he knew it was his father.

"Bastards should be grateful for what they are given," the figure boomed.

"I don't want yer damn money!" Dr Weeks yelled.

"Remember your place, boy!" the figure yelled back.

Dr Weeks suddenly felt his body being propelled backward, followed by the impact of landing on something soft. Dazed, he forced himself to regain his focus and saw a rectangular hole high above him. Miss Hicks, Dr Locke, and Inspector Conway stood at its edge, with a grey sky visible beyond them.

"What… what's happenin'?" Dr Weeks weakly enquired.

A vicar stepped into view beside Inspector Conway. "And so, it shall be in the end as it was in the beginning. Ashes to ashes, dust to dust."

"Nah…" Dr Weeks said as the first clumps of dirt fell upon him. "I ain't dead." Miss Hicks threw in more dirt, followed by Dr Locke. "I ain't dead!"

"Argh!" Dr Weeks thrashed against the dirt burying him but found he couldn't move his wrists. "I ain't dead!"

"Mr Weeks!"

"*Let me outta here*!" Dr Weeks yelled, kicking out.

"*Percy*!"

Dr Weeks stopped struggling and opened his eyes.

A deeply concerned Dr Colbert gazed down at him. "You were having a nightmare."

Dr Weeks looked down sharply and saw hands around his wrists. Following the arms, he realised they were Dr Colbert's. "They were buryin' me… I couldn't get out."

Dr Colbert eased his grip. "You're safe now."

Dr Weeks felt the cold dampness of his sweat-sodden nightshirt against the sheets. "Where am I?"

"Your room at the hospital," Dr Colbert watched Dr Weeks' reaction closely.

"Hospital…?" Dr Weeks turned his head left and right to take in his surroundings. To his right was a barred window. To his left was a sparsely furnished room dimly lit by gas light. Slowly, the fog separated in his mind and the memory of being brought there in a black maria took its place. "John… and Richard… they brought me here."

"Yes." Dr Colbert released Dr Weeks' wrists and sat on the edge of the bed.

A wave of nausea engulfed Dr Weeks, causing him to grimace and close his eyes. "I feel like shit." As he lifted his hand to his face, he felt the trembling of his fingers against his skin. "How long've I been here?"

"This is your second morning."

"It's mornin'?" Dr Weeks glanced at the window but saw only darkness.

"You've had a fever since you arrived, caused by the withdrawal from alcohol we've been obliged to impose upon you." Dr Colbert watched the second hand of his pocket watch as he felt Dr Weeks' pulse. Lifting each of Dr Weeks' eyelids next, he was pleased to see his pupils had returned to normal. His eyes remained bloodshot, however. "Do you have a headache?"

"Yeah." Dr Weeks closed his eyes and rested his arms by his sides.

"Nausea?"

"Yeah."

Dr Colbert pressed the back of his hand against Dr Weeks' forehead. "You don't seem to be feverish anymore, which is a good sign." He glanced at Dr Weeks' nightshirt. "I'll have some clean clothes brought in for you. Do you feel able to eat?"

Dr Weeks gave a curt shake of his head. "I jus' wanna sleep."

Dr Colbert stood and patted Dr Weeks' shoulder. "Sleep, then. I'll come back later to check on you."

"Thanks, doc."

"How is he?" Dr McWilliams enquired upon Dr Colbert emerging into the corridor.

Dr Colbert rubbed his eyes. "Better. His fever has finally broken and, although he feels nauseous, still, I think he is past the worst of it."

"You look exhausted, Neal. How much sleep did you get last night?"

"None."

"Go home and get some sleep," Dr McWilliams urged. "Please."

Dr Colbert glanced back at Dr Weeks' door and slowly nodded. "All right." His body felt like a lead weight as he walked with Dr McWilliams down the corridor. "If his condition changes, though—"

"I will send word to you immediately," Dr McWilliams promised.

"Thank you, Charles." Dr Colbert unlocked the doors into the entrance hall but couldn't gather the strength to push them open. Allowing Dr McWilliams to do it for him, he softly thanked him, again, and passed through, his feet barely lifting off the floor as he went.

FORTY-THREE

The train ride between the railway stations at Euston in London and New Street in Birmingham had been an uneventful one following departure. Prior to this, Mr Elliott had to convince the onboard conductor that Mr Snyder's first-class ticket was legitimate. Furthermore, they were friends, and Mr Elliott was in no way being threatened by Mr Snyder. The solicitor had thought it a sorry state of affairs when even a properly purchased ticket was insufficient to guarantee respect. The cabman had taken it in good humour, though, and brushed it off as one of those things.

Eating the last bite of his corned beef sandwich, Mr Elliott folded the paper into a neat, little square and slipped it into his overcoat pocket to dispose of later. "Please, pass on my gratitude to your wife. It hadn't occurred to me to pack some lunch."

"Thanks," Mr Snyder beamed. "She'll be chuffed to hear it."

"May I ask how long you've been married?"

"Goin' on twenty-five years now."

"And you have children, correct?"

"Five daughters for my sins." Mr Snyder chuckled. "Sally, my eldest, has started courtin'. 'E's a nice lad but not got much in the knowledge box." He tapped his temple. "Are you married, Mr Elliott? If you don't mind my askin'."

Mr Elliott usually avoided discussions about his personal life unless he'd instigated them. Yet, Mr Snyder had graciously answered his questions, so he had little choice but to do the same or risk appearing rude. "No. Marriage holds no interest for me."

"Not met the right woman, aye?"

The memory of the kiss he'd shared with Inspector Lee sprang into his mind, along with the feelings of desire, confusion, and unease which came with it. Pushing it aside, he looked out the window at the urban landscape sprawled out as far as the eye could see. "I've not sought any out."

"Birmingham!" The conductor shouted as he walked down the narrow corridor outside their compartment. "Next stop is New Street station, Birmingham!"

Mr Elliott and Mr Snyder put on their hats, gloves, and scarves.

"Do you have the address Miss Trent gave us?" Mr Elliott enquired.

"Right 'ere." Mr Snyder tapped his jacket's breast pocket.

"I'm expecting some resistance from the police, so we might want to check into our hotel first," Mr Elliott suggested.

"Can do. It's not far from the railway station."

A screeching of metal, coupled with an abundance of steam rolling past the window, prompted Mr Elliott to look outside. Upon seeing the wide platform approaching, he slid down the window and waited until the train had slowed before reaching out and gripping the external handle. As the train slowed further, he lifted the handle, retreated inside, and opened the door ajar. The same idea had occurred to the other passengers, who poured onto the platform whilst the train was still in motion.

Choosing to wait, Mr Elliott alighted once the train was stationary and looked along the platform. Seeing a second train slow to a halt on its opposite side, he watched as its passengers poured out to join the throng of the first. Everyone moved up the platform, weaving around each other and porters with luggage trolleys, only to be delayed by a bottleneck of people at the foot of the stairs. Just wide enough for two people, the stairs led up to a high-walled footbridge spanning the platforms in this part of the station.

During his earlier conversation with Mr Snyder, Mr Elliott had discovered this part of New Street railway station, the northern part to be precise, was occupied by the company whose service they'd arrived on: London North-Western Railway. Meanwhile, the southern part of the station—an extension completed in 1885—was occupied by Midlands Railway. Running between both parts was the carriageway Great Queen Street, a fact Mr Elliott had found quite astounding. Therefore, he could only assume the footbridge led to the LNWR ticket offices and station exit on Great Queen Street.

"Do yow have any luggage, sir?" a porter enquired in a broad West Midlands accent.

"No. Thank you," Mr Elliott replied.

Despite Mr Snyder also alighting from the first class compartment, the porter strode past him without uttering a word. Mr Elliott's lips pressed into a white slash upon seeing this, but he suspected Mr Snyder would prefer it if he didn't confront the narrow-minded man.

"Blimey, look who it is." Mr Snyder pointed toward the crowd. "Inspector Conway."

"Where?" Mr Elliott enquired, scanning the passengers' faces.

"To the right of the stairs."

Mr Elliott shifted his gaze and, sure enough, the grizzled policeman stood apart from the crowd, lighting a cigarette. He had his back to the train they'd alighted from, so Mr Elliott couldn't be certain whether he'd arrived on their service. He didn't appear to have any luggage, though, and wasn't behaving as if he were waiting for someone.

If Inspector Conway had still been at New Scotland Yard, Mr Elliott wouldn't have thought it unusual to find him in Birmingham. There had been multiple occasions when other constabularies had called upon the assistance of the Metropolitan Police detectives to investigate complex or high-profile murder cases. Yet, Inspector Conway had been reassigned to Bow Street and, as far as Mr Elliott was aware, detective officers from lower divisions were rarely sent outside London.

"I wonder why he's in Birmingham," Mr Elliott mused aloud.

"Don't know." Mr Snyder moved to approach him. "Let's ask."

"Wait." Mr Elliott lifted his arm to bar Mr Snyder's path. "Let's watch him first."

"The bloke's just havin' a smoke," Mr Snyder pointed out, a little confused.

"At the moment, yes, but I want to see what he does next."

"Why?"

"The likelihood of it occurring is small, but there's a possibility he's in Birmingham for the same reason we are."

Mr Snyder glanced at Inspector Conway, but he was looking the other way and smoking, still, besides. "We might as well ask 'im, then."

Mr Elliott's face tightened as he drew his eyebrows together. "I doubt he'd tell us."

"'E'd tell me."

"Not if he thought you would tell me afterward."

"Nah, John's not like that."

"Let us agree to disagree on what Inspector Conway is 'like,'" Mr Elliott cooly suggested. "As for watching him: please, humour me for a while?"

"I don't know what good it'll do," Mr Snyder scratched the back of his neck whilst shaking his head. "But, okay."

"Thank you, Sam," Mr Elliott briefly touched the small of Mr Snyder's back.

Inspector Conway, oblivious to the attention his presence had garnered, finished his cigarette and crushed it out under his shoe. He compared the time on his pocket watch to the station clock to confirm the former didn't require winding and approached the stairs. For as long as he could remember, he'd felt uneasy in crowds. Maybe it was the way people got so close to each other, and he couldn't see what their hands were doing that did it.

Pickpockets thrived in busy streets, and lots of bodies meant lots of obstacles when trying to chase a thief who'd scarpered with your things. Yet, as logical an explanation as this was, Inspector Conway wasn't convinced it was the catalyst of his aversion.

"I want to follow him," Mr Elliott quietly told Mr Snyder. "Are you with me?"

Mr Snyder agreed, if only to ensure Mr Elliott didn't get into trouble.

Mr Elliott watched Inspector Conway ascend the stairs and waited until he was almost at the top before walking toward them himself. Glancing sideways to confirm Mr Snyder was at his side, he quickened his pace when he saw Inspector Conway step onto the footbridge, turn, and move from view. Climbing the stairs two at a time, he felt his heart pounding in his ears by the time he'd reached the top. Expecting to find no sign of the policeman, he was relieved to see him talking to a railway employee. It appeared as though Inspector Conway had asked for directions; the employee was pointing into the distance, prompting Inspector Conway to turn and do the same.

"'E could be visitin' someone," Mr Snyder suggested as they watched and waited by the arched entranceway at the top of the stairs.

"Perhaps. Perhaps not." Mr Elliott watched Inspector Conway write something into his notebook and bid goodbye to the railway employee. "Come on."

Mr Elliott led the way along the footbridge with Mr Snyder following a few feet behind. Inspector Conway had once again moved from view, but Mr Elliott was confident they'd catch up with him on Great Queen Street. Therefore, quickening his pace, again, he weaved around the other passengers as he strode through the station and emerged onto the carriageway. Alas, when he looked up and down the road, he couldn't see any sign of Inspector Conway anywhere. Frowning, he conceded, "He's gone."

"It's probably for the best, lad." Mr Snyder gave him a pat on the back. "Our hotel should be along 'ere somewhere."

Mr Elliott scanned the faces of passing pedestrians but came up with nothing. Keen to learn the reason for Inspector Conway's visit to Birmingham, but conceding he never would, Mr Elliott felt frustrated as he followed Mr Snyder to their hotel. Yet no sooner had they left the vicinity of the station did he spot Inspector Conway up ahead. Gripping Mr Snyder's arm, he pointed to their quarry. "He's over there." He quickened his pace until he was practically running, as Mr Snyder jogged along behind. Determined not to lose sight of Inspector Conway again, Mr Elliott fixed his gaze upon the back of his head, thereby relying solely upon his peripheral vision to alert him to upcoming obstacles.

* * *

"Thou art fairer than the evening air, clad in the beauty of a thousand stars," Mr Stone softly recited as he brushed his fingertips against Miss Lily's cheek. Standing in a quiet corner of the backstage area, he had his back to the stage and his chest lightly touching hers.

"I adore Shakespeare," Miss Lily said, matching his tone.

"It was Marlowe."

"Oh."

"But I can teach you Marlowe." Mr Stone's gaze followed his hand as he slid it across her neck. "I can teach you many things. If you'd let me."

"Ronnie?" Mr Thurston enquired.

Mr Stone simultaneously closed his eyes, sighed, and dropped his hand at the interruption. Looking over his shoulder, he curtly enquired, "What is it?"

"Emmaline wants to see you," Mr Thurston replied.

"Tell her I'll be there in a minute." Mr Stone returned his attention to Miss Lily.

"She wants to see you now," Mr Thurston urged.

Mr Stone cupped Miss Lily's chin with his hand. "I'll see you later?"

Miss Lily nodded.

Mr Stone kissed her cheek and joined Mr Thurston.

"You ought to be ashamed of yourself," Mr Thurston whispered as they walked away. "You're old enough to be her father, for goodness sake."

"Don't get excited, old man," Mr Stone warned. "It's not good for your health."

Miss Kimberly met them at the entrance to the wings. She looked from Mr Thurston to Mr Stone and back again. "Where is Lily? I specifically asked you to fetch her, Morris."

Mr Stone shot Mr Thurston a black look.

"Did you? My apologies. I thought you said Mr Stone," Mr Thurston lied.

"Here I am, Aunt Emma." Miss Lily walked around Mr Thurston and Mr Stone but cast a subtle smile at the latter as she passed.

Miss Kimberly's gaze cooled as she caught the little exchange. Taking a firm grip of Miss Lily's arm, she marched her onto the stage. "You're late for rehearsals. Morris!"

"You can't prevent me from having her," Mr Stone quietly warned Mr Thurston.

Mr Thurston felt his blood run cold and his concern for Miss Lily intensify.

"*Mister* Thurston!" Miss Kimberly shouted.

"Y-Yes, Miss Kimberly!" Mr Thurston called back, hurrying onto the stage.

"Miss Kimberly?" Mr Benton called from the stalls.

Miss Kimberly turned and put her hands upon her hips when she saw Mr Benton standing in the aisle with the Lockes, Claude, Mr Heath, and a gentleman she didn't recognise. "We haven't the time for more discussions and investigations."

"Dr Locke wishes to speak to Miss Lily for a few minutes," Mr Benton explained.

"Lily is assuming Mina's part tonight. We must rehearse," Miss Kimberly stated.

"In that case, is it not preferable for Miss Lily to speak to us before her rehearsal?" Mr Locke enquired. "You have our word we shall not return and further disturb you for the remainder of the day."

Miss Lily stepped forward. "We may speak in my mother's dressing room—"

"They will speak to you here, with me present," Miss Kimberly ordered.

"Yes, Aunt Emma," Miss Lily sheepishly agreed.

"We may speak in my dressing room," Mr Benton informed Mr Locke and Mr Heath.

"Is Mr Stone around?" Mr Verity enquired from Miss Kimberly.

"I'm he." Mr Stone emerged from the wings. "Who are you?"

"Mr Virgil Verity, retired schoolmaster and member of the Bow Street Society," Mr Verity introduced.

Mr Stone narrowed his eyes. "What do you want?"

"A word. Nothing more, nothing less," Mr Verity replied in a nonchalant manner.

"I've told Mr Locke all I'm going to say." Mr Stone returned to the wings.

"A rude little beggar, isn't he?" Mr Verity quietly observed to Mr Locke.

"You may join me, if you'd like?" Dr Locke invited.

"Aye, that'll be nice, lass," Mr Verity smiled.

As Mr Locke, Claude, and Mr Heath followed Mr Benton onto and across the stage to his dressing room, Dr Locke put her arm around Mr Verity's and assisted him to Miss Kimberly and Miss Lily. Retrieving a stool for him as well, she set it down and helped him onto it. "Allow me to begin by offering my condolences, Miss Ilbert. Losing your mother in such an horrific way must be very distressing for you."

Miss Kimberly adopted a pinched expression. "Please, keep your questions brief and to the point, doctor."

Dr Locke adopted a hard tone. "I intend to." To Miss Lily, she enquired, "Were you in the wings when it occurred?"

Miss Lily hugged herself. "No. I only had a small part in the first act. I was changing from my costume in my dressing room when…" She pursed her lips until her emotions calmed. "I was afraid something would happen to her the moment she said she would disband the company. Everyone here," she glanced around her, "this theatre is their lives, and she was going to take it away from them. I thought someone might yell at her, or hit her, not… I *never* would have imagined anyone here could do something so *evil*."

"Sometimes the ends can justify the means," Miss Kimberly calmly observed.

"Murder can never be justified," Mr Verity countered.

"Mina was as good as holding a gun to our heads with her ultimatum." Miss Kimberly adopted a hard tone. "*I* have known what it is to be destitute, Mr Verity. To be cold, dirty, and starving. People turn their backs upon your suffering. They say your sins have brought misfortune upon you and demand you break your back for a meagre hunk of stale bread. Anyone not sick in mind would be desperate to spare themselves from such a fate. Murder is never the preferred option, Mr Verity, but, sometimes, circumstances make it the *only* option."

"By your logic, both you and Lily have a strong motive for murdering Mina," Dr Locke pointed out.

"A fact I don't deny," Miss Kimberly said.

"Aunt Emma could never have murdered my mother." Miss Lily was visibly shocked. "She was her oldest and dearest friend. *I* certainly could never… I *couldn't*. I *loved* my mother *dearly*."

"Has it been proven Mr Willis was competent in his work?" Miss Kimberly enquired.

Dr Locke gave a slight lift of her chin. "No."

"Then this conversation is redundant," Miss Kimberly said. "Lily, take your position, please." She strode across the stage and indicated a spot in its centre. "Remember, there will be dancers behind you."

"Who is your father, Miss Ilbert?" Dr Locke enquired.

"I… never knew him," Miss Lily replied.

"He died before she was born," Miss Kimberly interjected.

"May I know his name?" Dr Locke enquired.

Miss Lily looked nervously to Miss Kimberly for assistance.

Miss Kimberly's tone and expression softened. "Julian Raine."

Dr Locke noted the change in Miss Kimberly's demeanour. "May I know how he died?"

Miss Kimberly clasped her hands against her skirts and walked slowly toward the edge of the stage. "Prior to becoming stage manager here, Mr Stone managed the *Monolith Theatre* in Surrey. Mr Raine was his stage manager. One night, during a performance, a fire broke out. Mr Raine was below stage when it started. The theatre was quickly engulfed by flames. Mr Raine was trapped." She faced Dr Locke. "Mina gave Mr Stone employment here when she heard the fire had left him penniless."

"Was Miss Ilbert at the *Monolith* at the time of the fire?" Dr Locke enquired.

"No, but she would visit at weekends," Miss Kimberly replied.

"How do you know about Mr Raine and the fire?" Mr Verity enquired.

"I was part of Mr Stone's company," Miss Kimberly replied. "As an opera singer." She lowered her head as she walked, slowly, back to Miss Lily. "I, too, was caught up in the fire. My voice was so badly damaged from the smoke, I could no longer sing." She took Miss Lily's hand in hers. "Mina gave me the position of business manager." She looked to Dr Locke. "Much to Mr Stone's distaste."

She released Miss Lily's hand. "Lily was born six months after."

"May I ask how old you are, Miss Ilbert?" Dr Locke enquired.

"Eighteen," Miss Lily replied.

Dr Locke carefully considered the timeline. "Miss Kimberly, you, Miss Mina Ilbert, and Mr Stone have been part of the company here at the *Crescent Theatre* for all that time?"

"Mr Stone joined a year after the fire," Miss Kimberly replied. "When he had exhausted all other opportunities. Mina's offer was poorly received by him initially. But he soon had no choice but to swallow his pride and accept it."

"Thank you." Dr Locke offered a polite smile. "but the point I wanted to make was you have worked harmoniously together for seventeen years. Therefore, it's hard to comprehend why there's such disharmony now."

"Human nature, plain and simple," Mr Stone said from the wings, thereby drawing their attention to him. Walking out on stage, he had a cold demeanour as he continued, "We tolerated one another because it served our own interests to do so. It also helped Mina had never given us an ultimatum before. When she did, she was putting the proverbial cat amongst the pigeons." He turned hard eyes to Miss Kimberly. "I heard what you said about me, and you're wrong. I *make* my own opportunities; I don't seek them out. You'll discover that soon enough, and when you do, you'll regret making an enemy of me."

"New management, Mr Stone?" Mr Verity enquired. "It's what you told Mr Akers."

"You'll be manager of this theatre over my dead body," Miss Kimberly warned.

"Do your 'opportunities' include blackmailing the lead actor?" Dr Locke challenged.

Mr Stone narrowed his eyes. "I don't have to answer your questions."

"Ronnie?" Miss Lily enquired, visibly taken aback. "What is she talking about?"

"He is *Mister Stone* to you, child," Miss Kimberly admonished.

"Nothing." Mr Stone cast a glare at Miss Kimberly and Dr Locke in turn. "The Bow Street Society is just trying to blame someone else for Mina's death so they can get their money from Mr Willis."

"I resent that, lad," Mr Verity warned.

"Do you?" Mr Stone adopted a defensive tone. "I couldn't care less *what* you think."

FORTY-FOUR

The streets of Birmingham were awash with people, sounds, and odours. As vehicles vied for space on the roads, so, too, did pedestrians on the pavements. Amongst the latter, Mr Elliott weaved through the never-ending stream of oncoming bodies like a fish swimming against the tide. Mr Snyder, whose constitution was more accustomed to driving than running, took short, swift strides to keep pace with the solicitor. Fortunately, Inspector Conway was also incumbered by the mass of people and moved at a stroll several yards ahead of the Bow Streeters. When he reached the next corner, he stopped to consult his notebook, thereby granting Mr Elliott and Mr Snyder a small respite.

"Don't know why we couldn't of just asked 'im," Mr Snyder said. Panting and red-faced, he leant back against some railings and wiped the sweat from his face with his sleeve.

Mr Elliott kept his gaze fixed upon the policeman. "Because I don't trust him as far as I can throw him." He glanced at the cabman. "I know I'm the minority in the Society for thinking such, but it's an opinion I'll hold until, or unless, Inspector Conway gives me sufficient reason to change it."

"John's a good bloke. A bit too ready with his fists but still a good bloke."

"He looks after himself." Mr Elliott took in Mr Snyder's bruised face. "Like all policemen." He looked up the street in time to see Inspector Conway turn the corner. "He's moving, again." Continuing to weave around his fellow pedestrians, he was soon tracing Inspector Conway's footsteps. There was no sign of him on the next street, however. Mr Elliott pursed his lips and knitted his brow as he darted his gaze around the buildings for any clues to the policeman's whereabouts.

"Where is 'e?" Mr Snyder enquired upon joining Mr Elliott on the corner.

"I don't know." Mr Elliott looked to the street sign. "Newton Street."

"That's where we've got to go." Mr Snyder took out and reread the address. "Birmingham City Police, Newton Street." He showed it to Mr Elliott.

"Inspector Conway must have gone inside the police station, which means it should be further up the street." Mr Elliott continued walking, glancing at the buildings on either side of the road as he went. Suddenly, he caught sight of two uniformed constables conversing outside a door on the opposite side. He cast a sideways glance at Mr Snyder to ensure he was with him still, crossed the road, and approached the multi-storeyed building. "Good afternoon, Constables. Is this the office of Birmingham City Police?"

"It is, sir," one replied in a broad West Midlands accent. "Can oy help yow?"

"My friend and I wish to request an appointment with Detective Inspector Donahue," Mr Elliott replied. "May we go inside?"

The constables exchanged concerned glances.

"Oy don't know if yow'll get it, but go on," the first constable agreed.

"Thank you," Mr Elliott said.

Entering through the main door and holding it open for Mr Snyder, Mr Elliott did the same with a second inner door. Beyond this was a high-ceilinged room with whitewashed, plaster-covered walls, and dark-varnished wooden floorboards. Directly to the left of the door upon entering was a row of uncomfortable-looking wooden chairs. Opposite was a chest-high, wood-panelled counter that split the room in two. The width of the floorspace between the door and counter was approximately nine feet. A solid wooden door was perpendicular to the counter on its left and right ends. An open doorway behind the counter led into an office with wooden filing cabinets, and a constable sat behind a desk. A uniformed sergeant sat behind the counter, but it was the two men standing in front of it who caught Mr Elliott's attention.

The first was Inspector Conway; he had his back to the door, holding his trilby with both hands as he quietly conversed with the second man. He was in his early thirties, approximately five feet eleven inches tall, and broad shouldered. His weathered features were largely hidden by his dark-brown beard and thick hair of the same colour. The immaculate appearance of his cheap navy-blue suit and cream-coloured shirt hinted at him living with either a wife or spinster sister. The presence of a gold band upon his wedding finger immediately confirmed the former to be true, however. The remainder of his attire consisted of a dark-grey waistcoat, navy-blue tie, and polished black leather shoes.

"Yes, can oy help yow, sir?" the sergeant enquired.

"No, thank you," Mr Elliott replied.

Inspector Conway immediately turned his head to look at him.

"We've found who we were looking for," Mr Elliott added.

"What you doin' here?" Inspector Conway glanced at Mr Snyder. "Sumin' 'appen?"

"We saw you at the train station and decided to follow you," Mr Elliott replied.

Inspector Conway's face contorted into a scowl. "You what?"

"But we was comin' 'ere anyway," Mr Snyder interjected.

"What's your game, Elliott?" Inspector Conway demanded.

"No game, Inspector," Mr Elliott replied.

"We've come to see Detective Inspector Donahue," Mr Snyder said.

"Yow've found 'im," the immaculately dressed man said. "Who're yow?"

"Mr Sam Snyder, sir." The cabman offered his hand.

"And Mr Gregory Elliott of the Bow Street Society," the solicitor added.

"Yow's with Sidney Sloane's lot?" Inspector Donahue enquired, confused.

Mr Elliott and Mr Snyder exchanged glances as the latter withdrew his hand.

"Miss Trent briefed us on the case some of our fellow Bow Streeters investigated with the Birmingham Bow Street Society last year," Mr Elliott explained. "We're members of the London Bow Street Society, however."

"What do yow want to see me about?" Inspector Donahue enquired.

"We need your help in finding two people who we believe have travelled to Birmingham: Mr Jack Jerome and Miss Joanna Hightower," Mr Elliott replied. "They might have wed since, though."

Inspector Conway pushed his eyebrows together. "What do you want Jerome for?"

"We suspect he was involved in a scheme to blackmail Mr Luthor Ellis Benton, the lead actor at the *Crescent Theatre*, Strand," Mr Elliott replied. "We wish to confirm our suspicion and discover if anyone else was involved."

Inspector Conway lifted his chin slightly. "C Division said nothin' about blackmail."

"You've spoken to Detective Sergeant Dixon?" Mr Elliott enquired, intrigued.

"Yeah," Inspector Conway replied.

"About Miss Mina Ilbert's death?" Mr Elliott probed further.

"Yeah," Inspector Conway replied.

"I was told the police think it's an accident," Mr Elliott stated.

"We do," Inspector Conway said.

"Why speak to Sergeant Dixon about it, then?" Mr Elliott enquired.

Inspector Conway glared at him. "You're like a dog with a bloody bone, do you know that, Elliott?"

"It's my duty to be," Mr Elliott retorted. "Why did you speak to Sergeant Dixon?"

"I'm lookin' for Jerome, too," Inspector Conway begrudgingly replied.

"Also in connection with the blackmail?" Mr Elliott enquired.

"Blackmail, yeah, but not at the *Crescent*," Inspector Conway replied.

"At another theatre?" Mr Elliott enquired.

"Yeah," Inspector Conway replied.

"Which?" Mr Elliott enquired.

"*Royal Opera House*, Covent Garden," Inspector Conway replied.

Mr Elliott's gaze and tone cooled. "You're more difficult to draw information from than a defendant facing the death penalty."

"It's my duty to be," Inspector Conway retorted.

"Jerome was blackmail-ling actors in Bir-min-ham long before the arf-soaked Londoners," Inspector Donahue remarked with a hint of pride.

Mr Elliott recalled Miss Trent's warning about Inspector Donahue's prejudice against southerners.

"Bloke was gerron on my wick then," Inspector Donahue continued. "If he's back at it, I'll nick the little demon hell-raiser."

"Whether he is or he isn't, we still need to speak to him," Mr Elliott said.

"If the Birmingham City Police nick 'im, 'e's comin' back to Bow Street with me," Inspector Conway warned.

"It don't matter who wants 'im if we can't find 'im," Mr Snyder interjected.

Mr Elliott pursed his lips and softly exhaled through his nose, conceding the point.

"I've a Nark who'll know," Inspector Donahue informed Inspector Conway.

"May we meet them?" Mr Elliott enquired.

"No," Inspector Donahue replied firmly. "'E's a tuppeny 'apenny one who's two inches above upright.

Yow've got to talk to 'im all careful liok or 'e won't make a sound."

Inspector Conway knew how suspicious informants could be, especially with strangers. Therefore, he didn't volunteer to accompany Inspector Donahue either. The man knew what he was doing on his own patch. "While you're doin' that, Matthew, I've got someone to see. Should I meet you here after?"

"Will yow be want-ting to come?" Inspector Donahue enquired from Mr Elliott and Mr Snyder.

"Yes," Mr Elliott replied in an unequivocal tone.

"If you don't mind," Mr Snyder added.

Inspector Donahue took out his notebook and, leaning upon the counter, wrote out two copies of an address. "At six. The *Hope & Anchor* pub on Edmund Street." He tore off the two pages and gave one each to Inspector Conway and Mr Elliott. "I'll meet yow's there."

"Thank you, Inspector," Mr Elliott said with genuine appreciation.

* * *

"I had my reasons for not telling Dr Colbert about the assault," Mr Benton admitted.

"Which were?" Mr Locke enquired.

"I was afraid the police would intervene," Mr Benton replied.

"And cause you further trouble with Mr Jerome?" Mr Locke enquired.

"Precisely." Mr Benton's gaze drifted to the photograph of Mina on his dressing table.

Mr Benton was sitting at an angle to the table, the large mirror mounted upon the wall above it reflecting the back of his head. Innumerable letters, presumably from admirers, were glued to the wall on either side of the mirror. The dressing room at large was simply decorated with faded, dark-green wallpaper and an uneven tiled floor. Mr Benton's costumes were hung upon a rail spanning the wall opposite his dressing table. Mr Locke sat upon a stool next to the costumes, whilst Mr Heath stood beside him, and Claude waited outside the door.

"Forgive my next question, Mr Benton, for there is neither an intention to offend nor a desire to solidify a baseless supposition behind it," Mr Locke warned. "But could your reluctance to disclose the assault at Mr Jerome's hands have been due to another self-preservation-related reason? Namely, to prevent your involvement in the blackmail from being exposed? Thereby making you vulnerable to arrest alongside Mr Jerome?"

"You're right, Mr Locke. It is a baseless supposition," Mr Benton replied.

"Pardon me, Mr Benton, but you *did* propose to Miss Mina on many, *many* occasions and, well, one could understand why you'd grow weary of it and, for the lack of a better term, wish to 'take your revenge,' for the slight," Mr Heath observed.

"By damaging the reputation of what she loved the most?" Mr Benton demanded.

"You?" Mr Heath enquired.

"The *theatre*." Mr Benton stood, compelling Mr Heath to take a step back. "The *Crescent* was everything to her. She loved me, yes, but she loved the theatre more." He looked back at the photograph as a pained expression formed upon his face. "And I loved her." He picked up the photograph and, holding it in both hands, gazed down upon it with a great sorrow etched upon his features. "I proposed to her, and she declined, but I would've continued to propose to her until my dying breath." He rested the fingertips of one hand upon the photograph. "I should've reported Mr Jerome to the police. Perhaps, then, Mina wouldn't be…" He swallowed his emotions and lifted his head to meet Mr Heath's gaze. "But I didn't want to harm the theatre's reputation by bringing scandal to its door."

"An admirable and understandable decision," Mr Locke complimented.

Mr Heath stepped closer to Mr Locke for the sake of his own self-preservation.

"Do you know why Miss Ilbert declined your marriage proposals?" Mr Locke enquired.

"She was a formidable woman who liked things done her way." Mr Benton sat, the photograph still in his hands. "She possibly feared I'd try to impose my vision for the theatre upon her if we wed."

"Had she been married before?" Mr Locke enquired.

"Widowed," Mr Benton replied, setting the photograph down upon the dressing table. "To Julian Raine. He died in a fire almost twenty years ago."

"I presume Miss Lily is his daughter?" Mr Locke enquired.

"Yes, I presume so, too," Mr Benton admitted. "Mina never spoke of Mr Raine, and I never probed her about him."

Mr Locke allowed his gaze to drift around the room as he carefully considered his next question by weighing up the credibility of Mr Benton's answers thus far. Knowing Mr Benton professionally as he did, he knew both how highly respectable he was but also how highly skilled an actor he was. Consequently, it wasn't beyond the realm of possibility Mr Benton had simply been putting on a convincing act during their entire conversation. Mr Locke's instincts told him otherwise, but he knew it would be foolish to dismiss the possibility altogether. "Returning to the matter of the assault," Mr Locke began as his gaze slid back to Mr Benton. "I understand Mr Thurston intervened and prevented Mr Jerome from assaulting you further. Correct?"

"I didn't require his intervention but, yes, that is correct," Mr Benton replied.

"Did he give an explanation as to why he was by the stage door?" Mr Locke enquired.

"No," Mr Benton replied, furrowing his brow in confusion. His features relaxed as the penny dropped, however. "Ah, I see what you're getting at. Yes, it *was* unusual for Mr Thurston to be at the stage door at that hour."

"Could he be involved in the blackmail with Mr Jerome?" Mr Heath enquired.

"Morris?" Mr Thurston eyed him sceptically. "No. He's too mild mannered."

Mr Heath frowned. He thought it was a rather sensible question to ask.

"If Mr Thurston is involved in the blackmail, I shall eat my hat," Mr Benton added.

FORTY-FIVE

It had been some time since Inspector Conway had been in Birmingham. During his previous visits, he'd witnessed firsthand the squalor of an overcrowded court of back-to-back houses. Powerless to improve the conditions, he'd left with a fearful heart on behalf of another, concealed behind a tough exterior. Now, as his cab entered an area known as the Lozells, his fear eased. When, moments later, his cab turned onto Wheeler Street, his fear vanished completely. The red-brick-terraced houses reminded him of his own street in Hackney and, from what he could see, they were in reasonable condition.

"Here'll do, mate," Inspector Conway called up to the driver.

As the cab slowed to a halt, a group of children ran up to it to catch a glimpse of its occupant. A raising of the whip by the driver convinced them to back away, however. Alighting on the cab's opposite side, Inspector Conway paid his fare and a little extra to guarantee the cab's return later. The driver pocketed the coin and tipped his hat with a promise to honour their arrangement.

The children backed away further when the cab lurched forward and drove away. Yet, they continued to watch Inspector Conway intently as he consulted a handwritten letter and walked along the pavement. When he stopped at a house several doors down and glanced back at them, the children pretended to play. Smiling softly at their antics, he put the letter away into his overcoat pocket with one hand, whilst his other knocked upon the front door.

A woman in her late-thirties with long, dark-red hair pinned up into a messy bun and hazel eyes opened the door. She was evidently amid her weekly wash day because the sleeves of her dark-grey dress were rolled up to her elbows, and her lower arms were damp. The apron around her waist also had several damp patches, and there were droplets of sweat upon her forehead.

She was scowling whilst she opened door but, the moment she saw him, her eyes lit up, and her features lifted into a smile. Throwing her arms around him, she exclaimed, "*John*!"

"Hello, Mel," Inspector Conway replied, embracing her in return.

"Come in, come in," Mel encouraged as she stepped aside. "Gimmie your hat."

Inspector Conway removed his trilby and passed it to her as he entered the dark hallway beyond. It was modestly decorated and sparsely furnished but was still a far cry from the slums she'd previously existed in. He couldn't say 'living,' because no one could 'live' in conditions as bad as those.

Mel, or Mrs Melina Burgess to give her full name, hung his hat on a hook by the door and led him down the hallway, into the kitchen. Shirts, petticoats, and undergarments hung from the ceiling to dry by the warmth of the stove. The back door was open, and Inspector Conway could see the buckets of water, mangal, and other paraphernalia of laundry day in the yard beyond.

"You should of wrote to say you was comin'." Mrs Burgess pulled a chair out from underneath the table and closed the back door. "I've got laundry all about the place. I look a mess. The 'ouse is a mess."

"It was a last-minute thing." Inspector Conway took off his coat and, draping it over his chair, sat down. At her complaining, he retorted, "I'm your brother, not the Prince Regent. It don't matter what the 'ouse looks like."

"It matters to me." Mrs Burgess put the kettle on the stovetop to boil and dried her hands on a towel. "And it would matter to your wife, if you had one."

"Don't start."

"You're the only one out of us three who's not married, John. You know how Mum worries about you."

Inspector Conway glanced at the stove. "Any chance of a cuppa?"

Mrs Burgess tossed the towel at him. "*Don't* change the subject."

Inspector Conway smiled as he caught the towel.

Mrs Burgess took out two of her best mugs and set them down upon the table. "How long you 'ere for, anyway?"

"I don't know. A day or two."

Mrs Burgess hummed as she gave him a knowing look.

"What's that look for?" Inspector Conway enquired.

"You can't fool me, John Conway." She set the pot of sugar and milk jug down beside the mugs. "You've not come all this way just to see your little sister." She picked up the kettle as it began to boil and poured the hot water into the mugs through a strainer filled with tea leaves. "The job will be the death of you."

Inspector Conway added sugar and milk to his tea. Keen to change the subject, he enquired, "How's Todd and the boys?"

Mrs Burgess sat beside him and added sugar to her tea. "Todd's at work, and the boys are at school. Oliver's got a bit of a cough, so I'm keepin' an eye on 'im, but we're good overall." She cast an appraising glance over him as she took a sip of tea. "How are you? I read about your fight in the 'paper."

"I'm okay," Inspector Conway set down his mug and reached into his overcoat pocket. "I've got some coins for the boy."

Mrs Burgess put a gentle hand upon his shoulder. "Keep your money, John." She smiled softly. "Todd wouldn't like me to take it, and you need it, besides."

"I want to help, Mel."

"I know you do, and it's appreciated, but, honestly, it's not needed."

Inspector Conway frowned but returned the money to his pocket.

"I've got a nice lemon cake, just baked yesterday." Mrs Burgess stood and retrieved the tin from a shelf. "You can have some now and take some with you."

Inspector Conway gave a weak smile. "Thanks."

* * *

The afternoon air felt cold against Dr Locke's skin as she strode down the street with an umbrella in hand. Referring to her husband's copy of *The Era* the night before, she'd learned the newspaper's address was 49, Wellington Street, Covent Garden. As it was near to Bow Street, she'd decided to walk and allow Claude the use of the carriage to take Mr Locke home to rest. Mr Verity and Mr Heath had offered to accompany her, but she'd declined. As far as she was aware, neither knew of *The Era*'s article about her husband. Given it was commonly known she was the Great Locke's wife, she knew there was a high likelihood the article would be remarked upon at the newspaper office. This, coupled with her fellow Bow Streeters' ignorance, would've created an awkward situation she wanted to avoid.

The odd numbers between 45-49 were located within a commercial building on the corner of Russell Street and Wellington Street. The building itself had vertical stone corners lining its outer walls and an impressive turret upon its roof. Stone balusters, supporting a stone railing with cubed pillars in between, surrounded the turret. Atop each pillar was a stone figure. On the ground floor, three stone steps led to an arched doorway containing double doors on the building's corner. Excluding the turret but including the ground floor, the building was four storeys high in all.

After entering the building and locating the newspaper's offices, Dr Locke loitered by its door until a journalist attempted to leave. At which point she thrust out her calling card and said, "I'd like to speak to someone about your past editions, please."

"Doctor Lynette…" the journalist read aloud, his voice trailing off when he read the surname. Lifting his head to look at her, he lowered it again to reread the card, before lifting his head to look at her a second time. "Locke?"

"Yes."

"Excuse me, please." The journalist retreated into the office and exchanged a few hushed words with his colleague who, in turn, took the calling card into another office. A few moments later, the second journalist emerged empty-handed and exchanged more hushed words with the first who, in turn, crossed the office to Dr Locke. "If you'll follow me, please, doctor."

"Certainly." Dr Locke lifted her chin and locked her gaze upon the back of the journalist's head as she followed. She felt the eyes of the other journalists upon her and caught whispers about her being the Great Locke's wife. Yet, she paid them no need and was stoic when she entered the second office.

A man in his early thirties with chiselled cheekbones, square jaw, deep-set, dark-brown eyes, and short, blond hair stood to greet her from behind his desk. His attire consisted of a fashionable dark-grey, double-breasted suit with a grey and lavender pin-striped waistcoat, lavender tie, and white shirt beneath. "Good afternoon, doctor. How wonderful it is to meet you. I'm Mr David Ruggles, deputy editor here at *The Era*. Please, do sit down. Would you like some tea or, perhaps, something a little stronger? It's rather cold out, isn't it? I'm sure you'd welcome a little brandy. Mr Begg?"

"Yes, sir?" the journalist who'd escorted Dr Locke replied.

"Fetch Dr Locke a, eh, what was it?" Mr Ruggles enquired.

"Cup of tea, please. One sugar. Cream," Dr Locke replied.

Mr Ruggles dismissed Mr Begg with a wave of his hand whilst Dr Locke sat in the vacant chair before the desk. Lifting and moving his chair as close to the desk as possible, Mr Ruggles also sat and, flipping his notebook open, licked the lead of his pencil. "Of January," he mumbled whilst writing the date. "Three o'clock?" He consulted his pocket watch. "Yes." He wrote down the time. "Dr Lynette Locke and Mr David Ruggles," he said aloud whilst writing. "Past editions were mentioned to me. I presume you wish to discuss the recent article we ran about your husband?" He lifted his eyes but kept his head tilted downward. "Does he wish to make a statement?"

"No and no," Dr Locke replied.

"Speculation about the cause of the Great Locke's absence from the *Paddington Palladium* could be quelled if he did," Mr Ruggles pointed out. "Our readers are very concerned about his welfare."

"I'm sure they are," Dr Locke muttered in an ironic tone.

Mr Ruggles set down his pencil and sat back in his chair. "Your distaste for our newspaper is palpable."

Mr Begg opened the door, carrying the cup of tea.

"Take it away!" Mr Ruggles ordered.

Mr Begg halted and glanced at Dr Locke.

Mr Ruggles dismissed him with another wave of his hand.

"My opinion of your publication is irrelevant," Dr Locke said once they were alone. "For I'm not here as the wife of the Great Locke, but as a member of the Bow Street Society."

Mr Ruggles picked up his pencil and leant forward. "I'm listening."

Dr Locke fought the urge to roll her eyes. "I wish to see all articles, announcements, and/or advertisements featuring Miss Mina Ilbert in your archive. She may also be featured under her professional pseudonym of Lily of the Lyceum."

Mr Ruggles sat back in his chair and tapped his pencil against his fingernails. "*The Era* has something akin to an archive in a storeroom in the basement, but it's incomplete. It doesn't contain anything about Miss Ilbert, either."

"How do you know without looking?"

"Because someone has already purchased everything we had on Miss Ilbert."

Dr Locke's eyebrows lifted. "Who?"

Mr Ruggles gave a contrived smile. "She never gave her name."

"What did she look like?"

"Dark hair, fair skin. Beyond that, I couldn't say. She wore a black veil, you see."

"Was she in full mourning?"

Mr Ruggles hummed as he tilted his head a little to the side. "Yes. She was." He straightened his head. "She called upon us the day after Miss Ilbert's tragic death in fact."

Dr Locke wrote down the saliant points in her notebook. "Did she give a reason for her request?"

"She said she was a tremendous admirer of Miss Ilbert's and wanted to create a scrapbook commemorating her life and work," Mr Ruggles replied.

"Did she give payment on the same day?"

"No. She paid the day after when she collected the items." Mr Ruggles rolled the pencil between his thumb and forefinger. "She paid quite handsomely for them, too."

"Are there additional copies of the same editions elsewhere?"

"Yes. Like all newspapers, we send copies of published editions to the British Museum."

"I didn't know that." Dr Locke wondered if the unnamed admirer did.

"You're a woman, so why would you?" Mr Ruggles said in a condescending tone.

"And pray tell how my gender makes me ignorant?" Dr Locke challenged.

"I meant no offence, doctor," Mr Ruggles replied in the same condescending tone. "All women are unfamiliar with the mechanics of running a newspaper."

"Lady Katheryne Owston of *Truth* and *Women's Signal* would disagree with you."

"Those aren't *newspapers*!" Mr Ruggles scoffed.

"What are they, if not newspapers?" Dr Locke enquired.

"Poorly written mindless gossip."

Dr Locke could've said the same about *The Era*.

"Women *don't* know how newspapers are run," Mr Ruggles continued. "Otherwise, Miss Ilbert's greatest admirer wouldn't have paid fifty pounds for something she could've easily requested at the British Museum for free."

"I beg your pardon. *How* much did she pay?"

"*Fifty* pounds *in* pound banknotes," Mr Ruggles replied, proudly.

Dr Locke stood. "Thank you. You've been surprisingly helpful."

Mr Ruggles' gaze followed her. "I have?"

"Yes."

Mr Ruggles stood. "Well, if I can be of help again, please, let me know."

"I'll bear it in mind," Dr Locke said, intending to do nothing of the sort.

FORTY-SIX

The pawnbroker's window display looked like it hadn't been altered in years. A layer of dust covered the statuettes, tarnished brass, smoke damaged paintings, and sun faded fabrics. The window's glass was also covered in dirt and soot from the street. Pushing a strand of hair behind her ear as she pretended to peruse the goods on display, Miss Hicks bit her lower lip.

She'd been in two minds about Mr O'Hannigan after Miss Trent had forbidden him from visiting the Society's house. She'd spent the remainder of the night and all morning thinking about Dr Weeks, Mr O'Hannigan, and her future. Another illicit liaison with Mr O'Hannigan in the afternoon had then clouded her thoughts further.

Entering the pawnbroker's shop via a side door, she was immediately struck by the combined scents of mustiness and damp. The interior was also crammed full of boxes, clothes, and shelves filled with knick-knacks. Behind the narrow counter in the corner of the room was a man in his early twenties with slicked-back, greasy brown hair, and a pointed nose and chin. Tall and thin, his appearance seemed almost ghoulish in the gaslight.

Miss Hicks put a large carpet bag upon the counter and proceeded to empty its contents under the man's watchful gaze. First to come out was a red silk bustle dress with ornate beading and lace decoration. Second was a dark-green bustle dress of similar design. Third was a fox fur wrap. Finally, she added two pairs of black fur mittens to the pile and put the carpet bag at her feet. "How much for all this?"

The man carefully inspected each item, paying close attention to the fur wrap and mittens. When he spoke, it was with a nasally voice. "They're of *reasonable* quality." He checked the beading on the red and dark-green bustle dresses. "Rudimentary workmanship."

Miss Hicks' eyes narrowed. "Perce bought them from *Harrod's*."

"Really?" the man sarcastically enquired.

Miss Hicks moved to gather everything up. "If you don't want it, mate—"

"I never said *that*." The man put his hand on the pile. "Five pounds."

"Six."

The man gave a contrived smile. "Six, it is." He took some cloth from a shelf behind him and, tightly rolling the dresses, wrap, and mittens in it, pinned it closed. Next, he wrote out a ticket and duplicate which he blotted against a pile of sand in a nearby box and gave the duplicate to Miss Hicks. The roll of items was taken into a back room and, when he returned a moment later, he was carrying two banknotes: a £1 and £5. "*Pleasure* doing business with you."

Miss Hicks snatched the banknotes from him. "You, too."

Grinning from ear to ear, the man waved at her as she left.

* * *

Mr Elliott softly exhaled the smoke from his cigarette and sipped his dry sherry. He and Mr Snyder sat in a corner of the gentlemen only bar at the *Hope & Anchor* public house with empty plates and neatly arranged cutlery on the table before them. After checking into *The Stork Hotel* on Corporation Street, they'd decided to travel directly to Edmund Street and the *Hope & Anchor* for an early dinner. Mr Elliott had enjoyed a simple fare of bread, cheese, and cold meats, whilst Mr Snyder had opted for a beef and kidney pie with boiled potatoes, carrots, and gravy.

Upon arriving at Edmund Street, Mr Elliott was pleasantly surprised to find the *Birmingham Central Library* was the *Hope & Anchor*'s direct neighbour. He'd also overheard several conversations in the bar which hinted at the participants being councillors, or aldermen. Although their business deals could be considered dubious if one knew the wider context, their demeanours and language also appeared to be respectful and acceptable.

Mr Elliott and Mr Snyder were in a corner at the rear of the room. From their vantage point, the large, stone fireplace was on the right, and the bar ran along the opposite wall and curved around to the left, ending at a wall. A large bay window, comprising of small square panes of glass held in place by a wooden frame, filled the wall at the opposite end to the Bow Streeters. Between the window and end of the bar, standing perpendicular to both, was the door leading into the small entrance hall. On the opposite side of this hall was another door leading into the mixed bar room. On the right-hand side of the hall were the double doors opening out onto Edmund Street.

Directly outside the large bay window in the gentlemen only bar were two stone pillars which appeared to be supporting the main frontage. Noticing how they blocked the view, Mr Elliott had enquired about them from the landlord, Mr Joseph Astle, when he'd served their dinner. According to him, they had been added when the frontage was remodelled in 1893 by C.J. Hodson.

The walls of the gentlemen only bar room were decorated in a mustard wallpaper with a scrolling, brown leaf design. The floors were exposed wooden boards with innumerable dents, scuffs, and scratches. There was also a thin layer of sawdust on the floor, as one would expect to find in most public houses.

Mr Elliott stubbed out his cigarette on his plate and sipped some more sherry as he observed, "We've seen neither hide nor hair of Inspector Conway."

Mr Snyder sipped his pint of ale. "'E would of gone to see his sister."

Mr Elliott wondered how Mr Snyder knew such a thing until he recalled details of Inspector Conway's boxing past. "I forgot you knew one another when you were younger. Did you know his family well?"

"Nah." Mr Snyder put down his pint, rubbed the underside of his nose with his thumb and sniffed. "I only talked to his brother and sister when me and him fought the first time, but you hear things." He scratched his cheek. "Bobby's the oldest, Melina's the youngest, and John's in the middle, I think."

The door opened, and Inspector Conway entered. Taking his trilby off as he walked around the bar, he slowed to cast a glance over the room before increasing his speed, again, when he saw the Bow Streeters. He pulled a stool across and, setting it down beside Mr Snyder, sat on it. "Is Donahue here yet?"

"No." Mr Snyder put his pint in front of Inspector Conway.

"Thanks." Inspector Conway had two large mouthfuls and returned it to the cabman.

"How is your sister?" Mr Elliott enquired.

Inspector Conway looked from Mr Elliott to Mr Snyder and back again. "How do you know I was seein' Mel?"

"I didn't." Mr Elliott lifted his sherry to his lips. "But thank you for confirming it."

Inspector Conway turned his head away and muttered a curse under his breath.

Mr Elliott sipped his sherry. "Is she well?"

Inspector Conway glared at him. "Leave it out, Elliott."

"I was just trying to make conversation." Mr Elliott put down his sherry.

Mr Snyder knew the two didn't get along, but he could've done without their bickering. Therefore, he was pleased to see Inspector Donahue enter. The policeman approached the bar and, after exchanging a few pleasantries with the landlord, paid for a pint of Guiness that was duly served to him. He supped it as he walked through the room before making a beeline for the Bow Streeters' table. With the tips of his beard's moustache covered in froth, he said, "Eve-ning, all."

Inspector Conway retrieved another stool and set it down in front of the table.

Spotting the empty plates, Inspector Donahue felt his stomach rumble. "Wished I'd got some food now." He put down his pint and sat. "I'm starve-ing."

Inspector Conway took a hunk of something wrapped in his handkerchief from his overcoat pocket and put it on the table. "Some lemon cake."

"Ah *mate*." Inspector Donahue grinned as he unwrapped the cake and held it up to his nose. Taking a long sniff of it, he tore off a large piece and tossed it into his mouth. "Mhm. I luv a bit of lemon cake, I do." He tore off another large piece and, tossing it into his mouth, washed it down. "Can I 'ave all this?"

"Yeah," Inspector Conway replied.

Inspector Donahue took a large bite from the cake and, squinting as he chewed it, said, "Ah *mate*! That's good." He ate the rest and, again, washed it down. Licking his lips afterward, he gave the handkerchief back to Inspector Conway and licked his lips again. "*Mhm*." He wiped his hands on his own handkerchief and drank yet more Guinness. "I saw my Nark. A few pints and a few coins and 'e was sin-ging like a canary."

Mr Elliott sat forward. "What did he say?"

Inspector Donahue sat forward as well and lowered his voice. "Jerome's back in Birm-in-ham liok yow said, and 'e's got a wench with 'im. The Nark went 'round the Wrekin a bit but the gist is this: Jerome's back do-ing what 'e done before, harass-sing theatre folk for coin and give-ing them the bird when they don't pay."

"Is Miss Hightower involved?" Mr Elliott enquired.

Inspector Donahue nodded as he drank some more Guiness. "Jerome prostitutes her but not liok yow think. She's noice to the theatre folk and gets them to go with her to Baskerville Passage. Jerome gets there before any-thing 'appens, act-ting liok an angry husband. The actor gives 'im money to stay quiet about it and goes."

Mr Elliott frowned deeply. "And she is a willing participant in this?"

"I dunno," Inspector Donahue replied.

"Where's Baskerville Passage?" Mr Snyder enquired.

"Off Easy Row, by the old wharf," Inspector Donahue replied. "Jerome and 'is wench take their pick-gings from the folk of the *Theatre Royal* who go to *The Woodman* on Easy Row." He set his pint aside and drew a basic floorplan in his notebook. "This is what *The Woodman*'s liok inside." He marked the rear door. "'E might leg it out 'ere."

"I'll guard it," Mr Snyder volunteered.

Inspector Donahue considered whether using one of his own plain-clothed officers would be better. Unfortunately, run-ins with Mr Jerome in the past meant the braggard knew what they all looked like. Putting a uniformed constable there was also out of the question; Mr Jerome would spot him a mile off. "O-kay." Inspector Donahue put an 'x' in the main bar room and looked to Inspector Conway. "Yow and me in 'ere."

"Where shall I be?" Mr Elliott enquired.

"Yow's not come-ing," Inspector Donahue ordered.

"Mr Jerome knows both of you by sight." Mr Elliott glanced between Inspectors Conway and Donahue. "And, with all due respect, Mr Snyder, you don't have the appearance of an actor."

"Fair do's," Mr Snyder said.

"Neither Mr Jerome nor Miss Hightower have seen or met me," Mr Elliott continued. "If I were to allow them to think I was an actor, she might lure me to Baskerville Passage and Mr Jerome. You could follow us and make the arrest."

"I thought you wasn't the lyin' sort," Inspector Conway said.

"I'm not," Mr Elliott said. "I'll simply not correct their assumption."

"What do you think?" Inspector Conway enquired from his fellow policeman.

"I liok it," Inspector Donahue replied.

Mr Snyder tapped the 'x' on the floorplan. "Want me 'ere instead?"

"O-kay," Inspector Donahue replied.

"If it's only Miss Hightower at *The Woodman*, we'll be fine. She's not seen us before," Inspector Conway mused aloud. "If not, we'll have to keep our heads down."

"Do yow know what Miss Hightower looks liok?" Inspector Donahue enquired.

Mr Elliott took out his notebook and, turning to the relevant page, read out Miss Hightower's description from Miss Trent.

Inspector Donahue noted the key characteristics. "Thanks."

"Where does Baskerville Passage come out?" Mr Snyder enquired.

"Baskerville Place," Inspector Donahue replied.

"What if we want to get to Baskerville Place but not go through the passage?" Mr Snyder enquired.

"Wait at the end for Jerome in case 'e scarpers, you mean?" Inspector Conway enquired.

"Yeah," Mr Snyder replied.

"Easy Row onto Broad Street, then into Baskerville Place," Inspector Donahue replied. He scratched his cheek with the blunt end of his pencil. "I'll go that end." He pointed at Mr Snyder with the pencil. "Yow go at the Easy Row end." He pointed at Mr Elliott and Inspector Conway. "Yow's two in *The Woodman*."

Mr Elliott pursed his lips at the thought of putting his safety in Inspector Conway's hands. He suspected Inspector Conway's violent tendencies would be seen as an advantage by Inspector Donahue and Mr Snyder, though, as it meant he could protect them if a fight erupted. Furthermore, despite his well-founded fear Inspector Conway could be the catalyst for such a confrontation, he doubted the others would agree with him. Therefore, he resigned himself to the plan and the fact he was obliged to follow it.

"We ready?" Inspector Conway enquired.
Inspector Donahue and Mr Snyder finished their pints.
Inspector Donahue put his glass down with a thud.
"Let's go."

FORTY-SEVEN

Yellow light flooded Dr Weeks' vision. It was so bright, it caused him to look away in pain. Yet, no matter where he looked, the light remained. He could hear his own heavy breathing, accompanied by the rapid beat of his pounding heart. At the same time, though, he felt like he was watching and hearing it all from afar.

A head moved into his field of vision; the light's brightness made it appear narrow and without definition. A male voice, muffled like it was behind a wall, said, "He was found unresponsive in his room. We'll know more after the postmortem."

Dr Weeks instinctively knew he was talking about him.

"No superficial marks or injuries," the male voice observed.

Dr Weeks tried to move, but he was paralysed. He tried to speak, but his throat strangled his words. Couldn't they see he was breathing and had a pulse?!

"Starting the first incision now," the male voice said.

Dr Weeks tried to yell, but his vocal cords were frozen.

First, Dr Weeks felt the cold blade against his skin. Followed by the sharpest pain he'd ever felt leapt through his body like a lightning bolt. He screamed.

Dr Weeks' body bent in two from the pain in his abdomen, thereby lifting his upper body off the bed. Wrapping his arms around his middle, his muscles were so tense, the pressure from his arms increased the pain. He heard someone screaming, only to realise it was him. Cutting himself off, he gasped for air as his heart pounded so fast, his half-asleep, fog-filled mind barely registered it.

He stared at the wall, his mind's eye filled with the bright light, for several moments before the illusion vanished, and the reality of his surroundings snapped into his consciousness. He looked to his right and saw the barred window with the blackness of night beyond. He looked to his left and saw the sparsely furnished room and the closed door. Everything had the hint of familiarity, but his mind refused to give him the answer.

A second bolt of sharp pain caused him to double-over, again. Clenching his jaw shut, he hissed and moaned through his teeth as aftershocks of agony swept through his abdomen. Digging his fingernails into the flesh at his sides as well, he both waited and prayed for the pain to stop.

It finally did a few moments later.

Easing the pressure of his arms against his middle, he was immediately hit by nausea that caused him to twist his body and lean over the side of the bed. Only bile came up with each retch, though, and his stomach ached after only a few attempts. He pursed his lips and, swallowing against the rising sensation, took a few deep breaths before he felt able to move again without heaving. He eased himself onto his side and, bringing his knees up to his chest, wrapped his arms about his legs with a hard shiver.

The door opened, and Dr Colbert entered.

His face reminded Dr Weeks of where he was. He closed his eyes and softly groaned.

Dr Colbert closed the door and brought the chair up to Dr Weeks' bedside. Sitting, he ran an appraising glance over his patient. Despite the time which had passed since Dr Colbert had left, Dr Weeks remained unwashed and in his heavily soiled nightshirt. Dr Colbert frowned deeply with a mixture of disappointment and annoyance. Making a mental note to discuss the matter with Dr McWilliams, he put a gentle hand on Dr Weeks' shoulder and leant over him. In a soft voice, he enquired, "Percy, can you hear me?"

Dr Weeks groaned but kept his eyes closed.

"Speak to me. How are you feeling?"

"*Shit*," Dr Weeks replied, the dryness in his throat eliciting a cough.

"Have you eaten or drank today?"

"I ain't hungry," Dr Weeks mumbled. "I'll take a double whisky, though."

Dr Colbert's tone cooled. "That isn't amusing."

"Weren't meant to be." Dr Weeks briefly opened his eyes to look up at him.

"You need to keep your strength up," Dr Colbert warned.

Dr Weeks groaned as he eased himself onto his other side and assumed a position identical to the first. "Let me die in peace." A third bolt of pain caused his entire body to visibly tense, however, and again, he clenched his jaw shut whilst hissing and moaning through his teeth. This time, the aftershocks of agony which swept through his abdomen were enough to drive him to tears. Several slid down his face as he half-groaned, half-sobbed into his pillow.

Dr Colbert looked on with a furrowed brow and deeply concerned eyes. He'd seen such symptoms in his other alcoholic insane patients and so had a good idea what Dr Weeks was enduring. He could give him drugs to ease the pain, but Dr Colbert was wary of substituting one potentially addictive substance for another. Furthermore, he doubted Dr Weeks would be averse to resuming his drinking habits after release if he knew the process of weaning him off it was a relatively pain-free one. In short, Dr Colbert believed Dr Weeks had to fight to not only regain his sanity but keep it.

"I'll fetch you some gruel," he said and calmly left the room.

* * *

The Woodman on Easy Row was certainly the most striking public house Mr Elliott had visited, aesthetically speaking. The name's personification in the form of a stone statue, housed within an alcove above the main façade, made it easy to find and hard to forget. Within the establishment's Smoke Room, further dramatic décor was supplied in the form of intricately carved wooden pillars, panels, and archways. Booths with horseshoe-shaped benches upholstered in dark-brown leather lined one side of the room. On the other, square recesses separated by pillars, contained wooden-framed tub chairs with back rests and seat cushions upholstered to match the benches. Low, round-topped, dark-wooden tables were also dotted throughout.

An L-shaped bar with marble countertops and wooden panelling occupied the corner of the room. A man in his early forties with short black hair, sideburns, and moustache served. His attire consisted of a white shirt, black waistcoat, tie, and trousers, and an apron tied around his waist.

Sitting alone at a table facing the impressive stone fireplace, Mr Elliott saw Inspector Conway's reflection in the mirror mounted on the wall above. The policeman sat on the end of a bench in a booth close to the bar. Although he had his back to the door, Inspector Conway could also see its reflection, and anyone else's, in the mirror.

Unsurprisingly, the room's atmosphere was thick with tobacco smoke. The combined scents of burning coal, bodily odour, and stale beer also assaulted one's nostrils. Convinced he could taste everything in the back of his throat, Mr Elliott tried to wash it away with a sip of sherry, to no avail. Taking another sip, he slid the tip of his tongue between his lips and grimaced at the grainy texture he tasted there.

"Good evening, sir," a voice jovially greeted.

Mr Elliott lifted his gaze to find a man standing beside his table. In his early forties, he was approximately five feet tall with a round face, washed-out brown hair, and hazel eyes. His attire consisted of black trousers and a black frockcoat over a plum waistcoat and cravat and white shirt with starched Eaton collar.

"Good evening," Mr Elliott politely greeted, darting his gaze to the mirror. There was still no sign of either Mr Jerome or Miss Hightower, however.

The man thrust his hand toward Mr Elliott. "Crispian Hogarth-Huxley."

"Gregory Elliott." Mr Elliott gave his hand a brief squeeze.

"Would you care for some company?" Mr Hogarth-Huxley enquired.

"I—" Mr Elliott began.

"What *am* I saying? Of *course* you would." Mr Hogarth-Huxley sat.

"I appreciate your concern—" Mr Elliott began.

"*Think* nothing of it!" Mr Hogarth-Huxley looked to the bar and raised his hand to get the server's attention. "Being an *artiste* of note has *some* privileges." He made some hand signals and, satisfied his order was understood, smiled broadly at Mr Elliott. "I haven't seen *you* here before." He put his elbows upon the table and cupped his chin in his hands. "Are you seeking or merely looking?"

Mr Elliott's eyes widened a fraction. "I beg your pardon?"

Mr Hogarth-Huxley lifted his head and, resting his hands in his lap, turned sideways to lean in close to Mr Elliott. He lowered his voice and grinned. "You don't have to be coy with me, sir. I recognise one of my kind when I see him."

Mr Elliott narrowed his eyes and turned his head away. "I suggest you leave, sir."

"With you?" Mr Hogarth-Huxley teased. "But we hardly know one another."

The server set down two brandies upon their table. "With the compliments of the gentleman over there."

"Hm?" Mr Hogarth-Huxley enquired, confused.

When he and Mr Elliott looked to where the server was pointing, the latter was taken aback to see Inspector Conway give a small nod.

"Excuse me." Mr Hogarth-Huxley took his drink and wandered over to the policeman.

Mr Elliott stared at them, stunned, as Inspector Conway moved along and allowed Mr Hogarth-Huxley to sit beside him.

"Yow was lucky there, sir," the server told Mr Elliott. "That one's a mandrake."

"Yes. Thank you." Mr Elliott glanced at the server but immediately returned his gaze to the pair. Mr Hogarth-Huxley had his lips close to Inspector Conway's ear as he spoke to him, whilst Inspector Conway's gaze was locked upon Mr Elliott. Noticing him lift his hand to discreetly point at the fire, Mr Elliott looked and found a young woman matching Miss Hightower's description standing before his table. Taking a moment to gather himself, he greeted, "Good evening. May I help you?"

"I hope so," the woman replied, taking the seat Mr Hogarth-Huxley had vacated. "What's a handsome man like you doing sitting all alone?"

"Waiting for the right company," Mr Elliott replied.

"And have you found it?" the woman enquired.

Mr Elliott smiled softly. "I think so."

The woman ran a slow, appraising glance over him. "Me, too."

Mr Elliott glanced at the mirror and saw Inspector Conway lifting Mr Hogarth-Huxley's hand off his knee. Mr Elliott couldn't help but be amused at the sight and smiled. Fortunately, the woman interpreted it as being for her.

"It must be lonely, travelling around the country to perform," the woman said.

"It can be." Mr Elliott leant in closer and lowered his voice. "Sometimes."

The woman made a show of turning away as if shy. "*Sir*, you make me blush."

"In a good way, I hope?"

"Yes." The woman put her hand upon his. "In a very good way."

Mr Elliott pointed to the woman under the table.

Inspector Conway's reflection gave a subtle nod.

"We could go somewhere quieter, if you'd like?" the woman enquired. "More private?"

"I'd like that." Mr Elliott offered a soft smile. "I'm Gregory."

"Joanna," Miss Hightower replied, returning his smile.

"I'm pleased to meet you, Joanna." Mr Elliott stood and offered her his arm.

Miss Hightower held the crook of his elbow and followed him out.

Watching them leave, Inspector Conway waited a moment before exiting the booth.

"Where are you going?" Mr Hogarth-Huxley enquired.

Inspector Conway patted him on the shoulder as he passed. "Not tonight, mate."

Mr Hogarth-Huxley pouted.

Outside, Mr Elliott stalled to allow the policeman to catch up. "How far is it?"

Miss Hightower gave him a disarming smile. "Not far."

Mr Elliott felt her pull on his arm. "Then what is the hurry?"

"No hurry." Miss Hightower moved in closer. "Except a desire to be alone with you."

The door to *The Woodman* opened behind them and, upon seeing Inspector Conway, Miss Hightower pulled on Mr Elliott's arm for a second time. Glancing back at the policeman as well, Mr Elliott allowed her to lead them away since he'd detected no hint of her having recognised Inspector Conway, neither in her eyes nor her expression.

"You seem rather young to be doing this sort of thing," Mr Elliott observed.

"I know my business, sir," Miss Hightower said, a little affronted.

"I'm certain you do," Mr Elliott lied. "May I ask your age?"

"I'm eighteen, sir."

"Your accent. You weren't born in Birmingham, were you?"

"No, sir." Miss Hightower looked straight ahead. "Does it matter?"

"Where were you born?"

"Buckinghamshire," Miss Hightower lied. "It's just along here, sir."

Noticing they were moving up Easy Row, Mr Elliott sought out landmarks in case he had to return to *The Woodman* in a hurry. Distinguishing the outlines of tall, cube-like buildings with broad roofs, he felt reassured Miss Hightower was indeed leading them to the old wharf as per Inspector Donahue's intelligence.

"Do you have any family?" Mr Elliott enquired.

"My, you are a talkative one, aren't you?" Miss Hightower gently teased.

"I don't think of prostitutes as inhuman," Mr Elliott countered without thinking.

Miss Hightower halted. "You know I'm a prostitute?"

"I don't expect us to have a burgeoning romance," Mr Elliott replied in an ironic tone.

Miss Hightower continued walking. "No. I don't suppose you would."

Mr Elliott had heard too many accounts of gentlemen being ambushed and robbed in rookeries and passageways for him to be wary of such places after dark. If he hadn't the support and protection of Inspectors Conway and Donahue and Mr Snyder, he wouldn't have agreed to leave the relative safety of the public house with a woman he barely knew.

"Here we are, sir," Miss Hightower said.

They stopped at the narrow entrance of a long passageway with brown brick walls. A metal sign nailed to the top of the right-hand wall declared it to be Baskerville Passage. An iron bar, bent into an arch, spanned the passageway above their heads. A large wrought-iron lantern with glass panes hung from it with a single lit candle inside. The passageway beyond was in pitch blackness. The perfect setting for an illicit liaison, extortion, assault, and robbery.

Mr Elliott felt the hair lift on the back of his neck at the thought.

"Are you certain we shan't be disturbed?" Mr Elliott knew she'd expect the question.

"Absolutely, sir." Miss Hightower pulled him into the passageway.

The further inside she took him, the more isolated Mr Elliott felt. There had been no sign of Mr Snyder when they'd arrived, and he didn't know if Inspector Conway was behind them still. If he was indeed alone, he had nothing to defend himself with and only a few coins to buy his safety from Mr Jerome. Feeling a quivering in his stomach, he darted his gaze in all directions at the smallest of sounds. *There's nothing wrong*, he inwardly told himself. *Don't worry until, or unless, you have cause to*.

"We are finally alone, sir," Miss Hightower quietly said within the darkness.

Mr Elliott felt her hands upon his chest, guiding him backward, against the wall.

"Yes, so it would seem," Mr Elliott said, a slight shiver passing through him.

Mr Elliott felt her body against his, followed by her soft lips upon his dry ones. The memory of the kiss he shared with Inspector Lee last night sprang into his mind's eye. Suddenly, Miss Hightower had morphed into the policeman, and the hands which fumbled with his trousers were Inspector Lee's. Mr Elliott breathed in sharply as he felt a stirring, followed by a building fever. Giving the lips a stroke with his tongue, he pushed against them, demanding to be let in, as his breathing quickened and became louder. For the briefest of moments, he surrendered to the illusion and the feelings he'd suppressed for so long.

Suddenly, a man's voice tore through the darkness, shattering everything. "What're yow doin', bab?!"

Mr Elliott and Miss Hightower immediately pushed one another away. Feeling the cold air against his crotch,

Mr Elliott also hurriedly fastened his trousers, glad his obvious erection was hidden by the darkness.

There was a sharp firecracker like noise, followed by a burst of white light that illuminated the man's face. Around thirty years old, he had short, curly hair, topped by a bowler hat, and a large nose. His attire consisted of an open brown, knee-length overcoat, black waistcoat and trousers, green tie, and white shirt. In his right hand was the match, in his left a wooden club. He pointed the latter at Mr Elliott and advanced upon him. "Who are yow?!"

"Jack, please, it's not what it looks like," Miss Hightower pleaded.

The man shoved her aside and glared at Mr Elliott. "*Well*?"

"My name is Mr Gregory Elliott, Mr Jerome," Mr Eliott replied.

Mr Jerome tossed the match as its heat neared his fingers. "How'd yow know my name?"

The scrape of a shoe at the entrance of the passageway distracted him, however. Looking sharply in that direction, he saw Inspector Conway enter from the street and advance swiftly toward them. Catching sight of the policeman's face by the lantern's candlelight, Mr Jerome's eyes widened in recognition. "It's the coppers! *Scarper*!"

"But—!" Miss Hightower cried.

Yet, she was cut off by Mr Jerome grabbing her by the arm and pulling her in the opposite direction as he ran toward Baskerville Place. Their rapid footfalls echoed around the passageway, thereby preventing Mr Elliott from hearing Inspector Conway's approach until the last moment. Leaping back against the wall as a result, Mr Elliott simultaneously heard the policeman run past and smelt his combined scent of sweat and carbolic soap. Immediately feeling the breeze sweep across his face in the policeman's wake, he stepped into the passageway's centre and squinted into the darkness.

As one might expect, the young Mr Jerome and Miss Hightower were faster than the middle-aged Inspector

Conway. The pain of his broken ribs hindering his breathing also put the policeman at a further disadvantage. Nearing the long passageway's end in minutes, the Jeromes felt their hearts lift at the promise of imminent freedom. The moment they emerged, though, something caught their feet, sending them toppling forward.

Releasing a sharp cry of surprise, Miss Hightower landed with a roll upon the ground. Meanwhile, Mr Jerome gasped and threw his hands down to catch himself. Yet no sooner had he landed, did he hear a loud crack and felt his right arm collapse beneath him. This was instantly followed by an explosion of excruciating pain that sent shockwaves up and down his arm. Putting his hand upon the spot where the pain had started, he felt the jagged edge of his radius bone protruding from the torn fabric of his jacket. The colour drained from his face.

Inspector Conway emerged from the passageway and immediately skidded to a halt, narrowly avoiding Miss Hightower and Mr Jerome's prone forms.

A heartbeat later, Inspector Donahue emerged from the shadows to the right of the passageway's exit, with a "life preserver" in his hand. Made from a length of cane approximately a foot long, the weapon had a large ball of lead attached by catgut at one end and a leather loop hooked over Inspector Donahue's wrist at the other. He pointed the weapon at Mr Jerome. "Yow's nicked, yow little demon hell-raiser."

"Yow've broke my arm!" Mr Jerome cried.

Inspector Conway gently helped Miss Hightower to her feet. "Come on, lass."

"How… how did you find us?" Miss Hightower enquired.

"You was followed," Inspector Conway replied.

Inspector Donahue slipped the "life preserver" into its loop on the inside of his overcoat and, gripping Mr Jerome's lapels, hauled him to his feet. Taking a firm grip of his good arm, he dragged him toward the passageway. "Get move-ing, or I'll break some-thing else."

"Did my parents send you?" Miss Hightower enquired from Inspector Conway.

"No," Inspector Conway replied. "The Metropolitan Police."

Mr Elliott and Mr Snyder stepped aside to allow Inspector Donahue and Mr Jerome to pass, followed by Inspector Conway and Miss Hightower. Allowing some distance to form before following them, the Bow Streeters walked in silence.

To Mr Elliott's relief, his unexpected state of arousal was easing, and the darkness continued its excellent job of concealing his embarrassment. His mind whirled with thoughts of Inspector Lee and the question of why he'd allowed himself to succumb to his feelings. To say it was unlike him would've been the understatement of the century. To say he was confused would've likewise done an injustice to how he was feeling.

"Are you okay?" Mr Snyder enquired once they'd reached the passageway's entrance.

"Yes. Thank you." Mr Elliott looked up the street and saw Inspectors Conway and Donahue loading Miss Hightower and Mr Jerome into a black maria. "We ought to go with them to ensure Inspector Donahue doesn't break Mr Jerome's other arm."

"If we go, we'll be at the police station all night," Mr Snyder warned.

"It's a small price to pay to ensure justice is served, Sam," Mr Elliott countered.

"True enough," Mr Snyder agreed. Holding up his arm to signal to the policemen to wait, he walked over to the vehicle. "Can we come, too?"

Inspectors Conway and Donahue exchanged glances. The latter exhaled softly and replied, "Get in."

"Thanks." Mr Snyder climbed inside and, turning, gripped Mr Elliott's arm to help lift him inside as well. Upon noticing the indicative slight bulge in the solicitor's trousers, the cabman tapped him on the arm. When Mr Elliott met his gaze, Mr Snyder tapped the side of his own nose and gave a single nod, followed by a wink. Realising what he was referring to, Mr Elliott felt a prickling on his scalp and a heat in his cheeks. He swallowed hard and offered a weak smile of appreciation, before sitting on a narrow bench and covering his crotch with his frockcoat's skirt.

FORTY-EIGHT

Dr Weeks imagined sitting at a bar with a tankard of ale in one hand and a cigarette in the other. He imagined the lively conversations happening around him and the warmth of the fire. The vision dissolved, however, and he was brought back to the cold bedroom and the bowl of lukewarm gruel resting upon his lap. Dr Weeks' lip curled at its grey colour and oaty smell.

"It'll taste better if you eat it whilst it's still warm," Dr Colbert said.

"I ain't eatin' this slop." Dr Weeks put the bowl on the bed beside him.

"Yes. You are." Dr Colbert brought his chair close to Dr Weeks and, picking up the bowl, gave the gruel a stir. "You haven't eaten in days. This will be kind to your stomach."

Dr Weeks' gaze hardened. "I *ain't* eatin' it."

Dr Colbert lifted a spoonful to Dr Weeks' mouth. "Just a taste, then."

Dr Weeks clamped his mouth shut and folded his arms.

"You can't starve yourself simply to make a point," Dr Colbert chastised.

Dr Weeks lifted his chin in defiance.

Dr Colbert tossed the spoon into the bowl and sighed. "I'm trying to help you."

Dr Weeks' arm swept the bowl from Dr Colbert's hands. Landing on its edge, the bowl threw its contents across the floor before rolling and coming to a stop with a wobble.

"There was absolutely no need for that." Dr Colbert glared at him.

"I ain't eatin' until I get a drink," Dr Weeks stated.

Dr Colbert crouched beside his chair and used his hand to sweep as much of the gruel into the bowl as he could. "You'll eat something eventually." He stood. "You'll have to."

"No, I—" A bolt of sharp pain tearing through Dr Weeks' abdomen cut him off. Doubling over, he took short, shallow breaths as more aftershocks of agony swept through him.

"A partial cause of your pain will be your hunger," Dr Colbert said.

Dr Weeks lifted defiant eyes to him and growled, "If ya'll want me to eat, ya'll got to give me somethin' to drink."

"Your pain and nausea will continue as long as your stomach remains empty. You should also know I have limitless patience." Dr Colbert left the room but paused at the door to look back at him. "You might have won this battle, but I assure you, I'll win the war."

* * *

"Back here again, Jack?" the middle-aged sergeant enquired. "What's it this time?"

"Extortion," Inspector Donahue replied, maintaining a firm grip upon Mr Jerome's good arm as they stood before the wood-panelled custody desk.

Located at the rear of Newton Street police station, the room in which the desk stood was windowless with only two doors. Inspectors Donahue and Conway had brought the prisoners through the first door from the yard, with Mr Elliott and Mr Snyder following closely. The second door was solid iron and, presumably, led to the cells.

"In point of fact, Mr Jerome didn't demand any money," Mr Elliott stated. "He is wanted for questioning in connection with a murder and blackmail in London, however."

"Who're yow?" the sergeant enquired.

"Mr Gregory Elliott, solicitor and member of the Bow Street Society," Mr Elliott replied.

"Sydney Sloane's lot?" the sergeant enquired with distaste.

"No, myself and Mr Snyder here," Mr Elliott indicated the cabman, "are members of the original Bow Street Society in London."

"Do yow represent Jack?" the sergeant enquired.

Mr Elliott parted his lips to reply in the affirmative.

"You can't, Elliott," Inspector Conway warned. "You was involved in the crime."

"But that is my point, *Inspector*," Mr Elliott replied, matching his tone. "No crime has been committed against my person."

"What's she here for?" The sergeant indicated Miss Hightower.

"Prostitution," Inspector Donahue replied.

"*Again*," Mr Elliott said through a sigh. "No money exchanged hands."

The sergeant raised his brows. "She was with yow?"

"Yes, but—" Mr Elliott began.

"Is he being charged, too?" the sergeant enquired from Inspector Donahue whilst pointing his pencil at the solicitor.

Inspector Conway smirked.

"No," Inspector Donahue replied.

"I was only there to lure Mr Jerome and Miss Hightower," Mr Elliott stated.

"Mrs Jack Jerome, actually," Miss Hightower spoke up.

Inspector Conway's smirk vanished, that complicated matters.

"What are yow charge-ing them with, then?" the sergeant enquired.

"Suspicion of extortion for him and suspicion of prostitution for her," Inspector Donahue replied. He put Mr Jerome's club on the desk. "Have-ing a weapon for him, too."

"What's goin' to be done about *this*?" Mr Jerome demanded, lifting his broken arm.

455

"What happened?" the sergeant enquired from Inspector Donahue.

"He fell," Inspector Donahue replied.

"*Yow* hit me!" Mr Jerome cried.

"Prisoner injured due-ring arrest," the sergeant read aloud as he wrote in the logbook.

Mr Elliott's expression cooled at the blatant cover up. It was unfortunate he hadn't witnessed the assault. If he had, it wouldn't be Mr Jerome's word against Inspector Donahue's. Mr Elliott knew it was pointless attempting to argue the case on Mr Jerome's behalf, though, for the outcome almost always swung in the officer's favour. The lack of investigation into Inspector Conway's alleged assault of Mr Thaddeus Dorsey proved this.

The sergeant glanced at Mr Jerome's arm. "We'll get the doctor to look at it."

* * *

Gentle snoring filled the parlour, accompanied by the snap and crackle of the fire within its hearth. The pitter patter of rain against the window was concealed by drawn, heavy curtains. Sipping her cup of after-dinner tea, Dr Locke watched her husband as he slept in his armchair, his head resting against its side. Despite his apparent peace and comfort, her eyebrows were drawn together in worry. He'd eaten a hearty dinner but had struggled to complete their evening walk. He was yawning when Lyons had removed his outdoor accoutrements and had barely touched his own cup of tea.

Mr Locke's snoring momentarily ceased as he inhaled deeply and turned to rest against the chair's opposite side. With an unconscious smacking of his lips, he mumbled some gibberish and continued snoring.

Dr Locke glanced at the time on the mantel clock; it was almost half past eight. She finished her tea and set the cup down upon the wine table beside her chair. Her husband would usually have a warm bath around about now, but she doubted he'd need help sleeping tonight. Therefore, she'd told Claude it wouldn't be needed and to take the night off. It had been quite some time since she'd granted the attendant some proper rest, so he'd leapt at the chance. She stood and gently shook Mr Locke's shoulder. "Darling."

"Hm," Mr Locke half-grunted, half-groaned.

Dr Locke shook his shoulder a little harder, and Mr Locke awoke with a start.

"*Huh*?" Mr Locke blinked several times as he lifted his head and looked around.

"You fell asleep," Dr Locke replied.

"Did I?" Mr Locke sat up and rubbed his eyes. "I only intended to rest my eyes."

Dr Locke sat on the chair's arm and massaged his shoulders. "Are you tense?"

"A little." Mr Locke closed his eyes and grunted softly at her expert touch.

"I think you ought to resign from the case," Dr Locke said.

Mr Locke twisted his body to look up at her. "Pardon?"

Dr Locke rested her hands in her lap. "It's too tiring for you."

"But I cannot resign now, Lynette. Miss Trent and the others are relying upon me. On us."

Dr Locke picked up his cup of cold tea from his wine table and, standing, added it to her own. "Miss Trent and the others will understand you must do what's best for your health."

"But continuing with the investigation *is* what is best for my health. I have not felt this well in months."

Dr Locke sat on the edge of her chair and clasped her hands tightly in her lap. "Do you no longer trust my medical judgement?"

"*Pardon*?" Mr Locke did a double take. "Of course, I do."

"Then why are you choosing to ignore it?"

"I am not. I am simply explaining why I do not want to resign from the case." Mr Locke sat forward. "I am finally feeling like Mr Percival Locke the man, again, and not Mr Percival Locke the pitiful heroin addict." He placed his hand upon hers. "Is that not what you wanted?"

"You know it is," Dr Locke snapped.

Mr Locke withdrew his hand and straightened. "I did not mean to upset you, Lynette."

"And yet you have." Dr Locke swallowed hard as she felt her worry intensify. "I don't want you compromising your recovery over an actress—*again*."

Mr Locke lowered his head as the memory of the sandbag falling, reminding him of his mother's death on stage, replayed in his mind's eye. He quietly said, "I understand your concern." He lifted his head and, rallying himself, continued with greater fortitude, "But it is time I assumed responsibility for myself. If I feel I am becoming too fatigued, I shall rest. If I fear it is compromising my recovery, I shall resign. Either way, it should now be my decision to make, with you by my side."

Dr Locke tightened her hands' grip on one another as, with a quiver in her voice, she admitted, "I've fought too hard and too long to get you well to simply surrender control over your recovery now."

Mr Locke frowned, unsure of what to say, except, "I see."

"But I'm not a tyrant," Dr Locke went on. "If you feel strong enough to continue with the investigation, so be it. We shall see it through together. If, however, I think you require longer to regain your strength, I shall refuse whichever case Miss Trent wants to assign to us next. Agreed?"

Mr Locke's features lifted into a smile. "*Agreed. Absolutely and positively.*"

Dr Locke's heart warmed at the sight of his happiness, and so she permitted herself a small smile in return. "Good."

* * *

Mr Elliott strummed his fingers upon his knee as he watched the door Inspector Donahue had taken Inspector Conway through twenty minutes earlier. His lower back and hips ached from sitting on the hard wooden chair, whilst his core was chilled from the unheated air. Aside from him and the uniformed officer behind the counter, the Newton Street police station's public reception was deserted. Mr Snyder had left five minutes prior to seek out a cab to take the Bow Streeters back to their hotel. Furthermore, it was too early for the ruckus that usually accompanied closing time at the public houses.

Mr Elliott stood as the door opened, and Inspector Conway finally emerged. "Well?"

"'Well,' what?" Inspector Conway enquired in return.

Mr Elliott adopted a hard tone. "Are Mr and Mrs Jerome to be interviewed tonight?"

"No." Inspector Conway strolled over to him. "Donahue's not chargin' them with anythin'."

Mr Elliott eyed him with suspicion. "They're to be released then?"

"Into my custody, yeah. I'm takin' 'em back to London in the mornin'."

"By black maria?"

"By train. Donahue's comin' with us."

"You and the Jeromes?" Mr Elliott clarified.

"Me, the Jeromes, you, and Mr Snyder," Inspector Conway corrected.

Mr Elliott eyed him with cynicism. "You're allowing us to travel with you and your prisoners? Why?"

"I won't hear the last of it if I don't." Inspector Conway bid good night to the officer behind the counter and headed for the door, prompting Mr Elliott to follow. Releasing a soft sigh when the solicitor joined him on the pavement, Inspector Conway enquired, "Can't you gimmie a bit of peace?"

"On the matter of the Jeromes, yes. There's something else we need to discuss, however."

Inspector Conway took out a cigarette and walked a couple of paces whilst he lit it and took a deep pull. Stopping at the curb, he lifted his head and slowly exhaled the smoke. Lowering his head again, he took in a lungful of the cold night air through his mouth and steadily released it through his nose. He took a second, shallower, pull from his cigarette and swiftly exhaled the smoke. "I'm listenin'."

Mr Elliott joined him at the curb. "Mr Hogarth-Huxley."

Inspector Conway turned his head toward the road. "What about 'im?"

"You recognised the sort of man he was. How?"

"If you've been a copper as long as me; you get to know what people's actions mean." Inspector Conway took another shallow pull from his cigarette and swiftly exhaled the smoke away from Mr Elliott. "'E was actin' like a lovelorn pup with you."

"And so, you intervened to protect our plan," Mr Elliott thought aloud.

"Yeah." Inspector Conway flicked the excess ash from his cigarette into a drain at their feet.

Mr Elliott had his earlier suspicions confirmed. There was no need to continue the discussion. Yet, the part of him that had not only returned Inspector Lee's kiss but enjoyed it, demanded to know more. Not to hear the salacious details but to gauge how much of a potential threat Inspector Conway was to him both now and in the future. He lowered his voice a fraction as he enquired, "What did he say to you?"

Inspector Conway took a deep pull from his cigarette and, lifting his head, slowly exhaled the smoke as he carefully considered his answer. Deciding the solicitor would continue to interrogate him if he thought he wasn't being honest, he tossed his cigarette into the drain as he turned to face him. With a deadpan expression and serious tone, he replied, "I reminded 'im of his old boxer lover."

"And you didn't arrest him?"

"We was after the Jeromes."

"Afterward."

"What for?"

Mr Elliott despised the term, but it was the legal definition, so he was obliged to use it. "Sodomy."

"'E never got that close to me."

Mr Elliott's features tensed. "Answer the question."

"Why?"

"Professional curiosity." The next question toppled from Mr Elliott's lips before his brain could catch up. "Are you a mandrake?"

"Leave it out!"

"Then why didn't you return to *The Woodman* and arrest Mr Hogarth-Huxley after he'd made such a damning admission to you?"

"Because I don't care who 'e's got in his bed."

"You're a policeman. It's allegedly your sworn duty to uphold the law."

Inspector Conway's eyes narrowed. "I do."

"But not in this case?"

Inspector Conway stepped into Mr Elliott's personal space and lowered his voice, thereby increasing its already gravelly nature. "Tell me sumin', Elliott. What good would it of done for me to nick the mandrake? 'E was just some lonely bloke lookin' for company. No different to toffs payin' strumpets for knee-tremblers. If I arrested every bloke who got 'is pleasure by criminal means, I'd have half of London in my cells. Does *that* answer your bloody question?"

Despite the confrontational way the answer was given, Mr Elliott felt reassured by it. He remained convinced Inspector Conway was a man who resorted to violence more often than he should. Yet, after hearing his answer, Mr Elliott was willing to consider he might not be the animal he thought he was. Therefore, it was with genuine sincerity he replied, "Yes. Thank you, Inspector."

A cab trundled to a halt beside them, and Mr Snyder poked his head out the window. "Everythin' all right?"

"Yes, Sam." Mr Elliott moved around Inspector Conway to open the door.

"Want a lift, Inspector?" Mr Snyder enquired as Mr Elliott climbed inside.

"Nah," Inspector Conway replied. "Thanks."

"If you haven't a place to stay, we recommend *The Stork Hotel*," Mr Elliott said.

"It's outside of what the Yard's willin' to pay for expenses," Inspector Conway said. "My sister'll put me up."

"I'm willing to pay for your room," Mr Elliott said.

Inspector Conway stared at him. "You what?"

"It will save you travelling all the way back to your sister's, and we're going to the hotel now anyway," Mr Elliott explained. "Consider it a peace offering."

Inspector Conway pointed at Mr Elliott as he enquired from Mr Snyder, "Is 'e drunk or sumin'?"

"I'm *perfectly* sober, thank you," Mr Elliott tersely replied.

"I'd take the offer, if I was you, mate," Mr Snyder said, addressing Inspector Conway.

"You better not be pullin' my leg, Elliott," Inspector Conway warned.

"If 'e is, *I'll* pay for your bloomin' room," Mr Snyder said. "Get in."

Inspector Conway was still deeply suspicious of the solicitor but, feeling reassured by the cabman, climbed into the cab and sat down.

FORTY-NINE

Mr Jerome flinched in pain with each bump the hansom cab went over. His lower arm was covered by a cast and rested within a cotton sling upon his chest. The cast comprised of strips of coarse cotton cloth, rubbed with finely powdered plaster, which had been soaked in water and applied to his arm wet. The cast had then solidified as it had dried. The railway journey from Birmingham New Street to London Euston had proven equally as arduous. Each time the train had applied its brakes, the force had pulled his arm away from his chest, thereby causing more pain. It hadn't helped to be handcuffed to the man who'd broken his arm in the first place. Even now, he and Inspector Donahue sat shoulder to shoulder on the narrow bench with the handcuffs' chain resting between them.

In the cab behind theirs were Mrs Jerome and Inspector Conway. Handcuffed together in a manner identical to the others, she kept her head bowed whilst he kept a close eye on the other vehicle. She hadn't spoken since leaving the Newton Street police station but had promptly obeyed each order Inspector Conway had given. They'd shared a first class compartment with Mr Jerome and Inspector Donahue on the train. Although Mr Elliott and Mr Snyder had also been present, Inspector Conway was unsure whether Mrs Jerome's silence was born from fear or blind loyalty.

A third cab directly behind Mrs Jerome and Inspector Conway's held Mr Elliott and Mr Snyder. The former had paid for the Bow Streeters' railway tickets, whilst the remainder were purchased by Inspector Conway on behalf of the Metropolitan Police. The policeman had apparent cause to go to the trouble of escorting the Jeromes back to London. Yet, neither Mr Elliott nor Mr Snyder knew if Sergeant Dixon had been notified of their imminent arrival.

The convoy of cabs turned onto Bow Street and consecutively slowed to a halt outside the police station. Alighting from theirs and paying the driver, Mr Elliott watched Inspectors Conway and Donahue alight from their respective vehicles with their prisoners in tow. As Mr Snyder joined him, and they approached the others, though, Inspector Woolfe emerged from the police station and came down the steps toward them.

"What's this, a welcome committee?" Inspector Conway sardonically enquired.

Inspector Donahue looked up and down Inspector Woolfe's six feet four inches frame. "Yow're a big lad, ain't yow!"

Inspector Woolfe gave Inspector Donahue a cold look and turned to his friend. "I tried getting in touch, but you'd already left Newton Street."

Inspector Conway wrinkled his brow. "What's the matter?"

Inspector Woolfe indicated the Jeromes. "You're going to have to release these two."

Inspector Conway's voice raised in pitch. "You *what*?"

"The *Royal Opera House* don't want to press charges," Inspector Woolfe replied.

Inspector Donahue moved into Inspector Woolfe's personal space as he glared up at him. "Are yow tell-ing me I come all this way for noth-ing?"

Inspector Conway put his arm between them, but Inspector Donahue knocked it away.

"*Nah*, mate." Inspector Donahue shook his head. "I've left my Abi to come here."

"Excuse me." Mr Elliott stood to the side of Inspectors Donahue and Woolfe. "What of Mr Jerome's alleged assault and blackmail against Mr Benton at the *Crescent Theatre*, Inspector?"

A tightness entered Inspector Woolfe's mouth and eyes. "C Division didn't mention any outstanding complaints about blackmail or assault committed by these two."

Mr Jerome rocked back and forth on his heels as, deliberately raising his eyebrows, he told Inspector Donahue with a broad smile, "Yow'd better let me go, then."

Inspector Donahue thrust his fist close to Mr Jerome's face, obliging him to lean his head back. "Watch yow lip!"

"Inspector, *please*," Mr Elliott warned.

Inspector Donahue lowered his fist and, taking a step back, muttered under his breath.

Mr Elliott shifted his gaze to his prisoner. "I wouldn't be smug, Mr Jerome. You could still potentially be in a great deal of trouble."

Mr Jerome scowled. "And why should oy listen to *yow*?"

"Because I, and the Bow Street Society, are the only allies you and Mrs Jerome have," Mr Elliott calmly replied.

Inspector Woolfe narrowed his eyes and growled, "Get them out of my sight."

As Inspector Woolfe stormed back inside, Inspector Conway took the keys from his pocket with a soft sigh and removed the handcuffs from the Jeromes. "You heard him."

Mr Jerome put his good arm around his wife and guided her past Inspector Donahue whilst keeping a close eye on him and Inspector Conway.

"This way," Mr Elliott said, leading the Jeromes down Bow Street with Mr Snyder.

Inspector Donahue cast a glare in their direction as he strode into the police station. "One of these days, I'm going to get the little demon hell-raiser."

Inspector Conway followed Inspector Donahue as far as the door but stopped to light a cigarette and watch until the Jeromes and Bow Streeters had reached the Society's house. Taking a deep pull from his cigarette, he turned to enter the police station but stopped when he saw Miss

Hicks emerge from the Society's house carrying a carpet bag. The Jeromes, Mr Elliott, and Mr Snyder had gone inside, so Miss Hicks was alone. Intrigued, but also a little angry at the barmaid still, he descended the steps to intercept her when she walked past.

"Where are you goin'?" Inspector Conway enquired as he stepped into her path.

Miss Hicks stopped with a jolt and immediately clutched the bag to her chest. "What business is it of yours?"

"You're my mate's old lady," Inspector Conway's expression and tone turned cold, "who's carryin' on with another bloke while that same mate is in Bedlam." He glanced at the bag. "Doin' a runner, are you?"

Miss Hicks lowered the bag, squared her shoulders, and lifted her chin. "No."

Inspector Conway tossed away his cigarette and snatched the bag from her. "You won't mind me takin' a look then, will you?"

"*Oi!*" Miss Hicks tried to snatch it back, but he turned his back on her.

"Fancy dresses… lace… stockings," Inspector Conway said as he searched the bag.

Miss Hicks put her hands on her hips and tapped her foot.

Inspector Conway looked over his shoulder at her. "You sure you're not doin' a runner?"

Miss Hicks folded her arms. "If you *must* know, I'm takin' it to the pawnbrokers."

Inspector Conway faced her, a pair of stockings in his hand. "Here, you've not thieved this lot off Miss Trent, have you?"

Miss Hicks snatched the stockings. "Don't be stupid." She took the bag back and put the stockings into it. "It's things Perce bought me."

Inspector Conway's eyes became suspicious. "And you don't want to keep 'em?"

"I've got lots more." Miss Hicks fastened the bag. "And I want to give Becky some 'ousekeepin' money. And that's all you're gettin' from me, John Conway." She lifted her chin and began to walk past. "So go back to mindin' your own bloomin' business."

Inspector Conway grabbed her arm. "If I find out you've done a runner on my mate, I'll hunt you down. You *and* your bloke."

Agitated but doing her best to hide it, Miss Hicks tugged her arm free and walked away.

* * *

Breakfast had been served and eaten with little incident amongst the male patients. One was conspicuous by his absence, however. Discussing the matter with the head attendant Mr Corwin, Dr Colbert was informed Dr Weeks had refused to leave his room. Furthermore, Dr McWilliams had directed Mr Corwin to leave Dr Weeks be, as he would bring the matter up with Dr Colbert. Unfortunately, whether it be by choice or by circumstance, this hadn't happened, and Dr Weeks had missed the meal entirely. The last thing Dr Colbert wanted was for Dr Weeks to starve to death due to his stubbornness and their incompetence.

Emerging from the dining room with a bowl of fresh gruel and bottle of ginger-infused water in hand, Dr Colbert made his way to Dr Weeks' room. As per his earlier instructions, Mr Corwin and Mr Shayne were waiting for him in the corridor with a pair of soft gloves, a side-arm dress, and three large blankets. Padded to an approximate one-inch thickness, the gloves each had a wrist strap with a screw button. The side-arm dress was made from flannel-lined woollen material and had pockets attached to its sides. The three blankets were square in shape and made from thick, coarse wool.

"Are we all clear on the plan?" Dr Colbert enquired, his voice barely above a whisper.

"Yes, doctor," Mr Corwin replied as Mr Shayne nodded.

"Good." Dr Colbert faced the door and, taking a moment to mentally prepare himself, turned the handle. Yet, as he pushed, something on the other side prevented the door from opening. He pushed harder, but the door remained immobile against whatever was obstructing it. He furrowed his brow. "Strange."

"Allow me, doctor." Mr Corwin changed places with Dr Colbert and pushed. When the door wouldn't move for him either, he put his shoulder against the wood and pressed his whole weight against it. All he could manage was a few inches' gap, however. Peering through it, he spotted what the problem was. "There's a chair wedged under the doorknob."

"What the Devil…?" Dr Colbert looked over Mr Corwin's shoulder and saw the top corner of the chair's backrest through the gap. Side-stepping to get a better view of the room, he frowned when it was blocked by the door. He went through in his mind what was in there: the chair, a table, mattress, sheets, blankets. Suddenly, a chilling vision sprang into his mind's eye, and he pushed Mr Corwin aside to bang on the door. "Percy! Percy, speak to me!"

"What is it, doctor?" Mr Corwin enquired, looking between Dr Colbert and the door.

"He could've hung himself, man!" Dr Colbert cried. "*Percy*!"

"Fetch a broom," Mr Corwin told Mr Shayne who immediately hurried away.

"What good is a *broom* going to do?!" Dr Colbert cried, his heart pounding as the vision of Dr Weeks hanging from the ceiling by a makeshift rope plaited from sheets remained stuck in his mind.

"I might be able to knock the chair away with it," Mr Corwin replied.

"*Percy*!" Dr Colbert repeatedly banged on the door, desperate for an answer.

"Here." Mr Shayne handed the broom to Mr Corwin as he returned with it.

Mr Corwin touched Dr Colbert's arm. "Step aside, please, doctor."

Dr Colbert moved backward into the corridor and put his hand over his mouth.

Mr Corwin slipped the broom handle through the gap to gauge the angle before pulling it back a little and thrusting it forward as hard as he could. The chair shook but remained wedged. Pulling the broom handle back further, he gripped the external doorknob for balance and put his entire weight behind the second thrust. This time, the chair popped free, and Mr Corwin pushed it across the floor with a swift opening of the door.

Dr Colbert hung back as Mr Shayne followed Mr Corwin into the room.

For a couple of heart-wrenching seconds, there was silence.

Then Dr Colbert heard a cacophony of grunting and growling. Suddenly, Mr Corwin and Mr Shayne dragged a struggling Dr Weeks into view and wrestled him onto the bed. A wave of relief so intense it made him shudder swept across Dr Colbert at the sight. Entering the room, he moved the chair into the corridor and closed the door, whilst Mr Corwin and Mr Shayne fought to remove Dr Weeks' nightshirt.

"Get off me, ya damn sonsofbitches!" Dr Weeks snarled.

"This is for your own good, Percy," Dr Colbert said, standing behind Mr Corwin and Mr Shayne where Dr Weeks could see him. "You shouldn't have frightened us like that."

Dr Weeks kicked out at him, but Dr Colbert swiftly moved aside.

Mr Shayne pulled the nightshirt over Dr Weeks' head and tossed it onto the floor.

"What're ya doin'?!" Dr Weeks cried as he felt the cold air against his naked flesh.

"We're putting you into a side-arm dress and gloves," Dr Colbert replied.

Mr Corwin pinned Dr Weeks' left arm and upper body, whilst Mr Shayne put the dress over Dr Weeks' head and forced his right arm into the sleeve before slipping on a glove and securing it to Dr Weeks' wrist. They then switched roles to allow Dr Weeks' left arm to be forced into its sleeve and the second glove to be applied.

Dr Weeks arched his back and tried to pull his arms free as they were forced into the pockets of the dress and secured. "Ya can't do this! I ain't gonna be able to use my hands!"

Dr Colbert laid out the first blanket upon the floor. "That is the intention, yes."

Mr Corwin pulled the dress down to cover Dr Weeks' nakedness and wrapped his arms around his legs. Meanwhile, Mr Shayne hooked his arms under Dr Weeks', and, between them, they lifted him off the bed.

Dr Weeks tried to kick out, but all he could manage was a jerk of his hips as the attendants' grips remained firm. When they carried him over to the blanket and laid him down upon his back, his sensitivity to their touch increased, and his anger shifted into anxiety. He tried to pull his hands free, but his arms had turned to jelly. He tried to shrug their hands from his shoulders, but the weight only increased. He tried to wriggle against the blanket being wrapped around his body, but it was tightened, stopping his movement.

Suddenly, he realised how weak and restrained he was, and an overwhelming sense of vulnerability descended upon him. With it came a rapid heartbeat, a tingling in his fingers, and a tightening of his chest, preventing him from taking a full breath. His instincts told him he was having an attack, but he had no idea what kind. This second realisation caused his blood to run cold. A vision of his heart suddenly stopping under the pressure also exploded into his mind, intensifying his fear.

Sweating, pale faced, and shaking uncontrollably, he begged in a trembling voice, "*Stop… Please.*"

Yet, Dr Colbert, Mr Corwin and Mr Shayne appeared either oblivious or indifferent to his plea as the second blanket was laid out, and he was rolled onto it. The additional pressure of the floor against his chest made Dr Weeks feel like it was impossible to expand his lungs. Unconsciously holding what little breath he had, he felt his heart pound against his ribs and the tingling in his fingers move up his arms. By the time the second blanket was wrapped tightly around him and secured, his head was swimming, and his body felt utterly out of his control.

"Back onto the bed," Dr Colbert instructed.

Mr Corwin and Mr Shayne turned Dr Weeks onto his back, prompting a large and audible gasp from the surgeon as he finally released his breath and filled his lungs. Several short, sharp gasps ensured as he fought to regain control of his breathing and heartrate. Yet, neither attendant paid his obviously distressed state any heed. Instead, they lifted and carried him back to the bed, where they forced his body into a sitting position with his back against the headboard and his tightly bound legs sticking out in front of him. Mr Corwin and Mr Shayne finished their task by putting the third blanket across Dr Weeks' legs and tucking it firmly under the mattress to further restrict his movement.

"Thank you, gentlemen," Dr Colbert said as he approached Dr Weeks with the bowl of cold gruel and bottle of ginger-infused water. "You may return to your duties."

Dr Weeks bowed and repeatedly shook his head. "Ya *can't* do *this*… ya *can't* do *this*."

"I can." Dr Colbert set the things down upon the table. "I can also ensure you remain like this until, or unless, I'm satisfied you're willing to cooperate." He stirred the gruel and presented a spoonful to Dr Weeks' mouth. "Open wide."

Dr Weeks grimaced and leant his head back.

"I *said*." Dr Colbert tightly pinched and twisted Dr Weeks' nose, causing him to tilt his head sideways and cry out. Shoving the spoon into Dr Weeks' mouth the instant it opened, Dr Colbert slid it across the roof of his mouth to push its contents into the back of his throat before pulling it out. In a cold tone, he added, "*Open*. Wide."

Dr Weeks instinctively swallowed the foul-tasting mixture but immediately gagged on it before releasing a sound of disgust accompanied by a second grimace.

Dr Colbert presented another spoonful to his lips. "I expect you to obey this time."

Dr Weeks clamped his mouth shut.

Again, Dr Colbert pinched and twisted Dr Weeks' nose. Yet, the surgeon was able to keep his mouth closed despite emitting a sharp grunt of pain from behind his teeth. Dr Colbert's gaze cooled, and he twisted Dr Weeks' nose harder, causing tears to appear in his patient's eyes. "Do you want me to break your nose, Percy? Because I will if it means you eat something."

Dr Weeks flinched and released another sharp grunt of pain as Dr Colbert twisted his nose further. With tears flowing, his heart racing, and his stomach churning, Dr Weeks realised he was utterly powerless against the man with the spoon. Consequently, his crippling anxiety shifted into overwhelming humiliation, and he desperately wanted nothing more than for this latest ordeal to end. He closed his eyes and slowly opened his mouth.

Dr Colbert smiled. "A wise decision." He thrust the spoon into Dr Weeks' mouth.

Dr Weeks gagged at the first taste of gruel but forced it down anyway.

"Excellent." Dr Colbert's smile grew, and he released Dr Weeks' nose. "We are finally making some progress."

FIFTY

"I had a word with Sergeant Bird at Bow Street this mornin'," Sergeant Gutman put a tray of tea things upon Inspector Lee's desk. "He said Inspector Conway went to Birmingham yesterday but was comin' back today with some prisoners, an inspector from the Birmingham police, and Mr Elliott and Mr Snyder from the Bow Street Society."

"Inspector Conway's treacherous nature knows no bounds," Inspector Lee remarked. His thoughts were on Mr Elliott, however. The solicitor had neglected to inform him he was leaving London. Therefore, he'd called upon his office yesterday afternoon, only to be informed of his absence by one of his legal clerks.

Inspector Lee prepared his cup of tea and had a sip. "Send a message to Bow Street, inviting the Birmingham officer to visit New Scotland Yard."

At most, it would allow Inspector Lee to question him about the case Inspector Conway and the Bow Street Society had worked upon together in Birmingham. At least, it would give the officer something to tell his colleagues back home.

"Yes, sir." Sergeant Gutman sat at his desk and pulled across his notepaper, ink bottle, and pen. "Will you be signin' it, sir?"

"Yes." Inspector Lee had another sip of tea. "By the way, has Mr Hargreaves' search of the police records yielded any results since we last spoke?"

Sergeant Gutman abandoned his letter to consult his notebook. "Nothin' criminal, but Mr Percival Locke's name keeps comin' up as a witness in 'ousebreakin' cases."

Inspector Lee set down his tea. "As a house guest?"

"As a dinner guest, sir." Sergeant Gutman had a slight frown as he met Inspector Lee's gaze. "Seems all the victims had a dinner party one week, and their 'ouses was broke into the next."

Inspector Lee wrote in his own notebook. "And Mr Locke was a guest at each of the dinner parties?"

"Yes, sir."

"What were Mr Hargreaves' thoughts on the matter?"

Sergeant Gutman gave a one-sided shoulder shrug. "Said it was a coincidence, on account of toffs havin' a habit of goin' to other toffs' 'ouses."

"What was stolen in the burglaries?"

Sergeant Gutman turned back to his first page of notes. "Single jewellery items: necklaces, rings, that sort of thing. All the victims said it was their most valuable one."

Inspector Lee continued writing. "Were the items worn at the dinner parties?"

"Yes, sir."

"And they were never traced?"

"No, sir."

Inspector Lee looked to Mr Locke's section on their wall of documents as a theory formed in his mind. Alas, it was just a theory and not one he could ever hope to prove. "Anything else in the records, Sergeant?"

Sergeant Gutman's face fell. "No, sir."

"Instruct Mr Hargreaves to continue his search until all records have been checked."

"Yes, sir." Sergeant Gutman knew Mr Hargreaves would be displeased at the order.

A knock sounded upon the door, prompting Sergeant Gutman to stand and open it. Upon seeing who it was, he looked over his shoulder at Inspector Lee. "It's Sergeant Caulfield, sir."

"Let him in." Inspector Lee lowered his chin to have another sip of tea whilst following Sergeant Caulfield's approach with his eyes.

Sergeant Caulfield stood before Inspector Lee's desk and clasped his hands behind his back. With smooth features and a deadpan tone, he stated, "You wanted to see me, sir."

"Yes." Inspector Lee set down his tea and sat back in his chair. "It's been several days since I ordered you to find Mr Homer Fairbairn. Have you?"

Sergeant Caulfield felt a weight form in the pit of his stomach. "No, sir."

Inspector Lee adopted a firm tone. "Why not?"

"He's left the legal clerk profession by all accounts, sir," Sergeant Caulfield replied.

"Whose 'accounts?'" Inspector Lee probed further.

"All the legal clerks and solicitors I've spoken to, sir," Sergeant Caulfield replied.

Inspector Lee sat forward and pulled the undercover Mob Squad detective's report on Mr Elliott's background from the bottom of the pile. Referring to the account of Mr Fairbairn's departure from Mr Elliott's firm that Mr Elliott's current clerk Mr Warner gave, he read the part about 'murky circumstances' again. The memory of Inspector Lee and Mr Elliott's kiss replayed in the policeman's mind, reminding him of his earlier suspicion about the possible cause of Mr Fairbairn's termination of employment. He set the report aside and sat back in his chair, again. "Your next step is to make discreet enquiries about Mr Fairbairn at the molly houses, Sergeant."

Sergeant Caulfield was taken aback. "Sir?"

Inspector Lee glared at him. "It wasn't a request."

Sergeant Caulfield swallowed hard and shifted his weight between his feet. "Yes, sir."

"Well, what are you waiting for?" Inspector Lee demanded. "A kiss goodbye?"

"No, sir," Sergeant Caulfield mumbled.

Inspector Lee and Sergeant Gutman exchanged amused glances as he hastily left.

* * *

Visions of the kiss Mr Elliott and Inspector Lee had shared and the short, but heated, encounter with Mrs Jerome in Baskerville Passage whirled around the solicitor's mind. Framing them were imagined scenarios in which he was caught kissing another man, arrested, and put on trial. Even within this fiction, he felt the echoes of humiliation, degradation, and devastation. A possible future of imprisonment, followed by a foul existence as a destitute pariah of the legal profession, swept through his mind's eye like Dickens' ghost. He turned his back to the fireplace in the hope it would calm his inner storm. Yet, the sounds of voices in the hallway were a reminder of how isolated he was from his fellow Bow Streeters.

Miss Trent entered her office but stopped when she found Mr Elliott standing in the middle of the room. Closing the door, she went behind her desk and indicated the vacant chair. "Please, sit down."

"I prefer to stand."

Miss Trent lofted an eyebrow but remained standing. Casting an appraising glance over him, she detected the tension in his body. Concerned, she remarked, "You seem on edge."

Mr Elliott held his hands against his frockcoat's skirt and rubbed his left thumb with his right index finger. "I am."

"Why?"

"Something has happened," Mr Elliott admitted. "I didn't know who else to turn to."

Miss Trent recalled her earlier conversation with Mr Elliott and Mr Snyder in which they'd described the events which had unfolded in Birmingham. "Something else?"

"Yes, with Inspector Lee."

Miss Trent immediately came out from behind her desk. "What has he done to you?"

"A great deal and nothing at all." Mr Elliott averted his gaze. "We kissed, Miss Trent. Inspector Lee and I…" He grimaced and lowered his head. "We kissed."

Miss Trent's heart clenched. "Against your wishes?"

"No," Mr Elliott replied softly.

Miss Trent felt an initial burst of relief, followed by confusion. Doing her best to sound non-judgemental, she enquired, "I thought you despised him?"

Mr Elliott lifted his head to meet her gaze. "I do. He is a devious, manipulative, and arrogant individual. He represents everything I despise in this world."

"And yet you kissed him," Miss Trent gently countered. "Which is so beyond the bounds of your usual character, I can't help but think there's something you're not telling me."

Mr Elliott faced the window, but his gaze turned inward. "When I was eleven, I realised a courtship with a girl held no interest for me. When I was eighteen, I realised I was emotionally and physically attracted to a close male friend of mine. I was shocked and horrified. I tried to ignore it, to supress my feelings, but I couldn't stop thinking about him. He became engaged to a woman soon after, and it broke my heart." A pained look passed through his eyes. "I vowed I wouldn't be so vulnerable again. When I established my legal firm, it became imperative for my attraction toward men to be supressed, and it was, for many years, until *he* entered my life."

"You've known each other for several months, though, and expressed no attraction toward him until now," Miss Trent pointed out. "What has changed in these past few days?"

"Him." Mr Elliott faced her. "You were right; he is obsessed with me. I think he always has been but has managed to suppress his feelings until recently." He rubbed his temple. "I don't know if it's his new position as head of the Mob Squad that has allowed him to keep a closer eye on me, my friendship with Dr Colbert, or my role as the Society's solicitor that has intensified his feelings. Regardless of which it is, he's taken increasingly greater risks to be close to me."

Worry entered his eyes. "And I, who has supressed his natural inclinations for so long, has had his resistance worn down during those few stolen moments. Until, finally, we took the greatest risk thus far by kissing on my doorstep." He averted his gaze. "I knew we could be caught, so I tried to resist. But when he kissed me a second time, I relented. It was late at night, and the street was deserted." His lips curled in disgust. "I lost myself."

Miss Trent soothed, "You're only human, Gregory."

Mr Elliott vehemently shook his head as he turned and walked away. "No. Not me. Certainly not with him."

Miss Trent watched him pace. "Did anything else happen between you?"

"No. I pushed him away and told him to leave me alone."

"And did he?"

Mr Elliott rubbed his temple. "Yes, but he returned the following morning and invited me to dinner." He stood before her. "If I go to his house, something *will* happen—something illegal—and I *can't* allow it to. If the truth came out, we'd be imprisoned and ruined for the rest of our lives. But even if, by some miracle, the truth didn't come out, I can't trust him to not demand payment for his silence."

"I think it's unlikely he'd blackmail you if you were giving him what he wanted. However, the moment you refuse to give him more…" Miss Trent allowed her words to hang in the air.

"Precisely," Mr Elliott soberly agreed. "Which is why I hope you'll understand when I say I can't begin my research into his background by spending time with him."

"Of course," Miss Trent said unequivocally. "If looking into his background is going to be problematic for you, Gregory, I can—"

"*No.*" Mr Elliott briefly closed his eyes to calm his emotions. "I apologise, Miss Trent. I didn't mean to snap at you." He took a further moment to fully regain his composure. "I want to discover more about him. I need to." A sad look entered his eyes. "If only to understand why he is so attractive to me."

"I think you've partly answered that question already," Miss Trent said, gently. "But if things were to develop further between you—"

"They shan't," Mr Elliott insisted. "I can't allow them to."

Miss Trent lofted an eyebrow. "Just as you couldn't allow him to kiss you?"

Mr Elliott grimaced and turned away.

Miss Trent gently guided him to face her, however. In a low voice, she explained, "All I was going to say was: if things were to develop between you, it would be wise to know the full story about him. I agree he's an arrogant narcissist and master manipulator who's also old enough to be your father. But if you find something in his past that either redeems him enough so you can be happy with him or condemns him enough so you can walk away, I'll support you." She offered a small, reassuring smile. "In whichever choice you make."

"Thank you, Miss Trent. You've once again been a pillar of strength I can lean upon."

Miss Trent gave his arm a gentle squeeze. "I'm here any time you need me."

"And it's greatly appreciated," Mr Elliott said in earnest.

Miss Trent released his arm, grateful he'd shared his burden with her.

* * *

"There's little to tell, I'm afraid," Dr Colbert said.

"May I see him?" Chief Inspector Jones enquired.

With his gaze locked upon the policeman's, Dr Colbert lifted and lowered the fingers of his clasped hands resting upon his desk. Adopting a sombre tone, he was careful to choose his words as he replied, "No, Dr Weeks is prohibited from having any visitors."

Chief Inspector Jones looked puzzled. "Why?"

"Put simply: he's too volatile at present."

"And put complexly?" Chief Inspector Jones challenged.

"Dr Weeks is deliberately resisting all routines and treatments designed to support a stable, clean, and healthy existence. In doing so, he hopes to wear our patience down until we relent and give him what he yearns for most: alcohol. If I allowed you to visit him, he would undoubtedly tell you he was being mistreated in the hope you might arrange his release, thereby allowing him to indulge his vice at the nearest public house." Dr Colbert took a moment to calm his emotions and gather his thoughts. "When he realises you're not going to play by his rules, so to speak, he'll become incredibly agitated, and the progress we finally achieved with him this morning will be lost. No. I'm sorry, but I refuse to take the chance."

"May I remind you who brought him here, doctor."

"My mind is made up, Chief Inspector."

Chief Inspector Jones adopted a firm tone. "I'm under no illusions about his state of mind or the debilitating grip his addiction has upon him."

"I know you aren't," Dr Colbert admitted. "But Dr Weeks' cooperation is too precarious to allow him to see anyone at the moment."

Chief Inspector Jones considered proposing the option of seeing Dr Weeks from afar but, given Dr Colbert's adamance about no visitors, decided to abandon the idea. He averted his gaze and sat back in his chair, defeated. "Very well. I shall bow to your superior knowledge and experience in this matter."

The tension eased from Dr Colbert's face and voice. "Thank you."

"But I want to be kept informed of his progress, doctor," Chief Inspector Jones insisted. "Even if there's little to tell."

"Dr Weeks isn't the only patient in this hospital," Dr Colbert countered. "I shall endeavour to give regular updates, but I can't guarantee it."

"That is all I ask," Chief Inspector Jones agreed.

"Good," Dr Colbert said with a definitive tone. "As long as we're on the same page."

A worried look passed through Chief Inspector Jones' eyes. He'd hoped this visit would ease his concerns about Dr Weeks' current condition, but it had only increased them. Conceding there was nothing more he could do at present, he gathered up his things, bid goodbye to Dr Colbert, and left.

FIFTY-ONE

"We kissed, Miss Trent. Inspector Lee and I… we kissed," Mr Elliott's words replayed in Miss Trent's mind as she searched her memory of the past few days, weeks, and months for any indications of this eventuality. *"I don't like this shift in behaviour toward you; it's bordering on obsessive. For the time being, I don't want you to be alone with him,"* she'd told Mr Elliott only four days ago. To which he'd replied, *"I would rather put red-hot needles under my fingernails."*

She cast her memory back to November and the conversation she'd had with Mr Elliott at the Walmsley Hotel. He'd admitted to dining at Inspector Lee's house but had insisted nothing improper had occurred. Had it been a lie? Was he lying now? He was seated at the meeting room table, reading his notes, whilst awaiting the start of the meeting. Watching him for several moments, she wondered how a man as emotionally cold and rational as he could be seduced by someone like Inspector Lee. *"A deceptive man isn't incapable of telling the truth. One may even argue he knows it better than most, for he must be familiar with it to lie about it."* Those were Mr Elliott's words in defence of Inspector Lee, but was he also referring to himself?

The possibility of Mr Elliott growing closer to Inspector Lee disturbed her. Mr Elliott had confided his homosexuality during his interview for membership, so his feelings of attraction weren't a surprise. In all honesty, his homosexuality was irrelevant. He could've begun a relationship with a sailor, and she would've been happy for him. It was the fact it was *Inspector Lee*, possibly the most selfish and untrustworthy person she'd ever met, that disturbed her. If their relationship became physical, she could foresee Inspector Lee hurting Mr Elliott in a variety of ways, simply to serve his own interests.

"Miss Trent?" Dr Locke enquired in a low voice.

Pulled from her thoughts, Miss Trent looked to Dr Locke who, although seated, was leaning toward her with a concerned look in her eyes. "Yes, doctor?"

"Have you received any further news about Dr Weeks?" Dr Locke enquired.

Miss Trent gave a small frown. She'd temporarily forgotten about the poor surgeon. "No. I'm afraid not." *Polly hasn't returned either*, she realised. She'd seen her leave with a bag, but Mr Elliott and Mr Snyder's sudden arrival with the Jeromes had prevented her from questioning the barmaid. She hoped Miss Hicks hadn't run away with Mr O'Hannigan, for Dr Weeks' sake. *"Will you tell 'im I love 'im?"* Miss Hicks had asked Dr McWilliams to pass on the message to Dr Weeks. Yet, mere days later, Mr O'Hannigan was back in her bed. It was utterly immoral and selfish of the barmaid, and she'd had the audacity to try to justify her actions as 'survival.'

A great deal had happened over the past few days, and none of it entirely made sense to Miss Trent. People she thought she knew had shown different sides of themselves. Each new revelation had felt like a battering ram hauled against the Bow Street Society's very foundations. With Inspector Lee and the undercover Mob Squad detectives keeping such close surveillance of her, it was impossible to meet with Chief Inspector Jones. It also made meetings with Inspector Conway increasingly difficult. Consequently, the sense of isolation and vulnerability had gradually encroached upon her over the past few days.

"How's Miss Dexter doin' in Paris?" Mr Snyder enquired.

The pleasant memory of Miss Dexter's recent telegram filled Miss Trent's mind and brought genuine happiness to her breast. "Very well. She has visited the Louvre, and Lady Owston is accompanying her to her first ball."

Mr Locke took Dr Locke's hand. "Do you remember our first waltz, darling?"

"Yes." Dr Locke gave a wistful look. "I was the envy of all the young ladies."

Mr Locke softly kissed the back of her hand. "And I, the envy of all the young men."

Mr Elliott enquired in his usual monotone, "Shall we start the meeting?"

"*Yes.*" Mr Heath's eyes were bright with excitement. "*How* was Birmingham? Did you meet the *dastardly* Detective Inspector Donahue?"

"We did." Mr Elliott glanced at Mr Snyder. "He broke Mr Jerome's arm."

Mr Heath sat bolt upright. "I *say.*"

"We never saw him do it," Mr Snyder clarified.

"Unfortunately," Mr Elliott remarked.

"Me and Mr Elliott helped Inspectors Conway and Donahue find and arrest Mr and Mrs Jerome," Mr Snyder said. "Was Miss Joanna Hightower."

"Her mam and da won't want him as a husband for their bairn," Mr Verity said.

"Maybe," Dr Locke said. "But they will be pleased to hear she's safe."

"What were the Jeromes being arrested for?" Mr Locke enquired.

"Inspector Donahue's informant told him Mrs Jerome had been luring wealthy actors from *The Woodman* public house to the nearby Baskerville Passage for illicit liaisons," Mr Elliott replied. "Whereat Mr Jerome would 'come upon' them, express his anger at the actors, and demand payment by way of compensation."

"I see," Mr Locke said. "And how, pray tell, did you and Mr Snyder assist the police in locating and arresting them?"

Mr Elliott reached for the teapot to pour himself a cup. "I waited at *The Woodman* and, when Mrs Jerome approached me, I didn't correct her when she assumed I was an actor." He kept his gaze fixed upon his cup as he added cream and sugar. "She invited me to go somewhere more private with her. I agreed. She led me to Baskerville

Passage. When Mr Jerome arrived, Inspectors Donahue and Conway intervened to arrest them."

Amusement entered Mr Locke's eyes as he imagined the overtly prudish Mr Elliott with a woman of dubious reputation. "Was the arrest before or after the illicit liaison?"

"*Darling*." Dr Locke cast a glare at her husband.

Mr Elliott put the cup to his lips but lifted his eyes to meet Mr Snyder's. "Before."

"By Jove, I think you are blushing!" Mr Locke exclaimed in delight.

Mr Elliott's eyes snapped to the illusionist and lowered the cup. "I am not." He lifted the cup to his lips again and mumbled before taking a sip, "It's the steam."

"Do not worry, old man." Mr Locke smiled. "It proves you are human after all."

"Why were the Jeromes brought to London if they were arrested up north?" Mr Verity enquired.

"The City of Birmingham police had insufficient evidence to charge them." Mr Elliott dabbed his mouth with his handkerchief to hide his rosy cheeks. "Inspector Conway hoped to charge Mr Jerome with attempting to extort money from the actors at the *Royal Opera House* but, when we arrived at Bow Street, Inspector Woolfe informed him the complaint had been withdrawn."

"And the Jeromes are now in our parlour?" Mr Heath enquired.

"Yes," Miss Trent replied. "As agreed at a previous meeting, we need to speak to them about the blackmailing and assault of Mr Benton and their possible involvement in Miss Mina Ilbert's death."

Mr Locke took a cigarette from his case. "What are we to bargain with?"

Mr Heath looked puzzled. "Pardon?"

"One must have something to offer to gain something in return," Mr Locke replied.

"Yeah," Mr Snyder agreed. "Mr Jerome's not goin' to nark on his mates if there's nothin' in it for him."

"Our powers are limited, and we can't offer anything with certainty until we know the extent to which the Jeromes are involved in criminality," Mr Elliott explained. "However, it might be possible the police will allow Mr Jerome to turn Queen's Evidence, thereby making him immune to prosecution for the blackmail and assault, *if* his testimony secures the identification and conviction of Miss Mina Ilbert's murderer." He gave a slight frown. "Yet, even then, Mr Jerome's untrustworthy character and criminal background could prove too much of a barrier for the police to consider him a viable witness in any future trial."

"If one were to put it in simple terms, then, one would say we have very little to bargain with," Mr Locke put the cigarette between his lips and lit it with his silver lighter. Taking a small pull, he exhaled the smoke away from the others and watched Mr Elliott with expectant eyes. "Correct?"

"Correct," Mr Elliott replied with a sombre expression.

"Some hope is better than none," Mr Snyder interjected.

"Couldn't Mrs Jerome give us the information?" Mr Heath enquired hopefully.

"Yes, but as his wife, she couldn't testify against Mr Jerome in court," Mr Elliott replied.

"I suspect that was Mr Jerome's reason for marrying her," Dr Locke remarked.

"It certainly would not be the first time a criminal has used it to his advantage," Mr Locke interjected, taking another small pull from his cigarette.

Miss Trent glanced between the Lockes as the thought occurred to her Dr Locke couldn't testify against her husband either. Returning her attention to the question of the Jeromes, she said, "All we can do is ask our questions and see where they lead us. Sam, will you bring them in, please?"

* * *

Dr Weeks winced at the pressure in his bladder and tried to loosen the blankets by wiggling his feet. They were too tight for him to do anything other than rotate his ankles, however. Furrowing his brow as he tried to fathom a solution to this predicament, he pulled against the side-arm dress. Alas, the padding of the soft gloves, coupled with the pockets, prevented him from tugging his hands free. He released a soft growl and darted his gaze around the room for something, *anything*, he could use. Aside from the bed and the table, every piece of furniture had been removed following his earlier outburst. He glanced skyward and muttered, "Damn bastards."

A sudden bolt of sharp pain tore through his abdomen, causing his chest and stomach muscles to tense. His body tried to double-up at the same time, but it could only strain against the blankets. Growling and gasping as the aftershocks of agony swept through him, he felt his face grow hot under the strain. "*Jesus* H *Christ…*"

He heard the sound of distant footsteps in the corridor.

"Hey," he said, his dry throat causing his voice to be hoarse. Lubricating it with a few swallows, he called, "Hey!"

The sound grew louder as the footsteps came closer.

He stretched his neck toward the door. "*Hey*! In here!"

The door opened, and Dr McWilliams entered. "There's no need to yell."

"There is when ya can't move," Dr Weeks quipped. Realising this approach was likely to get him nowhere, though, he adopted a contrived, albeit polite, tone and said, "I need the bathroom." He frowned. "So can ya help a fella out?"

"I am afraid I am under strict instructions not to remove your restraints."

Dr Weeks stared at him. "Ya gotta be kiddin' me. I'm gonna piss all over this bed if ya don't get me a damn chamber pot right *now*."

Dr Colbert entered behind Dr McWilliams. "What is going on here?"

"Mr Weeks needs to urinate," Dr McWilliams replied.

"Do you?" Dr Colbert enquired.

"Yeah," Dr Weeks replied.

Dr Colbert responded to Dr McWilliams, however. "Instruct Mr Cowen and Mr Shayne to carry him to the bath."

Dr McWilliams left as Dr Weeks kept his head low and glared up at Dr Colbert. "I need a *piss*, not a *bath*."

"There's a commode in the bathroom." Dr Colbert removed the blanket pinning Dr Weeks' legs and draped it over the footboard. "I expect you to continue your cooperation. If you don't, you will not be permitted to use the commode, and you'll be brought back here. Understood?"

"I understand yer a heartless bastard."

"Insults will get you nowhere," Dr Colbert warned. "Recovery is only possible with discipline and cooperation. We guarantee both through either kindness or cruelty but, ultimately, which avenue we resort to is determined by the patient and his behaviour. In a nutshell, Percy, the quality of your existence depends upon you."

Dr Weeks' elbows shifted within the blankets as he tried to free his hands, again. Unconvinced by Dr Colbert's little speech, he mumbled, "Whatever ya say, doc."

Mr Corwin and Mr Shayne entered, and Dr Colbert moved away from the bed.

"If he cooperates, permit him the use of the commode and bath," Dr Colbert said. "If not, bring him back here in the restraints."

"And in the bath, doctor?" Mr Corwin enquired.

"Just the soft gloves," Dr Colbert replied. "Fetch me once he's in it."

"Yes, doctor," Mr Corwin agreed. He and Mr Shayne grunted as they lifted Dr Weeks and carried him into the corridor. As they passed Dr Colbert, Dr Weeks didn't hide his contempt. Yet, Dr Colbert either didn't see it or chose not to acknowledge it as he followed them out the room and spoke to another of his patients.

* * *

"Mr and Mrs Jerome," Miss Trent began. "You are here as guests of the Bow Street Society, and, as such, you're free to leave at any time. We'd be grateful if you could answer as many of our questions as possible, but you don't have to. Finally, you should know the Bow Street Society has no legal authority. In other words, we can't arrest you, hold you prisoner, or interrogate you for longer than is reasonable. Do you understand?"

"Yeah," Mr Jerome replied as his wife nodded.

"Would you like to begin, Mr Elliott?" Miss Trent invited.

"Yes. Thank you." Mr Elliott consulted his notes. "Mr Jerome, did you demand money from Mr Ellis Benton and, when he refused to pay, disrupt his performance until he left the stage?"

Mr Jerome smirked. "No."

Mrs Jerome lowered her hand and downcast her gaze.

"Were any of Mr Benton's performances disrupted in the days prior to Miss Ilbert's death?" Mr Locke enquired. When Mr Jerome's smirk grew, and Mrs Jerome didn't respond, Mr Locke probed, "Mrs Jerome?"

"No," Mrs Jerome quietly replied.

"Your parents will tell us if they were," Dr Locke said.

"And there'll be witnesses who'll confirm if Mr Jerome was the one responsible for the disruption," Mr Elliott added.

"Jack didn't do anything," Mrs Jerome said as she toyed with her fingers.

"Tellin' a bloke he's bad isn't a crime," Mr Jerome said with a lift of his chin.

"Mr Benton claims you asked him for money and hit him when he refused," Mr Elliott said. "Mr Morris

Thurston interrupted you during your argument at the stage door."

"They're lyin'." Mr Jerome helped himself to some shortbread. "Oy had nowt to do with eet." Taking a bite and chewing with his mouth open, he brushed the resultant crumbs from his clothes and onto the table.

"Mr Benton had repeatedly changed the time he was to arrive at the theatre to avoid you and your demands. Alas, you were always there. Which certainly suggests someone within the theatre, someone who Mr Benton trusted enough to reveal his intended time of arrival to, told you when to lurk by the stage door," Mr Locke said. "A person such as your wife, perhaps."

Mrs Jerome's head shot up, her eyebrows raised, and her lips parted. "I never did!"

"*Quiet*, Bab," Mr Jerome snapped.

Mrs Jerome turned desperate eyes to Mr Locke. "I never told Jack when Mr Benton was arriving because Mr Benton never told me, and I told Miss Ilbert that, and that my Jack had nothing to do with any of it, but she wouldn't believe me. I know my Jack isn't a saint, but he isn't a murderer, either."

"He is an extortionist, however," Mr Elliott remarked. "As your exploits in Birmingham prove."

Mrs Jerome curled her shoulders inward and lowered her head, unable to meet Mr Elliott's gaze.

"Who told you when Mr Benton would arrive?" Mr Elliott demanded.

Mr Jerome bit off a large piece of shortbread and spat crumbs as he replied, "*No one.*"

"You acted entirely alone?" Mr Elliott probed.

"Oy did nowt, and yow can't prove oy did," Mr Jerome replied.

"We cannot, but your accomplice could," Mr Locke interjected.

Mr Jerome squinted as his face contorted into a scowl. "What do yow mean?"

"Your accomplice could make a statement to the police, accusing you of blackmail, assault, and murder, in return for the police agreeing not to put them on trial," Mr Elliott explained. "It's called turning Queen's Evidence."

"Oy could do that," Mr Jerome scoffed.

"The word of a criminal is not as valuable as the word of a gentleman," Mr Locke said. "Even if the criminal is innocent, and the gentleman is guilty."

Mr Jerome glared at Mr Elliott and spat shortbread crumbs across the table at him as he yelled, "*Yow* said yow was my allies!"

"We are," Mr Snyder said.

Mr Elliott's lip curled in disgust as he brushed the crumbs from his person. "But we are powerless to help you without the whole truth."

Mr Jerome slammed the shortbread down, causing it to crumble. "Oy'm not a nark."

"Then you are a fool," Mr Elliott coldly stated.

Mr Jerome glared at him. "What did yow call me?"

"A fool," Mr Elliott repeated. "For that is what you'll be if you stand by and let someone else put your neck into a hangman's noose."

Mr Jerome stood and bent forward to thrust his good fist into Mr Elliott's face. "Yow're not goin' to put that on me!"

"Not I," Mr Elliott said. "Your accomplice."

Mr Jerome's glare intensified. "Yow don't know what yow're talkin' about."

"Enlighten me," Mr Elliott challenged.

"Why are you protectin' them, lad?" Mr Snyder interjected.

"Remember, there isn't just you to think about now," Dr Locke reminded Mr Jerome. "What would happen to Joanna if you were tried, convicted, and hung for a murder you didn't commit?"

Mr Jerome looked to his wife and saw her frightened eyes staring back at him.

"He doesn't care about her," Mr Elliott stated in a cool tone.

"Watch yow lip," Mr Jerome warned.

"If he did, he wouldn't have allowed her to go into a pitch-black, deserted passage with a stranger who could've as easily slit her throat as rape her," Mr Elliott said.

Mr Jerome pointed at his wife and insisted, "I *loive* her."

"Prove it," Dr Locke challenged. "Tell us the name of your accomplice so we may do all within our power to help both of you."

Mrs Jerome gripped her husband's good arm. "Listen to them, Jack."

Mr Jerome lowered his head and, with his face contorted into a scowl, glared at the table as he considered his limited options. The idea of refusing to say anything, walking out, and going straight to the *Crescent Theatre* was quickly dismissed. If the Bow Street Society had no power to arrest anyone, as they said, his request to tell them everything would undoubtedly fall on deaf ears. He glanced at his wife and thought of what he'd put her through in Birmingham to make ends meet. He'd never wanted that for her, for them.

"O-kay." Mr Jerome sat. "Oy'll tell yow." He looked to his wife. "For her."

FIFTY-TWO

The relief Dr Weeks felt upon using the commode was short lived. No sooner had he emptied his bladder, Mr Corwin and Mr Shayne dragged him from the chair and stripped and lifted him into the bath. At which point they manhandled him into kneeling and tightly strapped his gloved hands to the faucets. With only a few inches of tepid water in the bath, Dr Weeks' exposed flesh rapidly cooled in the freezing room. The lack of coverage from the water also meant his entire body was put on display for the indifferent attendants. Suddenly struck by the bleak realisation they'd calmly obliterated his modesty and dignity without a second thought, he attempted to regain both by sliding his knees into a crouching position. Yet, Mr Shayne captured his ankles, dragging them back and holding them tight to ensure he remained kneeling before the faucets.

"I can wash myself, y'know," Dr Weeks said as Mr Corwin dipped a bar of carbolic soap into the water beside him and rubbed it over a coarse wet flannel. The attendant showed no hint of acknowledgement, however. Instead, he slapped the flannel onto Dr Weeks' face and scrubbed his eyes, nose, mouth, and chin with it before gripping Dr Weeks by the hair and yanking his head back to scrub his neck. Wincing as the flannel made his skin sore, Dr Weeks growled, "Not so damn hard, ya sonofabitch."

Mr Corwin pushed Dr Weeks' face into the water and held it there against Dr Weeks' struggles whilst scrubbing his back and shoulders. Feeling his mouth and nose consumed by water, Dr Weeks did his best not to inhale, but the burning in his lungs made it increasingly difficult. Just as he was about to succumb, Mr Corwin pulled him out of the water by the roots of his hair. Water poured from Dr Weeks' mouth like a tap before he dragged the air into his lungs and violently coughed and spluttered, fighting to regain control of his breathing.

"You need to learn some manners, Mr Weeks." Mr Corwin released his hair to dip the flannel in the water. "It will make your stay with us far more pleasant."

"Go to hell," Dr Weeks croaked, his throat sore from being submerged.

Mr Corwin pushed Dr Weeks' head down and held it close to, but not in, the water. "We'll have none of that."

Dr Weeks gave a feeble growl as he tried to jerk his head free. Yet, Mr Shayne suddenly pulling his ankles wide obliged him to switch his focus to pushing against the momentum. His reduced strength, increasingly cold state, and awkward position meant he was no match for the man, however. Therefore, unable to resist Mr Shayne's manipulation, Dr Weeks felt his nausea return with a vengeance. Fearful he would vomit at any moment, he repeatedly swallowed against the rising sensation in his gullet and tried to imagine himself anywhere but here.

Mr Corwin's flannel-covered hand unexpectedly cupped Dr Weeks' crotch, causing the latter's body to jolt in response. Inhaling sharply at the same time, Dr Weeks tried to kick out, to move away, but Mr Shayne's grip tightened, and Mr Corwin's scrubbing continued. With every muscle in his back, shoulders, stomach, and legs tensing until he could do nothing but hold his breath against the pain, Dr Weeks felt like he was having an out-of-body experience. This sensation was instantly banished by Mr Corwin's flannel-covered finger forcibly penetrating Dr Weeks' behind, however. Reflexively clenching against the subsequent rubbing of his colon, Dr Weeks gritted his teeth as his heart pounded and his fingers tingled.

Mr Corwin withdrew his finger and stated in a matter-of-fact tone, "Almost done."

A second wave of nausea swept through Dr Weeks as Mr Corwin scrubbed the flannel between and over his buttocks. When the flannel moved on to scrub the back of his thighs and knees, Dr Weeks shuddered and felt his skin crawl. This was swiftly followed by hard shivering as his internal temperature dropped from the cold and shock of the ordeal.

Mr Corwin set the flannel aside and, filling a bucket from the bath, poured tepid water over Dr Weeks' head and back. Briefly tensing at the sudden impact, Dr Weeks' shivering shifted into violent trembling.

"What about his hair?" Mr Shayne enquired.

Mr Corwin refilled the bucket and poured it over Dr Weeks' head.

Dr Weeks released a sharp cry and dropped his head in response.

Mr Corwin inspected a strand of Dr Weeks' hair, "One more should do it."

"No… please," Dr Weeks begged; the trembling made it almost impossible to form words.

Yet, Mr Corwin either hadn't heard him or chose to ignore him, for he promptly refilled the bucket and poured it over his head.

"How are we getting on, gentlemen?" Dr Colbert enquired as he entered.

"We've just finished, doctor," Mr Corwin replied.

Mr Shayne released Dr Weeks' ankles and wiped his damp hands upon his uniform.

"Good." Dr Colbert smiled. "I imagine you feel a lot better for being clean."

Desperate to end this latest ordeal, Dr Weeks knew he could only do so by humouring the man responsible for his care. Therefore, he mustered a contrived smile and mumbled, "Yeah… I do."

Dr Colbert indicated the straps. "Take him out of the bath and put him back into the side-arm dress."

"Yes, doctor." Mr Corwin untied Dr Weeks' wrists.

The attendants next took an arm each and pulled Dr Weeks to his feet. Whilst Mr Shayne held him in place, Mr Corwin picked up the side-arm dress from the floor and put it over Dr Weeks' head. Between them, he and Mr Shayne slipped Dr Weeks' damp arms and body into the remainder of the dress and secured his gloved hands in its pockets. Finally, they hooked their arms around Dr Weeks' and took his weight whilst guiding him in stepping from the bath.

"You may return to your duties, gentlemen," Dr Colbert instructed.

Mr Corwin and Mr Shayne glanced at Dr Weeks but left without question.

"There, that wasn't so bad, was it?" Dr Colbert enquired with honest delight.

Feeling dirty without and numb within, Dr Weeks stared at Dr Colbert's feet. He couldn't think of another experience more humiliating and degrading than the one he'd just endured. Yet, Dr Colbert was acting as if they'd done him a favour. Utterly nauseated by the realisation, Dr Weeks grimaced, curled his shoulders, and pressed his chin against his chest, hoping Dr Colbert would take the hint and escort him back to his room.

Alas, the seemingly ignorant resident physician continued, "Dr McWilliams has finally arranged a fresh set of clothes for you. Provided you eat all your meals and don't cause any more incidents, you'll be allowed to wear the new clothes come morning."

"Great," Dr Weeks mumbled.

"In the meantime, you'll be allowed to move around your room in just the side-arm dress," Dr Colbert said. Putting his arm around Dr Weeks' shoulders, he misinterpreted his nervous flinch for surprise and so dismissed it without thought. "You'll enjoy having the same freedoms as the other patients." He guided Dr Weeks from the bathroom and back to the male ward. "We have a vegetable garden you can help maintain, a library you can read in, and even a newspaper you might want to contribute to. Naturally, you can't practise medicine while you're here, and I expect you to keep your opinions about our treatments to yourself. After all, you're proficient in postmortems, not illnesses of the mind." He gave a warm smile. "We're also obliged to address you as Mr Weeks and not doctor; it would confuse the other patients, you see." He opened Dr Weeks' door and let him enter ahead of him. "I'll also allow you some visitors once you've properly settled in."

Dr Weeks lifted his head sharply to meet his gaze. "Visitors?"

"Yes. Miss Trent, Miss Hicks, Inspector Woolfe, and Chief Inspector Jones have all sent their well wishes to you." Dr Colbert's smile faltered. "But I can't allow them to visit you if I think your behaviour and cooperation will deteriorate as a consequence."

If I can see Jones, I might be able to convince him to get me outta here, Dr Weeks thought. He wasn't as keen to see Miss Hicks, Miss Trent, and Inspector Woolfe, though. "Yeah… sure. I understand."

Unconvinced, Dr Colbert lifted his chin and studied Dr Weeks' face. "Yes, well, we'll see how things go, hm?" He headed out. "Have some rest, and I'll return later to check on you."

When Dr Colbert locked the door behind him, Dr Weeks was reminded of how much control he had over him. The painfully fresh memory of being bathed by the attendants was a further reminder of how little say he had over his own body. Sitting on the edge of his bed, he went to hug himself but the gloves and side-arm dress prevented it. Feeling the full weight of humiliation, isolation, and devastation descend upon him, he lay on his side, curled up as far as the restraints would allow, and prayed for the oblivion of sleep. Never, in all his years of abusing alcohol, had he needed a drink more.

* * *

"Mr Ronald Stone is our co-conspirator, then," Mr Locke mused as Miss Trent returned from settling the Jeromes in the parlour with a fresh pot of tea. "It does not surprise me. I knew the man was a rogue the moment I laid eyes upon him. His words merely confirmed my suspicion."

"There are now several points in favour of Mr Stone being responsible for Miss Ilbert's death," Mr Elliott said. Running his pencil down the list in his notebook, he read aloud, "Co-conspiring with Mr Jack Jerome to blackmail Mr Benton. Inconspicuous access to the metal plate as stage manager. Threatened with dismissal via Miss Ilbert's ultimatum. His statements about the *Crecent* getting a new manager. His anger and surprise at being told of the agreement Miss Ilbert had with Miss Kimberly. His blatant dislike for working for a woman. Mr Thurston's inability to locate Mr Stone the night Miss Ilbert died." He glanced around at the others. "Unfortunately, these are all circumstantial and couldn't withstand the scrutiny of a trial."

"You believe we require a confession?" Mr Locke enquired.

"Yes," Mr Elliott replied. "And, in order to acquire it, we may have to bring Detective Sergeant Dixon into our confidence."

"Unless someone else was involved in the blackmail," Mr Verity said. "You said yourself, Mr Locke; it's unusual for a prompter and super master to linger around a stage door."

"But Mr Jerome only named Mr Stone," Mr Heath pointed out.

"He mightn't have known about Mr Thurston," Mr Elliott said.

"Even if Mr Thurston was involved, it still leaves us with the problem of how to acquire a confession from either him, Mr Stone, or both regarding Miss Ilbert's murder," Mr Locke pointed out. "Personally, I am reluctant to provide the police with yet another opportunity to claim responsibility for the solving of a case when it is *us* who have conducted the investigation *they* ought to have done from the beginning. I am certain I am not alone in my thinking."

Mr Elliott recalled his conversation last October with Inspector Lee about the policeman taking the credit for solving the Cosgrove case. It had been done through deceptive means and was therefore another reason for Mr Elliott to dislike him. Nevertheless, the recent memory of kissing him replayed in his mind, reminding Mr Elliott of his conflicting feelings for the man. Having a sip of tea, he pushed the image away.

"With all due respect, gentlemen, we haven't yet reached the point where we can definitively state the remaining suspects are innocent," Dr Locke said. "Especially when I have two more to add to our list."

"Who?" Mr Snyder enquired.

Mr Elliott turned to a clean page in his notebook and sat forward, his pencil poised to write down the new information.

"First, an unidentified veiled woman who purchased *The Era* newspaper's entire archive on Miss Ilbert for the princely sum of fifty pounds in fresh banknotes two days after her death," Dr Locke replied. "Second, Miss Ilbert's husband." She placed a large leather-bound volume upon the table and, opening it at a page she'd previously bookmarked, turned it around for the others to see. It was the announcements section of the morning edition of the *Gaslight Gazette* from Wednesday 22nd September 1880. Dr Locke tapped an announcement in the top-right corner of the page. It read:

ANNOUNCING THE IMPENDING MARRIAGE
of
DARREL HOWARD GIBB & LILY ILBERT

Ceremony to take place at midday on Friday 24th September in the year of our Lord 1880 at St Mary le Strand, Strand, London. Invited guests only.

"Miss *Lily*!" Mr Heath exclaimed, taken aback, before a vision of Miss Lily Ilbert appeared in his mind's eye and caused him to frown. "But… wouldn't she have been rather *young* at the time?"

"Two years old," Dr Locke replied, amused by his error. "Miss Mina evidently used her stage pseudonym in the announcement."

"Lily of the Lyceum," Mr Locke reminded him.

"*Ahh*, yes. Of course." Mr Heath chuckled softly. "How *foolish* of me."

"She must not of married Mr Raine as everyone thought," Mr Snyder said.

"She could've been widowed," Mr Elliott said. "And married Mr Gibb later."

"Makes a lot of sense to me," Mr Verity agreed.

"Equally, the marriage to Mr Gibb mightn't have happened," Mr Elliott said. "This is only an announcement of the impending ceremony, not confirmation of it having occurred."

"I'll go to St Mary le Strand and see if the marriage is in the parish records," Mr Verity volunteered.

"I'll accompany you," Dr Locke said.

Mr Verity gave a brief dip of his head by way of acknowledgement.

"Miss Ilbert was using her maiden name when she died. Doesn't that prove she wasn't married?" Mr Heath enquired, confused.

"Actresses often continue to use their maiden name after marriage as it is the name upon which they have built their careers," Mr Locke explained.

Mr Heath hummed with a furrowing of his brow. "Logical, I suppose."

"Do we know anything further about," Mr Elliott referred to the announcement, "Mr Darrel Howard Gibb?"

"He is an American actor with exceptional good looks but mediocre talent," Mr Locke replied. "He auditioned for the *Paddington Palladium* once." He rested his elbows upon the arms of his chair and, steepling his fingers, glanced skyward as he continued, "If I recall correctly, he could impersonate an upper-class English accent rather well, but his acting was more wooden than a posser on laundry day."

"Darling, you wouldn't know a posser if you tripped over it," Dr Locke gently teased.

"I have seen it used on occasion," Mr Locke countered in a dry tone.

Miss Trent couldn't help but be amused by the exchange. It was a well-known fact Mr Locke, like almost all gentlemen, hadn't the first idea of how to dress himself, let alone how to do laundry. Hence the need for his valet, James.

"Were there any articles about a divorce between Mr Gibb and Miss Ilbert?" Mr Elliott enquired.

"No," Dr Locke replied.

"I might be able to discover more amongst the divorce court records," Mr Elliott noted his fellow Bow Streeter's answers. "But I'd like to examine Miss Ilbert's agreement with Miss Kimberly and her lease agreement with the building owner for the *Crescent,* first. If Miss Ilbert was still married to Mr Gibb, his status as her husband could persuade the building owner to grant him responsibility for the lease in place of Miss Kimberly. Do we know if he was in America at the time of Miss Ilbert's death?"

"I have not read of him appearing in any productions on Broadway of late," Mr Locke replied. "Or in any productions in the West End."

"If 'e was in London, 'e could of done in his wife to get the *Crescent*," Mr Snyder suggested.

"Which is why I'd like to add him to our list of suspects," Dr Locke said.

"I agree," Mr Elliott added.

Miss Trent wrote Mr Gibb's name at the bottom of the list.

"Returning to the veiled lady," Dr Locke said. "She told Mr Ruggles, the deputy editor of *The Era* newspaper, she was an admirer of Miss Ilbert's and wanted to create a scrapbook of her accomplishments." She consulted her notebook. "Her veil and dress were black, suggesting she was in mourning for Miss Ilbert. Aside from this, all Mr Ruggles could describe was her dark hair. Miss Kimberly and Miss Lily have dark hair." She used her pencil to indicate their names on the list.

"But it could of been another admirer we've not met," Mr Snyder interjected.

"Yes, it could," Dr Locke agreed. "Especially as I'm uncertain as to why either Miss Kimberly or Miss Lily would pay such a considerable amount for Miss Ilbert's archive from *The Era* without giving their name."

"Could we put an advertisement in *The Era* and *Gaslight Gazette* askin' for the lass to come see us?" Mr Snyder enquired.

"Yes, but I'm doubtful it would bear any fruit," Mr Elliott replied. "She wore a veil and didn't give her name. Therefore, one must assume she wishes to remain anonymous."

"Fair do's," Mr Snyder conceded.

Dr Locke placed a second large leather-bound volume upon the table and, opening it at a page she'd previously bookmarked, turned it around for the others to see. This time, it was an article from the evening edition of the *Gaslight Gazette* from Saturday 16th February 1878. It read:

MONOLITH THEATRE DESTROYED BY FIRE

The people of Woking, Surrey, have been left in shock this evening following a devastating fire at the *Monolith Theatre* last night that claimed at least forty lives. Early witness accounts suggest the fire began at the front of the stage and rapidly spread to the auditorium and backstage areas. The building was entirely consumed by fire within minutes

despite the valiant efforts of Woking Fire Brigade.

"People were running for their lives," one shocked witness recounted to your correspondent. "I think some people fell and were trampled by the others. It is such an horrific tragedy."

Your correspondent has since learnt from the physician responsible for identifying those who died that, in some cases, the damage is so severe identification is impossible. Although, local speculation suggests Mr Julian Raine, the highly respected stage manager at the *Monolith Theatre*, is amongst them. Survivors of the fire have claimed Mr Raine died while helping them to escape. Attempts to have this confirmed by the *Monolith*'s manager Mr Ronald Stone, have proven fruitless, however.

According to one of the theatre's ticket office employees, who wishes to remain anonymous, the *Monolith* has recently been experiencing financial difficulties. "Ticket sales have been declining for months. Everyone knows Mr Stone has fallen into debt because of it. We are surprised he can still afford to pay the insurance on the place." Further investigation by your correspondent has revealed an insurance policy was issued to Mr Stone last month by National Fire Insurance Corporation Ltd.

"Curious the article doesn't mention Mr Raine was survived by his pregnant wife," Mr Verity mused aloud. "It would've got the community behind her."

"It's possible Miss Ilbert knew Mr Stone had committed arson on his previous theatre to claim the insurance money. Furthermore, she might have used this knowledge to obligate him into accepting the position of stage manager at the *Crescent*," Mr Elliott hypothesised. "It would be an additional reason for Mr Stone to financially hurt Miss Ilbert by blackmailing her leading actor and physically hurt her by tampering with the metal plate. Were there any further articles about the fire?"

"Unfortunately, no," Dr Locke replied with a slight frown. "It would appear it didn't prove tantalising enough for the journalists of the *Gaslight Gazette* to pursue further." She closed both volumes and set them aside. "According to Miss Kimberly, Miss Lily was born six months after the fire, and Mr Stone became stage manager at the *Crescent* a year after the same."

"I think it is telling that he chose to return to London rather than rebuild his theatre in Woking using the insurance money," Mr Locke said. "The article suggests Mr Stone's insurance policy was common knowledge amongst the locals. Even if he were innocent of arson, individuals who gossip usually spread rumours based upon unfounded assumptions rather than taking the time to discover the mundane truth. Ergo, he could have felt he was no longer welcome in the town where so many of his productions had entertained."

"I believe the National Fire Insurance Corporation Limited was absorbed by the Royal Insurance Company," Mr Elliott said. "They may be able to confirm if Mr Stone's policy was honoured and the monies paid."

"I'll look up their address in the *Post Office Directory*. Mr Heath, could you call upon them after the meeting?" Miss Trent enquired.

"*Certainly*," Mr Heath replied.

"Mr Elliott, please outline our findings regarding Mr Stone to Sergeant Dixon after you and Mr Jerome have put forth your proposal," Miss Trent said. "If Sergeant Dixon decides to proceed with arresting Mr Stone on suspicion of blackmail and murder, based upon Mr Jerome's statement, please let me know as soon as possible."

"Very well," Mr Elliott agreed. "I'll call upon the *Crescent Theatre* later this afternoon. The agreements Miss Ilbert had with Miss Kimberly and the building owner are still worth examining regardless of whether Sergeant Dixon decides to pursue charges against Mr Stone. I may have to consult the divorce court records in the morning if I haven't the time today."

Miss Trent nodded as she noted the suggestion.

"I would like to have another conversation with Mr Thurston," Mr Locke said. "To either finally eliminate him as a suspect in the blackmailing of Mr Benton and the murder of Miss Mina, confirm he is guilty of one or the other or confirm he is guilty of both."

"You may accompany Mr Elliott to the *Crescent* later this afternoon," Miss Trent said.

"It will give you some time to rest in the meantime, darling," Dr Locke gently urged.

Mr Locke offered her a reassuring smile. "So it will."

"If there's nothing further, I'd like to end the meeting here," Miss Trent said, making a note of the time.

FIFTY-THREE

Prior to leaving the Society's house, Mr Elliott had enquired about Vine Street from Mr Snyder. The cabman had described it as a narrow, dead-end street off Swallow Street, the entrance to which was off the main thoroughfare of Piccadilly, past the Geology Museum and opposite the church. Miss Trent had also confirmed from the *Post Office Directory* the Metropolitan Police Force's C (or St. James) Division police station was at number 10, Vine Street. Both she and Mr Snyder had offered for Sam to drive Mr Elliott and Mr Jerome in the Society's cab, but Mr Elliott had declined on the grounds Dr Locke and Mr Verity were in greater need of it since Mr Locke and Mr Heath had taken their carriages elsewhere.

Vine Street police station was unremarkable compared to the grandeur of Bow Street and the provincial charm of Chiswick High Road. The uniformity of its brick façade, rectangular sash windows, and white stone window heads and ledges rendered it characterless and uninspiring. The only architectural clues to its function were thick iron bars on the ground floor and basement windows, and the standard blue lantern hung from an iron bracket between a pair of ground floor windows. A narrow, open doorway on the far right held a set of stone steps leading to the station's main door.

Upon entering the gloomy vestibule beyond, Mr Elliott felt Mr Jerome grip his arm. In a low voice, the latter said, "Oy don't think oy want to now."

Mr Elliott kept his expression plain. "Why not?"

Mr Jerome glanced behind them and lowered his voice further. "Oy'm not a nark."

"If you're arrested, your wife will be destitute."

"And eef oy confess oy *will* be arrested," Mr Jerome countered. "Oy don't trust coppers."

"I'll be with you every step of the way. You have my word."

"Yow was the one who got me arrested," Mr Jerome reminded him.

"Listen to me, Jack," Mr Elliott urged in a firm tone. "If you don't try to make this deal with the police now, Mr Stone will try to make the same deal with them later, only it will be you who is sent to jail, not him."

The door ahead of them opened, and a middle-aged man in a sergeant's uniform enquired, "Can I help you, sirs?"

Mr Elliott presented his business card to the officer. "We'd like to speak to Detective Sergeant Keith Dixon as a matter of urgency, please."

The sergeant looked to Mr Jerome. "And you are?"

"A con-cerned citizen," Mr Jerome replied with a sardonic edge.

"This way." The sergeant waited for Mr Elliott to take the door from him before leading them into a large room divided by a wood-panelled counter. The room's plastered walls were stained tobacco yellow and blackened by the gas lamps. The floorboards, although polished, were sun-bleached and heavily worn in places. Two of the barred windows overlooking the street were on the left-hand side of the room with the counter running between.

Behind the counter was a large open space with a door in the far-left corner. Mr Elliott assumed the door, along with the other located directly to the right upon entering, led to the police station proper. Shelves filled with files and ledgers framed C Division's beat map on the area's right wall, opposite the window. Lined up against the back wall were immense wooden filing cabinets filled with small, square drawers with brass handles and label holders affixed to their fronts. In the middle of the area, front to front, were two large desks. A third desk was positioned beneath the map, facing the wall. The remaining items of furniture in this area was a small coal stove and two hat stands. Hung upon the latter were three coxcomb police helmets adorned with the Metropolitan Police Force's silver crest, and three sets of heavy, leather capes.

"Wait here, please." The sergeant took the business card through the door on the right.

The limited space on this side of the counter was filled with people either already conversing with three uniformed constables behind the counter or waiting to do so. Conscious of the risks of Mr Jerome slipping away unnoticed and having his broken arm knocked, Mr Elliott guided him into the corner to their left and stood in front of him.

Several minutes passed, in which the exchange between a gentleman and one of the constables became increasingly heated. Apparently, the gentleman had had his pocket picked and lost a highly valuable pocket watch he'd inherited from his deceased father. It had occurred on the Strand during the busiest time of the day, and the gentleman hadn't seen the thief. Naturally, there was little the police could do under such circumstances, except take a description of the item and distribute it on a list they regularly sent to pawnbrokers, *etc.*, in the area. The gentleman, far from satisfied with this proposed course of action, demanded the police arrest and search every known pickpocket to find his property. Unsurprisingly, another gentleman who was waiting to be seen interjected with his thoughts, prompting the second constable to remind him to wait his turn. By the time the sergeant returned, a full-blown argument had erupted with the pickpocket victim even threatening to return with his solicitor.

Entering with the sergeant was a man in his late-thirties with short, dark-brown hair and moustache. He was attired in a dark-green waistcoat and tie, dark-grey trousers, and white shirt. The sergeant pointed to Mr Elliott, handed the business card to the man, and went behind the counter to calm the argument, whilst the man approached Mr Elliott.

"I'm Detective Sergeant Keith Dixon, Mr Elliott." The man offered his hand.

Mr Elliott gave it a firm shake and said in his usual monotone, "Good afternoon."

"Sergeant Camryn said you urgently wanted to speak to me," Sergeant Dixon said.

"Me and Mr Jerome, yes." Mr Elliott indicated the man.

Sergeant Dixon's demeanour cooled. "Hello, Jack."

"You know one another?" Mr Elliott enquired. Suddenly, Mr Jerome's renewed reluctance at the door made sense.

"Our paths have crossed a few times," Sergeant Dixon replied. "Still asking for money for not giving folks the bird, Jack?"

Mr Jerome lowered his head and downcast his eyes.

"You get to know rogues like him policing the West End," Sergeant Dixon informed Mr Elliott. "What do you want to talk about?"

"The murder of Miss Mina Ilbert," Mr Elliott replied.

Sergeant Dixon darted his gaze from Mr Elliott to Mr Jerome and back again. "Are you one of those Bow Street Society meddlers, Mr Elliott?"

"I'm a member, yes," Mr Elliott replied.

Sergeant Dixon lifted his chin. "I've already made our position clear. Miss Ilbert died in a tragic accident because of poor workmanship on the wires. There was no evidence of murder, except what the Bow Street Society conjured up to make a few bob from Mr Willis."

Mr Elliott knew Sergeant Dixon was trying to provoke him but was far too experienced in similar interactions in the courtroom to take the bait. Instead, he maintained a measured tone as he stated, "The Bow Street Society doesn't create evidence to fit the expectations of our client. In fact, we will readily investigate our client if we think it will help us uncover the truth. Even if it also means we lose our commission."

Sergeant Dixon scoffed.

"It's a shame the police aren't equally as scrupulous at times," Mr Elliott added.

"I resent that," Sergeant Dixon snapped.

"And I resent the fact the police are unwilling to investigate a blatant murder," Mr Elliott countered.

Mr Jerome smirked, amused by Mr Elliott's reprimanding of the policeman.

"We *have* investigated and found it was an accident," Sergeant Dixon stated.

"The Bow Street Society have several reasons to believe Mr Ronald Stone may be responsible for, or at least involved in, Miss Mina Ilbert's death," Mr Elliott said. "Mr Jerome, who I'm also acting as solicitor for, is willing to make a statement implicating Mr Stone in the blackmailing of Mr Benton in exchange for immunity to prosecution. His statement, alongside the circumstantial evidence we've discovered, should provide you with sufficient grounds to bring Mr Stone in for questioning on suspicion of blackmail and murder."

"I can't bring a man in on the word of a criminal," Sergeant Dixon rebutted.

"You can if it persuades Mr Stone to confess to murder," Mr Elliott countered.

Sergeant Dixon put his hands on his hips. "There's been *no* murder."

"Who is your senior officer?" Mr Elliott enquired.

Sergeant Dixon squinted at him, confused. "Excuse me?"

"Who is your senior officer?" Mr Elliott repeated. "If you shan't listen to reason, maybe he will."

Sergeant Dixon dropped his hands to his sides. "You can't see him."

"If it's not convenient now, I'll make an appointment for later," Mr Elliott said.

Sergeant Dixon's face and eyes became worried. "He's busy."

Mr Elliott moved toward the counter. "I'll ask Sergeant Camryn for his name."

Sergeant Dixon moved in front of him with his hands lifted. "*No.*" He forced a smile. "I'll listen to what you've got to say. Let me just find a quiet room, yeah?"

"Very well," Mr Elliott agreed.

Sergeant Dixon lowered his head and, releasing a soft sigh, ran his hand through his hair as he went back through the door.

Intrigued by the policeman's sudden change in demeanour when asked about his senior officer, Mr Elliott approached the counter and got the attention of Sergeant Camryn. Having defused the argument between the constable and pickpocketing victim, Sergeant Camryn came over to Mr Elliott at once. "Can I help you, sir?"

"Yes; could you tell me who Detective Sergeant Dixon's senior officer is, please?" Mr Elliott enquired.

Sergeant Camryn smiled softly. "Detective Inspector Tobias Witherspoon, sir."

"Is he a formidable man?" Mr Elliott enquired.

"No, sir," Sergeant Camryn replied with a slight shake of the head. "But he puts the fear of God in Sergeant Dixon."

"Why is that?" Mr Elliott enquired.

"He's his father-in-law," Sergeant Camryn replied with a low chuckle.

"I see." Mr Elliott gave an appreciative smile. "Thank you, Sergeant."

* * *

"I'm go-ing." Inspector Donahue closed the *Bradshaw's Rail Times* and returned it to Inspector Woolfe. "My Abi'll be pleased to see me home, at least." He stood and pulled on his coat. "Jerome's got more lives than a cat."

"Yeah," Inspector Conway still couldn't believe they'd gone to all that trouble and ended up with nothing. Sitting low in his chair with his legs sprawled out beneath his desk, he considered going home for a clean set of clothes.

"It was nice to meet you, Matthew." Inspector Woolfe stood and shook Inspector Donahue's hand. "Maybe the

Metropolitan and Birmingham City Police forces will have another reason to work together one day."

"I hope so." Inspector Donahue smiled.

A knock sounded on the door.

"Come in," Inspector Woolfe called.

The door opened ajar, and Sergeant Gutman poked his head around it before opening it wide and giving a respectful nod to Inspectors Woolfe and Donahue. "Sirs," he held out a small envelope to Inspector Woolfe, "I was asked by the sergeant at the desk to give this to you, sir." He held out a second small envelope to Inspector Donahue, "And Detective Inspector Lee invites you to visit him at New Scotland Yard, sir."

Inspector Conway became suspicious. "Why?"

Sergeant Gutman kept his back to him and, with a hint of contempt in his voice, replied, "To introduce himself as head of the Mob Squad and give a guided tour of the place to Inspector Donahue." He adopted a warm tone as he continued, addressing Inspector Donahue, "He thought you might find it interesting to see how things are done here in London, sir."

"Liok we don't know what we're do-ing in Bir-ming-ham?" Inspector Donahue challenged.

"The Birmingham City Police is as respected by the Metropolitan as any other, sir," Sergeant Gutman replied. "Inspector Lee merely wishes to be hospitable."

Inspector Woolfe grunted in amusement, only to suffer from a small coughing fit as a consequence. Having read Dr Colbert's name at the bottom of his note, he'd returned it to its envelope to read once he was alone. Loudly clearing his throat once the coughing fit had subsided, he told Inspector Donahue, "New Scotland Yard is worth a visit if only for the Crime Museum."

Inspector Donahue turned his head a little. "Oh yeah?"

"It's got pieces of evidence, weapons, and death masks from loads of different cases," Inspector Conway explained. "Only coppers and the odd invited guest are allowed in."

Inspector Donahue smiled and told Sergeant Gutman, "Gew on, then."

"I've got a cab waiting outside, sir," Sergeant Gutman said.

"Can I get a train to Bir-ming-ham from there?" Inspector Donahue enquired.

"I'll have a cab drive you back to Euston after, sir," Sergeant Gutman replied.

Inspector Donahue firmly shook the hands of Inspectors Woolfe and Conway. "This'll liokely be me gone, gents." He put on his bowler hat. "Keep in touch."

"You, too," Inspector Conway said.

Inspector Donahue followed Sergeant Gutman out and closed the door whilst Inspector Woolfe sat and opened a file. Pretending to read it, he casually remarked, "Are you not going home to put on some clean clothes? I didn't want to say anything when Donahue was here, but you're smelling a bit ripe, John."

"Yeah." Inspector Conway stood and retrieved his coat and hat from the stand. With a hint of annoyance, he rhetorically enquired, "With friends like you, Caleb, who needs enemies?" He put on his things and left.

Inspector Woolfe took Dr Colbert's note from its envelope as soon as he was gone. It read:

> Dear Inspector Woolfe,
> Thank you for your patience and understanding in this matter. I am writing to confirm my availability for our appointment at three o'clock today at the location we previously agreed upon. Unless I hear otherwise from you, I shall assume this time is convenient for you and will proceed as planned.

> Yours sincerely,
> Dr N. Colbert

Three o'clock, Inspector Woolfe thought and consulted his pocket watch. It was only an hour away. He considered whether he could get it done before Inspector Conway returned. Realising this could be their one and only opportunity to acquire J. Pettifoot's address from Miss Trent's records, though, he concluded Inspector Conway returning during their plan was a risk worth taking. He tore up the note, scattered the pieces around his ashtray, and set them alight with a match.

FIFTY-FOUR

There was an eerie silence in the *Crescent*'s auditorium as the Lockes, Mr Verity, and Claude made their way down its central aisle. The stage was empty, and only a handful of the lights were lit, giving the deserted, gloomy space a ghostly atmosphere. With the carpet also deadening the sounds of their footsteps, the Bow Streeters had the sense of being somewhere they shouldn't. As they neared the stage, they heard a door opening in the wings. Such a small sound would usually be drowned out by the noisy activity of a busy, functioning theatre. Yet, the current stillness meant it was magnified to the point where it instantly caught their attention, causing them to come to an abrupt halt.

"You disobeyed me," Miss Kimberly's voice said within the darkness. "I told you to stay away from him, but now you say you had *supper* with him?!"

"We were in a restaurant," Miss Lily's voice replied from the same direction.

"I do not care if you were on the dome of St. Paul's, the point remains you disobeyed me, child," Miss Kimberly's voice countered. "Mr Stone seeks pleasure first and is utterly uninterested in marriage. Not that I'd ever allow him to court you, of course. He's more than old enough to be your father!"

"We aren't courting, Aunt Emma." Miss Lily walked backward from the wings. "He was teaching me about Christopher Marlowe."

Miss Kimberly strode from the wings a heartbeat later. "Mr Benton can teach you about Marlowe, not—" She simultaneously cut herself short and stopped walking upon seeing the Bow Streeters. "How long have you been standing there?"

"Not very long," Mr Locke lied.

"It's rude to eavesdrop on others' conversations," Miss Kimberly strode to the edge of the stage. "What do you want?"

Dr Locke took two books from Claude which he'd been carrying under his arm. She informed Miss Kimberly and Miss Lily, "We've made a discovery we think you'll both be very interested in."

Miss Lily adopted an apprehensive tone. "You have?"

Dr Locke carried the books onto the stage. Placing the smaller of the two onto Mr Thurston's prompter desk, she opened the large one at a bookmarked page as Miss Kimberly and Miss Lily joined her. "This is from the *Gaslight Gazette* of Wednesday 22nd September 1880. It's an announcement for the upcoming marriage of Mr Darrel Howard Gibb and Miss Lily Ilbert." She looked to Miss Lily. "Your mother."

Miss Lily stared at Dr Locke, taken aback. "It's impossible. You must be mistaken."

Meanwhile, Miss Kimberly gripped the edge of the desk, her fingernails digging into the wood. At the same time, the muscles in her face and shoulders tensed, causing her expression to become pinched and the tendons in her neck to stand out.

"Read it yourself," Dr Locke passed the book to Miss Lily.

"I don't understand," Miss Lily admitted after reading the announcement. "Aunt Emma?"

Miss Kimberly's mouth formed a white slash as she pursed her lips.

Dr Locke retrieved the smaller book and opened it at a bookmarked page. "The marriage took place on Friday 24th September 1880 at the St. Mary le Strand Church, Strand, London. Here it is written in the parish record."

Miss Lily closed the larger book and, putting it down on the desk, took the smaller one from Dr Locke. After reading the passage, she shifted her weight from one foot to the other as she darted her gaze back and forth across the page to double-check specific details. "Was it a short marriage?" She momentarily lifted her head to look at Miss Kimberly, "Why wasn't I told of it?"

"You were only two years old at the time," Dr Locke explained.

"And we have yet to confirm whether the marriage ended in divorce, or if Mr Gibb and Miss Ilbert were merely estranged," Mr Locke added as he stepped onto the stage from the stairs, using his walking cane for balance and Claude's arm to lean upon.

In contrast, Mr Verity had chosen to save his energy by sitting in the stalls' front row.

Miss Kimberly dug deeper into the wood with her fingernails. "Your mother was married to Julian Raine. Your father." She swallowed against the tightening of her throat and adopted an accusatory tone as she challenged Dr Locke, "Why did you seek out these records? To discredit me? To ruin my reputation?"

"To uncover the truth," Dr Locke replied.

"To what end?" Miss Kimberly demanded. "Were you hoping to see me removed from the position of manager, thereby weakening the *Crescent* as the *Paddington Palladium's* direct competitor?"

"My dear lady, the *Crescent* would have to be successful for me to consider it worthy of sabotage," Mr Locke condescendingly rebutted.

"*Darling*," Dr Locke warned.

"I do not take kindly to my wife being accused of employing dishonest practises on my behalf, when I am perfectly capable of employing dishonest practises on my own," Mr Locke stated.

"The Bow Street Society instructed me to seek out the records, not my husband," Dr Locke informed Miss Kimberly. "Who appears to have forgotten his manners, so I must ask you to forgive him."

"I shall not," Miss Kimberly rebuffed. "I'm tired of your group's frequent visits and relentless insinuations."

"I am not," Mr Benton said as he emerged from the wings, thereby drawing all eyes to him. "I was coming from my dressing room when I heard talking. I am rather ashamed to say I have been eavesdropping for the past few minutes." A look of sorrow passed over his face. "Furthermore, I am heartbroken to hear of Mina's second marriage. It… explains a great deal."

Miss Lily closed the parish record and returned it to the desk. "Not to me, it doesn't."

"Nor us," Mr Locke interjected.

Miss Lily moved back from the group and hugged herself. "What do you mean?"

"A woman with dark hair, wearing full mourning attire, purchased the entire archive of articles featuring Miss Mina Ilbert from *The Era* newspaper in the days immediately after her death," Dr Locke explained.

Miss Lily glanced at Miss Kimberly's hair, then her own.

"She said she was an admirer of Miss Ilbert's who wanted to create a scrapbook of her life and career," Dr Locke added.

"Mina had many admirers," Mr Benton said.

Miss Lily bowed her head and stared at the floor as, becoming lost in thought, she twirled a strand of hair around her finger.

"The woman paid a princely sum for the archive but never gave her name," Dr Locke said. "Which has led us to suspect she may have had another reason for purchasing the archive. Rather than keeping it to look upon herself, she may have wanted to keep it to prevent others from looking upon it. Unfortunately, she was unaware of the, now standard, practise employed by newspapers whereby they send copies of each published edition to the British Museum."

Miss Kimberly tightly gripped her skirts with her free hand, and her voice was subdued by emotion as she demanded, "What *relevance* does *all* this have on *anything*?"

"If Mina and Mr Gibb never divorced, he would have legitimate grounds to petition the building owner for control of the lease agreement," Mr Locke replied. "If you knew of the marriage and had kept it a secret all these years, Miss Kimberly, you could have purchased the archive to, firstly, prevent the truth from being discovered, and, secondly, prevent Mr Gibb from acquiring evidence which would add weight to his proposal."

Miss Lily's head had snapped up at the mention of Miss Kimberly's name in connection with the archive. Looking swiftly between her and the Bow Streeters, she envisioned Miss Kimberly being unjustly arrested for Mina's death and felt a weight drop in the pit of her stomach. With an intense fear also rising within her breast, she blurted out, "I purchased it."

"I beg your pardon?" Mr Locke enquired.

"I-I purchased the archive," Miss Lily replied.

Miss Kimberly was taken aback. "Lily, why—?"

"I wanted to have something to remember Mother by," Miss Lily replied.

Miss Kimberly turned away with a pained look in her eyes.

"Where did you get such a sum?" Mr Benton enquired, confused.

The sudden opening of the auditorium doors distracted everyone, however.

"Good afternoon," Mr Stone greeted with a broad smile as he strode down the central aisle toward them. "And the Bow Street Society are also here. Fantastic."

At Mr Stone's side was a man in his early forties with defined cheekbones and dishevelled dark-brown hair. The last feature, coupled with his imperial moustache and goatee beard of the same colour, made him look like a character from Alexander Dumas' novel *The Three Musketeers*. His fashionable attire consisted of a knee-length, black woollen overcoat, cream-coloured shirt, brown trousers, tie and shoes, and a brown silk waistcoat embroidered with a golden paisley design.

Miss Kimberly glared at Mr Stone as he and his guest stood before the stage.

"Is Mr Kurtis here?" Mr Stone called over to her.

Miss Kimberly adopted a hard tone. "No."

"Who is Mr Kurtis?" Mr Locke enquired.

Mr Stone spread his arms. "The owner of *this* fine building."

"What do you need him for?" Miss Kimberly enquired.

"We have an appointment with him," Mr Stone replied with a smug look on his face.

Miss Kimberly looked puzzled. "No, I don't."

"Not *you*." Mr Stone gripped the shoulder of the man beside him. "*Us*."

Miss Kimberly's anger returned. "What is going on? Who is this man?"

Mr Locke discreetly held his wife's arm as he used his walking cane to point at the man beside Mr Stone. "Allow me to introduce Mr Darrel Howard Gibb; actor, husband, and, by all appearances, fellow co-conspirator in the blackmailing of Mr Benton and the murder of Miss Mina Ilbert."

* * *

"Yer a damn *filthy* whore, *Polly, and I ain't wantin' anythin' more to do with ya, d'ya hear? Go back to yer fella."* Dr Weeks' words bounced around Miss Hicks' mind as she remembered the look of utter pain in his eyes.

Next came Mr O'Hannigan's words on the matter: *"If you're now feelin' guilty, I'm sorry. But you weren't feelin' guilty when you bent over for me earlier. It's only your man findin' us that's got you feelin' this way."* She remembered his naked body against hers and felt a tingling between her legs. She'd told him she'd wanted him but didn't love him, and he'd said it was good enough for him. She'd asked Dr McWilliams to tell Dr Weeks she loved him, but she didn't know Dr Weeks' reply or even if her message had been delivered.

Releasing a soft sigh, she turned away from her window and sat at the dressing table in her room at Bow Street. She took the long drawer out and, reaching into the space behind, retrieved the pouch containing the money she'd raised thus far. The second visit to the pawnbrokers hadn't been as lucrative as the first, making her wonder if she ought to try another establishment for the third.

In any case, she had no idea what she would do with the money. She loved Dr Weeks, but he hated her. She desired Mr O'Hannigan, but he'd robbed her. She wanted to be close to Miss Trent, but she was disgusted by her. The prospect of going somewhere far away alone also filled Miss Hicks with dread. Releasing another soft sigh, she returned the pouch to its hiding place.

"Polly?"

Miss Hicks looked at the mirror and saw Toby standing in the doorway behind her. Feeling a little guilty over the way she'd spoken to him before, she put on a smile and turned to face him. "Toby. Come in."

Toby visibly relaxed and returned her smile as he entered the room.

"Do you want more help with readin'?" Miss Hicks enquired.

"Yeah, and…" Toby scratched the back of his ear. "Can I ask you sumin'?"

Miss Hicks moved along the stool and patted the space beside her. "Pull up a pew."

Toby plonked himself down and sheepishly glanced at her. "Are you goin' away?"

Miss Hicks felt her heart clench, but she did her best not to let it show. Instead, she gave a weak laugh. "What makes you think I'm goin' away?"

"Miss Trent's mad at you, and I've seen you takin' stuff out your room in bags." Toby looked her square in the eye. "I don't want you to go, Polly. I'd miss you too much."

Miss Hicks blinked. She studied Toby's face for any hint of deceit but found none. All at once, she felt flattered, blessed, guilty, and ashamed by the lad's admission. In truth, she hadn't given his thoughts or feelings about her leaving a second thought, which was terrible of her. Trying to make light of it, she put on another smile and said, "You don't want to be missin' a wrong'un like me, Toby. Besides, Miss Trent and the Society will look after you."

Toby frowned. "But you said you was 'ere to look after me. Was you lyin'?"

"No, but things change, love."

Toby downcast his eyes and bowed his head. "You are goin' away, then."

At a loss as to how to answer him, because she didn't know the answer herself, she put her arm around his shoulders and pulled him into a sideways hug. "No. I'm not."

When he returned the hug, she inwardly added, *Not yet, anyway.*

* * *

"I never had any part in blackmail or murder," Mr Gibb denied in a soft American accent. "I'm just here to claim what's mine."

"If one were a naïve babe in arms, one would say you coming to London so soon after Miss Ilbert's death was fortuitous," Mr Locke said. "The Bow Street Society is neither young nor naïve, however. Therefore, it would say you coming to London so soon after Miss Ilbert's death was not only planned but also highly suspicious, Mr Gibb." He slid his gaze to Mr Stone. "If Mr Kurtis grants control of the lease agreement to Mr Gibb, you will likely assume the elevated role of business manager since you are clearly the one who brought him here."

"Am I?" Mr Stone challenged with a smirk.

"Indeed, you are," Mr Locke replied with confidence. "For you remarked to Mr Akers, the *Crescent* would soon have a new manager. How could you possibly know that with any degree of certainty without being responsible for the change coming about?"

"It doesn't mean I murdered Mina," Mr Stone replied. "And I didn't blackmail Benton, either."

"I would argue otherwise," Mr Locke said.

"As would we," Sergeant Dixon announced as he walked down the auditorium's central aisle. With him were Mr Elliott and two uniformed constables. "Mr Ronald Stone, information has come to our attention that makes us view Miss Mina Ilbert's death in a new light. I must ask you to come with me to Vine Street."

"What 'information?'" Mr Stone spat.

Sergeant Dixon glanced around. "I think you'd prefer I didn't talk about it here, sir."

"Why does he need to go to Vine Street?" Miss Lily enquired.

"It's where the police station is, miss," Sergeant Dixon replied.

"The *police station*?" Miss Lily covered her mouth. "Ronnie, what have you done?"

"Nothing," Mr Stone replied.

"I have had about as much as I can stand of this." Miss Kimberly took Miss Lily by the arm. "You are going home, child."

"Will you come quietly, sir?" Sergeant Dixon enquired.

"Is Mr Thurston coming too?" Mr Stone challenged.

Sergeant Dixon exchanged glances with Mr Elliott. "Why?"

"He was the one blackmailing Mr Benton," Mr Stone replied.

Miss Kimberly released Miss Lily. "What did you say?"

"Morris Thurston was the one blackmailing Mr Benton, *not* me," Mr Stone replied. "He probably murdered Mina to stop her from finding out, too."

Miss Kimberly's face turned pale. "You're lying."

"Mr Thurston stopped Mr Jerome from hitting me," Mr Benton pointed out.

"Is Mr Thurston here?" Sergeant Dixon enquired.

"I will go and see." Mr Benton disappeared into the wings.

"With all due respect, Mr Stone, how does one know you and Mr Thurston were not blackmailing Mr Benton together?" Mr Locke enquired.

"With Jack Jerome as the bruiser," Mr Verity interjected.

Mr Stone looked at Mr Verity. "Jack Jerome?" He darted his gaze back to Sergeant Dixon. "Is *he* the source of your 'information?'" He glanced at Mr Gibb. "A *known* rogue."

"We will discuss it at Vine Street," Sergeant Dixon replied firmly.

"Wh-what's going on?" Mr Thurston glanced around the stage as he emerged from the wings. "Mr Locke?" He stopped when he saw Mr Stone surrounded by policemen. Recalling the stage manager's previous threats, his heart pounded, and his face and palms sweated. Envisioning Sergeant Dixon placing him under arrest and dragging him to the nearest police station, he glanced at the foyer doors behind him. There was no way he'd make it past the small crowd in the aisle, however. Wetting his dry lips, he quietly said, "Oh dear."

"There's the look of a guilty man if ever there was one," Mr Stone remarked.

Mr Thurston looked to Mr Stone, Sergeant Dixon, Mr Locke, and Miss Kimberly in turn. "What… am I s-supposed to be guilty of?"

"Blackmail, sir," Sergeant Dixon replied. "And possibly murder."

"Mm-mm-*murder*?" Mr Thurston repeatedly shook his head. "N-No. I would *never*…" He pointed at Mr Stone. "*Ronnie* was blackmailing Mr Benton with Mr Jerome's help! And I-I couldn't find him the night Mina died!"

Mr Locke caught Mr Stone and Mr Gibb exchanging a knowing glance.

Mr Thurston turned to Miss Kimberly with outstretched arms. "*You* know I wasn't responsible for Mina's death. Don't you, Emma?"

Miss Kimberly visibly tensed and darted her gaze between Mr Thurston and Sergeant Dixon. To the former, she replied, "Yes." She swallowed hard and added in a definitive tone, "I also know I can trust you, Morris."

Mr Thurston's features lifted with a smile. "You can. Absolutely."

"Are you willing to make a statement, Mr Thurston?" Sergeant Dixon enquired.

Mr Thurston turned his head sharply and stared at him, wide eyed. "Pardon?"

"About Mr Stone's part in the blackmailing of Mr Benton," Sergeant Dixon clarified.

"Oh…" Mr Thurston dry-washed his hands and, heading for the stairs, avoided making eye contact with Mr Stone. "Y-Yes. Of course."

Mr Stone lunged for him as soon as he approached. "I'm going to kill you!"

Mr Thurston released a high-pitched squeal and dived into a nearby row of seats. Bouncing off their arms and onto the floor with a hard grunt, he immediately rolled onto his back and threw up his arms to defend himself as Mr Stone tried to jump on top of him. Fortunately, the constables were quicker than the stage manager, and so they'd dragged him away from Mr Thurston in seconds. They pulled Mr Stone's arms behind him and, pinning his wrists against the small of his back, allowed Sergeant Dixon to apply the handcuffs.

"Excuse us," Sergeant Dixon said as he stepped between Mr Gibb and Mr Elliott, thereby obliging them to move aside, and left the auditorium. The constables, with Mr Stone held tightly between them, followed, as a nervous-looking Mr Thurston brought up the rear.

"I suppose I should cancel the meeting with Mr Kurtis," Mr Gibb mumbled once they'd gone. At Mr Elliott's questioning look, he explained, "the owner of the building."

"Actually, I would recommend you keep the meeting with him," Mr Elliott said.

"And you are?" Mr Gibb enquired.

"A solicitor who you would be wise to listen to," Mr Elliott replied. Taking a business card from his pocket, he climbed onto the stage and approached Miss Kimberly. "I'm Mr Gregory Elliott, a solicitor and member of the Bow Street Society. I was informed you have a signed agreement, between yourself and Miss Ilbert, that passes control of the lease agreement to you in the event of her death. May I see it?"

Miss Kimberly read the business card and glanced at Miss Lily and Mr Benton. "Yes. I keep it in the office."

"Thank you," Mr Elliott said. "Mr Benton, could I trouble you to verify Miss Ilbert's signature on the document?"

Mr Benton immediately stepped forward. "No trouble at all, sir."

"Mr Gibb, please wait with my fellow Bow Street Society members until Mr Kurtis arrives," Mr Elliott instructed the actor. "Please then bring them both to Miss Kimberly's office, doctor."

"Very well," Dr Locke agreed.

Mr Locke stepped up to Miss Lily and quietly offered, "My driver will take you home, if you would like to rest after all this emotional excitement."

Miss Lily gave a small nod. "Yes, please."

"Claude…" Mr Locke waited until his attendant had joined them. "Please, escort Miss Lily to the carriage and instruct Mr Lambert to drive her home."

"Yes, Mr Locke. Come with me, miss." Claude gently guided her away.

FIFTY-FIVE

"Mr Gibb, may I ask you a question?" Mr Locke enquired.

Mr Gibb, who'd taken a seat further down the row, leant forward to meet the illusionist's gaze. "What is it?"

"When did you hear of Miss Mina Ilbert's death?" Mr Locke enquired.

Mr Verity and Dr Locke, sitting between the pair, glanced from one to the other as they awaited the answer.

"Only, it has occurred to me you were not at all shocked when it was mentioned earlier," Mr Locke explained.

"Mr Stone told me," Mr Gibb said. "The day after."

"And when did you arrive in London from America?" Mr Locke enquired.

"You said only one," Mr Gibb rebuffed.

"Humour me," Mr Locke said.

"The same day," Mr Gibb said.

"As Mr Stone informed you of Miss Mina Ilbert's death?" Mr Locke enquired.

"*Yes*." Mr Gibb stood and headed for the foyer doors. "*Where's* Mr Kurtis?"

Mr Locke momentarily rested the handle of his cane against his lips. "Intriguing."

"What is?" Dr Locke enquired.

Mr Locke allowed the shaft of his cane to slide between his fingers and gripped the handle before it toppled over upon hitting the floor. "Mr Gibb lying to us."

"How do you know he was?" Mr Verity enquired.

"I saw him and Mr Stone exchange a rather telling look when the question of where Mr Stone was on the night Mina died was raised earlier," Mr Locke replied. "I suspect Mr Stone was having a clandestine meeting with Mr Gibb about the *Crescent Theatre* at the time, hence the look. If so, and I strongly believe it is, Mr Gibb has just lied about when he arrived in London. The question is, *which* day *did* he arrive?" He looked to his wife. "Did Mr Snyder choose to wait outside for you with his cab?"

"Yes," Dr Locke replied. "Why?"

Mr Locke leant upon his cane as he stood. "I wish to call upon his tremendous knowledge of London transportation, and beyond, to assist me in determining Mr Gibb's exact location in the days prior to, and the day of, Miss Mina Ilbert's murder. Darling, you may take our carriage back to Bow Street with Mr Verity. Claude!"

The attendant stood from his seat in the row behind.

"You are to come with us." Mr Locke shuffled along his row.

Claude looked to Dr Locke, who gave a subtle nod of approval.

"Yes, Mr Locke." Claude hurried along his row and, meeting Mr Locke on his, allowed him to lean upon his arm as they left the auditorium.

* * *

As Dr Colbert climbed the steps to the Bow Street Society's porch, his mind played out what could go wrong within the next fifteen minutes. Namely, a lack of synchronisation between him and Inspector Woolfe, and Miss Trent discovering their deception. Envisioning the latter intensified his apprehension, which surprised him. What he was about to do wasn't necessarily immoral; the clerk and Society's exploitation of decent people, for whatever ends, had to stop. Whilst it was true Miss Trent had impressed him on occasion, he remained against her intentional facilitation of irresponsible vigilantism. So, why was his reflection in the window grimacing?

"Focus, Neal," he mumbled and checked the time on his pocket watch. It was exactly three o'clock. *Go inside, ensure there are no other members around, discuss Dr Weeks, and make your request about the address*, he thought. Feeling his apprehension ease as he formed his strategy, he held his head high and knocked thrice on the door. In the ensuing seconds of waiting for it to be opened, he moved his lower jaw back and forth to loosen the muscles, thereby eradicating his grimace.

As he heard bolts slide and a key turn, he readied a polite smile, only to expel it when Toby opened the door. Parting his lips, he took a moment to consider his words. "Forgive me. I was expecting Miss Trent." He glanced over Toby's head, into the hallway beyond. "Is she receiving visitors?"

"Miss Trent!" Toby shouted. "Dr Colbert's 'ere!"

Dr Colbert heard a door open and saw Miss Treat walking into view from the direction of her office. Flashing her a smile that didn't reach his eyes, he greeted, "Forgive my unannounced visit, Miss Trent, but I thought you'd appreciate hearing the latest news about Dr Weeks firsthand."

"I do. Thank you." Miss Trent put a hand upon Toby's shoulder. "Have you finished clearing the grate in the parlour?"

Toby simultaneously rolled his eyes and turned upon his heel. "I'm doin' it now." He trudged off to the parlour and slammed the door.

"We're still working on his manners," Miss Trent said by way of an apology.

"Rome wasn't built in a day," Dr Colbert said by way of forgiveness.

"Please, come in." Miss Trent stepped aside and closed the door after him.

Dr Colbert glanced at the meeting room door as he removed his hat, scarf, and coat. "Are any of the other members here?"

"No. They're elsewhere investigating Miss Ilbert's death, still."

Dr Colbert silently thanked God for small mercies as he hung his things on the hat stand. "I must apologise, again, for my withdrawal from the case, but, as I'm sure you understand, Dr Weeks and his care had to be my priority."

"Of course." Miss Trent folded her arms. "When we were there, Dr McWilliams told Miss Hicks and I Dr Weeks was in danger of having a potentially life-threatening fit due to his alcoholic insanity. Is that still the case?"

"Thankfully, no. He is extremely fortunate not to suffer one, though, given the intensity of his dependency upon alcohol." Dr Colbert glanced at the kitchen door and up the stairs as he passed to join Miss Trent. "Is Miss Hicks here?"

Miss Trent recalled Miss Hicks hitting Inspector Conway. Not wishing for Dr Colbert to endure the same reaction, she lowered her voice and replied, "Yes, but I think I ought to hear the news first and pass it on after you've gone. Miss Hicks can be rather… passionate in her responses at times."

Dr Colbert smiled, partially in relief and partially in gratitude. "I understand."

"We'll go into my office." Miss Trent led the way and invited him to sit once there.

Dr Colbert was disappointed to find the infernally uncomfortable chair remained his only seating option. Releasing a soft sigh, he perched upon its edge and tried to focus on the matter at hand.

Meanwhile, Miss Trent closed the door and sat behind her desk. "You said Dr Weeks is no longer in danger of having a fit. How is he overall?"

"Weak, in pain, and suffering from terrible nightmares."

Miss Trent's eyes and expression turned sombre. "I see."

"He has only just begun to eat and drink again, but, before that, he was being stubbornly defiant in the hope we'd relent and give him alcohol to pacify him." Dr Colbert cast a discreet glance at the clock on Miss Trent's desk. It was almost ten minutes past three already. "However, I'm confident we've turned a corner with him and finally put him on the road to recovery." He held up his index finger. "Provided he continues to cooperate."

Miss Trent brightened. "I'm glad to hear it. Believe it or not, I've been very worried about him. He might be an arrogant and impossible cad at times, but he's also a brilliant surgeon and good friend. I would've hated for anything to happen to him."

"I believe it wholeheartedly. It's obvious you care for many of your members."

"I care for all my members, doctor. Including you."

Dr Colbert was taken aback. Had she guessed the truth behind his membership? "My good woman, there's no need to worry about me."

"I didn't say there was, but it doesn't mean I can't care about you as one friend to another."

"No." Dr Colbert offered a contrived smile as he inwardly breathed a sigh of relief. "That is true." He cast another glance at the clock. "I'll keep you regularly informed of Dr Weeks' progress. His recovery remains tenuous so, naturally, I must continue to prohibit visitors until I'm confident he isn't going to treat the interaction as a means of securing alcohol."

Miss Trent knew she'd never sneak alcohol to Dr Weeks, but she couldn't be as sure about Miss Hicks. Especially if the barmaid thought it could win back the surgeon's affections. "I understand. We'll respect your decision and take our lead from you."

"Thank you," Dr Colbert said with genuine appreciation. "There was another matter I wanted to discuss with you. I was wondering if you could add a second address to my membership record. My sister has a house in Devon that my family and I visit fairly regularly, and I wouldn't want to be uncontactable by you or the Society during those times."

Miss Trent adopted a defensive tone. "I don't expect you to always be on call."

"No, but I want to be involved in as many Society cases as possible."

"But if you're holidaying in Devon, the last thing you're going to want to do is abandon your family to investigate a horrible murder or the like."

Dr Colbert's expression turned serious. "Miss Trent, whilst I appreciate your concern, how I choose to spend my time is ultimately my decision and my decision alone. Please," he indicated the filing cabinet, "put the address on my record."

Miss Trent lofted her brow at his tone but relented, nonetheless. "As you wish." She stood and, taking a set of keys from a pocket hidden in her skirts, unlocked the filing cabinet. Dr Colbert noted the members were filed in alphabetical order by surname when she took his card from the drawer labelled *A-C*. As she sat behind her desk and reached for her pen, loud banging suddenly echoed around the hallway. Recognising the noise as Inspector Woolfe's interpretation of knocking, she excused herself from the room.

Dr Colbert watched her leave and, when he heard Inspector Woolfe's voice a few moments later, stood, closed the door ajar, and crept behind the desk. Thankful Miss Trent trusted him enough to leave the filing cabinet unlocked, he slowly slid open the drawer labelled *N-P* and thumbed through the cards until he found J. Pettifoot's.

Discovering it was the third one in, he pulled it out and slipped his fingers in the gap to hold its place whilst he read Pettifoot's address: *42, Kennington Road, Lambeth.* Dr Colbert's heart leapt with delight. *This is it!* His heart raced as he considered the significance of the information in his hand. *Finally, we can meet the mysterious J. Pettifoot!* Alas, aside from the address, the card only contained their first initial and surname. Reading the card several times over to memorise it, he returned it to its place and closed the drawer.

"I heard Miss Hicks is staying here," Inspector Woolfe said in the hallway.

Miss Trent put her hands on her hips. "She is. Not that it's any of your business."

"It is when her adultery puts a man in Bedlam."

Miss Trent lofted an eyebrow. "Why do you care?"

Inspector Woolfe narrowed his eyes. "Because it's not right."

"But not illegal. Besides, you're hardly a saint. You went out of your way to put the fear of God into Dr Weeks."

Inspector Woolfe's eyes hardened. "Only when I thought he was a Society member, and I was right, wasn't I?"

Miss Trent folded her arms. "What do you want from me, Inspector?"

Inspector Woolfe's gaze drifted over her. "Something you'll never give me."

"Finally, something we can agree on." Miss Trent returned to the door. "And since you have nothing sensible to discuss after all, I must ask you to leave." She opened the door. "I'm very busy."

Inspector Woolfe glanced at the office door. "Dinner."

"I beg your pardon?"

"Let me take you to dinner."

Miss Trent stared at him as if he'd grown a third eye. "*No.*"

Inspector Woolfe moved closer to her. "One dinner. In a public place. Nothing more."

"No, Caleb." Miss Trent turned her head toward the street. "Please. Leave."

Hurt penetrated Inspector Woolfe's eyes despite his hard expression. Striding past her and down the steps, he hoped for two things. Firstly, she didn't mention their conversation to Inspector Conway. Secondly, he'd given Dr Colbert enough time to find and memorise the address. Only time and patience would give him the answer to both.

Miss Trent locked her gaze upon the departing policeman to ensure he didn't loiter outside. Upon seeing him turn and head toward the police station, she closed and locked the door with an audible sigh. Rubbing her temple as she replayed their awkward and, honestly, uncomfortable, conversation, she muttered, "Unbelievable."

"Who was it?" Dr Colber enquired from the doorway of her office.

"Inspector Woolfe." Miss Trent joined him. "Social visits from the police are *always* a delight." She gave a wry smile.

"What did he want?" Dr Colbert returned to his chair.

"Nothing of any consequence." Miss Trent sat behind her desk and took a pen from the inkwell. "What is your sister's address in Devon, please?"

Dr Colbert's smile lifted his features as he gave it. Inspector Woolfe had played his part perfectly, he'd found and memorised the address, and Miss Trent appeared to be none the wiser. All in all, it had been a *very* good day.

FIFTY-SIX

"This is it." Inspector Woolfe gripped Dr Colbert's arm. In his other hand was the page, torn from Dr Colbert's notebook, containing J. Pettifoot's address. With rapt attention, he read and re-read the hastily written words, causing his smile to grow larger with each pass. His eyes also seemed to glow, making his face the most animated Dr Colbert had ever seen it. "It took us a while, but we've *got* it."

"What will be your next move?"

"Visit 42, Kennington Road in Lambeth." Inspector Woolfe pocketed the address.

Dr Colbert moved away from the door and looked to Inspector Woolfe as they heard footsteps coming along the corridor toward the latter's office. Briefly putting his finger to his lips to indicate he wanted Dr Colbert to remain silent, Inspector Woolfe sat behind his desk and indicated for Dr Colbert to sit across from him. No sooner had they done so, did the door open, and Inspector Conway entered.

"What did you do, soak in the bath for two hours?" Inspector Woolfe sardonically enquired as Inspector Conway halted upon seeing Dr Colbert. Appearing to notice where he was looking, Inspector Woolfe added, "You know Dr Colbert."

"Yeah." Inspector Conway watched him with wary eyes as he hung up his things.

"Hello, again, Inspector," Dr Colbert greeted. "How are your ribs?"

"Sore," Inspector Conway replied.

"He's here to tell us about Weeks," Inspector Woolfe said. "We were waiting for you to come back before we started."

Inspector Conway's expression turned grave. "I'm here now." He moved his chair for a clearer view of Dr Colbert and sat.

Coughing, Inspector Woolfe had a swig from a small, brown bottle on his desk. Coughing again afterward, he cleared his throat and coughed for a third time.

Dr Colbert watched Inspector Woolfe with concern. Despite prescribing a second bottle of medicine to the policeman, the cough hadn't seemed to wane any.

Inspector Conway's mind was on Dr Weeks, however. "How is 'e?"

"Out of danger," Dr Colbert replied. "He has been obstinate, arrogant, and wholly disobedient in the misguided hope we'd relent and give him alcohol. I'm pleased to say, though, as of today, he has decided to be compliant, humble, and obedient, allowing us to put him on the road to recovery."

"Can we see 'im?" Inspector Conway enquired.

Dr Colbert frowned with a furrowing of his brow. "I'm afraid not. Whilst he has turned a corner, his journey hasn't long begun. I fear any visit from a friend or family member might tempt him to coerce any one of them into bringing him alcohol on their next visit."

"I wouldn't do that," Inspector Conway rebuffed.

"All the same, I'd prefer not to take the risk," Dr Colbert said.

"We'll get to see him soon enough, mate," Inspector Woolfe said.

Regret entered Inspector Conway's eyes and voice as he softly replied, "Yeah."

* * *

It was raining when Mr Locke and Claude had emerged from the *Crescent Theatre*. Fortunately, Mr Snyder and his cab were parked at the curb directly outside the main door. Continuing to lean upon his attendant, Mr Locke approached his fellow Bow Streeter and gained his attention with a momentary lift of his walking cane. "Good afternoon, Sam!"

Mr Snyder's eyes were filled with warmth as, with two brief touches of his hat's brim, he greeted the illusionist and his attendant. "Good afternoon, sirs."

"If one were to travel from the United States of America, say, New York City, to London, how would one go about it?" Mr Locke enquired.

Mr Snyder looked skyward as he considered the question. "A *White Star Line* steamer from New York City to Southampton, then a train to London."

Mr Locke hummed. "Yes, I thought so." He indicated the doors of the cab with his walking cane by way of instructing Claude to open them. "Sam, would you be so kind as to drive Claude and me to the headquarters of the *White Star Line*?"

Mr Snyder adopted a serious tone. "I would, but it's a long way, sir."

"Oh?" Mr Locke envisioned the suburbs of London. "How long?"

"Liverpool," Mr Snyder replied.

Taken aback, Claude stopped what he was doing to witness Mr Locke's response.

"Ah." Mr Locke contemplated the journey. "Yes, that is rather far."

"There's a telegraph office on West Strand that's always open. If you sent a telegram to the *Oceanic Steam Navigation Company* at 10 Water Street in Liverpool, they can tell you about the passengers on any *White Star Line* steamer," Mr Snyder explained. "They bought the *White Star Line* house flag and name back when the first company went out of business in the '60s."

Mr Locke considered the feasibility of attaining the required information through such means. If he introduced himself and the Society, and briefly outlined the circumstances, the owners of the *Oceanic Steam Navigation Company* might be willing to cooperate. After all, as his last visit to Birmingham proved, the Society's reputation had already travelled further than London despite its relative infancy. He gestured for Claude to open the second door, "Let us be away to the West Strand Telegraph Office."

"Right-o." Mr Snyder touched the brim of his hat and readied the reins.

* * *

"Mina signed this." Mr Benton passed a page of handwriting to Mr Elliott.

Upon reading it, the solicitor realised it was a sweet and respectable love letter, in which Miss Ilbert praised Mr Benton for his loyalty and support. Examining the signature at the letter's end, Mr Elliott compared it to the signature on the agreement provided by Miss Kimberly. She sat behind her desk whilst Mr Elliott and Mr Benton sat in front. "I'm by no means an expert on such matters, but I'd be willing to testify under oath these signatures were identical. Would you agree, Mr Benton?"

Mr Benton took back his letter and compared its signature to the agreement's. "Yes."

Miss Kimberly adopted a hard tone. "I have always said it was authentic. My word ought to be sufficient."

"In social circles, it would be," Mr Elliott said. "The law requires greater reassurance, however." He read the agreement again. "With the provenance of Miss Ilbert's signature on the agreement confirmed by the signature on Mr Benton's letter, and Mr Benton's written statement confirming his letter's provenance, I see no reason why a court wouldn't grant you control over the building's lease agreement, which also appears to be in order. Pending Mr Kurtis' approval, of course. Regardless of who Miss Ilbert wished to assume control of the lease, the building remains Mr Kurtis' legal property. Therefore, the final decision is his."

Mr Benton's expression turned sombre. "Which means Mr Gibb could still acquire it."

"In theory, yes," Mr Elliott said.

"This theatre is Lily's future," Miss Kimberly said, firmly. "I shan't allow anyone to steal it away from her."

"Mr Gibb could argue he has a right to it if he and Miss Mina Ilbert were still married at the time of her death," Mr Elliott said. "I'll confirm whether this was indeed the case by consulting the records at the divorce courts. Is Mr Kurtis a conservative or sentimental man?"

"Neither." Mr Benton replied.

"All he cares about is living a comfortable and quiet life," Miss Kimberly explained further. "The income he receives from the *Crescent* enables him to live such a life. One saving grace in mine and Lily's favour could be his resistance to allowing a stranger to take over the *Crescent*'s lease agreement. For it would mean time spent here, and in the offices of financial men and solicitors, to amend the agreement to the satisfaction of both parties. He doesn't like to be away from his rose garden."

"I will see if he has arrived yet." Mr Benton left the room.

Miss Kimberly leant forward and lowered her voice. "Mr Elliott, may I be secret with you for a moment?"

Mr Elliott set down the letter and agreement. "That would depend upon the nature of what you have to say."

The tension eased from Miss Kimberly's features, and she lowered her voice further. "I believe I might have seen something of vital importance, on the night Mina died, but I am afraid to tell anyone of it because I suspect they will accuse me of trying to add another nail to Mr Stone's coffin. Especially now that his scheme with Mr Gibb has come to light."

"What did you see?"

Miss Kimberly sat back and downcast her gaze. "Mr Stone. Leaving the under-stage area. Shortly before Mina died."

"You're certain it was him?"

"His face was illuminated by the auditorium's lights." Miss Kimberly met his gaze. "Everyone here knows how

Mr Stone and I do not get along. Why should they believe my word over his?"

Mr Elliott considered the situation and conceded it appeared it be quite the predicament. "As a solicitor, I'm only interested in the truth, not unsubstantiated gossip." He sat forward. "My recommendation would be for you to provide a statement to Sergeant Dixon about what you saw and allow him to decide whether it is relevant to Miss Mina Ilbert's death. I'm certain Dr Locke would accompany you, if you didn't want to go alone."

"Yes." Miss Kimberly's appreciative smile failed to reach her eyes. "Thank you."

The door opened and, upon entering, Mr Benton announced, "Mr Kurtis and Mr Gibb."

FIFTY-SEVEN

The meeting room felt different to Dr Colbert as he sat with his fellow members around the table. *My fellow members*, he thought upon realising he'd not only put himself amongst them, but also perceived them as equals. *I'm not one of them in the way they think I am*, he reminded himself. *I'm here for a purpose that can't include friendships or alliances.* He looked to Mr Elliott sitting opposite, and his heart ached. He was the only one Dr Colbert wanted a deeper connection with, but his purpose made it impossible. Unless he took the solicitor into his confidence, but he doubted he'd understand or accept his point of view.

As he looked around the table, at the Lockes, Mr Heath, Mr Snyder, and Miss Trent, he doubted any of them would understand or accept his point of view. He wasn't sure about Mr Verity. They'd only been introduced tonight, so he'd yet to get the measure of the man. *Is this why the room feels different?* Dr Colbert mused. *Because I know they'd feel betrayed if they knew the truth?* But had he betrayed them? He was only doing what he thought was right, even if they'd probably never see it that way. There was no question in his mind they'd rally around Miss Trent. *But they might not once the mysterious J. Pettifoot is exposed.*

Toby entered the room and approached Mr Locke. "Can you show me another trick?"

Mr Locke reached behind Toby's ear and, as he withdrew his hand, a coin was between his fingers. "You ought to have a money box. Unsavoury characters like me might rob you if you continue to hide your money behind your ears."

Toby stared, wide eyed, at the coin. "*Cor*! How'd you do that?!"

"Magic, my dear boy." Mr Locke dropped the coin into his hand.

Toby put the coin between his teeth to confirm it was genuine.

"Perhaps Master Toby and Miss Trent would like to come to afternoon tea soon." Dr Locke looked to the clerk.

Toby's face and eyes came alive with excitement. "Can we?!"

"Yes, but *only* if you go to Miss Hicks and practise your reading," Miss Trent replied.

Toby pocketed the coin and left the room with a bounce in his step.

"Such a delightful young man," Mr Locke observed.

Miss Trent hummed. "When he wants to be."

"Reminds me of me as a boy," Mr Snyder said with a smile.

Hearing Miss Hicks speaking with Toby in the hallway, Miss Trent relaxed. Being occupied with Toby meant Miss Hicks couldn't be occupied with Mr O'Hannigan. Thoughts of their affair naturally moved onto thoughts of Dr Weeks, and Miss Trent resolved to give him the greater focus. "Before we begin the meeting proper, I'd like to invite Dr Colbert to give us the latest news about Dr Weeks' condition. Doctor?"

"Certainly." Dr Colbert sat forward and rested his clasped hands upon the table.

Dr Locke tensed with anxious anticipation as her gaze locked upon Dr Colbert.

Observing the change in his wife, Mr Locke slipped his left hand in hers and gave it a gentle squeeze. Feeling her hand tighten around his in response, he put his other arm around her waist to offer further support.

"Dr Weeks is a very sick man," Dr Colbert declared. "During his initial days at the asylum, he was in great danger of suffering a fatal fit. The risk of this occurring decreased as the hours and days went on. Due to his chronic dependence upon alcohol, I fear the risk will never be eliminated completely, especially if he bends to temptation."

"I presume alcohol is prohibited at Bethlehem Hospital?" Mr Elliott enquired.

"Yes," Dr Colbert replied. "We encourage sobriety amongst our patients."

"Is he in pain?" Dr Locke enquired, her voice subdued by emotion.

"At times," Dr Colbert replied. "However, I'm reluctant to prescribe medication he could become equally dependent upon."

"Who is paying for his care?" Mr Elliott enquired with a glance at Miss Trent.

"His Poor Union," Dr Colbert replied.

"Mr Thaddeus Dorsey, the client at the centre of the Society's first murder case, resided in this house under the supervision and care of an attendant in place of being admitted to an asylum," Mr Locke explained. "Could Dr Weeks not reside here under a similar arrangement? Aside from his dependence upon alcohol, he is otherwise sound in mind, is he not?"

Dr Colbert's expression turned grave. "I'm afraid not. Whilst I can't discuss the particulars of the circumstances which led to his admittance, I can tell you they convinced me of the fact his chronic alcohol dependency has made him extremely dangerous."

"Truly?" Mr Elliott enquired.

"Truly," Dr Colbert replied.

"I wouldn't have thought it of Dr Weeks," Mr Elliott remarked.

"Nor me," Mr Heath interjected.

"Dr Weeks in the asylum isn't the one you knew." Dr Colbert cast a glance around the table. "The alcohol has corrupted him beyond recognition. However," he drew in a slow, deep breath as he straightened, "his old self will gradually return with each passing day, and each offer of help he accepts."

"May we visit him?" Dr Locke enquired.

"No," Dr Colbert replied. "He needs time to settle into his new surroundings first."

Dr Locke lowered her gaze. "I see."

* * *

"How dare you ask me to perform after what has happened!" Miss Lily shouted.

"You've worked hard on perfecting Mina's routine. I shan't allow you to render it pointless for the sake of that-that *man*!" Miss Kimberly shouted in return.

"Ronnie isn't a saint, but he isn't a murderer either!"

Miss Kimberly advanced upon her. "*How* many *times* must I tell you, child?! He is *Mister* Stone to you!"

Miss Lily gave a defiant lift of her chin. "Maybe I want him to be Ronnie?"

Miss Kimberly's expression turned grim. "Not whilst there's breath in my body."

Mr Thurston entered the dressing room. "Lily, you're on soon."

Miss Lily tuned cold eyes upon him. "Here he is: the *other* traitor."

"*Lily*," Miss Kimberly scolded.

"It-it's quite all right, Emma." Mr Thurston polished his glasses with his handkerchief as he awkwardly shifted his weight from one foot to the other. "It's only five minutes until your cue, s-so I'd recommend getting in the wings now."

Miss Lily folded her arms. "I'm not going on."

Mr Thurston's head snapped up. "You're not?"

Miss Kimberly adopted a hard tone. "Yes, she is."

Miss Lily glared at her. "No, she isn't."

Miss Kimberly returned her glare. "*Yes*. You *are*."

"*No*. I'm *not*!" Miss Lily ran from the room. "And *you* can't make *me*!"

* * *

Mr Snyder added more coal to the fire whilst Miss Trent added a fresh pot of tea and refilled jug of cream to the table. Returning to her seat, she laid out the previous meeting's minutes, the current agenda, and the typed list of suspects in front of her. Next, she consulted her pocket watch and noted the time. "The first item on our agenda is Mr Ronald Stone. Sergeant Dixon took Mr Stone and Mr Thurston to Vine Street police station earlier. Have we discovered the outcomes of their interviews?"

"I called upon Sergeant Dixon on my way here," Mr Elliott replied. "He told me both men had denied having any involvement in Miss Mina Ilbert's death.

"Mr Stone alluded to being complicit in Mr Jerome's blackmailing of Mr Benton in as far as he suspected it was happening but chose not to intervene. He accused Mr Thurston of being the mastermind of the scheme, stating he wanted revenge on Miss Ilbert for refusing to read his play until recently. Mr Stone also alleged Miss Ilbert disapproved of Mr Thurston's fondness for Miss Kimberly, stating she sought admiration from all the men at the *Crescent* and didn't want them to put their affections elsewhere. When asked if he were one of the men who admired Miss Ilbert, Mr Stone scoffed and stated he preferred his women much younger, specifically Miss Lily's age."

Dr Locke made a soft sound of disgust. "Such a foul human being."

"I agree," Mr Locke added, taking a sip of tea.

"Mr Thurston also alluded to being complicit in Mr Jerome's blackmailing of Mr Benton in as far as he suspected it was happening but chose not to intervene," Mr Elliott resumed. "He also accused Mr Stone of not only being the mastermind of the scheme, but also the one who recruited Mr Jerome into it. He also provided Sergeant Dixon with a detailed explanation of how the scheme worked and Mr Stone and Mr Jerome's roles within it. Namely," he consulted his notebook, "Mr Stone informed Mr Jerome of Mr Benton's expected arrival time at the stage door. Mr Jerome would lie in wait for Mr Benton at the given time and demand money from him in exchange for allowing him to perform uninterrupted. If Mr Benton refused, Mr Jerome would become violent to persuade him."

"If Mr Thurston knew violence was highly likely, as he claimed in his interview with Sergeant Dixon, it would explain his loitering around the stage door," Mr Locke observed.

"Precisely," Mr Elliott agreed. "According to Mr Thurston, Mr Stone took seventy percent of all monies Mr Jerome extracted from Mr Benton."

"Why didn't Mr Thurston tell Miss Ilbert all this?" Mr Snyder enquired.

"He claimed he was frightened of Mr Stone," Mr Elliott replied. "He alleged Mr Stone had threatened him on several occasions."

"Perhaps, but I suspect another reason was his desire to retain Miss Ilbert's favour," Mr Locke said. "At the point at which she gave her ultimatum to the theatre company, she had agreed to put his play into production. If he had indeed revealed the extent of his knowledge about the blackmailing scheme to her, it is possible she would have seen his silence as a betrayal. Therefore, she would have withdrawn her offer to have his play performed and, possibly, dismissed Mr Thurston from the theatre company alongside Mr Stone."

"What did the sergeant think of their tales?" Mr Verity enquired.

"He thinks Mr Thurston is innocent of Miss Ilbert's murder, and he accepts his testimony as further evidence of Mr Stone's guilt in Miss Ilbert's murder," Mr Elliott replied.

"Are we in agreement with Sergeant Dixon about Mr Thurston's innocence?" Miss Trent enquired.

"If he was involved in the blackmailing scheme, it will be incredibly difficult for Mr Stone to prove without evidence," Mr Elliott said. "Personally, I suspect he was as involved as Mr Stone claims, but I doubt Mr Thurston will ever be brought to trial."

"In my opinion, Mr Thurston's temperament is far too nervous for cold-blooded murder," Mr Locke said.

Mr Heath looked thoughtful. "Yes. I'd agree. Given what I've seen of the man."

"Are we crossin' him off the list?" Mr Snyder enquired.

"I'd say so," Mr Elliott replied.

Miss Trent put a line through Mr Thurston's name.

"Returning to the question of Mr Stone's guilt." Mr Elliott consulted his notebook. "Mr Thurston's statement, alongside Mr Jerome and Miss Kimberly's, was sufficient to bring a charge of murder against Mr Stone, and he was formally arrested by Sergeant Dixon."

Mr Elliott glanced at the others. "To clarify, Miss Kimberly's statement concerns an admission she made to me earlier today, when we were alone in her office following my examination of the agreement she'd had with Miss Ilbert. Miss Kimberly alleged she'd seen Mr Stone leave the under-stage earlier, shortly before Miss Ilbert died. She claimed she'd kept silent about it because she feared people would accuse her of lying to remove her only rival for control of the *Crescent*." He consulted his notebook. "I'm satisfied the agreement was genuine. I compared Miss Ilbert's signature on it to a known sample of her signature provided by Mr Benton. It was a love letter she'd sent to him some weeks prior. They were identical."

"You suspect Mr Stone's motive was as we have previously discussed?" Mr Locke enquired.

"Yes," Mr Elliott replied. "He murdered her to avoid being exposed as the mastermind of the blackmailing scheme. In doing so, he also removed the threat of imminent dismissal for the entire theatre company and paved the way for Mr Gibb to assume control of the *Crescent* with Mr Stone's assistance." He looked to Mr Heath. "Did you call upon the *Royal Insurance Company* as arranged?"

"Yes, one moment," Mr Heath replied. Licking his index finger, he flipped through the pages of his notebook. "Here we are." He ran his finger down the page as he recounted his findings. "As we thought, the *Royal Insurance Company* procured the *National Fire Insurance Corporation Limited* who, in turn, had issued the insurance policy to Mr Stone for his theatre, *The Monolith*, in Woking, Surrey back in 1878. It took the clerks awhile to root through their archive, and I *assure* you their archive is *vast*! Why, I drank almost *six* cups of tea and ate almost a full bag of cherry drop sweets whilst I was waiting. Mr Greycloud, a *most* apt name for a man who works in fire insurance, wouldn't you say? Well, *he* came across the policy and was so very kind enough to permit me to borrow it to bring it to you all this evening." He pulled the document from his leather satchel and put it in the table's centre.

"Could you summarise it for us, please?" Miss Trent gently encouraged.

"Hm?" Mr Heath looked to her. "*Oh*! Yes, of course." He picked up the document and, clearing his throat, picked out the salient points. "The amount is seven pounds. It was issued in 1878 to Mr Ronald Stone. It insures against fire damage to the building and its contents. The building being *The Monolith Theatre* in Woking, Surrey." He put the document down and returned to his notes. "Mr Greycloud confirmed the policy was honoured and the monies awarded."

"Was there any suspicion of arson?" Mr Elliott enquired.

"The report from the time mentioned the possibility of an accelerant being responsible for the rapid spread of the fire," Mr Heath replied. "But *The Monolith* was still using a system of gas lighting at the time, so it was assumed it had caused the majority of the devastation."

"Whether arson could be proved or not is irrelevant, at least in the case of Miss Ilbert's death," Mr Elliott said. "The important point to make is: if she believed Mr Stone had started the fire at *The Monolith* deliberately and had confronted him about it, he could've taken her allegation seriously enough to perceive her as a further threat to his future. Therefore, the fire could've easily been yet another of his motives for her murder."

Mr Heath's eyes became bright with excitement. "Have we solved the case?"

"Yes," Mr Elliott replied.

"No," Mr Locke simultaneously replied.

"I beg your pardon?" Mr Elliott enquired, taken aback.

"We have not solved the case," Mr Locke replied and picked up the typed list of suspects. "There are two others on this list who we have yet to eliminate. Firstly, the veiled lady who purchased Miss Ilbert's archive from *The Era* newspaper. Secondly, Mr Darrel Howard Gibb."

"Mr Gibb can be ruled out immediately," Mr Elliott stated.

Mr Locke put down the list. "For what reason?"

"Several." Mr Elliott consulted his notebook. "His claim for control of the *Crescent* was rejected by the building's owner, Mr Kurtis, earlier today. More importantly however, he didn't arrive in England until the day after Miss Ilbert died."

"You are only partly correct," Mr Locke said.

Mr Elliott narrowed his eyes. "I was present in the meeting with Mr Kurtis."

"I am not referring to the lease agreement," Mr Locke said, allowing the weight of his words to hang in the air for a few moments before continuing. "But let us first discuss the veiled lady."

"She was an admirer of Miss Ilbert's who is irrelevant to the case," Mr Elliott stated.

"I do not agree," Mr Locke said. "Prior to your dramatic arrival at the *Crescent*, Miss Lily Ilbert claimed it was she who had purchased the archive. Yet—and I cannot claim any praise for this point as it was Mr Benton who asked the question, and an excellent one it was, too—

where did she find the money to make such a substantial purchase?"

Mr Heath raised his hand. "Savings?"

"On the small wage of an actress?" Mr Locke scoffed.

"She could've taken out a loan," Mr Elliott suggested.

"With what collateral, pray tell?" Mr Locke enquired. "She owns nothing."

"But the only other suspect it could've been is Miss Kimberly," Mr Elliott said. "Why would she purchase the archive?"

"I have not the faintest idea," Mr Locke replied.

Dr Locke stared at the list of suspects and furrowed her brow.

"But I am certain it was not Miss Lily," Mr Locke added.

"Even if it was Miss Kimberly, what relevance does the archive have on Miss Ilbert's murder?" Mr Elliott enquired.

"Perhaps she did not want Miss Ilbert's marriage to Mr Gibb to be known," Mr Locke suggested. "Speaking of which, did you find a record of their divorce?"

Mr Elliott frowned. "No."

"I see." Mr Locke lifted his chin as his eyes became curious. "How interesting."

"May we return to Mr Stone?" Mr Elliott enquired in a firm tone. "You're clearly unconvinced of his guilt, and I'd like to know why."

"Me, too," Mr Heath interjected.

"Me, three," Mr Verity added.

Mr Locke smiled. "Earlier today, when Mr Thurston said he could not find Mr Stone the night Miss Ilbert died, I saw Mr Stone exchange a knowing glance with Mr Gibb. This led me to enquire from Mr Gibb which day he had arrived in England. As you said, Mr Elliott, he claimed it was the day after Miss Ilbert's death. Furthermore, he had heard of her death from Mr Stone the same day. To satisfy my curiosity, how did you know his answer? You had already retired to Miss Kimberly's office."

"He heard me tell Miss Trent," Mr Verity volunteered.

"Yes, when we arrived tonight," Mr Elliott agreed.

"Ah yes, so you did." Mr Locke dismissed the matter with a small gesture. "Never mind." He leant forward. "As I was saying, I did not believe a word of Mr Gibb's account regarding his arrival." He sat back. "Therefore, with the unerring assistance of Mr Snyder, I sent a telegram to the parent company of the *White Star Line* in Liverpool. What was the name of it?"

"The *Oceanic Steam Navigation Company*," Mr Snyder replied.

Mr Locke snapped his fingers at him. "*Yes!*" He leant forward a second time and locked gazes with Mr Elliott. "I introduced myself and the Bow Street Society, outlined the context of my telegram, and asked four questions. One, the date Mr Gibb sailed into Southampton from New York City. Two, the name of the steamship he sailed in on. Three, the name, or names, of anyone travelling with him. Four, the address of the hotel in London he had his luggage sent to. Finally, I stressed the urgent nature of my telegram and expectation of a prompt response."

"And did you receive one?" Mr Elliott enquired.

"Certainly, I did." Mr Locke looked to his wife.

Dr Locke took a small envelope from her notebook and passed it to her husband.

Mr Locke removed the telegram from its envelope and read it aloud. It said:

```
DARREL  HOWARD  GIBB  SAILED
INTO    SOUTHAMPTON    ON
JANUARY          SEVENTEEN
EIGHTEEN NINETY-SEVEN ON
THE     ADRIATIC    STOP
TRAVELLING COMPANION WAS
MRS  RUTH  GIBB  WIFE  STOP
HOTEL  WAS  SAVOY  LONDON
STOP
```

"Mr Gibb sailed into Southampton three days prior to Miss Ilbert's death," Mr Locke said as he passed the telegram to Mr Elliott to read. "My wife and I took the liberty of calling upon Mr Gibb at the Savoy prior to our coming here. In light of the telegram, he admitted to arriving in England earlier than he had claimed but insisted he had no prior knowledge of Mr Stone's alleged plan to murder Miss Ilbert.

"Yet, he also insisted Mr Stone had met with him, in the lounge area of his hotel suite, on the night Miss Ilbert died. This was confirmed by Mrs Ruth Gibb who, by all appearances, had no knowledge of Miss Ilbert as Mr Gibb's first wife. To be certain, however, Lynette and I described Mr Stone to the doorman at the Savoy who confirmed the time Mr Stone had arrived at the hotel on the night Miss Ilbert died. It was the *precise* time she died."

"First wife?" Dr Colbert recalled Mr Elliott's answer about the divorce record. "Mr Gibb is a bigamist?"

"Yes," Mr Elliott replied. "But it only marginally affects his credibility as a witness." He frowned. "If Mr and Mrs Gibb are being truthful, and the doorman's testimony can be relied upon, Mr Stone has a strong alibi for the time of Miss Ilbert's murder."

Dr Locke furrowed her brow, again, as a theory formed in her mind.

"So does Mr Gibb," Mr Snyder pointed out.

Mr Elliott put down his pencil and sighed. "Neither could've committed the murder."

"Your reasoning was sound," Dr Colbert reassured.

"But based on incorrect information," Mr Elliott muttered as he took a sip of tea.

"Nevertheless, Mr Gibb exonerating Mr Stone presents another line of enquiry we must follow," Dr Locke mused aloud.

"Which is?" Mr Elliott enquired.

"Miss Kimberly," Dr Locke replied, meeting his gaze. "If Mr Stone was with Mr Gibb when Miss Ilbert died,

Miss Kimberly couldn't have seen him leave the under-stage area. Which can mean only one thing."

Mr Elliott's frown deepened. "She lied."

"Yes," Dr Locke felt the pieces of the puzzle fall into place. "And I think I know why." Her gaze slid to Mr Elliott. "But I shall need your help to prove it."

FIFTY-EIGHT

Thick, dark-grey clouds choked the sky, blocking out much of the mid-afternoon sun. The resultant gloom made everything feel small and enclosed, like the interior of a matchbox. It was the same in the Ilbert apartment, despite the open curtains. Before a large window in the morning room was a round table covered by a burgundy tablecloth and white lace. The upper body of the table's sole occupant was silhouetted against the subdued daylight coming through the window, as the pitter-patter of rain murmured through the cold air.

Sergeant Dixon opened the apartment's front door a few inches and peered inside. Initially thinking the room was empty, he stilled when he saw the silhouetted figure. It was his third surprise in a matter of moments. The first being the lack of response to his knocking, and the second being the fact the door was unlocked when he'd turned the knob. He held up his hand to signal to the others to wait in the corridor whilst he cautiously entered the room. The dim light and glare from the window made it difficult to distinguish any identifying features on the person sitting at the table. All he could say for certain was they were a woman. He therefore took a punt at the name, "Miss Ilbert?"

Miss Kimberly's emotionless voice responded, "She's in the bedroom."

Sergeant Dixon stopped halfway across the room. "Miss Kimberly?"

"If you wish to see Lily, you'll have to come back later," Miss Kimberly replied.

"Actually, it's you we want to talk to," Sergeant Dixon said.

"I thought you might." Miss Kimberly turned her head sideways, thereby allowing Sergeant Dixon to see her profile. "Who is 'we?'"

"Dr Locke, Mr Elliott, and me," Sergeant Dixon replied. "May we join you?"

Thunder rumbled in the distance.

"For a short while," Miss Kimberly replied.

Sergeant Dixon waved the Bow Streeters inside and approached the table.

"Sit. If you'd like," Miss Kimberly said.

Sergeant Dixon sat opposite her with his back to the window. Mr Elliott opted for the chair on the table's left side. It faced a second door that was also ajar. Light shone through the gap from the morning room, and, in it, he could see the foot of a bed with feminine-looking feet lying upon it. Meanwhile, Dr Locke closed the front door and sat in the remaining chair opposite Mr Elliott. Although she had her back to the second door, the mirror on the wall above the fireplace gave her an uninterrupted view of its top half.

Arranged on the table before Miss Kimberly was a small china teapot with a blue painted design, a matching sugar bowl filled with white granules, and a full teacup on a petite saucer. The design of the teacup and saucer matched the teapot and sugar bowl. Casting her eye over the items, Dr Locke was struck by the absence of a second teacup. After all, wouldn't Miss Kimberly be expecting Miss Lily to join her?

Sergeant Dixon took out his notebook. "May we ask you a few questions?"

The first in Mr Elliott's mind was why neither woman had answered the door despite Sergeant Dixon's loud knocking. Keenly aware they were only permitted to be present for as long as Sergeant Dixon's good humour lasted, though, he decided to remain silent.

"Not if they concern a certain stage manager." Miss Kimberly's expression was plain as she sat rigid in the chair with her hands resting on her lap and a faraway look in her eyes.

"I'm going to have to insist," Sergeant Dixon said.

"You shouldn't have withdrawn the charge of murder against him," Miss Kimberly stated. "You've ruined everything."

Sergeant Dixon parted his lips to remind her the blackmail charge remained intact. He changed his mind when he realised it was unlikely to go to trial, however. Mr Jerome's dubious character and Mr Stone's allegation about Mr Thurston's involvement meant the credibility of the witness testimonies was in question.

"Sergeant Dixon can't ignore the testimonies of Mr Gibb, the second Mrs Gibb, and the doorman at the *Savoy* which all state Mr Stone was at the hotel at the time of Miss Mina Ilbert's death," Mr Elliott explained. "Nor the fact you lied in your statement."

Miss Kimberly slowly turned her head toward the solicitor but spoke to the air rather than making direct eye contact with him. "I had no choice. He was seducing Lily. He is old enough to be her father; it's disgusting. I couldn't allow it to continue." She slowly turned her head back toward Sergeant Dixon but looked beyond him at the window, "And it wouldn't have, if the Bow Street Society hadn't meddled."

"We aren't in the business of allowing innocent people to be hung for murder because the truth is inconvenient for the guilty," Mr Elliott stated.

Miss Kimberly turned her head sharply to glare at him. "She's only a *child*."

"She's eighteen," Dr Locke said. "Many women are married with children at her age."

Miss Kimberly turned her glare upon Dr Locke. "What do *you* know of *motherhood*?"

"More than you think," Dr Locke countered. "For example, I know Miss Mina Ilbert wasn't Miss Lily's mother."

Miss Kimberly turned her head back toward the window as the cords in her neck became visible with the clenching of her jaw.

Dr Locke opened her notebook at a bookmarked page. "There were several instances which alluded to the truth, but whose significance I failed to recognise until recently. Instance one: when I asked you if Miss Mina Ilbert had included her daughter in her threat of dismissing the theatre company, your response was 'she threatened to dismiss Miss Lily if the conspirators didn't come forward, yes.'

"Instance two: when I showed the newspaper announcement and parish record of Miss Mina Ilbert's marriage to Mr Darrel Howard Gibb, Miss Lily asked you why she wasn't told about the marriage. Your response to her was 'Your mother was married to Julian Raine. Your father.' You also asked me why I'd sought out the records, and whether I'd done so to discredit you. One may only be discredited if one is caught out in a lie.

"As I said before, I hadn't realised the significance of these two instances until recently. You *had* been caught out in a lie but not the one we'd assumed. You hadn't lied about the marriage; how could you lie to Miss Lily about something she knew nothing about? No, you'd lied about the identity of Miss Lily's mother." She looked to the policeman. "If you noticed, Sergeant, Miss Kimberly didn't refer to Miss Mina as Miss Lily's mother in either of these two instances."

Mr Elliott put his satchel upon his lap and, opening it, took out two documents which he passed to Dr Locke who, in turn, passed them to Sergeant Dixon.

"These are the records of Mr Julian Raine's marriage in 1877 and Miss Lily's birth in 1878," Dr Locke said.

Miss Kimberly darted her gaze between Dr Locke and the documents.

"The bride and mother were not Miss Mina," Dr Locke continued. "They were you." She took the documents from Sergeant Dixon and put them in the middle of the table. "Miss Emmaline Kimberly."

Miss Kimberly's gaze locked upon the documents as her lips formed a thin line.

"We found them at Somerset House this morning," Mr Elliott explained.

"You and Miss Mina Ilbert have lied to Miss Lily her whole life," Dr Locke said. "She thought Miss Mina had married her father but, after her death, you remembered the announcement of Miss Mina's marriage to Mr Gibb in 1880. You couldn't risk Miss Lily discovering the truth, so you purchased the archive from *The Era* newspaper, but you didn't know the *Gaslight Gazette* had also carried the story. Furthermore, you were unaware *The Era* had also sent copies of those published editions to the British Museum."

Miss Kimberly first turned one record over, then the other. "You know nothing."

Dr Locke adopted a gentle tone. "You did all of it to protect your child."

Miss Kimberly lowered her head as she spooned the white granules from the sugar bowl into her tea and stirred.

Dr Locke consulted her notebook. "Instance three: you told Mr Verity, 'Mina was as good as holding a gun to our heads with her ultimatum' and 'murder is never the preferred option, Mr Verity, but, sometimes, circumstances make it the *only* option.' At the time, I thought you were being melodramatic. Now I see you were not only confessing but attempting to justify your actions." Her tone hardened. "You murdered Miss Mina to prevent her from executing her threat of dismissing your daughter alongside the rest of the theatre company. You altered the metal plate, and you flipped the switch when she stepped on it during her performance." Disgust entered her voice as she added, "You must have listened to her suffering from your hiding place beneath the stage."

Miss Kimberly turned hard eyes upon Dr Locke. "Mina *stole* Lily from me."

Sergeant Dixon and Mr Elliott exchanged concerned glances.

Dr Locke read aloud from her notebook. "'*I* have known what it is to be destitute, Mr Verity. To be cold, dirty, and starving. People turn their backs upon your suffering. They say your sins have brought misfortune upon you, and demand you break your back for a meagre hunk of stale bread. Anyone not sick in mind would be desperate to spare themselves from such a fate.'" Her gaze slid back to Miss Kimberly. "When your husband died in the fire at *The Monolith Theatre*, you were left destitute and pregnant with his child. Mr Stone, I assume, offered no compensation for the damage the fire rendered to your voice, making you unable to earn a living from the stage as you once did."

"The *snake* wouldn't even hold a benefit for the families of those who'd died," Miss Kimberly said. "Despite everyone *knowing* he'd set the theatre alight for the insurance money."

"But Miss Mina offered you a way to escape destitution?" Mr Elliott ventured.

Miss Kimberly glared at him. "She told me my child would be raised in a warm and loving home, and I'd be given the means by which to support myself. I *thought* she was being kind. But as soon as Lily was born, Mina had her ushered away and brought here, to her home. I tried to get Lily back—I begged and pleaded with Mina, but she kept saying we had an agreement. *She* was to raise *my* child as her own, and *I* would work as her business manager. How could a position in a theatre replace my child?!"

"Yet, you had no money and couldn't contest the arrangement," Mr Elliott said.

"No, and she made sure I never did," Miss Kimberly said.

"Which you, understandably, resented," Dr Locke said. "To Miss Lily, you weren't her mother, but an aunt."

"*Aunt Emma*," Miss Kimberly spat. "How I *loathed* the title, especially when it came from my daughter's lips. Yet, I tolerated it, and Mina's treatment of me in front of Lily, simply to keep the right to be in my daughter's life." She lifted her chin and swallowed against her rising anger.

"When Mina forbade me from comforting Lily and dismissed me from the dressing room like a servant, my tolerance finally ended. I resolved to remove her toxic influence from our lives permanently. Her ultimatum was further reason to set my plan into motion."

Sergeant Dixon's complexion had turned greyer with each word she'd uttered.

"Haven't you something to say, Sergeant?" Mr Elliott encouraged.

Sergeant Dixon looked at him and, for a moment, stared at him in dumb confusion. His thoughts then snapped back into focus, and he realised what the solicitor was alluding to. "Yes." He cleared his throat. "Miss Kimberly, I must tell you, after what you've told me, I have no choice but to take you to Vine Street for formal questioning."

Miss Kimberly drank her tea in one swallow. Before she'd even put the cup down, her face had flushed a bright red, and her fingers were reaching for the collar of her blouse. Her whole body tensed, causing the cup to tip over, as she gasped for air.

Recognising the symptoms of poisoning, Dr Locke leapt to her feet. "Fetch me some salt water!"

Mr Elliott stood, but it was already too late.

Miss Kimberly slumped back in her chair as her limp arms slipped away from her body and dangled at her sides.

Dr Locke held the back of her hand against Miss Kimberly's lips but felt no warmth or movement of air against her skin. Next, she put her fingertips against the main artery in Miss Kimberly's neck. Feeling no hint of a heartbeat, Dr Locke gave a subtle shake of her head. "She's dead."

"*What*?" Sergeant Dixon stood, visibly shaken. "How?"

Dr Locke picked up the teacup and sugar bowl. Wafting each under her nose in turn, she detected the faint scent of bitter almonds. "Tests should be conducted on the remaining tea leaves and sugar bowl to be certain, but I suspect she poisoned herself with cyanide."

"Dear God." Sergeant Dixon sat like a sack of potatoes.

"I'm surprised Miss Lily didn't wake up," Mr Elliott remarked.

The Bow Streeters locked eyes as a chilling possibility entered their minds.

Dr Locke bolted across the room. "Where is the bedroom?"

Mr Elliott ran after her. "Through there." He pointed at the second door.

Dr Locke threw open the door but halted at the sight that confronted her.

Wrapped in a blanket upon the bed was the body of Miss Lily Ilbert.

EPILOGUE

FURTHER HEARTBREAK FOR THE CRESCENT

The *Crescent Theatre* company have endured a second tragedy mere days after the violent death of its manager and leading actress Miss Mina Ilbert, known to many as Lily of the Lyceum. The theatre's business manager Miss Emmaline Kimberly and the promising young actress Miss Lily Ilbert died last night in what is thought to be a case of murder-suicide.

"We can't be sure until after the postmortems, but we suspect both women died from cyanide poisoning," Detective Sergeant Keith Dixon of the Metropolitan Police informed your correspondent. "We're seeking no one else in connection with these deaths."

Circumstances surrounding the deaths remain unclear, but your ever-diligent correspondent can confirm the police have reclassified the death of Miss Mina Ilbert as murder. They have also closed the case, citing Miss Kimberly as the individual responsible.

Your correspondent can also reveal Mr Ronald Stone, stage manager at the *Crescent Theatre*, has been questioned in connection with the extortion of lead actor Mr Luthor Ellis Benton. Notorious extortionist of theatrical artistes in the

West Midlands, Mr Jack Jerome, is said to also be involved.

A formal statement issued by Mr Benton this afternoon revealed he has assumed the position of manager at the *Crescent*. Furthermore, prompter and super master Mr Morris Thurston has accepted Mr Benton's offer of becoming the *Crescent*'s new business manager.

According to theatre sources, D H Gibb, who had laid claim to the building's lease agreement following Miss Mina Ilbert's death, is to leave for New York City in the coming days.

"What a waste," Inspector Conway mumbled with a small shake of his head as he put down the evening edition of the *Gaslight Gazette*. Sitting at his kitchen table, he addressed Miss Trent who occupied the chair diagonal to his own, "She could of just told Miss Lily the truth."

"She might have, before she poisoned her." Miss Trent watched him put a cigarette between his lips and light it with a match. "Unfortunately, we'll never know the whole story."

Inspector Conway discarded the spent match into the fire behind him. "Was Miss Kimberly expectin' Sergeant Dixon and the Society to turn up?"

"We don't think so."

"Was there a note?" Inspector Conway took a pull from the cigarette and exhaled the smoke away from the clerk.

"No. Sergeant Dixon, Mr Elliott, and Dr Locke went over the apartment with a fine-tooth comb."

Inspector Conway frowned. "It don't make sense. Why kill Miss Lily?"

"Based upon what she told Sergeant Dixon, Mr Elliott, and Dr Locke, we believe she was trying to protect

Miss Lily from Mr Stone. When Sergeant Dixon dropped the murder charge against Mr Stone, Miss Kimberly must have realised questions were being asked about her statement. If she was arrested for Miss Mina Ilbert's murder, and Mr Stone was released, it would leave Miss Lily vulnerable to his inappropriate advances." Miss Trent had a sip of tea. "Personally, I believe Miss Kimberly couldn't bear the thought of losing her daughter all over again, so she decided to take her with her."

"Yeah, maybe." Inspector Conway took another pull from his cigarette.

Miss Trent stood and, picking up her coat from the back of her chair, opened the pocket concealed within its lining. From it, she took a file that she passed across to him. "The final case report for Richard. I would like to see him, if it at all possible."

"I'll see what 'e says." Inspector Conway opened the file and cast a cursory glance over its contents. "I noticed there was nothin' about the Society in the 'paper."

"No," Miss Trent sat. "We agreed to suppress our presence for Sergeant Dixon's sake."

Inspector Conway thought it would've been nice if they'd done him the same courtesy but left it unsaid.

"Nevertheless, heated words were exchanged between Sergeant Dixon and Inspector Witherspoon when Sergeant Dixon returned to Vine Street with Mr Elliott and Dr Locke in tow," Miss Trent added.

Inspector Conway set the report aside. "I heard Witherspoon's had a dressin' down for not lookin' into Miss Mina Ilbert's death 'imself."

"But surely the fact Sergeant Dixon successfully solved the case should go in Sergeant Dixon's favour?"

"It should." Inspector Conway crushed out his cigarette on an old saucer. "If it does, is another question." He had a mouthful of tea. "What about Aaron Willis? What's happened to 'im?"

"He called in this afternoon to thank us. Mr Benton has exonerated him of any wrongdoing and reinstated his employment as chief electric man."

"Good," Inspector Conway glanced at the article. "And Jerome?"

"Sergeant Dixon expects him and Mr Stone to be given a month's hard labour by the magistrate," Miss Trent replied. "Mr Stone tried pointing the finger at Mr Thurston, but Mr Jerome's statement didn't corroborate his allegation." She pushed a strand of hair behind her ear. "We considered Mr Thurston a suspect in Miss Mina Ilbert's murder for a time, because of his close relationship with Miss Kimberly and the ultimatum. It turns out he knew all along Miss Kimberly was Miss Lily's mother, but he'd kept silent about it at Miss Kimberly's request. Sergeant Dixon thinks he's too nervous a person to commit cold-blooded murder, though, even on behalf of the woman he says he loved. We're inclined to agree as we'd already reached the same conclusion."

"Life in the theatre sounds as messy as life on the streets, if you ask me."

"It is." Miss Trent smiled. "It's one of the many things I love about it."

Inspector Conway finished his tea and glanced at her mug. "Fancy another cuppa?"

Miss Trent considered the offer. "I'd better not. Sam's waiting with the cab on the next street over."

Mirth danced upon Inspector Conway's lips. "Did you really drive here?"

Miss Trent lofted an eyebrow. "Don't sound too surprised."

"I'm not. I just don't peg you as the drivin' sort."

"Because I'm a woman?"

"Because you don't like gettin' your clothes dirty."

"I don't mind if they're the appropriate clothes."

Inspector Conway's smile grew. "I wouldn't want to get in your cab."

Miss Trent sat bolt upright. "And *why* not? I'm an *excellent* driver."

Inspector Conway chuckled, winced at the pain in his ribs, and chuckled some more.

Realising he was pulling her leg, Miss Trent gave him a gentle push. "Cheeky sod."

"I couldn't help it. You make it too easy."

"Only because I never know if you're being serious or not."

Inspector Conway continued to smile as he stood and, wrapping a cloth around the handle of the kettle, lifted it from its hook over the open fire to pour over the damp tea leaves in his mug.

Miss Trent watched him as her thoughts drifted to their mutual friend. He hadn't been mentioned since she'd arrived, but she wasn't sure whether it was because neither had news, or because neither wanted to broach a painful subject. Knowing it had to be, regardless of their feelings, she waited until Inspector Conway sat before enquiring in a cautious tone, "John… have you or Richard seen Dr Weeks since he was admitted?"

Inspector Conway's expression turned sombre. "No." He glanced at her as he added cream and sugar to his tea. "Have you?"

"No."

Inspector Conway rested his lower arm upon the table and, watching his tea as he stirred it, said quietly, "Probably for the best." His mind replayed the night he'd dragged Dr Weeks into Bethlehem Hospital, and a pang of guilt tore through his heart.

"I suppose so." Miss Trent watched him with worried eyes. "Will you let me know if you do see him?"

"Yeah." Inspector Conway had a large mouthful of tea. "Has O'Hannigan been back?"

"No." Miss Trent rested her folded arms upon the table. "Thankfully."

"And she's not run off with 'im?"

"Not as far as I know." Miss Trent eyed him with curiosity. "Why?"

Inspector Conway met her gaze. "I saw her with a bag on Bow Street. I asked her where she was goin', and she wouldn't tell me, so I got the bag off her and had a look. It was full of her clothes. She said she was goin' to pawn them to get some housekeepin' money for you."

"I've not had any of it." A hint of a frown touched Miss Trent's features as another possibility occurred to her. "I hope she's not planning on giving it to him to apologise for me throwing him out the other night."

"She's mad if she is."

Miss Trent released a soft sigh. "She's mad already for starting an affair with him."

"And heartless for carryin' it on."

Miss Trent frowned but couldn't disagree or defend her former lover. Therefore, she decided to change the subject to something less personal. "What do you know about Inspector Lee?"

"Is she carryin' on with 'im, too?"

"No, this has nothing to do with Miss Hicks."

Inspector Conway eyed her with suspicion. "Then why are you askin' about 'im?"

Miss Trent adopted a hard tone. "I'm tired of him and his officers hounding me and the members. I've tried to rise above it, to be professional, but it's only grown worse since he became head of the Mob Squad."

Inspector Conway downcast his eyes. "That wasn't my doin'."

"I know it wasn't." Miss Trent put her hand on his arm. "But it doesn't stop us from feeling frustrated with the situation. So," she withdrew her hand, "me and Mr Elliott have decided to do a little investigating of our own. Namely into Inspector Lee and his personal life. If he has any skeletons hidden away, we want to find them."

Inspector Conway met her gaze. "And get 'im thrown out of the police?"

"Yes, if it protects the Bow Street Society."

Inspector Conway sat back in his chair. "I don't know nothin' about Lee, apart from 'e was at Chiswick High Road and become a copper a few years after me."

Miss Trent studied him intently. "Why do I get the feeling you're not being entirely honest with me?"

Inspector Conway's expression and voice cooled. "You're askin' a copper about another copper, what did you think I was gonna say?"

"For an *incredibly* good reason."

Inspector Conway folded his arms. "I'm not gonna help you ruin a copper."

"Even if the copper is Inspector Gideon Lee?"

"*I'm* keepin' an eye on him. If he does sumin', I'll report it to Richard."

"And, in the meantime, we're supposed to just let him invade our lives?"

"As long as you're doin' what you should, Lee's guard's not up. 'E's bound to make a mistake eventually and, when 'e does, I'll be there to bring 'im down."

Miss Trent frowned. As much as she respected Inspector Conway, she knew it could be weeks, if not months, before his opportunity came. Adopting a calm tone, she said, "John, I appreciate everything you're doing but, surely, even you can see how likely it is we'll lose members if Inspector Lee's harassment is allowed to continue?" She put her hand on his arm again. "All I'm asking is for you to find out when he joined the police, where, and when he was born, whether he has any family, that sort of thing."

"You don't know what you're askin', Rebecca. If I'm caught with my nose in files it's got no right to be in, they'll cut it off."

"The survival of the Bow Street Society relies upon us finding out as much as we can about Inspector Lee. *Please*, John. You know I wouldn't ask if I had any other choice."

Numerous consequences whirled around Inspector Conway's mind as he looked in Miss Trent's pleading eyes. "I'll have to tell Richard."

"I'd be surprised if you didn't."

"Okay," Inspector Conway said through a loud sigh. "I'll try."

"Thank you."

"But I'm not promisin' anythin'. If I can't look at the file, I'm not pushin' it."

"Of course."

* * *

It was approaching seven thirty when Mr Elliott checked his pocket watch and considered whether to leave his office to find supper or work late. He had a new case to prepare for, but the date of the first hearing wasn't for another couple of weeks. Sitting back in his chair, he looked through the open doorway of his office and felt his heart sink upon seeing Inspector Lee. Mr Elliott's legal clerk, Mr Daventry attempted to intercept the policeman, but he simply walked around him and into Mr Elliott's office.

"I'm sorry, sir," Mr Daventry said as he followed. "I told him we were closed."

"It's all right," Mr Elliott said. "Please finish closing. This shan't take long."

"Yes, sir," Mr Daventry left the office.

Mr Elliott was grateful for Mr Daventry's presence. He couldn't trust himself to be alone with Inspector Lee anymore, a fact he found equally galling and unpleasant. Inspector Lee had awoken feelings he'd spent years burying, and the policeman's questionable character made it even more unpalatable. Deciding a formal approach would be best, he kept his expression emotionless as he enquired in a plain tone, "May I help you, Inspector?"

"Someone important to me is ignoring my telephone calls and messages." Inspector Lee approached the desk. "I was hoping you could remedy the situation."

"Perhaps they have good reason to ignore you."

Inspector Lee moved around the desk. "It did occur to me." He sat upon the edge of the desk, slightly to the left, facing Mr Elliott. "I wondered if they were embarrassed about a liaison they'd had in Birmingham."

Mr Elliott realised Inspector Lee must've spoken to Inspector Donahue whilst the latter was in London. Feeling annoyed at himself for not anticipating the possibility sooner and embarrassed by Inspector Lee knowing what had transpired between him and Mrs Jerome in Birmingham, he pursed his lips and cooled his gaze in a subtle but unmistakable glare.

Inspector Lee stood and, moving behind Mr Elliott, looked out the window. "I was surprised to learn who the liaison was with," he said in a low voice. "Given what I know about this person's preferences."

Mr Elliott remained facing the door, despite Inspector Lee's scent wafting past his nose. It was the same scent he'd smelt the night they'd kissed. Feeling an intense but unwelcome spark of desire at the memory, he tried to think of something dull, like accounting.

"But then I learned the liaison was part of a ruse and, suddenly, all made sense again." Inspector Lee put his hand on Mr Elliott's shoulder from behind. "But they've continued to ignore my telephone calls and messages." He moved directly behind Mr Elliott and put his other hand on his opposite shoulder. "What do you recommend I do next?"

Mr Elliott shrugged off his hands. "Maybe they just don't want any contact with you."

Inspector Lee released a soft sound of amusement and strode across the room. As Mr Daventry stood from his desk to greet him, he said, "Mr Elliott is working late. He said you may go."

"But—" Mr Daventry began.

Inspector Lee cut off his words by closing and locking the door, however.

"You have no right to give orders to my employees," Mr Elliott said.

Inspector Lee waited and listened. Only when he heard the outer door open and close did he look over his shoulder at Mr Elliott. "I think you'd agree it was necessary." He returned to the desk. "Especially since you can't trust yourself to be alone with me anymore."

Mr Elliott swallowed hard.

Inspector Lee put his hands upon the desk and leant forward so their faces were mere inches apart. "The truth is: I don't trust myself to be alone with you either."

"I want you to leave. Right now."

"And I want you on this desk, but we can't all get what we want."

Mr Elliott frowned. "Say what you suggest is true. Say I don't trust myself with you, how is coming to my place of work to confront me about it going to help matters?"

"I don't know, but I've succeeded in seeing you, which is half the battle these days."

Mr Elliott stood, obliging Inspector Lee to straighten. "You must leave me alone, Gideon. This, whatever it is, isn't good for either of us."

"But it's good enough for you and Dr Colbert?"

Mr Elliott looked confused. "What has Dr Colbert got to do with it?"

A hint of jealousy entered Inspector Lee's voice. "I saw you alighting from his carriage the other night."

"We'd attended a Bow Street Society meeting."

"And the regular afternoon teas? Were they Bow Street Society meetings, too?"

"Dr Colbert is a friend. Nothing more."

Inspector Lee hummed, but the look in his eyes showed he was unconvinced.

Mr Elliott suddenly felt uneasy. "It's time you were leaving."

Inspector Lee moved around the desk, obliging Mr Elliott to turn to face him as he came up behind him again. Stepping forward to keep Mr Elliott between the desk and himself, he immediately pressed his lips against his. Feeling Mr Elliott's hand pressing against his chest, he pushed it away and leant forward, obliging Mr Elliott to bend backward and put his hands down on the desk to steady himself. At the same time, Inspector Lee's tongue pressed against Mr Elliott's lips, demanding entry.

Mr Elliott initially resisted but, upon being encouraged into his new position, breathed in sharply as he felt Inspector Lee's body pressed against his own. Parting his lips as a consequence, he felt Inspector Lee's tongue slip inside, prompting a hard shiver to course through his body. His thoughts snapped back to the liaison with Mrs Jerome. He'd been playing a part to entrap her and Mr Jerome. He wished he was playing a part with Inspector Lee, too, but his emotional and physical reactions to the older man were all too genuine. Their strength had increased with each moment of closeness Inspector Lee had stolen with him and now, as he was kissed, Mr Elliott felt the last of his walls crumble. Gripping the back of Inspector Lee's head to keep him close, he returned his kiss with equal passion and pulled him down with him as he laid upon the desk.

* * *

"You realise you're being utterly unreasonable, don't you?" Dr Colbert enquired.

"I don't think I am," Inspector Woolfe replied.

They sat on either side of Dr Colbert's desk, but the gulf between them felt so great, they might as well have been sitting on either side of the Thames.

"Precisely what are you accusing me of, Inspector?"

"You've spent a lot of time with the Bow Street Society. Maybe you've started to come around to their way of thinking but, not wanting to upset the apple cart with me, pretended to get the address."

"There was nothing 'pretend' about the tremendous risk I took."

"As you say, but I only have your word for it."

Dr Colbert furrowed his brow and narrowed his eyes. "I retrieved the address using the method we agreed and at the time we agreed. It's not my fault it didn't lead anywhere."

"It led somewhere: the bloody telegraph office," Inspector Woolfe growled, which immediately brought on a coughing fit.

If the atmosphere wasn't so tense, Dr Colbert might've found the whole thing laughable. They'd both thought they'd struck gold when he'd retrieved J. Pettifoot's address of 42 Kennington Road, Lambeth from Miss Trent's filing cabinet, only for Inspector Woolfe to be met with a telegraph office when he'd paid the location a visit.

"It *was* the address on J. Pettifoot's card," Dr Colbert insisted as he watched Inspector Woolfe take a swig of medicine. "It was the *only* address."

Red-faced and sweating from the exertion of coughing, Inspector Woolfe demanded, "Why would Miss Trent have the address of a telegraph office on the card of the Society's suspected founder?"

"I don't know, but I swear to you, Inspector, I have *not* cheated you."

Inspector Woolfe pocketed the bottle of medicine as he studied Dr Colbert's face. Upon finding no hint of deception, he allowed himself to entertain the possibility he was telling the truth. In which case, they were no further along than they were before. "All right. I believe you."

Dr Colbert visibly relaxed. "Thank you."

"But I still don't like it."

"Nor do I," Dr Colbert admitted. "It's clear someone has gone to a great deal of trouble to not only conceal J.

Pettifoot's identity, but also the means by which they could be identified."

"Yeah; J. Pettifoot, probably."

Dr Colbert hummed in agreement as his face creased into a frown.

Inspector Woolfe rubbed his tired eyes. "I'll put a couple of plain-clothed lads on duty at the telegraph office in case J. Pettifoot turns up. It's all I can do for now."

Dr Colbert considered the problem. "There may be something else we can try." At Inspector Woolfe's questioning look, he added, "Sending a telegram to J. Pettifoot via the telegraph office and lying in wait for them to collect it."

Inspector Woolfe raised his bushy eyebrows. "Send a telegram to…?" His features slowly lifted as his mind processed the proposal. "We'd have to ask the clerk to give us a signal when J. Pettifoot arrived but," he gave a yellow-toothed smile, "yeah, I think it could work." He shook Dr Colbert's hand. "Let's do it."

Enjoyed the book?
Please consider writing a review

Discover more at www.bowstreetsociety.com

GLOSSARY OF TERMS

Actor's Bible	*The Era* newspaper
Athletic Droll	A comic performer of the music halls whose songs were interspersed with gymnastic feats.
Beef-headed	Stupid
Beer-eater	Large consumer of beer.
Blowsa-bella	A vulgar, self-assertive woman
Blue Pencil (To).	Cut down literature.
Born with a sneer	An implacable critic
Bug (To)	Abbreviation of bug-bear; a nuisance
Bum-Boozer	A desperate drinker.
Cabbage (The)	Savoy Theatre
Cannot show itself	Not equal to
Captain Macfluffer	Sudden loss of memory on the stage
Copping the brewery	To get drunk.
Cove	Individual.

Front	To cause outrage.
Knee-trembler	Sexual act conducted whilst standing.
Mandrake	A homosexual man.
Nark (Copper's)	A policeman's civilian spy.
Posser	A short stick used for stirring clothes in a washtub.
Round the Wrekin	Taking a long time to get to the point.
Shipwrecked	Drunk.
Strumpet	Prostitute.
Supers	Super-numerary actors, i.e., extras
Super Master	Manager of the super-numerary actors
Tararabit	Goodbye for now.
Toff	Someone who is wealthy, well-dressed or from a high social class.
Two inches above upright	Hypocritical liar
Tuppeny 'apenny one	A very poor and common sort.

Wench Term of endearment for a woman.

Notes from the author

Spoiler Alert

Before I begin, I feel I must address the proverbial elephant in the room. At the point of writing, it has been two years since the publication of the last Bow Street Society mystery, *The Case of the Pugilist's Ploy*. I apologise for the delay between instalments, as I've always aimed to release one a year. I've had difficult circumstances to deal with in my personal life, including the loss of my mum and working three consecutive jobs. I'm hopeful 2025 will bring calm to my personal life, so I may give greater focus to my writing and related projects. Another reason for the delay in publishing *The Case of The Fatal Flaw* was my determination to ensure I didn't shortchange the reader. Many I've spoken to about the books have expressed how they enjoy the characters' stories as much as the mysteries (if not more). Therefore, I didn't want to rush the process of writing this book and end up with something that was less than good enough. I hope, by giving myself the time I needed, I've delivered a seventh instalment worthy of my readers' love and praise.

New book, new year

With the seventh book in the series comes a brand-new year. Whereas the events between *The Case of the Curious Client* and *The Case of the Pugilist's Ploy* occurred in 1896, *The Case of The Fatal Flaw* begins in January 1897. I've always been mindful of allowing time to move forward in my books as I think this helps to strengthen the sense of time and place in the reader's mind. At present, the tenth instalment will conclude in 1897, but this might change if my characters decide they have other ideas.

Choosing a title

The Case of The Fatal Flaw was the third incarnation of the title for this book. The first was *The Case of The Deadly Dance*. I rejected this option as I didn't think it sounded catchy or dramatic enough.

The second incarnation was *The Case of The Fatal Finale*. This sounded catchy and dramatic but encountered a new problem. Despite this being only the seventh instalment out of a planned ten, my beta readers' initial reaction to the title was "is this the last one?" I realised the inclusion of the word 'finale' made the title misleading.

I finally settled on *The Case of The Fatal Flaw* because I liked how it was a play on words. Not only was the 'fatal flaw' the flaw in Miss Mina Ilbert's character, but it could also be heard as 'floor' when said aloud. As Miss Mina Ilbert is murdered by stepping onto an electrified metal plate, I thought this was rather apt.

Inspirations from Nineteenth Century Theatre

In the nineteenth century, there were female managers of theatres as well as male. Often, these managers were also performers who'd undertaken a theatre as a means of providing themselves with regular work (as they could put themselves in the starring roles). Unlike today, there were no funds or grants theatres could apply for to survive. The box office either made or broke a theatre, and the pantomime, which traditionally ran from Boxing Day until its popularity waned (sometimes months later), was the most lucrative time in a theatre's program. It was the manager's job to oversee all aspects of a theatre, including its finances and rehearsals. Some establishments secured additional funding by taking rental payments from companies who provided drinks and limited refreshments to audience members on the premises.

When the Bow Street Society enquires after what happened directly following Miss Mina Ilbert's death on stage, the Society is informed a police constable was sent to fetch Detective Sergeant Keith Dixon from Vine Street police station. The police constable in question is one assigned to the Crescent Theatre specifically. As in the real-life case of the Queen's Theatre in Long Acre, Covent Garden paying the Metropolitan Police directly for the use of Constable Bampton in 1871, the Crescent Theatre would've had a similar arrangement with C (or St. James') Division. Given London's theatrical West End would've fallen under this division's jurisdiction, DS Dixon would've been a familiar figure to the theatre managers and performers, hence why he is asked for by name. The fact a detective sergeant, and not a detective inspector, is assigned to investigate Miss Mina's death, is as suggestive of the commonality of tragic accidents within the theatre as it is of the police's attitude toward the case.

Mr Ellis Benton alludes to this heightened safety risk when he speaks of having witnessed someone being electrocuted on stage before. This is based on the real-life death of euphonium player Augustino Bierdermann. Whilst performing under the name of Mr Bruno in the orchestra at the Holte Theatre in Birmingham in January 1880 during the run of its pantomime, *Sleeping Beauty*, Bierdermann put his hands on the brass connections of the wires for the electric lighting. These wires led along the passage from the orchestra pit to the stage. Due to the lights being off at the time, Bierdermann was delivered the full force of the light's electric current, and he was said to have fallen back, unconscious. Tragically, he died before help arrived.

The lighting effect that is altered to cause Miss Mina's death, is based upon the real-life effect utilised by Miss Navette in her Danse Electrique at the Alhambra music hall in 1893. Like Miss Mina, she had metal plates on her shoes which were connected to wires running throughout her costume. These wires led to little lamps on her dress, in the flowers she carried, and the points of her parasol. When she stepped onto metal plates on the stage, the plates on her feet made contact with the sub-stage storage battery, thereby causing the lamps in her costume to light up.

Mr Heath enquires about the "candlepower" of the auditorium's lighting as this was the customary unit of measurement at the time. It wasn't until the 11th General Conference on Weights and Measurements in 1960 the Watt was accepted as a unit of measurement on the list of International System of Units (SI). Hence why it isn't applied within the context of 1897 in the book.

Her Majesty's theatre in 1897 had a switchboard that allowed a dimmer scale of 1 to 10; a stark contrast to the Off, ¼, ½, ¾ and On of the majority of controls for gas-lighting.

Electric lighting was confined to public buildings and wealthy households until after the First World War. Therefore, late-nineteenth century theatres were certainly ahead of their time. Yet, they continued to lack confidence in the new technology. As stated by Miss Kimberly in the book, most mimicked the Crescent's caution by maintaining their gas-lighting system as a back-up in case the electric system failed. Electricity supplied by an external company was also a relatively new thing, with publicly accessible electricity only being introduced in the 1890s.

I chose to use the words 'Electric Man' in the book as I thought they sounded more authentic to the period than 'electrician.' The 'chief' element of Mr Aaron Willis' job title is a reference to theatres of the period having a 'chief' (or head) assigned to each backstage area, e.g., carpenters, fly men, etc. These chiefs would report directly to the stage manager on behalf of their area.

Unlike modern day theatres, nineteenth century theatres adhered to the practise of keeping the house lights lit during a performance. Although some theatre managers were deviating from this by the end of the century, either for certain parts of the performance or certain types of production, e.g., comedies, it wasn't until the twentieth century when the industry standard shifted to complete darkness during all performances.

It must also be noted, whenever a manager lowered the lighting during a performance, it was often met with disdain by theatregoers and critics alike. For many, attending the theatre was seen more as an opportunity to acquire gossip than to watch a prestigious play or opera. Put simply, if the house lights were off, audience members couldn't see the man Lady Blackwood was with (who wasn't her husband), or what fashions other ladies were wearing. The theatre was also seen as an opportunity to socialise, with audience members continuing their conversations at a less-than-considerate level despite the actors attempting to deliver their lines on stage. No easy feat when one considers these were the days before microphones, and performers were obliged to rely on the natural acoustics of the auditorium to have their voices carried to the back rows.

The setting, suspects, and victim of *The Case of The Fatal Flaw* have been the most influenced by the findings of my research than any other Bow Street Society mystery in the series thus far. So much so, I could discuss the vast historical context for many pages more. I'll finish this section by highlighting the remaining elements featured in the book which were based on real-life examples:

- the use of carbon-filament bulbs.
- the use of on-site steam-engines and dynamos to generate electricity.
- the lift to raise the performer from below stage.
- the platform and system of pulleys and ropes Mr Akers utilised whilst painting the scenery.
- the scene-painters' dislike of electric lighting & their reasons.
- the use of three-dimensional scenery.
- the conflict between the theatre and religious moralists.

- the *Red Barn Mystery* as a popular, and frequently dramatized, story in nineteenth century theatres.
- *Her Golden Hair was Hanging Down Her Back* sung by Miss Lily.
- the application of the Theatres Regulation Act 1843 in 1897.

Birmingham, 'The Bird,' and Lost Buildings

The inspiration for Mr Jack Jerome, the blackmailer who torments Mr Ellis Benton at the Crecent's stage door, came from a passage in Nell Darby's book *Life on the Victorian Stage*, in which she states "in 1895 it was noted in the press that 'a system of blackmailing is being applied to pantomime artistes employed at two or more of the London theatres.' The best-known actors at one theatre were 'molested' when leaving after a performance one night and threatened with 'the bird'—the colloquial term for hissing and shouting complaints—unless the actors paid them to keep quiet." She then goes on to state it was noted in 1894 "Birmingham theatres were particularly notorious for incidents during the panto season." This made me wonder about a known blackmailer travelling from Birmingham to London to ply his trade. This, in turn, formed the inspiration for Mr Jack Jerome.

The Case of The Fatal Flaw isn't the first time a Bow Street Society case has involved a connection to Birmingham, however. In the short story *The Case of the Contradictory Corpse* in the *Brumology* charity anthology published in April 2023, Miss Trent is called to Birmingham by the Birmingham Bow Street Society; a 'copy-cat' group created in homage to the London original. This leads to Mr Locke, Dr Locke, and Mr Heath being assigned to the case and they meet Detective Inspector Matthew Rupert Peter Donahue for the first time.

DI Donahue is loosely based upon a good friend of mine, Twitch.tv streamer MattRPD, who was born, and lives in, the West Midlands. Therefore, I was delighted when I could legitimately write his character into a main Bow Street Society mystery, thereby making him a permanent part of the Bow Street Society canon. The inclusion of Birmingham in *The Case of The Fatal Flaw* also allowed me to introduce one of Inspector Conway's siblings, thereby giving the reader another glimpse into his life beyond his work.

According to information I received from the West Midlands Police Museum, the Birmingham City Police wasn't merged with West Midlands Constabulary until 1974. Furthermore, they were operating out of the Newton Street police station rather than the Moore Street Public Office in 1897. Additional research from John W. Reilly's book *POLICING BIRMINGHAM: An account of 150 years of policing Birmingham*, also confirmed the Watch Committee linked to the police had obtained 500 square yards in Newton Street alongside the Victoria Law Courts and Central Law Courts to build a central police station in 1891. Furthermore, that ten officers were added to the "burgeoning detective department" in 1883.

As usual, I wanted to include as many real-life locations in *The Case of the Fatal Flaw* as possible. Aside from the previously mentioned Newton Street police station, the Hope & Anchor public house on Edmund Street, the Lozells, The Stork Hotel, the Woodman public house on Easy Row, Baskerville Passage, Broad Street, and Baskerville Place were actual places in nineteenth century Birmingham. Unfortunately, some of them, specifically the Hope & Anchor, the Woodman, and The Stork Hotel, no longer exist. If you'd like to learn more about nineteenth century Birmingham, I highly recommend Roy Thornton's book *Lost Buildings of Birmingham*. I found it particularly helpful when describing the alteration to the frontage of the Hope & Anchor public house and that establishment's proximity to the Birmingham Central Library.

Another location worth noting is New Street train station. As described in the book, the northern (and original) part of the station was occupied by the London North-Western Railway Company, whilst the southern part of the station was an extension completed in 1885 occupied by Midland Railway. Later in 1897, a joint committee of London North-Western Railway and Midlands Railway was formed to operate New Street station, however.

Connections to the wider Bow Street Society universe

Aside from the previously mentioned connection to *The Case of the Contradictory Corpse* short story, *The Case of The Fatal Flaw* has many references to the wider Bow Street Society universe.

Firstly, the fictional Hampstead School Mr Verity and Dr Locke visit was featured in *The Case of the Impossible Implication* short story from the sixth volume of the Bow Street Society Casebook, *The Case of The Scream in the Smog & Other Stories*. There's also passing reference to the events of *The Impossible Implication* in *The Case of The Fatal Flaw* when Mr Verity and Dr Locke meet the headmaster of Hampstead School, Mr Jeconiah Rogers.

Secondly, Dr Colbert's colleague, Dr Charles McWilliams, was the Bow Street Society's client in the short story *The Case of the Devil's Dare* featured in the UK Crime Book Club's charity anthology *Criminal Shorts* published in November 2020.

Thirdly, the mention of Mr Gilbert Berry by the Gaslight Gazette's archive clerk is a direct reference to the short story *The Case of Mastermind Moss* featured in the fifth volume of the Bow Street Society Casebook, *The Case of the Fearful Father & Other Stories*.

The Private Life of Miss Rebecca Trent

When writing *The Case of The Fatal Flaw*, I made a concerted effort to give the reader further glimpses into Miss Trent's life beyond her work as the Bow Street Society's clerk. The driving lessons she receives from Mr Snyder is part of this (despite being connected to her work). I chose a dog cart for her learner vehicle as it's the one recommended for beginner drivers in Captain C. Morley Knight's book *Hints on Driving Horses (Harness, Carriage, Etc)* originally published in 1884. It should be noted, though, driving licenses weren't introduced until 1903, the first edition of the Highway Code wasn't published until 1931, and the driving test didn't become mandatory until 1935. Therefore, in 1897, Mr Snyder could legitimately (and legally) teach Miss Trent to drive on a public highway like Bow Street. If Miss Trent was learning to drive with a view to earning a living from being a hansom cab driver, though, she might've had to undergo a test at Scotland Yard, like Mr Snyder did, to acquire her operating license (if the police at the time would've permitted her do so, that is).

Aside from Miss Trent's driving lessons, the reader is also shown her private space within the Bow Street Society's house during *The Case of The Fatal Flaw*. I'd always imagined Miss Trent would have a bedroom and parlour etc separate to the rest of the house, so it was nice to have the opportunity to share this with the reader.

The new development of Toby living with Miss Trent was also part of my decision to shed the formidable clerk in a new light. She sees herself in the role of older sister to Toby, and he looks up to her in a similar way. Given the aims of the Bow Street Society, I felt it was a natural step for the group to take in an orphan who would've otherwise been homeless and destitute.

Same name, different fates

Whilst some readers might've rejoiced at the return of illusionist Mr Percival Locke after a prolonged absence, others might've been shocked by the downfall of surgeon Dr Percy Weeks. As Mr Locke steadily regains his strength, and love of his wife, Dr Weeks spirals into an alcohol-fuelled depression brought on by, amongst other things, Miss Hicks' adultery. Admittedly, I hadn't planned to lead Dr Weeks down this dark road when I introduced him in *The Case of The Curious Client*. Yet, lead him I have. Furthermore, I considered killing him off in *The Case of The Fatal Flaw*, as there was one point when he could've succumbed to a seizure brought on by his sudden abstinence from alcohol. I decided not to kill him, though, as he's a character I not only enjoy writing for, but one whose personal journey and development is far from over.

The idea of having Dr Weeks admitted to Bethlem Royal Hospital occurred to me when I was writing the scene between Inspector Lee and Dr Weeks at the end of *The Case of The Pugilist's Ploy*. At that point, I thought it would be a simple case of Dr Weeks attacking Inspector Lee, thereby causing Inspector Lee to accuse Dr Weeks of being insane and ordering Dr Colbert to admit Dr Weeks to Bethlem. Once again, though, my research proved this to be another erroneous assumption based on cliches.

I'd like to give very special thanks to David Luck, archivist at the Bethlem Museum of the Mind. His knowledge of the archive, the contemporary documents he supplied, and the additional references he pointed me to, were invaluable when I came to describing the complex process of Dr Weeks' admission to Bethlem. They, alongside other sources I'd found, meant the portrayal given in *The Case of The Fatal Flaw* was as historically accurate as possible.

Separate to the process of admission, I found E.C. Spitzka, M. D's book *INSANITY: Its Classification, Diagnosis and Treatment. A manual for students and practitioners of medicine* originally published in 1883 valuable when describing the process of diagnosing Dr Weeks' insanity. This, and the illness he is said to have (Chronic Alcoholic Insanity) were based upon the same term and associated symptoms outlined in Spitzka's book.

Dr Colbert's use of General Paralysis of the Insane is a direct reference to the identical term coined by many asylum doctors in the nineteenth century. According to an explanation given by Catharine Arnold in her book *BEDLAM: London and its Mad*, General Paralysis of the Insane (or GPI) was "a form of progressive dementia characterised by delusions of grandeur, failing memory, facial tics, slurred speech, and unsteady gait." Furthermore, it was classified by the Lunacy Commission in 1844 as "'incurable and hopeless' and caused by organic disease in the brain and noted that the condition 'seldom occurs in females, but mostly in men, and is the result almost uniformly of a debauched and intemperate life." Arnold then goes on to state "GPI was actually the result of a sexually transmitted disease: syphilis." Diagnosis of GPI would've involved an examination of the patient's genitalia, hence why Dr Colbert conducts this part of his assessment whilst Dr Weeks is in a cold bath.

The information I found in Catharine Arnold's book *BEDLAM: London and its Mad* regarding the use of mechanical restraint at Bethlem Royal Hospital, specifically an account by Dr George Henry Savage (1842—1921), president of the Medico-Psychological Association of Great Britain, informed Dr Colbert's use of soft gloves, a side-arm dress, and dry pack (the application of the blankets) on Dr Weeks.

According to the *Bethlem Hospital Rules & Orders* from 1905, "Both mechanical restraint and seclusion can only be authorised by the Resident Physician or the Assistant Medical Officer in the RP's absence. A register is kept of each instance of this, with the reasons for the restraint/seclusion included, and this register is presented to the Sub-Committee of the Court of Governors at every meeting." Therefore, as the resident physician, Dr Colbert could authorise and oversee the use of mechanical restraint, but he would've nonetheless been obliged to provide justification for its use to his employers.

Eagle-eyed readers might've noticed the asylum is referred to in these notes as 'Bethlem Hospital,' but is referred to as 'Bethlehem Hospital' in both *The Case of The Fatal Flaw* and *The Case of The Pugilist's Ploy*. The alternative 'Bethlehem Hospital' has been used on the basis it was the name given to the asylum in *The Queen's London: A Pictorial and Descriptive Record of the Streets, Buildings, Parks and Scenery of the Great Metropolis in the Fifty-Ninth Year of the Reign of Her Majesty Queen Victoria* published by Cassell & Company Limited in 1896. This demonstrates the "Bethlehem" and "Bethlem" names have become interchangeable over the years.

I recommend reading the *Sources of Reference* section for further information about how my portrayal of Bethlem Hospital in *The Case of The Fatal Flaw* is based upon my research findings.

With regards to Mr Locke's recovery, Dr Locke continues to follow the treatment plan outlined by Dr J.B. Mattison in his paper *The Treatment of Opium Addiction* originally published in 1885. Unlike Dr Weeks, Mr Locke has the benefit of Dr Locke's love, patience, and expertise to aid him. Mr Locke has also been allowed to remain at home in (relative) comfort, albeit with an attendant.

My aim of the conversation between Dr Weeks and Mr Locke, in which the former offers the latter heroin, followed by the description of Dr Weeks' treatment at Bethlem, is to show the reader how the experiences of patients suffering from mental health conditions in the nineteenth century could be both vastly different and eerily similar. Although Dr Colbert means well, the 'treatment' Dr Weeks endures at his hands and his attendants' is humiliating. Likewise, Dr Locke's heart is in the right place, but the fact her husband is at home means she can control every aspect of his life to ensure he doesn't relapse into addiction. In short, neither Dr Weeks nor Mr Locke are receiving effective treatment for their addictions but are instead enduring drugs and practises designed to alleviate their symptoms in the hope they might become good, honest people again.

If you'd like to discover more about the Bow Street Society, including its members, please visit the official website at www.bowstreetsociety.com. Please also consider writing a review on Amazon or Goodreads and telling your friends and family about this book and the other Bow Street Society mysteries. Thank you for your continued support, and feel free to reach out to me at info@bowstreetsociety.com with any thoughts / feedback you may have.

~ T.G. Campbell, *January 2025*

GASLIGHT GAZETTE

News about the Bow Street Society — Price: 1*d.*

SUBSCRIBE
to the
GASLIGHT GAZETTE
for...

- **NEWS** about **BOW STREET SOCIETY** releases

- **NEVER-BEFORE-SEEN** deleted scenes and unused drafts from past books and short stories.

- **FIRST LOOK AT NEW STORIES** Subscribers are first to read new casebook short stories

- **SNEAK PEEKS** of future releases...and **MORE!**

A FREE monthly publication delivered directly to your electronic mail box.

SUBSCRIBE *now:*
http://www.bowstreetsociety.com/news.html

SOURCES OF REFERENCE

Research has been conducted into the historical period *The Case of The Fatal Flaw* is set in. Aspects covered in this research include: the hierarchy & workings of west end theatres, hierarchy of, admission to, and treatments at Bethlem Hospital, Birmingham City Police, and numerous real-life locations. Though not directly referenced in this book, the research was used to form the basis of narrative descriptions and some character dialogue. I've therefore strived to cite each source used within my research here. Each citation includes the source's origin, the source's author, and which part of *The Case of The Fatal Flaw* the source relates to. All rights connected to the following sources remain with their respective authors and publishers.

BOOKS

Nineteenth century literary sources.

C. Morley Knight, Captain, Hints on Driving Horses (Harness, Carriage, Etc) (Digital edition by Read Country Books, 2020. Originally published in 1884).
Recommends Dog Carts for beginner drivers

Dickens, Charles, Dickens's Dictionary of London 1895—1896 (Seventeenth Year): An Unconventional Handbook, (c.1895, J. Smith, London)
London & County Banking Co. name, location, and current accounts.
Location of Charing Cross Hospital. Also, it's in-patient policy in cases of emergency and Electrical Department.
Location of The Era newspaper office.
National Fire Insurance Corporation Ltd being absorbed by the Royal Insurance Co.

Address of the Lambeth Telegraph Office referenced in chapter fifty-five and the epilogue.
Name & opening hours of the West Strand Telegraph Office.

Spitzka, M.D., E. C., <u>INSANITY: Its Classification, Diagnosis and Treatment. A manual for students and practitioners of medicine</u> (Bermingham & Co, New York, 1883).
Diagnosis of Dr Weeks' Chronic Alcoholic Insanity.

Mattison, Dr J.B., <u>The Treatment of Opium Addiction</u> (Originally published in 1885)
Mr Locke's ongoing treatment planned overseen by Dr Locke.

Richmond, Miss Lillie, <u>Domestic and Commercial Cookery Recipes with Special Hints on Gas Cooking</u>, (Cartwright & Rattray Ltd, London and Manchester, 1898)
Description of the gruel Dr Colbert serves Dr Weeks based on the recipe for Oatmeal Gruel in this book.

<u>The Queen's London: A Pictorial and Descriptive Record of the Streets, Buildings, Parks and Scenery of the Great Metropolis in the Fifty-Ninth Year of the Reign of Her Majesty Queen Victoria</u> (Cassell & Company Limited, 1896)
References to "Bethlehem Hospital" within the book in place of the "Bethlem Hospital" used in Notes from the author and acknowledgements.

Brewer, LL.D., Rev. E. Cobham, <u>A Dictionary of Phrase and Fable</u>, (Cassell and Company Ltd, London, Toronto, Melbourne, and Syndey, c.1800s)
Reference to the term "Cove" in chapter nine.

Modern literary sources.

Page, M.D., David W. The Howdunnit Series: Body Trauma: A Writer's Guide to Wounds and Injuries, (Writer's Digest Books, Cincinnati and Ohio, 1996), p.163
Deep burns at the site of the entrance of the electrical current and internal tissue damage, broken bones and ribs.

Stevens, Serita Deborah with Klarner, Anne The Howdunnit Series: Deadly Doses: A Writer's Guide to Poisons, (Writer's Digest Books, Cincinnati and Ohio, 1990)
Description of Miss Kimberly's symptoms of cyanide poisoning and the reaction time.

Arnold, Catharine, BEDLAM: London and its Mad (Pocket Books, London, Sydney, New York, Toronto, 2009)
- *p.235, Description of the soft gloves, side-arm dress and blankets Dr Colbert uses to mechanically restrain Dr Weeks, and the further explanation in Notes from the author.*
- *pp.242 - 243, references to the term "General Paralysis of the Insane" in chapter thirty-three and the explanation in Notes from the author.*

Ware, J. Redding, The Victorian Dictionary of Slang & Phrase (Bodleian Library, University of Oxford, 2013) (originally published 1909)
- *p.2, the term "Actor's Bible" in chapter three.*
- *p.11, the term "athletic droll" in chapter seven.*
- *p.24, the terms "beef-headed" in chapter six and "beer-eater" in chapter ten.*
- *p.36, the term "blowsa-bella" in chapter four.*
- *p.38, the term "blue pencil" in chapter four.*

- *p.44, the term "born with a sneer" in chapter four.*
- *p.53, the term "buggin'" in chapter seven.*
- *p.55, the term "bum-boozer" in chapter seven.*
- *p.60, the term "the Cabbage" in chapter four.*
- *p.63, the terms "cannot show itself" and "Captain Macfluffer" in chapter four.*
- *p.91 the term "coppin' the brewery" in chapter seven.*
- *p.92, the term "nark" in chapter forty-four.*
- *p.137, the term "front" in chapter forty-one.*
- *p.222, the term "shipwrecked" in chapter twenty-one.*
- *p.251, the term "tuppeny 'apenny one" in chapter forty-four.*
- *p.252, the term "two inches above upright" in chapter forty-four.*

Booth, Michael R., <u>Theatre in the Victorian Age</u> (Cambridge University Press, 1991)

- *p.33, the terms "supers" meaning super-numerary actors, i.e., extras, and "super master" in chapter four. Also, each area having a chief that reported directly to the stage manager, i.e., Mr Willis as the chief electric man.*
- *p.62, descriptions of the shape and construction of the auditorium, the auditorium being fully lit during the performance, and the audience members holding conversations at normal volume during the performance.*
- *pp.74-75, use of 3D scenery in the nineteenth century.*
- *p.77, description of lift for performer based upon the drawing and accompanying description in Booth's book.*
- *p.81, description of Mr Akers' framed canvas, pulleys, platform and mechanism.*

595

- *p.82, tiredness of scenery being highlighted by electrical lighting.*
- *p.83, reference to electric lighting being confined to public building and wealthy households until after the First World War in Notes from the author.*
- *p.88, theatres having the option to utilise the publicly accessible supply from an electricity company introduced in the 1890s.*
- *p.90, the Savoy Theatre being the first theatre to be entirely lit by electricity in 1881. Also, theatres maintaining their gas-lighting systems as a back-up for the electrical one.*
- *p.91, new carbon-filament bulbs in theatres and their power being measured in candlepower. Also, on-site steam-engines and dynamos being utilised by theatres to generate electricity and dimmers & dimmer scale/levels.*
- *p.92, reference & explanation of Miss Navette's illuminated costume in Notes from the author.*

Darby, Nell, Life on the Victorian Stage, (Pen & Sword History, Barnsley, 2017)
- *p.51, passage quoted in Notes from the author.*
- *p.54, references to PC Brampton and the Queen's Theatre in Notes from the author.*
- *p.138, reference to the electrocution of Augustino Bierdermann in Notes from the author.*

Reilly, John W. POLICING BIRMINGHAM: An account of 150 years of policing Birmingham (Think Digital Books Ltd, England, 2018)
- p.39, Existence of detective department at Birmingham City Police in early 1897 based upon the following

extract: "In 1883…The burgeoning Detective Department had grown by ten more officers"
- p.40, Birmingham City Police headquarters on Newton Street based upon the following extract: "In 1891, the Watch Committee obtained land uf 500 square yards in Newton Street alongside the courts for a proposed new to central Police Station."

Thornton, Roy, <u>Lost Buildings of Birmingham</u>, (The History Press, 2012)
- *p.85, Mr Elliott's reference to The Stork Hotel on Corporation Street.*
- *p.87, Inspector Donahue's reference to the Hope & Anchor on Edmund Street. Also, the reference to the Birmingham Central Library neighbouring the same establishment, and the references to the exterior of the Hope & Anchor, the year its frontage was remodelled, and who was responsible.*
- *pp.90-91, Inspector Donahue's references concerning The Woodman being popular with theatrical folk.*

* * *

WEBSITES

https://www.thecarriagefoundation.org.uk/item/dog-cart
Descriptions of the Dog Cart based upon photographs on the "Dog Cart" section of the Carriages of Britain website. The photographs show a dog cart manufactured in 1890.

https://www.gov.uk/government/publications/history-of-road-safety-and-the-driving-test/history-of-road-safety-the-highway-code-and-the-driving-test
Driving licenses were not introduced until 1903, the first edition of the Highway Code was published in 1931, and

the driving test didn't become mandatory until 1935. Therefore, in 1897, Mr Snyder could legitimately (and legally) teach Miss Trent to drive on a public highway like Bow Street.

https://www.hiddentrails.com/travelservices/good-to-know.htm#:~:text=All%20saddling%20and%20bridling%20is,and%20dismounted%20from%20that%20side.
Explanation of "off side of the horse": definition given on Hidden Trails website

https://fiveminutehistory.com/if-only-the-dead-could-talk-the-ghost-of-the-red-barn-murder/
The Red Barn Murder as a sensational story repeatedly acted out on the nineteenth century stage.

https://lawandreligionuk.com/2015/02/09/clerical-attire-officiants-and-safeguarding/#:~:text=There%20is%20no%20distinctive%20uniform,with%20the%20Church%20of%20England.%E2%80%9D
Description of Reverend Ananias Mullins' uniform based upon information found in above source that states there's no distinct uniform for Church of England clergymen.

https://www.crockford.org.uk/faq/how-to-address-the-clergy
Referenced form of address for Reverend Ananias Mullins.

https://bible.knowing-jesus.com/topics/Wickedness
Bible quote from Micah 2:1 referenced in chapter five.

https://www.biblestudytools.com/rhe/proverbs/passage/?q=proverbs+5:3-22
Bible quotes from Proverbs 5:3-5 referenced in chapters five and thirty-six.

https://bible.knowing-jesus.com/topics/The-Lust-Of-The-Flesh
Bible quote from Galatians 6:8 referenced in chapter five.

https://www.crossway.org/articles/10-key-bible-verses-on-sin/#:~:text=Yet%20John%20also%20makes%20it,14%3A18
Bible quote from Num. 14:18 referenced in chapter thirty-six.

https://www.kingjamesbibleonline.org/Bible-Verses-About-Unrepented-Sin/
Bible quote from 1 John 3:8-10 referenced in chapter thirty-six.
Bible quote from 1 John 1:8 referenced in chapter thirty-six.
Bible quote from 1 John 1:9 referenced in chapter thirty-six.

https://www.biblestudytools.com/topical-verses/bible-verses-about-gods-forgiveness/
Bible quote from Matthew 6:14-15 referenced in chapter thirty-six.

https://folksongandmusichall.com/index.php/and-her-golden-hair-was-hanging-down-her-back/
Lyrics referenced in chapter seven taken from the UK Sheet Music version of the song Her Golden Hair was Hanging Down Her Back written and composed by Monroe H. Rosenfeld & Felix McGlennon and first published in 1894.

https://www.archiseek.com/2013/1874-london-counties-bank-sevenoaks-kent/#:~:text=The%20Surrey%2C%20Kent%20and%20Sussex,was%20the%20largest%20British%20bank
London & County Banking Co. as the largest British bank by 1875.

https://www.natwestgroup.com/heritage/companies/westminster-bank-ltd.html
History of London & County Banking Co.

https://www.oldbaileyonline.org/about/the-old-bailey
Location, 1774 reconstruction, and 1824-1856 The New Court, Third Court and Fourth Court sections for description of the Old Bailey Courthouse in 1897, including the prisoners' quarters in the basement.

http://studymore.org.uk/3s.htm#Urgency
Requirement for a Reception Order via a magistrate, and two doctors' opinions. Also the police, i.e., Chief Inspector Jones applying for the urgent Reception Order instead of Dr Weeks' family, i.e., his mother.

http://studymore.org.uk/mhhglo.htm#1890ActWords
Requirement for a Certificate of Insanity.

http://studymore.org.uk/mhhglo.htm#GPI
Reference to General Paralysis of the Insane.

https://www.priorygroup.com/addiction-treatment/alcohol-rehab/alcohol-addiction-withdrawal
Symptoms of alcohol withdrawal experienced by Dr Weeks.

https://www.webmd.com/mental-health/addiction/delirium-tremens
Nightmares as a symptom of alcohol withdrawal experienced by Dr Weeks.

https://www.nurokor.com/blog/history-of-bioelectronic-medicine#:~:text=1840%20England%20Galvani's%20discovery%20leads,The%20start%20of%20Faradic%20Stimulation.
Electricity used in medicine from 1840 in the UK.

British Association for the Advancement of Science section of the article on https://www.iec.ch/history-si
The introduction of the "volt" as a unit measuring electricity.

https://britannica.com/science/International-System-of-Units
Reference to Watts and SI in Notes from the author.

https://bshm.org.uk/the-story-of-the-stethoscope/
Description of Dr Colbert's stethoscope based upon the image in this article.

https://www.medicalnewstoday.com/articles/curiosities-of-medical-history-the-controversy-of-using-cold-as-a-treatment#Cold-water-torture-in-psychiatric-institutions
Cold bath treatments for excitable patients (in Dr Weeks' case it was to lower the fever)

https://www.futurity.org/masculinity-book-boys-will-be-boys-2208512/
"Sunt pueri pueri, pueri puerilia tractant" Latin phrase spoken by Mr Rogers, and its meaning boys are boys, and boys will act like boys spoken by Mr Verity in chapter thirty-seven.

https://www.britannica.com/topic/feme-sole
Feme solo definition provided by Mr Elliott in chapter thirty-nine.

BBC News article Birmingham New Street station's changing face by Bethan Bell & Trystan Jones published on 20 September 2015
https://www.bbc.co.uk/news/uk-england-birmingham-34085505
Description of walkway and platform at Birmingham New Street train station in chapter forty-three based upon the photograph in this article.

New Street has seen significant changes in its history article on Network Rail website:
https://www.networkrail.co.uk/who-we-are/our-history/iconic-infrastructure/the-history-of-birmingham-new-street-station/
Northern part of Birmingham New Station being occupied by the London North-Western Railway Company in early 1897.

Steelhouse Lane Lock-up article by Corinne Brazier, archivist at the West Midlands Police Museum on the Prison History website:
https://www.prisonhistory.org/2019/04/steelhouse-lane-from-functioning-lock-up-to-lock-up-museum/
Birmingham City Police operating from Newton Street rather than the Moore Street Public Office in early 1897.

https://billdargue.jimdofree.com/glossary-brief-histories/a-brief-history-of-birmingham/victorian-birmingham/#:~:text=Town%20gardens%20and%20courts%20were,down%20into%20Digbeth%20and%20Deritend.
Extreme poverty in the courts and back-to-back housing in Birmingham alluded to by Inspector Conway in chapter forty-five.

https://billdargue.jimdofree.com/placenames-gazetteer-a-to-y/places-l/lozells/
The Lozells referred to in chapter forty-five. Also Wheeler Street having houses dating back to the nineteenth century.

http://epapers.bham.ac.uk/446/
Wheeler Street having houses dating back to the nineteenth century.

https://www.gale.com/intl/essays/ed-king-digitisation-of-british-newspapers-1800-1900
All newspapers depositing copies of their editions at the British Museum in 1897.

Hope & Anchor thread on the Birmingham History Forum
https://birminghamhistory.co.uk/forum/threads/hope-anchor-pub-edmund-st.35994/
Reference to Aldermen and Councillors doing dubious deals in chapter forty-six.

'OS Map name 014/05', in Map of Birmingham and its Environs (Southampton, 1884-1891), British History Online https://www.british-history.ac.uk/os-1-to-2500/birmingham/014/05 **[accessed 10 September 2024].**
https://www.british-history.ac.uk/os-1-to-2500/birmingham/014/05
Location of Baskerville Passage and its vicinity to Easy Row and Baskerville Place.

https://brumphotoarchive.co.uk/image/2363/Interior_of_the_Woodman_Easy_Row_Birmingham
Descriptions of the Smoke Room and bar at The Woodman on Easy Row.

Plaster of Paris–Short History of Casting and Injured Limb Immobilzation by **B. Szostakowski, P. Smitham, and W.S. Khan. Published online: 2017 Apr 17**
https://www.ncbi.nlm.nih.gov/pmc/articles/PMC5420179/
Description of the cast on Mr Jack Jerome's arm in chapter forty-nine.

https://www.1900s.org.uk/chamber-pots.htm
Commodes being used in early 1897.

https://sussexhistoryforum.co.uk/index.php?topic=16144.0;wap2
Reference to Woking Fire Brigade in chapter fifty-two.

https://eghammuseum.org/eghams-fire-brigade/

603

Fire insurance being a means of providing fire brigades to customers of the insurance companies, rather than as a way of rebuilding after a fire.

https://www.museumoffire.net/single-post/insurance-brigades-1837-to-1884
Fire insurance being a means of providing fire brigades to customers of the insurance companies, rather than as a way of rebuilding after a fire.

https://insurancehistory.cii.co.uk/collections_policies/national-fire-insurance-corporation-limited-1509/
National Fire Insurance Corporation Ltd issuing insurance policies in 1878.

https://www.encyclopedia-titanica.org/community/threads/white-stars-company-address.25629/ **that references The Times (London), 1 July 1929; Anderson's White Star; Mallett and Bell's The Pirrie-Kylsant Motorships.**
Reference to the registered office of Oceanic Steam Navigation Company in chapter fifty-six.

https://golocalise.com/blog/what-is-a-brummie-accent#:~:text=Sometimes%2C%20the%20letter%20'i',becomes%20an%20'ay'%20sound.
Phonetic depiction of the Birmingham accent.

https://www.timeout.com/birmingham/news/16-birmingham-and-black-country-slang-terms-explained-041315
The term "tararabit" in chapter seven.

https://www.dickens-online.info/the-pickwick-papers-page385.html#google_vignette
Mr Benton's statement referring to eating his hat included on the basis a variance of this was used in the Pickwick Papers by Charles Dickens published in 1837: "'Well, if I

knew as little of life as that, I'd eat my hat and swallow the buckle whole,' said the clerical gentleman."

https://welovebrum.co.uk/2023/09/11/brummie-accent-guide/#:~:text=Wench%20%E2%80%93%20Though%20the%20term%20is,endearment%20towards%20women%20and%20girls
Reference to the term "wench" used by Inspector Donahue as a non-offensive term in chapter forty-six. Also, the reference to the term "Round the Wrekin" in the same chapter.

https://greensdictofslang.com/entry/5xgnyxi#:~:text=1870s%E2%80%931880s%20n.p.%3A%20Mandrake%20A%20homosexual.
Reference to the term "mandrake" in chapter forty-seven.

https://www.oed.com/dictionary/toff_n
Reference to the term "toffs" in chapter forty-eight.

https://www.yourdictionary.com/articles/victorian-slang-terms
Reference to the term "strumpet" in chapter forty-eight.

https://www.oed.com/dictionary/knee-trembler_n#:~:text=The%20earliest%20known%20use%20of,a%20text%20by%20John%20S
Reference to the term "knee-trembler" in chapter forty-eight.

https://www.urbandictionary.com/define.php?term=knee-trembler
Reference to the term "knee-trembler" in chapter forty-eight.

https://www.dictionary.com/browse/posser
Reference to the term "posser" in chapter fifty-two.

Time and Date
The following sources are from the Time and Dates website:
https://www.timeanddate.com

https://www.timeanddate.com/sun/uk/london?month=1&year=1897
Time of sunrise on Monday 18th January 1897

https://www.timeanddate.com/calendar/index.html?year=1895&country=9
Day of the week and date referenced in chapter eighteen.

https://www.timeanddate.com/calendar/?year=1880&country=9
Day of the week and date referenced in chapter fifty-two.

https://www.timeanddate.com/calendar/?year=1878&country=9
Day of the week and date referenced in chapter fifty-two.

London Picture Archive
The following sources are from the London Picture Archive website:
https://www.londonpicturearchive.org.uk

https://www.londonpicturearchive.org.uk/view-item?WINID=1722765160561&i=25874
The Hightower's residing on Great Queen Street based upon the London Picture Archive image of Great Queen Street in 1879.

Catalogue No   SC_PHL_01_544_74_18808
Description of The Era newspaper office's exterior based upon the photograph contained within this catalogue entry.

Record No: 176308 Catalogue No:
SC_PHL_02_0183_2227
Description of the Vine Street police station's exterior based upon the photograph contained within this catalogue entry.

Dictionary of Victorian London
The following sources are from Lee Jackson's Dictionary of Victorian London website:
https://www.victorianlondon.org

Newnham-Davis, Lieut. Col., Dinners and Diners. Chapter 33: The East Room (Criterion, Piccadilly Circus) (1899)
Description of the interior of the East Room at the Criterion.

Timbs, John, Curiosities of London, (1867)
Location of Charing Cross Hospital.

Year Book of Philanthropy and the Hospital Annual (1900, The Scientific Press Ltd, London)
Founding year of Charing Cross Hospital in chapter twenty-three.

Gissing, George, *The Nether World*, (1889)
Description of the transaction Miss Hicks has at the pawnbroker's shop in chapter forty-six.

* * *

MAPS

Booth, Charles Booth's Maps of London Poverty East and West 1889 (reproduced by Old House Books) *purchased from* **Shire Books**
http://www.shirebooks.co.uk/old_house_books/

Location of Westbourne Terrace and its proximity to Cleveland Terrace, Bishop's Road and Westbourne Crescent.
The Hightower's residence based on the mixed, some comfortable, others poor classification on Great Queen Street on this map.
Description of landmarks and streets near to the police station on Vine Street.

* * *

THIRD-PARTY ASSISTANCE

Bethlem Museum of the Mind
The following sources were provided by David Luck, Archivist at the museum:

Luck, David, Emails to T.G. Campbell dated 1st & 2nd May 2024
Resident Physician being notified of Dr Weeks' arrival.
Bethlem Hospital recording existing injuries so it can't be held liable for them later.
Dr Weeks' physical examination by a doctor (the resident physician).
Penniless surgeons being uncommon amongst the hospital's patients.
Dr Weeks' formal admission to the hospital.
The expectation Dr Weeks would "go dry" due to the asylum promoting sober behaviour.

Bethlem Hospital Rules & Orders (1905)
- *Resident Physician being notified of Dr Weeks' arrival.*
- *The head attendant conducting the physical examination of the patient and submitting their report in writing to the resident physician who must immediately examine any injuries.*

- *Confiscation, safe-keeping, and recording of Dr Weeks' property and Inspector Conway's signing of the book is based upon the following extract: "A Book shall be kept in which all sums of money, or other property which may be found upon a Patient on admission, and shall be entered and certified by the persons bringing such Patient, and countersigned by the Steward, who shall have the custody of such property, which book shall be laid before the Bethlem Sub-Committee at every Meeting."*
- *Dr Weeks' formal admission to the hospital.*
- *The expectation Dr Weeks would "go dry" due to the asylum promoting sober behaviour based upon the following extract: "no provisions or liquors, under any pretence, shall be given to Patients by their friends, without the permission of the Resident Physician."*
- *Dr Colbert's use of mechanical restraint with Dr Weeks based upon the following extract: "Both mechanical restraint and seclusion can only be authorised by the Resident Physician or the Assistant Medical Officer in the RP's absence. A register is kept of each instance of this, with the reasons for the restraint/seclusion included, and this register is presented to the Sub-Committee of the Court of Governors at every meeting."*

Bethlem Hospital Floorplan
https://museumofthemind.org.uk/learning/explore-bethlem/floorplan
Small room referred to in chapter twenty-nine is based on the small room in the central administration block on the floorplan.

Sulphanol being used as a sedative based upon the following text on the "Baths" pop-up box on the floorplan: "In 1889, the superintendent physician Dr Smith welcomes the arrival of a new tranquilliser, sulphanol 'for the production of sleep and the control of excitement' remarking that a number of patients had recovered because of it."
Reference to the male patient gallery in chapter thirty-three.
Reference to the dining room in chapter forty-nine based upon the description under "Kitchen" on this floorplan.

West Midlands Police Museum
The following source was provided by the museum.

West Midlands Police Museum, Email to T.G. Campbell dated 5th September 2024
Birmingham City Police being its own entity in early 1897. Birmingham City Police operating from Newton Street rather than the Moore Street Public Office in early 1897.

* * *

UK LEGISLATION
https://www.legislation.gov.uk/

Theatres Regulation Act, 1843, pp.680-81
Play manuscripts being approved by the Lord Chamberlain on the basis of preserving the good manners, decorum and peace of the public.

The Married Women's Property Act, 1882
Mr Elliott's explanation of Miss Mina Ilbert's legal entitlement to retain the Crescent Theatre's lease as her own property under his act in chapter thirty-nine.

Printed in Great Britain
by Amazon